Join the Legions!

Sign-up for the Eagles and Dragons Publishing
Newsletter and get a FREE BOOK today.

Subscribers get first access to new releases, special
offers, and much more.

Go to:
www.eaglesanddragonspublishing.com

For Alexandra and Athena,

Who give me infinite joy and for whom I would battle a hundred hydras.

Για την Αλεξάνδρα και την Αθηνά,

Οι οποίες μου δίνουν απέραντη χαρά και για τις οποίες θα μαχόμουν εκατό Ύδρες.

KILLING

THE

HYDRA

EAGLES AND DRAGONS

BOOK II

ADAM ALEXANDER HAVIARAS

PROLOGUS

Beloved of Apollo...
Love! Blood! A sea of plots!
He bites at your heels...ravenous!
The Avenger is a harsh judge.
Keep her close. Empress. Your Empress!

Sands and forests.
South and North.
Where does your home lie?
Where does your heart lie?
Where does your sword lie?
Loyalty! Listen to the immortal!

Bravery and wisdom.
Eagles and Dragons.
Horses beneath.
They will come to you as thunder.
All scales...and death.
Use them...know them.
Upon the grassy mound...

Metellusssssssss...

A chilling voice rang out in the cavern, over and over and over, more insistent and violent with every utterance. The young warrior's arms shook as he fought back his fear, sword handle sweaty in his white-knuckled grip.

He struggled to keep his footing on the rocky steps that led further into darkness. A rank odour of salt and iron permeated the thick air through which the dreaded voice travelled.

"What do you want from me?" His hollow speech was swallowed by the shadows. Then, the rocky earth trembled and he pressed on, taunted by the same voice, the same words. He fell to his knees, panting and exhausted, darting eyes scanning the black walls. There was movement, sudden and swift from every direction.

The warrior ran, parrying ghostly blows. There were too many and he felt his flesh split and trickle. His body was thrown through the air to sprawl on jagged rocks like a helpless hatchling cast from a mountain peak. Mouth quivering with the taste of his own blood, he reached for a hopeful speck of light with one tremulous hand.

"Adara?" he sputtered. The walls began to crumble and he felt blood and heat wash over him. "Adara!" The light vanished and the warrior gagged and was swept away on the gory tide.

"Oi! Wake up, man! Tribune!" Rough hands were shaking Lucius where he sat on the trireme's deck, wrapped in his crimson cloak, leaning against barrels of fresh water. He started at the guttural, booming voice and looked up to see a grey-haired man in a brown tunic, old soldier's boots and a well-used military cloak.

"What?"

"Best stop that yelling, Tribune. People are starting to stare." Several disdainful heads were turned in their direction.

"Sorry. I was…having a nightmare."

"I don't want to know! Bad luck to speak of nightmares at sea. Here, let me help you up." He hefted Lucius with a grunt. "Name's Gaius. Used to be a centurion. Retired now."

"Lucius Metellus Anguis. tribune, III Augustan legion. Not retired."

"Ha! Humour! Good. It's a long journey." He slapped Lucius good-heartedly on the shoulder. "Aren't you a bit young to be an officer in that legion of veteran whoresons?"

"I suppose I am." Lucius' ego had long ago become acclimatized to remarks about his age and rank.

"Hm. No matter. You look like you could rip the head off a jackal." The old man looked Lucius up and down. Then his eyes fell on the blue bundle Lucius held. "Say, what's that you've got there?"

"A sword. My wife Adara had it made for me as a wedding gift," he said with fondness.

"Adara? That's the name you were calling out."

"I was?"

"Only the whole ship heard ya. Anyway, that's quite a gift your woman gave you." Gaius marked the gold pommel and dragon-headed hilt. "All my wife ever gives me are breeches! I should have your wife talk to mine. Is she aboard?"

"No. She isn't." Lucius felt a pang of hurt, regret, as he imagined his new wife far away, boarding ship in Brundisium, setting sail for Greece with her parents, Publius and Delphina, her sisters and his own sister, Alene. The length of their unwilling separation was undetermined. He could not bring her to Africa until he was sure it was safe.

"Pity," Gaius broke Lucius' thoughts. "My wife's lounging on couches mid-deck with all the other hens. Glad you're here though; I needed to get away. Garlic?" He held out several cloves of raw garlic which he had poured from a leather pouch.

"No. No thank you, Gaius." Lucius wrinkled his nose as the veteran popped a few into his mouth. He hoped he would keep it shut after that but it was a fool's hope.

"Suit yourself," Gaius replied, chewing. "Best thing a legionary can do is eat raw garlic every day! Always made sure my men had raw garlic, especially on the bloody northern frontier. Damn cold up there!"

It had only been a day since the fleet, led by the imperial and Praetorian ships, had left Ostia. Leptis Magna, Emperor Severus' home as well as that of Plautianus, Praetorian prefect and imperial kinsman, was to be the site of tremendous celebration. Emperor Severus had ordered all high-ranking military officers who had been in Rome for his triumph to accompany him to the prosperous African city.

Drusus, the Empress Julia Domna's man who had made sure Lucius was on the correct ship in Ostia, had teased the young tribune that he would get an earful of old war stories on the veterans' trireme. So far, Gaius had proved not to be a storyteller. Lucius was lost in thought. Septimius Severus always strove to keep his military happy, and close. The entire Praetorian Guard seemed to be going to Africa, leaving Rome to the senate for a time. That said, the emperor had stationed a legion not twenty miles from Rome in Albanum, just in case any die-hard Republicans got the wrong idea. Severus made sure the senate knew its place.

Lucius wondered how angry the Emperor's actions had made his own, hateful father, Quintus Caecilius Metellus. He did not care in the end, about his father or his boyhood friend, Argus; as far as he was concerned, he never wanted to see either of them again. *They're cowards*, Lucius thought. He hoped that his mother, Antonia, and his younger siblings, Quintus and Clarinda, would be all right.

His thoughts pulled once more to his cohort at their Numidian base in Lambaesis and the true duty ahead of him: to punish the traitors in his cohort and discover the truth behind the death of his dear friend and centurion, Antanelis. When the celebrations in Leptis Magna were at an end, Lucius would return to Lambaesis; he could not bring Adara to join him until it was safe. The Praetorians were watching him.

Gaius began to fidget where he leaned against the trireme's railing next to Lucius.

"Well, Tribune, we'd better sit down. It's still a long way to Africa."

"I'm sure it is." Lucius had made a friend from whom he could not detach himself. The animated veteran leaned back, hands clasped behind his head.

"You know," Gaius began, "this reminds me of the time I sailed up the Rhenus with my men…"

Lucius Metellus Anguis leaned back against his water barrel to settle in for the rest of the journey. While his friend

10

spoke, Lucius opened the wax tablet on which he had scribbled the Sybil's prophetic words. Cumae seemed like a dream, long ago. And yet, the words given to him in that dark cave lingered, had seeped into his nightmares.

Part I

THE LONELY ROAD

A.D. 203

I

LEPTIS MAGNA

Leptis Magna was the most gifted, blessed city of Africa Proconsularis. In its infancy it had been a prosperous Phoenician colony and as it matured, bowing to Roman control during the reign of Augustus, it flourished. When Trajan made it an official colonia, the settlement grew with the arrival of officials, traders and settlers in search of prosperity from all corners of the empire.

The city came to enjoy all of the comforts and pleasures that Rome had to offer. Leptis Magna had a theatre built by a local merchant, and the old forum had its own curia, a basilica, a Temple of Liber Pater, an Ionic Temple of Hercules and a Temple of Rome and Augustus. Hadrian also favoured the city with a huge bath complex that included a large palaestra where the inhabitants and troops would exercise and wrestle.

Eventually, Leptis Magna became one of the wealthiest metropolises in the Mare Internum with the richness of its exports going to the furthest reaches of the Roman world. Caravans from the desert interior came to the city's thriving market to sell everything from ivory and precious gems to slaves and exotic animals. The market was also renowned for its local products such as grain, olive oil from surrounding estates, garum and salted fish, local specialties.

When Septimius Severus became emperor, his home town reached a pinnacle of prosperity and sunned itself in the rays of the emperor's favouritism. Severus undertook massive building projects throughout the empire but nowhere more so than in Leptis Magna. In front of the Temple of Jupiter that faced the sea, a new circular harbour was built, complete with a large lighthouse and several warehouses where goods were stored before export.

A new forum, overlooked by large, peering Medusa heads, was built as well as a new Basilica of Severus. The latter was ornately decorated with a forest of red granite columns with white marble capitals, reliefs of acanthus, animal protomes and eye-pleasing mythological scenes. Beautiful statuary shone out from the many niches that adorned the walls where the use of different materials created a sense of sublime elegance. Most fantastic of all was the colonnaded road, sixty-five feet wide, that led from the harbour to a clear-sounding nymphaeum outside the baths. This roadway, unlike any other building project, was composed of six-hundred green-streaked marble columns that gleamed in the sun like blades of emerald grass. At the intersection of the main road through the city and the street leading up from the old forum stood a monument to Leptis Magna's beloved emperor. Locals and traders walked beneath and admired the newly erected, four-sided arch of Septimius Severus. Its friezes of political and religious scenes in honour of the imperial family were carved in a curiously new style that befitted the metropolitan atmosphere.

The weather had been perfect for the crossing, with crisp seas beneath a sunny sky during the day and calm, moonlit depths by night. A crossing that could have taken over a week in bad weather ended up as a journey of only a few days.

Moon and star had been Lucius' only companions on those lonely nights and the lulling splash of silky dark water against the hull of the ship doubled as the sound of his wife's breath in his ear. Many passengers had chosen to go below deck during the night, but he had opted to stay out, his cloak wrapped about him. Occasionally, he would walk the perimeter of the enormous deck to ease his cramped legs and clear his head.

That morning, when land finally came within sight, the sun rose from a blazing red sleep in the east. Lucius was one of the first people awake. He rose from his pile of ropes, splashed water from a bucket on his face and rinsed his mouth with wine. He put his helmet on his head, if only to get it out of the way, picked up his belongings and went to the prow of the ship to take in the view.

Sprawled out before him in the distance was Africa Proconsularis. At first, all he could see were smooth sandy beaches stretching along the limitless shore. As the ships drew closer, the land became green in places where settlements were safely nestled. The sun rose higher, brighter, until finally, like a single flashing diamond in neatly groomed garden grass, Leptis Magna appeared directly ahead of the fleet.

Lucius was surprised by the richness of the city as the gleam of white marble from its monuments began to reflect and shimmer like an oasis. Beyond the city was a backdrop of hills, slopes of green and bronze. The ship gently bobbed up and down as it entered the coastal currents. Then he spotted it. A haze beyond and between the mountains, limitless, opaque...and familiar. The city faded and his eyes were drawn to where it was beginning to bake in the waking sun. The desert.

Leptis Magna was hot and dry and the air was filled with all manner of smells; sea water, fish and drying dung from the animal market mingled with incense, spices and the tang of fresh fruit. The rustle of palm trees could be heard as a hot breeze came off the water, competing with exuberant shouts from the markets, the old and new fora.

Inside the circular harbour, the emperor's ship, flanked by the two Praetorian vessels, docked directly in front of the Temple of Jupiter. Slaves lined the quay awaiting baggage instructions; the city prefect and other officials came down the temple steps, where a wide path had been cleared, to greet the emperor. The ship for military officials moored next to one of the Praetorian ships and the passengers disembarked to watch the procession.

Clear sounding horns rang out, accompanied by flutes and drums as the emperor, Julia Domna, their imperial sons, Caracalla and Geta and the empress' sister, Julia Maesa, stepped onto land. Large crowds had gathered to cheer Septimius Severus, and the way was lined with young girls in Punic dress who cast flowers at the feet of the imperial family. Severus looked around and took in a deep breath; the air of his home was pleasingly familiar. After making an offering to Jupiter in a colossal tripod on the temple steps, thanks for a safe journey, the emperor and his entourage made their way up the colonnaded street to their palatial urban villa behind the new forum.

The emperor's limp and cough had worsened since his days in Alexandria. This did not, however, affect the way his countrymen perceived him; they loved him. As he hobbled painfully along, head held as high as he could, he showed that he was pleased with the results of the building projects, most of which had not been finished the last time he had come to Leptis Magna. He congratulated the city officials on their work and the procession moved along with an army of servants in the rear.

In the harbour, after the emperor had left, thousands of people, troops, returning locals, guests, merchants and slaves went about in a frenzy trying to get their baggage and move on to their respective lodgings. In front of the temple, Plautianus addressed his officers as to their orders for billeting and the construction of a camp to the south-west of the city where the bulk of the Praetorian Guard would be staying.

Lucius looked around. He found his chest of belongings where four slaves waited but he was not exactly sure where to go in all the chaos.

"Tribune! Tribune!"

"Oh, no," Lucius muttered to himself. He recognised Gaius' voice in an instant.

"I thought you'd gone already."

"No, I'm still here. Just not sure where to go. It's my first time in Leptis Magna."

"Well, well, just tell me what you're looking for. My wife and I live here. We've got a villa just outside the city walls."

Lucius looked at the scroll that contained his orders. "I'm supposed to be staying at an inn called The Camel's Hump."

"Tut, tut. That shit hole?"

"Gaius! Be civilised!" his wife shouted from a litter surrounded by their household slaves.

"Be still woman!" he yelled back. "Forgive me, Tribune. She doesn't listen so well as a century of troops. As I was going to say, you can't stay in that inn. Rubbish! You must stay with us!"

"Oh, I couldn't Gaius, really." *Apollo please help me out of this one!*

"I insist. No excuses. You'll be our guest. It's quiet outside the city walls and you won't be awoken by the sound of camel farts in the street below your window."

Lucius delayed an answer as long as he could but Gaius moved in, his garlic breath too close for comfort. "I suppose I could-"

"Tribune!" Drusus walked up to Lucius. He was not wearing his uniform now but a simple white tunic with a blue cloak that hid his sword and dagger.

"Drusus?" Lucius was thankful for the interruption. Gaius huffed and crossed his arms, waiting.

"Tribune, your accommodation has been changed." He eyed Gaius, saw no threat. "The empress has arranged lodgings for you in a domus belonging to a relative of hers along the main thoroughfare in the south-east corner of the city."

"Whoa, ho!" Gaius whistled. "Friends in high places, Tribune? I didn't know that the empress had arranged lodgings for you already. I must go now but I have to insist that you join us for dinner in two days. Our villa is outside the eastern gate along the small road."

"I look forward to it. Thank you," Lucius conceded.

"See you then." Gaius turned as his wife yelled to him again. "I'm coming, I'm coming!"

"Who was that?" Drusus asked as he watched Gaius leave.

"A veteran I met on the ship. War stories," he sighed.

"I see. Well, now that that's over, let me take you to your lodgings and get you settled." The slaves picked up the chests and followed Drusus who pushed his way through the crowd. Lucius was getting hotter and hotter in his armour.

"Hey! It's the young tribune, Metellus!" somebody yelled and pointed at Lucius' armour.

"You're right! I remember him when I was in Sabratha," said another.

"I've heard about him. May the Gods love you, Tribune!" praised a third.

That was something Lucius had not expected and did not know how to receive. The incident in Sabratha in which he had been forced to decimate an entire unit of auxiliary cavalry who had treated with the enemy was an event that had earned him much honour from some, and hatred from others, particularly his father. Sabratha was still too fresh, like a wound that would not heal. He smiled politely, gave a shy wave here and there. Drusus looked nervous now as a part of the crowd began to cheer excitedly with shouts of praise for "Tribune Metellus!"

On the stairs of the temple, Gaius Fulvius Plautianus, prefect of the Praetorian Guard, looked down to see what the commotion was and then heard what the crowd was saying. He spotted Lucius' horsehair crest moving through the crowd, some people even throwing any remaining flowers in the air.

"What in Hades?" Plautianus muttered, descending a few steps and dismissing his officers. It was bad enough that the emperor should have attention from the crowd in Leptis Magna instead of him, but that a sniveling young tribune from a dried up family should be cheered? That was too much. He watched as Lucius and the baggage slaves followed a man through the crowd and past a row of chained galley slaves waiting to be herded onto one of the larger triremes.

As Lucius passed, one of the galley slaves looked at him in disbelief. The short, hunched, dark haired man with a scraggly dark beard and black eyes began to mumble inaudibly, then started to shriek and curse, pulling on the chains that attached him to the other slaves who recoiled either side of him.

"Tribune? Metellus?" The slave began to shake his head uncontrollably, trying to catch a glimpse of Lucius. "You son of a whore! I'll kill him! I'll kill him!" He was silenced by the slave master's whip that came slashing across his face. Blood dripped from re-opened cuts but the man still tried to yell. "Whoreson! I'll kill him!" The slave master kicked him hard in the groin this time and the slave fell unconscious to the ground.

"You there!" said Plautianus, approaching the slave master with two Praetorians behind him. "Yes you! What's all this about? Can't you control your slaves?" The slave master cowered at the sight of Plautianus, tall and imposing, his eyes penetrating.

"Prefect!" The man bowed. "I don't know what got into him. I think he's gone mad or something. He just started yelling."

"What did he yell?"

"I didn't hear it all but I think he was yelling obscenities at that officer that went by."

"The one with the crested helmet and fancy armour?"

"Yes, sir! That's the one. I think so, sir." Plautianus eyed the slave master then looked at the slave on the ground. He bent over and grabbed the unconscious man by the hair, pulled his head up to look at his face, then dropped it. Plautianus saw that Lucius had obviously not heard the commotion. He had followed that other man up the street. "Do you know this slave, sir?" the slave master asked.

"No. But I want you to unchain him. Now."

"But, sir-"

"Do it! Or I'll have you take his place." The man hurriedly signaled to his two helpers who unchained the slave. Plautianus turned to the two guards behind him. "Take this slave to the camp. Gag him, clap him in irons in a hole covered by a dark tent. Don't feed him. I'll deal with him later."

"Yes, sir!" The men saluted and Plautianus went with the rest of his guard to follow after the emperor, the black crest on his helm cutting excitedly through the crowd like a shark's fin through bloody water.

"Here it is," said Drusus as they arrived outside a large set of bronze doors. Lucius had noticed that despite the busy nature of the streets they had taken, the city was extremely clean and well-cared for. Shining monuments, perfectly paved roads and brilliant colours greeted the eye in every direction. There was a permanent breeze, slight but constant, a gift from the sea and the wind to the people of Leptis Magna.

In the private neighbourhoods where Lucius had been led, facades were richly adorned with beautiful flowers, wall paintings and elaborately detailed doors. Roman styles and fashions were the most common, but the local Punic traditions crept in subtly almost everywhere. There was also a distinct lack of graffiti, unlike in Rome where one was hard put to find an area that had not been defaced by political slogans, etchings of fans' favourite charioteer or the latest gladiator to make a name for himself. Lucius thought that the fact that there was no graffiti was because this was the emperor's home. Then again, he also wondered if it wasn't because of harsh penalties inflicted on anyone caught defacing public or private buildings or monuments.

"This seems like an awfully large place for just one person to be staying in, Drusus." Lucius looked up at the tall atrium ceiling and beyond to where a palm tree towered above the central garden. He could hear the clear sound of fresh, gurgling water.

"My Lady wanted you to be comfortable during your stay, Tribune."

"That reminds me, Drusus. Why is the empress doing all this for me? I haven't done anything to merit this special treatment." Lucius knew that he should have kept his thoughts to himself since he did not know the man before him all that well. But it was too late.

"Hmm." Drusus kept on opening shutters casually as he answered. "I suppose it is because you are one of the emperor's tribunes, a good one at that. Loyal. The emperor is very busy with affairs of state, dealings with the senate and this trip. He wouldn't be able to see that everyone was looked after, so he leaves some things up to the empress. That's all, as far as I can tell."

"Fair enough." Lucius followed him up a staircase to a cubiculum where the servants had left his belongings. The floor was covered with an ornate mosaic depicting daily life in Leptis Magna: merchants, olive pickers, exotic animals in the market and fishermen. The walls were decorated with painted date palms and sand dunes; a reminder of what lay farther south. "What is there to do here in Leptis Magna, Drusus? Have you been here before?"

"Yes, I've been once before. There is actually quite a lot to do. The theatre is very good and I think they have a series of Greek plays that will be performed in honour of the emperor's visit. The bath complex is very nice. By the way, if you need someone to train with I'd be happy to help out. Have the steward send for me. The markets are always interesting too but be ready for crowds. If you wish to go to the temples, they are in the old forum. The Temple of Hercules is impressive."

"Sounds good. I need to stay occupied."

"I don't blame you, Tribune." He turned to Lucius "You must miss your wife very much."

"Yes I do. Are you married?"

"I was once but...she was, ah...killed in a riot in Antioch."

"Gods. I'm sorry, Drusus. I didn't know." Lucius felt terrible and could now understand why this man dedicated all his time to the empress and her errands.

"Not your fault, Tribune. How were you to know?" He shook his head as if to shake off painful memories. "At any rate. There are several functions for high ranking officials such as yourself at the imperial residence and the new forum over the next few weeks. I'll let you know when they are. For now just enjoy yourself, rest after the long journey. The baths are just down the street opposite the front door."

"Thanks for your help. I'm sure you'd rather be doing other things than showing me around."

"Not at all." Drusus walked to the door to leave. "One more thing. There is a small kitchen staff in the house, sent by the empress to cater for you. She's got an army of cooks in addition to all her learned friends. They have their instructions and will make whatever you crave."

"Excellent." Lucius went back down to the atrium with Drusus where the door slave saw him out. "I guess I'll see you around, Drusus."

"Oh yes. Good evening, Tribune." Drusus disappeared into the crowded street, more easily than most because of his short stature.

Lucius turned and was met by the staff that had been left at his disposal. There were four men and four women, cooks, maids, a body servant and the door slave. He suddenly felt alone and cold without anyone to confide in. The servants all had their heads bowed. It was a bit disturbing, the only others in the house were silent. So, Lucius asked their names. After some shocked and confused looks, the servants raised their heads. The man who was evidently the steward because of his neat attire stepped forward. He looked Egyptian. Indeed most of the others were either Egyptian or Greek.

"Tribune. My name is Jabari and I am the steward." He turned to indicate the others down the line. "This is Oba who watches the door." Oba nodded respectfully. "There are Acis and Ishaq who will do any errands you require. They also fix things and light the fires in the evenings. Over there are Briseis, Naeemah and Kesi; they can cook anything you like." The women smiled shyly.

"I've no idea what to eat ladies. Surprise me with local specialities."

"That we can do very well, Tribune," said the one called Naeemah, a tall lanky Egyptian.

Jabari continued, "And on the end there is Talia. She will be your body servant." The young girl stepped forward. She was dark, about twenty years of age.

"I do not require a body servant," Lucius pointed out. The girl looked disappointed, as if she were chided for doing something wrong. He felt badly.

"Of course. Talia you will help me and the others as needed then."

"Yes, Jabari." The girl looked at Lucius. "Is it true that…" Jabari looked shocked at the interruption and gave her an angry look but Lucius waved him off.

"What is it, Talia?" Lucius asked. The girl looked at the others, embarrassed, but pressed on.

"I was just wondering if…well…are you the one people call the Desert Dragon who passed through here almost two years ago?"

"What?" Lucius was quite taken aback by this question and Jabari took it for anger.

"Talia!" Jabari yelled. "I'll have you whipped!"

"No! No, Jabari," Lucius interrupted. "That won't be necessary. I'm just surprised at what she said."

"Forgive her, Tribune. It's just that word has gone through the streets that you are here in Leptis Magna. Your deeds are well known in these parts."

"They are?" Lucius asked.

"Yes. And remembered fondly too. You saved many of our neighbours from the nomadic raiding parties from the interior."

"Then you are the young tribune people are talking about?" Talia asked again.

"Umm, yes. I am. They call me Desert Dragon?"

"Yes, Tribune!" replied Jabari who joined in the excitement. All eight slaves smiled now. "We are honoured to serve you while you are here." They all nodded their heads. "If you have need of anything, anything at all, please let us know and it shall be done immediately."

"Thank you. I'm fine for now."

"As you wish," Jabari said. "If you like, dinner can be served in either the triclinium or the second garden in a couple of hours."

"The garden is fine. I'm going to rest until then."

"As you wish." Lucius turned to go upstairs to his cubiculum. Behind him he could hear them whispering excitedly.

Two hours later, Lucius emerged from his room, rested and lighter without his armour; he wore his blue and gold tunic and carried the bundle with his sword in it. The house seemed too big for just one man, too isolated, the surroundings foreign. However, the smells emanating from the kitchens cheered him. Now that he had rested, he found he was also famished, curious as to what the servants had prepared.

Jabari met him at the bottom of the stairs and led him through to the back garden which was even larger than the first. In the centre was a large pool lined with pink marble surrounded by a space of grass. On the grass, a plush couch had been laid out in front of a wide, low table. A few oil lamps burned to one side of the couch while on the other was a small pedestal table with a basin of fresh water and citrus oils for washing.

The pool of water was surrounded by young, delicate olive trees. Beyond that was a circular path lined with reddish stone that went around the garden. Directly behind the path, lining the peristylum were lemon and lime trees, their tangy fragrance enlivening the air. Because of all the trees, Lucius had complete privacy where he ate.

When Briseis, Kesi and Naeemah brought out the food, Lucius was delighted with the magnificence of the feast they had created. All of the red dinnerware was the finest Samian. Platters of various delicacies were brought out; shellfish covered in local garum and fresh herbs, rolled wheat mixed with lentils, boiled chicken stuffed with olives and onions. There was also a platter of local dates, figs and grapes that went well with the goat's cheese that had been put out. To wash it all down, a large silver pitcher of Cretan wine had been placed on the table. All that was missing was company. Lucius dined alone, knowing that he would never finish all the food. He certainly tried as it was too good to waste.

When the moon rose up in the sky and let its blue light fall down to the earth in a cascading coruscation, he thought of Adara. They should be in Brundisium by now. It seemed that he had been gone from her for an age. In fact, it seemed an age since he had last been in Africa Proconsularis. Not even two years ago! He could not believe it. He was between worlds at the moment, adrift in a dark sea. Odysseus indeed.

"What have I done?" He was alone on the other side of the empire, friendless, loveless. Now he discovered that he was well remembered, that everyone knew he was in Leptis Magna. He looked up at the moon again and it seemed to transform into Adara's face. He felt for the sword next to him and remembered when she gave it to him. The peace of Cumae filled his thoughts. Then, unwanted thoughts of the Sibyl broke into his reverie.

He shook his head, looked at the pitcher of wine and filled his cup again. The following months were going to be difficult; he was not ready to deal with it, not yet. He filled his cup again, then again. Leaning back on the couch, he gazed sad and glassy-eyed at the sky's waxing orb.

"Adara..." he whispered into the air. "I miss you..." A gentle breeze ruffled the olive and citrus leaves in the garden, encircling Lucius as he nodded off. At that moment, far away on a ship bound for Corinth, Adara sat on deck looking up at that same moon, whispering back and asking Venus to watch over her beloved.

The goddess had heard the plea of her favourite youths and went to Lucius on a caressing breeze to watch over him where he lay. She felt for them in their sadness, covered the garden with dewy droplets of lamentation while across the night sky Far-Shooting Apollo set stars to burning flight across the heavens.

Being back in Leptis Magna, home, Septimius Severus was in a perfectly beatific state of mind and body. He had forgotten how good the dry desert air was for him, how memories long past could be renewed by the sight of a certain plant, the smell of a certain street. Even the stars shone more brightly in Leptis Magna.

Julia Domna reclined on a couch, resplendent in a Tyrian purple stola with gold trim, her dark hair tightly braided in its usual manner. She watched her husband walk around the large fountain located in the centre of the second storey, open-air room.

"Husband," she called to him. "I know you are feeling better in this climate, but do be careful. The physicians said that you must take things slowly, especially with all of the public appearances you have planned." The emperor kept on walking.

"Oh Julia, come now! I haven't felt this good since before my illness. I have conquered many a warlike adversary, I can certainly conquer my own ailing feet!"

"You are hopelessly delinquent." She shook her head in feigned dismay. The emperor laughed, then started to cough.

"Ah, but you love your emperor nevertheless, do you not?"

"Yes. But as a wife it is also my duty to care for my husband." Julia Domna smiled lovingly at him, a man who trusted her with great responsibility. Despite rumours to the contrary, she loved the emperor dearly and was loyal to him, only him. It caused her great pain however, to be second to and overshadowed by Plautianus. Leptis Magna was his home as well, the people liked him, but did not love him. For the moment, Julia Domna had decided to bide her time and protect her husband in the shadows, ready, until an opportunity arose. When that might be, only the Gods knew. She was patient.

"Mother, would you please stop chiding him!" barked Caracalla from where he and Geta were playing a game of Tabula.

"I can fight my own battles, Marcus!" the emperor said to Caracalla from across the room.

"I prefer it if you call me Caracalla, father. You know that!" he said, his eyes still on the gaming board.

"Ha! I'm not going to address you after a piece of clothing! Your name is Marcus Aurelius Antoninus."

"Be still, Caracalla. You are upsetting your father," put in the empress.

"You're not helping much!" said the emperor as he came over.

"I win!" Geta yelled. "That's five in a row. Hand over that new Sarmatian bay you bought."

"Ach! You cheat, Geta!" Caracalla sat back and slugged his wine. "I'm finished playing."

"Suit yourself, brother. But your horse is still mine."

"You can have the horse but you'll still look like an ass Geta."

"That's enough, both of you!" chided their mother. "By Baal! One would think you were twelve years old again! Husband come. Our horoscopes are finished." The emperor came and reclined on the couch next to his wife in front of the small table where their astrologer sat.

"Well? What do they say?" asked Severus. The old man, a Syrian with a long curly beard, had been waiting patiently.

"For you, Emperor, the stars show great favour. It is a time of rejoicing. Words of love will come from the people's lips. The sun shines brightly on your city and threat from the outside will be easily crushed. Political changes ahead may not all be well received, but they will be adhered to. A great campaign is in the wind, in the future."

"That sounds promising. Is that all?"

"Yes, sire. That is all." He turned to Julia Domna. "For the empress, the sun's rays feel cool but light the way nevertheless. A new star will aid you if its light is harnessed and kept safe. You are a protector. People know your value and will know more as time and the stars tell it."

"Those were not as good as your last readings. Disappointing at best." The empress rose to walk around the fountain herself.

"My lady, the stars were out-shined this night, the skies weeping."

"It never rains this time of year," Caracalla insisted.

"It was a storm in the firmament, Caesar."

"Your work is done," the emperor said as he stood slowly. He was not exactly happy with that particular astrologer and dismissed him until another day.

"I will await your bidding, sire." The man gathered his things and backed his way out of the room, bowing.

"I don't know why you and mother believe in these astrologers so much, Father. They never make any sense and only speak in riddles."

"Because Marcus, the stars are ever our guide and those destined to lead must abide by them, listen to them. It is the Gods' way of speaking to us." The emperor snapped his fingers and a slave came running with his cloak. "I'm going now. I've asked Plautianus to apprise me of the situation with the Guard and the exploratory campaign into the interior. Apparently some of the nomadic tribes are raiding again."

"I thought Tribune Metellus had taken care of all that," Geta said sarcastically. Caracalla looked annoyed .

"He did, Geta, and very well too. That was a conspiracy. My scouts tell me that these latest raids are not connected at all. Just some goat raiding and a villa or two burned here and there. But, these rebels must be quelled, utterly crushed so that other groups do not rise up, thinking they are protected by the desert."

"Do you want me to come along with you, father?" Caracalla asked. He wanted to keep an eye on Plautianus, listen to what poison he poured into the emperor's ear. His mother looked their way when she heard this.

"Absolutely not! I know how you two are at odds." Caracalla thought his father did not know the half of it. "You can tend to your own affairs. Like Plautilla. Plautianus tells me his daughter is very unhappy in your marriage."

"Does he now?" Caracalla frowned, disgusted, angry.

"You're making things difficult for me by neglecting your wife, Marcus."

"She's a bore, father, and a bitch to boot!"

"That's enough! See to it!" The emperor stormed out of the garden with two more slaves running after him. Julia Domna came back to the couch and reclined.

"I'm off to the baths," Geta said merrily as he rose and left. The empress turned to Caracalla.

"It would be wise, my son, if you didn't always speak your mind. Who knows how many spies Plautianus has within the walls."

"I can't stand the woman."

"I know. She's abhorrent but your father married you to her because he wanted to keep Plautianus loyal."

"Pff!" Caracalla spat. "Loyal! He's an animal. He'd have a dagger in father's back if he could."

"As I've said before, we must bide our time. Plautianus is too power hungry and sure of himself and his popularity. He will make a mistake and when that moment comes…"

"We'll be ready," Caracalla finished.

"Yes." She poured herself some wine. "Now go to your wife, smile and use her however you wish, but on your way out send Drusus to me. He's waiting outside."

He got up, kissed his mother on the cheek and left, flinging his long cloak about his shoulders.

Drusus had been waiting for some time in the corridor to give his report to the empress. He was not bothered however, never was. Having lost his wife early on, he believed that life could never get any worse. When he had been drafted as a personal bodyguard and spy by Julia Domna, he had decided to dedicate his life to the task.

Though a short man, Drusus was strong as an ox and as quick as a tiger. His stature was more of a misleading guise than a weakness. When Caracalla told him to go in, Drusus found the room empty except for the empress. She never wanted any slaves around when she was speaking with him on matters of great secrecy and import.

She sat on her couch, calmness and serenity juxtaposed with a stern business-like look in her brown eyes. "Come here, Drusus," she called to him and he made his way over. "You look tired."

"My Lady." He bowed low before her. She motioned for him to sit on the couch directly opposite.

"What do you have to report?"

"Much, my Lady. I've been gathering information since we arrived."

"Go on."

"I have taken Tribune Metellus to the domus where your servants were awaiting us. He is settled in but is lonely and feels isolated. He is wondering why he should deserve such special treatment. I told him what you told me to say."

"Did he believe you?"

"Yes. Definitely. He is ignorant of politics and how things work. He's a soldier and that's all he seems to know about."

"Any talk of his family?"

"He spoke of his wife briefly but that is all. Nothing about the father."

"Very well. Go on."

"I have a man outside the domus in case Metellus goes anywhere. I also told the tribune that if he wanted to train with me at the baths he could let me know through the steward. He also asked what there was to do in the city and I told him about the theatre, the markets and the temples."

"If he does any of those things, have him followed or make sure you bump into him there."

"Yes, my Lady. I also mentioned that there might be some official gatherings to which he might be invited."

"That is fine but say no more of these for the time being. I want him to feel isolated a little longer. I will give you invitations to take to him when the time comes."

"Of course." Drusus was feeling slightly sorry for Lucius then. He liked him; the tribune did not put on any airs like most other Equestrian tribunes. "There are a couple of complications too." The empress lifted her head to look directly at Drusus.

"What?"

"He has met a veteran centurion on the voyage who has invited him to dine with him at his villa outside the eastern walls."

"Is he a threat?"

"No. Just an old soldier with a wife who henpecks him. Nothing to worry about."

"Keep an eye on him nevertheless." She pressed her bronze stylus to her lips in thought. "What else?"

"I went back to the harbour to gather some information and meet with my men. When I was there many people were talking about the Tribune Metellus."

"What were they saying about him?"

"It seems that he is quite famous in these parts because of that incident in Sabratha and the patrol he led. When I was leading him out of the harbour several people started to cheer and bless him until a large part of the crowd was praising him."

"How did he take it?"

"Oh, he was surprised, even embarrassed. He waived politely to some of the people who threw flowers at him."

"Does my son know about this?"

"I don't believe so, my Lady."

"Let's keep it that way if we can."

"Yes, my Lady." Drusus bowed his head. "There is one more thing…"

"Tell me."

"When the crowd cheered Metellus…Plautianus was on the Temple of Jupiter's steps. He saw and heard the whole thing."

"By the Gods of sun, moon and stars." She kept her voice calm but Drusus noticed her fist clench tightly. She was worried. "This is not good, Drusus."

"No, my Lady. I asked around the crowd about what had happened and some people said that there was a large disturbance with some galley slave yelling obscenities at the tribune and threatening to kill him. It must have been after we left the harbour because I never heard or saw a thing. People said that Plautianus had some words with the slave driver in charge. I tried to find the man to see what the prefect had wanted but he had gone with his slaves before I returned."

"This is extremely odd. We must be careful and be on the lookout. See what else you can find out about the slave driver and Plautianus' conversation. He's up to something, I know it." This last sentence was spoken more to herself than to Drusus.

"I shall do what I can, my Lady."

"Good. In the meantime, keep a close watch on Metellus. I don't want any harm coming to him or too much public attention around him. Plautianus' gaze must be led away from the tribune to keep him safe."

"I understand, my Lady. It's not safe with almost the entire Praetorian Guard outside the city."

"Precisely." She handed him a pouch of sestertii, the usual amount required for any bribing he needed to do. Obtaining information could be a costly undertaking. "Be careful, Drusus, and report as soon as you have any news. I shall send for you."

"Yes, my Lady." Drusus bowed, turned and walked to the door.

Julia Domna paced around the fountain several times to gather her thoughts. Around every corner Plautianus threatened to obstruct her, her plans. Lucius was but one possible ally she needed to woo. She had many such plots that were all, as she saw it, for the good of the emperor and the empire. The thought of being beaten by the prefect of the Praetorian Guard was too much. They could not afford another all-powerful demigod in charge of the Guard, for that is how Plautianus saw himself.

Once she had collected herself, the empress called for her slave who came out of an adjacent door.

"Send in Aemilius Papinianus and Domitius Ulpianus." The slave hurried off to fetch them. Papinian was a kinsman of hers from Emesa and a libellis to herself and her husband. Ulpian was his student, a jurist from Tyre. Both men were loyal to her and the emperor and both had a strong sense of equality that went with a strong hatred of Plautianus.

II

VINUM ET MUSA

'Wine and the Muse'

To Adara Antonina Metella
From Tribune Lucius Metellus Anguis

My beautiful wife,

You are most likely not in Athens yet, but I wanted to write to you so that you will have word from me upon your arrival. I know that it has only been two weeks since we parted, but I feel as though it has been many, many months.

Firstly, let me assure you that I am well and, though lonely, keeping busy. The journey to Leptis Magna was uneventful. On board I was befriended by an old centurion named Gaius. He can talk like Hades but is kind-hearted. He and his wife live in Leptis Magna and have had me over to their villa to dine with them several times. It is probably good that I am alone, as I have been eating quite a bit of garlic lately.

The city is quite beautiful and I am staying in a large domus along one of the main streets. The empress has arranged it for me. Actually, I do have one companion here. Drusus, our bodyguard from the journey to Cumae. He was to accompany the empress to Africa and she assigned him to show me around. We have been training on the palaestra together quite often which is good as I need to prepare myself for drilling my troops again.

Something odd happened. When I arrived at the harbour in Leptis Magna, some of the populace recognised me and cheered me. I don't have to tell you how shocked I was by this. I seem to be known and admired by a great many people. I have to admit this makes me uncomfortable much of the time.

I've taken to putting on a hooded cloak when I go out, despite the heat.

I have not been to the desert yet; though I feel its pull. The moon here is so different, feels different. One thing is the same: my thoughts of you whenever I look up at it or the sun. You are ever in my thoughts and prayers. Are you looking up at the moon every night, my love? I think you are because I can feel you closer then, hear your voice in my ear as you whisper me to sleep. At least I can see you in my dreams. That is one comfort.

In two days I am going to the imperial residence in Leptis Magna for a large banquet. All of the city officials and military officers are going, in addition to most of the region's prosperous merchants. I am not looking forward to it, but my presence has been requested. One of the few duties I still have at the moment. I wish you were at my side but it was my decision to come alone and I must deal with it.

Did you visit Delphi on your way to Athens? If you received any wisdom for me, a sign, please tell me. I could use some guidance. Daily I go over the Sibyl's words in my mind and they confuse me more and more.

I suppose I should stop writing though I could go on. I pray to Apollo and Venus that you are safe always and that our time apart will be brief. Do not worry about me Adara. I am safe and nothing seems to be amiss. I am prepared for whatever awaits me in Lambaesis. Thoughts of you and our love keep me strong and unafraid.

Please give my love to Alene. Tell her I am also sending a letter to our mother. Greetings also to your family, Emrys and Carissa, and please comfort Ashur with the fact that I am safe. Tell him I will speak his name to the desert soon. For you my beautiful wife, I send all of my love to you on swift winds, my heart to yours on one of Apollo's silver arrows. Continue to whisper to the night sky for me and know that I am yours forever. I will write again.

Your husband, Lucius.

Lucius rolled the papyrus, sealed it and put it next to the letter for his mother. Jabari had told him that the imperial mail and military correspondence went out the following day and that he could have it run down to the docks. Having written his letters, Lucius put his hooded cloak on over his tunic and went to the baths to exercise and wash his body; they were not usually crowded that time of day. It was also the time that Drusus habitually went too, when they would train together.

It was on that particular day that Drusus handed Lucius an invitation from the emperor and empress to attend an imperial banquet. At first, Lucius was not sure he wanted to go. Drusus pointed out however, that it would be an affair to remember with many important guests. Lucius conceded as he had been feeling extremely lonely locked away in the house. Besides, Drusus had said he would be there as well. Perhaps some friendly interaction with others would do him some good?

The day before the banquet, the imperial cooks and slaves had been in the markets of Leptis Magna buying out every fruit and vegetable stand, all the fishermen and meat sellers. Every amphora of fine wine was procured, as well as olive oil, and the best garum sauce. The army of chefs laden with provisions returning to the imperial residence was like a desert caravan all its own. There were even a few Praetorians overseeing the shopping to ensure everything went smoothly.

Where the triumphal banquet in Rome had been an event that was meant to impress upon everyone the emperor's greatness, this banquet was meant to be enjoyed by all like the final sips of a sweet nectar at the bottom of a golden cup. The emperor's aim was to illustrate his generosity, coupled with his greatness, to his countrymen and his clients.

Lucius sifted hurriedly through his wardrobe for his toga but could not find it. Drusus was arriving shortly and had said that because of the various entrances to the imperial complex he would show him the way. As Lucius had become used to his presence he thought it a friendly gesture.

"Jabari!" Lucius called out of his door. The steward came running. He had grown fond of the tribune and had come to see it as his honoured duty to look after their guest.

"Yes, Tribune?

"Where is my toga? It's gone missing."

"Oh, please forgive me, Tribune! I thought I had told you. It had become quite wrinkled during your voyage, so I had Talia clean and press it for this evening. I thought that you would want it."

"Very thoughtful of you Jabari, but where is it?"

"Here it is, master Anguis." Talia came rushing in the door with a neatly folded bundle and laid it on the bed.

"Ah. Good. Thank you. That'll be all."

"We'll leave you to ready yourself, Tribune." Jabari led Talia out of the room. She turned as he led her, admiring the work she had done cutting his hair. Lucius had complained of the heat and how his lengthening hair was making him too hot. When Jabari told him that Talia was good at barbering, Lucius agreed and now felt much more at ease in the heat.

It had been a long time since he had arranged his toga by himself and it took some time to get it almost correct. Alene had always helped him before, and then Adara. It seemed that women inevitably had an eye for arranging a toga just so. On an impulse, Lucius tucked his dagger securely inside the folds of his clothing. When Jabari called through the door that Drusus had arrived, Lucius went downstairs. The slaves had all lined up to see him out. They had adopted this custom for some reason. Lucius came down the stairs awkwardly, a fold of his toga falling over his tunic sleeve beneath.

"Drusus! How are you?"

"I am fine, Tribune. Are you ready?"

"Not sure. I can't seem to get this one fold correctly."

"Ha! Ha! I've never been able to do it either," Drusus laughed.

"Can any of you help me with this?" Lucius asked the smiling entourage. Briseis, Kesi and Talia stepped up and began fiddling with the toga as Lucius raised his arms horizontally. After a few moments of tucking, folding and careful draping, it was perfect. "Why, thank you ladies. I don't know how you did it, but thank you." They all smiled.

"We must be going." Drusus went to the door where Oba was holding it open for them.

"Right. Let's go." He nodded to the slaves and they went out into the street. The sky was reddening above as the day neared its end and they walked down the main street and turned north beneath the emperor's four-sided arch.

"The household slaves seem to have taken quite a liking to their new master," Drusus said as they walked.

"I suppose they have."

"I heard one of them refer to you as Anguis. Why is that?"

"Anguis is my cognomen. Lucius Metellus Anguis. It means Dragon."

"It's a very unusual name."

"It's thanks to my unusual grandfather, I suppose. He was very superstitious and, when I was born, insisted that I be given our true ancestral name." Lucius paused, his mind drifting, scanning the mysterious tales told in his youth. "It's a long story and not one I fully understand. Anyway, the slaves remember an incident I was involved in on a patrol through this region. That, along with my name and the unusual armour I wear, seem to have tickled their imaginations."

"More than that I think," Drusus added. "I've heard many people talking about the incident. What do you think of all this attention?"

"I don't think anything of it. I was doing my duty for the emperor and Rome at the time and that's all. To be honest I don't really want all the attention."

He is naïve, thought Drusus, *but honest and loyal.* "I suppose that fame, in whatever form, is more of a burden than anything."

"I guess so. I'm just glad I'm a soldier."

40

Drusus did not say anything more as they were about to arrive at the imperial villa. There were Praetorians everywhere, at the doorways, and in the surrounding streets. Drusus told one of the guards Lucius' name and they went with the rest of the guests.

The smell of food wafted through the long, marble corridors of the complex, dancing in and out of the nostrils to the soft tune of clinking cups and wine jugs as slaves went about pouring drinks for the mass of guests. This was evidently a more intimate affair than the previous imperial banquet in Rome; intimate because there were so many guests in a much smaller building than the palace on the Palatine.

Unlike an imperial banquet in Rome, this was a distinctly African affair. The walls were draped with beautifully coloured silks that fluttered in the breeze created by the current of guests making their way to the large garden. They would dine there beneath the stars, until the moon was high and bright. The colours, the smells and the general buzz of excited chatter reminded Lucius of the dye markets of Alexandria. As he followed Drusus, he felt many hands patting him on the back or shoulders. Evidently, people here had recognised him as well.

The enormous garden looked like the Field of Mars in the past, when quaestors would give feasts for the populace. People were not seated on couches but rather on mounds of richly decorated pillows and rugs that surrounded massive bronze dishes where the food would be served. There were perhaps a hundred such dishes with fifteen to twenty guests at each one. The largest mound of pillows, rugs and a few couches was naturally reserved for the imperial family and honoured guests, relatives of the emperor, and a few of the richest merchants. Surrounding Julia Domna was, of course, her usual entourage of learned men already engaged in heated philosophical discussions.

In the centre of the garden was a large round fountain with a sculpture of some Jupiter-like god, more eastern, holding up a monstrous dish. The god seemed to stand on the waves created by the flow of water, his muscles strained by the weight he held aloft. In the dish above his thickly curled hair, a blazing fire had been set so that it looked as though he was holding up the sun itself. As Lucius fell back among the cushions and rugs of his particular grouping, he noticed that the fountain's statue resembled the emperor slightly, although it was intended to be the Sun God Baal for whom the empress' father, Julius Bassianus had been high priest.

Horns rang out and Septimius Severus, with the help of his sons, rose to address his guests. The chattering mass of people fell silent as the emperor, their kinsman, stepped forward.

"Welcome to all of you, my dear friends, my family! It is good to be home again!" Everyone clapped and cheered. "This feast is for you! I want all of you to enjoy yourselves as my guests. Though I have been away for far too long, know that I have never ceased to think about the land where I was born, nor the people who bore me." He held up a bowl-like silver goblet. I drink to Liber Pater! Baal! Hercules and all of you! Leptis Magna!" The crowd rose and drank with him and then he spoke some words in Punic that Lucius and many Roman guests could not understand. The crowd loved it. As soon as he had finished, the emperor clapped his hands and the parade of food began from all corners of the garden.

The villa itself was an overflowing cornucopia. All courses were brought out at the same time and were constantly replenished. Lucius sat with Drusus and a couple of merchants, an augur, and some of his fellow military tribunes. The tribunes did not talk with him much, bored of hearing about him in the streets, and so they talked among themselves about how much longer they had to serve in the army before making it to the senate. When one of them asked Lucius what his plans were, he replied that he was content being a military tribune and had no wish to enter into politics. They turned up their noses and went back to their own private conversations. This did not go unnoticed by Drusus who was speaking politely with the augur, a relatively young one who had just come to Leptis Magna from Iberia. Lucius was not unused to such rudeness from his Equestrian peers, as most of the young men of his class aspired to a life of politics that would see them safely installed in their family homes in Rome. Military service for most of them was a stepping stone to greater things and more money. It had been so for his own father as well. Sometimes Lucius felt like the sole Equestrian dissenter.

When the slaves came with the food, Lucius and Drusus both swallowed hard at the explosive array of oddities before them. On one side of the dish was food from the sea; twenty types of cooked fish with herbs, grilled octopi and squid all covered with Leptis garum. On the other side of the dish in front of Lucius were piles of camel and goat meat prepared in a variety of ways and complimented with rolled grains. The fish and the meats were separated by bowls of ten varieties of olives, breads, dates stuffed with chicken livers, grapes, figs and oranges from Mauretania. Lucius would have tucked in eagerly but he was prevented from doing so by the camel head staring back at him from the top of the mound.

"Hmmm. I love these!" said one of the merchants as he reached over, plucked out one of the eyes with a skewer and bit it in half. Lucius averted his eyes quickly as the juice skirted all over the man's tunic. He reached for some fish and fruit instead just as the entertainment began.

The evening was to flow in conjunction with music, acrobatics and dancing performed by various groups. The first was a group of Nubian dancers and musicians who ushered themselves into the garden with an explosion of drumming that turned everyone's heads. Lean, muscled men with great feathered head-dresses pounded rhythmically with their bare hands as a group of naked women whirled and shook among the guests. Their skin was black and they stood almost seven feet in height. They mesmerised the gathering with their agility and exotic beauty.

Their dance reached heightened excitement when several Nubian men, dressed in lion skins and carrying long deadly spears, pounced into the garden as though hunting the naked dancers. The drum beats grew more intense, more driven, until finally the hunters had caught their prey and carried them off the scene in a rush of applause and thunder.

"Now that was something!" said Drusus, standing behind Lucius.

"Where did you get off to?"

"Just mingling. My legs were getting cramped. Look! I've heard this next group before. They're quite good." Drusus sat back down with a plate of goat meat and grapes as they watched and listened.

The soft sounds of a lyre, flutes, and the gentle tapping of a tambourine floated through the smoke-filled air. Diners craned their necks for a better view of the Greek troupe from Apollonia. Their soothing music seemed to tame the wild revellers the same as a menacing beast and all were calmed by the sight of the dancers when they appeared. There were nine of them, all young muses, all beautiful, all unearthly in their apparition. They were barefoot and wore only a very thin stola each, revealing flashes of supple skin when passing in front of firelight. They resembled butterflies as they danced, or swaying lilies in a mountain breeze. Heads of long gold, brown and red silky hair moved serpent-like, held by silver circlets with a single white feather around their foreheads. They moved in and around the guests, floating on air, and after pausing in front of the imperial gathering, they departed as they had arrived, like downy plumes on a gentle breath of Spring.

When they had gone, slaves came out once again to replenish the food and drink so that plates were not left empty, and wine continued to flow freely past everyone's lips. The usual reception line began to form of guests approaching the emperor to thank him as their host. Drusus tapped Lucius on the shoulder.

"Come, Tribune. We should thank our host."

"Right. I'd almost forgotten." Lucius rose uneasily to his feet. His legs were asleep.

The line moved quickly enough. For some reason, these reception lines always made him nervous. Being under the eyes of so many powerful people at once was unnerving, but he had learned to hide his discomfort well. The emperor was flanked by Julia Domna and Plautianus where they sat in the centre of the gathering. To the right were the prefect's kinsmen, clients and some of his Praetorian tribunes. On the left were Caracalla and his wife Plautilla, unhappy and scowling as usual, Geta, Aemilius Papinianus, Julius Paulus and Domitius Ulpianus the jurists. Also there, were Julia Maesa with her husband Julius Avitus Alexianus and their girls, Julia Soaemias and Julia Mamaea. Lucius concentrated on the emperor and empress.

Drusus nodded to Julia Domna as they approached. Plautianus, deep in conversation with another, saw Lucius approach and it seemed as though fire kindled in his relentless eyes. Lucius averted his gaze and looked only to the emperor and empress, bowed and offered his thanks for their hospitality.

"Ah! Tribune. It seems you are well known here." Plautianus suddenly broke off his conversation before Lucius could leave. The empress kept her calm.

"Prefect." Lucius bowed very slightly. He didn't like Plautianus; such a feeling of darkness emanated from him.

"People in the streets are speaking your name, Metellus. Is that not strange?"

"I do not have ears for talk in the streets, Prefect. I have heard the names of our emperor, our empress and of yourself spoken often enough and with great praise." Lucius stood up tall, having had enough of being cowed by Plautianus in front of everyone. He bowed his head to the emperor and empress.

"Never was such praise more fitting than in your honour. Thank you for allowing me to be a small part of your visit to Leptis Magna. This city shines like a jewel by the sea."

Well said young Metellus! thought Julia Domna as she met Lucius' gaze. *Go now before he questions you further.*

"Tribune Metellus," Plautianus began again. "I am happy that you are pleased with my home." He had a knack for sarcasm. "You must tell your father about it the next time you write to him." The tension rose as the empress became agitated by Plautianus' sly attack. Lucius wondered why he was mentioning his father so publicly.

"Tribune Metellus! Welcome." Caracalla had seen what Plautianus was about and decided to call him over. Lucius bowed once more to the emperor, empress and the prefect before going over to Caracalla. "Are you enjoying my father's home?"

"Yes, sire," Lucius replied, still wondering where to go and what to say. In the background he spotted Drusus. "It is a beautiful city, quite amazing really."

"I suppose it is! Though I much prefer Rome, it's always nice to come back here for a time." Caracalla rose and went over to his aunt Julia. "I don't believe you have met my aunt, Julia Maesa. Matertera, this is Tribune Lucius Metellus."

Lucius had forgotten how striking Julia Maesa was. He bowed to her and her family. She wore a bright yellow stola with a green silk shawl about her shoulders. Elaborate gold jewellery hung from her ears and from around her neck to drop between her breasts and out of sight. Her dark hair was more loosely bound than her sister's but was still tied up and combed in a wavy fashion, the way winds comb the sands during the night.

"Good evening, Tribune. I don't believe we have ever been properly introduced." She dipped her finger in her wine cup and sucked it dry. The action was very distracting to Lucius, as was Caracalla's silent laughter.

"It is an honour to meet you Lady Julia, Julius Avitus Alexianus, ladies." He bowed his head to Julia Maesa's husband and their two giggling young girls.

"Are you enjoying yourself at the banquet?" she asked.

"Yes, Lady. Very much." They stared lazily at Lucius, making him uncomfortable.

"That is all, Tribune," she suddenly said.

"Oh, of course. Sire, lady Julia." Lucius backed away and went back to his seat, relieved to be done with that. Drusus soon joined him.

"Don't worry about Julia Maesa, Tribune. She's a bit odd at times. I know her. She likes you."

"Funny way of showing it. I felt like an idiot standing there." Lucius was really annoyed but held back any more comments.

"Here." Drusus handed him his cup. "Drink, forget. There is one more act on the agenda tonight." Drusus really did feel sorry for Lucius and how they were playing with him, observing him like chattel at the slave market.

In front of the emperor stood a single man dressed in a long brown robe. He looked like a suppliant of some sort but then Severus bid him turn to face the crowd. There was a hush unlike any other as the simple man moved to begin. When his mouth opened, out came a sound of sadness and longing in a language nearly forgotten. The tone of his voice rose and fell, ululating in what can only be described as an heroic keening for something long gone. He was singing in Punic, the language of Africa Province before the advent of Rome and the final defeat of Carthage almost four hundred years before. Though he could not understand it, the song made Lucius want to weep. All around him people connected with something inward. The man did it with such ease, reached such tones and portrayed such emotion that Lucius wondered which god was speaking through him.

When the man finished, the emperor rose and embraced him to great applause. Drusus then told Lucius he had heard that the man was singing an ancient Punic song about the desert and all that had befallen his people from before the time of Queen Dido to the sad fall of Carthage. Though Severus was Emperor of Rome, he too had connected with the song of his countryman. What a strange destiny that should lead a man of Punic descent to the throne of the most powerful empire the world had ever known. The Gods did indeed have a sense of humour and justice. *It is ironic too,* thought Lucius, *that some of my ancestors were responsible for the final downfall of Carthage. Now I find myself in the land of the people they had overcome.*

By the time everyone had finished eating, drinking and talking, the night was already nearing its end. The streets were busy with people returning to their homes to sleep off the copious amounts of wine they had consumed. Lucius finally decided to go and rose from his seat. He wanted to be alone with his thoughts and so, pushing his way through the departing guests, he began to make his way up the street and back to the domus. Drusus had noticed too late that Lucius had gone and rushed out to find him.

The street Lucius had taken was between the eastern wall of the bath complex and the city wall. The early morning air from the sea began to clear his head of wine and smoke and he was feeling better when he heard a woman's screams up ahead. He ran up the street and peered around a corner where he saw one of the Greek muses from the banquet being attacked by what looked like an off duty Praetorian. He immediately thought of Plautianus and his anger rose.

The trooper was drunk and ripping away the young girl's clothing to take her in the street. She screamed and he slapped her hard across the face. She sobbed as he prepared to mount her.

Apollo give me strength! Lucius rushed out of the shadows and ran headlong into the man, sending both rolling off to the side and into a wall. The trooper didn't know what had hit him but he found his blade and started waving it around wildly. One swing got away from him, and he spun so that his back was to Lucius who took the opportunity and jumped behind him, locking his forearm around his neck to crush his throat. He tried stabbing at Lucius but missed.

Down the street, Drusus saw from afar what was happening and ran to intervene. He was too late. The trooper elbowed Lucius in the stomach so hard that he was knocked back against the wall, winded. The Praetorian turned, full of rage, his face red from the choke-hold and charged Lucius with his blade out. From the fold of his toga Lucius found the handle of his dagger, pulled it out and threw it in one swift motion from his chest so that it found its target in the man's sternum with a thump. So great was the assailant's momentum that he crashed into the wall head first and cracked his skull open on the stonework.

"Tribune! Are you all right?" Drusus came running up breathless.

Lucius ignored him and looked to where the girl had been huddled. She was gone. Not a trace of her remained, no blood or torn clothing, no hair.

"By Apollo! What's happening here?" Lucius hunched down against the wall, exhausted. His head spun and he vomited.

Drusus turned the man over and looked at him despairingly. "He's a Praetorian," he said hoarsely. "We have to get out of here." He didn't answer. "Lucius, let's go!" He pulled Lucius' dagger out of the man's chest, wiped it, and gave it back to Lucius who had by now picked himself up off the ground.

"Where's the girl?" Lucius muttered.

"What girl? Who?" Drusus thought Lucius was delirious.

"The girl! One of the muses from the banquet. He was going to rape her."

"Doesn't matter now, my friend. Let's just get out of here. If the guards find us like this we're both dead men." Drusus helped Lucius and they went swiftly around the corner.

When they entered the domus, Drusus told Jabari not to ask any questions, that Lucius had fallen and that was all. Once the two of them had taken Lucius upstairs and put him into his bed, Jabari led Drusus to the room next door where he could spend the night. He was happy for it to be over but as he wavered on the edge of sleep all he could hear was Lucius mumbling in the room next door.

"Apollo, Apollo. Where did she go? Muse. Adara, Adara!" Lucius muttered incoherently.

The sun rose not long after they had gotten Lucius to bed, where he slept much of the day away. Meanwhile, out in the streets beneath the sun, people were talking about the body of a Praetorian that had been discovered that morning. Troops scoured the lanes for clues or witnesses but none were to be found. The conversation of the day was an odd mixture of talk about murder, how magnificent a banquet it had been the night before, and how gracious an emperor Septimius Severus was. Plautianus was furious.

III

TREPIDATIO

'Trepidation'

The Praetorian camp that had been raised to the south of Leptis Magna was dark and silent in the stillness of the African night. While many troops slept in their tents, others kept the watch. Those off duty would go into town to carouse and gamble at the inns and brothels; the city walls contained any raucous noise so that only the swaying branches of tall palms and the crackling of fires between the rows of tents could be heard.

In a dark corner of the camp, behind a small walled enclosure, two Praetorians stood watch outside of a tent entrance. Their orders were to guard the tent-covered pit and the prisoner inside. No one was to approach without the watchword except the prefect. The two men leaned on their spears as they talked about the incident two nights before when one of their own men was murdered inside the city walls.

The Praetorians were in an uproar and the prefect was merciless in his search for the culprit. Several slaves had been tortured but they were not any closer to finding out the identity of the murderer. The men returning from the brothels and taverns were ordered to report any information they might have overheard during their time in the city, but nothing was forthcoming. The emperor had been told about the incident and was greatly disturbed and upset that such a thing had happened in his home city. That one of his own guard should be killed so brutally within walls upon which he had bestowed such rich adornments!

Severus told Plautianus that he did not want to become obsessed with the search for some wretch, so Plautianus was to take care of it himself, quietly if possible. Plautianus went about his business as he wished, as usual. Many whispered that he held the reigns of power, that he was not to be trusted, that he was brutal and scheming. Those who believed such things never disclosed them however. His spies were everywhere, he heard everything, knew everything.

While his men were investigating the murder, Plautianus decided that after almost three weeks in the pit, the slave-prisoner would probably be willing to talk. That is, if he wasn't dead.

As soon as the two guards heard the slow, severe footsteps in the dirt they stood to attention and stopped talking. From around the corner appeared the prefect's tall, dark outline. When he came closer, the men avoided his gaze. Few could look him in the eye, few did.

"Has he made a sound lately?" His voice was deep and steady.

"No, sir." the one trooper answered. "Not for a few days. Before that he was mumbling about killing someone. He might be dead by now."

"We'll see. Both of you step away from the door. Go to the end of the lane and make sure nobody comes this way. I'm going to question him myself." The two men went to their new posts as Plautianus swung open the wooden door and went in with a torch and a bucket of water.

The inside of the tent was putrid; the stench of urine and faeces wafted upward, out of the dark hole. Plautianus couldn't see anything, hear anything. He realised the slave might well be dead and, moving back the tent flaps, he held the torch above the pit. At the bottom in a pool of filth, lay a huddled mass with pocked skin and mud-caked hair. Plautianus couldn't see if he was breathing. He picked up the bucket of water, went to the edge of the pit and poured the contents over the prisoner. The slave jerked like he had been burned by fire. He was alive.

"Excellent!" Plautianus grinned. "You, slave! Wake up!" The prisoner turned weakly, shielding his eyes from the torchlight. When he realised there was water all over him and the ground he started licking at it, not caring that it mingled with his own waste. "If you co-operate, you'll have clean water." Plautianus teased.

"Huh?" The slave looked up, tried to see. "Who are you? Where am I?" He bent over to lick at a brown pool in the corner.

"All in good time. For now, I want you to answer some questions and if your answers please me you just might be allowed to live."

"I don't care," the slave muttered. "Kill me if you want."

"Very well. But then we would not be able to discuss the Tribune Metellus...or Sabratha." Suddenly the slave stopped drinking. His eyes filled with a fiery hatred. "Ah. I see that means something to you."

"Ahhhhh!" He was suddenly on his feet, yelling. "Metellus! I want to kill him! Kill him!" He pounded the side of the dank pit.

"What about Metellus? Who in Hades are you, slave? What's your name?" The slave still resisted saying anything. His thoughts of the tribune were rekindled. "Very well. If you don't want to answer my questions dog, then I can come back in three more weeks. But first," he reached for a small clay jar and removed the top, "here is some company for you." Plautianus tipped the jar and spilled six scorpions into the black pit.

The slave recoiled, tried to climb the dirt wall but couldn't. He began to panic. The scorpions unfolded their tails and began to spread out, finding areas of dry dirt amid the filthy pools.

"They can climb walls," said Plautianus, "you cannot. I'll see you in three weeks." Plautianus moved away with the torch, leaving the slave in darkness.

"Wait! Wait! I'll tell you what you want to know. Everything." The scorpions were coming closer but Plautianus kicked some dirt and pebbles into the pit to cover them.

"You had better tell me quickly before they dig their way out of the dirt. It won't take them long."

"What do you want to know?" he asked as he watched the ground for movement.

"First. Who are you?"

"Brutus Calvus."

"That's a Roman name. You're not Roman."

"I'm Egyptian born, by my mother. My father was a Roman merchant in Alexandria."

"Whatever. How do you know Metellus?" The slave's eyes narrowed evilly.

"I was commanding an auxiliary cavalry unit in Alexandria. We were assigned to the bastard for some patrol across North Africa."

"So. You're one of the traitors that survived the decimation and was sent to the galleys."

"Yes. And I've sworn every day that I would kill the boy who put me there!"

"Perhaps I should just let the scorpions kill you. After all, you plotted against the emperor and Rome.

"I don't care about dying anymore. The gods of darkness have said they will help me one way or another."

"Your gods have abandoned you, Brutus. You have nothing left. You're a traitor. The tribune was right to decimate the lot of you!" Plautianus' goal was to anger the slave, see how much he hated Metellus.

"No!"

"What were you before you joined the auxiliary cavalry?"

The man pounded the wall again. "I was a Praetorian until Severus, damn him, replaced the entire guard with his own men."

"Where?" asked Plautianus.

"In Germania."

"Were you a traitor then?"

"We had dealings with the barbarians." Brutus didn't care anymore. To Hades with the past.

"Hmm." Plautianus backed away leaving the slave in darkness as he went out to think in the fresh air. *The man's hate is strong but can I control him?* he wondered. *He's a traitor, unscrupulous. Might be a useful spy or assassin.* He heard a yell come from inside the pit and went back. Brutus was clawing at the walls as the scorpions found their way out of the dirt and filth.

"Why are you asking me all of this? Who are you?"

"All you need to know for now is that I'm the one who can keep you alive or kill you at any time. I can crush your dark dreams of vengeance in an instant, or give you the chance to see them through. If you do everything I say. It's my way or nothing. I don't need you, Brutus. I've broken a hundred slaves like you. But you need me." His voice was cold and unwavering.

"I'm listening. Just get me out of this stinking hole!"

"Not yet. I see the hatred you have for Metellus. I can use that."

"I see you hate him too." Brutus' eyes lit in the flame above.

"No. He's nothing. An upstart. But others may use him to block my way and I can't have that."

"What do you want me to do?"

"No. Not yet. I don't trust you. But I don't have to kill you. I can prolong your pain in this filthy hole for as long as I like." Brutus kicked at the dirt. "No. Save that anger for later. Think about what I've offered you. I'll be back in a couple of days for your answer." Plautianus backed out of the tent again and went outside.

"But I said yes! I said yes! Ahh!" Alone in the dark again, the slave screamed and Plautianus ignored him.

"Let him scream. Don't say a word to him or give him anything," he said to the guards outside. "I'll be back in two days to question him again."

"Yes, sir." they replied, distracted by the painful screams coming from inside the stinking pit.

Back in the Principia, Plautianus' personal secretary came into his study. "Send for Argus!" snapped the prefect. "Tell him to get here immediately!"

"Yes, Prefect!" The secretary scribbled a message in the usual code and sealed the missive with the prefect's seal.

The following day, an unusual amount of cloud had rolled in off the sea to block out the sun and flatten the bright colours of Leptis Magna. The inquiry into the death of the Praetorian was coming to a halt with no leads or clues. The clandestine search for information continued and an uneasy air filled the streets nightly, contrasted by the jollity and celebration of the daylight hours.

Lucius had remained inside for two days feeling ill, uneasy with himself and unsure of what had transpired over the last three. Jabari and the other servants worried greatly about him and did their utmost to make him comfortable. He had not mentioned anything of that night to anyone, not even Drusus. His friendly shadow had left the domus when he had awoken and had not returned since.

It was time for Drusus to report to the empress again, but he wondered how much he should report. He wanted to tell her everything but was unsure of her reaction, whether she would see it as a failure on his part. He decided that he would tell her, that because she despised Plautianus so much, it would not make a difference to her whether one of his men was murdered. When he was ushered into her presence in a small private garden, he found Julia Domna sitting beneath an olive tree reading a scroll, one of her latest philosophic commissions. She always seemed sad when clouds beset the sky and made it impossible to see the stars at night or the sun by day.

Drusus approached, clearing his throat so that she would not be startled, "My Lady."

"Come Drusus," she said, rolling up the scroll and placing it on a table. "Where have you been the past days?"

"My Lady, I have been around the city looking for clues. Much has happened of late and not for the better I'm afraid."

The empress crossed her hands on her lap, her brown eyes observed Drusus like a hawk. He rarely spoke in such a manner or felt uncomfortable with her. Something was definitely wrong. "What is it?"

Drusus looked around. "May I approach?"

"Of course."

Drusus knelt beside her couch staring at the ground as he told her what had happened. "First of all, my Lady, I went back down to the harbour and asked around for the slave master whom Plautianus had spoken to. I was told where to find the man and went to get some information. He was unwilling to talk at first but once I pulled out the jingling purse he was willing enough. He told me that Plautianus had taken the slave. It seems the slave was intent on killing Tribune Metellus. He had been ranting and cursing. The slave master said that he had never seen the wretch do that before, that he definitely recognised our young friend. He also mentioned that the slave had repeated the word 'Sabratha' several times."

"Great Baal." She put her hand to her mouth. "He must be one of the cavalry troopers that Metellus decimated for treason."

"It seems that way, my Lady."

"And Plautianus now has him somewhere. Most likely within the Praetorian camp."

"Most definitely. I'm afraid I can't get in there. It's too well guarded."

"Plautianus has this traitor who must hate Metellus very much. If he releases this man, it is sedition."

"Yes, my Lady."

"We are still at a disadvantage Drusus. We know nothing about this prisoner. If Plautianus knew that we had discovered he had this man, he would simply dispose of him before we could act. We need more proof."

"I will try, my Lady, but it will be extremely difficult. The man may be dead already."

"Possibly. Unfortunately, we must wait. Our hands are tied. However, if Plautianus decides to use this man, it is likely that young Metellus is in danger."

"Yes, my Lady. I believe he is in danger. I also believe that Plautianus has sent to Rome for some of his spies. The Praetorian transport set out early this morning. I cannot stay with Metellus all day and night to protect him; the tribune is not stupid. He is already suspicious of me, though he does trust me to an extent."

"Good."

"But…"

"But what, Drusus?"

"He is in graver danger than you know."

"Tell me."

He could feel her eyes on him. "My Lady, after the banquet, the tribune slipped away from me. I rushed out into the streets to look for him, but I was too late."

"Too late for what Drusus?" Her fears were not unwarranted.

"My Lady," he whispered, "it was Tribune Metellus who killed the off duty Praetorian in the street."

"By all the Gods, Drusus! You had better be sure of what you are saying!"

"I swear, by shining Baal, it is true. When I was looking for him in the street, I heard some noises and came running around a corner to see him fighting with the trooper. The man was drunk and had a knife and was waving it about. He charged the tribune when he was down and Metellus threw his dagger into the man's chest as he was running. He cracked his head open on the wall."

Julia Domna felt winded. One of her husband's guards murdered by the very man she needed and was trying to protect.

"There is more, my Lady. I did not see it but the tribune says that he attacked the man because he was raping one of the young Greek girls who danced in the banquet celebrations."

"One of the muses?"

"That is what he claims. But, I did not see any trace of a girl when I arrived."

"Perhaps she ran away? She must have been terrified."

"Perhaps. There is also another possibility."

"Which is?"

"I believe that the tribune may in fact be mad." The empress had a disbelieving look on her face. "My Lady, he was muttering the whole way back to the domus and then muttering all night in his sleep."

Julia Domna looked up at the sky, still cloudy. "What was he saying?"

"He was calling out to the god Apollo, saying things like 'Muse!', calling out the name of his wife and asking 'Where is she?' I tell you, my Lady, either he is touched by the Gods or he is completely insane."

"Hmm." The empress had risen from her couch and was looking at the leaves of the olive tree. When she was thinking deeply, she liked to look at trees as if they offered some advice. "I don't believe he is mad, Drusus."

"No, my Lady? Do you believe he actually is touched by the Gods?

"I don't know. Many of his line have risen to greatness. Their loyalty to the Immortals was well known long ago. Some were indeed believed to be gifted, others were accused of madness." Julia Domna remembered Lucius' cognomen, Anguis, the dragon constellation. She decided she would consult her private astrologer when the darkness overhead cleared.

"Whether mad or gifted, my Lady, it is not safe for him in Leptis Magna."

"You speak true, Drusus. We must get him out of here before Plautianus discovers his guilt and makes his move. The murder would only give him an excuse if he found out."

"And what of our divine emperor, my lady? Must he know of the incident?"

"I am in the habit of telling my husband everything, contrary to rumour. However, this attack was on Plautianus' man, a man who was violating one of the region's famed entertainers. Let us say there was a girl, shall we?" she said with a raised eyebrow. "The tribune was doing the honourable thing by protecting her. He has shown himself to be a young man of great fortitude and wisdom in the past. I do not want to threaten that. I still have hopes for him and our cause."

"I understand, my Lady."

"Good. For now you must continue to watch over him, keep him out of trouble and get more information about this slave that Plautianus is hiding. In the meantime I shall think of an excuse to get Metellus out of Leptis Magna and away from the Praetorians. I will send for you again shortly."

"Yes, my Lady." Drusus turned and went out of the garden as Julia Domna reclined back on her couch beneath the tree to watch the sky and wait for the sun.

When Drusus came to Lucius with a summons from the emperor, Lucius feared the worst. Although he did not remember a great deal from the night of the banquet, he knew that a Praetorian was dead and that he was there. It came back to him in a cryptic series of flashes and a tightness in his gut. He could tell that Drusus did not completely believe him and so decided to keep things to himself.

"Should I be writing any goodbye letters to my family before this audience, Drusus?" Drusus looked shocked by the insinuation. Lucius truly was in the dark.

"Not at all, Tribune. Believe me in one thing at least: You are safe. No one knows about the other night except you and I." He saw no reason to involve the empress. "Here, let me help you with that." Drusus fastened the buckles on Lucius' cuirass.

"Do you think it's too much to wear my full armour for this audience?"

"Not at all. In fact, you want to look as military as possible. A man of the legions."

"We'd better leave. I don't want to be late and who knows how many people will stop me along the way with this armour on. It seems everyone recognises it."

The street was almost empty as it was midday; the sun was back, high and blazing with heat. Only a few passers by waved and shouted greetings to Lucius as they went along the narrower lanes. At the imperial residence, Drusus led Lucius through the corridors to a small, innocuous room.

"In here?" Lucius asked, observing the plain door that looked more like the entrance to a storage room.

"You are to go in here first. I'll wait. Go," he whispered and knocked lightly before opening it for Lucius.

The room was larger than Lucius had thought from the doorway, but it was not the sort of room in which one met with an emperor. He reached for the handle of his gladius, then a shutter opened, flooding the room with sunlight.

"You won't be needing that, Tribune," a voice said.

"Augusta!" Julia Domna stood in front of the window, a purple veil over her head. Lucius dropped to one knee, removed his helmet and placed it under his left arm. "Forgive me. I did not know it was you."

"Rise, Tribune," she said. "I do not want anyone to know that I am meeting with you, but there are things that you must know. Listen carefully."

"Yes, Augusta." Lucius had never been this close to her. Her clove perfume was overwhelming and she was taller than he remembered.

"I know what happened the night of the banquet." Lucius gasped. "Do not worry. Drusus has told me alone. I have not even told my son. You must see this as a show of good faith on

61

my part, that you can trust me and what I tell you." She moved a little closer. "Now, the Praetorian prefect seems to have a problem with you and your family. I want to protect you, but you must help me too. As you probably know by now, Plautianus and I hate one another. I do not use the word 'hate' lightly. He seeks to undermine my husband and steal power for himself. There will be a time, some day, when he will make a mistake. When that time comes, I will need all the good men I can count on to aid the emperor, myself and my sons. I have been watching you for a while and I know your loyalties. I also know of the estrangement between you and your father. Plautianus has gotten to him as well, in what capacity I do not know, but be mindful of him, of whom you trust."

"Who can I trust Augusta? I do not have a mind for politics. I want only to serve Rome." Lucius' head was spinning with all of this.

"For the moment, you must trust me. You must leave Leptis Magna tomorrow. You wish to return to your duties?" Lucius noticed her words were half question, half statement.

"Ye…Yes?" he replied.

"You feel you must be back with your men to best serve Rome and the emperor?"

"Yes, Augusta." This was very strange, but Lucius believed he understood her insinuation.

"Very well. Be mindful, Tribune, and remember those you can trust." Lucius thought she smiled beneath her veil, but he couldn't be sure. She seemed to be observing him very, very closely, as if she were looking for something. "Drusus will show you out."

"Thank you, Augusta, for everything." Lucius bowed again.

"Gods go with you, Tribune." The door opened and Lucius walked out into the corridor again where Drusus was waiting. He did not speak but led Lucius further down the marble hallway to the official reception room. On a dais at the top of marble steps sat the emperor, finishing dictating a letter to his scribe. On either side of his gold and ivory chair were two other chairs; one was empty and in the one to the left sat Caracalla. Lucius gave his name to the guard at the door.

"Tribune Lucius Metellus Anguis, Divine Emperor."

"Approach!" the emperor bellowed back. He was not as friendly as in the past.

"Hail Caesar!" Lucius saluted sharply, his voice echoing in the marble hall. At that moment he spotted the empress entering from a side door, followed by one of her ladies in waiting.

"Tribune Metellus! Welcome." He coughed for a moment then resumed. "I suppose you are wondering why we have summoned you here."

"It is my duty and honour, Divine Emperor, to come when I am summoned."

"Of course." Severus pet his wife's hand as she seated herself in the chair next to his. "As you have probably heard Metellus, one of my Guard has been murdered in the streets of the city where I was born."

"I have heard of this, sire." Lucius began to shake and struggled not to show his discomfort under the emperor's questioning and the empress' gaze. Caracalla watched absently; he thought more about Plautianus and his spiteful daughter.

"My city has been ruined and the stars are not in my favour." This was an odd statement. Lucius continued to listen. "By that I mean, Tribune, that it is an outrage for one of my men to be killed here." Severus descended the dais and moved onto the floor. His limp had improved since being in Leptis Magna. "I see that you are wearing your full armour. I have always been curious about its design." He paused. "At any rate, it's good you are dressed for duty. I take it that you have spent enough time in Leptis Magna, Metellus?"

"It is a beautiful city, sire. Most splendid." Lucius glanced at the empress briefly, not unnoticed by Caracalla. "However," he remembered her words a short time before, "I am eager to return to my duties, sire, where I can best serve your divine self and Rome." The empress nodded approvingly.

"I see," said Severus. "You know, Tribune, the people of this city have been quite content with your presence among my followers. Is that not duty as well? To be where your emperor is?"

"Yes, sire."

"Yes. However," Severus continued, "you are correct in saying that you should return to active duty." He held out a dispatch. "I have just received word from your current legate, Gaius Flavius Marcellus, of more raids in Numidia. Nothing as large as before but they must be crushed immediately."

"Return to my men, sire?"

"Yes, Metellus." He coughed again. "The legate has requested your presence, if it can be spared, seeing as you were so effective against the nomads in the past." Lucius stood up straight.

"When do I leave, sire?"

"First thing tomorrow morning. You will take ship to Carthage before the first hour of daylight."

"Yes, sire."

"One more thing, Tribune." The emperor moved closer to Lucius. "Do not leave your wife in Greece for too long. I have passed a law that men of the legions may have their wives close by, especially the upper ranks. A good Roman should have his family with him at all times, no?"

"I agree, sire."

"Very well. Dismissed, Tribune, and may Neptune give you safe passage to Carthage."

"Hail Caesar!" Lucius saluted and bowed to the emperor, Caracalla and lastly the empress who nodded her head slightly as if bidding him remember her words. Lucius backed away several paces, turned and went out where Drusus awaited him.

That evening, after he had packed his belongings in the two trunks, Lucius sat down at the table in his room to write a quick letter to Adara about his plans.

Adara Antonina Metella
From Tribune Lucius Metellus Anguis

My Adara,

It turns out that I am to sail for Carthage with the morning tide. Much has happened here in Leptis Magna; I will tell you about it when we are together again. It seems that the legate at Lambaesis has asked for my help against some nomadic raiding parties. Do not worry for me. These raiders will not pose much of a problem.

I miss you so much and think of you every waking second. I try to picture what you are doing at a particular moment, if you are walking, reading, shopping or sleeping. I am happy to be returning to my men, and though I am unsure of their complete loyalty, it will be good to see Alerio again.

I wish I could write more but I must finish preparing to leave. This letter will leave with the early morning dispatch ship. I pray that it finds you in good spirits, healthy and filled with thoughts of us. This next journey I must make brings us yet another step closer together. My love to Alene and everyone else. May Venus and Apollo keep watch over you still.

Goodbye for now, my Adara. I love you beyond all things.

Your devoted husband, Lucius Metellus Anguis.

That final night, Lucius did not sleep at all, though not without trying. Morpheus proved as elusive as ever. He was alone with his thoughts of Leptis Magna, its beauty and the event that turned his stay into a nightmare. A man dead, a Praetorian, a wounded girl vanished into thin air, and cryptic warnings from the empress. The desert had decided to plague him with mystery yet again, its swaying palms singing an hypnotic song.

He was happy to be leaving and looked forward to setting things straight. However, Lucius realised that he did not know what kind of a mess he would be walking into, whom he could trust and those he could not. It was as the empress said, he should not trust a soul. Then again, he could always trust Alerio Cornelius Kasen. Alerio was Lucius' first centurion in the cohort and the one he had left in charge. He was also his best friend; having known each other for years Lucius knew that at least there, he would find trust, loyalty and fellowship. Alerio would help him sort through the detritus of his cohort, and then he would bring Adara to his side once more. These were the thoughts that passed in and out of his mind the whole of the long night until it was time for Lucius to collect his belongings and depart. All of the slaves, downcast at his sudden departure, were awaiting him at the doors.

Lucius had decided not to wear his armour for the journey. It was too hot during the day and he did not want to call undue attention to himself. Instead, he wore brown, knee-length bracae and his brown tunic with the gold thread borders. He packed his gladius, hung the sword that Adara had given to him over his right shoulder and tucked his dagger in his belt. Sandals were cooler during the day. To conceal himself, he put on his black hooded cloak until the city was far behind. Drusus had arrived and awaited Lucius as he turned to the servants.

"May the Gods smile on you, Tribune, and give you safe voyage," said Jabari for all of them. Lucius looked down the line of sad faces. He wondered how they could have become so attached to him. They were slaves, and yet, they cared for him!

"Oh, Tribune!" Talia threw herself at Lucius' feet and put her arms about his legs. "Don't go, Tribune! A shadow follows you!"

"Not again Talia!" Jabari said. "Naeemah please pick her up." The woman moved to coax Talia off of the floor.

"Come, Talia. The tribune must be going. It was just a dream you had, nothing more."

"Dream?" asked Lucius.

"Talia had a dream, Tribune," Jabari explained, "that you were beset on all sides, in the dark or something to that effect."

Lucius put his hand on the girl's head. "Don't worry, Talia. Apollo is my protector and I've been through many battles." Talia was not comforted. "Thank you all. I've enjoyed meeting you. Your wishes are comforting, but it is time for me to go." He looked at Drusus who nodded.

"Ishaq, Oba and Acis will help carry your things to the harbour, Tribune."

"Good." The door opened and the slaves went out with the trunks, followed by Drusus and Lucius who nodded one more time to Jabari and the four women beside him.

The streets were not yet flowing with people and in the harbour only a few torches flickered where the small bireme awaited its passenger. Lucius showed the imperial pass to the ship's captain who nodded and showed the slaves where to put the trunks. The emperor's secretary had given him the pass to board ship, procure horses in Carthage and obtain whatever other services he might require on his journey. He kept it in the satchel which he had slung over his shoulder.

Lucius pushed back the hood of his cloak. "I guess this is it, Drusus. Are you sure you're not coming with me by chance?" He had suspected for a long time that the empress had set him to be Lucius' shadow.

"No, Tribune. Not this time I'm afraid. Will you be all right?"

"Better than if I were to stay here, it seems." Lucius looked up at the Temple of Jupiter where a single flame burnt at the top of the steps. "Make an offering for me, Drusus."

"I will, Tribune. May he and the other gods guide you safely to your destination."

"Thank you, friend." Lucius clasped his forearm, the short, stocky man nodding as he looked to where the captain waited.

"They're ready for you. Go. You should be well away from here before the sun rises." Lucius turned, went up the gang plank and the ship pushed away from the quayside, its oars dipping into the calm water of the harbour to row out to sea and Carthage. Lucius' black-cloaked figure waved from the deck. Drusus raised his hand in farewell, knowing he would miss the tribune, that he worried for the innocent man he was. He hoped Lucius was not mad, but then a warrior so gifted with a closeness to the Gods was somehow even more frightening.

The slaves had gone back to the domus as soon as the ship had set off and Drusus, true to his word, went up the temple steps to throw a flower he had found on the steps into Jupiter's fire. "Safe voyage to him," he said as he tossed the red flower in, watched the petals singe, discolour and burn away.

Rarely did Drusus have moments of peace when he could let his guard down. He had forgotten how much he liked the sea. It looked so black and menacing in the dark, but during the day it became as bright and blue as the sky, the two of them joining on the horizon.

"To Hades with him and you!" The slurred voice came out of nowhere and the blow to the back of his head was sharp and biting.

Drusus fell forward, tumbling down the stairs of the temple, the back of his head agape leaving a trail of blood on the white marble. Trembling in the dark, Drusus felt for his dagger with a shaking hand as he crawled toward the water and away from whatever demon had come upon him. He tried to yell but his mouth only shook and curdled with blood. He felt a hand grab his cloak and flip him over. All he could see through his failing eyes was a dark shadow, all he could feel was another hand take the blade from his.

"I'll use this to cut his throat slowly," the sickening voice hissed. Drusus felt his neck pulled back and the bite of cold steel in his flesh cutting his gasping throat.

"Jupiter!" he called out in the blackness. There was no answer.

The body lay limp on the dock and the assassin cursed as he looked out to sea. Then he reached down to find the hand with the ring. It was the only sign that he was the empress' man, a ring she had given him for service. He cut the entire hand off with Drusus' dagger, punctured the body with several wide holes and pushed it over the edge of the quay into the black water.

Brutus turned and went slowly down a dark street. He was weak and sick. His feet were sore from stamping on the scorpions and his mouth was red, swollen and full of sores from when he had eaten them afterward. *Plautianus will be pleased with this!* he thought as he grasped Drusus' severed hand. *That should be proof enough that I'll do what he wants.*

When Plautianus had discovered, too late, that Lucius would be leaving Leptis Magna, that he had been spotted all over the city with the empress' man, he had decided enough was enough. Drusus was one reason she had always been one step ahead lately. The prefect's imagination ran wild with rage, so he decided to let the man in the pit prove his worth earlier than planned. If he failed, he would just kill him and be done with it. If he succeeded, he would still keep him in the pit of course, like a caged animal, but at least he would know if controlling him was a possibility.

Away in Rome, as the sun crept over the surrounding hills and the day spawned golden light over the rooftops, Quintus Metellus pater slept uneasily, alone in his bed. "What place is this?" he groaned as he found himself in a cold, dark cell. He realised the cell was his own house. Ravens cawed from the rooftop above the garden and hyenas circled in the streets outside, beyond his bars, slavering as they watched him. What had he done to deserve this? The wind howled back in answer to his cries as the sound of a whip lashed his soul. The Gods had forsaken him as he had always suspected.

His head spun with the pain, fear and shame of imprisonment. Quintus Metellus rolled in his bed, sweating, beset by sudden laughter. The faces all around him laughed at him. *Pathetic!* His wife, his daughters, his youngest son, his oldest, his bastard, his mistress, the Praetorian prefect, the senate, the empress and the emperor himself. Laughing, pointing, humiliating him. *No longer a dragon, never one!* The face of his son Lucius remained behind to spit at him, curse him, beat him.

"He'll kill me!!!" Quintus yelled from the room where he had been sleeping. "They're all laughing! Laughing!" He was alone in his sweaty, loathsome bed. No one to comfort him, no one to care.

IV

ATHENAE

'Athens'

"They're all laughing! Laughing!"

Antonia Metella came rushing in from the garden where she had just sat down with her children, young Quintus and Clarinda, for some food in the morning sun. The cubiculum was dark and the bed sheets wet and twisted.

"Quintus?" she called out. "What's wrong? Where are you?" The room was so dark she couldn't see a thing. When she opened one of the window shutters, she saw her husband's two darting eyes in a far corner of the room. He caught sight of her.

"Get out! Get out! Go away woman!"

"What's happened, husband? Tell me." She moved slowly toward him but stopped when he reached for a stool to throw. "I'm sending for a physician, Quintus."

"No! I don't need one! Go back to your laughing! I'm Paterfamilias, no one else! I can kill all of you if I please! Get out!"

Antonia rushed from the room, shaking and crying, full of fear in her ignorance of what was driving her husband to such madness and anger.

"Mama?" young Quintus asked as he came running. "What's wrong? I heard father yelling at you." Clarinda was crying in the background. "Are you hurt, Mama? Why are you crying?"

"I'm not hurt, but your father is not well. He wants to be alone right now so we are going to go to the Lady Claudia's for a visit. Get your sister and yourself ready to go out and bring your readings with you. We may be a while."

Young Quintus assumed an air of responsibility. "Yes, Mama. Right away." He went to get Clarinda and do as his mother had asked. Antonia went to the kitchen.

"Ambrosia?" she called for her most trusted slave girl.

"Yes, Mistress?" Ambrosia came out from one of the storage rooms.

"Ambrosia we won't be requiring any more meals today. The children and I are going to the Lady Claudia's. Also, do not disturb my husband. He is...not well today and wishes to be left alone. Just go about your cleaning duties. If he wants anything, he will let you know."

"Yes, Mistress. Are you all right?" Ambrosia saw where her makeup had run from her tears and that her eyes were red.

"No, Ambrosia! I am not all right!" She closed her eyes, upset with her loss of control. "Just do as I ask."

"Yes, Mistress. Oh by the way, this arrived early this morning." She held out a scroll. "It looks like Mistress Alene's handwriting."

"So it is." Antonia took the scroll to bring with her. "Quintus, Clarinda, are you ready?" The children appeared in the doorway.

"Yes, Mama," they said in unison.

"Good. Let's go." The three of them went outside and Antonia led them away from the domus as quickly as she could, trying to hold back any tears that rimmed her eyes. She could not let anyone see her so shaken in public.

Having arrived so unexpectedly at the Lady Claudia's home, the door slaves were not sure whether they should lead Antonia Metella and her children through the house or have them wait in the atrium for the mistress to come down from the upper floor. However, as soon as Claudia heard Antonia's voice she knew that something must have been wrong and she hurried downstairs to see her. Antonia would never have called on her friend so early, without an invitation.

"Come in! Come in my dear, children." Claudia immediately noticed Antonia's distraught face. "What a nice surprise!" She clapped her hands and ordered the servants to prepare a table of food in the garden next to the fountain. "Children, how wonderful to see you again!" she said, pinching their cheeks. "Clarinda, you grow more beautiful every time I see you!" Clarinda smiled and batted her eyelashes. "And little Quintus. You are growing more and more into a young man!"

"Thank you," said Quintus. "May we eat Lady Claudia, and sit? My mother is not well right now."

Claudia laughed lightly. "Ha, ha, but I see you are not so politic as a grown man. No seasoning of words for you! But of course, you are right. Let us sit. You know where the garden is, Quintus. Why don't you take your sister on ahead. We will follow." Quintus took Clarinda's hand and led her down the frescoed corridor.

"I am sorry for popping in on you like this Claudia, but we needed to get out of the house." Antonia sighed, trying to compose herself.

"Come, my dear. Let's sit and you can tell me about it."

In the garden, the children sat on one couch and Antonia and Claudia on another next to the fountain. The ladies talked in hushed tones, their voices hidden behind the splashing of the fountain, while the children delighted in the array of honeyed sweets that had been placed before them on a golden platter.

"Now dear, tell me. What has happened?" She did not have her usual gossipy voice but sounded genuinely concerned for her friend. Whatever Antonia told her would not leave the garden.

"Quintus has changed dramatically."

"So I've noticed."

"Yes but lately he has become extremely short-tempered, even violent. He keeps saying he is Paterfamilias and what he says is law."

"Is anyone challenging him? Are you?"

"No! That's what is so confounding. Lucius is the only one who ever stood up to him but he has been gone for weeks now. Quintus has his home to himself again, no more guests or parties. He simply locks himself away in his study when he is not in the curia."

"Very strange." Claudia did not know what to make of all of this. She had had three husbands herself but every one of them had been so much weaker, meeker than herself that she had never experienced such a thing.

"It is strange. He also wakes up in the middle of the night or in the morning, yelling out loud about killing and people laughing at him, cursing and all sorts of things. It is very frightening. This morning was the worst of it. He awoke screaming again while I was in the garden. I rushed in and he was hidden in a corner, his eyes mad with rage like a cornered animal. I asked what was wrong, said I was going to send for the physician and he turned on me saying he was Paterfamilias and that it was his right to kill any one of us as such." Antonia began to shake again and Claudia put her arm around her before pouring her some unwatered wine.

"I remember," Antonia continued, "when Quintus used to be so loving; he was always a strong and confident husband. Now, it's as though that man is gone and all he has left behind is an empty, fearful, dark shell of his former self. He's so jealous of Lucius and his achievements." Antonia's hand shook as she tried to drink. "He should be full of a father's pride."

Claudia did not know what to say to comfort her friend. She did not like Quintus Metellus and felt that he was unworthy of the family he had, of such a woman as Antonia. "There, there. Don't fret. We'll figure this out. You're not alone." Despite Claudia's attempts to comfort her, Antonia could not help but think the words her friend uttered were hollow. She felt that she was indeed alone in that moment.

After they had eaten some food and had a cup of wine, Claudia suggested that they go out to the fora to do some shopping and explore the animal markets where the variety of exotic beasts from around the empire would excite the children and take their attention away from their mother. Claudia had her slaves assemble out front of the house with two litters; one for herself and the children, and one for Antonia so that she could be alone and undisturbed, sleep if she so wished.

It was the end of Rome's summer but the city was still hot and vibrant, full of life. As Claudia and the children went from stall to stall perusing all kinds of imported oddities, Antonia remained in her litter. The sun shone pleasantly through its pink canopy and draping curtains, showering her in a private, peaceful light. Now that she was alone, she unrolled the scroll from Alene and read.

To Antonia Metella
From her loving daughter, Alene Metella

Dear Mother,

After a few weeks of travelling, we have finally arrived in Athens. The voyage was fine, the weather fair. It is much hotter in Greece than in Italy, but I like it. Though, I find that I must frequently cover myself with a cloak to keep from burning. My skin is unused to the sun here. Of course my wonderful new sister is as brown as a Greek olive. I always thought that a pale complexion was more desirable but I must confess that I am a little jealous.

At any rate, the voyage was very exciting. From Brundisium we crossed the sea to the Greek coast and travelled south until we entered the Gulf of Corinth. As Delphina hails from near the sanctuary of Apollo, we stopped for several days in Delphi, on the slopes of Mount Parnassus. Oh mother, what a beautiful place! The sanctuary is unlike any other I have ever seen. As I entered the precinct I could feel the god's presence and an overwhelming sense of peace came over me. It seemed as though music lingered permanently in the air. No doubt Apollo's muses sit atop the cliffs and peaks playing for him. The air smells sweetly of cedar, and delicate pines speak in hushed tones. Sacred groves of olive stretch out as far as the eye can comprehend, like a vast, glistening ocean in which the waves break occasionally on the tips of towering cypresses. The shadows of hundreds of years are cast to walk with the living, and soft muted breezes caress the ears like a warm bath. I think that all of the great poets must have been to this place. See what it has done to me!

There is a permanent line to see the oracle, the Pythia. It weaves its way down the mountainside, a truly amazing sight. So many pilgrims, for so long. Because Publius is a Roman official and the priests know Delphina, we were allowed to go ahead of the line to see the Pythia if we so desired. Adara went first, then myself and then Ashur. Publius and Delphina did not feel the need and Carissa and Emrys decided instead to look at the statues about the sanctuary. I cannot say what the Pythia told me for they say it is better to keep it to yourself. It is so cryptic anyway that I don't think I even understand what she said. Ashur stayed with her for some time and seemed almost distraught when he emerged from the inner sanctum. I hope it is nothing too serious.

Ashur has proved to be a true bodyguard, his eyes are watchful all the time. He also seems to be spending a great deal of time with Carissa; they have become quite close. I always thought that he was forbidden such intimacies for whatever reason. I am glad to see he is not and that he smiles widely when Carissa is with him.

From Delphi we departed by ship once more to Corinth where we hired wagons and slaves to take us by land to Athens. I was saddened to see the once magnificent city of Corinth in such a state. Though beautiful, it seems that our ancestors rather demolished it all those years ago. Sad really. Athens on the other hand is a beautiful city! I wish you could see it, Mother. It is surrounded by high brilliant mountains that bake in the sun. Then within the walls of the city is a vastness of green trees and gardens amid beautiful temples, arches, stoas and libraries. Out of the centre of this wondrous place rises the Acropolis. The Temple of Athena Parthenos dominates the city's skyline like a sanctuary in the clouds - brilliant and inspiring. You can see all of the city from the top. At night, the Augustus moon over Greece is larger and more brilliant than any I have heard of or seen. I'm sure it could challenge Lucius' desert moon.

Speaking of Lucius, I do not know if you have received your letter from him yet but there was one waiting here for Adara when we arrived. If you do not know already, Lucius is fine and doing well. So do not worry, Mother, for either of us. I hope that my absence is not too difficult on you and that father is treating you well now that Lucius and I are away. I wish you were here with me. The markets are truly exciting. And the Greek fashions! I am sending you some fabric I know you will love. In Rome we think that we have the latest Greek fashions but I must say that here there are things that women in Rome have not yet seen!

Oh I do believe I have run on quite a bit. I miss you very much Mother and I pray to Apollo that he keeps you safe and looks to your happiness. Kiss young Quintus and Clarinda for me and give my regards to father as you see fit. You have all my love and that of everybody here. I shall write again.

Your loving daughter,

Alene Metella

Antonia rolled up the scroll and dried the papyrus where her tears had made it wet. How she wished she were with Alene in Athens. It sounded marvellous. Instead, she found herself barred from her own home, lying alone in a litter, as she was carried through the streets of Rome. The litter bobbed gently from side to side and she laid back to sleep in the pink light of her own sanctuary, dreaming of her daughters and friends in a land far away, sunning themselves in ancient beauty.

Since their arrival in Athens, Adara had been busy showing Alene the beautiful sights, sounds and smells of her home. During Augustus the days were hot, the sun high and bright without a cloud in the sky. Publius Leander Antoninus, Adara's father, had a villa, near the eastern gate of the city, where Alene, Ashur, the mysterious friend who had followed Lucius from Africa, and the talented British sculptors Emrys and Carissa were welcome for as long as they wished to stay.

The villa was located on a slight rise in the land. Within a walled enclosure, the rectangular two-storey villa surrounded a courtyard in which a bevy of fruit trees, orange, lemon and pomegranate, provided soothing shade beneath the sun. Inside, every corridor wall displayed bright, colourful frescoes with images of anything from Cretan bull leapers and dolphins, to scenes of everyday life such as olive picking, sheep herding or fishing. When asked if she had painted the frescoes, Delphina responded with a humble "yes", that she had painted such things for the simple joy it provided her with. Every room had its own theme and statuary to match. The villa also included a farm that provided them with extra income and trade opportunities. Silver-leafed olive groves yielded plump olives which were processed into oil at their own press; Attic olive oil was a widely prized commodity. The servants on the land also cared for a flock of sheep, a herd of goats and four Thessalian horses.

Adara tried to show Alene how to ride but her Roman sister could not manage to stay atop the beasts, let alone get on. She was content to sit in the shade of an olive tree and watch Adara ride in circles on her favourite white stallion, Phoenix. When the party had finally reached the house at the end of their journey from Rome, Adara had gone directly to the stables to see Phoenix who had begun to neigh even before she had appeared. He always recognised her footsteps as she approached.

Some days the entire family would go into the city to shop in the Agora, go to the baths and the renovated theatre of Dionysus at the foot of the Acropolis. Emrys and Carissa made several visits to the sculptors' quarter to visit old friends and see what new techniques were in fashion, while Delphina, the girls, Ashur and Publius browsed in the markets.

For the most part, time in Athens was spent in slow enjoyment of the more leisurely pace that flavoured life in the ancient city. Alene had never been beyond the borders of Italy and so found herself swept away in art, music and a general state of newness that tickled her senses. Adara had tried to describe the life of the city during their voyage but she had not been prepared for the overwhelming feelings that such simple beauties could flush out of her.

"Oh Alene! You'll love it!" Adara had said. "It's so different from Rome. Hotter for one. The Gods have allowed the sun to shine brilliantly almost all the time. It's so bright, the buildings so pure and white, that you have to shield your eyes much of the time. Some people say that it's the presence of the Gods themselves, roaming about their favoured city, that makes it so luminous. From the top of the Acropolis, the smell of the sea reaches Athena's temple from Piraeus and you can see the heavenly beacons of the Temple of Aphaia on the island of Aegina and the Temple of Poseidon at Sounion, overlooking the sea. As you walk the streets you notice fallen fruit upon the ground, the scent of oranges and lemons tingeing the air. In the Agora, pine trees rustle with the Gods' presence, their cones crackling in salute to the sun, perfumed with the aroma of pine resin. This, mingled with the sweet smell of thyme, lightens you so that you want to lay yourself down beneath one of the sacred olive trees and dream." Adara could have gone on and on, not realising how much she had missed her home. However, the joy would be bittersweet without Lucius there, for now all her hopes and precious thoughts turned to him, paling the light of Athens.

"Does it ever rain?" Alene asked incredulously. "How do all these trees grow without water?"

"The Gods have made it so, Alene. A long time ago they chose to bless the city with the sun. But there are aqueducts throughout the city and it does indeed rain outside of winter."

"But you said that it doesn't rain during summer!"

"It doesn't...except for once."

"Once?"

"Yes. Every year there is a single summer storm, during Quinctilis or Augustus, that leaves the city clean of dust, polished. The mud and dust washes away completely and life smells strong and fresh." She hugged Alene, happy to share it all with her. "Oh Alene, I hope you can experience the summer rain! I used to go outside and jump around; it always made me feel purified."

Since their arrival in Athens, Alene had been up early every morning, eager to feel the world around her, not miss a moment. After a few days, Publius eventually had to return to his civic duties in the Agora and Delphina returned to her painting, time away having instilled her with new inspiration. While Emrys was hard at work, sculpting and teaching, Carissa passed much of her time with Ashur as he followed Adara and Alene about the city. Emrys had been upset at Carissa's slackening of her work, but he knew that she had been working diligently for many years. However, she had never smiled as he had seen her smile of late.

Publius had hired litter bearers to take his daughters, Alene, Ashur and Carissa wherever they wished during their stay. It was a short distance to the centre of the city, and there was much to see. At one point, Adara had told Ashur that he did not have to shadow them so faithfully, that he could be alone with Carissa, but in his loyalty to Lucius he had refused. With Hadrea and Lavena, Adara's younger sisters, clinging admiringly to Alene, going only where she would go, the six of them set out in two litters to see some more of the city.

The day was hot. The heat seemed alive as it moved about the streets, serpent-like veils in the torrid breeze. Alene, as was necessary, wore her green cloak so that her head would be covered; freckles had begun to form on her flawless face because of the sun's intensity.

Their destination that particular day was the Olympieion, the great Temple of Olympian Zeus, located just inside the old city walls. The monument could actually be seen from the villa, its glinting pediment rising to the sky. It seemed large enough from a distance, but as they drew closer and closer, Alene's head was permanently craned beyond the litter's curtains.

So this is it! she thought, *This is what wags so many tongues even as far away as Rome.* She rubbed her eyes, believing it to be a trick of the light and heat but it was not. The litter bearers stopped near the Arch of Hadrian. They were all immediately drawn to the Temple of Zeus as to an enchanted forest, feeling small and insignificant, inspired. Even Hadrea and Lavena stopped chattering.

The Olympieion was a tribute to Greek and Roman engineering, dedication and faith. Begun almost eight hundred years previously, the temple was finally completed by the Emperor Hadrian who had loved Athens. The one hundred and four Corinthian columns, rooted in the earth, seemed to explode skyward, flowers to the hand of Zeus himself.

Athenians mingled on and around the steps leading into the temple, discussing, arguing, revering the world of which they felt a central part. Inside the temple, the immense chryselephantine statue of the god peered down on all mortals who entered his sanctum. Honoured jointly with the god of gods was Hadrian, the emperor who had pumped life back into the city and shown it great favour and love.

They did not spend much time inside the temple, its grandeur along with Zeus' gaze were intensely humbling.

"I wish mother could have seen this," Alene said as she looked skyward to the flowering columns. "She'll never believe me when I tell her about it."

"Truly a marvel," Ashur added. "I had forgotten."

"Have you been to Athens before, Ashur?" asked Carissa.

Ashur smiled and held her hand. "Yes. Long ago..."

"Shall we go to the markets now? I would like to get mother another stola." Hadrea and Lavena's ears picked up as Alene said this.

"We know just where to take you!" Lavena clapped her hands excitedly.

"Adara?" Alene looked at her sister. "Is everything all right?" Adara had been quiet much of the morning and had been staring down, over the wall of the temple precinct at a gathering of trees by the river just to the south.

"I'm sorry Alene, I don't feel much like shopping today."

"Oh," she tried not to sound too disappointed, "it's all right. We can do it tomorrow when we go to the Hill of the Muses."

"Oh come now, Adara!" Hadrea chided. "You're letting down our guest!"

"No, not at all. We'll go another day."

"Hadrea, do you know the way to the markets?" Adara asked. "You won't be too long?"

"Of course we know where to go! You know how often we have mother take us there. We won't be long."

"Very well. Alene, do you mind going with Hadrea and Lavena while we go to the sanctuary?"

"Not at all. You do what you must and we'll see you back at the villa. We'll tell one of the litters to wait for you."

Alene, Hadrea and Lavena went off to shop and experience the sights and sounds of the Athenian markets while Adara, Carissa and Ashur went down the marble steps that led away from the temple's shadow.

Once down the stairs, they found themselves in a grove of trees beside the river Ilissos and one of the most sacred parts of Athens. Adara walked ahead of them, strolling in silent thought among groups of citizens gathered outside the ageing law courts and the Panellenion. She stopped when she came to the steps of the Temple of Apollo Delphinios. It was quiet at that time of day. Grateful for the peace, she purchased a vial of oil and went inside to make an offering to Apollo for the protection of her husband who was tortuously far from her. Ashur remained outside with Carissa, by the river's edge.

When Adara emerged from the temple, Ashur was sitting on a rock waiting for her while Carissa admired some of the statues scattered about the grove. This part of the city felt so much older than the rest. Not because the buildings were more aged, or because of the many times he had been there in the past. It felt more like the distant echo of a memory to Ashur; many things did of late.

"Ashur?" Adara came down the steps where grass sprouted from between the marble slabs. "Aren't you going in?"

"I do not think it would be appropriate at this time for me to go into Apollo's presence." He could not even look long at the temple. Adara thought he looked almost ashamed.

"But I thought you would like to come here. I'm sorry if..." She noticed him looking at Carissa, then shuddering in the face of the temple and the image of Apollo at its pediment. Adara sat on the rock next to him and pulled back her blue veil. "Ashur?"

"Yes?"

"What happened in Delphi? What did the Pythia say to you? I mean, I know that it's not good to say but ever since then you've not been yourself."

Ashur looked reluctantly up at the temple and then to Adara. Her look drew it out of him, though he did not want to say. "The Pythia...said nothing to me."

"Nothing? But you were in there so long?" Adara was remembering everything Lucius had told her of what he knew about Ashur and his connection with Apollo. "How can that be?"

"I don't know. After so many visits over the years, so many prophecies and riddles from her lips, nothing. The Pythia and Apollo uttered not a word. I waited and spoke and pleaded with him and still, nothing. I cannot bear to go into his presence unbidden."

"And you don't know why he is silent?" she asked.

"I suspect why." Ashur looked again at Carissa, his eyes following her every movement, his breath in time with hers, even from a distance. Adara understood.

"Ashur, I know not what mysteries you have had to deal with for so long, but from what my husband tells me you are Apollo's favourite, gifted by him. I am sure that he would not deny you something as healing and uplifting as love. For myself, I have felt him and Aphrodite working in concert. How can it be that he would deny you joy?"

"The Far-Shooter is kind and just, but he is also harsh and demands complete loyalty from his servants. In that I have failed him…and I am so far from my path that I do not care." At these words Adara covered her head with her veil as if to ward off the ominous words that Ashur had spoken in front of the temple. Carissa approached, luminous and smiling like a newborn wood nymph having drunk from the waters of a clear spring for the first time. "Come, let us go now *Minau*." He rose and they made their way back to the litter.

"*Minau?*" Adara repeated to herself. "I've heard that before." She remembered the word from her studies. It meant *heaven*, in Persian. She rose, bowed to the temple slightly, and followed after her friends.

Two weeks later, Delphina arranged for a special feast to be given at the villa in honour of their guests and invited some of the Roman officials in Athens, as well as a number of her closest friends. It was an evening filled with food, wine and laughter. An evening of stories and news from Rome and of Adara's wedding. Many of the guests had known her from a child and wanted to know everything about this mysterious Tribune Metellus.

Amid the array of couches, wine craters and diners, Adara answered every question that was put to her like a true aristocrat. Even though she wondered at people's audacity in expecting to know intimate details of this and that, who said what to whom, she answered when she thought it agreeable, and diverted the conversation when it grew too intrusive. Not that the gathering was full of bores and nuisances, rather the conglomeration was made up good, kind-hearted citizens whom she had long admired. The problem was that the world, no matter how vibrant or beautiful, friendly or admiring, left nothing but a foul taste in her mouth and an emptiness in her heart. Without Lucius, the sweetness of her life soured and the spirit within her wished itself far away, across the sea toward him.

Only that day, a letter from her husband had arrived informing her that he was now returning to Lambaesis and his men. He had obviously written it in haste, unable to say much except that he was well, that he would be fine and that he loved her. Yet she recognised an anxiety in his voice, in his handwriting.

"I'm going outside for some fresh air," she whispered to Alene toward the end of the feast. "Stay and enjoy yourself, I won't be long."

"Of course, sister. I understand." Alene knew of the letter from Lucius and how Adara had been worried about him, how she needed time to herself, especially at this time of night when the Augustus moon shone full and bright directly above the city.

Adara had begun a new ritual of going out into the garden to sit back in one of the carved marble benches and look up at the sky. That night however, she chose to go out of the villa, past the stables and into the olive groves to escape the sound of the banquet.

The world was peaceful at night as she walked amid the whispering trees that shed the day's heat and cooled beneath the silver light of the summer moon and stars. Her pace was meditative, serene as she pressed her lips against the ring of entwined dragons on her finger and thought of her husband. *Good evening, my Love...I am with you...* she intimated to the night, knowing that Lucius could somehow hear her voice.

Adara closed her eyes, tilted her head back and took a deep breath, inhaling the sweet, dry summer air. A cool breeze picked up and she could feel it caressing her bare arms and neck. For a moment she thought she heard chimes of a sort, as though every olive branch were made up of golden leaves. When she opened her eyes, she was adrift in a sea of twinkling lights within the trees. Thousands upon thousands of fireflies danced and hovered about her like flickering stars in the heavens. She waded through the lights, reaching out to touch them, missing as they floated by, their light reflected in the gold of a bangle that was wrapped about her wrist.

Several yards ahead of her, Adara thought she spied a form moving amidst the trees and made her way towards it, entranced by the moonlit grove. Something touched her on the shoulder; she turned quickly, but no one was there. When she turned back, however, the form was unmistakable. Love, the Goddess Venus, stood before her and smiled, radiant and beautiful as starlight in a golden vial.

"Goddess," Adara said, her voice hushed, her hand over her heart.

Love ran her golden hand over Adara's long hair and she felt her longing turn to joy. She said nothing with words at first, merely taking her by the hand and leading her deeper into the trees. As in a dream, Adara let herself be led by Love to a small clearing with a bench. In front of the bench, gazing up at the sky and leaning on a silver bow, was Far-Shooting Apollo. His blue cloak rustled in the breeze as he hummed to the night. The light all about them grew brighter but was not harsh, rather like swimming in a cool sea on a hot day, reposing.

Adara bowed, knowing the god could see her even if his back were turned, then Love led her to the bench and seated herself beside. Adara shook as she felt the heat emanating from Love, but the goddess put her at ease, comforted her, and soothing, cool breezes encircled them where they sat. *Is this real? Am I ill?* Adara wondered.

"You are not ill, dearest..." Love said in answer, her lips almost moving slower than her words as they left her mouth. "...nor are you dreaming. Lord Apollo and I are as real as the moon and the stars." Adara felt like weeping, so beautiful was the voice that reached her heart, like winged music. Then Apollo turned to face the mortal and the goddess seated before him, walked over and smiled, his eyes like two firmamental stars.

Welcome lady, he said without speaking. *We have heard your prayers and received your offerings.* Adara was transfixed, immobile in their presence. The god read her thoughts. *You wish to know about the Sibyl's message from me?*

"Yes...Lord," she managed.

"He has misinterpreted some of the message," he now said in harmonious tones. "I cannot reveal all for much is yet to pass. However, I say that you should soon be with your husband."

"When?"

"Soon, but not before." Apollo smiled and turned, drew a long-shafted arrow from his silver quiver and loosed it across the night sky. Adara could speak no more, only gaze in bewilderment as Apollo disappeared into the trees, into the night.

Next to her, Love remained, calm and thoughtful. She placed her arm around Adara like an older sister who cared

only for her happiness. "Let your heart be at peace dearest…"
Love comforted, "…for death and sadness are always
accompanied by life and joy. We are with you." She then
kissed Adara on the forehead, melting away her worries, and
smiled, tilting her head as if she had heard something in some
far land. Before disappearing into the moonlit night she held
her godly hand above Adara's stomach. The light all around
them grew to an intense whiteness and then all was dark again.

Adara found herself sitting on the ground, leaning against the
trunk of an aged tree. For several minutes she did not dare
move, for all her uncertainty as to what had happened. Then, it
hit. A sharp pain and a spinning sensation as the world about
her whirled, and whirled. She muttered Lucius' name and fell
over on her side.

Darkness had come once more in Rome as it did every other
day. Shops and stalls closed up for the night and the taverns
opened after the midday rest. Roaming gangs of youths
shuffled through the streets of the Subura looking for fights
and those who worked the night, prostitutes, murderers and
spies, went out of doors.
    As the shadows lengthened and grew darker, Argus'
footsteps upon the streets of Rome grew more silent, his
presence cloaked in black. Nightly, he went out to gather
information for the prefect or put his dagger to someone's
throat. He had become quite adept at his taciturn activity,
moving through the back streets to appear and disappear like a
shade in the night. *One day Plautianus will be emperor,* he
thought, *and when he is, those who have aided him will be
rewarded for their service.*
    That particular evening he found himself in very familiar
territory as he slipped through the Forum Boarium and up the
street to the Metellus domus. Of course he knew that Lucius
was in Leptis Magna and that his wife and family had gone to
Greece, but Argus wanted more information about Adara and

when she would join Lucius again. He wanted to know everything about the Antoninii: where they lived in Athens, any information that might prove useful to him at a later date.

When Ambrosia opened the door, Argus pushed his way through without admittance, reaching down to grab her crotch as he passed, laughing. Ambrosia cowered and ran away crying, unable to do anything. She had only seen him once before since he had left the house to join the Praetorians; she had been buying vegetables in the markets when Argus pushed her into an adjacent alleyway. She had been left in tears and in pain then too.

He pushed open the door to Quintus' study without knocking. "Where is your family, Father?" he scoffed.

"What in Hades are you doing here?" Quintus Metellus felt his heart pound hard in his chest at being startled so suddenly.

"You look old, Father," Argus said as he sat down in a chair and put his feet up on the table.

"Don't call me that, you swine! I never gave you the right to do so."

"You created me, *Father*, therefore I'll call you whatever I want. Got it, old man?" By his look, Argus was daring Quintus to oppose him, and Quintus knew it. He knew that Argus would not think twice before telling Antonia what he was holding above his head like a sharp blade ready to cut through the neck of a condemned man: that Argus was his bastard son by a woman who used to be Antonia's friend, before she and her husband were killed. When Argus had revealed his knowledge of his true paternity some months before, Quintus had known that he was cornered, that he could not risk the scandal. He cursed Argus' mother for having hidden a letter to her son in the few items he was to be given on his thirteenth birthday. Even in death the woman had betrayed Quintus.

"You'll go too far, Argus."

"Ha, ha! Please, you're in no position to threaten me, Father." Quintus hated Argus every time he used the word. "Besides the more you insult me, the longer I'll stay."

"What do you want?"

"Information."

"Of course. Scraps for your master, hmm?"

"When he is emperor, you'll wish you had given him more support."

"You live in a disgusting dream, Argus. He's no better than the rest of them. What information?"

Argus leaned forward, his elbows crushing a few scrolls that had been on the edge of the table, and became very serious. "I want to know about your other son's wife and her family, where they live in Athens, what they do, what their plans are. How long will Lucius be without her...or Ashur? Tell me everything."

"Why do you want to know all of this?"

"It's my business to know...and the price you pay."

"I can tell you what I know about the family, but I don't know when she will be joining Lucius again or where." Quintus then told Argus what he knew about Adara and her family, what they looked like (if he did not already know), where they had said they lived in Athens. Argus listened, his devious mind working round and round, gathering for his master.

The two of them had been in the study for some time, talking and arguing, when Antonia returned from the Lady Claudia's with the children. A red-eyed Ambrosia had opened the door for her mistress, shaking and sobbing.

"What is it Ambrosia?" Antonia whispered. "Has he hurt you?" She was of course thinking of her husband.

"No mistress. It ww...was...Argus is here." Antonia knew that she ought to be very careful at this point.

"Ambrosia, take the children up to their rooms and stay with them." The slave nodded and ushered the children away.

Antonia hung her own cloak on the hook by the door and stepped quietly down the corridor, past the row of ancestors. She heard raised voices and stopped, not wanting to be discovered. The voices got louder and she went past the study door and into a small room across the way, leaving the door slightly ajar so that she could listen.

"What else can you tell me about this woman, Adara? You're holding back information, Senator!"

"I've told you everything, you idiot! Oh, except one thing; she usually wears a long blue, hooded cloak. That's it! All right?"

"Fine, fine. But I'll be back for more information in a fortnight, so you'd better warm up to your wife and find out if she's received any letters, and what they say."

"Gods damn you, Argus! May your shade never rest!"

"They've already damned me!" Argus stood to leave. "Can't you hear them laughing at the irony of it all? Listen. They're laughing every time I call you *father* because they know how you hate it." Argus laughed at Quintus whose face was a vengeful crimson.

"Get out! Go! You'll always be a bastard!"

"A bastard I may be, Father, but I'm your bastard and I won't let you forget it." Argus slammed the door behind him and went back out into the night.

In the small dark room Antonia wept, frightened and confused while her husband destroyed his study, throwing stools, scrolls and anything else he could abuse. She felt angry as well. *What has he become?* she wondered. *What has he done?* She wiped the tears from her face and stepped into the corridor just as Quintus came out of his study.

"What was he doing here?" she asked. "Quintus?" He looked guilty, like a child who had been cutting the legs off of a bird he had caught.

"Get out of my way, woman! I'm not in the mood for this!"

"You seem to be well enough in the mood to betray your family!" she shouted back at him. "Why did he call you *father*?" Quintus turned in a fury, the back of his hand slamming into her cheek, sending her reeling into the wall where she knocked over the bust of Caecilia Metella.

"How dare you speak to me so impudently! I'm paterfamilias!" Quintus then grabbed Antonia's arm and dragged her down the marble floor to the edge of the garden at the bottom of the staircase. She cried out from the pain as he pulled her hair and slapped her again and again.

"Ambrosia, let me go!" Young Quintus yelled, trying to pull away and go to his screaming mother. "He's hurting her!" The young boy struggled in his anger as he remembered hiding in the dark in a mountain tomb above the Etrurian estate, unheard and unnoticed as he listened to the horrible words that were a secret between Argus and his own father. He had hated his father ever since then and could not hide while his mother was beaten. Ambrosia could not hold on to him so she let go, trying instead to cover Clarinda's ears as she wailed.

When young Quintus arrived at the top of the stairs he saw his father slapping and kicking Antonia, her cries growing weaker. "Leave her alone!" Little Quintus ran down in a rage, screaming like a gorgon. He leapt at his father from the middle of the stairs but Quintus pater moved so that his son crashed onto the ground next to his mother.

"You're all a disappointment! You hear me? All of you will learn to obey me. I'm paterfamilias!" Young Quintus grabbed his father's leg as he moved to kick Antonia again and bit into his ankle, the taste of blood filling his mouth. Quintus yelled out in pain and got free of his son's teeth. He then grabbed the boy by the neck, slapped him six times, and flung him against the wall where the boy's head slammed into the plaster and he fell motionless to the ground.

Mumbling incoherently, Antonia dragged herself to her son's side. Her husband spit at them, then dragged both to the small room where his wife had been hiding and locked them in.

"Clean up this mess!" he yelled at the house slaves who quivered in the garden. "If any of you opens this door before the morning, I'll kill you myself!" He went back into his study, feeling pathetically strong again, master of his home.

"Well? What's the diagnosis?"

"Senator, they are lucky to be alive," said the physician, holding back his shock and anger. "I cannot say that I condone such treatment of family but it is not my place to question, only to heal. Your wife's face is badly bruised and she has a broken jaw, a broken rib and a broken leg. The boy's skull is cracked; I've let some blood out to relieve pressure on the brain. He should heal…in time. He's lucky he did not hemorrhage to death. They should both recover after a couple of months, if lucky. Until then they must stay still and rest." Quintus hardly listened as the physician spoke.

"It was a hard lesson but they should learn after this. They'll recover you say?"

"By Aesclepius and Apollo's grace, yes."

"Hmmm."

"I must ask, Senator, that you do not call for my services again. I have done what I can for them with the gift I have, but I cannot bear to enter this house again to see such atrocities. My heart is not made of stone."

"You speak too freely, physician! Leave my home at once!"

"Good day to you, Senator." The physician calmly stepped out of the house, the door slamming behind him. He then allowed himself to shake with pity for the patients he had just treated and said a prayer to the Gods of healing to aid them.

One day, a couple weeks later, Ambrosia stepped into her mistress' rooms where she lay recovering alone in bed. Everyday, Antonia asked Ambrosia how her son was doing and what was happening in the house. Ambrosia now dedicated herself to caring for her mistress and young Quintus. She never left their sides, went back and forth from one room to the next.

At first, Antonia had found it difficult to speak, but she had adapted as best she could, as did Ambrosia in her attempts to understand her. Her bruised face was now a sickly yellow, but the swelling had gone down considerably. Daily, she asked Ambrosia to see if there were any letters for her and if she could get them to her secretly before her husband found them and destroyed them. On the tray that day, next to a bowl of broth, were two letters; one from Lucius and one from Alene.

Lucius' letter was brief, but did say that he was well and that he was now leaving Leptis Magna for Lambaesis where he was returning to duty. Antonia breathed a painful sigh of relief that he was all right and picked up Alene's letter.

To Antonia Metella
From her loving daughter, Alene Metella

Dear Mother,

I trust that you are well and not too lonely without me. I am writing because I had a worrying dream last night. I dreamt that you were attacked by savages in a wild northern forest, and that you were injured badly. I don't remember much else. I'm sure it is just the fact that I miss you so much. You know how I feel helpless if I am not there to make sure things go well. Don't mind me.

How right you were to talk me into going to Greece! I pray that someday you can come here and see the wonders that I have seen, smell what I have smelled and taste what I have tasted. I want nothing now but to see the world! There is so much beyond the walls of Rome. However, I doubt that I would find anything to match the beauty of this place.

Most days I have been going out with Adara and the girls to see temples or sanctuaries. Most of these monuments were built when Rome was but a village on the Palatine. This city is alive in so many ways; the people, the temples, the art and music all add to the flavour. Even the trees, the marble, and the fruit upon the ground enrich the surroundings.

The other day a most exciting thing happened. It rained! I know what you are thinking. Alene, it rains all the time in Rome. But this is different, Mother. It does not usually rain here from Aprilis to November except for one summer storm in which the Gods cleanse the land with a furious downpour. The other day, this storm occurred. It was most astonishing. We were in the Agora of the city under a clear blue sky and hot sun. Suddenly, as if conjured out of nothingness, the sky darkened with whirling black clouds. Zeus himself cast fiery bolts across the sky to strike the surrounding mountains and Poseidon leant the sea to the skies, for it rained unlike anything I have seen before.

We took shelter in one of the stoas in the Agora and waited for two hours as the city was lashed with the Gods' fury. I believed the stoa would fall in upon us but things here are well-built. When we went outside again there was not a cloud to be seen. The world all around us was changed. It was a blessing not a punishment, for I had to shield my eyes from the brilliance around me. Every layer of dust and dirt that had covered the white marble of the city during the dry, hot summer months was completely washed away.

I thought we had been swept away to Mount Olympus everything was so bright and heavenly. There was a sweet smell in the air, most likely the lingering presence of the Gods. All was strong and fresh and breathtaking. I wish you could see what I have seen.

Forgive me, Mother, for writing such a lengthy work yet again. I hope that I have not bored you with all of my raving. If only the Gods could wisp you away to us here in Athens!

If you do not know already, Lucius has departed for the legionary base in Numidia. He says he is well and that he will write again when he arrives.

Once again you have the love and wishes of everyone here, especially myself. I love you, Mama. I don't know if I have said *it enough. Perhaps Aphrodite has inspired me here. I shall write again soon. My heart is with you. May the Gods bless and protect you.*

Your Loving Daughter

Alene Metella

Antonia rolled up the letter, tried not to sob; the pain in her rib caused too much pain. She placed the scroll beneath her pillow and called for Ambrosia to take away her tray and bowl.

"How is my son, Ambrosia?" she asked.

"He is sleeping mistress, peacefully."

"Good. I shall sleep for a while now."

"Shall I close the shutters to block out the sun, mistress?"

"No, not this time. I like the feel of the sun on my face. Just close the door behind you."

"Very well, mistress." Ambrosia closed the doors to both rooms and seated herself on a stool in the hallway outside. If either of them needed anything she wanted to be there to help.

Antonia leaned back slowly, her breath shallow and pained. The sun warmed her face as she lay her head on her pillow and closed her eyes. She thought of Alene and tried to picture her in Athens as she had done so many times. The thought comforted her, brought her closer to her daughter who helped her to escape through her long letters.

Sighing, she nodded off to restful sleep, dreamed of Alene and Greece, temples, warm cradling sunlight and rain.

V

IN ITINERE AD CIRTAM

'On the Road to Cirta'

After three days at sea, unfavourable winds and scorching sun, Lucius' ship finally made berth in the circular, military port of Carthage. The ship's captain had attempted to make for the city by hugging the coastline westward before turning north, but a summer storm had swept them off course, followed by no wind at all for an entire day. The captain, Lucius and the rest of the crew breathed a collective sigh of relief when they finally moored the ship.

As they made their approach through the first harbour full of merchant vessels, Lucius stood on the prow looking out over the city he left almost a year before. So much had happened since that day when Alerio, Antanelis and the others had stood on the dock to see him and Argus off. Now he thought of it, the reality of all that had happened since was harsh and biting: Argus was much estranged, there was the threat of mutiny within his cohort and Antanelis was dead. Good and bad, much had changed; now that he had met Adara, there was much more to lose. As they eased into the harbour, he spotted where Antanelis had stood, strong and proud, face scarred, saluting. He remembered what his friend's father had told him. If Antanelis had not written his father, asking him to warn Lucius of the plots against him in the cohort, Lucius would be walking blindly into danger.

"Ready to disembark, Tribune," the captain said as some of the crew lowered the gang plank. "We'll be staying here for a day. If you want to leave your belongings on board until you find accommodation and hire a wagon, you may do so. I'll set a watch here so none of the locals wander onto the ship looking for something to steal."

"Thank you, captain, I'll do that. Shouldn't take too long for me to find quarters." Lucius strapped on his sword and dagger, put on his cloak and picked up the satchel containing his imperial pass. He recalled as he walked onto the docks that in a few days it would be the time of the Ludi Romani, the games held in honour of Jupiter Optimus Maximus. Carthage was said to put on a good show on this occasion; finding quarters might prove more difficult than he had thought.

The smell of the sea mingled with the scents of incense, dung and sand that trickled down the long straight avenues from the markets and fora. The few times Lucius had been in Carthage, the same sense of eerie uncertainty had come over him. Many said that the streets of Carthage were haunted by the shades of the Punic dead who fell by Rome's will. Whispers seemed to come out of walls and an undead populace emerged at night to sow seeds in the salted earth where they would never grow. Now however, Carthage was one of the empire's most illustrious jewels. But, under the beauty and prosperity, there was always something to remind the citizens of a brutal past. The jewel's setting was sad and black.

The immense Antonine bath complex came into view as Lucius made his way up the main thoroughfare that led from the baths to the theatre of Carthage. There were several inns along the street, many of them located above small shops and taverns. From one window a bare-breasted prostitute whistled at Lucius and from another across the street an old woman held up bunches of grapes to sell. He nodded politely to both women and moved on. The old woman promptly made an obscene gesture to the prostitute, a sign against bad luck and competition, and the naked woman squeezed her own wares in return.

Eventually, Lucius came to an inn called *The Centurion* that looked much tidier than the rest and had a tavern located on the ground floor. He walked in the main door and went directly to a counter where an old veteran sat on a stool going over his accounts on a wax tablet. The man was about fifty-five with pale, receding hair and tired, green eyes. He noticed Lucius and looked up from his accounts.

"Tavern's closed right now," he muttered.

"I'm not looking for food," replied Lucius seriously. "I need a room for the night."

"Sorry young one, officers only at my inn. Try the one down the road with the naked woman hanging out the window."

Calmly, Lucius reached into his satchel, produced the imperial pass and laid it, seal up, on the counter. "I would like to stay here if you have the room."

The man looked at it and as soon as his eye fell upon the seal, he jumped up from his stool. "My apologies! Centurion, is it?"

"Tribune Metellus. I'm travelling on an imperial pass. Is it good here?" Lucius knew the answer to that of course; anyone who refused an imperial pass could be shut down.

"Of course, of course, Tribune. Hail Caesar and all of that! My name's Curtius and you're welcome here. We only have one room left due to the games but I think you'll find it satisfactory. It's on the top floor and gets a nice breeze from the sea. Small but comfortable for a night's stay."

"Good. I'll take it." Lucius rolled up the pass and put it back in his satchel.

"Do you have any bags, Tribune? My sons can help you with them."

"My two trunks are on my ship in the harbour. Can they come with me to get them?"

"Of course." The man turned to yell into a back room. "Titus! Fulvius! Mazentius! Get the wagon and go with the tribune here to the harbour to get his belongings!"

"Yes, Father!" a voice yelled back.

"So Tribune, you're only staying one night?"

"Yes, afraid so. I need to get back to Lambaesis."

"Oh, Lambaesis. I've got a couple of cavalry officers staying here who are headed that way tomorrow too."

"Really?"

"Yes. Strange ones they are though. Two tall fellas with reddish hair, dark skin and untrusting grey eyes. Auxiliaries from some north-eastern country. Keep to themselves."

"Hmm. Well maybe I'll see them in here later."

"Father? We're ready to go now." A young man stuck his head in the front door. The three of them were waiting outside with a mule-drawn wagon. Lucius followed him outside. They were three young men under twenty and much resembled their father. Titus was the only one who spoke. "Are we going to the military harbor, Tribune?"

"Yes." Lucius followed Titus as they walked in front of the other two boys in the wagon behind.

"Hello boys!" the friendly prostitute called to them from her window and waved. All three of them tried not to look up or wave as she fondled herself and invited them in by name. She obviously knew them *very* well.

"I'm telling your father!" said the old woman across the street. Little did she know that it was their father who had introduced his sons to her as part of their 'education'.

After Lucius had settled into his room at the inn and arranged for a wagon and two horses to take to Lambaesis the next day, he went to the baths. All the people of Carthage had piled themselves into the enormous edifice, or so it appeared. Lucius had hoped to relax quietly in some remote corner of the complex and train by himself on the palaestra or in the gymnasium, but as the sun reached its peak and the day burned, those who were not sleeping or eating were there. Every hall of the complex echoed with the voices of men and women. Lucius paid the small fee at the main entrance and went through to the large hexagonal changing room where he found a small niche to put his things. He had brought a fresh tunic in which he had carefully rolled his dagger and placed it at the back of the niche behind his sandals.

On the outdoor palaestra, after three bouts of wrestling, Lucius decided to train his spear arm by throwing a few javelins at a target that had been set up at the far end; that particular skill needed attention as it had been some time since he had practiced. Once physically exhausted, it was time to head to the tepidarium where he cleaned the dirt from his body with strigil and oil and soothed his muscles in the warm waters. The pool was relatively small and he found himself almost cheek to cheek with two Punic women and one man who had waded over. Lucius felt something tickle his thigh underwater.

"Bathing is always more pleasurable with more bodies, don't you think?" said the woman on his right in horrifically accented Latin. The other woman said something else in Punic that Lucius did not understand but from the feel of her hand and the smile on her face, she agreed. Feeling uncomfortable and unrelaxed, Lucius decided to go to the caldarium next. The two women and the man observed his naked body as he got out of the water and walked down the hall to the hot pool.

"Romans are such prudes," laughed the women's male companion. Their laughter echoed in Lucius' wake.

In the thick steamy air of the caldarium, Lucius found some respite from the crowds. There were many people in the hot pool but because of the steam and size of the pool, he was able to feel more alone, close his eyes and remember Cumae when he and Adara had lain on the beach, undisturbed. He imagined that the water on his chest was the lapping sea as they swam naked and without care. How he missed her. He wanted to bring her to Numidia with him, but that reminded him of the task he had avoided thinking about. His muscles tensed and he sweat profusely as he thought again of what Antanelis had written to his father before he was apparently killed by a lion while hunting. Lucius prayed that Alerio had handled things and not revealed too much to anyone. Garai, Eligius and Maren would help also he hoped, if they could be trusted. He doubted everything, decided to clear his mind before he went mad. He had a long journey by himself to think about all of it, and so went back to his thoughts of Adara and how he loved to lay next to her beautiful body as she whispered softly that she loved him.

Feeling light-headed after having spent too long in the steamy water, Lucius left the caldarium and walked along the mosaic floors to the immense, rectangular frigidarium. He jumped right in, invigorated by the cold water that came down from the mountains outside Carthage by way of the aqueducts. He felt completely revived after swimming back and forth a few times and made his way eagerly for a deep rubdown with scented oil by one of the slaves.

There was much to do in Carthage during the games; the theatres were staging performances, the shows in the amphitheatre went on all day and there were chariot races in the circus. Crowds could be heard all over the city cheering and clapping, merchants cajoled unwary buyers and the forum buzzed with local politicking. Overlooking the city streets was the monumental centre of Carthage where the Capitol and other religious buildings had been erected in the spot where the Punic palace and temple of Eshmoun had once existed.

The smell of fresh dates reached Lucius' nose as he passed a street leading to the markets. He realised that he needed to bring provisions along with him for the journey, some food and a couple water skins that he could refill along the way. He turned off the street and walked for a while until he came to a square where vendors had their produce displayed for the milling crowd.

"Come, come! Fresh figs! Figs! Very Juicy!" yelled one man.

"Dates! Olives! Spices!" called another.

Lucius walked along the fragrant rows full of colour and life, like a sweet-smelling garden in full bloom. First, he bought the water skins, then some figs and dates. He stopped at an open air oven where a woman was making fresh bread and bought several flat loaves at a good price. He had forgotten any Punic that he had learned in the past, but made due with a curt Latin phrase if anything was too expensive, and if that did not work, then a sharp wave of the hand indicated he would not be had. The trick was always to make like he was going to walk away without a care and inevitably the merchant would pull him back by the sleeve for a better price.

He then purchased some dried goat meat and some cheese although the latter would not last terribly long before going bad in the intense heat. Even in September, the land was hot and burning, at least up until the green uplands of the mountains. Lucius passed quickly by the rows of sheep and cattle heads that hung from wooden beams where they dripped, leaving pools of blood on the cobbles, vacant eyes betraying their escaped souls.

Finally, with just about as much as he could carry, he made his way out of the market, arms full of food, and returned to *The Centurion* for the evening.

"Welcome back, Tribune!" said Curtius as Lucius entered the tavern door. "Spent the day at the baths did you?"

"Yes, well, part of it anyway." Lucius went through the room where several groups of men were eating. The two men sitting in one corner staring at him did not go unnoticed but he decided to make his way to his room and unload his purchases. Suspicious too, he wanted to have his sword close by and pulled it out once he entered the room.

The days had begun to grow shorter in length, the light slipping away. However, that did not mean that the city went to sleep early too. In fact, with the Ludi Romani for the next couple of weeks, Carthage would sleep during the hot hours. Lucius had already prepared his belongings and set aside his travelling clothes: his blue tunic, grey breeches and his crimson cloak. He did not want to show off his rank but did want to show some sign that he was in the military to warn away any would-be assailants. However, he needed to be discreet as he would be travelling by himself. He sat on the edge of the bed and decided upon his route; out of the northern city gate to the westward road to Cirta through the passes. Then, he would turn south to Thamugadi and then push on to Lambaesis. It would be a long journey.

Perhaps it would be best to travel at night, he wondered. He had quit Leptis Magna in such a hurry and in such secrecy that there had not been any time to arrange for a detachment of his troops to meet him in Carthage. Besides, considering the events in Leptis Magna and the level of uncertainty he faced in Numidia, it was probably safer to travel alone and mix as little as possible with anybody. As he sat there he was reminded once more of the two men downstairs and figured that they must be the auxiliary officers to whom Curtius had referred.

Lucius felt ashamed hiding in that room. He was fed up with skulking in corners. The two men had given him a strange feeling; his soldier's gut sat uneasily for some reason. He was hungry but did not want to eat into his supplies for the journey, and so he decided to go downstairs and introduce himself to them and see what they were about. *No more waiting!* With his dagger and sword hidden beneath his cloak, he made his way down.

"Ah! Tribune, you're back. Good. Would you like something to eat and drink then? We have some good stew, fresh bread and an excellent wine," Curtius said joyfully.

"Yes. Thank you, Curtius." Lucius leaned forward over the counter and spoke beneath the laughter from surrounding tables. "Are those the officers you spoke of, Curtius?" The innkeeper nodded. "Good." Lucius turned and walked directly to the table where the two men sat. He smiled before speaking. "It appears, gentlemen, that we're headed for the same destination." The men looked at each other, then at Lucius, but said nothing. They continued to sip their wine. Lucius decided to ignore the insult and continue. "Are you not going to the legionary fortress at Lambaesis?"

"Yes we are," said the older of the two. Curtius had been right about their appearances; they were indeed tall, even when sitting and had unusual reddish-brown hair. Their eyes were grey but not so much untrusting as uninterested.

"Here's your food, Tribune." Curtius came up behind Lucius with a large tray. "Where would you like it?"

"Please set it down here, Curtius, thank you." Lucius pointed to the table next to the one where the cavalry officers sat. The innkeeper set the food down on the table, poured the wine and left Lucius to his meal after clearing the two men's empty plates.

"You are a tribune?" asked the younger of the two, obviously surprised by Lucius' rank. The older officer might have been about forty-five to fifty years of age and the younger about twenty-two.

"Yes," replied Lucius. "Tribune Metellus, stationed at Lambaesis with my cohort."

"What are you doing here?" asked the older one.

"I've been away in Rome for some time." Lucius did not want to say that he had just come from Leptis Magna. The fewer people who knew that, the better. "What are your ranks and names?"

"My name is Dagon," said the young one with great pride. "I am the standard bearer for our ala unit."

"And yourself?" Lucius asked the older man who was giving Dagon a look urging him not to volunteer any information.

"I am Mar. I am the ala commander." He too seemed very proud of his position, as this was the only time he had shown any feeling or emotion up to that point.

"I've not come across names such as yours before," Lucius said, "where do you hail from?"

"North of Pontus," answered Mar.

"That covers a large area." Lucius decided to push things and not be intimidated by Mar's coolness. "What country?"

"We are Sarmatian," Dagon put in, unable to hold back.

"Sarmatian?" Lucius asked again. He wanted to make sure, having only ever heard of the Sarmatians and how they were one of the fiercest foes Rome had ever faced. Emperor Marcus Aurelius finally defeated them and afterward used them as auxiliaries. Lucius had never seen any. "Is your ala entirely made up of Sarmatian cavalry?"

"Yes," Mar answered. Lucius tried not to look surprised.

"*Mar* and *Dagon*...what do your names mean in your tongue?"

"My name means *little fish*," said Dagon.

"And yours Mar?"

"It means *lord*."

"Are you a lord?" Lucius pressed.

"In my own land, yes." By this time, Mar was visibly annoyed and rose from his seat, Dagon followed immediately. "You ask too many questions, Roman," he said. The tavern grew quiet. "Good night to you." They picked up their belongings to go to their rooms but not before Mar paused to stare at the hilt of Lucius' sword and the two golden dragon heads that protruded.

"We should travel together back to base," Lucius suggested as they went.

"We travel alone," Mar said over his shoulder.

Lucius sat back and finished his meal. He had not wanted to ask to travel with them but they did not seem like they cared enough about him to kill him. An assassin would have been friendlier and accepted the invitation to travel. These two kept to themselves.

"You see what I mean, Tribune? Odd aren't they?" said Curtius as he cleared the table.

"You could say that, Curtius. Odd indeed."

Before a brightly-coloured dawn, Lucius' covered cart and two horses were waiting out front of the inn for him. Curtius' groggy sons helped him to load his belongings. He thanked them and his host and drove the cart through the streets of

Carthage to the northern gate where he eventually turned west onto the road to Thugga.

The morning was brisk and Lucius wrapped his cloak about himself as he drove his team out of the sandy plain and into the green hills that rose before him. The miles ahead seemed to be covered with interminable rows of olive and fig trees. He felt anxious surrounded by trees in the darkness where he would be vulnerable to ambush by bandits. However, his fears were allayed with the rising of Apollo's sun, its red light glistening on the dew-covered earth as the cart rolled on at a steady pace. The horses he had been given were by no means pure stallions, but they were strong and managed well enough on the increasingly steep roads.

To the south, Lucius could see the snake-like expanse of the aqueduct that supplied water to Carthage from the mountains. Hours had passed, the sun having risen higher and higher. As there was not a soul on the road, he decided to stop at a roadside shrine with a fountain to water the horses and top up his own supply. While the horses drank their fill at a trough, Lucius took out some of the cheese and bread he had bought for the journey to suppress the grumbling in his stomach. Chewing hungrily, he stepped onto the road to look around and stretch his legs. He was thankful for the direct route of a good Roman road, for without it, the journey would be three or four times longer. It was peaceful; birds cooed in the groves of trees and shepherds emerged from their dwellings with their flocks. Lucius jumped back into the wagon to continue the journey. He would reach Thugga in two days, but first he had to make his way over the hills. The wagon creaked as it climbed behind the horses and the groves began to give way to dense shrub, cedar and pine.

That first night there was not an inn in sight and so, as the sun made its descent to disappear behind the hills, Lucius chose to make camp in a small, hidden clearing that was partly sheltered by a looming rock-face. He kept his fire small so as not to attract any unwanted attention besides that of the local god whose shrine rose up at the top of the hill to overlook the countryside. Having fed the horses and tethered them to a root at the centre of the clearing, Lucius rolled out a small mat next to the fire, placed his sword and dagger on the ground beside it and leaned up against one of the wagon wheels. He looked up at yet another starlit sky and thought of Adara, far away in Athens, sighed and spoke her name to the air.

Sleep came upon him quickly and before he realised it, dawn was upon him; the horses roused his dreaming mind with their snorting and stomping of heavy hooves. Lucius relieved himself and took some breakfast from his provisions before hitching them to the wagon and setting off once more. The day was good for travelling with a light breeze from the north. He had already reached the highest peak of the range of hills and now the road began to descend into a green valley accompanied by a small river. A few villas belonging to rich farmers dotted the landscape. Slaves busied themselves in the olive orchards, caring for the year's yield, to be harvested in a few months time. They paid little heed to the lonely traveller as he passed through. Here and there they sang Punic songs, some resembling a sad wailing, others happy. Lucius could picture them during harvest time busily knocking the fruit out of the trees with their long sticks to be caught in nets around the base of trees, their songs in tune with the gentle whacking of their work.

A day later, after another damp night out of doors, Lucius passed the milestone indicating that Thugga was a mere eight miles away. The sun was somewhat blotted out due to the low clouds that encircled the surrounding hills as he drew near to the city. It seemed odd that such a large and prosperous settlement should be found in so remote and quiet a region. The road was extremely well-kept and was flanked with many impressive shrines and tombs the closer he came to the settlement. Finally, the city came into full view, its vast array of bright buildings cutting through the cloud, foremost among them the tall peak of the Capitol with the image of an eagle soaring above the streets.

Thugga overlooked vast olive groves that blanketed the rolling land. It was a prosperous city with many new buildings in evidence; it even had an arch recently dedicated to the emperor through which Lucius passed as he entered the city on the Carthage road. As he looked up, he was struck by how the buildings radiated from the Capitol at the top to cover the sloping hill like the surrounding olive groves. To the south of the city limits stood a lonely Punic mausoleum jutting out among the trees.

The streets were densely packed and Lucius could hear noise from the theatre at the top of the hill and the hippodrome to the north. Beautiful temples stood all around the walls providing the citizens with pockets of peaceful silence away from the forum and places of entertainment. Just inside the eastern gate, along the main road, Lucius spotted a large inn with stables in the rear and decided it might be a good place to spend the night as he could not take the wagon further into the city.

The inn was at the corner of two streets. Lucius left the wagon with the slave out front to whom he gave a denarius to watch his belongings. The man nodded, planted himself next to the horses and held the reigns tightly in his hand while Lucius went inside. He was welcomed by a man of Punic origin who was gaudily dressed in purple, gold and orange robes. His bangled arms clanged as he raised them in greeting to the traveller.

"Come, come inside, oh weary traveller!" he said in what must have been a completely new version of Latin. Lucius struggled to understand him. "You need a room for the night, two nights, a week?" His groomed eyebrows pointed upward curiously as he looked for a money pouch at Lucius' waist.

"Just one night."

"Very well, very well. I have a room for you. Only twenty denarii!"

"Twenty!" *He must be putting me on?* Lucius wondered.

"Thugga is a prosperous city, citizen, and very expensive during the games."

"Very well." Lucius laughed to himself as the man continued looking for a money pouch. "I'll take it as long as you stable my horses and wagon for the night. I set out early in the morning."

"Very good! Excellent!" The man clapped his hands and rubbed them together briskly. "You do have coins, do you not?"

"Something better, my good man!" Lucius reached into his satchel.

"Gold!" The proprietor was practically jumping up and down like a child awaiting honeyed sweets. "You have gold! Oh, may the Gods bless you!"

"No. Not gold. Here." Lucius produced the imperial pass and handed it to the man whose giddiness soon vanished as if he had lead weights tied to his feet. He frowned and huffed. Evidently, he had seen this sort of thing before and was clearly disappointed.

"Not another!" he said to himself. "I knew I should have opened an inn in the area closer to the forum! Everybody has coin there. But here? No! Travellers passing through with imperial passes!"

"I can go elsewhere if you do not wish to honour the emperor's seal," Lucius said sternly. The man lightened up slightly.

"No! It is fine. I honour the emperor's seal." He knew that if he did not, he would have trouble from the local magistrate. "Come with me to your room." Lucius followed him up some stairs to a small room with a single bed and a small table. Not the most luxurious room in the house, but good enough for one night. "Here it is. The stables are around back. I keep them guarded all the time, so do not worry about any belongings," he said curtly.

"Good. Are there baths in the town?" Lucius asked.

"Of course there are baths in the town!" The man looked greatly insulted. "Thugga has three baths! There is the large one down the road you came in on, there is the one at the brothel up the street in front of this inn if that is to your taste..." He winked at Lucius who ignored him. The man cleared his throat and stepped back. "Or, if you prefer, the family of the Licinii has recently constructed a beautiful bath complex toward the centre of town. Very nice, that one!"

"That sounds good." Lucius then followed the man downstairs and took his wagon to the rear of the building where he stabled the horses and hid the wagon as best he could, covering the trunks with some loose planks of wood so that they were not evident in the dark. They had locks on them, but one never knew who was about at night.

With a change of clothes in his satchel, Lucius left the inn and walked up the street. At the second intersection, he found himself in the shadow of a giant marble phallus that protruded, very erect, from the front of a small complex. The brothel.

"By Bacchus!" Lucius laughed. He could hear giggling from within, mingled with moans and pitched screams of some form or another. A half-dressed man came running out into the street smiling and entered the next door where the public latrines were located. Soon after, he emerged quite relieved and re-entered the brothel beneath the giant phallus. Lucius moved on to the new baths. Just as he turned, a woman appeared in the doorway of the brothel.

"Hellooo!" she said in a feigned sultry voice. "Looking for company, Roman?" She was of an average height, dark and slender. She would have been beautiful if not for the thick layer of stibium around her eyes, the scent of previous customers and a musky oil that emanated from her body.

"No, erm, thank you," he said politely as he turned to go.

"Don't leave so soon!" She skipped after him, her silver anklets and bracelets jingling as she went. "I'm only being friendly!"

"Sorry, but I really must go now. Thanks for the offer." Lucius continued walking, embarrassed by the unwanted stares he received by passing locals. The girl was unperturbed.

"My name's Dido," she said.

"Of course it is."

"What's yours?"

"Aeneas."

"Ha! You're playing with me, Roman! What's your real name?" she persisted.

"Titus." Lucius did not want to give his real name to her. He walked faster to escape her strong smell but she was fleet-footed.

"Oooo. I like that name. Titus, how would you like to play with me? Half price for the entire night. You look like you could do that." She poked Lucius in the side and he stopped.

"Look here, *Dido*! I've been travelling for two days, I'm tired and there's only ever one woman on my mind or in my bed: my wife! So, if you don't mind, I'd like to be alone, understand?" He continued walking and she followed him up the wide marble avenue that curved around the baths up the hill.

"Oh ho! You're a feisty one! I like that. But since when is being married something to prevent a man travelling by himself from having a little fun?"

"Since *me,* woman! All right?" He stopped outside the doors to the baths. Dido lowered her head a little, either in disappointment or embarrassment. "Look," said Lucius, feeling badly he had raised his voice to her so loudly. "I'm tired, filthy and otherwise extremely happy with my situation. Thank you again for your offer, but I'm sure that there are plenty of other men who would welcome a night immersed in your pleasures. Just not me." Dido raised her head and smiled understandingly, her eyes glistening behind the dark stibium.

"Forgive me, Titus. It's rare that a man like you passes through Thugga. I respect your situation and though my offer still stands, I understand your reasoning. Good evening to you and may Baal protect you on your journey." With that, she turned and went back down the white street, her bare feet smacking on the marble to the tune of her jingling jewellery.

Once clean and refreshed, Lucius made for the market where he hoped to buy more food for his journey. Thugga was indeed pleasing to the eye and curious in its construction as a myriad of private homes blended in with public and official buildings to create a plan as elaborate and varied as the mosaics he had seen. In the market, he purchased some food and a small skin of wine in addition to some fresh sprigs of rosemary which he intended to offer to Jupiter, Juno and Minerva at the Capitolium overlooking the forum and markets.

As he made his way up the steps of the temple, he could hear the clapping emanating from the theatre up the road. A part of him longed for some entertainment to distract his mind but he knew he needed sleep if he was to leave before the sun lit the sky.

The temple was empty. Lucius entered the inner sanctum and went over to a three-sided altar to the Capitoline Triad. He placed the sprigs on it, prayed to the three gods for a safe journey and thanked them for protecting him thus far. When he went back outside, he stood at the top of the steps and breathed deeply of the clean night air. The clouds had cleared, it would be a stunning night of brilliant stars and a bright moon.

Lucius enjoyed his slow walk back to the inn, admiring various buildings along the way and bathing in the moon's light. This time he took a different route that led between the temples of Concordia, Bacchus and Pluto. That particular street was very quiet, dark except for a single torch that flickered near the Temple of Pluto. As he walked slowly, looking up at the sky, Lucius heard several hushed voices coming from a narrow alleyway between the temples. He stopped, not in the mood to expose himself to the local ruffians.

"Shhhh. Keep it down, all of you!" said a husky voice around the corner.

"Well? What did he say? Does he have lots of gold?" asked another voice.

"Probably. My friend said that this traveller just arrived today and is setting out on the Cirta road before the sun rises. He says that he has two big chests in his wagon."

"They're probably full of valuables!"

"Let's hope so," said the leader.

"Where should we ambush?"

"I've sent ten men to wait for him where the road passes close to the wooded mountainside. I don't want anything happening close to the city."

"I agree. Killing some hapless traveller is one thing, killing a military officer is quite another."

"Not even a military officer will be able to beat off ten armed men," the leader mocked. "Two of my men are expert archers." They all laughed together.

Lucius peered around the corner. He wanted to rush them then and there, catch them unawares, but from his quick glance at the situation, he noticed about eight to ten men, perhaps some slaves. *Damn!* he thought. *If it's not one thing it's another! I can't risk running into an ambush.* Lucius slowly backed off and returned the way he had come to get onto the main street again and take the longer way to the inn so as not to be spotted by the conspirators.

It seemed that the innkeeper had a big mouth. Lucius was tempted to wring his fat neck, but he didn't want to cause an incident, he just wanted to move on, get out of Thugga. But which way? There was only one road that led directly to Cirta. The other road to the south would take him the wrong side of the mountains. He was alone and did not know a soul in the city. There was only one possibility for help.

"Achh!" He stomped his foot as he realised what it meant. "Dido!" he said her name as the erect phallus of the brothel came into view glistening in the silver light from above. "By all the Gods! The one time I'm really stuck and my only option is a pleasure mistress named 'Dido'." He stopped several feet from the entrance, the usual array of sounds floating out of doors. He walked in.

Lucius found himself standing on a colourful mosaic floor looking down a stairwell that led directly to a colonnaded garden with a small pool in the middle. The air was heavy and humid, hazy with the smoke of strong incense. He walked into the garden, unable to suppress a cough due to the smoke. He felt light-headed. Giggles and sighs crept through curtained doors.

"What do ya want?" came a woman's voice from his right. An old voluptuous woman painted thick with makeup stood in the garden, arms crossed, eyeing Lucius suspiciously. He realised that he must have looked odd standing in the brothel with a satchel and groceries.

"I'm looking for Dido," he said, clearing his throat.

"You moving in?" She eyed his bundles.

"No, I just want to see her." Lucius winked for effect, knowing that only paying customers were allowed to go any further. The woman said nothing, simply stared, that is until she heard the jingle of coin in his satchel.

"Go on in!" she grumbled, her chins shaking with speech. "Fourth door on the left."

"Thanks." Lucius nodded to her and went around the edge of the garden until he came to the door indicated. It had a pink-dyed curtain that brushed the ground.

Lucius pulled back the curtain slightly and peered inside. The small cubiculum was dark except for a single lamp that burned on a small table. In a bed in the far corner, he could see a woman sleeping beneath a single sheet that hugged her body loosely. He had been trying to hold his breath but realised that she did not have the same scent as before. Evidently, she had taken a bath at the end of the day. He cleared his throat and knocked on the plastered wall inside.

"Not now..." she mumbled, "...too tired, I'm sleeping."

"Dido?" Lucius whispered.

"Not here…" she said again, pulling the sheet above her head so that her long legs were bared.

"By Eros! Dido, wake up!" he said a little louder. The girl pushed herself up on one elbow, then slowly dropped her feet over the edge of the bed, her hair in disarray, like a serpented Medusa.

"All right, all right! I'm up." She reached for the oil lamp on the table and stood up completely naked. Lucius tried not to look and cleared his throat again. Dido walked toward the door holding up the lamp to his face.

"Titus!" Dido exclaimed full of shock. She smiled, then realised she was naked and grabbed the sheet on the bed to cover herself. "Titus, what are you doing here?" Lucius regretted telling her his name was Titus. He hated that name.

"This is a nice way to wake up." She put her hand on his cheek. "You've come to accept my offer?"

"No." Lucius removed her hand and stepped back. She smelled much better than before, like orange blossom. "I need your help."

Her face grew serious. "What is it?"

"I'm in trouble and you're the only person I can trust at the moment."

"Of course you can trust me, Titus. Here, put your things down and tell me." She helped Lucius with his things and gave him a stool to sit on before slipping a loose, long tunic over her head. "Well? How can I help?"

"I'm travelling to Cirta but I can't go along the main road next to the mountains."

"Why not? It's a good road."

"Because there are several men waiting to make sure I don't get very far."

"How do you know?"

"I just do. Now, do you know this area very well?"

"Of course I do! I grew up as a slave on an estate not far from Cirta."

"Do you know of another road I could take with a two-horse wagon?" Dido thought for a moment then nodded as though she remembered something.

"Yes," she said with certainty. "There's a smaller road that runs along the other side of the river for several miles. It's used mostly by shepherds and goatherds but a wagon could move along it. It's flat and runs among the trees so that it should be well-hidden enough. There's a bridge just a mile out of town that can take you to the other side of the river."

"Does it avoid the point where the main road passes closest to the mountain?"

"Hmm. Yes, it does."

"Tell me how to find the small road."

Dido looked at Lucius, around her room and at the small table where her few belongings were scattered: a bone brush, an old tarnished bronze mirror, her jewellery and a charm of some sort. She picked up a small worn leather bag and swept the items into it.

"What are you doing?" Lucius asked.

"I'll show you myself," she replied.

"Oh no! I'm going alone. Just tell me how to find the path."

"Listen, Titus. It's been years since I've taken the path. If it's overgrown you'll never find it. It will be easier if I show you."

Lucius paced the floor impatiently. He knew that the sooner he got out of town, the better. Travelling in the dark was safer for now. "Just tell me. I don't want to endanger you or take you away from your life here."

"Oh, gods forbid I should leave all of this!" She waved her hand around the room in a dramatic gesture worthy of the theatre. "Besides, I could use a little excitement and perhaps I could even see my brother in Cirta. If he's still alive that is."

"Who said anything about going as far as Cirta with me?"

"That's my price, Titus! If you want my help, you get me to Cirta."

Lucius saw no way out of it. She was the only one who could help him. "Fine, fine. But only as far as Cirta."

"Agreed." She smiled, took up her bag and went to the door. "Let's go." They went out into the garden and made their way to the stairs to go out when a voice came out of the darkness.

"Where are you going?" the chins flapped.

"Oh, well, this traveller feels confined in my cubiculum. He wants me to pleasure him in the olive grove," Dido explained, indicating with one hand that Lucius was a little off, a little perverted. "He's even got a picnic."

"Well, whatever!" She waived a fat finger at Lucius. "But it's going to cost you extra!" Lucius nodded in return and Dido led him outside.

Lucius was relieved he had not left anything in his room at the inn; there was not a bolt on the door. Therefore, he and Dido went stealthily down the street and around the back of the inn to the stables. Lucius looked around the corner to where the so-called guard sat, snoring away as he leaned up against a stack of hay. Nobody else was around.

"Wait here," he whispered to her as he placed his bags on the ground and drew his dagger. Dido covered her mouth to avoid gasping. She wondered if it was such a good idea to go with someone who would kill so easily. Lucius tiptoed through the shadows to where the guard was sleeping. His dagger gleamed coldly in the moonlight as he raised his hand above the man's head. With a hard thump, Lucius hammered the pommel on the back of the guard's head knocking him unconscious so that he fell down into the hay. Dido sighed in relief and went to Lucius when he waived for her to come. He uncovered the wagon quietly and hitched up the horses. Thankfully the trunks were still there, locked. With the girl beside him in the cart, Lucius nudged the horses forward. Unnoticed by unfriendly eyes, they rolled down the street to join with the main road.

The night was cold, a dewy mist hovered amidst the olive trees and the silence was broken by the occasional bleating of sheep. Lucius heard Dido's teeth chattering at one point and realised that she did not have anything except the thin tunic.

"Here, take this." Lucius reached behind and handed her his black cloak. "This will keep you warm."

"Thank you," she said, grateful for the added warmth.

A short while later they spotted the river, silver in the moonlight. "There!" She pointed. "The bridge is just past that group of trees. See?"

"Yes," he said, pleased she had known what she was talking about. When they arrived at the crumbling stone bridge, Lucius doubted that the wagon would actually fit. Luckily it only just fit, the wheels rubbing gently on the stone. Once across, they picked up the pace to try and get as far as possible before daybreak. The cloudless night allowed for the road to be lit by moon and stars, enough to see and avoid crashing into any trees along the way. Lucius hoped that the assailants would not be able to see them from the other side of the river.

Rested and still, Dido awoke to see the orange light of the morning sun cutting through the misty air of a grove. She jumped up when she realised that the wagon was stopped and that Lucius was missing. Panic began to set in but she did not yell. She stepped down out of the wagon and looked around. He was nowhere to be seen. The dewy ground was cold to her bare feet as she walked through the trees. On the other side of the river she could see the mountains rising up and heard voices in the distance where smoke was coming from somewhere in the rock-face. The figure of a man came walking down the grassy slope to the river, whistling and swinging two water skins. A large recurve bow was slung across his back along with a quiver of arrows. Dido stepped backward slowly, worried that they had gotten Lucius, wherever he was.

"Oh Titus…" she whispered. Suddenly a strong arm came around her chest and a hand covered her mouth as she was yanked back behind a fallen tree. Lucius held her down, her mouth covered until he was sure she recognised him.

"It's the men who were to ambush me," he whispered in her ear. They watched as the man at the river looked their way. "Hades! I think he's spotted the wagon," Lucius mumbled. The man at the river put down the water skins and stepped into the water to get a better look. He unhitched his bow from his back. "He's coming." Lucius' heart was pounding. "You stay here. Don't move, don't get up."

"Where are you going?" Dido grabbed his tunic sleeve.

"If he alerts his friends, we're finished. This is no sleeping guard." Lucius crawled through the long grass to another log and then to hide behind the trunk of an old tree. The man waded across and came up onto the riverbank. He had also drawn an arrow from his quiver. Lucius wondered what to do, for if he charged the man he would have an arrow in his chest before he got close enough to run him through. The man stood still at the river's edge, cautious. Lucius looked on the ground at his feet and found several good-sized rocks. He picked up two of them, one in each hand. "Far-Shooting Apollo make me fast and accurate. Guide my hand." Lucius breathed deeply, steadying himself as the man came closer.

Quickly, he jumped out from behind the tree, and with all the power he could muster, he wielded the first rock so that it hit the archer on the side of the head. Stunned, the man grasped his head but did not fall. He spotted Lucius, but not before the second rock landed square in his face sending him reeling backward into the river where he floated away with the current. Lucius ran forward, picked up the bow the man had dropped, and ran back to Dido.

"Let's get away from this place before they realise he's been gone too long!" She got to her feet and they rushed back to the wagon. He threw the bow in the back and they set off at once.

Several hours later, sure that they were out of danger, Lucius stopped the wagon to water the horses and have some food. Dido had been silent most of the way, shocked by the morning's events. Once they set off again, however, she felt more comfortable and spoke freely.

"So Titus. Who are you?"

"Who am I? I told you."

"All you said was that your name was Titus. That's it. What else? Are you some kind of warrior, spy? No merchant throws rocks like that."

Lucius did not want to tell her anything. But, she had helped him quite a bit really and perhaps, he thought, she deserved to know something about him since she was risking her life to help him. She was utterly changed from the first time he had met her and not only how she smelled. She had pretty eyes the colour of dates, which were much more visible now that most of the stibium had worn off. Her dark hair was cleaner and fluttered in the breeze like a ship's sail on the Nile. He decided to amuse her. After all, they had a long journey ahead of them.

"I'm in the army," he said.

"Are you a legionary or something else?"

"Uhm, a tribune." He ignored the shocked look on her face.

"A tribune! Baal's great head, Titus! A tribune?"

"Yes. So?"

"So why are you travelling all alone across Numidia? Should you not have some sort of following, troops, slaves, that sort of thing?"

"Not this time."

"Why not, Titus?" Dido pressed. One of the horses at that moment purged its bowels, fouling the air as if it sensed Lucius' intended lies to the girl.

"Because...because...it's a long story, and I can't really go into it. Suffice it to say that the fewer people who know I'm travelling this way, the better. At least until I reach Lambaesis." He had not planned to let the latter slip.

"Is that where you're based? Lam-bae-sis?" she said the word slowly to get it right.

"Yes. That's where I'm based, where my men are."

"I see. How many men?"

"By the Gods, Dido, you're like a child with all of these questions!"

"Oh, come now, Titus!" She nudged his ribs. "We've got a long trip and should talk about something. How many men?" she repeated.

"A tribune usually commands about four-hundred and eighty men."

"Have you fought many battles?"

"A few."

"Where?" Her eyes were large and curious.

"Uhm, Parthia, across Africa province and in Numidia."

"Numidia? Here? Was it a large battle, that one?"

"Yes." Lucius did not want to relive the memories now that he was returning there.

"Did you lose many men?"

"Several."

"Have you killed many men? Besides this morning."

"Yes, many." Lucius grew quiet. Dido changed the topic. If she had learned anything from the array of clients she had had over the years, especially soldiers, it was that when a man did not want to talk about something serious, he meant it. This was more true for soldiers than other men, for they saw things that most people would never see, or want to.

"What about yourself Dido?" asked Lucius finally. "Where are you from and how did you get to be, well, how did you come to be in Thugga?"

"Are you sure you're interested Titus?"

"Yes." Although he wished she could stop calling him Titus.

"Very well. I was actually born in Hippo Regius, by the sea. My parents were both slaves. I have a brother, as I have said. I also had two sisters but they died along with my father aboard our master's ship during a storm."

"I'm sorry."

"Yes, well, I was only three years old then. After that, my mother, brother and I were sold to an oil merchant in Cirta. I haven't seen the sea since then. We lived in the house of our new master in Cirta for many years, fifteen actually. My mother's heart gave out during that time however, and she died. Not long after that, the master died too and there were no relatives to take over his affairs or property. So, my brother and I decided to get away from Cirta while we could; too many people there knew our faces. We decided to go to Thugga. I found work at the brothel, but my brother, he wanted more than just to pick olives. He went south to find something more."

"When was the last time you saw your brother?" Lucius was feeling much pity at her sad story but was also amazed at the strength and resilience she was showing after so much tragedy.

"I saw him about three years ago, I guess. He'd come back to Thugga to tell me he was going back to Cirta where a Punic merchant had hired him as a freedman. He never wanted to work for Romans."

"So how old are you then, Dido?"

"That's a good question, I think I'm about twenty-four, though, I seem to have lost track of time along the way. What about you, Titus?"

"Twenty-five."

"And your wife?"

"She is twenty-four."

"Is she beautiful? Where is she from? Rome?"

"She's from Athens, in Greece and yes, she is very beautiful."

"What's her name?"

"Adara." He could lie about his own name but not about his wife's. He enjoyed talking about her, saying her name.

"It is a pretty name."

Eventually, night began to fall once more and they needed to find a place to make camp. There were no inns along the minor road through the groves. Lucius looked about for some high ground but there was none, so he decided to go into the trees, away from the river where there was a small clearing protected by thick-trunked olive trees. He unhitched the horses to let them graze and built a small fire. Dido sat by the fire playing with blades of long grass while Lucius went to look at the surrounding area to make sure nobody was about. When he returned, he found she had laid out some of the food for them to eat.

"I hope you don't mind, but I thought I could help out in some way."

"Not at all. Thank you." Lucius looked around before sitting on the other side of the fire. "It seems safe around here. Not a soul about. I think we can sleep easy tonight."

"Good. Although, among my people, it's said that the shades of the fallen walk among the ancient olive groves. We should keep the fire lit all night."

"At least we'll be warm. If it keeps the shades away, that's good too."

"The shades...and lions."

"Lions?" Lucius repeated. "This far north?"

"Occasionally," said Dido matter-of-factly.

Shortly after, Lucius and Dido fell asleep on their opposite sides of the fire. Dido slept wrapped in Lucius' cloak while he slept too, however uneasily, sword in hand, trying not to think of shades and lions.

The following day they crossed into Numidia. The relatively flat, gentle slopes of Africa Proconsularis gave way to a rockier terrain, and the land now came in shades of red sand

and skin rather than green and silver. Wild flowers sprung from between rocks and ahead of them the mountains rose up jaggedly. Somehow, Numidia smelled more familiar to Lucius, to Dido as well. The travelling had been slow the last two days but the following day they would rejoin the main road.

To Lucius' surprise, Dido had proved to be an excellent travelling companion. The sexual temptress and businesswoman had been left behind in Thugga. Instead, he found himself in the company of a sweet and quick-witted young woman who glowed with the thought of returning home to see her brother. Both enjoyed talking as they went and Dido even entertained Lucius and the horses, whose ears perked up, with songs in her native tongue.

The nights passed quietly and the days sped by. At one point, Dido asked about Lucius' family and to his astonishment he went into his problems with his father. She listened attentively, trying to understand such a foreign world in which fathers would insist upon their sons doing one thing instead of another, and all for the good of the family and its political standing in society. In one way, she pitied the life he had to lead, but she did not say as much.

"What gods do you pray to?" she asked one night as they ate by the campfire.

"For myself, I pray to Apollo and Venus."

"Have they been good to you?"

"Very good. They guide and protect me at all times. They brought my wife to me...they will bring her to me again."

"I pray to Baal mostly."

"Does he hear your prayers?"

"Sometimes. I've been praying to him that I may see my brother again and now, I will. That's also thanks to you, Titus." Lucius hung his head low. After so many days in her company, with her honest opinions and unwavering character, the guilt was too much. It did not feel right.

"Dido? I have something to tell you."

125

"What is it, Titus?" she looked at him with sweet, friendly eyes.

"My name's not Titus."

She said nothing but continued to stare wide eyed, brows peaked pointedly in surprise and curiosity.

"What *is* your name then?" Now her arms were crossed.

"Lucius…Lucius Metellus Anguis."

"Hmmm….tut, tut, tut…" she clicked her tongue, "that is…much, much better suited to you. Lucius," she said to herself. "I like it!"

"You're not angry?"

"Not at all! I'm not surprised you gave me a different name with all that's going on around you. Besides, I was coming on a bit strongly in Thugga. I must apologise also."

"Oh don't worry about that," Lucius said happily. "It was nice to talk to someone after so long on the road."

"No, not for approaching you."

"For what then?"

"For telling you my name is Dido when it's really…Sara."

"Sara?"

"Yes. Sara." They both laughed at the absurdness of the situation.

"Well, you can call me Lucius now, and I shall call you Sara."

"Actually, Lucius," she said, "I would prefer it if you called me Dido. I like it more and it's the name I made up when we met."

"Very well, Dido it is." Lucius smiled.

"Do you want me to continue calling you 'Titus'?"

"Actually, no." He shook his head.

"Why not?"

"I hate the name Titus." Lucius cringed and Dido laughed so hard that she fell off the log she was sitting on.

Several days later, having passed over the range of rocky hills, Lucius and Dido came within sight of Cirta. The journey had been relatively pleasant since the road followed the river for most of the way allowing them to stop periodically to wash and cool themselves from the heat.

Lucius knew very little of Cirta except that it was known as the birthplace of Marcus Cornelius Fronto, the skilled orator, former consul and tutor to Marcus Aurelius and Lucius Verus. He had also been a friend of Emperor Severus' father, Publius Septimius Geta, who spent the final years of his life in the prosperous city.

Long ago, Cirta had been one of the capital cities of the Numidian kings until it was conquered by Julius Caesar. It was the strongest point in Numidia, a convergence for all of the military roads in the region. One of the richest cities in the southern empire, Cirta's wealth came largely from grain production. As they descended the steep road out of the mountains, Lucius and Dido looked upon the much-varied landscape surrounding the city. A deep gorge ran along the side of the city, so large that it seemed one of the Titans had slashed through the red and brown rock with a god-forged weapon. At the bottom of the layered gorge ran a river that was fed intermittently by small waterfalls. The extremely rocky landscape about the city was accented with fields of grain, pine and eucalyptus forests that sweetened the dry air for miles.

"Cirta is much bigger than I expected," said Lucius in amazement as they came closer. "Will you be able to find your brother in all of that?"

"Oh, yes. If I can find some people we used to know. I'll find him. Many people know him around here." Dido fidgeted at the thought of seeing her brother after so long. "Will you be spending the night here?"

"I was thinking of pushing on but it'll be another two days at least to Thamugadi. I suppose I should spend the night here. Perhaps there's another inn along the road."

"Actually there are several near the southern gate, along the road you need to take. You won't have a problem finding a place to stay." Dido was quiet for a time, as was Lucius. Neither of them really wanted to part company; they had become good friends over the last few days.

"Where will you stay Dido?" Lucius really was concerned, and it surprised him.

"Oh, when I find my brother we'll have much to talk about. I'll stay with him."

"I see." Lucius looked ahead as the road straightened out and led to the city's eastern gate. Monuments began to line the road on either side as the wagon creaked along. The day was hotter now that they had come out of the mountains, the sun intense as it beat down on the red earth. "Where do you want me to let you off?"

"Just outside the gate is fine. You can't take the cart within the walls at this time of day so you'll have to follow the wall around to the southern gate to find the inns. Right over there is fine." Dido pointed at a grouping of tall monuments near the gate and Lucius reigned in the horses as he drew even with them. He felt sad for some reason, perhaps the loss of friendly company, someone who had helped him get out of Thugga alive. He was happy, however, to help her leave the brothel and reunite with her brother. That would leave him feeling good.

"Well, Lucius, I suppose this is goodbye." Dido looked at the ground, making lines in the dirt at the side of the road with her bare foot.

"Thank you, Dido... for helping. I won't forget it. I wish you well in life, and may Apollo keep you and your brother safe and together from now on."

"Baal bless you, Lucius Metellus, and see you safely across the sands, you and your Adara."

Lucius hopped down off of the wagon so that he stood in front of her. He took her hands in his for a moment. Dido kissed his cheek quickly, turned and walked toward the gate without looking back. He watched her disappear into the crowd beyond, until the jingle of her silver jewellery could no longer be heard.

"Well, it's just us now boys!" Lucius said to the horses as he slapped the one on the rump. The horse's behind hissed with a profuse release of gas. "Phew!" Lucius waived his hand. "I think I'm feeding you both the wrong things!"

Once back in the cart, he followed the path around the city walls. On the bench next to him lay the black cloak that he had given Dido to use. He had wanted to let her keep it since she had so little but had forgotten.

The path skirted the gorge dangerously close. At times the horses stopped, unwilling to go further, but after some coaxing they went forward. When they came to the southern gate of the city, Lucius was greatly relieved. He was also happy to see a profusion of inns along the road, and his eye was drawn immediately to one that displayed the mark of the legions. He would definitely stay the night there. *No more fat innkeepers and ambushes, thank you very much!*

This inn, called *The Crested Helm*, was much better than the previous one. The proprietor was an extremely welcoming, old veteran who was happy to accept the imperial pass and even had two slaves carry Lucius' chests up to his room for him before taking the horses around the back to feed, water and brush down. Impeccable. Lucius realised he had been travelling in the wilderness for far too long. After settling into his room, he went into town to visit the baths and get more provisions.

That night he slept well, despite his roaming thoughts of Adara and the rest of the family, Lambaesis, and whether Dido had been able to find her brother. For the first night in several days he did not have anyone to talk to; it actually felt strange without the crackle of a campfire or the gentle nightly breezes. Lucius got out of bed and opened the window shutters to let in the breeze and some of the moonlight. Soon after, he fell asleep.

When morning came, he was awoken by the sound of a cock crowing. Having slept longer than he had wanted to, he washed his face, dressed and gathered his belongings. He would eat on the road. The horses were already hitched up to the wagon when he went downstairs to thank the innkeeper who had the slaves load up Lucius' belongings.

The road stretched orange and pink into the distance with the rising sun to his left. He could hear the faint song of the waterfalls far below in the gorge. The wagon moved along once more for the final part of his long journey and Lucius looked around at the large number of monuments that crowded the area either side of the paving slabs. Apart from the sounds of a few goatherds leading their flocks to the city market, the road was quiet in the early morning light.

Lucius felt refreshed and turned his thoughts to dealing with his cohort. He had been away for so long, he hoped that he still held some measure of respect among his men, or at least a large portion of them. His thoughts were broken, however, by a tremulous sobbing in a field to the far right. He stopped the wagon and looked to see the outline of a huddled figure at the base of a pitiful memorial stone.

"Dido!" Lucius gasped. He pulled the cart to the side of the road, grabbed the black cloak and ran over to where she was. "Dido, what's wrong?" She said nothing. Lucius went next to her and knelt down in the wet grass. She had been there all night and was shivering. He looked at the carved block but could not make out the Punic lettering. He put the cloak around her shoulders and she jerked slightly as if only just noticing that someone was next to her.

"He's dead..." she muttered, "gone."

"Your brother?" She looked up at Lucius, her eyes bloodshot from crying.

"Yes. They told me he died in a great battle against the Romans to the south...almost two years ago." Dido bent over the sad memorial to her brother in despair, her tears wetting the cold stone.

As Lucius had his hand on her back, holding the cloak in place, a terrible thought came into his mind. *A battle to the south, almost two years ago? By Mars! Not the one I fought in…the one for which my men and I were decorated?* It was unbearable. He prayed that it was not his hand that had cut down her brother. Only the Gods knew that. He tried to push the thought far away, guilt-ridden at the sight of the young woman before him, mourning for the loss of the last person that meant anything to her in the world.

"Dido," Lucius spoke softly to her. "Come dear, come with me." He knew he had no idea what he would do with her, but he could not just leave her there. No. He had to help her. "Dido. Please get up." She did not move but sat there, shivering and crying inconsolably.

"Leave me here! Please, Lucius. I can't go on any more." Her hands shook as she waved Lucius away weakly.

"I'm not leaving you here." Lucius bent down and laced his arms beneath her legs and arms and lifted her limp body up effortlessly. Her head buried in his neck as she wept tears that burned his skin, he carried her back to the wagon and laid her down behind the bench. He then wrapped her in the cloak and put his own on top of her to give her extra warmth. "Rest Dido. You'll be all right." He hoped that were true at least.

As they drove on, Dido cried herself to sleep while Lucius wondered what to do. In two days they would reach Thamugadi. Of course there was no way he could bring her to base. He would have to leave her in Thamugadi, but where?

"Ah! Marius Nelek! Yes!" He remembered his father's old friend who had welcomed him into his home when he had first arrived at Lambaesis. "Maybe he'll know what to do." Dido stirred quietly in the back, and Lucius stopped talking to himself, not wanting to wake her. The sun was higher in the sky now as the wagon moved down the straight road that ran across the plains. Ahead, dark mountains pierced the horizon, blanketed by a clear blue sky where eagles soared on the winds.

VI

DIDO

Lucius' passenger seemed lost, trapped in a sorrowful slumber. Tears fell from her eyes as she slept curled in his black cloak. From the time he met her, Dido had appeared strong and unshakeable, as if nothing could mar her friendly demeanour or rattle her confidence. She was utterly changed and Lucius supposed that at some point, even the strongest will, no matter how many hardships one has endured, has a breaking point.

He wondered if the Gods had some plan in bringing them together. He also wondered whether it was kind or cruel of him to be bringing her with him, closer to the army that was no doubt responsible for the death of her lamented brother. He felt somewhat responsible, even though her brother had taken his life into his own hands in opposing Rome.

Dido slept the entire first day of the journey from Cirta. They had passed a couple of inns along the way but Lucius decided to camp outside on a small hillock that lay off of the road. They would rest only for a few hours anyway. After caring for the horses and starting a fire with some dry wood he had collected, Lucius laid out some food and the wine and went to the wagon to wake her.

"Dido." He squeezed her shoulder. "You have to eat something. Come, I've got a nice fire going to keep you warm."

Without saying anything, Dido got up and allowed Lucius to help her down out of the wagon and over to the fire. She sat down and he brought her some cheese and dates on a small piece of linen, and an unwatered cup of wine. She accepted them and ate slowly, staring at the fire.

"You should have left me in Cirta, Lucius. You can't take me with you where you're going. You have duties back at your base." It was good to hear her speak again.

"I wasn't about to leave you weeping in that field, was I? Besides you helped me out of danger before. Now, it's my turn."

"You got me to Cirta. That was the bargain," she said stubbornly.

"Yeah, and look where that got you. Listen, Dido. I want to help you because I see you as a friend now, a friend I can help in some way. In Thamugadi I know a very kind family and they may have some contacts. There are a lot of fabricae and shops there, perhaps they might know someone who needs help?"

"Help doing what? I'm a common whore, that's all."

"I don't believe that for a moment. You did what you had to do at the time, but I see more strength in you than in most men." Dido looked hard at him, trying to push back any feelings she might have developed, knowing full well that they would only cause her further hurt. The truth of it was that he really was the only one whom she trusted, who seemed to care for her at all. She could not be hard on him, not now, not even after losing her brother.

"I'm sorry for being like this. I know you want to help me and I'm grateful for your kindness."

"You've just had some terrible news. I understand completely. If there's nothing for you in Thamugadi, then I'll take you back to Cirta or Thugga myself."

Dido smiled for the first time that day. "Who would have thought that after our first meeting we would become such good friends."

"Who would have thought indeed." Lucius paused briefly. "I'd better check around, make sure we're alone." He picked up his sword with his left hand; the dragons on it and his ring glowed sharply in the light. "Finish your food and get some rest." He put his crimson cloak about his shoulders and went into the surrounding darkness where he looked up at the moon as he prayed to Apollo and spoke to Adara. Now that he was drawing nearer and nearer to Lambaesis and duty, he felt a greater need for guidance.

The distance they had to travel the second day was much shorter than Lucius had expected. Before he knew it, the milestones indicated ten, five and then one mile to Thamugadi. He had forgotten how large this particular colonia was. In the centre of the immense plain surrounded by distant mountains, Thamugadi sprawled over the flat, rocky earth like an oasis full of red sandstone trees, terracotta fruit and straight limestone rivers. Rising out of the forest came whiffs of smoke from the fourteen baths.

"It looks more like a military base than a city," said Dido, a slight tremble in her voice. Lucius worried what she might be thinking.

"It looks like that because it was built by Rome over a hundred years ago for retired veterans." He put his hand on her shoulder comfortingly. "Don't worry. I wouldn't bring you here if I thought that you'd be in any sort of danger. Most of the inhabitants are Roman, yes, but most have married with the local population and just want to settle down into comfortable, peaceful retirement in a trade of some sort. Actually, there are many baths, a library, markets and temples inside and outside of the walls. There's even a theatre, look." Lucius pointed to where they could just see the natural impression where the theatre had been built on the south side of town.

"I trust you," she said, curious at the sight before them. "Actually, I have a good feeling about this place." Dido was more and more like her old self again.

Lucius thought he remembered where the Nelek domus was; somewhere down a smaller street along the west wall. They entered the vast grid of streets through the northern gate that led onto the cardo maximus. It felt strange to Lucius to see so many Romans so far from home, but then the empire was a vast and varied realm where home could be almost anywhere. No one really paid them any attention so long as he kept the horses and the wagon on the large streets and did not roll over any unwary pedestrian's feet.

They turned right onto the east-west running decumanus maximus, in the shadow of the colonnaded forum. Lucius slowed the horses so as not to annoy any locals on this busier street. People were returning through the west gate laden with goods they had obtained at the markets of Sertius, just beneath the powerful arch of Emperor Trajan. This western gate and road led to Lambaesis.

Lucius stopped the wagon now, unsure of which direction to go to find Nelek's home. Dido looked down from the wagon at a small fountain that adorned that particular intersection. It was marble with ornate floral mosaics at the bottom that shimmered like water lilies.

"There's a fountain at almost every street corner!" she exclaimed.

"Romans do like their fountains," Lucius agreed. "They need them in this heat though, and it's not even summer anymore." Lucius got down and walked into the street to look around. He spotted a strong, leathery old man with a head of excited white hair. The way he walked told Lucius he had been a soldier with years spent marching.

"Good day to you, citizen! May I have a word?" Lucius asked as respectfully as possible. The man stopped, a large loaf of bread under his arm. He observed Lucius carefully.

"What is it?" he replied after deciding Lucius was not a threat.

"I am here to visit a good friend of mine, well, actually a friend of my father's, but I can't remember which street he lives on. I was wondering if you would know him."

"Listen here, sonny." This was one time Lucius wished he had his uniform on. "There are a lot of people here, all shapes and colours. What makes you think that I would know your daddy's friend? Hmm?" The man's white hair danced atop his head in the hot breeze.

"Well, I supposed that since you are one of our noble veterans of the III Augustan, that you might know another of the local veterans. I am only asking because I would like to visit my friend before returning to Lambaesis and my cohort. Duty cannot wait, you understand." The mention of his rank did not go unnoticed for the man's demeanour changed in an instant.

"By all means, of course. What is your friend's name?" he asked, all smiles.

"Marius Nelek."

"By Juno's sweet eyes! He just cheated me out of several denarii last night when we were gaming at dice!"

"So you know him then?"

"Of course! Just go down to the last street before the arch and turn right. His name is outside the door."

"Will the wagon fit down that street?"

"Well, they don't usually like folks bringing wagons and such down the smaller streets, but so long as you're just dropping things off it shouldn't matter much. Old Marius will know where you can leave the horses and wagon."

"Thank you very much indeed." Lucius nodded gratefully and got up into the wagon.

"One piece of advice!" the man shouted back. "Don't play dice with him. He's a rascal and he cheats!" He turned and went off grumbling to himself, annoying his white hair.

The wagon had just been able to turn onto the street and there was still room for people to pass by on the side if they ran into anyone. They pulled up in front of the house where the engraved plaque read 'NELEK' in red letters.

"Here it is," Lucius said. "Maybe you should wait here while I go and knock."

"Probably a good idea. I don't want to shock anyone," Dido agreed, feeling awkward.

Lucius jumped down, pushed his cloak back, straightened his hair and cleared his throat. He hoped the old family friends would remember him as it had been several long months since he had seen them when he first came to Lambaesis. He knocked on the solid door three times. He heard nothing for a few moments. Then came a grumbling from behind the door.

"I'm coming!" The door swung open and Marius appeared. For a moment he looked upon the caller with suspicion and caution, as men who have families are wont to do, before recognition dawned on his ageing brow, throwing his eyes wide. "By all the Gods! Lucius Metellus! You're back!" He put his hands on Lucius' shoulders and shook him happily. "I almost didn't recognise you without your stylish armour on. What brings you here?"

"I'm returning from Rome to Lambaesis and-"

"Papa? Who is at the door?" A little voice came from behind Marius.

"Look, Tulia! Do you remember who this is?"

The little girl with olive skin and long dark hair moved in front of her father. "Tribune Lucius!" She rushed to him and clamped onto his legs. "You've come back!"

"Yes, Tulia. I've come for a visit, if that is all right."

"To play? I am seven now! Much older than when I was six you know."

"And all grown up into a young lady." Lucius laughed. Marius spotted the wagon and the woman sitting there smiling in silence at the reunion. Tulia spotted her too.

"Tribune Lucius, who is that? She looks like she would like to play with me."

"Forgive me." He looked at Marius and went over to the wagon to help Dido down. "This is my friend, Dido. She saved my life on the way here." Tulia went over to Dido.

"You must be very brave!" Tulia stated.

"Well, any friend of our young tribune is welcome," said Marius, smiling again, "especially one who has aided him. Please come inside."

"Thank you." Dido went in behind Tulia who introduced her to her mother, Octavia, and her brother Aeneas as 'Tribune Lucius' friend that saved him'. Dido felt a little awkward now that she was meeting someone actually called Aeneas. The young boy gazed adoringly at her. Octavia, ignoring the fact she had no sandals, welcomed her and led her to the atrium.

"So, Lucius," said Marius once the ladies had gone in and they were alone. "Who's this young woman?"

"It's a long story, Marius, but the short of it is that I met her in Thugga where she helped me to avoid an ambush that was lain for me by some local bandits. I wouldn't have made it out of there alive. Anyway, she helped me and in return I was to take her to Cirta to her brother. Unfortunately, her brother has died and now she has nothing. I felt it my duty to help her and thought that perhaps there was something she could do here in Thamugadi."

"I see." Marius rubbed his tanned chin. "We'll talk more of it. You did the right thing. Honourable like your ancestors, Lucius. For now though, we should get this wagon out of the way. We can stable the horses outside the west gate. How long are you staying before returning to base?"

"Two days, if that's all right with you and Octavia."

"Fine, fine. Here, let's get those chests of yours out of the wagon." They went over and removed both chests carefully from the wagon and carried them one at a time to the spare cubiculum. Marius then led Lucius inside to greet Octavia and Aeneas, who were both happy to see him again, before they went to stable the horses and the wagon.

They returned a short time later to find that Octavia, Tulia and Dido had set out a meal in the triclinium for all of them. Marius and Octavia sat on one couch, Lucius and Aeneas on another, and Dido sat next to Tulia. The eating was silent for a time until Marius finally spoke.

"So, Lucius! What news from this past year? What about the family, how are they?"

"Lots of news all around. Hmm..." Lucius wondered where he should start. Tulia was keeping Dido entertained so he felt he had the time to update them. "Well, I returned to Rome for the emperor's triumph and games. Truly a spectacular site! While in Rome, I met a woman."

"Oh ho! Did you now? What is her name?"

"Adara Antonina. Actually she could be called Metella now." Lucius smiled. Dido pretended not to hear him as Tulia plied her with questions.

"You're married!" Marius yelled.

"Yes."

"Oh congratulations, Lucius!" exclaimed Octavia.

"Then here's to your marriage!" Marius raised his cup and drank.

"Where did you hold the wedding?" Octavia asked. "In her home?"

"No. She and her family live in Athens. The priests in the Temple of Apollo on the Palatine Hill allowed us to hold the ceremonies there as well as the banquet."

"That's quite an honour. Your parents must have been extremely proud."

Lucius looked down. "My mother was extremely proud," Marius's great brow wrinkled. Lucius had told him of the rift between himself and his father on his previous visit.

"Well it's a fine and ancient family she hails from. A strong name!"

"Tribune Lucius?" began Tulia. "Where is she now?"

"Oh, erm, well Tulia, she is in Athens at the moment. I will send for her soon, hopefully, but first I needed to take care of some things at my base."

"Things?" Marius asked.

"Problems," answered Lucius.

"Ah. Better wait then, I agree." He looked then at his other guest. "And yourself, Dido, where do you come from?" Lucius had hoped they would not ask questions but it was only natural to know something about a person staying beneath your roof.

"I was born in Hippo Regius but spent most of my life in Cirta and a few years in Thugga."

"Hmm. And what do you do?" Marius asked. Lucius felt for her. He wanted to interject but she was ready to answer.

"Well, I was-"

"Oh father!" Tulia interrupted. "Isn't it obvious? She makes her own jewellery!" Tulia rolled her big brown eyes and pointed to Dido's silver necklace and anklets. "Are they not pretty?"

"Yes indeed," Octavia agreed, "very pretty." She looked at Marius. "Husband, won't you help me get something from the kitchen? It is much too high on the shelf for me to reach."

"Oh, certainly." Marius followed his wife out.

Lucius looked across the room at Dido who seemed to be shaking, a little upset. "Did you make those yourself?" he asked her.

"Yes," she answered as Tulia played with the silver making it sing.

"Well, I suppose that is a craft, a wonderful skill to have. Something to do?" Dido said nothing but smiled broadly at him and nodded. He had given her an idea as to what she might do in Thamugadi. Something she enjoyed and loved.

"Marius, my husband," Octavia chided, as she rarely did, once they reached the kitchens. "Why did you ask the girl what she does? And in front of the children." She kept her voice as low as possible.

"What in the name of Jupiter are you talking about? What's the matter?" Marius threw his arms up.

"Do you honestly think that she made jewellery for a living in Thugga?"

"Perhaps? I don't know. It looks nice enough."

"Marius, she has little or no clothing to her name, stibium stains under her eyes and prances around barefoot."

"So? She seems rather nice."

"That's the soldier in you talking. She may be nice but she was evidently a prostitute in Thugga. Maybe that's where Lucius met her? Did you think of that?"

"Listen here, Octavia," Marius was now upset, a redness creeping into his tanned leather skin. "Lucius Metellus is a good lad, better than his father I dare say. If he says they met in the street, they met in the street. I may be old and blinded by youthful beauty these days but I refuse to believe that he would bring a stranger into our home if that stranger posed any sort of danger to us or our children."

"But Marius-"

"I'm not finished," he cut her off. "Furthermore, if she indeed saved his life, then we owe it to him and his family to show her every kindness. Surely we've not become so isolated here that we've lost all sense of hospitality?"

"You sound like me, Husband." Octavia smiled once more, knew she was wrong in her harsh judgement. "I suppose it is a good sign that the children seem so smitten with her. Tulia especially can tell if someone is not right."

"Yup. She's like a good hound our little girl, can sniff out the bad ones. Don't worry though, Lucius is staying for a couple of days and that gives me the time to go about town and see if any of the other shop owners I know might need some help."

"All right, Husband. You win." She hugged him lovingly. "It seems as though you are growing kinder and more hospitable in your old age."

"Just don't tell any of the other ladies that, or their husbands will be by here calling on me for favours whenever the wind blows right."

"Fine. Now can you get me that clay container filled with honeyed sweets up there? We need to go back with something." Octavia pointed to the top shelf.

"What's it doing up there?" Marius asked as he reached up with one arm, steadying himself on the tabletop with the other.

"I found Tulia trying to stick her head inside it to get a better whiff of the honey. She had it all over her hair. Oh, don't worry, I checked it for any strands. It's clean." Marius got it down and they went back into the triclinium.

"We're back," said Octavia as she carried the container.

"Hmmmm. Honey!" cried Tulia.

"You'll wait your turn, little one," said her father. "Our guests go first." Octavia offered some sweets to Dido first and then to Lucius. The children, when they finally got theirs, licked the honey off of the thin pastry and sucked their fingers.

After everyone had had their fill of sweets and fruit, Marius began to speak again.

"I know that the city has fourteen baths but if either of you would like to rinse the road's dirt from yourselves, feel free to use our small bath after the meal."

"That is very kind of you, sir. Thank you," Dido said.

"Oh, please my dear, call me Marius. I'm too much of a grunt to be called *sir* by anyone."

"And you can call me Tulia," put in the honey-covered sprite beside her, "because that's my name." Dido laughed with a childlike joy that was contagious.

"Oh you are a cheeky little one!" said her mother. "Come now, let's get you both washed before our guests wish to use the baths themselves."

"Mother! I'm thirteen years old!" Aeneas protested. "I can wash myself."

"Yes, fine," Marius said, "but until you have a beard of some making, and not one made of honey, then you will wash yourself when you are told." He tried to be serious with his son but he was so proud of him that a faint smile crept in upon his lips.

"Yes, father," Aeneas laughed. "But when I have a beard, I'll do as I please." He jumped off the couch and made a hasty getaway before his father's mocked spanking reached him.

"Good night, children!" Lucius called after them before turning to Marius. "So how is your business going, Marius?"

"Oh, rather well actually. I've got a steady supply of orders from the base and a lot of private clients, mostly veterans who like to keep their sword arms in shape. I've also begun to make farming implements and tools. Not as exciting as weapons, but with all of the olive farmers and grain growers in the region, it provides a steady income. Keeps me busy too, so that I don't get bored and grumpy. But we shouldn't talk business in front of a lady."

"I don't mind, really!" she said. "I'm just enjoying being in your beautiful home. It's so quiet and welcoming."

"Why thank you, dear. You're the first to say such a thing." Marius was beginning to like her more and more, as he would an older daughter. "Speaking of business, Lucius mentioned that you might, if you so desire, be staying in Thamugadi for a time. If that's the case, then I may be able to make some inquiries around the city with some of the local tradesmen to see if they could use any help. Would that interest you?"

Dido could hardly contain her excitement. "Oh yes! It would very much, thank you." She beamed as she smiled and Lucius thought even more that it was the Gods' will that he bring her here and felt better about the decision.

"Good. So, I'll do that and we'll see what happens. I can't make any promises of course, but I know how to handle these veterans. I may not have been a tribune like our young Metellus here, but I was an optio. I could always get the men to do what I said."

"I'll bet you had them quaking in their caligae!" Lucius could just imagine the scene.

"Of course. Praise Mars." Marius laughed as he remembered a few incidents.

"We are finished with the baths!" Octavia called from the garden as she herded the children to their rooms amid a cacophony of protestations.

Dido finished the last of her wine and then rose from her couch. "I know you both have much to talk about so I'll say good night." She turned to Marius. "Thank you again for your kindness."

"Not at all, my dear. Sleep easy."

"Good night, Dido," Lucius said.

"Good night."

Marius then went over to the door and closed it so that they could talk frankly. Lucius poured them both more wine. "Time for soldier talk!" Marius clapped his hands. "So, Lucius, do you regret being married after running into this charming woman?" The question was blunt and to the point. Soldier talk indeed.

"Not at all." Lucius felt quite at ease because of the wine but also because he had come to think of Marius as a sort of military mentor. "I'll admit, Dido is a beautiful, exotic woman," Marius nodded approvingly, "but Adara outshines all other women in beauty, intellect and spirit."

"A true daughter of Venus?"

"To say the least. The Gods have blessed me."

"Why, by Jupiter and Venus' golden breast, did you leave her in Greece?"

"I suppose I have the time to tell you now if you would like to hear."

"Do tell. I'm all ears." Marius settled back to listen to the turn of events from the time Lucius arrived in Rome: how he and Argus had become estranged, as well as he and his father, and how he had been attacked several times. Lucius told him about the death of Antanelis and what he had said in his letters to his father about dissent within the cohort. His listener's fists clenched.

Marius listened to the account of the Sibyl's prophecy (soldiers were notoriously superstitious) and he believed every word, making a gesture of protection against ill omen. Lucius spoke of his burgeoning relationship with the empress and Caracalla, and the murder of the off-duty Praetorian, the reason for his quick escape from Leptis Magna. At this particular incident Marius closed his eyes and shook his head. When Lucius had finished, Marius leaned back, painfully sobered by this account.

"You were right to leave your wife in Greece." He rubbed his tired, old eyes. "Lucius my boy, you are also right to worry."

"I know it. I don't know who to trust here besides your family, my first centurion and Dido."

"That's quite an odd mix of allies to say the least."

"Gods know."

"Have you thought about what you're going to do when you rejoin your men?" Marius avoided talking about the Sibyl.

"I suppose I'll discuss things with my centurion first, Alerio, and then with the other centurions before anything else."

"You'd better. But don't let on how much you might know. Hopefully this Alerio fellow has done the same. He's still alive so that must mean something."

"Now you're scaring me."

"I know. But it's not uncalled for. Be secretive and cunning in your investigation and when you discover the guilty parties, strike quickly and without mercy. I know your legate and, though an old codger, you can trust him. Just don't say anything to him until you're sure. All it takes is one poisoned olive in your plate and you're done for, out of the way!" Lucius gulped at the thought and looked at the bowl of olives on the table. "How times have changed," Marius mused.

"Really? Times have changed so much?"

"Well, not really. It just seems that way to every successive generation of veterans. Someday you'll probably say the same thing." Marius waved his hand in the air. "Enough of this unpleasantness for now. How do you get along with your new side of the family?"

"Very well, gods be praised. Adara's father has been much more of a father to me than my own."

"I'm glad for you of course," sighed Marius, "but it pains me to hear you say this. Quintus seems too far changed. Are things really so bad between the two of you?"

"Worse I'm afraid. He thinks I'm an embarrassment to the family and a disgrace. We won't speak again. I told him as much when we parted last."

"Quintus, you old fool." Marius hung his head like the branches of an aged willow. "I'm very sad to hear it Lucius, for both your sakes." I cannot replace your father, nor would I want to, but if ever you need my help in anything, I'm here in whatever capacity. I want you to know that." He gazed steadily at Lucius, rising on shaky legs from his couch. "Now, I must go to sleep. You've given me much to think about, too much as I am also prone to brooding in my old age."

"Thank you for listening, Marius." Lucius helped steady him.

"Not at all. Oh, and don't worry about your friend Dido. We'll see what we can do for her about a job and a place to stay somewhere in the city."

"You're very kind, all of you."

Marius pat Lucius on the back and went out the door.

Alone, Lucius sat back to have another cup of wine before going to wash. He had much on his mind and Marius' concern for him made him all the more anxious about his situation. For the moment, Lucius tried to forget. When he finished his wine, he extinguished the brazier in the triclinium and headed for the bath. His head spun slightly but he was still aware of everything around him. He thought Dido should be finished by then and sleeping away in one of the guest cubicula. As he turned into the baths, he bumped into someone who let out a slight shriek.

"Lucius, you scared me!" Dido laughed nervously. She was still dripping and had a large linen towel wrapped about her body. The long twist of her dark hair dripped where it curled down the front of her chest.

"Sorry," Lucius said. "I thought you were already asleep."

"I spent a while washing. It felt very good to get clean. Are you going in now?"

"Yes, not for long though. Do you have everything you need?"

She nodded, a couple droplets falling from her long lashes. "They are very nice people. Thank you for bringing me here."

"It's the least I could do. Now, let's get some sleep. I'm tired and a little drunk. I'll see you in the morning."

"Good night, Lucius," she said as he went into the first small washing room. She watched him go and forget to close the door. Inside, the red walls, decorated with blue waves, were lit by a four-headed lamp that hung on a wall sconce. The light flickered and the waves seemed to move back and forth across the walls as Lucius removed his sandals, unbelted his tunic and pulled it over his head. Dido watched admiringly as he stretched the tired limbs of his tall, muscular body. He swayed a little on his feet and she smiled to herself.

A part of her wanted to go back in, to immerse herself in the warm water with him amid scented oils. Her heart pounded in her breast in a way it had never done before, but the other part of her prevailed that night, the part that Lucius called his 'friend', the part that admired him for his strength and loyalty to the woman he loved. To mar such a beautiful thing would be a sacrilege to the goddess of love. The dripping of water reverberated off of the walls as Lucius ran a sea sponge over his scarred muscles and rolled his stiff neck backward, side to side. *He's beautiful*, Dido thought. She took a step forward to the open door but stopped, wrenched herself away from the bath and Lucius, and went to her room to lay down to sleep, naked on the soft mattress, alone with her dreams and memories.

The following morning, despite an aching head, Lucius rose before anyone else was stirring. Dressed in a fresh tunic, he strapped on his sword and dagger beneath his extra cloak and went out of doors to make his way to the Capitol at the south-west corner of the city. The Gods had been extremely protective of him on this journey and it would have been unappreciative of him not to acknowledge their kindness and mercy.

Orange light crept into the near-deserted streets as the sun began to rise above the distant mountains. Apart from a few delivery wagons, Lucius was alone. He stopped at one point to listen. It was the spot where he had been attacked before by the nomad assassins, where Ashur had appeared out of the darkness and saved his life. Lucius instinctively felt at his thigh where he carried a long scar from an attacker's blade. There were no assassins now, but he did wonder how his friend was faring in Athens. Lucius moved on, thinking of how Ashur was smitten by the unassuming Carissa and how things had progressed since. A part of him hoped that Ashur was not so much in love that he forgot to watch over Adara and Alene; though this thought caused Lucius some guilt, it would not go away.

As he moved onto the main street, the smell of fresh bread hovered in the morning air from the bakers' district nearby. He felt his stomach rumble, tempting him to change direction, but he wanted to make an offering at the temple before anything else. The Capitol was quiet as Lucius made his way up the stairs and onto the pronaos where he stood at the base of six ornate Corinthian columns. He had brought along a small phial of rosemary oil to offer as a libation. The view from the top was beautiful in the morning; sunlight suffused the usually brown, drab landscape. With such a rising, there seemed to be a humming in the air from some far away source that called out to awaken life.

The temple was dark inside except for a few small braziers, one beneath an image of each god. Stopping at each of the three altars, Lucius said prayers of thanks to Jupiter, Juno and Minerva and made his offerings beneath their steady gaze. It always seemed to him that he could feel their presence,

148

especially at this time of day when he was alone. Then again, the Gods lived everywhere, their sight was far-reaching. Lucius asked for help in the coming days. He would be tested, would have to prove himself a worthy leader.

Upon his return to the Nelek domus, Octavia greeted him. She stood in the atrium watching Dido play with Tulia in the garden, pleased that for once she could ease into the morning calmly while someone else entertained her energetic daughter.

"Ah, good morning Lucius," Octavia said as he walked up, a beaming smile on her face. "You are stirring early. I trust you slept well."

"Very well, thank you. I had forgotten how beautiful mornings could be in this part of the world when the sun comes out." He stood beside her to watch the girls playing.

"I must say that I was a little shocked to see you bring this woman into our home yesterday," Octavia said candidly as she watched Dido put a small crown of flowers she had made on Tulia's head.

"Do forgive me," began Lucius, highly apologetic. "I had no wish to inconvenience you or cause discomfort in your home."

Octavia put her hand on his shoulder. "You mistake me, Lucius. What I was going to say is that I was wrong in my first impressions of this girl. Quintus explained everything to me about her, how she helped you and what she has been through. And, well, after seeing her with the children, especially Tulia, it would behove me to say that she is always welcome here, as you are." Lucius' hostess shone like a proud mother in admiration of her daughter. A serene sense of safety brought out happy wrinkles at the sides of her eyes.

"I'm relieved to hear you say this." He breathed deeply as though releasing unexpressed worry. At that point, Tulia skipped over to where Lucius and her mother stood watching. Lucius bowed to the young princess and she bowed just enough so that the crown of flowers did not fall from her dark head.

"Do you like my crown, Tribune Lucius? Dido made it for me." Her playmate came walking up behind the young girl, preceded by the now familiar jingle of her jewellery and the soft sound of her bare feet on the flowery mosaic floor.

"You look like a princess, Tulia," Lucius said, smiling at Dido. "A crown of flowers suits you."

"Do you really think so?" she asked excitedly. "Did you hear that, Dido? Tribune Lucius thinks I look like a princess!"

"He's right but even princesses need to wash the dirt from their feet," Dido said to the little girl who looked thoughtful.

"You are right," Tulia decided. "Come, let's go to the baths and wash our feet." To her mother's shock, Tulia walked, princess-like, to the baths and Dido followed laughing.

"Yes," Octavia said, "I like her very much."

"Beautiful morning!" Marius burst in through the front door behind them, flung his cloak onto a peg on the wall and walked over.

"Good morning, Marius," Lucius greeted. "I just returned myself."

"Yes, I saw you walking toward the Capitol, but I didn't want to interrupt; a man's time with the Gods should be private. Anyway, I've been out visiting some friends of mine who make jewellery, gold and silver cups, ornaments and the like. I wanted to get to them before they were too busy."

"And? Did you find out anything?" his wife asked.

"Yes...and no. Well, to make it short, all of them have enough craftsmen working for them at the moment and can't afford any more. Others refuse to hire a girl, especially one of Punic origin." Marius waved his hand like he was swatting flies angrily. "They're all idiots! All of them, except one."

"Really?" Lucius wanted to know more, and Marius always seemed to drag things out.

"Yup! His name's Calvinus Orban and he has a workshop near the east gate."

"What is he like, Husband? Can he be trusted with a young girl? We don't want to put her in any danger." Octavia seemed suddenly quite protective of Dido.

"Oh, ho! She'll be safe all right!" Marius laughed. "Besides being as old as I am, Calvinus is, how shall I put it? He's one of those fellows who prefers the company of men."

"You're right about that then, Marius. Dido will definitely be left alone to work." Lucius smiled, trying not to laugh. "Thank you for looking."

"Not at all. Happy to do it! I told him that we would bring her by later this morning to meet him and show him her work."

"Where are we going?" Dido asked as she and Tulia emerged from the baths.

"Ah, my dear." Octavia walked to meet her. "My husband has found a man who may wish to hire you to make jewellery. Would you be interested in going to meet with him this morning?"

"Um, yes, of course," Dido replied somewhat hesitantly, looking to Lucius. His smile eased her worry. "Thank you very much for this."

"Please, please dear. You'll make an old man blush." Marius cleared his throat. "I can't make any promises but I think you'll get on well with Calvinus."

"Well, before we go out," Octavia put in, "we should break our fast. I've put out some food." She led them all to the triclinium where Aeneas was already sitting, waiting impatiently to eat. He had placed himself on the couch where Dido had sat the night before, but when they entered, Marius barked at him to move.

"Not until you have your beard!" his father said.

Late morning the streets were extremely hot but that did not prevent the citizenry from going out to do whatever shopping and bargaining they needed to. Summer was over and so was the worst of the heat for the year. This was simply a pleasant, early-autumn morning in Thamugadi. Marius had decided not to open his shop for the day, opting to use his time to show Dido and Lucius around and help them out.

They walked along slowly; the women browsed at various wares along the way and the men talked of the army, business and the like while young Aeneas listened, learned. Lucius kept an eye on Dido even though they were completely safe; his sense of responsibility for her safety was there to stay. It was almost as if, with the absence of his own wife and sister, his protective energies were concentrated on his new-found friend.

At one point, Octavia spotted Dido admiring a pair of plain Punic-style sandals that hung on display with fifty other pairs at a stall. Dido preferred not to wear anything on her feet but she was finding that Thamugadi's streets were quite hot under the sun where it stood in the middle of the plain. Octavia watched the young woman caressing the shoes like a fond memory and felt for her.

"Do you like these, my dear?" she asked.

"My mother used to have some like this, long ago." Dido wiped away a tear, as a thought of her mother inevitably led to one of her brother. She turned to continue walking but Octavia stayed.

"How much are these?" she asked the shopkeeper.

"Ten denarii," the seller said from behind a cracked wooden counter.

"You're a thief! You should be ashamed! Two denarii!" Octavia countered.

"Ha! Five!" returned the shopkeeper.

"The Gods would punish you for such robbery! Three denarii or nothing at all!" Octavia made to leave while the seller thought about it.

"Wait, wait!" he finally said. "All right, three."

"I suppose I'll take them," she feigned disappointment. "But next time I expect a better price!" Octavia tossed the three coins to the wide-eyed seller and took the sandals.

She caught up with Dido a couple of stalls up from that one.

"Here, my dear." She handed Dido the sandals. "A little present for you as our guest." Dido blushed, tried to say no and back away but Octavia wouldn't have it.

"No, no I really couldn't!"

"Oh stop now. Please take them!"

"Yes, please take them!" echoed Tulia, tugging on Dido's clothing.

"See them as a gift from your new friends in your new home." Octavia's face was so kind, genuine and motherly that Dido acceded to her generosity.

"I don't know what to say." She tried not to weep. "Thank you."

"You are welcome," Octavia said happily. Dido put on the new sandals and they continued their walk to the workshop.

Calvinus Orban's shop had a small front with a pristine olive-wood counter shaded by a pale blue awning. A few pieces of exquisite jewellery hung on display guarded by a lounging cat, a bald Egyptian breed so disconcerting that none would dare approach to handle the valuable goods. The unpretentious storefront did not betray the vast workshop concealed within where upwards of twenty craftsmen and apprentices worked under the artistic owner.

As Lucius and the rest approached, the faint sound of delicate hammering could be heard until the bald cat on the counter meowed and sat up, a small blue bell in the shape of a scarab beetle jingled about his neck.

"Let's stop here," Marius said. "That cat looks mangy but I saw him scratch a thief's hand to Hades one day. Beastly looking thing!" The cat meowed again, staring at them. "Ho! Calvinus! Come out here!" yelled Marius.

"Coming!" came a voice in return from the darkness beyond the counter. The group waited a moment before Calvinus Orban appeared. He was a tall thin man, about Marius' age, but wore a short chiton of the sort that younger men wore. "Marius! Welcome back. I see you've brought everyone." Calvinus' voice was high and melodic and his bald head sweat profusely as he went over to his equally bald cat and pet it. "There, there Ptolemy, these are friends," he reassured.

"Calvinus," Marius began, "this is a good friend of ours, Tribune Metellus." Lucius nodded. "And here is the young lady I spoke to you about earlier, Dido."

Dido came forward feeling awkward under Calvinus' intense stare. She bowed her head slightly, unaware that what he was really looking at was the jewellery around her neck, ankles and wrists.

"Very nice," he muttered, "very nice indeed." He lifted her chin with his fingers and smiled a huge, friendly smile beneath batting eyelids. "We are going to get along famously!" he squealed. "Did you make all of these yourself?"

"Yes, sir. I did," replied Dido.

"Oh, call me Calvinus, please dear. So Marius tells me you are new to Thamugadi and would like to make some money making jewellery here."

"Yes, I would like that. If you will have me, that is."

"All I expect is that you work hard and improve constantly. I always expect my employees to move into new creative realms so that our shop provides items that cannot be found anywhere else." Calvinus had suddenly switched to a very business-like tone of voice. "I will provide you with all the raw materials and tools you require and pay you well for work that I like, thirty percent of the selling price."

"That doesn't seem very fair to me!" Lucius said, stepping forward to the counter where the cat stood up suddenly. Calvinus was unperturbed.

"Trust me, Tribune, if you knew the prices people pay for any one of my items you would know that thirty percent will provide well for anyone." Calvinus stopped speaking. Lucius looked at Dido, eyebrows up questioningly. She moved to his side to calm him.

"I have a good feeling about this, Lucius. You don't have to worry so much about me anymore. I am fine now."

"I would be delighted to show you all around the workshop and introduce you to the craftsmen if it would ease your minds," Calvinus offered.

"Yes," Dido replied. "That's a good idea."

"Very well, follow me." They all followed Calvinus into the back where they found themselves walking down a long corridor. The entire length of it was flanked by small rooms that housed two artists each. "I like for my employees to be able to work quietly and undisturbed so that they can offer up their full attention to their individual muses." Dido walked beside Calvinus as he showed her around. The craftsmen consisted of either young boys, too shy to look over at any new face, or of old men too stubborn to let themselves be distracted by newcomers.

When they arrived at the end of the corridor there was an opening in the roof that allowed sunlight to pour in. On either side of a fountain in the form of a gold and silver palm tree were two altars, one to Apollo, god of arts and master of the Muses and another honouring Vulcan, god of the forge and patron of smiths. They all stopped to admire the shrines and Calvinus took Dido gently by the hand and led her to the fountain. All that could be heard was the sound of water trickling down the branches of the tree.

"Now Dido, no craftsman or artist can create beauty without the help and inspiration of the Gods. It would be extremely arrogant of us to believe that we do anything without some help, in whatever form it may come. Apollo and Vulcan are important to us here and I expect that every morning when you arrive and every evening before you depart, that you give thanks and make an offering, no matter how small, to the gods of our workshop. It does not matter if they are your gods or not; what matters is that we show them the respect they deserve in this place and the part they play in your creativity. Do you understand?" Calvinus still held her hand but she was not inclined to take it away. He seemed to her a man inspired and she did not feel any malevolence in anything he said or did, nor in the way he looked at her.

"I would very much like to work here," Dido said with certainty. She then looked at Lucius who smiled as he thought that any place or person that so honoured Apollo was good and to be trusted.

"Excellent!" Calvinus clapped his hands, his voice high again. "You may work in this cubiculum here." He pointed to an empty room off to the side, not far from the shrines. "You will be able to work alone at first, until you find your own inspiration and guidance. I see a lot of potential in you, Dido." As she looked in the room, she felt somewhat at home, a feeling she had not had in some time. Her heart leapt.

As they walked back down the corridor and outside beneath the pale blue awning, Lucius found himself troubled, wondering why a part of him felt odd about Dido's new position. Of course he knew she would be better off and the happiness now on her face painted a thousand pictures, but still, something inside him wished it was himself who had given her this smile and not a bald-headed craftsman. Realising the absurdity of his ridiculously childish thoughts, he joined in everyone's happiness and congratulated her. It had not taken Calvinus more than a few moments to realise Dido's potential, and as a result, she would start working the very next day.

The following morning, Lucius walked Dido to the workshop. He had one more day in Thamugadi before his inevitable return to base.

"Here it is," Lucius said to Dido as they walked up to the workshop. "Are you nervous?"

"Yes and no." She shook her head. "I mean, I'm happy to have found something to do and, Calvinus seems nice enough don't you think?"

"Yes, he seems like a good man," Lucius acceded.

"But..." Dido looked up at him with her big eyes, some unsaid emotion within. "...I am worried for you Lucius. Some of the things you have told me are, well, mysterious and frightening."

"I know." He looked up at the blue sky, sighed. "I know. The things we don't understand always frighten us more." Dido's face was sombre and he did not want to leave her there, anxious and worried for him when she was beginning a new life. "I'll be fine, really. We'll see each other this evening back at the house. Perhaps by then Marius will have found you a place to live? Now, go in there, make an offering to the Gods, and show Calvinus what you can do."

"I will." Her smile returned. "See you tonight?"

"Yes, tonight." Dido turned and went into the workshop, passing the cat as she went. It appeared the little guardian knew that she was to be admitted.

The day passed slowly. Lucius spent his time going through his things, rearranging his chests more neatly as they had been jostled about quite a bit during travel. He lifted the eagle feather from his childhood, a reminder of the Gods' gifts, and the wax tablet on which he had written the Sibyl's words. It made him shudder and he avoided reading them again. However, the thought of Cumae warmed him. He wished he could go back to that point in time with Adara whenever life seemed too unbearable, when the strength needed to move forward just seemed out of reach.

His armour was still neatly wrapped, polished. It had been in Lucius' mind to go back to base in full armour but the thought of arriving on a wagon so bedecked did not sit well with him. He decided he would wear his clean travelling clothes and his cloak. After placing everything back neatly, he closed the chests and went to the garden to sit for a time with his thoughts and a scroll of an account of Alexander's campaigns. It helped to read about so great a man, what he accomplished and how his men looked up to him, how they would have followed him into Hades itself. Lucius knew he was not an Alexander but he believed that there were still some of his men who loved him, or had before, and he would use that to reclaim their loyalty and trust.

A short while later, as he lay sleeping in the garden chair, the scroll curled up on his lap, Lucius was awoken by children laughing. Aeneas and Tulia, hidden behind a bush, had watched his head bob up and down in a most unrefined manner. When he awoke and saw them, they giggled and ran down the corridor.

"You're going to need your sleep before you start rising for drills again," Marius said, looking down at Lucius. "Are you unwell?"

"I'm fine. Just nodded off reading Arrian." Lucius rolled up the scroll.

"Ah yes. I remember reading that too while I was on campaign," Marius said nostalgically. "I always found comfort in the account…somehow made the world seem full of possibility, less mad."

"Any luck today around the city?" Lucius had also been wondering whether Marius had found lodgings for Dido.

"Unfortunately, no. Not a thing. They're building some new tenement blocks in the north-east corner of the city but it'll be a while before they're habitable." At that moment, Octavia came into the garden. Lucius stood up.

"Please sit, Lucius. We shall join you," she said as she put a tray on a small table. "Here, have some wine." They all poured a cup and sat back.

"So what…I mean…I brought her here for nothing." Lucius felt terrible but Marius spoke quickly.

"No! Not at all. In fact Lucius, well, Octavia you tell him."

"Marius and I have decided to ask Dido if she would like to live here with us for as long as she likes or until suitable lodgings become available in the city."

Lucius was shocked, awed by their generosity. He was sure that they knew what Dido had been before but was amazed that it did not make a difference to them.

"I see you are surprised," Octavia observed. "We have thought about it quite a lot. Dido seems to be a hard worker, she is intelligent and kind. Most importantly the children adore her and frankly, I could always use the extra help around here."

"If Dido will agree to this," Marius added.

"Of course, if she agrees."

"I wouldn't dream of asking such a thing from both of you. I really had no right, or thought for that matter, to leave her with you," Lucius said guiltily.

"We know that, my boy." Marius sipped his wine. "You did what you thought was right, and it was."

"Now, we are doing what we feel is right. More so, it is something we *want* to do." Octavia smiled.

An hour later when Lucius returned with Dido, having escorted her home from the workshop, they found the children skipping happily about the house. Delicious scents floated out of the kitchen. Marius led Dido to the triclinium where a wonderful meal had been set out with their best dishes and cups.

"What is all this?" Dido asked.

"A celebration," he bellowed happily, "in honour of your first day in the workshop."

"Sit with me, Dido!" Tulia grabbed Dido's hand as she passed.

"Yes, everyone sit. The food is ready." Octavia came in with a steaming platter of meats mixed with lentils, olives and dates. Aeneas followed with steaming flat breads which he placed on the table next to an overflowing basket of fresh fruit. The wine was poured and Marius held up his cup.

"To Dido and her new life!" Everyone toasted the blushing guest and set to eating.

"So how was your first day, dear?" Octavia asked her.

"Very good!" Dido answered excitedly. "I met all the other craftsmen and received my own tools to use; much better tools than the crude ones I had used before."

"Was Calvinus decent with you?" Marius raised an eyebrow.

"Oh yes. He explained different things to me, how things work. He showed me the forge and the gold and silver stores and told me what new techniques he wants me to learn to improve my work. He knows so much."

"Excellent!" Marius clapped his hands, pleased with himself for talking to Calvinus.

"Aren't you going to tell her, Papa?" Tulia asked, unable to control herself. "If you do not want to, I can!"

"Tut you! Your mother can tell her."

"Tell me what? Did you find a place I could rent?"

"Well not exactly," Marius said. "Actually, I couldn't find anything."

"Oh." The first thought that came to Dido's mind was that she had to return to Cirta or Thugga.

"We have a better idea, my dear," stated Octavia, reaching to hold Dido's hand. "Marius, myself and the children would like for you to come live with us." The room was silent. All waited for Dido to speak.

"I...I...I couldn't possibly..."

"Yes you can!" prodded Tulia.

"But you are a family! I'm a stranger."

"We would not ask you if we were not sure my dear," Octavia spoke softly. "Unless of course, you do not want to stay with us. That is different."

"No! I would love to but...how would I repay such kindness?"

"Kindness itself is payment enough. You are a good girl, Dido. The children love you and we enjoy your company."

"For how long?" Dido's mind raced and she looked to Lucius, but he simply smiled for her, knew that he should keep out of it.

"For as long as you want," stated Marius.

"For as long as I want? I would insist that you have me work here in the house. I want to be useful to you, not just a lodger."

"Any help would be welcome," Octavia acquiesced, "but remember that you also work for Calvinus and will need your rest."

"Please, Dido! Please, please, please say yes!" Tulia performed like a tragic actress, she would die if the Gods did not hear her entreaties. Dido laughed happily, cried for the kindness.

"Yes. I would love to stay here!"

"Wooohooo!" Tulia yelled out in joy. Aeneas smiled and clapped his hands. Marius drained his cup, Octavia hugged her new family member, and Lucius remained silent, smiling at his friend whose eyes met his from within the immense hug Tulia then wrapped around her.

When the meal was over and the dishes cleared, Lucius went to Dido where she stood in the garden.

"Are you pleased with everything?"

"Oh, Lucius! You startled me." She had been looking up at the stars, familiarising herself with the view from within the garden. "Yes, I am. I just can't believe the Gods have been so kind to me these days, despite the news of…my brother. They have taken me away from Thugga, brought me here to Thamugadi, given me wonderful work I can enjoy and a new family."

"That certainly is quite a bit to happen in a few days." Lucius too looked at the stars, searched for the moon but he could not spot it from that angle.

Dido looked at him. "They have also given me you, Lucius." She put her hand on his chest.

"Me? What have I done?"

"Don't you know? Without you my...friend..." she had wanted to say something else, "...none of these wonderful things would have happened to me. I would still be in Thugga, a slave."

Lucius looked down at her, wanted to pull away through guilt or fear, but could not. He willed his heart to stop beating so obviously, but it would not listen. She reached up to put her arms about his neck, pressed herself against him and kissed him on the cheek, just shy of his mouth.

"Thank you for everything Lucius Metellus. I thank the Gods for our meeting, for the pain and joy it has brought me." Lucius said nothing but kissed her hand and left her to stare at the night sky from the garden in her new home.

Dawn rose up in hues of red, orange and brown, colouring the Numidian morning. When Lucius had dressed, armed and finished packing his belongings, he found the wagon and horses already awaiting him outside in the street. Marius had decided to go early to the stables and prepare them for the journey.

Tulia, having left Dido's side for a short time, now followed Tribune Lucius about the house, sad at his leaving.

"Please don't go, Tribune Lucius!" she pleaded.

"I have to, little princess." Lucius hoisted her up into his arms, her little limbs wrapped about his neck. "I'll come and visit though."

"You promise?"

"Yes, Tulia. I promise. Lambaesis is not a day away. I can come often." He put her down and she held his hand.

"Do you hear that Dido? He can come often to visit!"

"Yes. I heard. I am happy for it." Dido did not smile this time.

"Here is some food for your journey, Lucius." Octavia came up and handed him some food wrapped in rough linen.

"Thank you."

"You are most welcome, and do please come any time you wish. Though I know that you no doubt have much work ahead of you, you are always welcome."

"I will remember."

Marius came behind Lucius and put his crimson cloak over his shoulders. "You'd better get going before the streets get too busy."

"You're right."

"Here, I'll help you with your chests." Marius and Lucius hoisted the chests into the wagon before Lucius said goodbye to Octavia, Aeneas and Tulia. Dido followed Marius and Lucius outside where Marius took him aside. "You remember what I told you: be secretive in your investigations and when you discover the guilty parties, hit'em hard and without mercy, before they hit you. Marcellus will back you."

Lucius clasped the old man's forearm in friendship. "Thank you, Marius. Truly."

"Think nothing of it. And remember, I'm not far away if you need help or a place to retreat to. All right?"

"All right," Lucius replied.

"Good. Mercury guide you safely there." Marius turned, let Dido through and went back into the house to leave them alone.

"If you need me, Marius knows how I can be reached." This time she did not approach Lucius but stood back a little as he mounted the wagon. The closeness of the night before had been too tortuous, too overwhelming. "Will you be all right here, Dido?"

"Yes," she said uncertainly. "I should be fine but there are…things I would say…to you…but cannot. The Gods would be upset and I don't want that."

"Best not to say anything then."

"Yes, except that I want you to know that I want only for you to be safe. Thank you, Lucius."

His heart plummeted in his chest with the look on her sad, beautiful face. His love lay with someone else but he knew that he owed Dido his life and had to be content with the thought that he had perhaps given her something in return.

"I will be ever-thankful for what you've done for me. Fortuna love you Dido, and may the Gods protect and inspire you." Lucius smacked the horses with the reigns and the wagon rolled down the cobbled street. Dido watched as they turned the corner onto the Decumanus Maximus to go out of the gate beneath Trajan's arch and on to Lambaesis.

Dido stood in the street for some time, trying to put an end to the tears that slid down her dark cheeks. After a while, Octavia, who had noticed the restrained love the girl had for Lucius, came out and put her arms about her shoulder and led her inside, speaking soft words of comfort that only a mother could devise.

VII

OFFICIUM

'Duty'

Lucius tried, with great difficulty, to set aside all of the things that he would rather have been thinking about, those thoughts that inevitably proved far more enticing, more comfortable than the fears and uncertainties that came to his mind when the uniform stone walls of the III Augustan legion's base came into view. There it was before him, little more than a mile away, covering an enormous portion of the plain, a city unto itself.

Smoke fumed from the legion's bath complex and fabricae at the northern end of the base and outside the walls there was the familiar sight of dust rising into the sky from the parade ground. As it was afternoon, most of the troops were out on drills; this gave Lucius a chance to settle into the officer's quarters before running into too many people he knew.

The final stretch of road was long and straight, leading directly to Lambaesis' eastern gate and the via Principalis. Traffic to and from the fort increased as Lucius got closer; Lambaesis controlled one of the few natural routes through the mountains. Guards at every gate monitored traffic and trade that came from the southern desert, the high eastern plateaus, the mountains to the south-west and the plains in the north.

Happy to pause for a few minutes before going on, Lucius pulled the wagon to the side of the road in order to allow a large caravan to pass. He waited, watched the camels pass, bundles of salt and spices tied to their backs. He had forgotten the smell of camels, did not miss their constant groaning along with their tendency to foam at the mouth and spit at any unwary passer by. Once the tail of the caravan cleared, Lucius moved back onto the road to approach the walls. It seemed to him that the size of the vicus outside the walls had increased dramatically since he left. Small stone houses, shops, taverns and brothels surrounded the walls. Many of the troops' wives and children lived there as well as businessmen and merchants who had come to settle down more permanently, hoping to make a living out of supplying the legion with clothing, luxury goods and extra food to supplement their military rations. In Numidia, even on the edge of the desert, there was always someone willing to help you part with a well-earned denarius.

"Hold!" said the trooper at the gate as Lucius stopped the wagon. "State your business." Lucius realised he had taken off his military cloak and therefore bore no sign of his status. He reached into his satchel next to him and pulled out his imperial orders, handed them to the trooper. The man said something but Lucius could not hear for all the racket created by a herd of goats being shuffled across the road behind the wagon.

"What's that?" Lucius asked.

"I said welcome back, Tribune Metellus," he said a little louder, saluting sharply to Lucius who nodded back.

"Is the legate in the Principia or out on the parade ground today?"

"Not sure, Tribune. He should be somewhere in the Principia this time of day. Just leave your wagon out front on the street. I'll give orders that it is not to be moved." The man spoke to one of his inferiors behind him who went through the gates to give the orders. "You may go through, Tribune."

Lucius thanked the man and the wagon rolled beneath the high double arches of the guard-tower. The trooper eyed Lucius as he passed, thought it odd that a tribune was travelling in such a state.

It had been so long, and so much had happened, that Lucius felt like it was his first time within the walls. Everything seemed foreign to him at the moment, the sight, the smells, the presence of so many troops and so few women. The Principia's tiled roof floated above the surrounding structures where it stood in the centre of the base. Lucius realised that he should have taken the time to wash and make himself more presentable to the legate but he did not know if his quarters were prepared yet. Besides, they didn't really know he was coming.

The guards at the Principia gate awaited him and took the reins of his horses when he pulled up. Lucius put his cloak back on and jumped down from the wagon. The large courtyard was empty at the moment. The large tripod in the centre, in which the sacred incense burned, filled the space with a strong, bluish smoke. His footsteps echoed among the columns around the edges as he approached the main, two-storey building. He passed beneath the larger central arch, came to the legate's offices, and gave his name to one of the two guards. The man went inside and emerged moments later bidding Lucius enter.

Flavius Marcellus sat behind a large table amid an array of curled maps and official documents, numerous but neatly ordered. Lucius remembered his etiquette as he approached his commander.

"Hail, Legate Commander!" Lucius stopped several feet from the table and saluted sharply, oddly aware of his appearance. Flavius Marcellus looked up from his work, motioned to his secretary to leave.

"Hail, Tribune Metellus. Welcome back." He did not smile. Lucius remembered he rarely did, but his voice was friendly if not a little tired. He looked older.

"Forgive my appearance, Commander, but I thought I should report immediately." Lucius placed the imperial pass on the table. Marcellus set it aside.

"Quite right of you, Tribune. Please sit." Marcellus motioned to a stool on the right. "We've been expecting you for several days."

"Really?" Lucius was surprised. "I didn't realised the emperor's orders had reached you so quickly."

"Oh no, I haven't received anything of the sort yet. Two new auxiliary commanders came in the other day and said they had met you in Carthage some time ago."

Lucius remembered. "Ah, was it the Sarmatians?"

"Yes. I know I had requested your presence to combat the raiding parties popping up again but it seems they've ceased their activities for the moment. Our cavalry auxiliaries are more than enough to take care of it. Wine?" Marcellus motioned for his slave to pour them some watered wine. Lucius felt the drink moisten his parched mouth and lips. "So," continued the legate, "did you enjoy your time in Rome?"

"Very much, sir. Thank you."

"I hear you got married. Your centurion told me."

"Yes, Legate."

"That's good. Marriage makes a man more responsible and sensible. I can see you did not bring her with you but we won't get into that right now. I'm sure you are tired from your journey and in need of some rest before getting back to your duties tomorrow. Are you in shape for it, Tribune?" Marcellus had a slightly playful smirk on his face.

"Absolutely, Legate!" Lucius lied of course.

Marcellus could tell he was not as muscular as he had been before but decided to give Lucius a chance to prove himself again. "Good. That's what I like to hear. Your quarters are ready for you. Your centurion moved out and had them cleaned from top to bottom as soon as he heard you were on your way. You will also have to acquaint yourself with your new centurions; Alerio chose them to replace...well, to replace your fallen comrade, as well as Centurion Argus."

"I expected he would, sir. I'll meet with my centurions this evening."

"A lot has happened since you left, Tribune. We'll talk of it later." Lucius thought Marcellus gave him a sort of knowing nod but did not acknowledge it for fear he was wrong. "For now, as all of my officers are returned from Rome (you are the last) I would like to have all of you to dine with me in the Praetorium tomorrow night. Would you be amenable to that?"

"I'd be honoured, Legate."

"It'll help you to get re-acquainted with your peers." He paused. "Well, Tribune, it's good to have you back. We can always use a *good* man. Good commanders keep the ranks together. For now, go and get settled and report to me tomorrow morning for roll call and orders." Lucius stood up from the stool.

"Yes, Legate. Until tomorrow." He saluted, turned and went out.

Marcellus watched Lucius go, shook his head in dismay, sensing something was not right; his gut never lied. "I can always smell politics on a good man," he said to himself. "Like a fetid smell, it clings."

Since the tribunes' quarters were a short distance down the street, one of the Principia guards helped Lucius unload his chests and take them into his quarters before taking the wagon and horses to the legion's stables.

Lucius was pleased to have forgotten how large the tribunes' quarters were, even larger now that they were empty. The newly washed limestone courtyard gleamed in the afternoon sun as he paused in the centre of it to look around, try to remember. Inside, the sounds and smells of the base were a world apart.

"Tribune Metellus! Gods be praised you are back among us safely." Lucius turned around to see the old slave Xeno hobbling over to him in his usual hunched way.

"Xeno! How are you?" Lucius asked.

"I am well, Tribune, thank you for asking. How was your time in Rome?" he asked with a hint of awe for a place he had never seen.

"Very good, thank you. How was my centurion with you while I was away?"

ADAM ALEXANDER HAVIARAS

He nodded and smiled. "Centurion Alerio was very decent. An honourable man he is, without a doubt."

"Glad to hear it, Xeno. And your wife?" Lucius remembered he was married and thought to ask.

"Oh, my poor Tertia passed away. Her heart gave out on her." Xeno had evidently come to terms with the loss but Lucius felt terrible nevertheless.

"I am sorry for you. Forgive me, I did not know."

"The Gods' doing is not always an easy thing to bear, Tribune. She was in pain for some time. It was a blessing."

"You are a brave man, Xeno."

"I do my best, Tribune. But let us speak of happier tidings. I hear from Centurion Alerio that you married in Rome!"

"Yes I did." Lucius felt awkward talking about it after Xeno's news but the old man was full of happiness for him.

"That is wonderful!" He smiled. "I wish you every happiness and many children. But is she not joining you here?"

"Not yet, Xeno. But I hope to bring her here once I...settle in comfortably."

"Yes. A good idea, Tribune. Make the nest warm and safe first."

"Indeed, Xeno."

"Well, I should let you settle in, Tribune. I shall prepare your dinner shortly while you are arranging your things. If you need me for anything just call out and I'll come a' running."

"All right. Thank you, Xeno." Lucius smiled at the old man, laughing inwardly. He knew running was not something Xeno could even come close to. Such a kind old man.

Lucius settled first into his cubiculum where the bed in the corner had been laid out with fresh linen sheets and a flickering brazier beside for light. The room was unbearably empty, so Lucius set to unpacking his belongings in an effort to make it into something resembling a home. First, he unpacked his clothes and hung them along one wall where a long wooden pole was suspended horizontally. There were several pegs protruding from the wall on which he placed his cloaks. Once he had finished with his clothing, he chose a space along the wall next to his bed where he decided to arrange the altar to Apollo. He placed it on the small shelf that stood there; on one side of the altar he positioned the statue of Olympian Apollo and on the other side he laid the eagle feather, one of a pair given to him when the two eagles had visited him on the day he became a man. He had given its twin to Adara for protection before leaving. On hooks above the sacred items he hung the corona aurea and the hasta spear he had been awarded for saving the legate's life during the nomad attack on Lambaesis the previous year. Having been remiss in his prayers to his patron god, Lucius thought Apollo would be pleased with these offerings. After placing these revered items, he then arranged the statues of other gods: Jupiter, Mars and Venus.

Next, he went around to another corner and picked up the wooden frame on which to hang his armour, sword and dagger and placed it adjacent to the entrance. He unwrapped the greaves from their linen coverings and did the same with the helmet, affixing the crest once more, and then the cuirass. The dragon gleamed upon his breastplate as well as the cheek protectors of his helmet atop which the red horsehair crest fluttered like flames. Once these had been placed upon the T-shaped frame, he hung his gladius from one arm and his pugio from the other. Against the wall behind his armour, he leaned the bow he had taken from the man who had lain in ambush near Thugga; he thought he could learn how to use it later on.

The sword given to him by Adara, he hung between his bed and the altar. He hefted it lovingly in his hand and sat on the edge of the bed to remember, feel with closed eyes, the warm sensations of Cumae. He would write to her that night, let her know he had arrived. "Cumae," he said to himself. His mind rushed back to the acropolis there, the cave and the Sibyl. *Forget not...* Lucius jumped at the words that seemed to come as a whisper out of the close air of his quarters. "Who's there?" he said, but no answer came. His eyes fell upon the satchel containing his things, including the wax tablet with the Sibyl's words.

Immediately, Lucius went over, removed the tablet and placed it in front of the altar, open to Apollo, hoping that He would help him decipher his own message. He lit a chunk of incense, offered it into the carved dish on top of the altar and stepped backward. That was enough for his sleeping quarters for the moment. He picked up his collection of scrolls and maps and carried them with both arms to the room next door.

The meeting room was spotless. The large table surrounded by tall stools was empty, except for a small plate of cheese and olives and a cup of wine that Xeno had laid out for him until the meal was ready. Lucius laid the scrolls on the table, took a sip of wine and a bite of food, and began arranging. The scrolls he placed in the pigeon hole cupboards on the far left wall; histories, military accounts and tactical treatises, philosophical works, dramas and poetry. He had forgotten how many he had, mostly thanks to his old tutor, Diodorus, who had left them to Lucius before he passed.

The only map already on display was the large map of the immediate region, painted on cow's hide and stretched out in the midst of a rectangular wooden frame. His own maps, he placed neatly on a small table next to the pigeon holes. On the main table there were also fresh sheets of papyrus, blank wax tablets and several different styli. Alerio had left everything in impeccable condition. He hoped that his friend would come before the others so that they might speak privately.

After unpacking and arranging, Lucius went to the baths where Xeno had already lit the fires of the hypocausts. As the baths were small, it had not taken long for the temperature in the caldarium to rise. It felt good to relax a little; he knew that this would be a much-needed evening ritual when he began drilling the troops, for his body was unused to the intensity of the drills he wanted to inflict upon them.

Having bathed and oiled himself, Lucius put on a fresh tunic and went to the triclinium where Xeno had put out the evening meal. It consisted of wholesome fare: some rolled grains mixed with olives and lentils, a cooked chicken, flat breads, some fresh fruit and of course, a pitcher of wine. He would refrain from having too much of the latter, as he wanted to be aware and coherent when he met with his centurions. It was lonely eating but he realised that he would have to get used to it for a time. That made the wine all the more tempting.

Lucius finished his meal and found himself full and content, if not a little tired. Xeno had begun to clear away the dirty dishes and returned a second time for the remainder.

"Tribune, Centurion Alerio is here to see you. He said he would wait in the meeting room." The old man smiled, knowing how much each man was looking forward to this reunion. He would wait around to see that Lucius and Alerio had everything they wished before he left. Xeno did not want to be around when the others arrived, he did not care for them much.

"Thank you, Xeno. You can retire whenever you like." Lucius jumped up from his couch and went quickly into the courtyard before stopping himself. He had to be composed. Although he felt that Alerio was loyal to him, he had to make sure. But how? Lucius looked up at the rising moon, not yet at its pinnacle. *Apollo, I beg you, make it so that I can still trust him.* Before going into the meeting room, Lucius went to his cubiculum to hang Adara's gift across his shoulder and put on his cloak.

When he arrived in front of the open door to the meeting room, Alerio's back was turned where he stood in front of the hide map. His head was down, as though he was not really looking at it. His mind was elsewhere, and he tapped his right foot nervously in sync with the tap tapping of the polished vinerod upon his leg. Lucius watched him for a moment or two. The room felt heavy.

"Alerio," he said evenly. His friend turned immediately, not surprised but rather almost relieved.

"Lucius. My friend." Alerio smiled, gazed across the room at a man he feared he might not see again. Lucius smiled back and felt a pang in his chest. His closest friend looked tired and worn out. He still stood tall like himself and his body seemed strong, solid as before, but his features betrayed an exhaustion of another sort. Alerio's shortly cropped black hair now had small hints of grey, and he had lost weight in the face. Most of all, Lucius noticed the darkness beneath his tired eyes, their once piercing golden lustre dimmed of their light, shaded and ready to weep upon seeing him. *How could I have doubted his loyalty?* Lucius thought. The unspoken joy Alerio expressed at seeing Lucius dismissed any suspicions.

"It's good to see you."

"The Gods bless you, Lucius," he replied, reaching for Lucius' forearm and clasping it tightly in welcome friendship with both hands. "It's been too long."

"Far too long." Lucius hugged him like a brother. "How are you?" he asked, though the answer was apparent. Alerio sighed as Lucius pulled up a stool for him and poured the wine.

"Tired," he said plainly. "To be honest I'm happy to hand command back over to you."

"Your health." Lucius raised his cup.

"Likewise." There was so much he wanted to tell Lucius but they did not have the time, the others would be arriving soon. "Congratulations on your marriage. I drank a toast to you when I heard."

"Thank you. I decided not to bring Adara with me. Not yet." Lucius looked for a reaction.

"That was wise of you." Alerio's voice lowered. "We have a lot to talk about, there are things…you need to know. But…"

"But not now. Not yet." Lucius tried to look calm, determined, in an effort to lend his friend some measure of comfort that he was no longer alone, that he had an ally.

Lucius thought that if things were as bad as he suspected, Alerio should have been dead already. It was either a gift from the Gods or a sign most of his men were still loyal to him that Alerio was even alive in that room. "We'll talk about it when the time's right. For now tell me briefly what the cohort's makeup is, where we stand in the legion."

Alerio put down his vinerod for the first time. Of late, it had been a sort of talisman for him to ward off harm and inflict punishment. "The legate decided that since we were going to be here for a while, the cohort would become part of the main body of the legion. Tertius Sabinus has replaced Cornelius Ciceron; he and Balbas Ascanius command the legion in rotation. That means we're now in Sabinus' position – our cohort plus a few extra men that survived Ciceron's disaster."

"How is Sabinus filling the role?" Lucius had never liked Cornelius Ciceron, though he felt a chill at the memory of seeing Ciceron's cavalry turn on him, cut him down during the battle against the nomads.

"He's capable and communicative. A good man. In the beginning he was having trouble adjusting to the responsibility, but he seems to have adapted. He asks after you all the time."

"He was always nicer to me than the rest. What about Ascanius?"

"Huh!" Alerio laughed. "He's a tough bastard but good on the troops. He balances Sabinus' sense of justice nicely with hard discipline. They work well together."

"Everything sounds good on that level of things then." Lucius took another sip and leaned forward. "What about our men? Besides the…things…we'll discuss later."

"I've been drilling them ruthlessly, keeping them busy-"

There was a knock on the door.

"Your pardon, Tribune, Centurion." It was Xeno. "I just wanted to bring you some more wine and this platter of fruit." He walked in and placed the things on the table. Xeno stepped back and looked at the two men. "It's good to see two friends reunited."

"Thank you, Xeno. It is indeed. Are the others here yet?"

"No, Tribune. But as soon as they arrive I shall show them in." Xeno left again.

"Continue," Lucius said, as he picked up a fat date.

"I've kept discipline harsh. There's been some grumbling but nothing mutinous. They've all been too busy to get up to anything. Many of the men have married and now have wives outside the walls."

"That's a relief. Briefly, how have the others, our centurions, been treating you as their superior?"

"We've butt heads a few times, but recently, things have been pretty quiet. I've spent most of my time here alone. Sometimes Eligius would come for a drink but other than that I only see them on duty."

"Odd. I'm sorry I didn't take you to Rome, Alerio."

"I have to admit, at one point I wished very much that I hadn't told you to take Argus instead."

"Who have you appointed to replace...I mean...to take over Antanelis' century?" The mention of their friend's name seemed to fall heavily in the room, like a stone in the sand.

"That was the task I relished least of all while you were gone. I did however, decide on someone."

"Who is it?"

"His name's Paulus Valerus."

"Valerus...Valerus," Lucius repeated the name. "That name seems familiar to me." He snapped his fingers. "Didn't Antanelis mention him before? I've been away too long."

"He was Antanelis' optio; they were good friends."

"What's he like?" Lucius felt badly for not remembering Antanelis' own optio, a man he was apparently friends with.

"He's a couple years our junior, short, but deadly strong and fast as lightening. Valerus has adapted well to the role of centurion and keeps his men in top form. Right now they're the most disciplined."

"I'm impressed. Sounds like a good choice. The fact that he was Antanelis' friend might work for us."

"That's what I thought too. He was hard hit by Antanelis' death and kept coming to me to see if there was anything he could do to help in an investigation. I said no to him at the time though he assured me he would help in any way he could. I think he believes that if he runs his friend's former century well, then it might appease his shade." Alerio shivered from a chill that went through his body. Talk of shades was never a good thing to undertake.

"What about Argus' century?"

"This one I'm not certain about. His name's Favonius Pephredo. Iberian, from Hispania. Not short, but not huge. Maren suggested him when word came that Argus had joined the Praetorians. He keeps to himself most of the time but has an extremely tight reign on his men. Ha!" Alerio chuckled. "He's already broken a few vinerods on some backs."

"Is he a problem?"

"Not yet. Both he and Valerus seem to be doing well." They heard footsteps in the courtyard and several voices. "That's them now," Alerio confirmed, standing up and grabbing his vinerod tightly. Lucius stood too, behind the table, in front of the map. He was nervous, his heart pounded as he tried to stand tall. The voices came closer and closer. Xeno opened the door for the rest of the cohort's centurions.

They came in talking, Maren and Garai first, then Garai's brother, Eligius, and finally Paulus Valerus and Favonius Pephredo, the latter two quiet like children at their first day of tutoring. Valerus and Pephredo both saluted first, perfect. Garai laughed, smiling at Lucius, and then the others followed suit. Eligius was the first to round the table to welcome Lucius.

"Hail Tribune, and friend. Welcome back!" Lucius clasped his arm and looked into his green eyes.

"Eligius. Good to see you." Lucius looked at the others. "Garai, Maren."

"Welcome back, Lucius," Garai said. Maren nodded in agreement, silent as usual. "How does it feel to be back in Numidia?"

"Good. Happy to get back to things." He did not want to let on that there was any hesitation about his coming back, that he would rather have been anywhere else. Lucius looked at the two young men, still in uniform, standing by the door. He decided to walk around the table to meet them. He thought he recognised them. After all, they had been in his cohort from the beginning, but after so much time and so many faces, he could not place them. "You must be Pephredo."

The young man stepped forward, nodded. "Yes, Tribune." Lucius could tell he was a man of few words. Favonius Pephredo was of medium height and build with jet-black hair and near-black eyes. His armour was brightly polished. Lucius noticed splintering on his vinerod. Evidently he had used it that day.

"How have you adapted to your role as centurion?" he asked Favonius.

"Very well, Tribune. I've straightened the men out nicely. If they get out of line, I put them back." The young centurion spoke with pride.

"I can see that." Lucius pointed to the vinerod.

"Just discipline, Tribune."

"Discipline!" Garai laughed out loud. "He beats the shit out of them any chance he gets!" Everyone was staring at Pephredo.

"That's fine," said Lucius. "So long as they deserve it. By all means use discipline, but don't kill or injure every man in your century, otherwise we'll be even more short-handed." Maren's eyebrows went up, surprised to hear Lucius talk that way. He was always more caring about his men. Lucius then turned to the other centurion. "And you must be Valerus."

"Yes, Tribune." The short blond man in brilliant armour saluted sharply once more, his voice high-pitched, so much so that Lucius' eyes went wide for a moment. "Welcome back to you, Tribune," he squeaked with an odd accent.

"Where are you from, Centurion?"

"Gaul, Tribune. Lugdunum."

"I see. And how have you settled in?"

"Very well, Tribune. The men are excellent. Antanelis taught us well and always held discipline. He always talked about how good it was to serve as centurion under you and I must say I am honoured to have the chance to do the same, even though I would rather he were alive and continuing his job." Everyone in the room went silent.

By the Gods this boy is eager, and blunt. I like him, Lucius thought. Lucius looked around the room at everyone, either head down or feet shuffling, they felt uncomfortable. Alerio stood behind Lucius, unmoving.

"Careful pipsqueak! Kissing ass won't get you anywhere in this room!" said Maren disrespectfully. Valerus ignored him, stood still at attention before his tribune. Lucius put his hand on the man's shoulder.

"We could all learn from Antanelis' example, Valerus." The young man nodded once, confident. Lucius stepped back behind the table. "Now! Alerio has informed me that things have been going well, that you're all in shape." Xeno entered with a tray of five extra cups for the other centurions and left. Lucius noticed that as he had entered, his hands began to shake nervously until he put the tray down. "Thank you Xeno." Lucius put in as the men poured themselves some wine. Valerus refrained. "Tomorrow, after I report to the legate, I'll come out to the parade ground to watch your drills and see what you've been up to."

"Are you ready to get back to drills, Lucius?" Garai asked. "You look like you've lost some muscle there. Being in Rome hasn't softened you, has it?" Lucius stared across the room at him, then smiled.

"Oh, I'm ready." He was silent for a moment.

"We should drink a toast to you, Lucius," Eligius said. "After all, you got married while you were away!" He raised his cup, Paulus hurriedly poured himself a little to toast with. "Congratulations on your marriage and may the Gods bless you!" Everyone repeated and drank together.

"Thank you," Lucius said graciously.

"So where is the newest Metella?" Maren asked. "Did she not come with you?"

"Well-," began Lucius but he was interrupted.

"Probably in Athens," Garai blurted.

Inside Lucius panicked but he tried to hide his fear. *How did they know that? Must have been Argus who told them.*

"How did you know my wife was in Athens, Garai?" Lucius stared evenly at him, voice deceptively calm.

"Uhm, well, you know how word gets around. All the men have been asking for news about you and someone must have found something out." He fidgeted. "Anyway, you must be happy?"

"Very." An awkward silence hung in the room for some time before Eligius broke it.

"Well, my friend, you must be exhausted after your journey. We should let you get some sleep for your first full day tomorrow."

"Yes you must be tired," echoed Garai.

"Tribune," Valerus stepped forward, "thank you for inviting us into your home. We shall see you tomorrow. Good night to you."

"Good night, Valerus." Lucius nodded to him. "Pephredo."

"Good night, Tribune." The two newcomers went out of the door and back to their barrack blocks. Shortly after Maren, Garai and Eligius followed.

"Are you coming, Alerio?" asked Eligius.

"No, go ahead. I have some orders from the legate for Lucius. I'll see you in the morning."

"All right. Good night." Eligius' voice echoed in the courtyard and then the main door closed with a thud behind them as they went back to barracks.

Lucius and Alerio sat down, more relaxed now. Lucius unhooked the sword Adara had given him and placed in on the table. Alerio put down his vinerod again.

"By Vulcan, Lucius! That's a beautiful sword!" Alerio almost had to shield his eyes from the brightness of the hilt. He also noticed Lucius' ring. "I see dragons have proved to be a good thing."

"Yes. The sword was a gift from Adara after our wedding. She gave it to me in Cumae."

"It's magnificent. Do you have a likeness with you of her?" Alerio asked. Lucius had not even thought of it before leaving. Adara was so vivid and alive in his mind, with him always.

"No actually, I don't." He remembered the statues that had been their wedding gift back in Rome. No likeness would ever compare to Emrys and Carissa's work but until he had made a larger home for the two of them, they would remain there. Little did he know that his mother wept almost daily at the base of his own likeness once she was able to leave her bed.

"So what do you think?" Alerio asked.

"About what?"

"About the men."

"What do I think?" Lucius repeated. "I think Argus has been writing to some of them, that's what I think."

"Yes. I've heard his name mentioned a lot, that's he's some kind of big man in the Guard now or something. Did you see him much in Rome?"

"Not much after he left to join the Guard. He popped up at my wedding with the Praetorian prefect."

"Plautianus?"

"Yup. Now that's one despicable man." Lucius didn't want to tell Alerio about Leptis Magna and the empress. It would be safer for him if he did not know anything about it, at least for now. The fewer who knew the better.

"What about Ashur?"

"I asked him to stay with Adara and my sister for their time in Athens. Someone to look over them while I'm away."

"Good idea." Alerio rubbed his eyes. "Sorry I'm so quiet, Lucius. There's just so much spinning around in my mind, things I want to tell you. The Gods have given me sleepless nights, for what reasons I don't know. All I know is I'm glad you're back."

"Me too, my friend. Me too." Lucius reached over and pat him on the shoulder.

"Oh, that reminds me!" said Alerio more awake. "I have something for you."

"What?"

"I can't say right now. All I'll say is that it's a late wedding present."

"Alerio, you shouldn't have done that. You should save your pay. Don't *you* have a wife hidden away in the vicus?"

"Ha!" Alerio waved his hand. "Who has time for love? Besides, I haven't seen anyone remotely interesting. Just me and Lady Venus in my dreams when I do manage to sleep but even that doesn't happen often."

"Speaking of sleep," began Lucius, "we should both get some."

"You're right. Lots of time to catch up on things later. Tomorrow, after drills, I'll give you your present."

"All right." They went outside into the courtyard. "I'll meet you out on the parade ground around the second hour of day. Give myself some time to stretch my limbs before going."

"Good idea. I'll see you tomorrow." Alerio turned at the main door. "It's good to see you. I feel better now. It'll be just like old times, no?"

"Once we straighten things out," Lucius said confidently.

Alerio stepped out onto the via Principalis and turned down one of the smaller streets to go to his quarters in the barracks; it would be his first good night of sleep since Antanelis' death.

The night sky was clear and the stars danced around the white moon, shedding creamy light onto the cobbles of the courtyard. It seemed to Lucius that something was missing and he decided that it might be a good idea to have a tripod set up in the centre of the yard where he and any visitors could make an offering to the household Gods. He did not know what dark thoughts any of his visitors might be carrying within themselves. A ritual purification before entering the rooms would be beneficial, appeasing.

In the meeting room, Lucius made space on the table to do what he had been wanting to do since he arrived: write to Adara. He unrolled a sheet of papyrus, put small pebbles on each corner and dipped his stylus into the inkpot.

To Adara Antonina Metella
From her loving husband Lucius Metellus Anguis,

Forgive me, my Love, for having taken so long to give you news of myself, my whereabouts. The journey from Leptis Magna was long and broken. Know now that I am safe and sound, having arrived in Lambaesis this very day.

My centurion, Alerio, has kept things running. He remains a good friend and ally, one whom I can trust with my life. There are some things that I must look into and so I cannot yet send for you, though I want nothing more in this world than to have you here with me, close.

I trust that you and the others are well. One night, I don't remember how long ago, I felt that you were in pain. I have been praying that you are well and that Apollo and Venus are looking over you. If your heart is screaming as much as mine, then that must be what I felt. I am trying to be strong, truthful in my actions, but I find myself fighting anger being here. I resent it. However, I know my duty, to you and to Rome. Reconciling the two proves difficult but never doubt that my truest loyalty, love, is to you.

I promise that I shall write more often now. When you get this, please send word to me, news of yourself, Alene and the others. I will feel better if I know what is happening.

The moon is almost full this night and I shall go to sleep dreaming of you, as I always do. I am with you every moment. Make an offering for me in the great temple and I shall whisper your name to the sky and stars. I love you.

Your loving husband, always,
Lucius

The lamp on the table was flickering wildly now, the last remnants of oil burning away. Lucius had wanted to write more but he was tired and needed his rest. After sealing the letter, he blew out the lamps and went to his cubicula where Xeno had replenished the brazier and put out fresh water in a basin. Lucius closed the door, bolted it. He removed his tunic and sandals and placed them at the foot of the bed. When he climbed beneath the fresh linen sheets, his eyes closed almost before his head was down. He pictured Adara's face in the sunlight, green eyes sparkling. In one hand he grasped the sword she had given him.

The Gods did not grant Lucius sleep for long. He had gone to bed with a vision of his wife, a vision his mind tried desperately to cling to but it was not the Gods' will. After no more than an hour of rest, his mind began to whirl, his body tensed, sweat glistened upon his brow. To the incessant ringing he remembered from the Sibyl's cave, Lucius revisited the inner sanctum, saw Adara kneeling over him, weeping. He found himself in the desert once more, walking barefoot among the dunes, the powder-like sand cool between his toes.

The ringing ceased and a strong wind picked up. The moon blocked out the sun, the desert dark. Ahead of him, Lucius spotted a figure beneath a tall, lonely palm. He walked over, the fine sand turning to mud beneath his feet. The figure was cloaked in crimson, glistening red curls protruding from the hood. *Who are you?* Lucius mouthed, no words coming forth. The figure did not turn or speak, but pointed to the side where a massive lion came charging toward him. Lucius braced for the deadly impact but the beast stopped short and walked over to the cloaked figure.

The crimson cloak fell to the sand like a pool of blood revealing a body torn apart. Gashes ran up and down the sides where ribs protruded. *Antanelis!* Lucius yelled into a soundless void. The figure turned, a reflection of what the young man had been. The eyes, set in a mauled face, looked pitifully upon Lucius as he trembled, now on his knees in the mud. The light of the eclipsed sun burned his eyes but he forced himself to look as the lion rubbed against Antanelis' leg, like an affectionate kitten. A bloody hand pet the beast and the two walked away as friends. Before disappearing over the dunes, the figure raised a hand in parting.

The sun appeared once more and the mud turned to sand. Crawling to the palm, naked and alone, Lucius wept.

He awoke weeping, unaware of where he was. The bed was soaked with sweat and his limbs ached.

Lucius felt better after bathing quickly and eating but he had not slept well. The day would be that much more difficult. In his cubiculum, he put on his thin-striped tunic beneath his full armour. He would be inspecting all his men for the first time that day and needed to command respect. Once he had put on his doublet and pteruges, Xeno helped him to strap on his breastplate.

"I always wondered at your armour, Tribune," said the old man. "It makes me want to look up at the sky for some reason. I'll leave you now, to finish getting ready." Xeno walked out into the courtyard where the first rays were angling their way onto the roof tiles.

The small ironwork windows of his room began to brighten slightly and Lucius took a deep breath. He was glad for the morning, the day. He went over to the altar he had set up, lit some frankincense. Holding the eagle feather to his chest, he bowed his head.

"Wise and mighty Apollo, hear me. Today I face my men for the first time. Let them still be *my* men, the men I trained with and bled with. I have led them through many lands and they have stayed by me. Let not the memory of so much be blown away like so many grains of sand, gritty and stinging. As I work here, in this place, I would ask that you guide me truthfully. I would also ask that you keep my wife safe, my family." Lucius kissed the ring on his finger. I commend myself to you, Far Shooting Apollo, to Lady Venus and to Mars, God of War that I may go on in wisdom, love, and strength." Lucius replaced the feather next to the altar and backed away.

It was a short walk to the Principia and the legate's offices. Lucius' hobnailed boots clicked on the cobbles of the via Principalis as he walked. Men saluted him as he passed; the base was already bustling with the sounds of the legion's troops going about their assigned duties for the day. A lone cornu resonated hauntingly from the Principia's courtyard where one of the cohorts was going through morning inspection. The horn's hum was followed by crisp orders, another horn blast and then the unified stomping of soldier's boots upon the flagstones as the company was dismissed.

Close to five hundred men flowed out of the large double gates, the centurions barking orders as they filed past.

"Good morning, Tribune!" the guard at the gate greeted Lucius and saluted. "The legate is expecting you, sir." Lucius nodded and went in. The great tripod in the centre of the courtyard crackled as the newly offered cedar branches burned and smoked, mingled with the oil that had been poured on top. Lucius realised the courtyard seemed ten times bigger when it was empty; how else could so many men gather there? In less hospitable climes, the assembly space of the Principia tended to be in a covered basilica but as the weather in Lambaesis was bearable most of the year, it had the advantage of an outdoor space.

Once inside, Lucius was informed that the legate was busy with one of the other officers and that he would be several minutes. So, he decided to make his way into the lower level of the structure where the legionary vaults were located but more importantly where the aedes sacrae were under constant guard.

The aedes sacrae were the sacred rooms where the legion's standards were kept. It was quiet except for the flicker of flames and Lucius' footsteps as he descended the stairs. Two more guards saluted but said not a word, for it was treated as a temple. Rooms on either side of the floor contained the standards of the various cohorts and directly ahead, up a flight of stairs and behind bronze bars, were the III Augustan's standards. Altars stood on either side of the entrance and Lucius picked up a beaker of scented oil and poured some on one of them in offering.

He had never been down there before, wished he had, for it was a place of peace and reflection. Standing there alone offered one the opportunity to think on what it was to serve Rome. Lucius was filled with a sense of duty in that moment and thought of his wife and family, that to serve Rome's emperor willingly was to make the world a better place for those he cared about. He had not always believed this but in that place he could see it, feel the majesty of the mightiest empire since Alexander.

Before him were the imagines, silver images of the emperor atop a long spear, a reminder to the legion of their oath. Other standards as well as statues of Septimius Severus and Marcus Aurelius flanked the central object of sacred importance: the Aquila. Upon their creation, each legion was gifted with one of these brilliant golden eagle standards, carried into battle by the aquilifer. The eagle, Jupiter's envoy, was central to the legion's life. For it to be lost in battle was utter disgrace; men died for the Aquila.

"Tribune Metellus, the legate will see you now," the guard whispered to Lucius.

"Thank you." Lucius removed his helmet, put it beneath his left arm and went directly. The room was empty of attendants. "Hail, Legate Commander!" he saluted to his superior. Marcellus was dressed in his parade armour, as he would be observing the men from the dais on the parade ground that day.

"Good morning Metellus. Have a seat." Lucius sat in the usual stool while Marcellus finished writing some dispatch. "So, you met with your centurions last night?"

"Yes, sir."

"Everything in order then? The two new centurions seem fine?"

"They appear to be good men. Alerio chose well, I think."

"I think so too. Good! Now, orders to get you back into things here after life in Rome. Three weeks from now we are going to have a mock battle to keep the men tuned; it will be a good substitute for not fighting the raiding parties. I'll also order training marches for the cohorts; these will also serve as patrols so that we can show our presence over a greater area. Build full camps at night for these marches. When the men are based somewhere permanent and they don't have any wars to fight for some time, I find that this sort of exercise is just the thing. So, once you get reacquainted with the men and see where they're at, I want you to drill them harder, make sure they can wheel and form up with one blow on the horn. Then I want you to take them out on field exercise to prepare for the march; have them dig a ditch and palisade befitting your numbers. They'll curse you for it but later on they'll thank you. Any questions?"

"About the drills no. Everything is clear, Legate, but I do have a personal request for you." Lucius wondered if he was being too bold but he had to ask.

"Yes. What is it?" Marcellus put his elbows on the table and laced his fingers.

"I would like to request your permission to undertake my own investigation into the death of Antanelis, my centurion." Marcellus did not look at all surprised, even though Alerio had already done this same thing.

"I thought you might," he said gravely.

"You did, sir?"

"Yes." Lucius was not sure what to say next but Marcellus spoke first. "Permission granted. I won't say I haven't had my suspicions about the incident but I thought it better to leave it up to your centurion. He's a capable man. However, it wouldn't hurt for you to conduct another. But! I want you to keep it quiet; if you tread lightly upon the ground, the jackals won't suspect your coming. Heavy feet scare away the prey, correct?"

"Yes, sir." Lucius nodded.

"I want you to report anything you discover to me alone. If word were to get out in the legion about this sort of thing, we'd have more incidents on our hands."

"Understood, Legate." Lucius stood up at attention as Marcellus rose.

"Good. Now, you had better go out and inspect your men on the field. I'll see you this evening in the Praetorium for dinner."

"I look forward to it, sir."

"Dismissed." Lucius turned and went back outside into the courtyard. When he stepped out, he was awaited by a trooper holding a vexillum standard. The trooper had a leopard skin hanging over his head and down around his armoured shoulders. He saluted Lucius as he came into the growing light. The tall standard he held was comprised of a long shaft affixed with a large, red square banner flanked by two long strands of bronze roundels that swayed in the breeze. On the banner was a yellow-gold dragon similar to the one on his breastplate.

Lucius stopped. "What's this, trooper?"

"I'm your vexillarius, Tribune. Centurion Alerio said I should meet you here and accompany you to the field." Lucius looked at the man, at the banner. He liked it.

"I didn't have a vexillum before."

"No, Tribune. But, after you left for Rome and we were made a part of the legion, the cohort was granted one. I was promoted to the position by Centurion Alerio who asked me to make this as I had some skill." Lucius looked at the man, tried to place his face and name like a teacher trying to remember the name of a pupil returned from the wars. "Does it please you, Tribune?"

"Yes it does…Frontus, right?" he remembered the name.

"Yes, Tribune. Antonius Frontus."

"So, you will be following me around the field from now on." Lucius replaced his helmet.

"Yes, Tribune. Always, and might I say, sir, that…" he was afraid he was speaking out of turn, "…it's good to have you back." Lucius realised he would have to get used to the idea of a standard bearer following him around.

"All right then, Frontus, let's go." The vexillarius waited for Lucius to walk in front and then followed directly behind him, hoisting the standard high above his head so that the bronze strands jingled lightly, and the leopard skin swung rhythmically behind him as he marched.

"Halt! First row! Pila Iacite! Second row! Pila Iacite! Scuta Portate! Gladios Destringite! Forward!" Alerio shouted his orders with ferocity from where he stood on the parade ground as he drilled the troops before Lucius' arrival. The morning sun cut through clouds of dust where the pila crashed into the earth. He wondered what was taking Lucius so long, busied himself and the troops with pre-emptory drills before their inspection. It did not matter if they were a little dusty, things were always dusty, dirty, on the Numidian plain.

Finally, he spotted the vexillum coming through one of the gates of the parade ground and smiled to himself. "Form up for inspection!" he yelled. More than four hundred and eighty troops immediately gathered into neatly ordered centuries each marked by their own signum standard. Five of the centuries' signifers carried long shafts decorated with four large, silver discs above a tasselled hand guard and each topped by a larger silver spearhead. Alerio's century was marked by a signum with a tasselled guard, a crescent moon, four discs and an upraised hand instead of a spearhead. The men were lined up in perfect rows and had done so very quickly. Alerio wondered if they had done it for the other tribunes and the legate who had come riding up to the dais earlier to watch the proceedings.

Lucius had disappeared into clouds of dust for the moment as the wind picked up violently, whirling about in an orange haze. The horizontal crest of Alerio's helmet shivered with each gust as he waited for Lucius to appear. Then he spotted the tall crimson crest and vexillum with the dragon.

"Cornu! Salutate!" Alerio ordered Balbus, the cornicen, to sound out the return of the cohort's tribune. Alerio felt a chill as his friend approached. Lucius' crimson cloak whipped in the wind, almost in imitation of the dragon's wings upon his standard. The men's faces were stern, still, silent. The cornu sounded a long, high-pitched note as the tribune came to stand in front the cohort. "Hail, Tribune Metellus!" Alerio called out, turning to salute Lucius.

"Hail, Tribune Metellus!" the men echoed into the dusty wind and saluted.

"Inspection!" Alerio yelled, indicating that the tribune would walk the rows. "Ready for this?" he whispered to Lucius.

"I'm ready." Starting at the back rows, Lucius and Alerio, followed by Frontus and Balbus, walked among the men. Lucius eyed each of them intently, greeted those he remembered as exceptional and received greetings. He told a few men to fix parts of their armour, broken hinges or splintered pila handles. Alerio followed closely, his vinerod tucked under his arm. He realised that many of the men who had given him some trouble before, now cowered with Lucius there. They still talked of Sabratha.

When they had finished inspection, Lucius moved to the front of the men where a small dais had been set up. With a vantage point overlooking the cohort, he addressed his men. Before beginning, he took several deep breaths to slow his heart and calm his nerves.

"It's good to be back among you men! I've been away for some time but I can see that you've kept yourselves in top condition. I'm glad of it! I feel better being here, at your head, and it gives me great pride to see you all so well turned-out. We've got a lot of work ahead of us. The legate has given us orders to train and drill harder than ever in preparation for intense exercises to be held in several weeks. I know you will not disappoint." Lucius paused to look at the faces, see if there were any disapproving looks. None that he could spot.

"As for those who are no longer with us," he continued, referencing Antanelis intentionally, "terrible as it is, it was the Gods' will that it be so. The Gods' will is inevitable, their justice is harsh!" Alerio gripped his vinerod as he stared around at the men. "We must accept this fate. All of us. What I demand of you is that you perform your duties with truth, honour and intent. If you do this, the Gods will be pleased! Now! Show me what this cohort can do!" Several cheers went up calling Lucius' name as the cornu sounded the resumption of drills.

"Show me what they've got, Centurion!"

"Yes, Tribune!" Alerio answered. "Form up! Together! March!" he yelled, the horn relaying the orders to the signifers who led the men. Where he stood, stern-faced, severe beneath his new banner, Lucius rejoiced inwardly at the sound of Alerio's harsh, commanding voice. He had missed it. The men marched, wheeled, hurled their pila and drew their swords, over and over and over again on the dusty field.

This is for you Antanelis, Lucius thought as he took his command.

VIII

REDIRE AD CASTRUM

'Back to Barracks'

Lucius' first day of exercises on the parade ground of
Lambaesis was spent mostly in observation from the central
dais beneath the statue of Emperor Hadrian. He had thought to
go out onto the plain for the entire day and sweat with the
troops but decided against it. He agreed with Alerio; it would
not do him any good to be so painfully sore on the first day
that he might not be able to raise his weary limbs from bed the
following morning. Besides, the other tribunes were observing
from the dais with the legate who gave orders or advice as
called for.

The legate did not speak with Lucius on that first day, as he
wanted to allow him to settle in. He knew Lucius was a good
commander who could think clearly and quickly. When
exercises came to a close in the afternoon, the winds having
died down and the dust settled, Lucius dismissed his men for
the evening and congratulated them on their work. He knew
early dismissal would be appreciated, was sure many of the
men wanted to get back to their wives and children in the vicus
outside the base walls, gamble in some of the scholae or go to
the baths. Alerio remained behind with Lucius as the men
marched off the field century by century.

"What do you think?" Alerio asked once they were alone.

"I think you've done an amazing job with them. Mars must
be pleased. I just hope I made the right decision by staying up
there," he pointed to the dais, "and observing."

"You did," Alerio reassured him. "For the most part,
they're a good bunch of men, the same men that followed you
across Africa, but it will take time to get used to you. It's

better that you get involved slowly before rubbing their noses in it."

"I hope you're right." The two of them walked in companionable silence for a time.

"Do you like the vexillum?" Alerio asked. "I thought it was about time that you had one. You're a decorated commander after all and it'll stress your rank to the men."

"It's fantastic, Alerio, really. I just have to get used to the idea of having it follow me everywhere. Frontus seems like a good man."

"He is. He's always been a big help, so I thought the promotion was deserved."

"It was." Lucius smiled as they walked, a childlike glint in his eye. "So, what about this wedding present?" Alerio smiled too as it had been on his mind for a long time; he knew Lucius would be shocked. For so long he had saved up his soldier's pay in the Principia vaults. He thought his best friend's wedding was the perfect opportunity to use it.

"How much time do you have before going to the Praetorium?"

"Plenty."

"Well then, follow me." Alerio led the way as they entered the fortress walls.

"I haven't been in this part of the base for a long time," Lucius said as they made their way through some of the narrower streets in the north-eastern sector. The smell of hay and dung was strong in the air, not an unpleasant smell, but one that was more than noticeable. "Where are we going?" The smell was familiar, reminded him of when they had first arrived at the base, of quiet mornings and evenings spent brushing down Pegasus, the stallion he had lost in battle against the nomads.

"Almost there." Alerio waved at someone where the narrow street opened onto a larger area. On either side of them were the stables where all the auxiliary horses were kept in neat rows. The hammering from a blacksmith's forge broke into the peaceful setting where only moments before the neighing of horses could be heard. "Wait here. I'll be right back." Alerio went around the corner of one of the larger stables next to a large round enclosure.

Lucius removed his helmet to let the breeze cool his head. He realised that he needed to wash and shave before going to the Praetorium; he would be dining with some of his fellow Equestrians as well as some high-born aristocrats. Lucius walked the rows of horses slowly. Most of the animals ignored him, some perked up their ears questioningly.

There was a sudden commotion behind him near the round enclosure. Alerio called out: "Lucius! Over here!" He waved for him to come over. He had said something else but Lucius had not understood due to a loud, intense neighing and pounding of hooves. Alerio was facing Lucius, leaning against the wooden beams of the enclosure. A huge smile cracked his face. "Congratulations on your wedding!" Lucius approached in silent awe, unable to speak at what he saw before him. "What do you think?"

"I...I..." Lucius stopped, looked from his friend to the enclosure where the beast ran round and round. "This can't be, I mean, Alerio is this what you were talking about?"

"Ha! Ha! For once I've got you speechless. Excellent!" Alerio rejoiced at the look on Lucius' overwhelmed face. "Yes it is. This is your wedding present. I've trained him myself, well, with a little help from one of my men from Toletum. Say something!" He gave Lucius a playful punch in the arm.

"This is too much, Alerio. You shouldn't have done this."

"Camel dung! You're my best friend! If anyone deserves this, you do. I know how much you miss Pegasus. You should be riding at the head of your cohort, not walking." The animal continued to charge around in circles. "Are you going in?" Alerio asked, laughing to himself.

"In there? Are you mad? He'll crush me!"

"Trust me. He's just stretching his legs."

"He's magnificent." Lucius put his helmet on a bench and leaned on the beam to admire his gift. The stallion was young, big and strong. As he bounded back and forth, kicking up dust, his muscles pulsed and flexed like a Titan's. He held his head high, throwing back a solid, thick neck. His colour was one of the most beautiful Lucius had ever set eyes upon; beautiful dapple-grey from head to foot with both a long, flowing mane and tail of purest black. The tall stallion was not at all skittish but rather aware, confident, full of power. "What breed is he?"

"Iberian." Alerio gazed proudly on the creature he had trained and nurtured in honour of his friend. "I bought him in Cirta."

"What's his name? Did you give him one already, or should I?"

"I gave him a name. Had to in order to properly train him but I gave him one I think you'll like: Lunaris." The stallion paused briefly on the other side of the enclosure as Alerio whispered the name to Lucius.

"Hmm. Lunaris," Lucius repeated as he looked at the animal. "*Of the Moon*. It's perfect." He smiled. It was indeed perfect, for the stallion's dapple coat was a cool, clear silver, slightly spotted like the full moon.

"So what are you waiting for? Go in." The horse began to charge around once more.

"I don't know about this."

"By all the Gods, Lucius. Trust me. Here, take off your cloak." Alerio began to undo the brooches and remove Lucius' cloak. "Now, give me your sword and dagger so they don't get in the way." He took them and laid them on another bench. By now, a few men had gathered a short distance behind them to watch. Lucius thought they took wagers on whether the horse would throw him. He ignored this. "Go on. Climb over slowly, move calmly. As you approach, say his name gently but louder than before." Lucius looked doubtful but decided to trust him.

He climbed up and over the top beam, set his foot down in the soft sand and turned to face his gift. The stallion eyed him

197

curiously but did not stop moving. Once, he even rose up on his hind legs to tower above Lucius.

"Lunaris." The instant the name left Lucius' lips the stallion stopped, waited, stomping the occasional hoof in the sand and nodding its head.

"Now," said Alerio, "turn your back to him and walk around the enclosure slowly. No sudden movements. Let him adapt to your presence."

Lucius did as he said, turned his back to the horse and walked around the enclosure. He hummed a little, partly to ease his nerves, partly because he thought it might calm the horse. He could hear gentle steps in the sand behind him. The third time around he felt hot breath on the back of his neck.

"Now Lucius, move to the middle and stop. Let him look at you and then turn to face him." Alerio didn't doubt what would happen; he had never seen the horse so calm, not even around himself.

Having stopped in the middle of the sand, Lucius felt a gentle, almost playful, nudging in his back. The horse moved back from him for a moment, watched Lucius and then returned. "Can I turn now?" Lucius asked.

"Yes. Turn." Alerio smiled at the sight of the two of them meeting eye to eye for the first time.

"Lunaris," Lucius soothed as he looked up. The eyes were a lively hazel, large, full of life. "Yes, you're magnificent...Lunaris," he repeated, enjoying the way the name rolled off his tongue. "A good name. Yes." He slid his hand along the strong neck, felt the smooth mane. Lunaris remained still. His new master was amazed at his strength and height. It would take some effort to climb onto his back.

"Do you want to try riding him?" Alerio asked. "I've had a saddle made for you as well as a new harness." He waved to the stable master who came over with the two items and slung them over the top beam. "Don't worry, he's already had them on and doesn't mind so much. He really likes you!" Lucius nodded and walked over to get the harness and saddle. Lunaris followed.

Alerio climbed over too, let Lunaris decide he was acceptable and then draped a tasselled crimson blanket over his back. The saddle was the usual four-horned type with soft leather padding for comfort. Lucius put it on Lunaris' back and passed the strap underneath to Alerio who buckled it. A new harness had been made of red leather with bronze phalerae and strap ends for decoration. On the forehead was a gold disc with the image of a dragon on it. Lucius noted that Alerio had spent far too much on all of this. He was also happy to see that the bit was not the usual contraption that, when the reins were pulled, inflicted severe pain on the roof of the horse's mouth. It was a straight bit with bronze discs on either side of the mouth. Lunaris accepted the bit without complaint and kept his head still as it was strapped on.

"Good boy," Alerio said, patting Lunaris on the neck before climbing back over the fence. "All right Lucius. He's all yours." Lucius walked back to the centre of the enclosure away from the fence, with Lunaris following again. By now, even more men had gathered and watched keenly to see if they would win their wagers.

It was a long way up to get into the saddle. Lucius had to reach for the horns. He had not been on a horse for some time. "Lunaris, I'm getting on now," he warned. The stallion nodded its head vigorously and steadied himself when Lucius took hold of the saddle-horns. He pulled hard and jumped at the same time and before he knew it, he was in the saddle, thighs held firmly in place between the saddle horns. He took the reins in his hands and squeezed gently with his legs. Lunaris began to walk, his head held high as though he was proud to show off his new rider. "Does he know the usual commands?" Lucius asked Alerio as he passed.

"Yes! But you only need to nudge him lightly. He'll listen very easily to you. Try it!"

Lucius kicked twice very lightly with one leg and Lunaris went into a canter, his hooves pounding on the sand in a smooth rhythm. In the centre, Lucius pulled gently on the reigns and Lunaris stopped immediately. Now Lucius felt at ease with his new friend. Together the two of them proceeded to move sideways and back, wheel tightly and without flaw. The dust rose as they darted back and forth with precision. At one point, Lucius dismounted while riding and ran beside Lunaris, who remained perfectly even with him, and swung back up onto his back while moving. In battle, this could prove-life saving. Eventually, Lucius grew tired and reigned in at the fence in front of Alerio.

"I guess you haven't forgotten how to ride. Been mingling with the Goddess Epona lately?"

"No Alerio. The horse goddess and I aren't on speaking terms yet. After this though, I think we might be." Lucius pat Lunaris on the neck and dismounted. "Thank you for this, my friend," he said to Alerio. "You overwhelm and honour me." Alerio did not answer, simply smiled at the sight of Lucius and Lunaris; they already seemed like long-time friends.

"Come, I'll show you where his stable is with the officers' horses." Alerio opened the gate, picked up the cloak, helmet and weapons and Lucius walked out with Lunaris.

The officers' stables were twice the size of regular stables and each horse had its own space. Lunaris walked directly to his own, turned and waited for the saddle and harness to be taken off. Lucius began to remove the items while Alerio got a fresh bucket of water and some straw. Lunaris enjoyed being brushed down, seemed to sigh and twitch a muscle here and there.

When they had finished, Lucius closed the stable door. "Lunaris." The stallion came up to the low door. "I'll see you tomorrow." The big eyes blinked. Lucius stroked his forehead for a moment before putting his sword, dagger, cloak and helmet back on. Lunaris watched the transformation curiously then resumed eating his meal once the two men had turned the corner.

The moon was up and near full, the desert air fresh. Silver light was cast onto the limestone street as Lucius made his way to the Praetorium. The moon brought Adara to the front of his mind, as it always did. He wished she was with him and hoped that the other tribunes were not bringing their wives.

"Metellus!" a voice called from down the street. Lucius strained his eyes to see who it was. Three men in togas came toward him followed by a large litter and several slaves. Some of the other tribunes, Miles Octavius, Idaeus Ignatius and Tertius Sabinus approached. "Hail Lucius Metellus!" Sabinus greeted him.

"Hail, Tertius Sabinus!" Lucius returned.

"Welcome back, Metellus!" Ignatius said.

"Ignatius, Octavius." Lucius greeted the others.

"Shall we all go together then?" Sabinus said happily. "The others are already there."

"Let's," Lucius replied, nervous already.

"So how does it feel being back here, Lucius? Any regrets?" Sabinus enquired while the other two tribunes walked behind them talking.

"Feels good. No regrets at all. I already feel at home." That was a lie of course, but he was growing weary of the same questions over and over again. There was an audible giggling from the litter several paces back; they had brought their wives.

"Congratulations on your marriage in Rome, Lucius! Good news."

"Thank you, Sabinus."

"I hear it was a good match. An Antonina! Is she not coming this evening? I told my wife she would have a new friend to talk with."

"Actually, she's not even here in Lambaesis. She's in Athens."

"That's a pity. Did you hear that, Martia? Metellus' wife is in Athens!" he called back.

"Oh no! What a shame!" came a distressed and disappointed voice from within the litter.

"She'll be here soon though," Lucius added, hoping that that were true.

"Good. Martia is expecting soon. She's six months along now."

"Congratulations, Tertius! That's wonderful news!" Lucius was genuinely happy for him. However, for himself, having children was not something he had given much thought to of late. It seemed like a distant dream at the moment.

"We're here!" Sabinus called out as they came to the Praetorium's double bronze doors. The slaves put the litter down and three women slid out. The first was Martia, showing her pregnancy quite well, wearing a loose, elegant green stola that complimented her gold jewellery. The other two women, Octavius' wife Laurissa and Ignatius' wife Jasmina were much older, like their husbands, but no less elegant.

Lucius stepped aside, bowing to the ladies who greeted him as they passed into the house where several slaves waited to care for the guests.

"I'm so sorry your wife is not here, Tribune," Martia said. "It would be nice to have a younger woman to speak with." She smiled genuinely as her husband helped her up the short flight of steps. Lucius sighed, took another look at the moon and went in last. He hoped the evening would not be too long.

The Praetorium was, to say the least, almost palatial in its size and elaborate decoration. Lucius felt as though he was back in Rome in some aristocratic domus, transported away from the frontier's edge and back to civilisation. The atrium's columns alone were two storeys high. Voices became hushed as they were led down one of the many corridors. There were ornate rooms everywhere, either for public or private functions, and in the middle of the house was an enormous central garden and courtyard with paths and fountains; there were even peacocks roaming amidst the foliage.

The walls and floors were covered in multi-hued marble from around the empire, black with red veins, green, yellow and gold, pure white, rich red. Lucius wondered at the expense of the place since marble was hard to come by this far into Numidia. However, being a Roman senator and aristocrat, Gaius Flavius Marcellus, as legate of the III Augustan, was entitled to the finest accommodation...even in Numidia.

Everyone was led to a large reception room that opened onto another smaller garden. There, in the middle of an elaborate mosaic floor, stood the legate and the other tribunes: Aufidus Brencis and Balbas Ascanius, as well as the camp prefect, Lartius Claudius and his wife. Waving his strong arms about with enthusiasm was the legion's primus pilus, Spurius Renato, a career soldier with a scarred face that resembled a slave's lashed back. The white toga he wore did not soften his appearance in the least. The veterans were enrapt in some discussion of a military nature; as they talked, Marcellus' wife came over to greet the new arrivals.

"Welcome to you all," Aelia Sophonisma greeted her guests warmly. Lucius was always surprised how a woman of such advanced years could still look so elegant, her movements utterly smooth, fluid and unhurried. She had managed to retain her beauty with far more success than had the other older women in the room. Where the latter were fully decked out in all their gems, the hostess' long neck was only slightly jewelled, her face made up without any trace of vanity and her muted grey hair arrayed modestly with gold thread. She greeted everyone personally, one by one and bid them to join her husband and the others for a cup of wine before they settled down to dine. The last to come in was Lucius whom she honoured with kind words. "I am glad that you arrived in time to join us for this evening, Tribune Metellus."

"Lady Aelia Sophonisma," Lucius bowed earnestly. "I am very grateful for the invitation to dine with you."

"I hear that congratulations are in order."

"Thank you, my lady."

"I am sure you are tired of being asked when your wife will arrive, so I will refrain from doing so." She smiled kindly. "Suffice it to say that when she does arrive I would enjoy meeting with her. It is always difficult to live on the frontier and she may find comfort, as I always have, in socialisation with the other women who share in the plight of being married to an army officer." Surprisingly, she laughed gently at her intended joke, putting Lucius at ease. "Please, accept a cup of wine and join the others."

Lucius should have been quite adept at socialising in this small aristocratic circle, especially after his doings in Rome. Banquets on the Palatine Hill were more intimidating by far. However, it took him some time to stop sweating beneath his toga and engage confidently in some meaningful conversation with the other guests.

The triclinium was no less elaborate than any of the other rooms, with each guest being accorded a small couch to themselves. The men were grouped together so that the women could discuss their own matters without being set upon by boredom. Inevitably, when dining with soldiers, especially experienced ones, the conversation always seemed to drift back to this or that battle. Thoroughly unappetising.

Lucius, reclined on his satyr-legged couch, found himself sitting between Sabinus and Ignatius and across from Renato whose scarred face and intense gaze drove away any remnants of hunger he might have had. This was a pity since the food was fantastic - the best Lucius had had in a long time. The wine was even better, and he had to restrain himself from drinking too much of it; it would not do to go glassy-eyed and slur his words in front of his peers, the legate and his wife. He sipped slowly.

The conversation went on steadily course after course. The women seemed louder than the men as they discussed the gossip from Thamugadi and beyond. Lucius noticed that there was not much talk of the emperor; perhaps there was not much to say with the emperor vacationing in Leptis Magna. Nothing new there. Lucius just hoped they didn't ask about his time there, if they knew. The thought of it sent chills down his spine; relating the story of how he murdered an off duty Praetorian in an alleyway was not his idea of getting into the conversation. Frankly, he was not sure anymore if that had happened. He pushed the thought aside by looking at Renato's face.

The face talked back. "So, Metellus, did you enjoy your time off in Rome?"

"Yes, I did. Quite a display the emperor put on for the triumph and the games that followed."

"I was there too," Renato stated proudly as one of the few centurions to have received the imperial summons. "I think I saw you at the Palatine banquet. You were there, weren't you?"

"Oh yes." Lucius noticed that other conversations had died down a little. Some of the others were listening. Renato started to laugh deeply as if remembering something. Lucius tensed up.

"Ha! Ha! I remember now! You went up to the emperor with some woman."

"My sister," Lucius said sternly.

"Right," Renato continued. "You went up to the emperor and in front of the entire imperial family addressed him as 'Parthicus Maximus'!" Renato laughed amid titters from the other tribunes and their wives. Lucius was happy to see that Sabinus did not laugh. The legate stepped in as Lucius' face flushed red.

"Metellus did the right thing in giving the emperor his due credit." His voice was commanding, his language faultless. "Who would expect that the emperor would not take the name of the conqueror after such a victory? Unusual. No? Metellus acted correctly. He did not know not to use the title only because he has the sense to stay out of politics, despite his Equestrian status." Everyone had been silenced. The legate gave Lucius a knowing look. Indeed, the legate himself was unusual. He had the right to stay in the senate, comfortable, accepting bribes from city officials, living it up, but he had opted for the soldier's life far from Rome. Some men loved it, and by the surroundings in which Lucius found himself, he could understand why.

Renato continued. "It's no matter any way. Metellus was soon distracted by some girl for the rest of the evening. Struck through by Eros it seemed. Who was she, Metellus?" Renato had had too much to drink and it was showing now.

"My wife," Lucius said with pride and strength. The women at the other end of the gathering sighed.

"Oh how romantic!" Martia chimed. "Is that where you met, Tribune?"

"Yes."

"Oh my! She must have been beautiful for you to notice her in that huge gathering," wondered Ignatius' wife.

"Well, this is something!" began Aelia Sophonisma. "A soldier who is not afraid to sing the praises of his own wife in the company of others. The Gods reward such boldness and honesty. A pity there are some who do not see the merit in it." She threw a glance at Renato that could have sent him reeling from his couch. Lucius enjoyed that; in a situation where it would have been improper to pommel someone like Renato, it was better to let the women take care of him. The next several minutes were spent watching the ladies henpeck the Primus Pilus.

The legate soon put a stop to it, quite slyly, by beginning a conversation about cavalry versus infantry. A brilliant manoeuvre as it brought a moan from the women who promptly turned to discussing the theatre and the latest poets to make an inspired splash. Lucius heard Longus' name mentioned and smiled. It seemed like ages since Longus had graced his family with his poetry at their house in Rome during the festival of Venus.

"What do you think about it, Metellus?" Lucius had been thinking of his time in Rome when the question was put to him. The legate had been addressing him.

"I beg your pardon, Commander?"

"What do you think of the use of cavalry?"

"We all know what Metellus thinks of cavalry," Ascanius put in. "He decimates the lot of them. And I agree! No need for them!"

"We all know what you think, Balbas," the legate said calmly. "I'm asking Metellus his opinion."

"Well, sir, it's true that I've had my share of problems with cavalry auxiliaries, but that was due to the calibre of men, not the fact that they were cavalry. I think cavalry is an essential part of a battle plan and we could probably use more of them. In his account of the conquest of Gaul, Julius Caesar recounts how he made extensive use of cavalry at key moments to turn the tide of a battle. In fact, much of the work is taken up with accounts of cavalry manoeuvrings. Quite fascinating really. And of course, Alexander the Great led cavalry himself."

"Quite right, Metellus!" the legate began again. "Both excellent examples. I read those accounts myself, often, but let's stay with our Roman example: Gaius Julius Caesar." The conversation went from there. Lucius' remarks had sparked heated discussion among the veterans there, and it reached such a fevered pitch that the women actually withdrew to another room to finish their wine and their gossip. Lady Aelia Sophonisma allowed this sort of thing to happen occasionally under her roof as she very much enjoyed the spark she could see in her ageing husband's eyes when he got into heated military discussions. That much she could allow him.

By the time the servants had begun to clear away the empty dishes, the women were enjoying poetic recitations in the small garden; a young Greek slave in a short chiton eased the company into the night with images of far off lands, turquoise waters and tales of love. In contrast to this, the men had remained where they were, continuing the ongoing discussion of cavalry. At times, it had become quite heated. When the Sarmatians were mentioned, tempers rose. Some believed that they were an invaluable part of the auxiliary forces - the best cavalry ever. Those opposed to the latter point of view held that the Sarmatians were a too recently defeated foe and not to be trusted, especially because of their brutal strength. Lucius wondered where the Sarmatians were. He had not seen any of them since he arrived. He later discovered that Marcellus had been making efficient use of them by sending them out on small punitive expeditions to areas where there were whispers of nomadic resistance. The legate too, had his own network of spies in the southern desert.

The wine eventually got to Lucius and he excused himself to go to the latrines; a slave had to show him the way. On his way back to the gathering he turned into the large courtyard garden where the moonlight was blue upon the footpaths and fountains. He was unused to soldierly converse and needed a few moments of fresh air and peace. He inhaled the sweet smell of jasmine, listened to the trickle of water coming from somewhere to his left. Adjusting his toga, he moved along the path. It amazed him that at that very moment he was actually standing in the middle of a base and not in Rome.

The peace was not to last as a shrill squawk pierced the air behind him. He jumped and turned quickly to see one of the peacocks scuttle across the path and into a facing bush.

"Damned insolent creatures they are!" The legate came walking up to Lucius, the broad senatorial stripe of his toga almost black in the shadows. "We keep them here because it reminds Aelia of her family's villa along the Tiber."

"Legate, forgive me. I was just getting a little fresh air."

"At ease, Tribune. This evening is intended for us all to relax and set aside duty for a short time. You're welcome to roam about while the others talk. I often come out here to help me see beyond the walls of this fortress. I'm sure you understand. You're young, but your career has already taken you across the empire. Remember the broader scope of things and then everything on your doorstep will seem that much smaller and less insurmountable."

Lucius thought he understood what his Commander was saying. Duty could envelop a man too much, so much so that it becomes unbearable.

"Perspective," Lucius muttered, more to himself.

"Exactly. You have it there. One word, that's all. We all have our perspectives: the Gods, emperors, soldiers, merchants, slaves. Everybody has a perspective of some sort, but the key is to maintain a healthy perspective that will enable us to live as efficiently and truthfully as possible." Marcellus was gazing up at the moon. Lucius had never imagined the battle-hardened commander could be so calm and philosophical. He gazed admiringly at the moon and it seemed to Lucius then that one could not be posted out there in the desert for any length of time without being drawn to it.

"I understand you, Legate."

"I know you do. That's what I like about you. You're good with a sword, but you can think beyond the tip of that sword, beyond the confines of the fortress where it's safe. That's what makes a good commander. Perspective and the ability to see the Gods' broader scheme." He looked up at the moon again. "The moon is ivory tonight and Mars' eye is not upon us." He sighed. "Another thing a good commander should not do; he should never hope for battle but savour peace while it lasts. Inevitably, battle will come when it comes, and then, there is no turning from it."

The conversation had gone somewhat astray and Lucius wondered, not unkindly, whether the fine wine had gone to Marcellus' head also. The man had evidently lived through much in his life and, therefore, had earned himself the right to philosophise beneath the moonlight to a young officer after a few cups of wine. Lucius would remember what he had said.

"Husband?" Aelia Sophonisma's voice came softly through the cool garden air. She came up the path to where the legate and Lucius stood. "Forgive the intrusion Flavius, but our guests are anxious for your presence."

Marcellus smiled at the sight of his wife in the moonlight. "I'm coming, my dear. I was just speaking with the tribune." He took his wife's hand in his. Lucius felt awkward and decided to go back to the gathering.

"I'll go and tell them you will be along shortly, sir."

"Thank you, Metellus." Lucius bowed to both of them and went back down the path, careful not to step on any of the peacocks' tails that might be sticking out of the bushes. Before turning the corner he looked back at the legate and his wife. He admired them greatly. Some might have rushed back to the guests in a hurry, but the two of them took a moment together to look up at the night sky from their garden as they held hands.

In that moment, Lucius could envision himself growing old with Adara. He knew that age mattered not, so long as they had love and each other.

It was quite late when the last of the guests, Lucius included, left the Praetorium. Though they all could have stayed much longer, the early morning roll call would not be delayed. Lucius needed his sleep, as did the others. Walking back to the officers' quarters, the tribunes chatted idly about the exercises that were to take place and whether their men were up to the challenge. Being a legion of veterans, the common response was that they were ready for anything and had been for years.

The following days were spent drilling the troops. When he had spare time, Lucius went to the gymnasium to train, strengthen his body and harden his limbs to the pain that he had been feeling all over since exercises with the men had begun in earnest. His legs especially burnt due to the amount of hard riding he was doing atop Lunaris as he raced along the ranks ensuring each was doing his part, that the centurions gave the correct orders, and that the standard bearers knew their commands. He was more involved than any of the other tribunes and though many a remark was made by them from the central dais on the parade ground, Lucius continued to push himself.

One evening, after ordering an altar from one of the fabricae for his courtyard, Lucius went to Loxias in the hopes of obtaining a remedy for his aching limbs. He hid his pain well in front of the men but it came to the point where he had trouble sleeping because of the cramping. Loxias sympathised with the young tribune, having always liked him, and gave Lucius a pot of a special ointment that he said was his own secret cure.

Back at his quarters, Lucius hurriedly undressed and opened the pot of ointment. It looked like garum sauce and he hesitated before sniffing it. Luckily, the predominant scent was of strong mint coupled with bee's wax and some flower varieties, though he knew not which. It did not matter. Several minutes after he rubbed the mixture on his shoulders, arms and ailing thighs, there was relief. He sighed.

"Shall I leave you alone with yourself for a while?" Alerio stood in the doorway of Lucius' room, chuckling.

"By the Gods, Alerio. Don't you knock?" Lucius was not angry or embarrassed, for the relief he was feeling caused him too much happiness.

"It's a good thing the men don't see you rubbing yourself down with that scented cream! Ha, ha!" It was good to joke sometimes. Lucius laughed too. "Still in pain?" Alerio was the only one Lucius had told about his discomfort.

"Alerio, I don't think I've ever felt such pain. It's like having daggers jammed into my legs. Loxias gave me this ointment. Seems to be working already."

"Hence the, erm, sounds. Well, I just wanted to give you some news. I'll wait in the meeting room while you get dressed."

Lucius threw on a tunic and laced up his sandals. He smelt of mint, like some country girl having fallen asleep in the fields. But what of it? He felt better. When he went into the next room, Alerio was pouring the two of them some of the wine that Xeno had brought in.

"All right, what's this news?" Lucius took a seat across from his friend and they drank.

"I was just at the Principia seeing to the cleaning of the standards. The legate saw me and asked me to let you know that the cohort is getting the next two days off. He said you've been working them and yourself hard and that we could all use the time. He thought it would be better for the cohort's morale. He also asked that we assign two centuries of men to escort the Lady Aelia to Thamugadi for shopping."

"Well, I won't say I'm not happy with the time off!" Lucius exclaimed rubbing his legs. "Good. I'll leave it to you to notify the men."

"Already done. I passed the word on to the others and gave the escort orders to Eligius and Garai; they were happy with that as they'll be able to relax in town anyway." Alerio sipped his wine and poured more. "Actually, I thought that since we have some time, you and I could ride out and..." He paused, rose from his stool and looked at the map. "I just thought that you may want to see the spot where...where they found Antanelis." Alerio gazed at the map of the surrounding area, absentmindedly ran a finger over an area south of the base, near an oasis. Lucius set his cup down. It would mean a lot of riding but it was something that he had to do.

"I think we should. You're right. You've carried this burden yourself for too long, my friend. Tomorrow we'll ride out and survey the ground."

"We'll need to camp for the night so come prepared. I'll see to our provisions and then meet you at the stables before dawn."

"Fine. Get some sleep and I'll see you tomorrow."

IX

MANES DESERTIS

'Shades in the Desert'

The day emerged with a sense of calm, the rising sun's golden brow winking above the eastern horizon. Lucius, however, was gripped more by apprehension from the time his lids shot open as he pondered the task ahead. The oasis was far and before setting out he wanted to pay his respects to Antanelis. The memorial stone that Alerio had had erected was outside the base's southern gate.

Lucius wore his full armour as a sign of respect to the shade of a friend who had been dear to him and had risked much to warn him of a possible threat. He was somewhat reticent about the journey, had not been out in the desert for a long time. It called to him, he could feel its pull, but journeying to a place of death made him uneasy. Sword and dagger would not leave his side in the cold night. He felt better knowing he would be with Alerio, that they would finally be at ease to speak openly and alone.

"Apollo watch over us and keep my mind clear," he prayed in front of the altar in his room before picking up his things and leaving.

As he walked to the stables, his satchel slung over his shoulders, it was quite cool and he was glad for the crimson cloak over his shoulders. He nodded to a sleepy guard every hundred paces.

Alerio was not yet at the stables when Lucius arrived, the stable master dozed on a cot in a far corner. As he approached, Lunaris rose from his straw bedding; he had already learned to recognise Lucius' footsteps. The bond between horse and rider had grown stronger with each successive day from the time they had met in the circular enclosure outside the stables.

Lucius had cared for Lunaris himself at all times, and in return, the stallion had come to be his truest friend and companion. Just as Lucius had finished strapping on the saddle, Alerio came around the corner, also dressed in full armour.

"Morning," Lucius said. "I thought *I* would be the one to be decked out."

"Respect for our friend." Alerio nodded, the horizontal crest of his centurion's helmet waving, "But also some measure of protection. I don't know what we might run into out there." Alerio had developed a distrust of the desert while Lucius had been away. That, coupled with his sense of superstition, made him extremely cautious. Alerio saddled his horse, a white Arabian that he had been using whenever he had need of a mount.

"I never thought I'd see the day when you'd enjoy riding." Lucius watched him and smiled. Alerio had changed his mind about horses and their reliability.

"I see horses differently now, after training Lunaris." He stroked his mount's neck gently. Alerio picked up two bundles, one full of food, the other a tent. He handed one to Lucius to strap onto Lunaris' back and he did the same. "We can fill these up again at the oasis." He handed Lucius a large water skin. "Ready?"

"Let's go." The two of them mounted up, rode out of the stables and made their way out the southern gate. There were several memorials on the road south; many soldiers and their families had died over the years in Lambaesis.

"It never ceases to amaze me how many there are," Alerio said in a hushed voice as they rode between the monuments. The necropolis was not his favourite place.

The sun was beginning to show now, casting the riders' elongated shadows across the tombs on the right side of the road. Finally, they reached the end of the rows and turned to face the one they were looking for.

Here lies Antanelis Brennius Crispus, Centurion.
He defended Rome and his men,
Willingly. Faithfully.

The letters seemed freshly etched in the golden African marble of the memorial, its base covered in soft sand and dried twigs. Alerio stood back with the horses.

Lucius stood in front of the memorial, silent for a moment, sad. He felt cold. "I'm sorry I wasn't here to help you, my friend. Can you hear me from across the dark river, Antanelis?" He placed a sprig of olive branch he had brought on top of the memorial and looked at the carved image of Antanelis wearing his corona, the palm tree, the lion. His hands shook as he wiped the tears from his eyes. He heard Alerio calming Lunaris who tried to move toward him. "I won't rest until I discover the truth. May the Gods grant you rest and may they guide me..." Lucius bowed his head, his hands on the memorial as he knelt. A small breeze picked up from the north, blowing sand about the necropolis. Alerio looked around uneasily. Lucius finally rose, saluted the memorial and went back to Alerio. "We can go now."

The two men came through the southern pass between the mountains where the terrain opened up and sloped away. Alerio's horse reared nervously at one point and they had to stop until he calmed it. Lucius looked around, at the ground, the rocks above. They were on the battle plain where their cohort had proved its worth to the legion. The air became thick, heavy, and it seemed to Lucius that the cries of man and beast could be heard on the dusty breeze. He spotted the area where the legate had been when the nomads had charged him, where Lucius and his men had intervened. It all came back to him like a rushing tide, row upon row of nomadic warriors. Light horse and camels, the treacherous Numidian cavalry...assassins descending upon him. The images were as clear as a memory of the day before. Alerio unsheathed his sword; it made him feel better among the souls of the wandering dead upon the field. They rode on, their need to leave the field suddenly immediate and overwhelming.

By midday, Lucius and Alerio had eased into their journey. The day was clear with a soft breeze from the north-west. It was time to discuss matters. How had Antanelis died? They reviewed. Antanelis, Garai and Maren had gone hunting for lions and jackals in the desert, south of the mountains. Garai's report stated that while he and Maren were finishing off a jackal, Antanelis spotted a lion that had approached them, attracted by the smell of blood. Antanelis grazed it with his spear and went after it when it bolted into the desert flats, away from the oasis.

Antanelis' horse broke its leg and threw him onto some rocks beneath a large palm. The lion turned on him in a rage, attacked. The fall onto the rocks would have hurt Antanelis a great deal, winded him. He and the lion fought like titans but Antanelis died first. The lion died a mile away from blood loss and a crushed throat. It also had a broken leg.

"You said in your letter, Alerio, that Garai stated he and Maren rode hard after Antanelis when they saw him go after the lion?"

"Yes. That's what the report said. They were too late though."

"Must have been too far. Did you visit the site before?"

"No. Garai and Maren brought the body back themselves. It was obvious that a lion had done that. Claw marks everywhere."

"Hmm." Lucius scratched his chin, remembered what Antanelis' father had said. "Did Antanelis ever tell you anything about...treason in the ranks? The cohort?"

"No. He was pretty quiet is all. Actually, I was so busy in your place that I didn't really have the time to notice. Come to think of it, he had been a little apprehensive about talking, even when we were alone. He kept looking around and staring at the small barred windows in your rooms when we would meet." Alerio had a sudden fear. "Lucius, what did Antanelis' father tell you?"

"It's been on my mind constantly. He said that Antanelis had written him, several times, that some of the men in the cohort had very bad feelings toward the upper ranks. I can assume that means you and me. He also said that in his last letter, Antanelis' tone was very secretive and fearful. He warned his father that if anything happened to him, he was to tell me, if he saw me...warn me. Antanelis was worried about something."

Great feelings of sadness came over Alerio as Lucius spoke. Had he not been Antanelis' friend? Why had he not told him about his fears? If he had, perhaps he might have aided him, prevented his death. But it *was* a lion. No treachery there! A lion in the desert.

"I know how you feel, Alerio," Lucius comforted. "We both wish we could have helped him but...the Gods' plan was otherwise...it was his time."

"But why didn't he say anything to me about it?" Alerio's head was spinning with dark, confused feelings and thoughts. He wanted to yell, scream, but the tightness he felt in his chest was too great.

"I don't know. Maybe he wanted to protect you, as he did me. You know how selfless he was."

"I know. What about the lion though?"

"A coincidence? Not sure." Lucius really did not know, could not make the connection. "I'm hoping we'll find something out when we get to the oasis."

Alerio was silent, lost in thought as they rode. There were too many questions now. Inwardly, he asked Nemesis for aid.

By late afternoon they had reached the unending dunes of the deep desert. Another world lay before them, their eyes peering into the distance for some sign of life, the oasis. The terrain was vast, dry and burning, yet beautiful in its soft flowing contours. Lucius stopped to look. The view was like an infinite seabed, an underwater world derelict of ancient creatures, long forgotten by the Gods. Neptune's desertion left behind a desolate world of fire and death. And yet…and yet, to Lucius, some attraction still held in that world, though only the strongest of living things survived therein. The road had become sand-covered, swallowed. They squinted, searching.

"There it is," Alerio's voice was swallowed by the air as he pointed to the south-east. "See those trees?"

"Finally." Lucius was relieved. He wanted to have some time to look around before it got dark. They galloped in that direction, left the dim road to course over the dunes in a cloud of dust.

They found the oasis to be much larger than it had appeared before, extremely long. Palms surrounded a large pool of water and several rock outcroppings peered out of the foliage. The two men did not enter immediately but skirted the edge, their eyes searching the darkness within. If there were lions, which seemed odd considering how far out they were, the beasts would be within the oasis.

"Are you sure this is the oasis Maren mentioned in his report?" Lucius asked.

"I'm sure. I asked him several times when it happened, checked the maps, asked some of the nomad guides the legion uses. This is the only oasis of any size around here."

"Seems rather far out no?"

"Well, they did go hunting for three days."

"I suppose. Let's keep riding." They continued along the edge of the trees until they reached its southern tip. From there they could spot a singular, broad-leafed palm swaying in the breeze among the dunes. "Do you think that's where he was thrown, Alerio?"

"Likely. I don't see any others outside the oasis. Kind of odd looking all by itself."

"It is. I think we should make camp beneath it." Lucius had a bad feeling about the oasis, felt a shudder run through him.

"Wouldn't it be better to shelter ourselves in the oasis for the night?"

"I don't think so. Over there is better. The wind is gone and the air is still now. There won't be a storm tonight."

"But Lucius! That's…that's where Antanelis was killed."

"Do you prefer to be attacked by lions in the night in there?" Lucius nodded toward the dark oasis.

"By Hades, what a choice! All right, let's set up camp out there." The two of them rode out to the palm tree where it towered above the sand. When they arrived, they found that it was actually much larger, that the high dunes around it actually hid the base. The dunes were so high that from the base of the tree, they could not see anything but sky.

"This doesn't look like the tree I've been picturing," Alerio said as he dismounted.

"No. It doesn't." Lucius dismounted too, thought for a moment. "You know Alerio, the distance between the oasis and here isn't at all what I was thinking either. This tree is perfectly visible from the oasis."

"You're right! It's only about two stadii. We rode at an easy pace and got here in no time."

"Let's get the tent up before we look around." In a matter of minutes they had the tent up, one end tied to the palm the other to a stake in the ground, the four corners secured. After that, they watered and fed the horses.

"I've noticed something else, Lucius."

"What's that?"

"Do you see any rocks here?"

Lucius looked around. "No. I don't. Maybe the sand has blown over them." They proceeded to walk around the site from the top of the dunes to the base of the tree, kicking up sand and poking the tips of their swords into the soft ground. Nothing.

"This just doesn't make sense." Alerio paced the area. "Antanelis was thrown from his horse and landed on rocks.

That's when the lion attacked him." Lucius was standing at the top of the dune.

"Let's go back and have a look at the oasis edge to see if we can find the spot where Garai and Maren killed the jackal and where Antanelis spotted the lion in the brush. Lunaris!" Lucius called Lunaris who stopped drinking and charged up the sandy slope to his side. Alerio untied his mount from the tree and rode up to join them.

On the way back to the oasis they galloped faster to see how long it would take. No time at all. They looked for the rocks on the edge of the trees where Garai and Maren would have been able to corner a jackal and found one spot, facing west and in view of the palm out in the dunes.

"Well, you could certainly corner a jackal here if you were fast enough. The rock is high, so it couldn't scramble up and escape into the oasis."

"Hm. You're right." Lucius dismounted, sword drawn, and looked around the ground. There were some faint stains of blood on the rock-face. Any tracks had long been rubbed out by the desert's breath. "Hey!"

"What?"

"Didn't you say that Antanelis spotted a lion in the brush, sneaking up on the others, attracted by the smell of the jackal's blood?"

"That's what the report said. Yes."

"Where are the shrubs?" They looked around and Lucius climbed up the side of the rocks to look at the top. "There isn't even any tall grass here. Just the rock, some sand and tall trees above. Too tall for a lion to hide in."

"What in Hades is going on?" Alerio burst out. He was angry now, not afraid, angry. "Garai's got some explaining to do about that bogus report!"

"Hold off just now! Wait, let's think." Lucius was surprised at how calm he was being. He thought that this journey was going to be very painful, that he would not be able to think out here, but he could. "Let's look at the sequence of events from here." Lucius mounted his horse. "Now, let's say we are Garai and Maren. We're here and have cornered a jackal. There's the blood. A lion sneaks up from somewhere - where I don't know. No shrubs or cover. Perhaps he charged from somewhere? But aren't lions supposed to sneak up as close as they can to attack?"

"Yes, usually. And I don't think they would attack something that is surrounded by three mounted horsemen."

"Unless it was starving. Perhaps a lion would chance it. Who knows? Anyway, let's assume that Antanelis was here. He saw the lion and threw his spear. The lion bolts. Where?"

"Into the desert, to the palm?" Alerio wasn't sure about it now.

"What's wrong with that?" Lucius asked.

"Considering the denseness of the oasis, I would think the lion would run for cover in there, not into the open."

"I would think so too. For now, let's assume it was really spooked and ran the other way, to the palm. Antanelis races after it. Now, there's no way that Garai and Maren would not have seen this. They were right next to him and from here we can see in a straight line to the palm. Imagine he and the lion have taken off. Let's chase after them. Now!" Lucius took off in the direction of the palm, Lunaris flying over the sand, Alerio close behind. Shortly after, they arrived at the dune overlooking the base of the tree where their tent was.

"That was fast Lucius. Really fast." Alerio breathed excitedly.

"Definitely! We arrive shortly after Antanelis. Now, they were supposed to arrive after the lion has already mauled Antanelis…" Lucius paused, swallowed. Now he was shaking at what he was imagining. "They said they caught his last few breaths before he died."

"In the short time that it took us to race here, there's no way that Antanelis could have chased the lion, been thrown from his horse onto the supposed rocks, fought with the lion, and bled to death after it fled. Impossible!"

"It seems so, doesn't it?" Lucius rubbed his spinning head, felt a vein throbbing at its side. "There are no rocks."

"No." Alerio grit his teeth. "So what happened then, if Garai has lied? Antanelis was a lion himself. Nobody could get close to him and kill him easily. No one! He was younger but vastly stronger than most of the others. What happened?"

"I don't know. We'll find out. For now though, I think we should get a fire going and settle in for the night so we can think about all this calmly."

"I don't know how calm I can be, but I'll get the fire going."

While Alerio saw to the fire, Lucius unsaddled the horses, tied them to the tree and brushed them down. After that he removed his breastplate and threw his black cloak around his shoulders to ward off the growing chill of the desert air. He kept his sword and dagger on himself.

A night in the desert, between sand and starry sky, is as peaceful as life can get for a soldier. Even though the tributaries of Lucius' mind ran with a steady flow of longing for his wife, revenge for a lost friend and an inescapable duty to Rome, along with all the political intrigues that entailed, he was yet able to find peace in the quiet of the desert. Leaning against a small sand drift wrapped in his cloak, he listened to the crackle of the small fire Alerio had built. They ate in silence for a time, enjoying the bread, cheese and dried meat they had brought, tossing the wineskin back and forth.

With the anger he now experienced, the colour seemed to return to Alerio's face, his eyes regaining some of their golden lustre. Lucius wondered whether this would be a problem; he knew that Alerio's anger, as well as his own, would have to be controlled.

"What are you thinking?" Lucius asked from across the circle of orange flame in the sand.

"My mind is racing." Alerio shook his head as though upset with himself. "I've let them play me like a damned Ostia whore!"

"You're not that easily played," Lucius joked.

"You know what I mean! I could've come out here myself when it happened. Instead, I believed the whoresons the whole time!"

"What else could you have done? You made your inquiries and they panned out. Short of coming out here, you did everything you could."

"I should have come out here!" Alerio was really beating himself up now.

"Who with? Garai and Maren? Then it'd be you lying face down in the sand." Alerio did not speak to this. He knew Lucius was right.

"We still don't know how he was killed. How did they manage it with the lion? Was it just a coincidence?"

"Maybe they remembered wrong, were too shaken by events to notice that there wasn't a rock or brush for the lion to hide in? Perhaps the ride here from the oasis seemed longer than it really is? You know how it is in an intense moment; the world seems to move with slowed motion so that thirty seconds becomes thirty minutes."

"I can't believe you're so inclined to believe them now!" Alerio pounded the sand with his fist.

"I'm not!" Lucius insisted. "I just want to be certain before we make our move. No mistakes on this one." Alerio held his tongue, knew that his blood was up.

Meanwhile, the moon was making its transit across the firmament. "We should get some sleep so we can get up early to look around tomorrow."

"You go ahead. I'm going to sit here a little longer."

"All right." Alerio got up, brushed the sand from himself and went to lie down on his roll beneath the tent. "Good night," he muttered from beneath his cloak.

223

Lucius stared into the crackling flames. He leaned back and looked up at the sky. Alerio was already snoring. Lucius laughed, remembered how Alerio was always the one to snore in the barracks during their training. So long ago.

Lucius' lids became heavy as he watched the stars enveloping the bright moon. *Adara.* He hoped she could hear him, somehow. He prayed that Apollo and Venus would stay with him, not abandon him at this time. He needed them more than ever, his heart told him. He needed Adara too. *Not yet,* he thought. *It's too soon.*

The stars overhead quivered, blurred, he felt the sand shifting beneath him. Lucius looked over at Alerio but he slept soundly, the horses were still too. Then one of the stars grew larger, brighter. It moved. He rubbed the sand from his eyes and shielded them from the firelight. It did not help. The star whirled about the heavens in a silver and blue light and plummeted into the sand beyond the encampment.

Lucius jumped up in wonder, an inkling of fear. *What sort of omen is this? A star falling to Earth?* He crawled up the dune, looked back to see that Alerio was fine, sleeping. He was. He peered over the dune's crest, searching the soft landscape. The oasis was dark to his left, a patch of black. To his right, further into the desert, a cloud subsided, leaving what he could only describe as a radiance in the sand. He could not see, but could tell it was not a great distance.

The sound of his sword unsheathing broke the stillness of the air. It was cold but the closer he came to the light, the hotter he became, though his breath still quit his mouth in puffs of steam. The stars above seemed to sing, each of its own accord and yet all of them together sounded in perfect concert. He felt his heartbeat slow, his every movement languid. The light became more intense, the music louder, clearer. His sword weighed heavily and he had to sheathe it to free his hand so he could clamber up the remaining dunes.

This is a mistake, he thought.

No. It is not, answered a deep, clear voice. Lucius' heart beat louder and louder, so loud that it hammered in his ears. In a final rush, he strode up the final dune reaching for his sword and then...blindness. The light was so intense he dropped his sword as his hands went up to shield his burning eyes. He stumbled and rolled down in the sand.

He found himself on his knees, the sand gone from his eyes. It was quiet, the air perfect. For a moment, he shook uncontrollably, but that ceased when a hand touched his head.

"Rise, Metellus," said a voice like running water in a stream. Compelled to rise, Lucius brought himself to his feet. "You are safe. Open your eyes and heart to me."

"Apollo?" Lucius sounded surprised; in fact, his voice did not sound his own. He rubbed his eyes but they were not lying. Before him, glowing in light of blue and silver, was the Far-Shooter himself, leaning on his great silver bow. His blue cloak hung about him like a waterfall and his grey eyes were deep like twin moons seen in a glassy lake. "Forgive me for not knowing it was you." Lucius felt ashamed to have drawn his sword. The god was silent for a moment, then smiled.

"A sleeping dragon, when awoken, rushes into danger, sword drawn. Your preparedness is a quality. You are forgiven."

"Thank you, Lord."

Apollo gazed at Lucius expectantly. "It was you who called to me. Speak."

"I called?"

"Yesss." His smile was gone. "You worry that I will abandon you?"

"No Lord, I...I..." Lucius had no words.

"You do. It is in your heart."

"Yes, Lord. It is."

"Do you think I reward loyalty and sacrifice with abandonment?" Lucius began to shake under his chiding look but breathed to calm himself.

"No, my Lord. I do not think that. I am simply awed by the events around me, the course of my life."

"You are on the correct path though you have misinterpreted my messages."

"I have?"

"Sybil…" The word seemed to hiss forth from his mouth. "She advised you well of my words. *"Keep her close. Empress.* Your *Empress!* Do you remember?"

"Yes, but the empress sent me away."

Apollo arched a dark, questioning brow. *"Your* Empress," he repeated.

"My Empress…" Lucius fell to his knees, his shaking hands over his face. "Adara." He had been wrong about the Sybil's words. His empress, the one who ruled him utterly was not Julia Domna, but rather his own true love. He had not kept her close, he had sent her far away from him. "Forgive me. I did not know," Lucius pleaded. "Protect her for me. Keep her safe."

Then a cool breeze came from the north, pleasant and soothing. Lucius felt a thousand hairs on the back of his neck stand up. Apollo smiled. Lucius looked up to see…Adara…walking toward him, barefoot in the sand. At first he wept, thinking she was dead, her shade before him. The outpouring of his heart yielded to the gentle touch of the hand that caressed his cheek and the pausing voice that spoke his name. *Lucius*…

It was not Adara. "She is safe," Love said with care and compassion as she cradled Lucius' head to her breast, her golden hair raining down. "She is safe," she soothed. Lucius felt strength and warmth re-enter his body and heart. He looked up at Love, his tears glistening gold in her light.

"Lady Venus." He spoke slowly, smiled. "Adara is well?"

"She is." Her voice sounded like wind in golden wheat. "She needs to be with you. Call her to you. You will see why." She caressed his dark hair, held her hand to his cheek.

"He must not know all," Apollo said next to them; his brilliance illuminated the space even more. "It is for him to chose the way. Come." He reached down to take Lucius by the arm and raise him to his feet. His touch was strangely warm and cool at once. "The night is short for you. You cannot linger long in our light."

"What shall I do to make the way safe?" Lucius did not know what to ask, how to ask it?

"Finish your present task. Look to the oasis," Apollo advised.

"And call her to you." Love smiled knowingly.

"I will. Thank you." Lucius knelt, his hand upon his heart.

Apollo turned before leaving, came back to Lucius and put his strong hand upon his head. Within, Lucius heard him speak. *The Red planet is restless, and the Avenger has his eye upon you. Sacrifice your foes to him.*

Apollo returned to the side of Venus and the two disappeared in a flash of blue, silver and gold light entwined.

"Lucius? Come on, wake up. It's dawn."

"What? Where? Oh, Alerio it's you."

"What do you mean it's me? Who else would it be? You fell asleep looking up at the stars." He reached down and brushed the crumbs of cheese off Lucius' cloak. "Looks like you fell asleep eating too. Breakfast?"

"No. I'm not hungry. You go ahead." Lucius got up, quickly felt for his sword. Still there. He walked up the slope of the dune to look into the distance. Everything was the same. "By the Gods."

"What'd you say?" Alerio called up.

"Nothing! Nothing." The morning was as cool and quiet as the night, and the sun's pink beginnings pressed in the east. He looked at the oasis, felt a chill. He went back down to the fire to sit with Alerio. "I think we should check out that oasis."

"Good. Let's do that and get out of here." Alerio finished eating and began packing up his things.

Shortly after, the horses were saddled and their satchels tied up. Lucius took one last look around the tree; no traces of blood on the trunk, no rocks to fall on. They rode to the top of the dune and toward the oasis. When they reached the edge of the trees, they paused. It was still dark within, the sun was not at a great height yet. They retraced their steps to the small rock face, where they figured the jackal was speared, and stopped.

"Well, let's go in," Lucius urged, unsheathing his sword. Alerio did the same. It was a world apart within the oasis; there was a trickle of water coming from a small stream where it poured into a pool. They stopped at the pool to fill their water-skins. The horses were restless.

To Lucius, the oasis was nothing like a desert sanctuary. He shivered, felt a constricting sense of dread, of evil. Nothing in that place was sacred. The horses whinnied violently.

"What's wrong with them?" Alerio grabbed the reigns of his mount so he could get back on.

"Alerio look out!" Lucius pointed to the rock behind him where a coiled snake had risen up, surprised by the horse's movements. Alerio's gladius slammed down onto the rock cutting the snake in half. The sound of the metal upon the rock echoed in the oasis. "There are more!"

"What in Hades…there are bloody asps everywhere!"

"Let's get away from the water! They're gathered all around it." They rode farther in. Lunaris jumped up, trampling a snake beneath him.

"Let's keep our eyes open for anything unusual." They rode some more until they found a trail coming from the eastern side of the oasis. "Let's follow this, see where it leads." Lucius followed Alerio. After a short time, they stopped.

"I'd say this is unusual. Look Lucius. It's a cage. Big one too." Lucius rode around. It was indeed a cage, broken and abandoned. On one of the planks of what was the door were claw marks.

"Look at this." Lucius dismounted, his sword drawn.

"A lion's?"

"Could be…" Lucius stepped back.

"Who brings a caged lion out here?" Alerio looked at the cage and its broken wheels. He followed Lucius who was still stepping back. "Whoa! Lucius!" Lucius slipped but Alerio caught his forearm in time. "I've got you!" he pulled him up.

"What in Hades…it's a pit!"

"Somebody's covered it up with palm branches." The two of them brushed aside the palms covering the large, rectangular pit.

Alerio stepped back. "Look at that." The two of them peered over the edge to see the bones of a lion in one corner. A snake was wrapped up in one of the eye sockets.

"Look, there are four arrows sticking into it." Lucius walked around to the other side of the pit, stared into the darkness below. Something caught his eye, something in the dirt glistened. "Alerio, get me one of the longer tent ropes."

"What do you want it for?"

"Lower me down."

"Are you mad? There are probably more snakes down there." He tossed a rock into the pit, nothing moved. "All right but it's your ass they're going to bite, not mine." Alerio gripped the rope tightly and lowered Lucius slowly into the bottom. He could just see the top of Lucius' head and shoulders. "See anything?"

"Yes," Lucius said to himself as he uncovered a broken arrowhead with blood on it, then another. "I found something!" he called up. He dug around with the tip of his sword. Dirt, small animal bones, more dirt, but he stopped when the blade caught on something soft. A piece of cloth from a legionary's crimson cloak. Lucius felt sick. His head spun. "Pull me up! Now!"

Alerio grunted as he pulled hard to bring Lucius out of the pit, the urgency of his voice worried him. "You all right? What is it?" Lucius took a moment to catch his breath. He held out his open palm with the two bloodstained arrowheads; the shafts were broken near the end.

ADAM ALEXANDER HAVIARAS

"There's blood on them."

"And this." Lucius held out his other palm to reveal the shredded crimson fabric. Alerio reached for it with a shaking hand.

"You don't think…it can't be. Antanelis'?"

"Did he have his cloak on when they brought him back?"

"Yes, well…part of it." Alerio gripped it tightly; his hand turned white.

"If it was our friend who was thrown in here with that poor beast over there," he pointed to the lion's bones, "I'll send whoever's responsible to the deepest fires."

"Not if I do first." The two of them stood there, each imagining Antanelis thrown into the pit with a lion. Whether he was shot with the arrows before or after didn't matter now. "Let's get out of this accursed place and purify ourselves back at base." Alerio was superstitious but he was also right. To touch the place of a death so brutal, and of one's own friend, was not fitting. As they rode hard from the oasis, Lucius thought he could hear the roar of a lion mixed with Antanelis' screams emanating from that dark pit and into the swaying trees, to be lost on the sandy wind. The men who watched that would pay for it dearly.

"How are we going to go about this?" Alerio asked as they travelled back to base.

"I don't know. The impact of it all has me rattled. Cautiously, for one. If they, whoever *they* are, killed Antanelis then they won't be averse to killing you or me."

"Let the bastards try!"

"We need more proof. Not just two arrow heads and a piece of cloth that every trooper wears. Did the autopsy say anything about arrow wounds?"

"We didn't do one. At the time, it seemed so obvious that it was a lion attack. Probably wouldn't have shown anyway. His body was pretty torn up."

"Well, the two who were with him are the main culprits. Garai and Maren. From Antanelis' letters to his father, there should have been more men in on it. But who?"

"We'll just have to be patient," Alerio spat the word, "and keep our eyes open for any signs of guilt, any more clues."

"In the meantime, I'll talk with the legate about it."

"Are you sure you want to do that?"

"We can trust him. He already told me I could undertake a new investigation to be kept between us and him alone."

"What a wonderful old goat!"

X

ALERIO CORNELIUS KASEN

"Testudinem facite! Unus! Duo! Tres! Quattuor!"

As senior centurion of the cohort, Alerio led drills for Lucius as he always had done. His harsh parade ground voice reverberated in the men's ears as the first, second, third and fourth ranks locked their shields together to form a tortoise shell. They had been having trouble with the drill in the past days and Alerio was growing increasingly impatient with them. "No, no, no! Halt! Do it again! Unus! Duo! Tres! Quattuor!" He watched them intently, tapping his vinerod on his greaves, willing the rhythm of their steps. "Balls!" he muttered to himself. "They'll never get it."

At that moment, Lucius came riding up. "You all right, Centurion?" He spoke lowly so that the men would not hear him.

Alerio looked up at him through the sweat stinging his eyes. "No, I'm not all right, Tribune. They should have this drill perfect by now. We've been doing it over and over and there are always two or three whoresons out of time with the rest."

"They'll get it right, Centurion, don't worry. Just keep at it until they do. Stay calm." Lucius winked at him and rode off.

Stay calm? Alerio thought. *How the bloody hell can I stay calm?*

In fact, Alerio had not been able to rest his mind, his body or his conscience for over a week now, ever since he and Lucius had returned from the desert. Where he had once revelled in drilling the troops, the reliability of it, the pride he had in honing their skills, he now grew impatient and eager to return to his barracks to be alone. Now he hated being on the dusty field, hated to look at them, especially Garai. Alerio thought constantly of the bogus report, and it frustrated him that Lucius was constantly telling him to be patient, to wait for the right moment. *What further proof does he need?*

"Balbus! Sound the command to halt and form up."

"Yes, sir!" The cornicen blew a series of notes on the horn and Alerio stood back to allow Lucius to address the men on their performance. As the tribune spoke, Alerio adjusted the phalerae, his awards, on the leather harness about his torso.

"Claudio," Alerio called to his signifer when Lucius finished with them, "you lead the centuries back to barracks."

"Yes, sir," the signifer answered calmly.

Every night in his quarters, Alerio locked himself away to be alone with his thoughts. He polished his armour in a ritualistic manner and sharpened both his gladius and the harsh thoughts that goaded his mind. In the lamplight, he could see the outlines of the items on one of his tables: the arrowheads and the piece of torn, bloody cloak that he and Lucius had found in the pit with the lion bones. Lucius had wanted to keep them in his quarters but Alerio had insisted on taking care of them himself. In truth, he wanted them as reminders. His golden eyes observed the harsh, sad looking objects. He was never without his dagger now; the bolt on his door was always locked.

That evening, when he had finished polishing his armour, he went over to the same table and swung open the cedar doors of the small shrine he kept. He lit a piece of incense and placed it in a dish before an image of Mars and a newly acquired likeness of Nemesis. He then crumpled some dry bay leaves on the smoking embers.

"Mars, Avenger, I've always been faithful, fearful of you. Aid me in this. When the time comes, guide my hand to make those guilty of the crime pay for their treachery. I always reward honour and bravery among my men. So too must I punish dishonour and cowardice. I humble myself before you, God of War. Show me my faith is not misplaced."

Alerio shook with resolved anger as he prayed. He then took his dagger and reopened a cut on his forearm to let the few drops of blood fall onto the crisp leaves of his offering. *And to you, Nemesis, Goddess of retribution. With you on my side, the red-handed culprits will suffer justly. I don't know if Lucius' plan will work, whether you Gods are laughing at us, but if it does not, help me to send them into darkness so that they suffer your wrath.*

Alerio finished his prayers, sat back on the edge of his bed and watched until his bloody offerings burned away. He had his doubts about Lucius' plan; it was really the first time he had ever doubted his friend's judgement. *How can he appear so removed from all of this?*

The plan, as Lucius had told it, was simple. "Using the pretext of the marching drills," Lucius said, "we'll take the men out into the desert for a few days to carry out the legate's orders: patrol, drill, and make camp every night. On the second or third night, we'll end up camping out and drilling at the same oasis where Antanelis was killed. When we're there, we'll observe the suspects for any reactions."

"That's it? That's your plan?" Alerio did not think it would work from the beginning. "I don't think that's the way to go, Lucius."

"It'll work." Lucius seemed serenely confident. Alerio wondered if inside, he really believed it would work.

The centurion closed the cedar shrine and laid himself down for another sleepless night.

In the courtyard of the Principia two mornings later, Alerio stood with his century and the others of the cohort for inspection. After that was completed, Lucius sacrificed a cockerel to Mars before they marched out onto the field for drills. *They'd better get it perfect today,* Alerio thought as he watched Lucius slit the animal's neck, *or else I'll break my vinerod over their backs.*

Alerio found himself remembering the past a lot and thought about this as they marched to the parade ground. He had seen much since he joined the army all those years ago in Rome. Different lands and peoples. He had been witness to some wonderful sights, smells and sounds. He also had the misfortune to have been too close to some horrendous moments, massacres, torment and treachery.

He had seen much that he did not understand, especially in his time with Lucius. He had been exposed to some very mysterious and inexplicable occurrences. He felt sure that there were some things that Lucius just did not tell him during their quiet evenings over a beaker of wine in the tribune's quarters. That was fine with him, he supposed. Some things he did not want to know about; some things should be left to the Gods alone. Alerio believed that men were not meant to understand all there is in the world, or the otherworld - prophecies, demigods, destiny and messages in the stars. "Leave that to augurs, priests and soothsayers," he would say. But, that day on the parade ground was different.

The men were practicing their pila drills with the legate and tribunes looking on. Lucius was charging up and down the ranks. The men were hitting the mark every time and Alerio began to feel a measure of relief, a satisfaction that he had not felt for a while. This momentary respite was shaken when there came a sound unlike any other the men had heard before. There was a rushing of wind, howling in the distance, growing nearer and nearer. The men rustled on the field in uncertainty. Someone thought it was a sandstorm, others that Jupiter was unhappy with the men's efforts and was voicing his dismay. Alerio felt a twinge of fear; apprehension crept up his spine as he tried to calm the men.

The howling grew louder and louder. On the podium, the legate was still, calm. Then, there was the sound of thunder. Lunaris reared up but Lucius managed to bring him under control as he looked around uneasily. Then, they arrived.

235

Cavalry, hundreds of men, charged through the southern gate of the parade ground. They came out of the desert with clouds in their wake and rode like faceless furies. At their head were two men, although to the Romans they did not resemble anything like men. Their faces were covered. The commander wore a helmet with a bronze mask that looked like some deathly shade. A long strand of golden horsehair sprouted from the top. Next to him, his pace ever quick, was another rider, masked and faceless. He was the source of the howling wind. High above his head was their standard: a long flowing silk of red, gold and green attached to the massive head of a dragon. When he rode at speed, the dragon howled fearfully.

"Sarmatians," one of the men in Alerio's century observed.

"Quiet!" Alerio yelled as he watched uneasily. *Where the hell did they come from?*

The Sarmatians had in fact been at the base for some weeks by then, but most of the men had not seen them in action. They always left the base before dawn and returned in the night. This time was different. The legate had them out patrolling for raiding parties, and it seemed they had news to report. Their leader went directly to Marcellus on the podium to give him news.

Lucius, Alerio and the rest of the men there noticed that the Sarmatians seemed to shine in the dim, dusty light, that there were glistening patches on their bodies. Then they realised what it was: blood. There was blood everywhere upon the bronze scale armour that covered their bodies. They looked like creatures from some titanic age long gone. The men were nervous and began to whisper and point. However, the legate seemed happy with what they had told them; they had slaughtered a large force of nomad raiders to the south-west, outside one of the fortlets there.

What happened next disturbed Alerio. The Sarmatian commander looked about the field from his horse as though he was eyeing and thus challenging each man there. His gaze finally rested on Lucius who rode out to meet him with

Frontus running after him with the vexillum. The two men reined in inches from each other. The Sarmatian standard bearer followed behind.

No one could hear what they said, but they appeared relaxed. The commander was older and proud, and the standard bearer carrying the draconarius was a strongly built youth. Alerio realised they must be the ones Lucius had met briefly in Carthage. He ordered the men to rest for a few minutes while he watched Lucius and the two strangers. After a time, Alerio approached Lucius.

"What in Hades was all that about? What do they want?"

"Nothing, Alerio. Just greetings is all." Lucius seemed dazed, lost in thought. He stopped Lunaris and looked up at the sun for a few moments. "They will come to you as thunder...All scales...and death," he said to himself.

"What did you say?"

"Nothing, Alerio. Nothing. Let's get on with drills."

Alerio tried to forget the nonsense Lucius had said to himself, but he could not; he muttered it the whole way back to base. The words reminded Alerio of the Sarmatians' bloody armour and the sound of that ghostly standard. He wondered what forces guided Lucius in his life. He knew that there was still so much that he did not know about his best friend. He loved Lucius as a brother but he found that he also feared him and the darkness that seemed to follow him. He feared what he did not know about Lucius Metellus Anguis.

When he laid himself down exhausted on his cot that night, he was unable to shake the day's events from his mind. Images of Sarmatian warriors charged toward him, the howling wind at their head and blood on their scales. Lifeless faces in shadow and dust plagued his dreams.

XI

LIBERI APOLLINIS

'Children of Apollo'

Night in the eternal city was no longer hot, and with the change in season, more and more clouds appeared on the blue canvas of the sky above Athens. Rain had, as yet, not made weekly appearances and the days were still pleasantly warm and bright. Cool night gave way to dewy morn which led to the dry days of early autumn. The branches of olive-laden trees bent and swayed under their fruitful weight, while the scent of honey trickled into the air as the Attic hives were opened.

Adara stepped from the villa onto the moist grass of the olive grove for her morning walk in the fresh air. Her smooth dark curls were tied back from her face. For weeks she had been forced to rise early from her soft bed to vomit in a bowl on a table next to where she slept. The sickness was most unpleasant to her, but not unexpected. She knew why it was upon her and was happy for it.

Dressed in a long white stola and wrapped in her favourite blue cloak, she tip-toed down the corridor and outside. She kissed her ring in morning greeting to her husband far away; it never left her finger. A faint mist hung in the grove, the sun had not yet peered over the mountain tops surrounding Athens. All was peaceful before the cock's crow and the donkey's bray. Adara sang softly to herself, to the world about her. The fresh air filled her lungs; it felt good against the bout of dizziness she had experienced since that special night when she believed Venus and Apollo had appeared to her.

Her voice was tender as she chased away the frightful dreams she had had that night, of Lucius suffocating in a cloud of purple as he struggled in vain against a cloaked and faceless figure. "Just a dream," she told herself.

She strolled on the wet-beaded blades of grass to the ornate well at the far end of the grove. Adara always walked to that point before returning. At the wellhead, was a glistening serpent coiled about the base. Her foot brushed a patch of earth and it slinked away at her approach, disappeared into the adjacent field beyond the trees. The well water was clear and cool and Adara cupped her hand to bring some of it to her mouth. It moistened her dry lips, tasted sweet.

The sun was rising beyond the hills now, their ridges outlined in orange and pink. Alone, she thought only of Lucius and missed him. She wondered if she should write to him; she was torn. Alene was pressing her to tell him, but Adara knew that it would only strain her husband. She knew he was prone to worry and she did not want him to make a rash decision, rush whatever it was he had to do. If he knew, his mind would be bent toward her and not his own safety. A difficult decision.

A day would come, hopefully soon, when she would leave Athens, perhaps for good, to go to him and to whatever place the legions led him. For now, that place was Numidia. Adara looked around her at the beauty of her birthplace, and knew in her heart that she would miss everything about Athens. But, she missed Lucius infinitely more. In the distance, a cock crowed and one of the donkeys brayed. She sighed. The world was waking up. It was time to walk back.

As Adara approached the house she spotted her father at the main gate and an army messenger riding away. *A letter from Lucius?* she wondered. It had been some time since the last one and she had been worried. Publius Leander came striding down the path wearing only a tunic and sandals, his hair dishevelled from sleep.

"Father? Is everything all right?"

"Yes, my dear. Everything's fine." He was smiling, inwardly relieved for his daughter that Lucius had finally written. He hoped it was good news. "It's from Lucius."

239

Publius handed the scroll to his beaming daughter who held it to her heart. "Well? Are you going to read it?"

"Yes. Of course!" She ripped open the seal excitedly like a child at Saturnalia and read carefully. She touched the paper where his hands had touched. "He says that he's arrived safely at Lambaesis…that all seems well but that there are other matters which he must look into." Adara paused, her sadness and disappointment clear upon her face. Publius had thought it was too soon for Lucius to call for her but he had not wanted to dash her hopes. "He hopes we are all well and says that he will write more often." Adara omitted the loving words that were for her ears alone.

"I'm sure he has your best interests at heart, my girl." Her father tried to soothe her. "Lucius is a man of honour; he always thinks ahead. I'm sure his reasons for delaying are very good."

"I know, father. I know. Besides, this letter was probably sent weeks ago. Perhaps by the time I receive the next letter, things will have changed?"

"Anything's possible." He put his arm around his eldest girl. "Come, let's go inside and join the others for the morning meal. You need to keep your strength up." Adara leaned against her father as he led her inside the stirring villa.

Adara was solemn at breakfast. Everyone knew why and they tried to keep her talking, to console her. The letter was undoubtedly loving, yes of course, but ever so short. She wanted to hear more, pages and pages that she could read over and over again. Not this time. Alene eyed her sister sadly, critically, as they ate. She was becoming frustrated with Adara's reluctance to tell Lucius the news.

"I think you should tell him, Adara!" Alene finally burst out. "He should know."

"I'm not sure for now," Adara replied unconvincingly.

"I think you are. You want to tell him, I know you do. I'm positive that if he knew, he would call for you immediately.

He would finish up whatever business he has and bring you to him." Alene tapped the cushions on the couch impatiently.

"I need to think about it more," Adara responded automatically.

"Daughter," broke in Delphina, "sometimes you can think too much on something, wait too long. Lucius is a bright, strong young man and would not make a wrong decision. He should know. I agree with Alene."

"Will you all stop pushing her!" Publius said. "Adara knows what she must do." Delphina cast her husband a cool look, but not without love. She knew his reasons for saying this. Though he was quite happy about his daughter's match, he was reluctant to let her go, to see her move to a far corner of the empire where he would never see her. She allowed Publius this fatherly sentimentality.

"Look everybody," Adara cut in, "I appreciate your concern but I know what I must do for the moment. Now, can we enjoy our meal and the beautiful day?" Everyone acceded and set themselves to talk of the events surrounding the upcoming Festivals of Venus Victrix and Juno Moneta. While the others conversed, Adara thought inwardly about what she should do. She was not sure after all; she wanted to tell Lucius.

That afternoon, while lying on a couch that the servants had set out in the orchard for her, Adara unrolled a papyrus and dipped her stylus in the inkpot. In the background, a few remaining cicadas hummed the last of the year's songs amid the tree branches. Alene would be joining her soon, so with stylus pressed to her lips in thought, Adara decided what she would say.

To Tribune Lucius Metellus Anguis
III Augustan Legion
From Adara Antonina Metella

My dear husband, my love,

I am sitting in the olive grove outside our home in Athens, alone for the moment. I received your letter early this morning and I am grateful to the Gods that you are safe and returned to Lambaesis unharmed. It is so long since we parted, an eternity. I know it is so for you as well. I don't know what I would do without our sister. Alene gives me such strength. Of course she is worried about you, as am I, but she doesn't let on. I suppose she wants to instill in me confidence in your abilities, though I do not need help for that.

I know what a strong, blessed man and warrior you are. I know that Apollo and Venus are watching over us. The world seems so changed, as though I walk constantly in dreams in which I hope that you will appear to me in the flesh, around the next tree or the next column. That I will hear your determined footsteps along the corridor outside my cubiculum. I miss your touch and the soft warmth of your voice in my ear. I can hear you speaking to me in the night as the moon waxes and wanes with the passing days. I know in my heart that you love me more than anything, that you would do all in your power to protect me from harm, from danger, but I would risk a terrible death in the black waters of Styx to be by your side.

I am being dramatic, perhaps, but these feelings are more real than anything on this earth. You said that you felt that I was in pain some time ago, and you were right. I was. But it was not the sound of my heart crying out in sadness at your absence, though that does happen daily. It was something else. Something so wonderful that you must know it. I must tell you before my courage disappears.

Lucius, my husband, I am with child.

I know this must come as a shock to you, that we had not spoken of it before but...is it not wonderful? A gift from the Gods, of that I am sure. For several weeks I have been carrying our child. Life has welled up within me. So, you see now why I would be with you? I want you to be there for the *birth of our child, to be the first to lift him up to the light of the world as yours. Oh Lucius, I love you so much!*

I know that your mind must be spinning at this moment. I had actually thought not to tell you until you sent for me, but Alene and my mother and sisters have been pushing me to say so. I could possibly have held out but for the pain and longing in my heart, the knowing that you should not miss this. So do not worry further; know that the physicians say that I am extremely healthy. All the omens are good. Alene and the others do all they can to help me too. She has not told your mother yet, at my request, because I wanted you to know first.

I could write forever at this moment. Truly. But I want this to reach you with all possible speed. Autumn is here and soon winter will be upon us. The sea will not be navigable in two months' time and I do not think I can wait until the spring to see you. Please send for me, my love. I...we...should be with you.

I will await your response and I know that you will do what you believe is right. For now, take care, be strong and may the Gods keep you safe for me and for our child.

You have all my love.
Your adoring wife, Adara.

That was it. She had done it, and was sure of her decision. Around the edges of the papyrus she dabbed some of her favourite perfume, the one she was wearing when they first met. Now that the letter was written, she felt lighter, that a burden had been lifted. The letter was sealed and ready to go out with the next shipment of official mail from Athens; her father would see to that. Her father. Adara knew he would be very sad to see her leave, her mother too, but for all the tears they would shed, she knew that they would understand. They had loved as she loved. There was an inner peace in simply knowing you had found your true love. They would not deny her that. She smiled to herself, looked about the grove and felt the sun on her face and shoulders. *What is it like in Numidia?* she wondered as Alene came down the path with a servant who carried watered wine and a platter of fruit and cheese.

"How are you feeling?" Alene asked, spying the sealed letter.

"I'm feeling wonderful!" Adara smiled cheekily, knowing full well that her sister was dying to know what she had written. "Oh good, food! I'm starving!" Adara reached for a fig and split it open.

"Well?" Alene pressed.

"It's very juicy! I swear, that fig tree behind the villa grows the best figs in all of Greece!" She took another bite, trying not to laugh. Alene sat on the carved bench next to her, sipped her wine and tried not to give in to this little game.

"All right! Fine. You tell me what you wrote to him when you want to. I don't want to know. Really! I'll just sit here, drink, eat and enjoy the sun beneath this big hat of mine."

"Yes, quite wise of you. Your Roman skin is too soft and creamy for our sun." Alene darted a wild-eyed glance at Adara who proceeded to giggle and then laugh uncontrollably. Soon Alene gave in to the urge as well and their laughter echoed amid the trees. The departing servants looked back down the path, shaking their heads and wondering if the two women had gone completely mad.

"Must be the wine," said the one to the other.

"I can't bear it anymore, Adara! Did you tell him?"

"Yes. I told him. I asked for him to send for me if he saw fit."

"Good!" Alene clapped her hands. "He'll send for you, you can be sure of it." She took a drink of wine and ate some cheese. "You know, I'll be hopelessly lost without you. I don't know how I shall handle it." She had smiled when she said it but behind the giggling façade, tears welled up. It had not hit either of them until this moment.

From the time they had met in Rome, a year past, Adara and Alene had become the best of friends, sisters. Alene now loved Adara as much as she loved Lucius. Now, the thought of parting ways for who knew how long was insufferable. Adara too felt this and she shifted on her couch to make room for Alene. Together, the two women leaned back, hand in hand, silent.

"You could come with me?" Adara suddenly said.

"What?"

"If Lucius sends for me, you could come too!"

"I couldn't. You're husband and wife. What would I do in Numidia except be a nuisance to you and my brother?"

"Nuisance? Don't be ridiculous! Lucius loves you and would be overjoyed to have you close again after so many years."

"I...I...what about Rome? My mother?"

"You know as well as I that your mother would tell you to go. As for Rome, you've lived there all your life. Why, just the other day you were going on about how much you wanted to see other parts of the empire. What better place to start than where your brother is stationed?"

"I don't know." Alene shook her head. "Let's first wait until we know what Lucius' answer will be. Then we can talk about it."

"Promise you'll think about it, Alene?"

"I promise."

Alene helped Adara up from the couch after a few more figs and they slowly made their way up the path to the villa. It was about time for their daily visit to the Temple of Apollo. Outside the gates, the litter bearers were awaiting their master and his guests to go into town. Adara looked around for Ashur but realised that he had probably gone ahead with Carissa to meet with Emrys in the sculptors' quarters. He did not visit the temples anymore. She had not asked why. It was obvious.

"Carissa? Did you not hear me?" Emrys' stern voice sounded in the warehouse. They were in a far corner of the sculptor's quarters visiting an old friend of his, learning a new technique for polishing marble. The group of young apprentices who gathered about Emrys and his friend waited impatiently for the girl to answer. Her mind was not in it, work had no real importance to her. She was too busy making eyes with the dark foreigner who stood off to the side with his arms crossed. What else could one expect from a woman? That was the question in the minds of the apprentices. The colour rose to Emrys' face. "Carissa!" he barked, making her jump.

"Yes, Master. What did you say?"

"I asked you if you understood the way the technique works. We could make good use of this."

"Yes. I understand. It's nothing new to me. I'll wait outside." Carissa turned to join Ashur and the two of them strode into the sunlight together to wait. Emrys was mortified. Carissa's behaviour in front of an old friend of his, who was good enough to share knowledge with them, was atrocious.

"Stephanos, my friend, forgive me. She has grown impertinent of late. I assure you her skill surpasses her manners by far."

"Don't mention it, Emrys. You always did pick odd apprentices. It's nothing new. I'm sure that her skill is good if you are her teacher. Perhaps next time you should teach one of our local young men and not some straw-haired Celt." The apprentices surrounding the two men laughed, but stopped when their master raised a hand.

"Good advice," said Emrys, accepting the slight upon himself and his own apprentice as payment for her rudeness to their host. "Please go on with your demonstration."

As Stephanos went on speaking to the group, Emrys made every attempt to concentrate on what was being said, but his mind kept wandering out the large main door to where Carissa sat under a tree with Ashur. A part of him regretted bringing her to Rome. Ever since she had met Ashur, Carissa had not been herself. Her work had suffered, and she was inattentive. The last glimpse he had caught of her exceptional skills as an artisan was when they had sculpted Lucius and Adara's

246

statues. Emrys thanked the Gods for that at least; there was far more to those magnificent creations than mere marble. With their skill, they had breathed life into the images; it was the best work they had ever done. Emrys wondered if those two sculptures were Carissa's final testament to her skill.

When he finally emerged from the warehouse, Emrys wore many strained emotions upon his bearded face: anger, embarrassment, frustration and sadness. The latter was the most apparent. He had loved Carissa like a daughter, had taken her under his wing when he had spotted her potential. With him, she had seen the world and created many beautiful things that had drawn many an adoring gaze, even the emperor's. Her shunning of all that she had learned was poor payment indeed.

Emrys walked past the tree where Carissa and Ashur had been waiting without speaking. He could not even bear to look at them, simply began the long walk back to the villa on the other side of the city. Carissa and Ashur exchanged looks momentarily before rising and following after him. She let go of Ashur's hand and skipped on after Emrys.

"Is something wrong, Master?" He did not respond. "Please Emrys, answer."

"What do you think the matter might be, Carissa? Tell me." He continued to walk hurriedly, hoped Ashur would stay behind them, allow them to speak privately for a change.

"Are you upset because I did not remain for the entire demonstration?"

"Quite more than that, I assure you."

"Tell me," she said. He wondered briefly if she really did have any clue what she had done.

"Do you enjoy sculpting any more, Carissa?"

"Of course I do, Master."

"Then why is it that, for several weeks, months, you have shown no real interest in anything related to the craft?"

"I am interested!" she protested.

"Are you? Truly?"

"My mind may have been on other things from time to time perhaps, but…"

"Oh, I know your mind has been on 'other things' as you put it." He looked back at Ashur whose dark eyes followed them. "That would be fine, except that you have no room for anything else in your life anymore. I love you as though you were my own child and I have always been exceedingly proud of you, but lately…" Emrys paused, thought out his words.

"Lately?"

"Lately, all you think about is Ashur. Ever since you met him at the Metelli's domus during Verticordia, you are forever in his company. The only thing you care about is Ashur!" His voice had risen too high, he quieted himself, his temper rising. "In the beginning, I was overjoyed for you - both of you. He's an honourable, interesting man. But now, your blatant disregard for anything other than Ashur is very hurtful to me… even to our hosts who constantly look for your presence at dinner and rarely are rewarded with it." Emrys stopped. He was on the verge of tears, could not go on like this anymore. Carissa's eyes already ran wet as she looked up to meet his gaze but he would not look at her. It would be too painful.

"I've always been grateful to you for everything, Emrys. Truly I have! I promise I'll do better, apply myself, work harder."

"No."

"No?" She began to shake.

"No, Carissa. You are in love and that, unlike art, cannot be so easily cast aside. I'm returning to Rome, alone."

"Rome? No, Master! Please," Carissa begged. "Take me with you!"

"No. Your place is not with me anymore. I'm going alone and I will finish the work we started in the imperial palace."

Carissa, tears flowing freely from her eyes, stopped in her tracks, sobbing in the middle of the road as Emrys, strode onward without stopping. He too cried, unable to stay the emotions that overflowed within.

Behind Emrys, Ashur had come to Carissa's side, wrapped his cloak about her shoulders, comforted her. It angered him to see her weep so. He wanted to charge after Emrys, to berate him. But Carissa held on to him, and Ashur knew that it was between them.

For some time they stood in the middle of the road as the sun began to go down. Carissa wept and Ashur attempted to soothe her aching heart. Eventually, he convinced her to walk with him and they made their way to the city's eastern gate. When they passed the great Temple of Olympian Zeus, Ashur stopped and looked beyond to the stairs that led down to the Temple of Apollo. Taking Carissa by the hand, he led her in that direction, a stern look upon his face.

Having gone down the stairs, they approached the temple. Ashur felt a pain inside as he looked at Carissa's sodden eyes. The woman he loved was hurt. He had never loved before and now within himself, the anger he felt at her sadness vied with his love for her. A raging torrent of the spirit overcame him.

"Please stay here. I won't be long." Ashur sat Carissa on a rock just outside the temple, and then strode up the steps and into the darkness of the god's inner sanctum. His footsteps echoed in the darkness. Only a few braziers burnt near the altar. Ashur's eyes focused on the statue of Apollo. It seemed angry, menacing. He did not care. He was beyond that. Standing before the image of the god, Ashur Mehrdad spoke.

"Mighty Apollo. Long have I served you, been ever loyal in your bidding. I have never asked for anything. No. I have been a true servant for as long as I can recall. Now, I want something from you. I *demand* something of you. Speak to me of love and what I must do to keep it." Ashur closed his eyes, listened inwardly for an answer as he had done for so many lifetimes. He listened, waited. No reply came. The god was silent in the flickering light of the flames, stern and severe.

"Why do you not answer me? Am I not deserving of love? Father?" Not a word, not a sound. "SPEAK TO ME!" Ashur yelled out, his pleading voice shaking the rows of columns on either side of the temple.

Still, no reply. "Very well. As you remain silent I am no longer yours to command. Do you hear me, oh Far Shooter? I will go my own way from now on." Ashur paused. A part of him still hoped the god would respond. He did not. "To Hades with you then!" Ashur spit upon the altar before turning his back and striding out of the darkness.

Outside, Carissa jumped to her feet when she saw Ashur coming down the stairs. "Are you all right, my love? I heard you yelling."

"Let's leave this place." They hurried away, went up the stairs and toward the eastern gate of Athens. As they walked, dark clouds began to roll in overhead, casting dark shadows over the city. The sound of thunder rumbled for several minutes and then the rain began. It fell in angry torrents upon the earth, lashing Ashur and Carissa as they ran back to the villa. The autumn rains had begun and Ashur held his arms about Carissa to protect her from the raging skies.

The house in Rome was quiet as a mausoleum, its usual state, for weeks and weeks; an eternity it seemed. For Antonia Metella, it had become a prison. At first she had been restricted to her rooms because of the injuries she had sustained at the hands of her husband, too sore and frail to move from her bed, but now she was simply not permitted out of doors. Quintus had discovered a brutal side of himself, a side he now seemed to relish. For the moment, Antonia judged, it was better to play it safe.

Besides, her main concern was for the children still living under her roof. They needed her. Clarinda had been traumatised by the violent episode that had rung through the house; she was now prone to fits of fearful crying and nightmares. Young Quintus, who had come so swiftly and bravely to his mother's aid, was still abed. His headaches had grown worse, the excruciating pain all too much to bear.

Ambrosia had taken to sleeping on a cot within his cubicula; she had grown quite adept at mixing pain relieving tonics which she would give to Quintus whenever he would wake screaming in the middle of the night, tortured by the pain in his head. Twice more the physicians had come to make a small hole in his skull to allow relief of the intense pressure. On these occasions, Antonia had hobbled over to his room to sit by her son's side for the procedure. She wished with all of her heart that she could do more for him, anything at all, but she was still weak and speaking did not come as easily and clearly as it once had.

All this time, on the main level of the domus, the servants cowered under Quintus pater's increasingly violent commands, afraid that he might well make good on his threats to kill them. They reasoned that if he was wont to beat his own wife and son to near death, then it might be a simple pleasure for him to do away with one of them. The rumours suited Quintus fine; it made life in the home more bearable.

Quintus Metellus' days now comprised of daily sittings in the senate, making social ties that he might find beneficial in the near future, and then returning home in the evening to go over work in his study. He even found the garden enjoyable, now that he was able to enjoy it alone, undisturbed. He had, however, been forced to move the two unseemly statues of Lucius and the girl from his sight. They were too large, too distracting, and so he had some of the slaves cover them with rough-woven throws and place them in the storage area. Antonia had wanted them in her room but he had denied her that.

With every day that Antonia spent in her bed, with every letter she received from Alene or Lucius, the more determined she became that they should stay away. It was for their own good that she never even hinted at what had occurred to her and their younger brother. If Alene knew, she would return in an instant, as would Lucius; the first to play nursemaid to her and also risk a beating, the second probably to kill his father.

She did not want her eldest son to be branded a parricide by society, to condemn himself and the family he would one day have. No. Antonia Metella knew her silence was crucial. She could do no less for her children.

Several times she had had dreams of young Quintus' death. She worried for him, deeply, as he flowed in and out of consciousness like the tide in a quiet bay. She prayed to every god she could think of, called upon their grace, their pity. A kindly look from above would not hurt his recovery. She had even sent Ambrosia to the temples to make offerings on her behalf. The servant had done all she was asked without protestation and as a result had greatly endeared herself to her mistress.

The days had grown colder in Rome. Dried leaves from scattered gardens were whisked by increasing winds through the streets and though the sun still shone, the rains had begun, accompanied by a crispness in the air. The growing gloom of the season had been difficult to bear for Antonia. The sun that had shone intensely through her window weeks before now went quickly by, leaving her to thinking. Aside from her concern for her children, one thought that plagued her mind as it strained to rest, to forget, was what had passed between Argus and Quintus on that terrible day, and what had been said.

Antonia reproved herself incessantly. How could she have been so blind? Having believed that Quintus loved her, having loved him, she had allowed herself to be deceived like a naïve country girl. They - Argus' supposed parents - had been two of their closest friends! People they had helped through very difficult times. "Why?" she asked herself over and over. She had been a good wife, had given her husband two sons and two daughters, all healthy. It seemed now, in hindsight, that none of that had mattered. She wondered if her friend's husband had known, even that he might have planned it that way so that later on, pressure could be applied to Quintus for some kind of inheritance. No matter, they had taken Argus under their roof anyway, in the end.

Antonia wept, her jaw clenched. She was torturing herself. *So stupid! So ashamed!* she thought. Blind for so long, so long. And yet, to think of her own children, how noble they were, the joy they had given her. They had made it all worthwhile. All the suffering and pain she now felt could melt away if she concentrated on them. Alene, Lucius, young Quintus and little Clarinda, they were all of them by far more worthy of their ancient and noble ancestry than their father.

One autumn day, when the sun had decided to grace the city with its heavenly rays, Ambrosia came running into the room, a letter in her hand.

"Mistress, a letter from Athens! From mistress Alene!"

"Quiet, my dear! Is not the senator within?"

"No, Mistress. He said he would be gone for some time. This letter just arrived." Ambrosia handed it to Antonia who smiled as best she could manage with the slight jaw deformity she now had.

"Thank you, Ambrosia. I'll read it while you check on my son. He's been quiet today, so do not wake him. Let him sleep if that's what he is doing. Otherwise, see if you can get him to eat something."

"Yes, Mistress." Ambrosia closed the door behind her and Antonia opened the letter.

Her eyes scanned every word carefully. She smiled, observing that Alene's writing had grown more and more poetic with every letter. The Athenian air evidently agreed with her. Then her eyes came to a small phrase the stopped her dead. She re-read it again and again to be certain her mind was not playing tricks. It was not. She had read correctly; Adara was with child and they were waiting to hear from Lucius about his decision to send for her or not.

Antonia wept. As her husband was away at the moment, she even allowed herself the luxury of joyous laughter out loud, the first to sound throughout the house in some time. Life did indeed go on. She felt uplifted, wished she could go to Adara and share in her joy along with Delphina and Publius Leander who were good people.

Antonia read on, noted that Alene was debating whether or not she should go to Numidia with her sister-in-law to join her brother or return to Rome to be with her. There was no question! She had to go with Adara. She must not return to Rome, not for the moment. As soon as Ambrosia returned, having fed young Quintus and even walked him around the house, Antonia asked her for some ink, a stylus and a papyrus sheet. She wanted to have the letter sent before her husband returned and quickly jotted down a brief but loving letter to her daughter to express her joy for Lucius and Adara and that she thought it was a wonderful idea that she should go to Numidia. After all, she had developed a fondness for travelling. *Besides,* she wrote, *I am perfectly well here in Rome. Busy as usual with all manner of social occasions.*

She hoped that Alene would listen to her words and that Lucius would invite her. She had to stay away from Rome, away from her father and the sight of her mother and brother, the cries of her sister. She would be safer with Lucius; she was sure of it. A feeling of triumph within, Antonia rolled up the scroll, sealed it and handed it back to Ambrosia who took it off immediately to be sent to Athens.

"I don't know if I can bear it Delphina. To see our daughter go? So far away too! I know I shouldn't have a problem, that she's found a man worthy of her, something I never thought possible but…I shall miss her."

Delphina put the paintbrush down, laid aside the pallet and went over to Publius where he sat on the window sill outlined in golden sunlight. He had been watching Adara and Alene through the window as they walked around the courtyard, arm in arm. He could not believe his eyes to see his eldest girl, still his little girl, heavy with child.

"Did I ever tell you how wonderful a man you are?" asked Delphina as she leaned against him, shades of coloured paint in her dark hair. Her smile melted his heart, and each time she smiled, he was reminded of why he loved her. Her tenderness and understanding, her understated strength.

"You can tell me again so that maybe someday I'll believe it." He smiled. "Look at her. Where has the time gone, Delphina?"

"The same place it always has; upon the winds that encircle us, carrying our hearts and minds and our winged memories."

"I don't want to forget a thing."

"You don't have to, Publius, but you do have to let go. Don't you want Adara to be as happy as we have been?"

"Of course I do. We've been blessed."

"And so has she. You will not forget and neither will she. We will all move on together, and no matter the distance between us, we will always be together."

"Wise and beautiful! I think I'm the most blessed of all." Publius tenderly wiped some orange paint from her cheek with his thumb, kissed her softly. Delphina blushed, happiness radiating from her eyes as she turned to look back at the wall she was working on. "And how is your mural coming along?" her husband asked. Delphina studied the wall intensely, looking over what she had done thus far.

"Well. I've finished the scenes of the desert and the banquet, though they still need more work. I want to get started on the central wedding fresco now, work out the colour scheme." Publius looked over the whole thing admiringly.

"It's absolutely beautiful, my love. Truly." He kissed the back of her head. "I'll leave you to it. I've got to go into the city to take care of some things. I'll be back soon."

"Be careful," she called back.

"Aren't I always?" As Publius stepped out, Delphina smiled to herself before dipping her brush into a spot of flame-coloured orange on her pallet. Delicately, where the temple steps were faintly outlined, she put her brush to the wall in exact strokes. Her daughter's sacred wedding robe, the flameum, had to be perfect in order to draw the viewer's eye into the scene. Delphina stepped back, looked again, dipped her brush once more and painted again. A broad smile spanned her face as she revelled in her art, her creation, and the memories of that special day. She could never forget that.

XII

DOMINI ET SERVI

'Masters and Slaves'

The slave's hands shook with uncontrollable fear, he fumbled clumsily with the golden goblets and pitcher filled to the top with the finest wine from the cellars beneath the imperial residence in Leptis Magna. He had almost dropped the heavy amphora as he carried it up the stone steps from the dark recesses below. Luckily, one of the other kitchen slaves had helped him carry it the rest of the way.

"What's the matter with ya? You've done this before a thousand times!" That didn't help the slave, his ears were ringing far too loudly to hear anything other than the blood pumping in his head. "Hey! You deaf? What's going on with you today?"

The slave put the pitcher safely on the large tray that sat on a table and turned. "The Praetorian prefect is in the emperor's chambers with him. He asked me to fetch them something to drink."

"So? What of it?"

"Have you ever met the prefect?"

"Nope. Seen him from a distance, though."

"Then you wouldn't understand a thing I'm saying."

"You've gone off, that's what you've done! Talking nonsense like some deranged desert holy man."

"Laugh if you like, camel-dung-for-brains, but I'm telling you, you haven't felt evil till you've had that man's eyes on you. You can feel his thoughts, like he's thinking of how he might torture you for information...for nothing...anything." The slave's voice was now a whisper, his listener silent. "They say the prefect turns men into eunuchs for the sheer pleasure of it. He gorges himself on babies taken from the female slaves and drinks until he vomits...then eats some more."

"You're daft! By the sand beneath my feet, you're mad!"

"Oh really?" The slave was quite confident now as he spoke, pointed at the other slave. "Just you wait until you have to serve him, wondering whether he'll cut your balls off and have 'em for his din dins. Did you know he's going to be made Consul?"

"Consul? What's that mean?"

"Not sure exactly, but I think it means he'll be almost as powerful as the emperor. I heard some of the others talking about it last night. He'll be able to do whatever he wants to us."

"Ha! They need us to serve them at all hours!" the kitchen slave said naively.

"You're a fool, you are. They don't need us. They could kill us for fun at their banquet and then replace us with any other slave. Makes no difference because they don't see us as people. We're things to use and then toss away with the morning rubbish. Take it from me." The kitchen slave was now shaking, his voice caught in his throat as he tried to say something but could not. "I'd better take this in." The slave took up the wine, hands still shaking, sweat upon his brow, and went down the corridor from the kitchens, past several offices and turned through the servants' door that led into the emperor's chambers.

The light was dim and it took the slave's eyes a moment to adjust to the change. He looked around but the emperor and the prefect were not where he had left them. Then, he heard voices from outside and moved nervously toward the silk curtains that separated the seaward balcony and sunlight from the darkness within. A guard pulled aside the curtain for the slave to pass. The sun was blinding; he stopped to steady the tray, tried not to fall over.

"What's the matter with that slave?" said a deep voice, harsh like a knife cutting through bone. "I asked for that wine half an hour ago! Get over here and serve it before I have you whipped." The slave tried with all his might to stop from shaking, took slow, small shuffling steps to the squat table that was between the emperor and the prefect. He averted his eyes, setting the tray down, grateful for not spilling anything. "Hurry up damn you! Septimius, you really have to get better slaves. This one is useless," the prefect said.

"I suppose, Gaius, but must you speak so loudly all the time? It's really unpleasant, especially with this wonderful view of our home." The emperor swept his arm in front of himself, indicating the view of Leptis Magna and the sea. The slave poured the wine and offered it to the emperor first. When the golden cup was held out to the prefect, he snatched it violently, spilling some wine.

"Now look what you made me do!" The slave shuddered in the moment before the prefect's hand came smashing into his face, sending him to the tiled floor.

"By the sun's light, Gaius! Calm yourself."

"Ha!" The prefect spit at the slave, ignoring the emperor's words.

"Leave us," Severus said to the slave as he rose from the ground. Once beyond the curtain he ran back to the kitchens as fast as he could. His shaking turned to stunned shock as he put his hand to his left eye.

"You're bleeding!" said the other kitchen slave when he returned. "Here, let me help." He dipped a cloth in a basin of water and dabbed his friend's eye to soak up the blood that ran from the deep cut made by the prefect's ring.

"See? I...told...you..." the slave managed to say through his laboured and terrified breath.

"As I was saying," Plautianus continued, filling his cup a second time, "if you make me Consul now, then I can return to Rome ahead of you to get stuck into things."

"And what things, my friend, might those be?" Severus held up his hand anticipating Plautianus' protestation. "There is no need for you to leave. I've already made it public that you will be Consul. For now, stay, enjoy being in our home again. You are too taken up with work, Gaius. You need to enjoy the comforts of Leptis Magna before taking office again. Being home refreshes and reminds us all of better times...of youthful..." Severus coughed harshly for a moment before continuing. "...youthful pursuits."

"I don't have time for that, Septimius. I'm too busy keeping you on your throne."

"My dear prefect, if I had not won a civil war there would be no throne, no emperor. Remember, if you will, that your friend managed to preserve this empire, and secure its borders. Give me some credit at least!"

Plautianus smirked. "Whatever you say."

"I do say." Severus took another sip. "Now, I was talking of youthful pursuits. Do you remember, when we were boys, the time our fathers went away and we decided to play legionaries with their old equipment? You know, in our courtyard, in the old house."

"Vaguely," Plautianus recalled bitterly. "I remember you almost sticking me with a pilum. I thought you wanted to kill me."

"Ha, ha! Of course I didn't! I didn't know how to use one, let alone lift it. You just got in the way, like you always did."

"Yes well, I gave back at you when we first trained in pancration didn't I?"

"Almost broke my jaw..." Severus rubbed his chin. "There was a lot of competition between us then. But you see, Gaius, those are things that brought us closer together. Then they seemed like harsh lessons but now we can laugh at them because we are closer than ever. That's what brotherhood is all about."

Plautianus stared out over the city remembering something else. "What I remember most is when your parents were gone to one of their estates south of here and we were left alone at your house with the servants. Do you remember when we took the serving girls into the baths?"

"I've tried to forget that detestable night. We should be ashamed we treated them like that." A broad frown crossed Severus' forehead as Plautianus smiled.

"Oh, come now, Septimius. You enjoyed that as much as I."

"You may speak for yourself, Gaius. When I was old enough, I gave those serving girls their freedom as recompense."

"You didn't!" Plautianus was almost angry, insulted.

"I did."

"I wonder..." Plautianus sat back on his couch, smiled to himself, his teeth forming in a malicious grin.

"What do you wonder?"

"I wonder if you have ever told Julia about that incident, seeing as you tell her everything."

"You can leave my wife out of it, Gaius." Severus turned his head, eyes flashing in the sunlight. "Besides, I don't tell her everything. A man must have some secrets, just as a woman must."

"I'm still convinced she's no good for you." Plautianus' rude bluntness was nothing new to Severus and, though hard to take, he had grown used to his friend's loose tongue. "The Syrians just wanted to weasel their way into power. They only care about money."

"Don't be ridiculous! She's as loyal to me as you are." Plautianus enjoyed the irony and ignorance of the words. "Her father was a good man, a respected high priest of the Sun God. I do not worry about my wife."

"Don't say I didn't warn you, Septimius. I'll leave it at that."

At that moment, out in the corridor before the main entrance to his father's chambers, Caracalla approached the Praetorians guarding the doors. They were four big brutes, talking of gambling and their sexual prowess, each apparently better than the other. Caracalla flung back the hood of his military cloak to reveal his face to the guards. The men saluted haphazardly and stood to attention. The slight did not go unnoticed and Caracalla knew that the prefect must be within. *A good time to listen in*, he thought.

"Stand aside, men, I'm here to see my father." Caracalla's look was fierce, permanently angry.

"Sorry, Caesar," began the top ranking soldier present. "Orders are that no one enters until the prefect leaves."

"Yes, I understand that, oaf, of course. But that doesn't apply to myself. Let me through, or I'll have you flogged."

"Again, sire, we can't let you pass. Orders are orders." The trooper stood his ground, and Caracalla hated him for it. He wanted to run him through then and there, but he did not. They meant business; that much was evident by the two spears crossed before the doors. They were four and he was one. Praetorians had killed emperors in the past. Caracalla backed off.

"It is really quite admirable how you perform you duties with such fervour. When I'm emperor, I'll see fit to reward you for your loyalty." Caracalla smiled, turned and left the guards looking puzzled, all except the one who had spoken; he watched the cloaked figure of the young Caesar step confidently back down the marble corridor.

In a room facing west, where she could see the sun clearly at that time of day, Julia Domna lay sunning herself in the privacy of her intimate rooms. It was a place of contemplation for her, where she could rest assured that no one would disturb her in the least. The small rooms were reached by a hidden door located behind a wall panel in a storage room and only she and her son Caracalla knew of it. He rarely came there and so she found herself in rare serenity, wearing only a thin white stola, the sun covering her entire body in its warm rays. She had let her hair down too. She enjoyed the feeling of its dark wisps dancing in the warm breeze. Soon, cool autumn would be along and the opportunity to sit outside in the warmth of the sun would die away for yet another unbearably long winter.

Her world and her position as Augusta had, of late, grown ever more precarious. She had not thought that possible, but it was. *Plautianus made Consul!* How was it possible that the scoundrel could have played her husband so easily? It hurt her, for she knew what the prefect was up to, what he said about her to her husband. That he could even say such things was absurd but that he could get away with his life after having said them was abominable.

She was happy that her sister, Julia Maesa, had consented to return to Rome with her husband and daughters under the pretense that she had had a terrible dream that one of the children would die if they did not see their particular physician in Rome. The empress needed a trusted pair of ears in Rome to stay informed of what was going on. Trust was a word that she had been unable to comprehend of late as most officials and others had been bribed or threatened by Plautianus in some way. Julia Maesa hated him too and so her sister knew she could at least trust her.

She sighed and sipped her favourite date wine from a silver cup. She missed Drusus, his reassuring presence something she could always count on. She wished she had treated him with greater kindness, given him more. There was an emptiness, a feeling of dread, since his body had been found in the harbour. Caracalla had recounted to her how the body had been found: a hand cut off, several stab wounds, and a head injury. If the body had not been churned up by the rudder of a heavily laden merchant vessel, she might never have known what had befallen him.

Poor Drusus. He had performed his duty until the last breath. She had been told by her husband that the legate of the III Augustan had written to say that Tribune Metellus had arrived. The threat of nomadic raids had decreased but he was grateful nevertheless to have a skilled commander returned to duties. If not for Drusus, Metellus would never have made that journey.

Soon after she had received news of Drusus' murder, Julia Domna had written a brief letter to the young tribune to warn him. That was all she could do for the moment. Metellus was on his own. After all, she had her own things to worry about. The tribune was insignificant for now. The Praetorians had apprehended some poor fellow, a drunken sailor, for the murder of their comrade. They tortured him, tried him, and executed him all in one day! Of course she knew that the claims were false, knew who had really killed that Praetorian in the night but she was not about to say anything. The Guard and Plautianus had saved face, killed their scapegoat and calmed the storm.

Now she was left with her thoughts of what to do, tried to remember the meaning of the word 'trust'. If something should happen to her husband...well...that did not bear thinking about. She would be finished. Plautianus still held too much power. Her husband's health was unstable; his cough had begun to re-emerge and his ability to walk with greater ease would leave him once winter set in and they returned to Rome. Politics, plotting, deception, murder; it was all too much to think about at once and so she returned to the scroll that Philostratus had sent her to lose herself in sophistry.

"So this is where you've been all day! I've been looking all over for you, mother." Caracalla appeared from one of the small rooms behind her, an angry look on his face. Julia Domna, her reverie broken, covered her body with the light cloak she had thrown over the chair next to her couch and tied her hair back neatly as her son came to sit beside her. Caracalla poured himself some date wine.

"Hades! I hate the man!"

"I suppose, my son, that I do not need to guess which man you are referring to." She took up her own cup and sipped casually, not wanting her son to see how distraught she had been. She had grown quite adept at hiding it.

"Yes. Plautianus, the bastard!"

"What happened now?"

"He had the audacity to post guards outside of father's chambers while they spoke, with orders to prevent anyone, including myself, from entering."

"And that surprises you?" She placed her cup back on the table and put her hands in her lap. "You forget that he even prohibited your father from visiting him before, unless the emperor left his own guards outside. It is a step down to do something similar to you."

Caracalla creased his brow in angry thought; his mother spotted something sinister behind his eyes. "It will all get worse once he's officially made Consul, you know that, don't you?"

"I know that, yes. I also know that we are not yet out of favour with the Gods, that the stars still provide glimpses of hope. I also know that he gets bolder and bolder. Your aunt tells me that there are now more statues of Plautianus than your father in Rome and that most of them have been erected by the senate!" She rubbed her temples, feeling a headache emerging. "She also wrote to tell me that public prayers have also been offered to honour him."

"Sole, permanent Praetorian prefect *and* consul! You know what's next don't you?"

"Hold your tongue! We're not done yet. That would be sacrilege and we can't afford an affront to the Gods. Let Plautianus do that on his own."

"Yes well, we're going to have to make our move soon, mother. We all know money buys troops and troops can get you anything, including the throne. If father has taught us anything, it's that."

"What is your point now, my son?"

"My point is that for years, and much more recently, Plautianus has been amassing vast wealth, draining and plundering the provinces, taking or accepting funds from those who wish to impress him or be safe from him."

"How did you find this out?"

"I have my sources too."

Julia Domna looked at her son for some time after that. She had not known he was up to his own little games of espionage. Of course she knew that he had sources but he seemed rather well informed.

"Has your wife been telling you things?"

"Plautilla? Ha!" He spat. "She's an imbecile. I'm tempted to slit her throat in bed and have done with it."

"That would not be wise at this time. She's harmless enough. I agree, she is a little, well, dull, but she is definitely not a threat. Her father only used her to ally himself more closely with your father. That's all."

"Someday I'll be rid of both of them."

The empress did not speak at that. She knew her son, knew his looks and how he said things. He had meant that. For the first time, she felt an inkling of dread at the sight of him, something that told her he was capable of more than just talking about terrible things.

"So, what do we do now?"

"Have you spoken with your brother on the matter?"

"Geta? He's too busy whoring with his gladiator friends to care."

"He is Caesar too, you know."

"Yes. I know."

"And you also keep company with gladiators, especially when your father's troops are not around."

"Yes, but at least I know when to stop fucking around and get down to business. Geta is incompetent. He's not a good Caesar."

Julia Domna took up her cup again, sipped. Though she did not say so at the time, she feared that Caracalla was right in what he was saying. Perhaps that was why she confided more in him than in her other son.

"So what's our next move?" Caracalla asked again.

"We remain still. So long as Plautianus does not return to Rome without us we can keep him in check."

"I'll try and convince father that we should all return to Rome together. The sooner the better, I say."

"We'll both convince him of that." She nodded. "We have to keep our eyes on the prefect, perhaps postpone his consulship if possible."

"That won't be easy, especially when he has half the bloody senate in his pocket."

"No, it will not be easy," the empress said calmly, "but we have to try."

As the pink light of dusk blanketed the sands about Leptis Magna, the evening air grew quiet, still. Torches were lit within the Praetorian camp and the watch was changed. Four troops guarded each of the four gates at that particular hour. For several weeks the Guard had been on angry edge, but that was done now as the murderer of the one guardsman had been found and put to death. Not many had wanted to admit that one of their own had been sent to Hades by a common sailor; it just was not supposed to happen. Still, better a sailor than some raggedy-ass merchant who spent his evening keeping his camel warm in the dust and dirt.

Laughter emanated from the mess within the camp as the evening's gambling got underway and the guards at the north gate winced, wished they were in on the action rather than protecting the fort against shepherds and olive merchants. The centurion posted to that gate paced back and forth, his vinerod tucked neatly under his arm as his three inferiors sat on stools to either side of the gate. One polished his sword, another chewed on a piece of dried camel meat. The third watched the centurion and wondered what was going on in his mind. He had thought not to speak at all, for fear of a stern beating with the rod, but could not help but wonder why the centurion seemed so nervous.

"Something the matter, sir?" the man asked. His comrades looked up. The centurion said nothing at first, paced a few more times then stopped to gaze up the road to the city.

"What's it to you? You bored, trooper? Maybe you'd rather clean out the latrine? Hmm?" The centurion's beak-like nose protruded from beneath his horizontally-crested helm, and his scarred forearms were crossed in front of his broad, decorated chest harness.

"No, sir. I'm fine here, sir. I was just wondering if we should expect any action tonight is all, sir."

"Action? You want some action. How about if I shove this vinerod up your ass? Would that be any better?"

The trooper shirked at the thought of it. He was not getting anywhere and so decided to give up his questioning, opting for silence rather than three feet of discomfort. The centurion paced once more after no reply came, his mind busy with something. Then he spoke.

"Truth is lads, we're expecting some sort of important visitor to come through this gate tonight."

"Important? How so? Is it the emperor or some senator?" asked the trooper who had been chewing on the camel meat.

"How, by Mars' iron balls, am I supposed to know? All I know is that the prefect told me I should be here with you and then bring the man directly to him. I don't know who the man is but if the prefect has such an interest in him, then he must be important. Got it?"

"Aye, sir. Got it," they replied.

"Good! Now, get your lazy asses off those stools and stand at attention. If this person gets here and you look like that, then he might say something to the prefect and then we'll be knee-deep in shit. As for myself, I'd like to get back to Rome as soon as possible, and in one piece." The men got the message and stood up immediately on either side of the gate as the centurion went back to his pacing and the sun began its final descent into the western abyss.

The Praetorian Principia was a large and luxurious affair even for a temporary camp. However, the light within was dim, especially when the prefect was holding interviews; secrecy was paramount. His own personal guards were posted all around the perimeter of the structure but kept a safe distance from its walls so that they could not by chance overhear what was being said inside. It was said that once the prefect had cut out the tongue of a man he suspected of overhearing a particularly significant conversation. Luckily for the trooper he could not read or write; otherwise, he would have had both hands cut off.

The prefect was in there at the moment and the men outside tried very hard not to hear what was being said. Unfortunately, the man he was talking with was very loud and annoying. It was hard to miss his voice. Plautianus sat in a padded, high-backed chair, his eyes flashing in the light of the brazier to his right. He dipped his finger into his wine and sucked it; the sound was quite annoying to the other man there. He had not been offered any wine.

Walking about the room, anxious for something, the other man began to annoy the prefect who promptly told him to shut up and sit down. The man did as he was told, without question. Plautianus had been pleased with the control he had managed to exert over this fellow. There had been a time when he thought he would simply have to cut his throat and dump his body into the sea, but he had been pleasantly surprised. No matter how much he beat or starved him, the man did as he was told. After all, he was treated well enough, given occasional food, clothes, and sometimes a woman to satisfy his aggressive nature. *What an animal*, the prefect mused.

He studied his property, his slave, with a satisfied grin. The object of this study knew the man before him was powerful, knew that he could kill him with a word, and so he obeyed. How long he had to put up with it was a question to which he did not have the answer. He did not care; anything was better than pulling an oar in shit and urine-stinking darkness. He turned the ring on his finger, the only object he owned. The gold flashed on his dark skin, against his black clothing, yellow gold with blue inlay. The prefect had allowed him to keep it for his well-completed task in the harbour but he knew, and was not allowed to forget, that it was more like a shackle than a piece of jewellery. His new master had only wanted to see it, to be sure that the empress' man, the one called Drusus, was dead.

"Brutus, I really must allow you to bathe again," Plautianus sniffed. "You stink." The slave said nothing to this, huffed his annoyance and that was all. "Trust me, Brutus, you'll enjoy this little surprise I've arranged for you."

"What the hell kind of surprise?" Brutus realised he had raised his voice and corrected himself, with his head bowed. "I mean, Prefect, for what, or who, are we waiting for?"

"Ah, ah, not yet. You'll find out soon enough. Here." Plautianus tossed a piece of bread at Brutus who caught it desperately and devoured it in an instant. "Still hungry?" Brutus nodded. "I'm sorry I don't have any scorpions to give you at the moment."

"That's fine, sir, I'll do without." The memory of that made Brutus shiver with dread. It would not be below the prefect to do such a thing again. He had eaten the scorpions out of shear starvation; he hoped it would not come to that again. The sores that had surrounded his mouth had gone away although they had left distinct marks. His feet too had healed, though the recollection of walking at the time was so vivid he thought he could still feel the pain when he walked. Brutus looked up at the prefect. "When are you going to have another assignment for me, sir?"

"Eager, are we? Well, you'll find that out tonight." Plautianus looked over to a table where a water clock counted down the time. "Won't be long now."

"Am I going to receive a weapon this time or will I have to steal one again?"

"We'll have to wait and see about that, won't we?"

270

Brutus gave up. He was not going to get any information out of the prefect; he did not want to try, for the consequences of a wrong phrase could put him back in that black pit again. That was not an option; being locked in a small room with a straw mattress every night was fine for the moment.

At the north gate of the camp the guards stiffened as their centurion spoke to them in hushed tones.

"Here he is, lads. Attention." The centurion stepped forward to the edge of the fire's reach. Where a slight mist had flown in from the sea and now hovered above the patches of grass and sand, an imposing figure seemed to emerge out of the darkness, moving like a shade through the mist. The centurion could not see a face, only that the man was tall, broad, and evidently very strong. He moved with stealth, no footsteps could be heard at all, likely a skill practised over and over. This was someone who had perfected not being seen. The only reason they could see him now was because he allowed them to. The men behind the centurion levelled their spears and took up their shields. One uttered a prayer to Mars beneath his breath, hoping it was a man and not something else approaching.

"Hold!" the centurion called out, his hand raised. "State your business!" The figure in black stopped where he was, several feet from the centurion, his grey eyes peered out at the men before him.

"I've come from Rome to see the prefect." The voice was deep and even; it seemed unnatural to the soldiers at the gate.

"So you say, stranger." The centurion tried not to sound intimidated. "But you're not getting through this gate without giving me the watchword for tonight. If you're to see the prefect, then you must have it."

"*Monster*," said the stranger, his grey eyes glinting from under his hood. The centurion nodded.

"Follow me." The centurion turned to his men. "I'll be back shortly. Keep an eye out while I'm gone or I'll thrash you."

The men nodded as the centurion went through the open gate and down the via Principalis with the stranger following. As he walked, the centurion felt ill at ease with this man behind him and so kept his right hand wrapped tightly around the handle of his gladius. He did not trust men who would not show their face.

The camp had grown quiet by the time Plautianus' guard had told him that his visitor had arrived and was waiting at the entrance. He told Brutus to leave and wait in the back room until he was called for. If he moved or made a sound, he would kill him.

The prefect sat himself back in his chair behind his table and twirled a dagger on its tip. He was enjoying the sound of the iron spinning when the visitor was shown in.

"Leave us," the prefect said to the guard without looking up. The guard saluted and hurried back to his post outside the building's walls. The visitor waited a moment then drew back his hood, his face cold and lifeless when it appeared.

"Hail, Prefect!" the visitor saluted sharply and then bowed low as though he were before the emperor himself.

"You're late, Argus," Plautianus said evenly. "I don't like to be kept waiting, monster."

"Forgive me, Prefect. The crossing was not as easy as the captain had hoped. I came as soon as we landed, outside the city walls so that no one would see me, as you ordered."

"Exactly as I ordered. And that is why you are here. Rise. Sit down on that stool." Argus removed his cloak to reveal his plain brown and black tunic and breeches. He adjusted the sword and dagger at his sides and waited for his superior to speak. Plautianus rose from his chair and proceeded to walk around the room, behind the chair, along one wall and then directly behind Argus. Even to Argus, the prefect was imposing, although that was mostly an illusion created by the terror he exuded. Every time Argus was in Plautianus' presence the memory of that agonizing scourge ripping his flesh tortured him, the memory of the dark, filthy pit hidden away in Rome's Praetorian camp utterly terrifying. The Praetorian prefect had an iron hold on Argus and there was no escaping, only the possibility of honour and promotion if he pleased him.

"What do you have to report?"

"Well, sir, when I left Rome, the support of several more senators had been secured by...special means. They've erected several more statues of you throughout the streets and fora."

"Excellent." Plautianus smiled as he imagined his likeness adorning the streets and public places of Rome even more than the emperor's. "What else?"

"I also paid a visit to my...to Senator Metellus who will be co-operative from now on in every way." Argus caught himself before the word 'father' slipped from his lips; he did not want that, did not want the prefect to hear him use it. He paused and licked his lips nervously as his superior's eyes stared at him so deeply that he felt as though he were being cut to the bone.

"How did you manage that?"

"Simple blackmail, a threat to ruin his family or, more to the point, himself."

"Point the dagger at a senator's family and he'll think...point it at his own throat and he'll bend over for you in a second. Good. What did you offer the old shit?"

"Just what you instructed me to say; that if he supported you fully in the senate you would see to it that his voice, his opinion, would resonate loudly, be heard and respected."

"Did he buy that rubbish about me considering returning to a Republic again?"

"Outwardly he did. In his mind, I'm not sure. What I am sure of is that he will support you, Republic or no. He hates the emperor. With the opportunity for him to raise his family to prominence again, his greed has come to the fore."

"And what of his informing on his family? Any news there?"

"He did tell me that the tribune's wife and his nomad companion are in Athens. I was about to go there myself to take care of that business but then I received your summons and came here. I did however, tell the senator that if he had any information for me, to notify my man in Rome who would then tell me."

"You did well, monster. The woman is insignificant at the moment. I need you here." Argus nodded his head in obeisance as Plautianus thought for a moment. "What about the empress' sister? Any problems?"

"Not as far as I can tell. All she does is go to a different party every night. Nothing new."

"Hmm. She's got to be up to something. Who's she visiting?"

"Oh, just the usual crowd. I've got a man shadowing her in case anything happens while I'm gone."

"Good. Because you'll be gone for some time." Plautianus slapped Argus on the shoulder, squeezed hard. "You seem to be learning your trade quite well. I'm pleased. What of the…problems…I asked you to clear away?"

"All done. A couple poisonings, a drowning in the public baths, a viper under the sheets. The usual fare."

"Fine. Fine." The prefect looked pleased for some reason; he smiled as he looked to the curtains that separated their room from another one. "Now, I haven't asked you yet of the tribune himself."

"Sir?"

"Your brother." The prefect smiled again, enjoying the look on Argus' face as he stoked his anger. "You thought I didn't know, didn't you?"

"But…how…"

"Don't be an idiot! Of course I knew you are the senator's bastard. I make it my business to know. What I *want* to know, monster, is whether your dedication to this task is as fervent as ever or if you are experiencing any misgivings." Argus didn't speak for a moment. "Well?" The prefect was now standing directly in front of Argus, leaning over him so that his breath filled Argus' nostrils.

"By Mithras, I'll cut his throat as soon as I have the chance!" Argus hardened his features to show his determination. In actual fact, he had not thought of Lucius for some time as his thoughts were more taken up with his parentage and the fact that he had revealed his knowledge to his *real* father. He had been enjoying the power and influence he had been given over Metellus pater. As for Lucius, his half-brother, Argus resented his success more than any man's and still hated him deeply. But he had stowed that hatred, until now. "I want him dead, sir."

"Glad to hear it, Argus, because the time has come for you to hunt this shit down. He's become quite a thorn in my side. It appears that the empress herself is watching his back. She smuggled him out of Leptis Magna before my new man could kill him."

"New man, sir?" Argus had not expected that. "I thought you had told me the task of killing Lucius was to be mine and mine alone."

"I did. Are you questioning me?" Plautianus gripped Argus by his tunic and lifted him out of his chair. "Are you?"

"No, sir! Not at all."

"You'd better not be." He released him. "I did say that before, yes, but it has come to light that you are not the only one who...hates...the young tribune."

"Who is this new person then, sir? Do I know him?"

"Oh, your paths have crossed, I believe. He's to be your new partner."

"But I work alone, sir."

"Not any more. You'll do as I say and work with this trash...unless you would like to visit my dark little building back in Rome?"

The memory of that place, of darkness and torture and pain crept back into Argus' mind like a poison. He felt reduced to a quivering child and wanted to cry. But he did not.

"I didn't think so. Now, wait here a moment and I'll get the scum." Plautianus went to the curtains at the back of the room and disappeared into the darkness for a moment. Argus paced around the room, waiting. Then the prefect returned with a hooded man behind him. Plautianus went around the back of his table, picked up his dagger and watched. Argus looked at the man approaching warily.

When the newcomer pulled back his hood so that he could see, time itself stopped dead. For a moment Argus looked at the man curiously, at his scarred face and the starved, hateful look about him. When recognition set in for both of them, Argus felt the blood pounding in his ears so loudly that he heard nothing, felt only rage.

The stranger's eyes went wide also, his teeth bared themselves and spittle leaked from the corner of his scarred mouth as he went to speak and no words emerged. Plautianus laughed out loud. "So you do recognise each-" Before he could finish, the two men lunged furiously at each other. Argus, forgetting about Plautianus, torture and darkness, wanted only to strangle Brutus and managed to deflect several forceful punches from the man before landing a crushing blow into his stomach and moving behind him to lock his neck against his bicep.

Plautianus observed the display coldly, watched as Argus, by far the stronger of the two, squeezed and squeezed, almost lifting his prey off the ground. Brutus on the other hand, seemed immune to the lack of air reaching his lungs, hate filling his eyes as he spat and wailed like a jackal against a lion. His every thought of Argus was reduced to the day when he had been sentenced, beaten and thrown into the darkness of the galleys by the man who now was choking him. He did not care. His fists flailed and he cursed but Argus' grip was iron clad.

"All right! That's enough!" Plautianus came over, his short sword levelled at the two struggling men. Argus ignored him, could not even hear him. His reaction was automatic, second nature. When Brutus' eyes began to roll back in his ugly head, Plautianus raised the butt of his sword and knocked Argus on the side of the head with the pommel. The two men fell in a heap on the dusty floor, Brutus unconscious and Argus struggling to get to his feet, his head spinning. He felt a sharp pain as the prefect kicked him in the side for good measure. "Want to be a gladiator, do you? You prefer that? I can arrange for you to go into the arena instead."

Argus gasped for air and wiped the blood on his lip where Brutus, still unconscious, had hit him with his head. "I can't work with him! Can't trust him!"

"Trust?" Plautianus laughed. "You're in the wrong business for trust, you idiot! Get yourself up." Argus struggled to rise on one elbow and find his feet. Slowly he moved to the chair and sat down, staring at the slave on the floor. "You can't trust anyone but you can rely on the fact that they will do as they are told."

"Not that one, sir."

"Oh really? Do you remember your dark little room?" Argus nodded painfully. "Well, that animal on the floor got it far worse for far longer. He'll do as he's told," Plautianus said confidently.

"Where did you find him?"

"That's my business. Your business is to work with the swine. You're going to travel to Numidia as soon as I leave for Rome to be made Consul."

"Numidia? All the way there?"

"Problem?"

"No, sir."

"Good. You, and that lump of shit," he pointed to Brutus with his dagger, "are going to Numidia to hunt down the tribune. When the opportunity arises, you'll kill him. Feel free to make him suffer for all his upstart insolence. Do you still have your men inside the cohort?"

"Yes, sir."

"Can you still count on them?"

"Absolutely."

"Good. They took care of that one meddlesome centurion nicely from what you reported before. Something similar for our tribune would be highly entertaining. Do you have the stomach for it?"

"Yes. I do, sir. But I still don't understand why we need him." Argus pointed to Brutus.

"Because he hates the tribune even more and cares more about killing him than he does his own life. Use him how you will, Argus, and once the deed is done…" Plautianus made a gesture like he was drawing his dagger across his throat. "Understand?"

"That part, I like." Argus looked forward to the moment when he could slit Brutus' throat but first, he had much more to do and had to do it with the man lying on the floor.

"Excellent. My suggestion is that you avoid sleep when he's around; if you do nod off, keep your sword in hand."

"I thought I didn't have to worry about him, that his fear of you was strongly inflicted."

"Yes but sometimes, hate can be far more powerful than fear." Argus nodded and looked down at Brutus who began to groan. "For the moment you'll find yourself rooms in the city, something inconspicuous, and report to me everyday. You and he will have to get used to each other before you set out. That might take some time, but I want no mistakes in this mission. Got it?" Argus rose to his feet, recognising his dismissal.

"Yes, sir!" He saluted.

"Fine. Now get out of here and tell the guards outside to come in and take this piece of shit out of my room and back to his cell."

"Yes, sir! Right away." Argus turned on his heel, went out of the Principia, and pulled his cloak over his shoulders and head as he went. Behind him, Plautianus laughed as he tried to picture the two of them working together. They were in fact both expendable, and it did not matter which one died, so long as the job was done.

The night air was cool when Argus left the Praetorian camp shrouded in mist. He was not happy to be back in Africa. It held too many memories, most of them churned up by his encounter with Brutus and the mission the two of them had been given.

He managed to find a room hidden conveniently amongst the brothels near the harbour. It was dark and stank of urine but he was used to living in such places, having changed quarters every three weeks in Rome so that no one could track him down except his superiors. By the light of a small lamp that gave off more black smoke than light, he opened his satchel and took out some of the stale oat bread he always had with him. He sucked on it until it softened, and swallowed. It would not always be like that, he believed, once Plautianus rewarded him for faithful service and promoted him to a higher rank in the Guard itself.

Once he was promoted as promised, he would be able to enjoy his own lavish quarters in the Praetorian camp, rich food to eat every night and the company of clean, well-born women whenever he chose. These thoughts drove him on, always. Plautianus was hard, he knew that, but he maintained the solid hope that if he completed his duties as ordered, the prefect, soon-to-be consul, would remember him. He just had to complete this one mission, that was the key to it all now. Everything he wanted.

In the darkness of the room, as he lay on the mat he had rolled out on the floor, Argus slept uneasily beneath his black cloak. Visions of Brutus' ugly face floated before his eyes. He dreamt of the people he had thought for much of his youth to be his true parents and then of Quintus Metellus, his real father. Any sense of home that he had had over the years, of brotherhood or family, had been dashed, burned away in the sacrificial flames of his life.

He tossed and turned and wept in his sleep, tortured by thoughts of his mission. His wounded mind returned evermore to the darkness and pain of that sealed, brick building where he had become Plautianus' slave. He awoke in the middle of the night, sweating and weeping with the realisation that he was no less the man's slave than was Brutus. *What has it come to?* he wondered. *Complete the mission and it will all end,* he told himself in the dark.

XIII

ANIMA

'Life'

"Why do you insist, my young friend, on asking me about my kingdom?" The Sarmatian commander looked coolly at Lucius from across the table. This was the second time that Mar, their leader, and the younger standard bearer, Dagon, had been invited to share wine with Lucius and Alerio in the tribune's quarters.

"Why do you not tell him, my Lord?" Dagon asked. He wondered why his superior was insisting on being so harsh to a man who had been nothing but hospitable toward them. "We have shared wine and broken bread with them. Surely that merits some tale from our glorious past."

Mar eyed the young man grimly. "You, *little fish*, will hold your tongue when it comes to matters you do not understand." Dagon crossed his arms and obeyed. "You speak of the 'glorious past' of our people, and yet, here we are servants to another."

"I meant no disrespect, truly." Lucius felt awkward, wanted to lighten the tense mood. He knew that Alerio, next to him, had his hand on his dagger beneath the table. Lucius continued. "I have invited you here as friends. It's merely honest curiosity to know more about you as friends, that brings me to ask. Forgive me if I've been too forward."

The hefty Sarmatian breathed deeply, felt slightly ashamed at his defensiveness, and looked to his young countryman whose eyes pleaded for peace. Alerio watched all of this in silence. He had not wanted to come. He did not trust the Sarmatians, but he did not want to leave Lucius alone with them. He knew that ever since the day they had ridden up to Lucius on the parade ground, they had been on his friend's mind. Lucius talked of omens and prophecies in conjunction with their name. Alerio liked the young one, Dagon, because he was actually quite friendly, keen to know about Rome and Romans. He wanted to be Roman, and yet as a Sarmatian cavalryman, his martial prowess was equalled only by that of Mar who had supposedly been a king of some sort in the lands north of the Black Sea.

"I too ask your forgiveness, friend," Mar conceded. "I have been harsh and unfair to you. I am sure you understand that it is difficult for the conquered to speak openly of their past life, especially when that life no longer exists."

"I understand completely," Lucius sympathized. "If you don't wish to speak of it, I will no longer ask."

"No, no. It is fine. My impertinent young kinsman is correct, *this time*." Dagon bowed his head to Mar. "There is no harm in relating to you our story." Alerio sheathed his dagger quietly. "So, now that our weapons are stowed away," he smiled at Alerio who smiled curtly in return, "I can tell you something of how we got here."

Mar reached across the table for the pitcher of wine and filled his cup again before beginning. The other three men leaned back as Mar rose from his chair and went over to the map of the empire and traced his finger along the lands north of Pontus and Dacia. His pleated ankle-length robes, the traditional garb of his country, swayed as his arm moved across the hide map, as he remembered. With his back to the others, he spoke.

"Sarmatia lies here." He pointed. "A land of forests and mountains in the south, vast windswept plains to the north. Our people came from the east ages ago to settle. Our elite, our warriors, sit atop strong, spirited horses. We are called the 'lizard people' by some because of our armour and because the totem of our people is the dragon, all-powerful and wise."

Lucius and Alerio listened intently to the tale that hinted at a longing felt deep within its teller. His voice was like wind across the plains of which he spoke and his eyes looked upon some distant memory far beyond the confines of the Roman fort in which they sat. Dagon looked upon his lord with pride as he continued.

"We have many gods of our own; the highest is our god of war, whose sword is sacred to us. He favours those who survive battle, especially single combat, for that is when a warrior looks deep into the enemy before him and is forced to look deep within himself or herself."

"Herself?" Alerio raised a hand apologetically. "Are you saying your women fight?"

"Yes. That is what I am saying, Centurion. The women of our land are brave souls. We do not lock them up before the hearths of our homes. They are free to ride with us and wield the sacred sword. Some are priestesses and others have been gifted by our gods with foresight. Sarmatian women are nobler than what your Latin word 'noble' implies."

Lucius filled his cup again. He felt the hairs on the back of his neck stand on end as he heard all this. It fascinated him, spoke to something inside. "What of you, Mar?" Lucius asked. "You've told me that your name means 'lord' in the ancient tongue. Were you a king of your people?"

"I had my own vast lands, and many servants and followers, but I was not a king over all of Sarmatia. I was lord over my domains, hailed from one of our ancient bloodlines. A line that had been one of the first to be granted the right to fight mounted and lead cavalry."

"What happened to your realm?" Alerio asked, genuinely curious.

"What happened?" Mar reiterated. "Rome happened." He paused, and pain entered his features. "When all the Sarmatian tribes decided to rebel against Rome over thirty years ago, I had been lord of my people for only five years. The lords of Sarmatia, myself included, had taken the decision to invade the Roman province of Pannonia across the blue waters of the Danube. The earth shook under the hooves of our horses as thousands of us rode to battle. The women took it upon themselves to remain behind to protect our lands from the barbarians to the east in our absence...

"When we crossed the Danube, we met the forces of Emperor Marcus Aurelius." Mar closed his eyes. "I can still hear it...the sound of our charge, the howling of our dragons in the wind. Things did not turn out the way we had hoped. Unlike all of our previous foes, the Romans did not turn and flee before us. They held fast, maintained their discipline. For days the battle went on, and there were numerous skirmishes for miles and miles along the river. But the Emperor Aurelius, an admittedly noble man, commanded a superior force and so we were left defeated. Many of my countrymen died upon the field that day and the survivors were left at the mercy of Rome."

"What happened then?" Lucius asked.

"The Sarmatian commanders and nobility were brought before the emperor not as slaves but as friends. We were told that he greatly respected us and our strength and he offered us peace. Peace," he repeated the word. "As a lord of many, I had not only my own fortune to consider but that of my people. The terms were this: that every Sarmatian noble was to provide one thousand heavy cavalry to serve as ala units alongside Rome's legions. In return, we were allowed to return home to our lands to bid farewell to loved ones and see to our estates. I wish I had declined the emperor's offer, but I did not. I accepted the terms for my people, so that my family might live on."

"Why did you say you wished you had declined the offer?" Lucius poured more wine for Mar who nodded his thanks.

"When we returned home to levy troops and supplies to form up the ala units, I found only desolation on my doorstep." Mar was gazing at the map again. "In our absence, a large force of raiders from the east had attacked our lands and settlements. Our women and younger men had fought bravely but...had paid for it with many lives, including..." Mar's voice shook, "...including my wife. I found her and our newborn son and daughter when I returned. The children had been cut to pieces and my wife used, then skinned and nailed to the wall of our home. Her sword had been broken ritually. About her lay the slashed bodies of ten of the enemy that she had slain before being overcome."

The room was silent, sorrow and gloom hanging in the close air. Dagon wept as he listened to his lord's tale and Lucius and Alerio sat with their mouths agape, rapt with all manner of feelings from sadness and guilt, to awe and respect. Mar turned toward them, his eyes dry but evidently seeing the painful past.

"That is why I wished I had denied the offer. Because I would have been dead and not seen the destruction of my family. Dagon here," he put his hand on the young man's shoulder, "is the last of my true relations, my sister's son - she also died in the raid on our home. She had hidden him as a babe in a dark recess of one of the stables, somewhere the enemy had neglected to look. The gods of our people had left me alive for a purpose which, I believe, is to protect this young man at all costs."

"I am grateful they saw fit, Uncle," Dagon said, and kissed his lord's hand.

"As am I, *little fish*, as am I." Mar turned to Lucius and Alerio. "So there you have it. That is how I came to be where I am. I no longer have a kingdom or homeland. My life is in the saddle, fighting as our people were meant to and now, I fight for Rome and her emperors wherever I am needed."

"The men of your ala unit, are they your kinsmen?"

"Yes, Centurion, they are the men of my lands that survived war with Rome, or survived the raid back home as children. Their loyalty is unquestionable and their skill in battle beneath the windy wings and howling voice of the dragon is unequalled."

Mar sat down again and Lucius excused himself to ask Xeno for food for his guests. When he returned, Mar looked at the sword Adara had given Lucius where it hung at his side.

"I have answered your questions as a friend, Tribune. Now, might I ask something of you?"

"Of course. It's the least I could do in return for your frankness. What would you like to know?"

"Will you tell us of your first experience of battle?" The question was a little odd, unexpected.

"You want to know about the Parthian campaign?" Alerio asked.

"No, Centurion. I wish to know about the tribune in the Parthian campaign. There is nothing more telling of a man than the tale of his first experience of battle."

Lucius shrugged his shoulders. "If that's what you would like to hear about. It's rather a long tale."

"The hour is of no consequence. In our country, the best of tales are told around the evening fires. Please, tell us." Mar sat down next to his nephew and the two of them watched Lucius intently.

The Roman took a sip of wine and began. "Well, I was just a green recruit when we set out for Parthia. Alerio too. None of us, at least of the men in our century, had ever been there. We had, of course, heard the stories. Two hundred and fifty years or so before, Marcus Licinius Crassus led seven legions into Parthia in order to annex it to Rome. It was a massive force, but in the end, Crassus suffered a crushing defeat and was killed. We could imagine the rich man himself lying dead in the Parthian soil."

"The Roman Marcus Antonius also marched into Parthia, did he not?" Dagon asked excitedly. Mar put his hand on his shoulder; it was rude to interrupt someone telling a tale.

"He did, Dagon, yes. Marcus Antonius marched on the Parthians with thirty-two thousand troops. The enemy had only eleven-thousand. Only two thousand Romans left the field alive." Dagon whistled. The numbers were staggering. "Not all was lost however; the emperors Trajan, Aurelius and Verus managed to conquer much of the Parthian realm in later years, including the capital of Ctesiphon along the Tigris river. But, the tales of what had happened all those years before are what stuck in our minds. Needless to say we were scared. This was our emperor's second campaign there; the previous victories never sat well due to internal strife at the Parthian court and their support of Niger in the civil war. We knew that our emperor was taking us there to finish matters. In summer, we crossed into the province of Osrhoene." Lucius stopped for a moment. He realised that he was lecturing as Diodorus might have during a history lesson. Mar wanted to know about *his* experiences. The trouble was that it was all a bit of a blur really, fragmentary memories. Mar spoke.

"Some things are harder to remember, Tribune. You have probably never related the tale before, am I right?"

"Come to think of it, yes."

"What images flash back to your mind the most clearly from the day of battle? Take your time."

Lucius thought for a moment. "The first memories of that day are more of sounds, smells and feelings really." Lucius remembered the blistering sunlight as the ranks stood waiting on the banks of the river. They could not see much at the time. "While we were waiting for the command to move forward, I could hear the engineers yelling as they secured the pontoon bridges across the Tigris. I remember the dry smell of the cracked earth at my feet, the feel of sweat running along my jaw while we waited."

Lucius moved toward the map as he thought, his listeners silent as they waited for him to continue. He saw the route the army had taken across the Syrian desert, past Dura Europus to Seleucia, and then to Babylon, ghostly and deserted. "I recall having thought I could feel the shades of the past watching us: Xerxes, Darius, Alexander, even Crassus and Antonius. There were no more palaces, or hanging gardens, no fountains or springs fed by the trickle of fresh water...

"Then, the enemy arrived. We thought it was a sandstorm at first but the giant cloud that billowed up from the earth with the sound of thunder was no storm. It was cavalry, tens of thousands of Parthian cataphracts and mounted archers. I was afraid." Lucius leaned on the table to support himself and his memories. Alerio watched him curiously; he thought Lucius looked younger, almost childlike at that moment. Vulnerable.

"Go on, Tribune," Dagon urged him softly.

"I remember the smell of the burning sacrifices our priests had made but the good omens didn't comfort me much. I remember gripping my two pila so tightly. Men began to march beneath the hissing of arrows as we shuffled forward to the bridges. There were screams and splashes but we could see very little." In his mind, Lucius could hear the ululating war cries of the Parthians over the battlefield like it was yesterday. "We got across the bridge and formed a testudo. My knees were weak. Arrows crashed down on our shields. The sound of cavalry was everywhere." Lucius turned back to face his listeners. "At one point, I remember walking over the bodies of Roman dead as we pushed our way forward, Decimus, our centurion, yelling. Some Parthian cataphracts managed to slice their way through our legion's ranks, straight for our century. This is the moment I remember from battle: I couldn't hear anything and all movement about me slowed perceptibly. Strangely though, my limbs felt lighter, quicker and faster than ever. I suppose our training took over because I didn't think, I just fought. Our unit was in disarray. I must have swung my sword hundreds of times. Then I saw a spear point burst through the face of our centurion as a Parthian rode in toward me. I brought him down with my sword; I don't remember how exactly. We struggled on the ground. I couldn't see his face but I slashed and swung and killed him, my sword planted in his head. It was the first man I ever killed, I remember thinking that. I remember trying to pull my gladius out of his cloven face." Lucius sat back down with the others, and took a sip of his wine for his dry throat.

"The rest of the century was being attacked by other enemy riders so I rushed back to join them. I was an easy target by myself. It was then that I ran to help one of our friends." His voice caught. "Luckily, I was able to help him, that time. It was then that one of the tribunes asked me where our centurion was. When I told him Decimus was dead, he put me in charge, and told me to get into formation in case the Parthians came back for another offensive."

"What happened then?" Mar asked.

"Nothing. The Parthians fell back, and retreated. I couldn't believe it. From where we were, it seemed that we were being slaughtered and that we were finished. But we weren't. There was no more fighting that day. We all stood there, numb, the smell of death all around us. I remember my hands caked and clotted with blood, the dry ground moistened with offal. The odd thing is that, though it all passed so quickly, as I stood there on the plain, I felt more alive than ever before."

"That is natural, friend." The two Romans looked at Mar oddly.

"How is that natural?" Alerio leaned forward.

"Have you ever wondered why animals such as lions or tigers fight so viciously in the wilds, on the hunt or in the arena? Why do they appear so spirited, powerful, almost elegant in those moments before their deaths?" Lucius and Alerio shook their heads. "It is because, for the mightiest of animals, every fight is a life-or-death situation. They never do it half-heartedly, as humans do, but rather with every measure of strength that they can muster from deep within. That is how most men fight in their first battle: with purity, with truth, with an honest will to live." Mar waited for a moment, looked at Lucius who nodded. He could see that the tribune knew exactly what he was saying. "One of the most appalling acts of this age, for me, is when the fat masses sit in the seats of amphitheatres to laugh and howl whilst these noble beasts are cut to bloody pieces. It is truly disgusting to me." Mar did not take his eyes off of Lucius. He wanted to know one more thing. "Tell me, Tribune, what was the *worst* thing you remember of that day? It was not the battle itself, was it?"

"No." *It definitely wasn't*, Lucius thought. "The most horrible memory of that day was when we sacked the city, Ctesiphon. We'd won a great victory but it wasn't over. When we took Ctesiphon, the legions spent the night plundering the capital and slaying the populace, 'finishing the job' as some men joked. Any survivors were sold as slaves. Our 'discipline' crumbled and chaos took hold. What I remember was my disgust, Mar." Lucius now addressed the Sarmatian directly. "I walked the streets dazed, angry at what was happening." Lucius had not forgotten, never would forget, the sound of flames eating up ancient shrines and palaces, the clink of Romans with loads of booty in their arms, and the chilling cries of civilians being hacked to pieces, burned alive, and tortured. Babies tossed from the walls. The sight of Parthian boys, girls and women being raped by one or more of the troops. He remembered the stinging taste of vomit in his mouth as he purged his guts in an alleyway. "I was ashamed of the disregard for life, the arrogance that had taken hold of the men I was so proud to have fought beside." Lucius looked now at Alerio and knew that he too remembered that night, how the two of them and Antanelis had stood outside the walls of the city, still and sad before the giant, flaming pyre that was Ctesiphon. Alerio looked up at Lucius, his eyes red and moist.

"Your tale moves me, Tribune." Mar sighed. "It is indeed strange, one of life's great illusions. When you set out for war, you are consumed with the idea that you are riding to glory and honour, when in truth, all that awaits you upon your return are pain, loneliness, and desolation."

"But, Uncle-" Dagon made to protest but Mar knew his mind.

"You did not see what I saw back in our village...nor what the tribune and centurion here saw in Parthia."

"But Mar," Lucius began. "Why do you continue to go to war?"

"Because...it is what our people were born to, and..." Mar looked sad, almost beaten for a moment. "It is why Rome lets us live. That is the price of being the vanquished." Lucius could see then that were it not for Dagon, his nephew, his sister's son, Mar would sooner quit the world than go on living in it. The old Sarmatian cleared his throat. "That night, in Ctesiphon, Tribune..."

"Yes?"

"*How* do you remember it?"

"I remember it more clearly than any other moment of that part of my life."

"Then you understand, Tribune, why I was reluctant to speak of my kingdom. Of all the joy and love I have known in my life, that is the way I remember my wife...how I last saw her when we returned from battle. Clear and terrifying." Mar tried to hold his head up nobly, as he always did, despite the heavy sadness of loss that pulled him into the dirt. He looked around the room at Alerio, Lucius and Dagon. "Careful, young men. Too much remembrance can weaken even the strongest among you."

The four men ate the remainder of their meal in silence, and sipped their wine in thought. The evening had been one of revelation, of getting to know each other and the sort of men they were. Lucius thought of Mar's story, of his own memories. He did not want fear and death to dominate the recesses of his mind as they did for Mar. Lucius wanted only to remember Adara and their hopes and dreams. He looked at the Sarmatian and felt great sadness for him, for what he must have felt. *Gods protect me from such tragedy, I beg you*, Lucius thought to himself as he tipped a little wine onto the floor. Lucius noticed Dagon staring at his sword and ring.

"Are you well, Dagon?" Lucius asked.

"As well as I can be after such sad tales, Tribune. Actually, there is something I'm curious about."

"What's that?"

"From the time my uncle and I met you in Carthage, I have been curious about your weapons and armour."

"What about them?"

"Upon your Roman cuirass and the cheek pieces of your crested helm, you wear a powerful symbol: the winged dragon. The hilt of the magnificent sword you wear at your side is adorned with the heads of two dragons. Even your ring is made up of two intertwined dragons. Where did you come across these items and do you know of their significance?"

Lucius' armour had always attracted attention but never with the honesty that Dagon was showing. "The armour has been in my family for some generations. The dragons are the symbol of my particular branch of the Metelli."

"Your ancestors are well known to us. Many a Metellus has left their mark on the pages of Rome's history," Mar added. "But what branch of the bloodline do you hail from? Are you a Caecilius?"

"No. Though my father has always falsely claimed so. He even named my younger brother Caecilius."

"What is it then?" Dagon leaned forward, his thick elbows on the table.

"A much lesser known branch. My grandfather insisted I be given that name because he had a dream. *Anguis* is the name: Lucius Metellus Anguis." Mar and Dagon were silent and exchanged looks. Alerio wondered why they were behaving so strangely all of a sudden.

"You carry a powerful name, my friend," Mar said softly. "*Anguis*: the dragon constellation, the great serpent. Now I see why your armour bears the symbol. But what of the sword and your ring? Are they heirlooms?"

"No, actually. This," Lucius held up his hand, "is one of the rings my wife and I exchanged on the day of our union at the Temple of Apollo on the Palatine Hill in Rome. And this," he unsheathed the sword and laid it on the table, "was a gift from my wife. She had it made." Mar and Dagon gazed in wonder and respect at the blade, the intricate, skilled design of the hilt.

"It's magnificent!" Dagon reached but stopped himself from touching.

"Yes," Lucius acknowledged. "I wear it always."

"A truly ancient design." Mar looked upon it with great reverence. Lucius thought of Adara, when she had given it to him and the song the sword had made when he had unsheathed it for the first time. "A wonderful gift," Mar continued. "Your wife must be quite a woman."

"She is." Lucius walked around the table lost in thought.

"It is indeed an astounding thing to be married, is it not?"

"It is, Mar." Lucius smiled at the older man but could see that he was somewhere else. Talk of wives had become too much of a burden for him and he rose, prepared to leave.

"I must be going now. I am tired and we have another patrol to go on at sun-up. I thank you for your hospitality, Centurion." Mar bowed his head respectfully to Alerio, and went to the door. "Tribune." He held out his hand to Lucius. "Good night to you. Thank you for sharing your tale."

"To you also." Mar turned and followed Xeno, who had been outside waiting to lead the guests to the door. Dagon remained behind for a moment to finish his wine.

"Is your uncle all right?" Alerio asked.

"I have never heard him speak of the things he told you this night, not to anyone. I myself had only heard the tale once before and that was because I was a little pest full of questions."

"He's been through a lot," Lucius said, watching across the courtyard where Xeno was closing the door behind Mar. "Your uncle is a strong and good man."

"There is none better." Dagon rose to take his leave. "Thank you both for this evening. It is nice to meet people such as yourselves for a change." He bowed to the two of them, went to the door and turned back. "For him to tell you these things…well…it means he has a respect for you that very few men have the privilege of sharing. Good night to you both."

Once Dagon was gone, Lucius and Alerio both sat down again to finish their wine. They had drunk a lot but it felt needed.

"That was interesting, wasn't it?" Alerio said as he reached for a small branch of dates.

"Definitely. They're very interesting people."

"I have to say that I feel a bit better about the Sarmatians after talking to them. They're probably not all like Mar and Dagon though."

"No. Those two are different."

Alerio wondered what was going on in Lucius' mind, but did not want to ask. He was not in the mood to hear more talk of prophecies and omens, especially on a night with a full moon.

"Erm," he cleared his throat. "So, has the legate told you why the mock battle has been postponed?"

"Not in great detail. He just figured the men needed more time to prepare and that there were still some nomadic raiding parties to be taken care of."

"But our plan, the march, is still on, right?" Alerio's features had hardened. He had thought of little else since their trip to the oasis weeks ago. He had been watching Maren and Garai carefully, Eligius too.

"Yes. It's still on and I've told the legate about it."

"Was that wise, Lucius? I know he's our commander and all but to tell him about the plan? What if he speaks of it to someone?"

"Marcellus? Alerio, aside from you, he's the only other one I trust in this whole legion with the information. He needs to know ahead of time in case charges are laid."

"I just want to make sure I get my hands around the necks of Antanelis' murderers."

"Easy now. We have to play things out patiently, intelligently. I don't want anyone alerted to this."

Alerio rose from his chair and threw on his cloak. "I'd better get back to the barracks and make sure the century is locked down for the night."

"Careful going back."

"Don't worry." Alerio unsheathed his sword. "My hand never leaves this."

Alerio waived Xeno back to his stool, indicating he could let himself out. Lambaesis' streets were quiet, empty except for the men of the night watch making their rounds. They politely saluted Alerio as he walked back to his rooms, bolted his door and readied himself for sleep. Every night he thought only of the march and catching the traitors. In five days, he would have his chance.

Two days later, the base stirred with its usual morning fervour just as the first rays of sun had begun to streak into every open window and lane. The stables were quiet at the time, for the Sarmatian cavalry had set out early the day before for a long patrol. Lunaris stood in his stable patiently waiting for Lucius to come for him. His ears perked up as his master's footsteps became audible around the corner and he huffed and neighed at his approach.

"Good morning, boy." He stroked the stallion's forehead gently. "Did they feed you yet?" Lucius looked around for the stablemaster and spotted his long, narrow head jutting out above one of the other distant stables. The man saw Lucius looking at him and came over.

"Morning, Tribune."

"Croesus, good morning. How's he doing?"

"Fine, fine, Tribune. I've already brushed and fed him for you. He's all set to go."

"Thanks for that. Good to save some time today." Lucius set about saddling Lunaris. The stallion's hooves echoed on the cobbles outside the stable and he stood still as Lucius looked him over, playfully nibbling at his helmet's crest. Once mounted, Lucius went out through the southern gate to go for a little ride so Lunaris could stretch his legs. The dapple stallion was pleased and charged back and forth at his rider's bidding without complaint or hesitation. They had learned to ride together in perfect unison; each had grown loyal and fond of the other. When he had the time, Lucius enjoyed rising early to do this before getting down to work.

As he rode around to the west side of the base, he stopped short where the legion's archery range was located. There were two men and for a moment he thought he recognised them. The blonde hair protruding out from beneath their centurion's helmets was unmistakable. Lucius rode over to greet them and see what they were up to.

"Eligius, Garai? Good morning to you both. You're up early today. Already in uniform even before breakfast." The two brothers turned quickly, saw Lucius and saluted.

"Lucius! Eligius called back. Morning! Come on over here." Each of the two brothers held a long recurve bow and had a quiver of arrows leaning up against a post that stood between them. "Watch this!" Eligius said as Lucius rode up behind them. The target was a good sixty paces away. Eligius' green eyes concentrated and focussed as he pulled the bowstring back to his cheek, sighted and let fly. The bowstring snapped a humming tune as the arrow arched its way to land at the base of the target.

"Ha! You'll never get it, Eligius. Watch how it's done." Garai pulled a long-shafted arrow from his quiver and notched it on his bowstring. His bow seemed longer to Lucius, harder to pull back, but he managed to hold it steady as he sighted. He loosed the shaft and the arrow whizzed through the air to plant itself so deeply within the target's centre that it tipped backwards and over. Garai stared for a moment, pleased with himself, victorious. "That's how it's done, Eligius. You buy the wine tonight."

"Of course. But you know," he looked at Lucius, "his bow is much stronger than mine." He looked back to his brother. "It's not fair really, is it?"

"Well then brother, you'll just have to either get used to losing or get a better bow. What do you think, Lucius?"

"I think archery is for auxiliaries. When did you two start practising?" Garai looked away as if something else had entered his mind. Eligius spoke.

"Oh, a few months ago. Thought it was better for hunting lions. No point in getting too close if you don't have to, I say."

"Not a very brave fight. The lion doesn't have a bow or arrows." Lucius stared at Garai for a moment until the centurion's eyes came up from the ground.

"If it's them or us, Lucius, I'll make sure I get out alive." Lucius did not speak as Garai removed another arrow from his quiver. Eligius and Lucius watched but before the arrow flew, Lucius noticed something about the arrowhead. He dismounted.

"Those are interesting looking arrows. Long," he said. "Are they usually that long?" The question was simple and a little stupid, but he wanted something. Lucius reached down and drew one of Garai's arrows from his quiver. The long shaft was thick and the arrowhead long, narrow and razor sharp. Deadly barbs angled out of the sides. "Have you killed anything with these yet?"

Garai stopped, unhooked his bowstring and took up the arrows, including the last one in Lucius' hand. "Couple jackals, a lion or two."

"Garai's a lot better at this stuff than me, Lucius. I can't hit a moving target whereas Garai can knock a jackal off its feet at a hundred paces. I saw him do it once."

"We really should get going, Eligius," Garai put his helmet back on. "The men will be done eating by now."

"Will we see you on the parade ground then, Lucius?"

"Of course, Eligius. I'll be there shortly. Just going to give Lunaris a little more time before standing around to watch the lot of you."

"See you there, then," Garai said as he walked on with his bow slung over his shoulder and the quiver of arrows in his hand. Lucius stayed there a moment watching the two brothers leave and wondering what was going on inside their golden heads.

The arrowhead. Something about it. When they were out of sight, he rode up to the target they had been shooting at. Stuck in the ground he picked up the arrow shot by Eligius and looked at it - a short squat arrowhead. It was very different to the one he pulled out of the target, the one belonging to Garai. Lucius looked up at the sky, now in its transformation from pink to pale blue, and realised he had little time before the men were assembled. He mounted Lunaris, tucked the arrowheads he had broken from their shafts into a small pouch that hung beneath his cloak and spurred his stallion on toward the parade ground where the dust was beginning to rise.

The day had passed slowly it seemed, more so for every day that approached the march to the oasis. Lucius had asked Alerio to come to his quarters by himself that night but not for dinner this time. In fact his tone had been quite serious and Alerio wondered why, though he could only guess that it was something to do with the march. When he entered Lucius asked him to sit down.

"Did you bring them?"

"Yes I did," Alerio reached into the fold of his tunic and put down the arrowheads he had taken from the oasis. They still carried the blood of their friend and the two men stared at them for a moment before Lucius went over to a small table and picked up the arrowheads he had taken that morning.

"Here." Lucius held out the arrowhead that Eligius had shot. "Recognise this?" Alerio examined it and looked at those on the table.

"No. Should I?"

"How about this one?" Lucius then held out the other hand with Garai's arrow. "See anything similar?"

"But...it's the same as these!" Alerio pointed to the ones he had brought. "Where did you get these?"

"This morning, I was out riding when I found Eligius and Garai out on the archery range practising."

"You saw what?" Alerio pounded his fist on the table.

"You heard me, my friend. That first one there was from Eligius' bow, the second from Garai's."

"Garai's looks exactly like the arrowheads from the oasis."

"It seems that way. We must be cautious here in our judgement though. Aren't there a whole slew of styles of arrowheads? Barbed, straight-edged, short and long?"

"I suppose, Lucius, but...come now, this isn't a coincidence." Alerio stared at him for an uncomfortable space of time before Lucius spoke.

"I know you're right. It's just that, now it comes to it, the closer we are to figuring all this out, ending it, the harder it is to think about nailing them. These aren't some rag tag auxiliaries or mercenaries Alerio, these are men who have fought side by side with us, to Hades and back. We've lived with them, bled with them. The more tangible revenge seems, the more wrong it all feels." Alerio stood up then. His face was crimson as he thought about what he might say to Lucius.

"Lucius, listen to me. I've thought long and hard on this. While you were away, I lived in constant fear of having one of my own men shove a knife in my back. I didn't know about how Antanelis died then, but I could sense things weren't right. Now that I know for sure what happened to him...there can be no doubt about what we have to do. For me, Lucius, this is about revenge and peace for the shade of our friend."

"It's about that for me too, Alerio."

"Yes, of course, but for you it must be about more. Your resolve has been ironclad up to this point and it can't flag now. Lucius, you're our tribune, our commander, and for very good reasons. The Gods favour you. I haven't always understood your gift, or wanted to. I see things in you that are beyond my comprehension but I do know some things: you were born to lead men, to inspire them with your courage and sense of honour. The example you set is one each of us aspires to but almost never reaches. We all have the urge for revenge but for you it's got to be about more than that. This whole tragic situation has arisen because there are men who will *never* be like you. For you, as a friend, as our leader and as a Metellus and a Roman, setting this right is about your duty...duty to Antanelis, to those who look up to you and to Rome. I had a taste of what it was to carry the responsibilities you do and I tell you, more than once I almost slit my wrists. I don't envy your position."

Lucius sighed, rubbed his face hard. Alerio had never spoken to him so openly or frankly. In the company of men, such words rarely came easily. But at that moment, his friend's words reached deep within him to awaken some untapped reserve of courage.

"You're not alone in this though, I promise you. You're my tribune, but you're also my best friend, Lucius. I'll stand by your side through whatever test the Gods send your way. These past days I've felt them watching...waiting. The time is fast approaching when we'll help our departed friend." Alerio reached for two cups and a pitcher of wine, filled them and handed one to Lucius. "To Antanelis!" Alerio raised his cup and Lucius stood from his stool.

"To our friend and to duty!" They then spilled a portion of wine to the Gods and drank deeply. Always, it had been Lucius who had spoken winged words to pick up his friends' spirits but then, in that very room, Alerio was the one who had re-instilled in Lucius his sense of accountability and reminded him of who he was.

The day before the march arrived, and the cohort had been given a welcome break from drills in order to prepare their kit for the expedition. The men grumbled slightly, many wondered where they were headed. Information had been given out only on a need-to-know basis. The only persons with any knowledge of their destination were Lucius, Alerio and the legate.

The previous afternoon, Lucius had gone to report to the legate commander about his plans, and to inform him exactly of what was to transpire. Marcellus had been quiet at first. Lucius worried that he might call a halt to the whole thing, but he did not. Gaius Flavius Marcellus paced the room, rubbing his grizzled chin as he went over the possibilities of Lucius' plan and what could go wrong. He had dismissed his servants and staff so that they could be alone without risk of being overheard.

"Are you sure about this, Metellus? I don't want your reputation marred by making false accusations. You need solid proof. These men you suspect…they all have solid records. This is a dangerous game now."

"I realize that, Commander, but it's something that must be done. The only proof thus far is what's out there and what the men's reaction to it might be."

"What if they don't show any sort of reaction? What then?"

"I'll make sure they react. We'll make camp there, spend some time…eventually, someone will do or say something."

"Still doesn't sound solid enough, Metellus." The legate paused, leaned on the back of his chair. He went over his own impeccable record in his mind. Years of dutiful service full of glory and honour. He knew that if he was connected in any way with the false imprisonment or execution of innocent men, his family name would be disgraced. He stared evenly at Lucius for a moment. "All right, Tribune. You have my approval to go ahead with your plan. I see you're determined to do this. After all, they're men who have been in your command for some time. It's no easy thing to have the worry of treachery around every corner. Still, I must make one thing clear to you." The legate walked around the table so that he stood very close to Lucius, his voice but a whisper. "If things go amiss in all of this. If you are wrong…" he heaved a great sigh, clearly torn by what he was saying, "…if you are wrong, then I can't appear to have been involved in any way. If it all goes to Hades, Metellus, then you must accept full responsibility on your own as though you did it all without my knowledge."

"Sir?" Lucius was surprised that Marcellus, a legate and man of undoubted honour, would remove himself from responsibility and ask others to lie. He could see that it pained the legate to say such a thing, something that could be construed as cowardice, but it was a harsh lesson nevertheless. A man could spend a lifetime fighting for Rome, covering himself in glory, commanding the loyalty of thousands of men, but one wrong move could destroy it all and bring a career to ruin. Politics and honour, Lucius realised, were uneasy bedfellows and the fear of destruction loomed large at all times.

"I'm sorry to say this. I know you are a good man and I believe what you are saying and what you think you must do. However, you are young. You feel indestructible, protected by the Gods who favour you and your ancestors, but when you are older, when you've spent a lifetime building up what you consider to be a life of success based on dedication, sweat and blood and loss, perhaps then you will understand what I'm saying."

Lucius stood silent and gazed into the legate's tired eyes. For the first time the man before him seemed his age. He had only been in command of the III Augustan for two years but prior to that he had seen a lifetime of war and service. It was understandable, Lucius thought, why he should be so reluctant. The only difficulty in accepting the legate's words lay in the fact that he had to be absolutely certain about things, strike fast and with complete accuracy, or else he would lose everything.

"I understand, Commander," Lucius said, bowing his head slightly.

Marcellus smiled, slightly sad and worried at the bravery of the young man before him. *Perhaps politics has not corrupted him as much as I feared*, he thought to himself. "May Nemesis smile kindly on you, Metellus. Go now. Finish your preparations for tomorrow. Good luck."

"Thank you, sir!" Lucius saluted and turned to go out of the Principia.

"Metellus!" called the legate before Lucius stepped from the room. "I hope you nail the whoresons."

"I will, Commander." Lucius nodded, placed his helmet upon his head and went back to his quarters.

As Lucius walked down the via Principalis, lost in deep thought and not a little inkling of doubt, a trooper came running.

"Tribune! Tribune Metellus!" the man called, holding something above his head. Lucius stopped in front of his door and turned to face the man.

"Yes. What is it, soldier?" The man stopped in front of him, saluted and held out a rolled papyrus.

"This was found this morning on the floor in the imperial mail room. Seemed to have fallen behind a table some time ago. I was ordered to bring it to you immediately." Lucius held out his hand and accepted the small scroll. It was a discreet missive, no ribbons, only a small seal.

"Things like that should not be happening. Especially with imperial mail." Lucius nodded and made to leave but the trooper held up his hand.

"A moment, sir. This also came for you this morning." The man held out a larger scroll and Lucius accepted it eagerly. He recognised the seal as that of Publius Leander Antoninus. A letter from Adara, Lucius was sure of it.

"Thank you, trooper."

"Sir." The man saluted again and went back to his duties.

As he sat down with some wine, cheese and bread that Xeno had set out for him in his meeting room, Lucius' heart leapt at the thought of a letter from Adara. He looked forward to them, enjoyed touching the paper she had touched, smelling the sweet scent of the perfume she dabbed along the edges. First, he decided to read the small mysterious, letter that had come late to him by way of the imperial mail. He was curious, broke the small red seal and began to read. The writing was small and there was very little of it. It was a brief message but weighty news.

Things have taken a bad turn. You must be cautious.
Drusus' body was found in the harbour of Leptis Magna.
He is dead. Murdered after your departure.
His hand was cut off, his ring taken.
This warning is all I can give to you.
I must see to myself.
Spies are on the move, perhaps for you.
Be careful and may the Gods, sun and stars protect you.
Your loyalty is not forgotten and one day will be rewarded.
Burn this.
J.D.

Lucius read and re-read the cryptic message four times before putting it down. *Drusus dead, spies on the move.* Who else could have written the message than the empress herself, Julia Domna? She had wanted to warn him but how long had that message lain undiscovered in the mail rooms?

This was not what Lucius wanted at the moment. Too much was at stake and the last thing he needed was to have to be looking over both shoulders, with traitors on the one hand and assassins or spies on the other. *Poor Drusus.* Lucius realised that he must have been murdered just after the ship left, meaning he only just escaped with his life into the dark night. An image of Drusus, bloated and pale, came to Lucius' mind and he quickly chased it away.

Lucius chided himself for losing sight of the task at hand. On the morrow he would march out with his men once more but this time it was not to fight a foreign enemy, it was not even a real exercise. This march was a punitive one, an investigation into his own men, their loyalty, and perhaps his own abilities as a commander and leader. Thinking of all of this, Lucius folded up the small missive and placed it on top of the brazier in the corner of the room where it dissolved in flame.

That done, his mind reeling with thoughts of duty and death, he turned his mind to the letter from his wife, hoping for some uplifting news but fully expecting sad words at their separation. It did not matter, he told himself, so long as it was from Adara it shed light on his world and his heart. He held the paper to his nose and inhaled her fragrance, his eyes closed. He missed her more than anything. Lucius broke the seal eagerly, unrolled the papyrus scroll and read slowly and carefully, not wanting to miss one word from his wife's lips.

The beginning of the letter was more full of longing than usual but Lucius also detected a strong sense of determination in her words. There was something more to this letter than all the others and he paused, unsure of whether he should continue or not. He did, knowing he would not be able to stand *not* knowing. His eyes hesitated as he tried to read into the words but he knew that she was always honest and open with him, that she was only ever able to speak her heart. She had been like that from the moment they had met.

She spoke of pain and Lucius' heart stopped, full of fear but he read on. What he read next, he did not believe at first. *Something so wonderful*, were her words. Lucius nearly fell off of the stool on which he sat. His face beamed with smiles, his heart leapt for joy as he stood up and read the words again: *Lucius, my husband, I am with child.*

A love strong and deep burned within his breast as he read the words again to be certain that he was not dreaming, that it was not some long-held wish that trickled into his mind so that he mistook her real words. However, he was not wrong, and he thanked the Gods with all his heart for such joyous, blessed news.

Xeno came rushing into the room wondering what the racquet was all about and why the tribune was laughing all to himself.

"Tribune? Is something the matter?"

305

"No Xeno! Nothing is the matter. Wonderful news!"

"What is it, Tribune?" the old man asked, visibly very curious. His bushy eyebrows pushed up.

"I'm going to be a father, Xeno! A father!" Lucius poured some wine and thrust a cup into the old man's hand. "Drink with me, Xeno. To my wife!" The old man smiled shyly and raised his cup to meet Lucius' and the two of them drank.

"I am most happy for you, Tribune. It is wonderful news when one receives it." Xeno savoured the fine wine in his cup, unused to such a luxury, and smiled in gratitude. He was happy to share a moment with the young man he had grown to admire and respect. "Unfortunate though that the lady is so far away from you." Xeno realised he had spoken too frankly and waited for Lucius to say something but he was caught up reading the rest of the letter. "Thank you for the wine, Tribune, and congratulations." Xeno put his cup down and left Lucius alone to finish the letter.

Lucius put the letter down again and drained his cup. The news was joyous indeed and he shook with exhilaration. But worry crept into his mind. He had not thought of sending for Adara until all the dangers about him had been cleanly swept away. There were of course, many wives at the base. Adara would have no lack of socializing, but how could he be sure of her safety and the safety of their child? He stood and paced the room; his right hand swinging his sword to help him think.

Firstly, he had to quell the mutiny, if there was one, within his cohort; that was the most immediate danger. Secondly, Adara was far away from him; perhaps she would be safer where Lucius could keep an eye on her and know where she was. This would be possible if he succeeded in the first. Thirdly, there was the danger of which the empress had warned him; if they could get to Drusus, they could get to anyone, and if they found out that Adara was in Athens...Lucius stopped that thought the moment it entered his mind. Adara had not spoken at all of Ashur in her last letters and Lucius wondered why, whether he could count on his old friend or not.

Then, like a flash of light it came back to him, the words Apollo had spoken to him in the desert. He knew he had not dreamed them; the words had been too real, and had struck too deeply. Now that the memory of those words had come back into his mind so vividly, his decision was obvious. The Far-Shooter had advised him that his wife should be at his side; that he should keep *his* empress close to him. Adara was the true ruler of his heart and his most absolute duty was to her and the life she now carried.

A new sense of responsibility had been instantly thrust upon Lucius' shoulders the minute he had read that letter. He would send for her. But what if things went wrong in the next three days? He could be in graver danger than he was now. He thought about the time it would take for the letter to travel to Athens, for the amount of time Adara would need to assemble all her things, hire guards and make the voyage to Africa...it would take perhaps two months, even if the Gods granted a smooth passage.

He would, he decided, have enough time to write a second letter telling her to remain in Athens if everything went wrong. She would receive that before leaving Greece. If everything went well on the patrol, then the sooner the letter left, the sooner she would be with him. Immediately, Lucius took a fresh sheet of papyrus and began to write to his wife.

To Adara Antonina Metella
From Tribune Lucius Metellus Anguis

My beautiful wife,

I have just received your letter and I am overwhelmed with myriad emotions. I can't possibly express in words the joy that I feel and the longing that is now stronger and more unbearable than ever. To think that you are carrying our child fills me with a will to live, to protect you and be with you. That is why I have decided that you should come to live with me here in Lambaesis, with all possible speed, before the winter storms make Neptune's realm unsafe.

I am grateful to the Gods that you are feeling well and healthy and I wish I was with you to help you in all things. But that time will come soon enough. I have almost finished my work here; our home must be safe for you and our child. Tomorrow, I leave on a patrol that will, I hope, clear away all dangers of which I was so fearful before. I feel the Gods are on our side and watch over us, as you have told me so often.

As soon as you receive this letter and make preparations for your voyage, send word to me with all haste to let me know which port you will be arriving at and when; Hippo Regius is closest. Though at this time of year, the passage over the high mountains will not be pleasant. There are more ships making berth in the port of Carthage but Hadrumetum is probably the best choice if you can get there. It is a large port also and the road from there to Lambaesis will be easier. Your father will know which is best. Be sure to keep Ashur close, and hire a guard as escort for extra security during the voyage.

Oh, my love, I can't tell you how wonderful I feel at this moment and though I know I yet have much to do before you arrive, I know I will succeed. I will pray and make offerings daily for your safe journey until I hold you in my arms again, something I imagine every moment I am alone.

Kiss Alene for me. I miss her dearly. And give my love to your parents. I too could write forever at this moment, but I have to attend to things. Know that I love you more than life and comfort yourself with the thought that within two months, come Saturnalia, we shall be reunited. And then, my Adara, not even the Titans will be able to separate us. Venus and Apollo watch over you, my love.

Your loving husband, Lucius.

XIV

AMBULATOR TACITUS

'The Silent Walker'

"Apollo, accept these offerings and watch over me these next days. Guide my mind to wisdom and my sword to justice. Let the fear be bled from my body so that I am unaffected by its fallout. Give me strength. I am your servant. Mighty Far-Shooter, often you have come to me in the desert, your forgotten realm beneath sun and full moon. Do not forget me when I am knee deep in the sands. I honour you above all others. If you see fit to leave me to the will of the Fates, then I ask only that you and Lady Venus maintain your caring watch over my wife and unborn child. I will do right by them, by you, and by my ancestors who worshipped you."

Lucius bowed to the floor in front of the altar in his sleeping chamber and poured the oil over the sprigs of rosemary and cedar that were his offerings. The lamp flickered next to the image of the God of the Silver Bow with his outstretched arm extended as he directed a battle. This time, he directed Lucius to his task.

Amid the smoke and scent of burning incense, Lucius prepared himself. It was yet more than two hours to the time of their departure, long before the cock's crow. The night had been sleepless as the tribune had tossed and turned, wrapped in thoughts of his expectant wife and the days ahead. Had his life come to this? Was it to be measured by this one sequence of events? His judges in this, he felt, would be more than men, Caesars, generals or legionaries. Out there, in the deep desert, the Gods themselves would be watching and judging him more harshly than any mortal.

Lucius had asked Alerio to join him before he saw to his century, to help him arm and to have a quiet breakfast before the drama unfolded. After his offerings, he put on his white thin-striped tunic over his matching knee breeches. Beneath the tunic, he placed the eagle feather; he was comforted by the fact that his wife carried its twin. He sat on the edge of his bed, laced up his boots and strapped on his greaves, assured they were snug, comfortable. Then there came a knock at his door and Xeno emerged with a burning lamp in his hand.

"Good morning, Tribune."

"Good morning, Xeno. Is Alerio here?"

"Yes, Tribune. Shall I show him in?"

"Please do." Xeno went out for a moment and then returned behind Alerio who was fully decked out. His armour was polished to such a shine that it lit up the room with reflected lamplight. He removed his helmet and placed it on a small table near the door.

"Shall I arrange food for you in the meeting room, Tribune?"

"Yes, thank you, Xeno." Alerio approached Lucius, noticing the offerings on the altar and stifling a cough from the incense.

"Sleep at all?"

"Barely. You?" Lucius answered, rubbing his eyes.

"Not a bloody wink." Alerio went over to the altar, took a small sprig of cedar from a basket in the corner and placed it on the top. He was silent for a moment, his head bowed, before he turned back to Lucius who was smiling at him. "What?" Alerio asked. "I think we could use all the help we can get the next few days, don't you?"

"Absolutely."

"Ready to arm?"

"Yes." Alerio went over to the wooden stand that displayed Lucius' shining armour and removed the cuirass carefully while Lucius slipped his padded corselet over his tunic. "Is it cold outside?"

"Yes, quite."

"Good. Then I won't get too hot with all this on." Alerio helped Lucius slide his arm through one side of the breastplate and tightened the straps on the other side so that it was firmly in place. The layers of pteruges hung down uniformly from Lucius' waist and shoulders and Alerio made an adjustment to assure that the stripes of his Equestrian class showed clearly at the sleeves. Alerio went back to the wooden stand, removed Lucius' pugio and gladius, and helped him strap them on properly.

Usually, Lucius was well able to arm himself with a little help from Xeno with the buckles in the hard to reach places, but that day of all days, he wanted it to be perfect and knew that Alerio was an expert when it came to detail. The men of his century were always in tip-top form, every strap in its position, every buckle and hinge polished.

Lucius went over to the peg on the wall, removed his military cloak, and laid it on the bed so that Alerio could tie the knotted crimson sash about his torso. The sash ended in a perfect knot just beneath the wings and head of the dragon on his cuirass. Alerio stepped back to take a look.

"Perfect. They'll tremble."

"Let's just hope they obey and follow orders. I'm not going to give them a cushy march. We've got to make this whole thing believable."

"Oh, they'll believe it all right," Alerio answered as he draped the cloak over Lucius' shoulders and fastened it with the blue and red enamelled brooch. "I know you haven't been using it all that much lately, but are you going to wear the spatha, at your back like you used to?" He went over to the rack and unhooked the long cavalry sword, hefted it in the air and felt its perfect balance. Lucius thought about it for a moment.

"No. Not this time. I'll wear this across my back." He went over to the side of his bed where the sword Adara had given him rested against the wall. "Its straps are designed to go around the waist or across the back. I'll hang the spatha from my saddle."

"All right." Lucius handed the sword to Alerio. "Let me help you with that." After a minute, the sword hung comfortably and safely so that Lucius could reach for it easily with his right hand if he had to. "Looks good."

"Aye. Now, we'd better eat something."

Lucius removed his crested helmet from the stand and picked up his spatha and a satchel he had packed for the journey. Inside the bag were the arrowheads, the possible proof they had found in the oasis and those he had taken from the archery range.

"Are you bringing that?" Alerio pointed to the bow and quiver of arrows in the corner of the room that Lucius had taken from his assailant on the road from Thugga.

"No. Haven't had the time to learn how to use it."

"Might have been a good idea that," Alerio wondered. "Ah, doesn't matter. You have everything then?"

"Yes."

The two men went out into the courtyard where the stars and moon still shone quite brightly and went into the meeting room where Xeno had set out watered wine, fresh, hot bread, steaming bowls of millet porridge, some fruit and goat's cheese. They were grateful for the meal because they knew they would need all the energy they could get. Rations always smaller on the march, and though they had packed some extras for themselves in their satchels, they relished the meal.

When they had finished the millet and started into the dates and grapes, Lucius stood up to review the map and the route they were to take.

"Did you make all the preparations I asked you to?"

"Yup. Yesterday. Everything we need to build a marching camp every night. Each man will have his shovel or pick axe, two stakes for the palisade and everything needed for them to cook their food. Rations aplenty."

"Good. What about artillery? Any luck with the quartermaster?"

"That's where it gets a little complicated. Because we're heading into the desert and areas where there aren't any roads, we can't possibly take wagons. I've got several pack horses to carry the tents, animal feed and other equipment. As for artillery, I obtained two of those new, small ballistae and a load of the short heavy bolts they fire."

"Will they go on the back of the horses?"

"Not a problem. The base disassembles so each one can be tied to the back of a horse."

"Excellent. Hopefully we don't need them but they're always good to have." Lucius sat back, thinking of anything else he might have forgotten but Alerio had taken care of everything. He yawned.

"So, why couldn't you sleep? Same as me...eager to get the whoresons?" Alerio gritted his teeth.

"Yes that, but also...I got some news yesterday." Alerio wondered what on earth Lucius could be smiling about, and whether there was actually something to be happy at.

"What news is that?"

"I received a letter from Adara yesterday."

"What did she say?"

"She said, my friend, that I am going to be a father." Lucius beamed each time he thought of it, and even Alerio could not help but break into a smile for him.

"By the Gods, Lucius! I'm happy for you. A husband first and now a father. May you have every happiness. Only a shame she's not here with you, that you'll miss the birthing."

"Oh, I won't."

"What? What do you mean?"

"As soon as I finished reading her letter, I sent one back telling her to come here."

"But Lucius..." Alerio flushed with doubt, "are you sure that's wise? I mean, there's so much going on. It might not be safe."

"I thought about that, a lot. It'll take three days to clear this mess up and two months for Adara to get here. We have time to change plans if needed. Besides, I can't miss the birth of our first child. She'll be safer with me here at the base."

"Whatever you say, my friend. All I know is that we have all the more reason to make this 'patrol' work. If we fail in this, then…"

"We can't fail Alerio. We won't." Lucius tried to smile confidently.

"Well," Alerio raised his cup, "to your family and to our success. May the Gods grant it."

As the first rays of light stroked the morning sky, the men of Lucius' cohort were already assembled in perfect ranks on the cobbles of the Principia courtyard. They were silent as their tribune and centurions went up and down each row checking every detail of their armour and kit. Each man carried his own provisions and tools including the two stakes for the marching camp. Weighed down by all that equipment it was obvious that the march would be a brutal one if they found themselves off of the roads.

The cohort had not yet been told where they were headed and so that was the question on every man's mind. It was apparent from what they had been ordered to bring that they were going to be gone for a few days and that they were going into hostile territory, hence the artillery on two of the pack horses. But where? When Lucius had finished the inspection and looked each man in the eye carefully, he moved to the tripod in the centre of the courtyard and poured a handful of powder into the flames as an offering to the Gods for their journey. Each man said his own inward prayer then, the silent personal whispers that soldiers were wont to do when they went into uncertainty.

Now, standing on the podium to address his men, Lucius looked out over the assemblage and felt everyone's eyes on him. Alerio was pleased when many of the men's glances reflected a long held awe and admiration, something he had not seen for a long time. Lucius breathed deeply before speaking.

"Men! I know you've been wondering where we're headed. It had been undecided until now due to the intelligence brought back by our cavalry squadrons. Once we pass over the battlefield south of base, we will be marching for three to four days to the southwest. We will follow the road through the mountain pass to the last frontier fort and then leave the road." When Lucius said this there were several sighs of disappointment among the ranks; these were quickly silenced by barking centurions and the smacks of their vinerods on the plaintiffs' backs. "I know it will be a hard march but I have faith in you lot! We've come a long way together. If we can cross the whole of Africa from Aegyptus to Numidia, we can do this!" At this there were a few, permitted, cheers of encouragement. Lucius continued. "We're one of the youngest cohorts in the legions, certainly the youngest in Lambaesis but we are also one of the best, strongest and most loyal!" Lucius let these last words hang in the air until they dropped to sink in. "Men, it has always been my privilege to lead you and I will for a long time. We are brothers! Keep your chins up and hold your packs and standards high. Show the Gods watching us that we are men and that we are Romans!"

"Hail, Metellus!" many of the men then yelled and saluted as Lucius' standard was raised behind him. Lucius walked over to where a trooper was holding Lunaris' reins for him and hefted himself up into the saddle. The stallion neighed with excitement and reared, raising Lucius even higher above his men.

"Move out!" he yelled, his voice echoed chillingly by Balbus who blew a long, lingering note on his curved, polished horn. Lucius led the way onto the via Principalis toward the west gate, followed by Alerio and the first century and then Eligius, Garai, Maren, Valerus and Pephredo's centuries. Beside each centurion, each century's signum was held high and proud for all to see, as the column marched down the road; their hobnailed boots echoed on the paving slabs beneath the light of the first day of their march.

Each man was happy for his cloak in the early morning, for in the desert, the crispness of night lingered until well past the fourth hour of day. Every hour, Lucius allowed his men a short rest to relieve their shoulders of the heavy burden of packs and stakes that they bore. Water skins were refilled every time they stopped at a well.

Originally, Lucius and Alerio had planned on marching directly to the oasis without wasting time, but then Lucius had had misgivings. If either Garai, Maren or any of the other guilty parties recognised the terrain, which they most certainly would, then their suspicions would be aroused. That could not be risked. The entire plan rested on secrecy and surprise, or delayed knowledge at the very least. Alerio had turned out to be an accomplished actor, thrice having come to Lucius with the other centurions to ask about the plans for their march. Three times Lucius had refused to say anything on the matter, said that he was waiting on intelligence reports.

By the time evening began to approach on the first day, the cohort had marched twenty miles to the south-west along the Roman road. It was time to look for a decent site to make camp. The terrain was still rocky where they were, though the larger mountains were behind them now. Tomorrow, they would leave the road and go into the desert. Lucius rode ahead to look at a peculiar rise in the land; it was the highest point for some distance and the ground around could be dug up easily enough. He rode back to where Alerio and the others had the men standing to attention.

"I want a castra aestiva put up on that rise over there!" Lucius pointed to the spot and immediately the centurions began giving orders. With efficiency and speed, the ground where the camp was to be was leveled. In the centre, the cohort engineer set up his groma, the standard instrument with four plum lines that set up the camp fortifications and throughways for tents at ninety degree angles. Once that was done, each legionary shed his pack, weapons and armour and began to dig the fossa - the v-shaped ditch that would surround the outside of the camp.

Eligius approached Lucius. "Tribune?"

"What is it, Centurion?" Lucius looked down from his mount.

"The ground is too hard to dig to the usual depth for the ditch."

Lucius thought for a moment. He did not want to make it easy for them. "Have them dig it as deep and as evenly as possible then. Enough for a decent amount of earth to be piled up for a rampart, and for the stakes to be driven into the ground. That should suffice."

"But Tribune, they'll still run into rock."

"Then they can just work around it, work the rock into the fortifications. We've done this before, Centurion. Haven't we?"

"Yes. We have." Eligius saluted and backed off. He could see Lucius' mind was set and that he seemed a little on edge. He marched off to pass on the orders.

When put to it, the men worked efficiently enough. Four gates with titula had also been created on each side of the camp; these smaller walls were built up in front of the entrances to break, or at least slow, any assault. Individual mounds were dug up to flank either side of the gates to serve as watch towers. On two of these mounds, one to the south and one to the west, the ballistae were set up.

As dusk began to descend, the last of the tents had been put up in even rows according to century. In the centre of the fort, the larger campaign tent was reserved for the tribune; a guard, selected from among men Alerio trusted was posted outside. They stood on either side of Lucius' vexillum.

Lucius removed his armour and paced back and forth in his quarters. The entire day he had been wondering whether he could trust the two new centurions, Valerus and Pephredo. Once, Valerus had said he would do anything to help Lucius find out what had happened to Antanelis. Lucius wanted to believe that and so he sent Alerio to bring the man to him. Alerio came in first, leaving Valerus outside for the moment. The camp was quiet now, the men down on their mats for the night, getting rest for the hard day of marching on the morrow.

"Tribune." Alerio addressed him formally when others were around.

"Centurion, come here, I need a word with you." Alerio approached.

"I've brought him," he whispered. "What is it you wanted with him, Lucius?"

"Alerio, I've been thinking, we need to know if we can count on others. I know that Pephredo was part of Argus' century and was suggested by Maren. So that leaves him out of the question. But what do you think of Valerus? He seems like a good lad. He was a friend of Antanelis, but can we trust him?" Alerio looked back at the entrance to the tent to make sure the young man was still outside and had not wandered in.

"I think so. I mean, he was pretty upset over Antanelis' death and you saw how he didn't care about Garai or Maren when you first met him back at base. He seems eager to help."

"I just don't know if it's a good time. Tomorrow night we'll be encamped near the oasis, just out of sight. The morning after we'll hatch things out."

"I know, it's coming closer to it. The men have been good today. Lucius, in the end you're the commander of this cohort. It's your decision. Valerus is a good man, I'm sure. We just have to make him swear to silence."

"Bring him in," Lucius said.

Alerio went back and called for Valerus who had been waiting at attention. When he came before Lucius, he saluted.

"Hail, Tribune!"

"At ease, Centurion. Wine?"

"No thank you, sir."

"I don't know you that well, Valerus, and I'm always a little wary around people I don't know. Can I trust you?"

"I...um..." Clearly the question had taken the centurion by surprise. "Of course you can trust me, Tribune."

"Good, then come closer." The centurion approached and found himself between Lucius and Alerio. "Valerus, do you remember when you said you would do anything to help me find out about how Antanelis died?"

"Antanelis," he whispered too, following Lucius' lead, "was my friend, Tribune, and yes, I do remember what I said."

"Do you still mean that, or have you lost your initiative?"

"I'll never lose that initiative, Tribune. There was something not right about the whole thing."

"You're right about that, Centurion. Now, before I go on you have to swear that anything we tell you right now will stay between the three of us, understood? If you don't want this responsibility then you can leave and be none the wiser for it. I would, of course, be grateful for your support in this."

Valerus stood tall, as tall as a short man could, and looked Lucius and Alerio each in the eyes. "Tell me what I can do."

Lucius looked at Alerio who nodded his approval. "You can be ready for anything that might happen out there." Lucius realised that he was being too vague.

"What's going to happen, sir?"

"It's our belief that Antanelis was murdered."

"Murdered?" the young man repeated.

"Yes. And, by someone within this cohort."

"What? But-"

"Did Antanelis ever share his misgivings about certain members of the cohort? Did he ever say anything about treachery?"

"No, Tribune." Lucius was relieved to hear genuine surprise in the centurion's voice. "He seemed thoughtful a lot toward the end I suppose, but he wouldn't tell me what was wrong."

"He was probably trying to protect you. At any rate, we're marching toward the oasis where we believe he was murdered and it's likely that those responsible for his death may react there."

"But who did it, Tribune? Who should I watch?"

"I can't tell you that yet. I just want to know that you'll back us up if anything does happen, that you and your men will be ready for anything."

"I will, Tribune, you can count on it."

"Good. Just watch Alerio and myself for our lead. Don't tell your men a thing but have them ready all the time."

"Oh, they'll be ready, Tribune. You have my word, and by Antanelis' shade, we'll get them." Valerus blew a whiff of his blonde hair out of his eyes.

"Glad to hear it, but remember, act as though you know nothing. If the culprits are alerted to anything, we're lost in this. Agreed?"

"Yes, sir. I won't say a word to anyone and I'll act as always."

"Good man. Now, get back to your tent before anyone notices you're in here too long."

"Yes, Tribune. Good night to you both." Valerus turned and went out. His mind was racing now as he relished the thought of finally avenging his friend's death. His suspicions had been correct; he found comfort in that, now that his doubt was dispelled. But who was it? Though he continued to play the part of the dutiful centurion the whole of the following day, inside he raged with apprehension over each man in the cohort.

In the morning, after a quick meal for each trooper over their individual fires, the camp was broken down. The tents were packed up and the ditches filled in so that enemies could not make use of them at any time later on.

Each man had had ample rest, much needed for this second day. Only an hour after they had set out, the cohort quit the Roman road and began moving directly southward over the sand. It was hotter than before. Wells in the desert became more and more sparse and Lucius decided to allow the men extra time at each one in order to drink and fill their skins again before moving on. It was an unwanted delay but it was in his best interest to keep them hydrated and content.

Along the way, the only other travellers they spotted were part of a caravan coming out of the desert to the west. Lucius approached them warily but it soon became obvious that they were simply poor merchants going to the smaller settlements outside Lambaesis to try and sell whatever trinkets they could get a coin for. As they passed by the marching column of troops, it was obvious that many of the traders wished to approach in search of possible buyers but they were held back by fear. Yes the troops carried coin and would probably have bought something but they were close to five hundred armed men and would just as likely take what they wanted. When they passed without incident, Lucius breathed a sigh of relief to himself. He did not want to have to discipline anyone, not yet.

After a long day, Lucius called a halt and looked out at the horizon to the east. No sign of the oasis. He began to wonder if they had gone too far south and west, even though he had made sure to curve eastward earlier in the day. He wanted to continue the march but he could not ask that of the men after trudging through the soft sand in the blazing sun. They would have to make camp where they were. The ground was uneven except for a small area to their right where if they placed the tents closer together, they might just be able to entrench themselves.

"Centurion!" Lucius called to Alerio. "Let's make camp. The day's too far gone to keep going and the men have worked hard."

"Yes, Tribune!" Alerio acknowledged.

"I'm going to take a ride around and check things out." Lucius gave a nod to Alerio. He too had been wondering if they were close yet to the oasis and watched as Lucius charged off over the dunes.

"What in Hades are you all gawping at?" he shouted at a bunch of troops staring at Lucius ride away by himself. "You heard the tribune! Make camp right over there! Move!" The men were shocked back to and quickly set about levelling the sandy ground, planning and digging.

The dunes were high and many, and Lucius cursed himself for not having turned east sooner. Ahead, he spotted a particularly high dune and spurred Lunaris toward it. The dappled stallion surged up the steep, soft slope until he reached the top. Lucius reigned in. In the distance, dark and shadowy, lay the oasis, about two miles away. Lucius dismounted and rubbed Lunaris' neck. He felt a momentary wave of relief pass over him.

"There it is, boy. That's the place." Lucius looked to the south of the oasis and there he spotted the top branches of the giant palm. "Definitely the right place. Gods help us." Lucius turned around and looked at the setting sun, orange and pink on the horizon. The wind began to pick up and Lucius shielded his eyes. The light in the west became hazy and blurred. "We'd better get back before we're missed and this wind gets too strong." Lucius mounted up, looked one more time at the oasis and returned to the camp.

When he returned, he found Alerio standing on a high dune looking out for him. Visibly relieved when Lucius rode up, he took Lunaris' reigns. "So? Is it there?"

"It is. About two miles east over the dunes. You can't really see it until you're about a half mile away. In this wind and at night however, nobody will see it."

"The Gods are with us, Lucius. Jupiter has conjured up this wind to hide that place until tomorrow."

"I just hope He doesn't bury our tents in the process." Lucius rubbed his eyes. "Is the camp about ready?"

"They're just setting up the tents now. They should just fit."

"Good. Let's get everyone inside before this turns into a damned sand storm. Tell the men we have a short march and drills tomorrow."

"Lucius, one more thing."

"What is it?"

"Perhaps we should all meet in your tent this evening. I'm worried that the other centurions are feeling left out."

"You're right. We have to keep up appearances. Bring them. We'll talk."

That evening, after eating a small meal of crusty bread, dried meat and dried fruit, Lucius looked over all the hinges and straps of his armour and sword belts to make sure nothing was ready to break. He unsheathed his pugio and other swords and sharpened them all except the one Adara had given him; its blade always gleamed, even in the darkest of places. He wondered if he would be forced to test its metal.

Lucius felt oddly at peace by himself even in the midst of all his plans and upheavals. Sitting directly across from his cuirass, he looked upon the emblazoned dragon and thought of how many campaigns it had seen, how many victories. He wondered how much blood had been smeared across it in the killing fields across the empire. Now, it was his, the symbol of his ancestors, a symbol that had led him on an unusual path to a yet unknown destiny. *Eagles and Dragons*, the Sybil had said. The words were burned onto his mind. She had spoken of bravery and wisdom too, words that held much more meaning for him that very eve.

Lucius thought often of what the Sybil had prophesied, but he did not speak of it often, did not understand most of it. Someday, he figured, the knowledge of what Apollo had meant as He spoke through the Sybil, would come to him. Until that time, however, he had to be mindful and aware of both his thoughts and his actions, lest that which the Sybil had uttered pass him by.

323

There was laughter in the camp, sounds of men sitting about their campfires with their tent-mates as they threw dice and recounted tales of sweethearts, family and home. The desert did that to men; it somehow made them feel smaller and more philosophical. Through a crack in the stitching of the side of his campaign tent, Lucius felt the cold moonlight on his cheek. A break in the swirling, windswept clouds had revealed the full, silver orb and it drew Lucius' eye like a beacon in the night. However, as quickly as it had appeared, it disappeared, covered by cloud once more.

The wind picked up and the sides of his leather tent wavered spastically. Outside, some of the men cursed; the fine desert sand doused fires, whipped and wove itself among the rows. Then, a lonesome note rang out, blown by the cornicen on duty, and Lucius realised that Alerio and the other centurions would arrive shortly. He hung his sword over his shoulder and threw on his black cloak as he prepared to meet his men and keep up the pretence of friendship, as much as that pained him.

Voices outside the tent entrance told him that they had arrived, punctual as usual. He called for them to enter and all six men came in pushing back the hoods of their cloaks and shaking the sand from their hair.

"The Gods are pissed tonight," Eligius said to no one in particular as each of them came in. "Where in Hades did this windstorm come from?"

"You ought to be used to sandstorms by now, brother. We've been in this forsaken place for so long I can't remember the last time I felt rain on my face." Garai gave Eligius a brotherly push that was immediately returned. In the meantime, Lucius had been pretending to look over some papers that he rolled up and set aside before speaking.

"At ease," Lucius said. "There's some wine for you if you want it." Lucius pointed to a large wine-skin and some small cups. Garai, Eligius and Maren poured themselves some while the others declined. Alerio had told himself he would not drink, not until all was resolved. "I called you all in here," Lucius continued, "so you can give me a sense of how the men are taking this march, if they have expressed any ill-feelings toward you, the cohort, or myself. Anything."

"I can only speak for my century, Tribune," began Valerus as he brushed more sand out of his blond hair. "I can assure you that they are up for anything. They'll follow any order." Garai rolled his eyes. He had grown quite impatient with what he saw to be Valerus' obvious attempts at winning favour with those of higher rank.

"What about the rest of you? Anything you can tell me?" Lucius looked from one to the other, taking each of them in. Eligius shifted uneasily beneath his gaze but managed to answer that his men only complained about the sand in their eyes.

"Good, Eligius. What about you, Garai, Maren, Pephredo?"

"Well, Lucius, you know how it is with these men," began Maren, half smiling. "They're sick of wasting away the days and nights on this desolate edge of the empire when they could be getting more action on the eastern and German fronts."

"Have you punished those who have expressed these views aloud?" Lucius crossed his arms and stared at Maren. Alerio wondered where he was going with this but remained silent. He was treading a thin line between his normal, disciplined self and unusual behaviour. "Who are the men, Maren? What are their names?"

"You have much more important things to do, Lucius, I'm sure." Maren eyed Lucius, defiance glinting behind his deep blue eyes. He had always taken duty very seriously, but now he seemed almost apathetic about it, all of it. "I'll take care of things tomorrow, don't worry. They'll listen to anything I say." This last statement stuck in Lucius' mind as he looked at Garai.

"I suppose," Garai began, "that *my* men are just doing what they've always done; going about their orders whether they like it or not. Everything is getting done isn't it?"

"Yes," Lucius said. "It is. And you, Pephredo?"

"Nothing to complain about, Tribune. Anyone gets out of line in my century I crack my vinerod across their back. Simple as that."

"Is it, Centurion?" Lucius walked behind them, around the circle they formed.

"Yes, sir," Pephredo answered and nodded his black, shaggy head once.

"Well, it seems everything is under control then. Now, I wanted to tell you what we're going to be about tomorrow. I know that I haven't told any of you where we are going but that is because I haven't known myself all that much. We were meant to march to the south-west for a day and then south and east. I thought it would be a good idea to practice drills in the desert sand where we don't have the advantage of a large, flat, unimpeded view, and where we can't rely on solid ground underfoot. We haven't been tested all that much in soft sand for some time and I thought we should be ready just in case we're called into action. There are still occasional reports of nomadic raiding parties and if there is a very large one, I want us ready for it. If you have any complaints or concerns you wish to voice, do it now. I insist on giving you all the opportunity to be a part of this cohort." The centurions looked from one to the other, Alerio and Valerus were playing too. None spoke. "Very well then," Lucius said. "Tomorrow we'll march only for a short distance and then do some drills. I want every trooper to be perfectly equipped with nothing extra for hunting."

"What extras would they have?" asked Garai.

"Oh, extra daggers, slings, bows that sort of thing. Only army issue weaponry." Lucius watched Garai and Maren who looked annoyed by this ridiculous request. "You can strap your bows to the pack horses, set an example."

"What for? My men wouldn't say a thing about anything to me," Garai insisted.

"I just think that as centurions, you should set the example to your men. Agreed?"

"Anything you say, Lucius," Eligius agreed. "Odd request but you do have a point."

"Good. Now you'd all better get some sleep tonight. I want to break camp during the first hour of day."

Everyone put back on their cloaks and hoods, saluted and went out of the tent to make their way back to their centuries.

"What in the name of Mithras was all that about?" Garai asked Maren as the two of them walked with Eligius in tow along the dark rows to the edge of the encampment.

"I don't know, Garai, but it seems he's losing it. Lucius hasn't been the same since he returned from Rome. He's grown soft."

"Argus is right about him. He's not fit to command anymore." Maren glanced sideways at Eligius as Garai spoke.

"Watch what you two say around here! If anyone hears you say a damned thing like that, you'll be up on charges. No matter how much you intimidate your men, there's always someone willing to report you, hoping to take your place. Besides, you're both full of it."

"Ease up, Eligius!" Maren said. "You're too sensitive. We're just talking. How about you go get some sleep?"

"I am, and you two should as well. Just keep your mouths shut and I'll see you in the morning. Good night." Eligius walked off, looking about to make sure that no one had heard what his brother and Maren had said.

"Maybe we shouldn't have said that in front of your brother, Garai."

"Ach, don't worry yourself about him. He's just been grumpy these past few days. He'll sleep it off. Besides, he knows we're right about Lucius, that's why he gets so upset when we talk like that. He really agrees with us."

"Well, maybe we should just stop talking about it for now. Don't mention Argus."

"Fine, fine. Let's get some sleep then."

"Yeah, we'd better." Maren kicked some sand into the air and it was instantly carried away on the wind. "I can't believe he's going to have us do more bloody drills tomorrow. I just hope this wind dies down."

"It should. I'll see you in the morning." Garai turned to go after his brother and have a quick word with him, calm him down, while Maren went directly to his own tent to drink some more wine and fall asleep.

Back in his tent at the centre of camp, Lucius felt relieved they had all gone and wondered whether it had been a mistake having them come. The thought that he may have to seriously confront any of them the following day was more difficult to bear now that he had seen them face to face in private, the way they used to gather on campaign as friends.

How many of their own men have turned against me? Lucius wondered as he tried to spot the moon once more through the rip in the tent wall. He was not tired yet, so busy was his mind that he would simply toss back and forth were he to lay himself down. The camp was quiet, most of the troops either asleep or talking within their own tents. The only others that would have been out were the sentries on duty around the perimeter of the encampment. They would be suffering out there in the gritty wind.

Lucius pulled on the hood of his cloak and went outside, informing the guard that he was going to inspect the camp and see to some things. The guard saluted and nodded his understanding.

What had been an unpleasant hissing had now turned to an unearthly howl and groaning on the air as the wind seemed to attack them from every direction. Lucius' dark figure passed slowly in front of the tents until he reached the southern gate of the camp where the two troopers there did not see him until he was directly beside them. They were shielding their eyes from the sand but once one of them spotted the black-cloaked figure approaching, he nudged his mate and they levelled their pila.

"Ho there! Password!" demanded the smaller of the two.

"Nemesis!" Lucius called back. Alerio had thought that would be a fitting password for the evening when they had arrived at the site that afternoon. The men saluted when they heard Lucius' voice and saw his face as he came to stand on the raised mound between them. "Thought I'd come and see how you lads are doing. Nothing amiss?"

"No...no, Tribune. Nothing except this stinging wind." The trooper looked at his friend who was clearly confused by the presence of the tribune on the ramparts, alone on a night like this.

"I hope it stops soon, Tribune," began the other trooper. "Bit hard to see any enemies coming."

"Yes, it is." Lucius looked up at the sky for a glimpse of the moon but it was nowhere to be found. "If you ask for a good day tomorrow men, perhaps the Gods will hear you." The men blinked and looked around.

"Do you think they'd listen to us, sir?"

"Out here? I think that they can hear us all the more out here." They were all three silent for a bit before Lucius smiled and turned to leave. "I'll make sure you get extra rations tomorrow for your duty this night."

"Thank you, Tribune!" said the larger of the two men who saluted as Lucius disappeared into the sand-choked air behind them. As he made his way around the entire perimeter of the camp, Lucius checked on every group of sentries. It was the same with all of them: no trouble from without except for the strange storm that refused to yield. The men were even more wary, their superstitions more intense and remembered, when they were deep in the desert. Because of the desolate violence of the night, many of them expected an attack at any moment and were on edge. But Lucius put them at ease, instilled confidence, and told them they had the Gods' favour and that the storm would soon pass.

At every station, the men were both surprised and pleased to see the tribune. Commanders above the rank of centurion rarely made the rounds like that, certainly not in the middle of the night. When Lucius left them each time to continue his walk, the men felt confident, uplifted, and their apprehension about the desert put to rest.

He had hoped to speak with more of the troops but all were inside their tents, hidden from the whirling sands. He had wanted to get a sense of how they felt toward him if, on the morrow, he needed their help. For many, many months he had wondered about their loyalty; following orders on the parade ground was one thing, but coming willingly to his aid out in the desert was quite another. He had wanted to determine the extent of their loyalty; but that, as it now seemed, was evidently in the hands of the Gods wherever they were beyond the choking, wind-swept air.

He closed the tent flap behind him and removed his dusty cloak before going over to a basin full of water and washing the sand from his face. As he laid himself down on his cot, Lucius pictured the giant palm swaying out there in the storm. The palm, sacred to Apollo, the tree under which the Far-Shooter had been born. He imagined that tree, near to where Antanelis had been killed, and prayed to Phoebus Apollo for wisdom and guidance on the day to come.

Eventually, Lucius managed to settle down to a surprisingly restful sleep sometime during the night, and when Alerio arrived to rouse him before dawn, it took him several moments before he realised where he was and what they were about to do. Once awake, however, his limbs strengthened themselves with the resolve he now felt. It was a point of no return for them.

As Alerio helped Lucius to arm himself in full panoply, they decided on their course of action. The men would pack up camp and they would march for two miles south and then turn east for two miles before stopping. There, each century would perform their usual drills among the dunes. Then, they would begin to move northward in their drills until they came upon the oasis from the south. With the entire cohort there, the suspects would not make a false move. Lucius would order water to be retrieved from the spring in the oasis, and once there, he and Alerio, with the support of Valerus and his men, would take Garai and Maren to the pit. He still was not sure about Eligius but could not afford to keep the brothers together. He did not know what would happen, only what he hoped would happen.

"It's not a pretty plan, Lucius. Sloppy come to think of it," said Alerio as he strapped on Lucius' cuirass.

"Don't I know it, but we have little choice. We have to get them to the spot itself to see any sort of reaction. They're smart, they won't let on easily." The two of them were silent for a time as they ate some food.

"Antonius Frontus is already up too. He's out front feeding Lunaris."

"He's a good man, Frontus." Lucius smiled as he looked through the tent flaps to see Frontus polishing the vexillum he was charged with guarding at all times while Lunaris ate oats from a feed bag that hung around his head. Each of the buckles and discs on the stallion's harness had been polished and they flickered in the light of the brazier next to them. Lucius had grown fond of his standard bearer; he respected how seriously Frontus took his duty, the dedication he gave to each task no matter how minor.

"Glad that wind has died down," Alerio said as he handed Lucius the sword to sling across his back.

"That was quite a night. I went out for a walk because I couldn't sleep. Thought I'd talk with all the sentries."

"You did? What about?"

"Nothing in particular. Just told them they were doing a good job. Oh, that reminds me, extra rations for all those on duty last night."

"Done. They'll love you for that if nothing else."

"Well, it was a night in Hades for them. They deserve it for standing out there for so long."

"A night in Hades it was, but look now, Lucius; the sun is rising, and the winds have all gone home to their caves." Alerio and Lucius went to the tent opening to feel the soft light that streaked across the sands from the distant east. Soothing rays of orange and scarlet lit up the earth beyond the tent walls to reveal a world changed.

"By the Gods, Alerio, would you look at that." Lucius stroked Lunaris. As the two men stood there, they gazed out to take it all in.

During the sleepless night, what had been a deafening world choked with wind and sand was transformed into one of beauty and repose. The serenity of the surroundings was like the odd quiet after a battle. The soft, flour-like sand dunes and the sky above echoed each other in texture and symmetry; both appeared to have been raked brutally by the malformed claws of some unknown desert-dwelling god during what must have been a battle of sorts in the heavens above. The gashes in the sky, like wounds, seemed to bleed with intense fluid colour where the god had marked his passing fury. The respite afterward gave way to a sight none of the men in the camp expected to wake up to. Likewise, the dunes had shifted, tossed and turned like a seabed thrashed after a spell of Neptune's rage; smooth lines flowed in perfect unison wiping away any trace of previous passage.

As men emerged from their tents, they gazed in awed delight at the horizon, the sand and the scarred sky. There was a pervasive sense of gaiety in the troops' talk too. Many whispered of the tribune's passing among the camp sentries in the eye of the storm, his talk of Gods, of men and the desert. Some superstitious soldiers even attributed the peace they now enjoyed to the Tribune's discourse with the Gods themselves. Word of this spread so quickly that as Lucius led the way southward, his vexillarius holding the dragon banner high above his head, he was met with either smiles and heartfelt salutes or humbled looks of dread.

XV

CONIURATI

'The Conspirators'

It had not taken long to march the men to the area south of the oasis where Lucius had decided they would commence drills. In fact, many of the men had wanted, inwardly, to continue their march as each new step in the soft, churned sand was a discovery in itself. Those at the head of the column were as discoverers of, what was to them, an untouched world.

The air was neither hot nor cold, and each man carried his kit without discomfort or excess exertion. Once the pack-horses had been hobbled, the various centuries organised themselves separately to begin the first round of drills; the men marched in formation: up and down the giving dunes for a distance of half a mile before turning back to do the same at a quick-step. The sand made it more difficult due to its nature under foot but Lucius was pleased to see that the men still gave it their all under his watchful eyes as he charged along with them. The next drills involved three centuries at a time moving in formation, wheeling with varying blows on the horn. The centurions led the way for their men, pushing themselves to stay at the head of their formation.

Eventually, they came to drills involving the entire cohort as they perfected their responses to blows upon the horn and commands issued by the tribune. Lucius' cohort had always been expert at their testudo formations, their shields perfectly locked. By midday the cohort had earned a deserved rest and they broke out their meal rations before heading north. Alerio made sure that the sentries of the night before received their extra rations as Lucius had ordered. Each centurion rested with his men while Lucius walked off alone a short distance to clear his mind. He had been present throughout the drills and given his orders, but for the duration of the exercises his mind had been elsewhere. This was inevitable; the time was approaching and he now concentrated on the oasis.

Valerus had proved a tremendous actor, worthy of a Euripidian play as he convincingly hid his eagerness and his anger. Lucius could see that the young man was intensely vengeful when it came to talk of Antanelis and what had befallen him. He controlled his anger well, but would Alerio? Would he? Lucius wondered if he would be able to. However, it was imperative. *You're a leader, Lucius*, he told himself. *You must stay calm.*

Lucius ordered the cohort to get their gear back on and prepare to leave. They would, he announced through his officers, call a halt early that day as a reward for their outstanding performance. Their final task would be to make camp before they could settle in for the evening. That is what they were told, and there were waves of cheering in response.

When the giant palm and the oasis came into view just ahead of the column, a half mile distant, Lucius made sure that he was riding beside Garai and his century in the middle. As they peaked a large dune, the swaying palm and green expanse stretched out like a fresco before the cohort as the sun was just passing midday.

"Good!" Lucius proclaimed so that Garai could hear him. "Centurion!"

"Yes, Tribune?" answered Garai, his eyes fixed directly ahead. For a second he tripped himself up as he hesitated; something was beginning to gnaw, but he recovered quickly.

"We'll make camp here for the night," Lucius stated.

"But Tribune...we could go on much further today, no?"

"Yes we could, Centurion, but the men have worked hard this morning and they deserve a rest. Besides, that oasis there looks pleasant enough. *He notices it, I know he does!* We could replenish our water supply." Garai's blue eyes looked up at Lucius.

"I'll see to it, Tribune."

"Good. I'll ride ahead and find a suitable area to start digging in." With that, Lucius spurred Lunaris along the ranks until he reached the first century and Alerio. "We'll make camp up ahead."

"Aye..." Alerio smiled, his fist clenched around his vinerod. "Just tell us where to start, Tribune."

The dunes were high and steep-sided in many areas. It was nearly impossible to find a spot that would offer an unimpeded view of the surroundings. Lucius looked about for the highest point possible and finally decided on an area to the west of the oasis where the dunes were smaller and less obtrusive. The men would have to level the ground quite a bit to have the most commanding view. The cohort set itself to the task; with every load of sand, each man glanced eagerly at the green of the oasis, imagined the cool watery respite that lay in wait for them beyond those first trees.

Within a few hours, the uniform camp was laid out and fortified with the ballistae placed at the south and west gates. Pephredo's century was posted to guard duty while the rest of the cohort settled in to cook their evening meals. Lucius took the opportunity to speak privately with Alerio. They sat in the command tent, the arrowheads spread out on the table before them.

"What now?" Alerio asked as he fixed his eyes upon the blood-encrusted barbs.

"Have either Garai, Maren or Eligius said anything to you about being here?"

"Not a word. Business as usual. To be honest, I don't see any sign of recognition from any of them."

"No. But when the oasis first came into view I was with Garai and I definitely spotted something in his behaviour. He recovered himself quickly."

"So what happens now? We really don't have that much time, you know."

"I know, I know. I think in our eagerness to put an end to all this, Alerio, we haven't thought this thing through nearly enough."

"I told you that before, but we've come too far now to stop. We can't stop! Antanelis is out there and he'll be watching." Alerio felt a shiver go down his spine. "How do we go about this?"

"For today, we'll say nothing at all. The men can rest and the guilty parties can stew quietly. For our part, we'll feign ignorance. Tomorrow morning, we'll make our move. Before breaking camp I'll order Eligius' century to remain on guard at camp while I go with you, Garai, Maren and your respective centuries to get water in the oasis. We'll approach from the rock face and then go in to the spring for water. Remember the snakes though! From there, we'll pass through the oasis to that bloody pit. We'll stop, have a curious look, make sure they look."

"What will Valerus and Pephredo's centuries be up to at the time?"

"I'll order them to patrol the surrounding area around us and make sure that Valerus keeps his men close to the giant palm."

"What's going to happen there?"

"Once we're out of the oasis, Garai and Maren's men will practice drills between the oasis and the palm but I'll tell them to ask their optios to see to their men while they come with me to discuss the route back to base. You'll be with me of course."

"Then what?" Alerio had doubts, had countless questions. *This won't work! How are we going to do this?*

"When we reach the bottom of the giant palm, hemmed in by the dunes, private, I'll accuse both of them. From there, it's in the hands of the Gods."

Alerio hung his head in thought, wondered whether the plan was either brilliantly simplistic or utterly naïve. "What about my men? We should keep them close. You know how violently Maren will react."

"I'll take care of Maren."

"But if either his or Garai's men hear a struggle, they might come running to help their centurions."

"True, they might. Then again, they might not. To be safe though, have Claudio drill your own men as close as possible to our position. If you think you can confide in him, then tell him what might occur and that he should keep a watchful eye. If any of Maren or Garai's men make a move to run at us or away, they should apprehend them and bind them."

"Will do." Alerio stood up and put his helmet back on. "By Nemesis, we'll get the bastards!"

"We will."

"I'd better get back to my men, see if I can have a quiet word with Claudio. We can trust him like a Vestal Virgin."

"Good. The watchword for tonight is," he thought for a moment, "gladius."

"*Gladius*. Fitting. Will you be wandering about again tonight?"

"I may." Lucius rose and clasped Alerio's forearm tightly. "Don't worry, my friend. We'll get through this charade and Antanelis will rest easier for it. He's with us in this."

"I know." Alerio nodded with sad certainty as he departed, gripping his gladius in his fist.

The full moon hovered in the heavens, an icy silver and blue, its ethereal splendour seeped into every tent, every cup of water left next to lingering embers. Star and moonlight glistened in the helmets of men on sentry duty as they struggled to stay awake, staring into the distant emptiness. To some, it was almost preferable to be unable to see out in the desert, for when the sky was clear and the dunes lit with the Gods' candles, the world became much more mysterious, foreign and lonely. Each man was silent in his watch and all that could be heard besides the beating of their own hearts or the breath from their lips was the strange song that seemed to come from every star in the firmament. In that place, each man's god was watching him.

In his cot, Lucius turned uncomfortably in his armour. The only things he had removed were his helmet and the sword at his back which lay on the ground next to him. Tears seeped from beneath his lids and he murmured incoherently as images from the beyond danced in his mind like leaves on the autumn wind.

His arm shot out to grab his sword but he realized he had been dreaming. "Gods rid me of these dreams," he said lowly as he wiped his eyes and stood up. It was the middle of the night, a beautiful night at that from the looks of things, as he peered out his tent. Lucius threw his cloak over his shoulders, slung his sword across his back and put on his helmet. As he stepped out of the tent, he startled the guards who had been leaning on their pila next to a small fire.

"At ease, men. I'm just going for a walk. Be back soon."

"Tribune." The men saluted and watched him make his way down the path. "Where's he going?" asked one man.

"I don't know. All's I know is that I wouldn't want to go beyond the defences on a night like this. Look there, I can see his crest moving out of the camp." The trooper pointed to where Lucius walked beyond the titulum and disappeared into the dark.

"What in Hades is Lucius doing walking about?" wondered Garai as he and Maren sat in his tent, looking out.

"Who cares? You know how he is, Garai."

"And what the bloody hell are we doing in this place? How did we end up here?"

"Would you shut your fucking mouth about it! It's pure chance that's led us here, that's all. It's only natural he'd pick camp next to an oasis during the march so that the men have fresh water. It's the bloody desert!"

"You watch yourself! I'm not one of your slap around whores, Maren. I'm just concerned. We killed him here, the

Gods know it! Of all the places we could pass by, we pass here. Something's not right."

"You have to calm yourself. Don't be a fool! They suspect nothing! They know nothing! Lucius wasn't even here and Alerio's not as smart as he looks. We did what Argus asked us to do. Antanelis was going to report what he heard us saying about Argus getting rid of Lucius. If Antanelis had said anything…" Maren's voice was now a low, angry whisper, "we'd have been crucified where the vultures could peck out our eyes and tongues. Does that sound better to you?"

"Of course not! I'm just saying-"

"No! Don't say anything. Don't do anything. Tomorrow we'll break camp after drills and be on our way and never see this place again."

"You'd better be right about that, Maren."

"I am. Now go back to your own bloody tent so I can get some sleep. Let Lucius walk about as he chooses."

"Garai poked his head out of the tent to ensure that no one was watching and picked his way carefully back to his tent at the end of the rows occupied by his century.

Lucius stopped beneath the giant palm, and leaned up against its massive trunk, the base of which was bathed in cold light. The stars flickered about the moon and he sighed out loud trying to chase away the images he had dreamt: Antanelis' pained expression in the darkness of the pit, his bloody teeth gritted against the pain of gruesome death. The lion's cries as it was riddled with arrows by the men looming over them, weaker men bent on destroying two titans.

The images haunted Lucius and he fell to his knees in the sand. He called out to Apollo who had come to him in that place. The air was still.

"All you Gods of the Pantheon," he whispered. "I honour you. I honour my ancestors and the blood in my veins. Give me strength tomorrow." Lucius did not know what else to say. He was at a loss for words, he had said all there was to say up to that point. Now, his feelings were his prayers; his actions would be his offerings. With his hand, he felt the dragon upon his chest, searched for that inner strength and mastery of self that he knew dwelled within.

His mind drifted back to the days of soaring eagles and omens, of love and of wars. He thought of cool breezes upon his neck and glimpses of earthly goddesses. Black pathways and murder, sandstorms and uneasy peace…what did it all mean? What purpose did his life serve? Too much had happened for it to end there, at the edge of an oasis in the deep desert.

A star glowed brighter than all the others then, in the heavens, a red star that drew in Lucius' eye and mind. He thought of the cave at Cumae, of broken words and riddles, *The Avenger is a harsh judge…Eagles and Dragons…* Lucius shook his head. If he did not keep his wits, things would go ill. They were watching from beyond, all of them, from the slopes of the sacred mountain, from across the black waters. They would be watching…judging. The stage was set, and one way or another, there would be an outcome.

Dawn broke into the world with a solemn light that morning. The stars were gone and the full moon faded into the sky. Balbus blew a series of long and lonely notes on the cornu as he stood outside Lucius' tent beneath the vexillum. The dragon banner fluttered in the kissing breeze, its ornate hangings jingling as they swayed.

Frontus, the paws of his leopard hide tied neatly across his chest, had already harnessed and fed Lunaris who awaited his master, patiently eating his morning oats. When the cornu had sounded, Lucius had just roused himself. In the pit of his stomach he felt a tightness; it would not be possible to forget what day this was. He splashed some water from a small basin on his face and neck before nibbling at some dried bread dipped in watered wine, dates and nuts. He was not hungry;

the need or want of food quit his body. When he had finished, he put on his cloak, sword and helmet and went outside.

"Good morning, Balbus, Frontus." The two men immediately stood to attention and saluted.

"Sir!" they said in unison.

"Has Centurion Alerio been by yet?"

"Yes, sir, he has," answered Balbus. "He said that he would go around the camp to give the morning's orders. Told us to tell you that when you awoke."

"Fine." Lucius took a deep breath of the desert air.

"Sir?" asked Frontus.

"Yes?"

"What *are* the orders today, sir? Centurion Alerio said that we're not breaking camp right away."

"That's right. I want to take advantage of the good weather while we're out here and have the men drill some more. We also need to collect water for the return journey." He removed the feed bag from Lunaris' head and stroked his soft muzzle. "And how are you this morning?" The stallion prodded Lucius in the side and neighed loudly. "Eager to get going are you? Ha, ha. Good boy, always ready." Lucius turned to the cornicen. "Balbus, sound the assembly in half an hour."

"Yes, Tribune."

"You'll remain in the camp for the morning with Centurion Eligius and his men. Frontus?" Lucius turned to his standard bearer.

"Yes sir?" The vexillarius moved to Lucius' side as he mounted Lunaris.

"Meet me with the standard outside the eastern gate when Balbus sounds the cornu. I want you to stay close to me at all times today."

"Of course, Tribune. I'll be there."

"See you then." Lucius instantly set off on Lunaris to find Alerio. Men saluted him all along the rows of tents in the golden light of early morning.

The troops wondered slightly at the odd order of things that morning, but for the most part, it was dismissed. The majority were content to stay where they were; drilling, rather than returning to base where they would probably be conscripted to build yet another length of road, raise another bath house or escort some officer's wife to Thamugadi for shopping. The day was fine, not too hot, and the sun was shining between softly broken clouds that added to the beauty of the sky.

Once Eligius' century was posted at the camp and Valerus and Pephredo's men had begun their perimeter march of the area, Lucius led the remaining three centuries to the oasis to search, he said, for water and any animals they could find for food. Alerio's heart rose in his throat as the dark oasis came into view and they came to a halt in front of the rock face.

"I want each century to cover a different area of the oasis. Keep your swords drawn, and when you find water, fill up both your water skins!" Lucius cantered in front of the three centuries where they formed up, giving his orders. "Look out for snakes or lions too, lads. You never know! Centurions, you'll stay with me." Lucius looked down at Alerio, Garai and Maren. "All right, set them to it and come back here."

The centurions began yelling their orders for the men to form up into individual contubernia with their tent mates before moving into the darkness of the oasis. Meanwhile, Lucius waited in front of the rock face peering down at the blood stain that was now very faint indeed. When the three men returned to find Lucius gazing down at that spot, there was no reaction, only silence as they waited for him to speak.

"Odd place this is," he said absently. "I suppose we should go in with them." From within, they could hear faint yells of surprise and then the swing of swords as men stumbled upon the area of snakes that lay near the spring. "Sounds like they might have found something."

"Don't you think, Lucius, that we ought to go in there and be with our men instead of lingering out here?" Maren's words were sarcastic and biting.

Lucius looked down at him, reassured by the weight of the sword on his back.

"We'll go in together, Maren, and have a look for ourselves. The men will be fine."

"Lucius, you've been acting strangely lately."

"Have I, Garai?" Lucius shrugged his heavy shoulders. "Just a lot on my mind lately is all, you know: duty to Rome, one's office, one's friends, that sort of thing. Come on, let's go in toward the southern end of this forest where the men haven't yet been."

Lucius walked on. Lunaris was jumping, impatient at their slow progression. Alerio, Maren and Garai walked to his side, all of them silent. Shortly after they cut inward, Lucius dismounted and led his horse by the reins.

"Dark in here," muttered Alerio. "Like some kind of tomb."

"You've always been so superstitious, Alerio," chided Maren, who was unaware of the wrath that Alerio had at that moment.

It took Alerio all of his strength and will to stop himself from reaching out and lacing his fingers about Maren's neck and squeezing. All he could see was Antanelis' face when they had brought his body back to base. All he could hear, as they walked beneath the canopy of palm leaves to the pit, were the cries of his friend in the final moments of his life as the lion mauled him. They were deafening.

Through the foliage they could see groups of troopers picking their careful way to the spring. Lucius looked back to see his vexillarius following closely behind them, the banner hoisted in one hand, his sword drawn with the other. Frontus hated snakes.

"What's that over there?" Lucius suddenly asked as he surged forward with Lunaris following. Garai's blue eyes shot wide with fear and Maren slapped him harshly on the back.

"Scared of a few snakes, Garai? Ha, ha. You're like that pipsqueak Valerus."

"Bugger off, Maren!" Garai grumbled and shot him a worried look.

"Shut up, both of you!" barked Alerio. "Lucius seems to have found something." Alerio pointed to where Lucius stood next to a broken cart that seemed to have had a cage on top. The tribune's arms were crossed; his features were dark and half-hidden by the cheek guards of his helmet. He stared into the blackness of the pit where only a few stray rays of sun penetrated the bottom.

Garai stopped in his tracks but Maren continued to Lucius' side with his sword still drawn. Alerio stopped next to Garai but kept his eye on Maren.

"Garai? What's the matter with you?" Lucius called. "It's just a big black hole." Garai forced himself to walk, though the last place he wanted to be was standing above that pit. He began to shake, tried to hide it. He thought of that hunting expedition when they had planned to take Antanelis out into the desert, confront him, and then...

His guilt and torment were too much for him and he seemed to weep as he remembered something. That something was the twang of his bowstring and the thud when the arrow's barbed head penetrated Antanelis' flesh. He remembered Maren laughing as the younger man cursed them just before they released the lion. It was all too clear, fresh, and bloody in his mind. He had offended the Gods and knew they would not allow him to get away with his actions.

Maren, on the other hand, had hidden his guilt well. He was proud of it, defiant in the way he stood directly above the blackness below. Lucius wanted to push him in there, leave him for dead, but knew that he needed more. Maren had not shown the least amount of emotion.

"Looks like there are some bones down there. Look." Lucius pointed to the lion bones at the bottom where they were spotted with sunlight.

"Aye, so?" Maren answered as Garai approached hesitantly, Alerio behind him.

"Seems some bastards had some fun torturing this poor beast," Alerio put in. Garai's head whipped around. "Gods know what else they did here. Savages! Probably some nomads feeding babies to the beast. What do you think, Maren?"

"I really don't care, Alerio." Maren turned his fierce eyes on him. "Fact is, we're wasting time here touring the oasis when we should be tending to our men and back on drills."

"There'll be time enough for that later," Lucius interjected. "Maren, I'll lower you down there so you can get a better look. Here, I've got some rope on my saddle."

"I'm not going in that hole, Lucius!" Maren spat and frustration coloured his face. "Go yourself if you want to."

"Come now, Maren." Lucius put his hand on Maren's back and the centurion instantly levelled his gladius. But he pulled it back quickly. "Ease up and sheathe that sword before you make a mistake, Centurion." Lucius forced a smile. "I'm just joking with you."

"I'm getting out of here!" Garai pushed his way past the three others to the edge of the oasis and vomited.

"Wonder what's wrong with him?" Alerio asked. "Garai! You all right?"

"I guess he doesn't want to go in there either," Lucius said to Maren, nodding at the pit.

"You're both out of your fucking minds!" Maren hissed as he followed Garai.

Lucius nodded to Alerio. It seemed they had some sort of proof after all. It was time to confront them.

"Centurions!" Lucius yelled after the two men who stood conversing in whispers on the edge of the oasis where the sand began. "Go order your troops to drill over there!" Lucius pointed to the area between the oasis and the great palm. "Have your signifers lead the drills. I want to have a word with you." Garai and Maren looked over at Lucius angrily as he rode out of the oasis on Lunaris, towering above them. "Get to it!" Lucius looked as the two men walked along the edge of the oasis to where their centuries awaited them with their full water skins. Alerio walked the shorter distance to where Claudio stood at attention with his men; he had already briefed his signifer secretly on what would transpire. Claudio nodded when he saw his centurion give him the signal to move to the area where they were to drill.

Lucius looked to the south-west and spotted the dust rising from Valerus' century where they came to a stop just west of the giant palm. Pephredo, he knew, must have been patrolling his designated area on the eastern side of the oasis. Lucius led his mount to the top of the largest dune overlooking the area at the base of the palm whose branches rustled in the increasing breeze. Frontus made sure to stay close, and hold the vexillum high to be spotted from any point. Garai and Maren's centuries came to a halt a short distance away where they left them in charge of the signifers Gratian and Camilo. The troops seemed confused by this order but went about their business nonetheless. The signifers kept a watchful eye on their respective centurions as they made their way to the tribune.

"Frontus, you stay up here for now." He then looked at Garai and Maren. "Right. Let's go to the bottom here," began Lucius, "where we can stand in the shade." He made his way down the steep slope, the two men following, each looking at the other questioningly.

"What's this about?" whispered Garai.

"Don't know," Maren gripped his sword. "Just be ready. I don't trust him."

"Ah, beautiful day isn't it?" Lucius dismounted and led Lunaris to the other side of the palm. "Sit down if you like, *friends*, we need to talk." Lucius paced slowly, and Alerio stood stock-still, staring at the two of them.

"We'll stand thanks," Garai muttered. "What did you want, Lucius?"

Lucius stopped in front of them. He was happy to see their backs were to the steepest slope of the dune. His armour glinted, sending malformed reflections in every direction. He sighed an unhappy sigh, then spoke.

"Do you remember when we first set out from Alexandria on that patrol?"

"Yeah, what of it? That was a long time ago, Lucius." Maren's voice was defensive, uncaring.

"Longer than you think, I suppose." He was now staring at both of them. "Those were good times. We'd all been newly promoted, all friends; us four and Eligius, Argus…and Antanelis." He paused, looked down at the sand, and then up at the tree. "Argus and I have parted ways and I'm not sorry to say that. He changed for the worse but then again, you two would know that since you keep in contact with him. Don't speak!" Lucius held up a hand. "That's fine if you want to remain friends with him, it's your prerogative. He was a traitor to his brothers, his friends, and he left his men behind…that was his prerogative."

"He might say the same of you," Maren said.

"Aye. That he would, I'm sure of it. Truth is, I don't care about him. He's a coward, riddled with jealousy because he was never good enough. He'd stab a friend in the back if it meant his path would be made a little easier."

"I'd like to see you say that to his face, *Tribune*." Garai looked in horror at Maren as he challenged Lucius who ignored him for the moment.

"Garai, what would you say of a man who betrays his friends, his brothers?"

"I…I…I wouldn't know about that."

"But you write to Argus? You must have some insight, no?" Garai said nothing but Maren did.

"What are you trying to say?"

"I'm saying that I miss one of my truest friends. You remember Antanelis don't you? Of course you do." Lucius moved closer. "Antanelis was the best among us, don't you think? Maren?"

"He was a kiss-ass kid. Nothing more."

"He could have bested either of you in a fair fight!" Alerio spoke for the first time.

"Yes but," Lucius held him fast, "the fact is that his life was cut unfairly short." He eyed the two men harshly. "Do you recognise this place we're in?"

"Yes," Maren admitted. "It's where we were hunting when Antanelis was attacked by the lion."

"Ah yes. The lion. I remember reading your report when I returned from Rome. It said something about Antanelis charging after the lion and being thrown from his horse onto some rocks at the base of a giant palm outside the oasis before the lion mauled him." Lucius looked at the ground about them and shook his head. "To be honest, my friends, I don't see any rocks at all."

"Maybe this is the wrong oasis?" Garai offered meekly.

"But Maren just said with certainty that this was the exact one." Nobody said anything and Lucius continued. Alerio wondered how far he was going to go with it and realised that he wanted them to make a move first. "Did you know Antanelis wrote to his father just before he died? He did, you know. Did you also know I paid a visit to his parents back home to pay my respects and hand over his belongings to them? Well, I don't need to tell you that they were very kind and that their hearts were broken when I told them about their son. At any rate, before I left, Antanelis' father told me that his son wrote to him about treachery within the cohort and ill feelings toward me! I was shocked to say the least, and when I returned to base all those months later, Alerio and I took a little trip into the desert and ended up right here." Lucius stopped talking then. He let the silence sink in while he decided what he would say next.

"Alerio and I found that pit we were just looking at…found some disturbing things in there. Aside from lion bones, we found this," Lucius held up the bloodied part of Antanelis' cloak, "and these." He nodded to Alerio who threw the arrowheads onto the ground.

"What are those supposed to be?" Maren scoffed.

"We found those in the pit with this piece of cloak. Antanelis had a cloak like this, didn't he?" They said nothing. "We found these along with the lion bones and that cage that might well have held a lion. Interesting isn't it? I suspect, *friends*, that you saw the pit in that oasis before too."

Lucius' heart was pounding faster than lightening and he thought he would pass out but for the swelling anger. Alerio stepped to his side, ready.

"Why did you do it?" Lucius asked, almost pleadingly. "Why did you kill Antanelis?"

"It wasn't our idea, Lucius, it was-"

"Shut up, Garai! We don't have to stay here and listen to this shit!"

"I'm afraid you do!" Lucius rose to his full height; he was taller than any of them. "I accuse you of cowardice, of treason and treachery! I accuse you of murder! Both of you!" There was an intense silence in that moment as eyes flashed side to side, assessing, waiting for someone to move.

The first action came from Garai who ran toward Lunaris and jumped into the saddle to spur the stallion up the steep slope. Lucius turned to run after him and called out the stallion's name. Hearing his master call, Lunaris reared at the top of the slope sending Garai head over heels behind the saddle into the sand at the top of the dune. Maren saw his chance; he drew his gladius and dove for Lucius' back but Alerio slammed into him in mid-air and the two centurions fell into a heap of sand and dust, their deadly blades stabbing sporadically at each other.

Lucius called out to Frontus to signal Claudio where he stood with Alerio's century and the group came running. Seeing this and suspecting foul play, Garai and Maren's signifers ordered their men to move toward the palm.

"Garai! It's over! You can't go anywhere now!" Lucius drew the long sword from his back and levelled it at him. Meanwhile, on the ground at the base of the palm, Alerio and

Maren were locked in single combat, like a god and a giant - each strong and hateful of the other.

"Ahhh!" Alerio dodged one of Maren's stabbing blades but received the tip of his dagger on the cheek. Maren smiled and lunged again but Alerio charged first before Maren's blade could close fast enough and butted his face with the forefront of his helmet. Maren flew backwards, blood flowing down his chest.

"Garai, put that sword down! You don't want to fight me!" Lucius shifted his stance to face his opponent but the sun was in his eyes. Everything seemed to happen at once. Just as the three centuries arrived to see the fighting going on from above, there was a mass of yelling, most of it for the tribune. The men gawped in awe as their officers fought. Garai and Maren's signifers turned and ran for the oasis along with four other men. Seeing this, Claudio ordered half his century to pursue them.

From the camp, the sound of Balbus' cornu rang out the alarm. Lucius turned to look back briefly at the scene. When Garai ran at him, he sidestepped and tripped his attacker sending him face first into the sand.

"Move and I'll kill you!" Lucius put the point of his sword to Garai's neck. He looked down to see Alerio stumbling against the tree and Maren coming at him with a deadly swing. "Alerio!" he yelled as his friend parried the blow with what strength remained in his limbs and grabbed hold of Maren's neck. The rest of Maren's men did nothing to help their centurion, and neither did Garai's.

Alerio's golden eyes burned with a fire that told of long-held fury, prayers to Nemesis and endless nightmares in the dark. He burned with rage as he squeezed. Maren's sword fell to the ground, his eyes rolling back in his head. "Alive Alerio! Keep him ali-!" Lucius yelled down but was cut short. Several of the troops on the opposite dune fell flat in an explosion of blood. The cornu sounded louder, more desperate in the distance. A hissing sound passed by Lucius' ear and he felt the flesh of his left arm tear loudly, sending him reeling down the steep slope of sand to the bottom of the palm.

"ATTACK! ATTACK!" The words stirred Lucius as he heard Alerio's voice and an arm pulling him up. "Lucius! We're under attack!" The tribune opened his eyes to see arrows hissing by and a dust cloud created by hundreds of horsemen. "Garamantians! Claudio! Get the men formed up!" Alerio was giving commands from Lucius' side. "Lucius! Get up!"

"Where's Lunaris? Lunaris!" Lucius called. The stallion came running down the slope of the dune to their side. "Alerio, help me up!" Alerio hefted Lucius onto his mount's back and handed him the sword he had dropped. The arrows continued to hiss and from their terrible position, Lucius could see that Claudio's men were attacked on all sides. The only thing keeping them alive were their locked shields. "Alerio! You're in command of them." Lucius pointed to Garai and Maren's men. "Have some of them guard Maren while you see if you can lure the riders closer to the ballistae."

"What about you?"

"I'll be fine. Frontus stays with Claudio! Where's Valerus?" Lucius charged to the top of the dune to see Valerus' century surrounded on all sides. "By the Gods! Where'd the bastards come from?" Lucius felt the blood trickling down his arm as another stray arrow deflected off of his cuirass. "Mars! This day is yours!" he yelled as he charged in to get closer to the horse archers and take them down at the gallop before they annihilated his cohort.

The enemy had come from four directions. Claudio tried to push his men to the top of the sand dune above the tree so that their backs would be more protected, while the two centuries Alerio had taken command of began to surge forward in a testudo to the edge of the camp where Eligius watched panic-stricken from the southern gate.

"Ballistae!" Eligius commanded.

"Sir! We have to go out and help them!" Balbus yelled.

"No! We can't leave the camp undefended. Sound the order to reinforce the gates! Any man with a bow to the ramparts now!"

Back at the base of the palm, eight men had tied Maren to the tree and stood guard. They were pinned down. At the top of the dune, Garai crawled on his hands and knees and made to run when one of the troops at the palm ran to apprehend him. Garai turned and plunged his dagger into the trooper's belly, beneath his lorica, and ran in the direction of a horse that had thrown its rider. He pulled himself into the saddle and charged away, swerving in and out of the attacking enemy until he started to pull away from the action. As he rode south of the oasis, Pephredo's century rounded the southern edge.

"Garai!" Pephredo yelled, but Garai charged on and on, never looking back. "Forget'em! Testudo! Forward at the run men!" the young centurion yelled as they rushed to help their comrades.

Mars' bloody fist pounded the earth on which the battle took place, unrelenting, until the sand was laced with crimson rivers about the cohort's formations. Lucius fought alone, out in the open against ten riders of the enemy. Lunaris' silver coat was clotted with blood as he charged about and the men watched as their tribune's sword piled up bodies. Many men there wanted to run to fight at his side. The Gods were with him in his struggle but he was still outnumbered.

The losses on the Roman side were heavy and they were pinned down, separated, having been taken unawares. The ballistae had done some damage but not nearly enough to slow the enemy substantially. Lucius attacked where he could to help his men, but he was only one, charging vainly like a winged fury, his war cry heard all over.

He managed to reach Claudio and ordered him to attempt to form up with Pephredo and Valerus so they could stand back to back behind a wall of shields. After heavy fighting they managed to do so. Lucius, with fresh wounds to his legs and arms, spotted enemy horsemen riding to the base of the palm where the few men had been set to guard Maren.

He charged as fast as Lunaris could carry him across the sand hoping that they had not all been slaughtered. When he crested the topmost dune, a heavy bowshot to his chest knocked him into the air. All he could see as the world spun and howled about him was Adara's face, and all he could hear was his whirling prayer to the Gods, unsure of whether the next blow would end it all. He stumbled to his feet just as one nomad charged him. He drew his gladius and, in the same upward motion, drove the point under the attacker's chin where it lodged. Several paces away he spotted his golden-hilted sword and ran to grab it.

Several horsemen spotted him standing alone, while the remainder of his fellows at the base of the palm fought off others in a desperate last stand. The horsemen charged at Lucius, now alone and on foot. Time seemed to stop and the clash of battle turned to the Gods' cursing in the wind. They came faster, closer, but all was quiet. Was that what happened in the moments before death? Lucius blinked, blood dripping from his forehead where his helmet had dug in.

Then a loud ringing reached his pounding ears.

The sky was blue and cloudless above and yet the sound of thunder rang loud and clear. A piercing howl shattered the air, war cries echoed across the bloody sand, and the long, flowing standard of a magnificent dragon cut through the enemy like a ship through the sea. In a deadly, unstoppable wave of four arrowhead formations, the Sarmatian cavalry broke the enemy's onslaught, their scales awash in blood and offal as they harried the nomad cavalry like harpies.

From the arm of Mars himself, four spears seemed to ride upon swift winds to impale Lucius' four attackers as they were thrown and hacked by the passing horsemen.

"Anguis!" a voice called behind him. Lucius spun, his sword up to see two riders and the flowing banner held high.

Their faces were masked and lifeless, but then the standard bearer lifted his visor.

"Dagon!" Lucius cried out. The young man, beaded with sweat, smiled broadly.

"Mount up, Anguis. We've got them!"

"Lunaris!" Lucius called out fearfully. "Lunaris!" Then beyond the palm he spotted the silver stallion, his shanks painted red, charging toward his master. As he passed, Lucius grabbed hold of the saddle horns and leaped up. Dagon rejoined his formation and the howling of the dragon standard resumed, sending the enemy into a fearful flight.

The men at the palm were losing fast and Maren, tied to the tree, now struggled to free himself. As they were about to be overwhelmed, Lucius charged down the slope of the dune and clashed with the three riders there, struggling to give his men a fighting chance. When they saw the opportunity, the five remaining men leapt to their commander's aid. They pulled the riders from their saddles and killed them.

Lucius rode back up the slope to see how the battle fared with the rest of the cohort. Several small fires burned in the encampment and many Roman bodies lay about the sand. But for the most part, the enemy was either defeated or on the run being pursued by the Sarmatian cavalry, cut down to the last man.

"Hail, Metellus! Hail!" came a cry that began small, and then grew louder and louder like a roiling wave that begins far out to sea before crashing on the unsuspecting shore. "Hail Metellus! Hail!" Lucius turned to see the remainder of his men cheering. To his left, several Sarmatian riders approached now and the men quieted. Lucius rode to meet them and stopped as the commander removed his helmet.

"Four units pursue the rest before they get away. Report back when you have them."

"Lord Mar!" Lucius exclaimed, his breath heavy. "Your timing was well met."

"Tribune." Mar rode to Lucius' side and reached out to steady him. "You have a victory."

"Nonsense, Commander. The victory is yours." Lucius sheathed his sword at his back and wiped the blood from his face. "If you hadn't arrived when you did, I'd be lying dead in the sand."

"It is not your time yet. Your god of war is appeased, it seems, and has decided to allow you to live. For my part, I have seen today a desperate stand worthy of the greatest Sarmatian warrior. Your men performed bravely and held the enemy until our arrival."

"Lucius!" Alerio came running over to his friend's side.

"Thank the Gods you're alive, Alerio."

"Thank you Mar, Dagon." Alerio nodded his head thankfully.

"I think, Centurion," Mar said, "that you should get the tribune to his quarters for care. He's lost a lot of blood."

"Lucius, he's right. Come this way. Commander. You're welcome to station your men here. I'll come to you later."

"Very well, Centurion." Mar motioned to one of his riders. "My physician will go with you to care for our young dragon. He fought well." The physician followed Lucius and Alerio as they passed between the ranks of men. All of them saluted Lucius, cheering as he passed, bloody and half-conscious.

XVI

CONSECUTIONES PERDUELLIONIS

'The Consequences of Treason'

Two days had passed. Two days in which the winds took their rest, in which the hoary gloom of violence and death dissipated from the dunes and returned once more to Hades. A sorrowful silence settled instead on the cohort's camp as the troops made every attempt to cleanse themselves of the Gods' fury, and their fallen comrades' blood.

While the wounded fought off impending death or slept to regain some measure of strength, the living laid the shades of the dead to rest through offerings and prayers. Men who did not usually pray, fell to their knees when they were alone at night, calling out to gods they had long neglected; men who habitually offered prayers, prayed twice as much. All this transpired as the flames of massive byres rose to the starlit sky, engulfing the bodies of dead Romans placed upon the Gods' altar, their payment for the Boatman inside their silent mouths.

In the command tent, upon a cot, Lucius Metellus Anguis lay sleeping, dreaming of the faces he longed to see again, of the gods who had never left his side and of those who had allowed him to go on living. But, even from the brink of the black waters that lapped at his feet, he had to fight back to the world outside. As he shook in fevered slumber, muttering, his truest friend leaned over him, only leaving his side when the physician appeared so that he might see to other matters. The embers on the sand outside the camp were dying down and Lucius awoke to see Alerio sitting next to his cot, smiling.

"Alerio?" He reached for his friend's hand. "You don't look so good," Lucius said lightly, seeing the black and swollen eye that protruded from Alerio's face.

"You should see yourself," he chuckled. "How do you feel?"

"I don't know. Weak? Hungry? How long have I been here?"

"You've been sleeping for two days."

"Two days!" Lucius tried to prop himself up but the pain was too much for him to do it on his own. Alerio helped him get his feet over the edge of the cot.

"You have to take it easy, Lucius. Don't move too abruptly or else the stitches and staples holding your wounds together will split." Lucius winced as he felt intense pain on his left arm, both thighs and his forehead. He held up his hands to look at the cuts on top, his ring was still there.

"So we're still at the oasis?"

"Yes. There's no way we could have left here. Too many wounded."

"How many?"

"We'll meet with the others later. For now, you really need to rest. Shall I get you some food?"

"Sounds good. Thanks. After that though, I want to go and see the men."

"Fine. If you're up to it." Alerio stood up. "I'll be right back."

Lucius sat there waiting, hesitant to rise in case his legs could not hold him. Minutes later, Alerio returned with some bread and a bowl of odd smelling broth that the physician had told him to give Lucius once he woke up.

"Whoa! This stuff stinks of feet." Lucius' nose retreated from the steaming bowl.

"Yup. It does indeed, but the physician says it'll speed your recovery. You should regain enough strength to walk one hour after drinking it."

"One hour?"

"That's what he said. Go on, eat up while I get you some clothes." Alerio went over to the other side of the tent where Lucius' newly washed tunic had been hung to dry along with his knee breeches. "You can still wear your boots; good thing you had your greaves on or else your legs would have been hacked to bits by those whoresons."

"You're probably right." Lucius shook his head, as he finished the last of the broth and bread. "Sorry, my head is spinning with questions right now, Alerio."

"I know. But I'll tell you everything in time."

"How are the men, first of all?"

"Well, we had a lot of losses and so, naturally, morale has been a little low. They've been asking after you though. In every century there is concern for you and wishes for your recovery."

"Hmm." Lucius remembered hearing cheering; the last thing he remembered before everything went dark. "And what about you, my friend? How are you?"

"I'm fine. Can't see out of this puffy eye right now but the physician says my sight will return as the swelling goes down. I'm just glad it's all over. Glad to see you awake."

"Me too. Although I would have preferred waking up to my wife's face rather than your ugly mug."

"Poor substitute, I know. You'll see her soon enough."

"Are the Sarmatians still here?"

"Yes. They've put up their camp next to ours. They've been an enormous help and the men have come to admire them greatly. After all, you, Mar and Dagon are the heroes of the hour."

Lucius looked down at the floor as a terrible thought broke into his mind. "Lunaris was wounded I think. Is he…I mean did you have to…"

"Don't worry, he's fine and on the mend in Mar's camp. The Sarmatians know a hell of a lot about horses. He had a gash on his left shank but it'll heal well. You'll be able to ride him in a couple of days."

"Good. Good. Here, can you help me with my tunic?" Alerio helped Lucius to pull his tunic down over his head, minding his arm in the sleeves, and then helped him get each leg into his breeches before tying the laces of his boots for him.

"You sure you want to try to walk so soon?"

"I really should get out to see the men and take stock of everything. Besides, I think that foul smelling broth really is working. I just need you to help me get up and find my feet again."

"All right, here we go." Alerio helped Lucius to his feet holding him by his right arm to steady him. The ground felt oddly foreign but his legs held him up. He took several slow steps around the tent.

"That feels fine. Good. Just stay by my side in case I start to keel over."

"Always."

Lucius looked around the tent for his armour and spotted it in a corner, cleaned and polished, free of any trace of blood. The sword Adara gave him hung next to his spatha and his gladius; the latter had been retrieved from the body of a dead Garamantian on the field. As they moved to the tent flaps and spread them wide, the sunlight blinded Lucius momentarily and he had to stop so that his eyes could adjust. With his other arm, he gripped the shaft of his vexillum.

"Good to see you well, Tribune." Balbus saluted Lucius and smiled.

"Thank you, Balbus. Are you well?"

"Yes, sir."

"Good." Lucius turned to Alerio. "Where's Frontus?"

"He's in the infirmary."

"Is it bad?"

"He's lost an eye. Broken spear tip punctured it."

"Damn."

"He'll be fine besides. Tough bastard continued to hold up the banner even after he lost his eye."

"That's Frontus. I'd like to go to the infirmary before we start getting down to business."

"Right. It's over near the west gate." Alerio held Lucius' arm as he moved into the tent rows; the sight that met him stirred something wonderful within. Despite all the pain and loss, each contuburnium of men stood outside their individual tents and saluted Lucius as he passed. He asked the men how they were, looked them in the eye and offered his thanks for their hard-fought battle.

Eventually, Lucius was able to walk unaided, though Alerio stayed close. Many a man that saw him was humbled at the strength he was showing, especially considering the wounds he had sustained and the blood he had lost; blood they had all seen at the end of the battle as he rode past them back to camp. They had all seen him fall from his horse when he had fainted; the wounds appeared horrific.

The infirmary had had to be enlarged in order to accommodate all the casualties after the battle. As Lucius and Alerio approached the entrance, the sound of moaning could be heard from within. Before going through the tent flaps, Lucius paused to catch his breath.

There were about forty men laid out in four long rows upon campaign mats cushioned by the soft sand. Rays of intermittent sunlight lit the area where they had been treated by the Sarmatian physician who stood at the far end examining one man. He was tall and thin and wore a long robe stained with blood. When Lucius and Alerio entered and he spotted them, he finished changing the soldier's dressing and walked slowly to meet them.

"Biton," Alerio greeted the man as he approached. "The tribune has found his strength thanks to your interesting broth."

The physician's gaze was removed and academic, fixed intently on his patient and the wounds that were visible to him. After a moment, he looked up, and a thin, subtle smile crossed his mouth.

"You should recover quickly, Tribune. None of the wounds have become infected."

"I am in your debt, Biton. Thank you for your aid to me and my men." The physician held up a hand in protest.

"You owe me nothing, Tribune. It is my duty, my oath as a healer that I remain true to."

"Nevertheless, you have my personal thanks and gratitude," Lucius insisted. Biton bowed his head. "How are the rest of my men doing?"

"These men here will pull through. Some of them have severe wounds that will take time, but they will mend. The shock of the whole ordeal is what seems to have been the most difficult obstacle. There were others here two days ago but…it was not their time to live."

"I understand." Lucius looked at the faces of those before him; he recognised several and moved along the rows to speak to those who were awake. Some of the men spoke, others nodded or groaned in pain but they were alive. Lucius reached out to many of them, gave others water to drink from skins. To his amazement some of them even asked how he was feeling, even though he was much better off than they were.

At the far end where the physician had been when Lucius and Alerio had first come in, Lucius spotted Frontus. Half of his face was hidden behind bandages. When he heard Lucius' voice nearby his head turned slightly in that direction but he could not see him for the bandages and the drainage that seeped from his hollow socket. Lucius moved to a position where the man could at least see his outline.

"Frontus. Thank the Gods you're alive."

"Tribune," he replied. "I thought we'd lost you."

"No. I'm still here, as are you." Lucius wanted to kneel down at his side but he knew that if he did his wounds might rip open. He stood closer, wondering if he should acknowledge the man's wound or not. Some men preferred to ignore such things, to feel as though life were the same. Losing a finger or hand was one thing but to lose an eye, to be robbed of the full measure of beauty that still existed in the world, was quite another.

"I'm sorry you lost your eye," Lucius said finally.

"Me too, Tribune. But, at least I still have the other." Frontus managed an optimistic smile behind the strings of bandage that crossed over his face.

"True. For now, get your rest. The standard will be awaiting you when you're ready."

"Thank you, Tribune." Lucius backed away and turned to Alerio.

"Alerio, let's leave these men to get some rest." The two of them walked out of the tent again into the sunlight. "I want to meet with the centurions, Mar, and Dagon, to discuss the situation. I need to know what's been happening. Where are they?"

"They're probably in the Sarmatian camp. We've been meeting there so that you could rest in peace in the command tent. It's a bit of a walk though."

"That's fine. I can make it. I also want to see Lunaris. I'll wait at the gate while you tell the others about the meeting."

"All right, Lucius, but there's one thing you should be prepared for."

"What's that?"

"Eligius. He's in quite a state and has been demanding to speak with you. I've had to try very hard to keep him away."

"I'll deal with it. Have him come a little later so I can speak with the others first. Go now, I'll wait for you."

As Alerio went to notify his fellow centurions of the assembly, Lucius made the short walk to the southern gate of the fort and waited just on the outside of the ramparts. He looked out over the dunes between the camp and the oasis and saw where the charred remains of the byres had blackened the sand. Soon the desert would claim the remains, and the blood that had spilled would be swallowed as though nothing had transpired.

He spotted the Sarmatian camp made up of several tents behind a ditch and rampart, along with rows of horses where they were hobbled or tied to cut boughs taken from the oasis. The smoke from several cooking fires rose up. In the centre of the camp was a tent larger than all the rest - Mar's tent. Lucius assumed that was where they would meet.

"Ready, Tribune." Alerio returned, using Lucius' title in front of the sentries. "Valerus, Pephredo and Eligius will meet us there."

"Good. Let's go." Lucius began to walk, negotiating the softer, uneven sand of the area outside the camp. In several spots before the gates the sand was pocked with areas of red and pink where blood had been spilled. Little did he realize that much of it, leading to the gate, was his own.

In the distance surrounding their immediate position, Lucius could see the dust rising where riders patrolled the area constantly, day and night. Mar, Alerio had told him, had ordered groups of three six-man squadrons to patrol the area to avoid any other unwelcome surprise attacks of retribution, if any of the nomads had lived out the day of battle.

When they arrived at the Sarmatian camp, Lucius was received with great respect and a sense of equality that the Sarmatians were not prone to bestow with any ease. The two Romans were ushered into the main tent where a small fire burned in the middle, beneath a hole in the roof that allowed the smoke to escape. Beyond the fire was a chair raised on a mound of packed sand. The chair, Lucius noticed, was more like a throne of some sort, one that apparently came apart in sections of plank that fit together like a puzzle. Two guards entered the tent and held the flaps open as Mar and Dagon entered.

"Tribune!" Mar actually smiled, which stretched the creases on his aging face. "I am most pleased to see you up and doing well." Behind Mar, Dagon stood smiling broadly, his youth shining through the serious nature of his armour. He had just returned from patrol.

"If I'm alive, Mar, it's thanks to you and your men, including your physician. Quite an amazing fellow he is."

"Biton? He has been with me for many years and truly is one of the greatest physicians I have come across. He was trained at the sanctuary of the God Aesclepius on the island of Kos and takes his work very seriously. Too seriously sometimes, for he cannot abide the thought of losing one patient. It has been a difficult couple of days for him."

"Well, I am extremely grateful to you all." Lucius bowed as low as he possibly could and winced when he had gone too far. Mar came to his side and helped him; Dagon had never seen his uncle show such esteem toward a Roman before.

"How are you feeling, Tribune?" Dagon asked.

"Well enough to stand and walk about a little. Which is more than I can say for about forty of my men at the moment."

"They will heal quickly with Biton attending them," Mar assured. "There were, actually, many more of them." He moved to sit on his chair while Lucius and Alerio were shown to stools nearby.

"Lord," said a guard at the tent entrance.

"Yes."

"The centurions, Valerus and Pephredo." The guard stood aside as the two men came in, dressed in full armour, their helmets tucked neatly under their left arms. First they nodded their greetings to Mar and then turned to Lucius and saluted.

"Hail, Tribune!" they said in unison. Lucius looked them over and was shocked by their appearances. Pephredo's head was bandaged as well as one arm. Valerus' face had changed altogether. He seemed to have aged several years since the last time Lucius remembered seeing him. Across the young man's face was a deep, vicious looking cut that had miraculously missed both of his eyes. Lucius' heart caught in his throat as he was reminded of Antanelis.

"How are both of you?" he asked in fatherly tones.

"Alive and well, Tribune," Valerus answered.

"And you, Pephredo?"

"Can't complain, sir!"

"Good lad. I hear you both commanded your men exceedingly well out there despite the situation."

"Thank you, sir," they said. Pephredo grabbed for his head.

"You all right there?" Alerio asked.

"Yes, sir. Just that I feel dizzy and nauseous at times." Mar indicated that they should also be brought stools. Pephredo accepted it gratefully.

"And you, Valerus? That's a nasty looking slash. Going to be quite a scar there." Lucius saw the young man's face darken.

"I know, Tribune." He was young and evidently conscious and concerned how it had changed his good looks. Valerus had not been one to avoid women when they crossed his path.

"Well, you know, Valerus, that scar on your face looks almost exactly like the one Antanelis carried."

"Really?" the young man's face lit up upon hearing this.

"Really," affirmed Lucius. "Wear it with pride." Valerus sat down so that the meeting could commence. Mar stood up.

"I suppose we should begin now. As I understand it, your centurion Eligius will be along shortly?" He looked at Lucius who nodded. "Right then. It has been an interesting few days to say the least, not without sorrow and, it seems, other matters that do not necessarily concern myself or my men. Therefore I will leave it to Centurion Alerio to update Tribune Metellus and give us the final numbers. Centurion."

"Thank you, Mar." Alerio got up from his stool, as Mar sat down again, and moved in front of the fire to face everyone. "As we all know, we were meant to be out here on drills - a standard patrol. That's only partly true as you will see. Some time ago, Tribune Metellus uncovered a plot within the cohort which led to the murder of Centurion Antanelis." As Alerio spoke the words, there was a gasp, a look of shock on everyone's face save his and Lucius'. "Now, we had come intentionally to this place because this is where the murder was carried out. We wanted to confront the traitors after verifying their guilt from their reactions. Well, they did react. Valerus and Pephredo, you were on patrol in the surrounding area at the time this took place. Needless to say, there was an altercation once the tribune accused the guilty parties."

"Who were they?" Pephredo blurted, evidently in total shock and surprise. "Forgive me. It's just that, I had no idea that…"

"Not to worry, Centurion. We could not tell anyone for fear that word would reach the culprits' ears. It's now safe to tell you, and indeed you have a right to know as an officer in this cohort. Those whom we suspected were the centurions Maren and Garai, and, as it turned out, a few of their own men - their signifiers, Gratian and Camilo, who were slain when they tried to help them, and four others." Alerio let them think about it for a moment while he gathered himself. Mar and Dagon looked on with stern, thoughtful expressions.

"I can't believe it!" Pephredo said again.

"It's true," Lucius said from his seat. "When I accused Garai and Maren, Garai attempted to flee and Maren attacked. Did either of you know about their plans or hear anything about it?" Lucius asked the two younger centurions who shook their heads. "Pephredo. You were recommended by Maren to take over command of Argus' century. Do you swear by the Gods' grace that you knew nothing about this?"

"Of course I swear, Tribune." Pephredo looked almost hurt, his pride wounded. "I knew nothing about any of this."

"Did you know about their communication with Argus?"

"No, Tribune. Truth is, I never even liked Maren and Argus. Frankly, I hated the both of them, as did the rest of the men in the century. Both he and Maren broke far too many vinerods over our backs to endear themselves to any of us." Lucius stared at the young man for a long time, trying to see any trace of guilt or deception. There was none.

"Glad to hear it, Pephredo." Lucius turned to Alerio. "I assume that both Maren and Garai are in custody and under guard?" Alerio looked at the others and then down at the ground.

"Maren and four others are in custody, but I'm afraid that Garai escaped."

"What?"

"He escaped. When the nomads attacked, remember? You'd been hit by an arrow and went down. He laid there until a stray horse came along. He took it and rode into the eastern desert. Pephredo saw him riding hard and fast but didn't know what was going on. He was more concerned with reaching us to provide reinforcement." Alerio looked at the centurion who bowed his head in shame. Lucius spoke.

"You did the right thing, Pephredo. If he was on horseback you would never have caught him." Lucius turned to face Mar. "Your men didn't find him?"

"Sorry to say they did not, Tribune. We finished off all the nomads but by the time we had arrived, I assume your missing centurion was long gone."

"Damn!" Lucius almost slapped his thigh but stopped, realised he would have hit his wounds. "Forgive me."

"It's doubtful that he would survive in the deep desert for any length of time, Tribune," Dagon said. "He had no food, no water and the sun still burns hot during the middle of the day. Besides that, if starvation and sun don't get him, the nomads will."

"I suppose." Lucius was disappointed by this news, but he did remember his altercation with Garai now, and how he had him pinned just before the attack. After that, he was too busy fighting off the enemy to be concerned with Garai. "I'll go see the men in custody later."

"Perhaps we should have them executed before the troops, Tribune." Mar suggested, knowing that he was exceeding his rank as an outsider.

"No." Lucius shook his head. "No. These traitors will be tried by the legate back in Lambaesis. I've already executed enough men in my career, short as it is. They'll go back to base in irons and I'll make my report." Mar nodded, conceding to the proper course of action. "What else Alerio?" Lucius motioned for him to continue.

"As Lord Mar said, they finished off the nomads. We gained a number of horses from them that we can use to carry the supplies and wounded back to base. Enemy bodies have been burned without ceremony."

"What of our fallen men?" Lucius asked.

"Forty dead, sixty-three severely wounded including yourself."

"Hmm. I thought it would have been more, considering."

"We were lucky. It would have been more if the Sarmatians had not shown up."

"By the way my friends, how, in Mars' name, did you manage to be there at that moment?" Lucius looked amazed now that he thought of it. Mar turned to Dagon to answer.

"We were out on patrol to the west when we came upon a large force of nomad cavalry. Mostly Garamantians. We'd been following them for days, harrying them off and on, but then we lost them in some of the passes to the west. We tracked them for a day and a night, and when we finally caught up with them they were attacking you! It's most likely that they simply stumbled onto your position and decided to attack and take you by surprise."

"They certainly did." Lucius shook his head. "We were spread out, the men drilling, and Alerio and I taking care of matters with Maren and Garai." Lucius closed his eyes a moment, remembering that Garai had got away.

"Eligius and Balbus saw the dust cloud from the enemy cavalry from the gate tower at the camp and sounded the alarm, but it was far too late by the time any of us realised what was happening." Alerio sat down again.

"They just came from what seemed to be four different directions, Tribune," Valerus said. His scar dripped a little blood onto his lorica. He accepted a cloth from Dagon.

"We just have to accept that we were taken badly by surprise," Lucius said, "and be glad the Gods were on our side...and that our horse-bound friends arrived when they did." The Romans in the room nodded in agreement.

"Stand fast, Centurion!" a guard suddenly yelled at the tent entrance.

"Out of my way, Sarmatian! I'm here to see the tribune!" There was a loud, desperate voice.

"Let him enter," Mar called as the armed centurion rushed through the tent flaps.

"Lucius! Where's my brother? What's happened to Garai?"

Out on the sand, as another orange sun dipped into the horizon, Alerio, Valerus and Pephredo stood back as Lucius walked with Eligius a short distance off; they stayed within easy reach and sight. Lucius knew immediately it would be a hard task to calm Eligius and so decided to talk with him away from any of the men except for the three other centurions behind them.

As they walked over the sand, Lucius went slowly so as not to trip. Eligius' face was twisted up in anger and distress; his green eyes flashing and his complexion crimson. When they had gone far enough, the oasis in view, Lucius stopped and turned to his centurion.

"All right, Lucius!" Eligius began before he could say anything, "Someone had better tell me what in Hades is going on here! I've been hearing men in the cohort talking about Garai, calling him a traitor! What's this all about?"

"Eligius." Lucius was not sure how to begin to tell him about his brother. "This isn't easy for me to say to you, but you have a right to know now. This patrol was a hoax. It was all intended from the beginning as a trap to catch traitors within the cohort."

"Traitors? What traitors, Lucius? My brother?"

"Let me finish!" Lucius calmed his anger, knew it would not help the situation. "Did you like Antanelis?"

"What?" Eligius appeared shocked. "What's he got to do with this?"

"Everything. Just answer the question."

"Of course I liked him. He was a good lad. Why?"

"Did you know he was murdered?"

Eligius' face clouded over. He did not know what to make of this as his mind reeled from the crushing emotions he was feeling. "Murdered? By whom? Where? Lucius, I don't understand why you're telling me this. I just want to know what's happened to Garai, where he is and why people are saying terrible things about him. It's a dishonour to our family - lies. I won't take any of it!"

"I'm afraid you have to, my friend." Lucius put his hands on Eligius' shoulders and looked into his eyes. "Antanelis was murdered by some of our own men, right here, in this oasis." Lucius pointed to the swaying palms, "He was murdered by Maren and by…Garai, for trying to warn me about a plot against my life."

"You lie!" Eligius pushed him back, and Lucius struggled to keep his footing, not to show the pain he felt in his wounds. "It's a lie! He would never do that!"

"He would. He did, Eligius."

"You know nothing! You never liked him!"

"You're wrong. Listen to me."

"I'm done listening to this." He turned to walk away but Lucius grabbed him roughly by the neck of his lorica with both hands, and shook him violently.

"Your not believing it doesn't make it any less true or less real! You see that rock face over there?" Lucius shook him again and turned him to face the oasis. "Garai's report said that Antanelis was attacked by a lion while he and Maren had cornered a jackal in front of the rocks. Listen to me!" He shook him again. "There was no jackal, no lion that was going to attack them. When they had their opportunity, they shot

Antanelis with arrows against the rocks. His blood is still there, for Jupiter's sake! After that they dragged him, our friend, to a pit over there." Lucius pointed to that part of the oasis. "They threw him into that pit, wounded, like cowards!"

"Stop it!" Eligius howled, tears coming to his eyes.

"Then, you know what they did? They released a lion into the pit with him. The cage is still there if you don't believe me! He was mauled to death in that black hole while Maren and your brother stood and watched him die, torn to pieces while he fought for his life!" Lucius let go of Eligius. The pain in his leg and arm wounds was unbearable. "Alerio and I confronted them about it and their reaction was to attack us and flee."

"Damn you, Lucius! Why did you have to bring us out here?"

"Because it was my duty! My duty to all of us and to Antanelis! By Apollo, this wasn't an easy thing for me to do but I had to do it. They conspired to kill Antanelis who discovered they were trying to get to me and who knows how many others."

"It's madness what you say! Where's my brother?" Eligius cried out, his eyes wet and red.

"He fled during the attack, Eligius. He confessed his guilt, took a horse, and rode into the desert by himself leaving the rest of us to fight it out."

"NO! You lie!" Eligius turned and ran, ran fast, stumbling over his own feet, crying, towards the darkness of the oasis.

Alerio and the others came running up to Lucius where he watched Eligius go. "Lucius! Your legs and arms are bleeding!" Alerio came up to him and held him. The blood was showing through his clothes. "Let's get you back to your quarters. It's getting dark."

"What about Eligius?" Valerus asked. Lucius seemed drained all of a sudden, swayed on his feet.

"He'll come back. He's a better man than his brother. Come. Valerus, Pephredo, tell the men to keep a watch out for him."

"Yes, sir," they replied, gazing out to the oasis and Eligius' shape as it disappeared into the trees.

Upon returning to the base and his quarters, Lucius was cared for by Biton who was clearly displeased with the tribune's lack of regard for his orders to stay calm so that the wounds would not open. When the physician spotted the blood staining his patient's clothes again, he ordered the tribune to lie down and stay put for the remainder of the day and night. More foul smelling broth was brought in and clean dressings were applied. Within minutes of finishing his broth, Lucius fell to heavy slumber, his lids too weighty even against the thoughts churning in his head.

Alerio, in command again until Lucius awoke, asked Valerus and Pephredo to notify him as soon as Eligius returned. He did in fact return, sombre, sullen and quiet as a tomb. He gave a few curt orders to his signifer, a man named Elvio, and spent the remainder of the night alone in his tent. For Eligius, the day had been more difficult than any he could have imagined. His brother was not dead, not even simply missing in action. No. Garai had been marked as a traitor - a murderer. *How could he have done such a thing?* his brother wondered by the light of the small oil lamp he carried with him.

Eligius hoped with all his heart that the accusations were false, and unfounded, but he had just been to the oasis and seen the pit, seen the blood upon the rock face. He had read the report his brother had filed regarding the tragic hunting excursion. From what he remembered, the terrain did not match exactly. But, what if this was the wrong oasis? He was hopeful for a moment, but then remembered that Garai had all but confessed outright with his flight from the field and the attack on Lucius and Alerio. *Why did he have to run?* he asked himself. *A plot on Lucius' life?* It just did not make any sense. Who would conjure such a thing and why? These questions and more burned him as he lay awake all through the night.

373

"Argus!" his voice gasped in the dark of his tent. He remembered Garai and Maren talking often about Argus, the Praetorians and the possibility of promotion to the Guard. Could it be that Argus was behind the death of Antanelis? It did not make sense for Garai to think that up on his own, nor even Maren, at least not without some coaxing from someone who had reason to hate and envy Lucius to the point of wanting to kill him. Eligius decided he needed to talk to Maren, without delay, and went out of the tent to make his way to where the prisoners were being held under guard.

He walked through the camp to the north-east corner until he reached the designated area and stopped in front of the guards on duty. Behind them, he could see Maren and the four other men. Maren was sleeping in the corner of the holding enclosure. His black hair was matted with sand and blood, and his nose was broken, swollen and crooked.

"No one is to see the prisoners, Centurion, not until tomorrow after daybreak." The first guard held up his hand.

"I'm here to question that prisoner there," he pointed to Maren, "at the request of the Tribune." The man looked at Maren and back at Eligius.

"I've had no such orders, sir."

"Nevertheless it's true. Shall I have you flogged for being insubordinate?" The man stepped back as Eligius raised his vinerod above his head to strike him.

"Point taken, sir. You can have a few minutes with him." Eligius said nothing, pushed past the man and went to the edge of the enclosure where Maren was sleeping.

"Maren!" Eligius hit the makeshift bars with his vinerod. "Wake up, I've got some questions for you."

"Eligius? Get out of here!" His voice sounded different because of his broken nose.

"No. Not until you tell me your side of the story. What's happened to my brother?"

"Good question, Eligius. What *did* happen to him? Seems to me that he took off like a coward and left me here to rot."

"Did you two kill Antanelis?"

"What's done is done, Eligius. Go back to your tent, forget about your brother and forget this place. You'll sleep better for it."

"No!" He slapped the side of the bars again. "Why did you do it? He was a good man, Antanelis." Maren rolled his eyes.

"He was an informer," Maren growled.

"What did he inform on? Your little plot to kill Lucius? Is that it?"

"You're either very stupid or very naïve and gullible, Eligius. You buy everything they say."

"Lucius has never lied to us, Maren." Eligius glanced over at the guards who were trying to listen, pretending not to look. "Did Argus put you up to this? He convinced Garai to do it, didn't he? Garai would never do this thing."

"You *are* stupid!" Maren laughed, and Eligius lunged for the bars to strike the prisoner. "Fuck off, Eligius! To Hades with you, your brother and your precious tribune. I'm not telling you anything. That way you can suffer from not knowing. Did Garai kill Antanelis or didn't he? Was your brother going to kill Lucius or Alerio, or *you* even?"

"Ahh!" Eligius punched Maren in the head, but not hard as his fist was slowed as it passed between the wooden bars. "I'll kill you, Maren! You ruined my brother, you whoreson!"

"Sir! Get away from there! Sir!" The two guards who had been watching were now using all their strength to pull Eligius away from the cage as his muscled arm strained and reached for Maren's head. The two men finally managed to push the centurion away and he tumbled into the sand. "Sir!"

"All right! I'm going!" Eligius began to walk but turned again to Maren, his face hideous in the torchlight. "I'm going to kill you, Maren. Some day."

"You'll have to wait in line for that!" Maren laughed again as he saw the frustration he had caused Eligius. "Pleasant dreams," he called after him.

When morning broke, Lucius was feeling much better. After a small breakfast, he had Alerio help him arm, and the two of them went immediately to the prisoner holding area. The guards coming off duty gave him their report of what had occurred the previous night. Lucius was assured there was no friendly banter between Eligius and Maren and was somewhat comforted as it meant two things. One, Eligius was back; and two, he had had no part in the plot with Maren and his brother. But had Eligius known they were communicating with Argus? He would speak to him about that later.

Maren and the other four men were disappointingly, but not unexpectedly, less forthcoming with any information. In fact, they chose to remain silent knowing full well that whether they spoke or not had no bearing on the outcome of their lives if they were given a military trial in Lambaesis. Lucius informed them that that was indeed what would happen; he had proof in the form of the arrowheads, the bloody piece of cloak, the bogus report, and most importantly, the fact that they had either tried to escape from or attack their fellows upon being confronted at the scene of the crime. Maren had, before Lucius arrived, pressured his fellow conspirators to remain silent and that if they got out of the present situation in which they found themselves, he knew people who would be *very* grateful for their silence.

The four men were not sure whether to believe Maren but conceded out of fear of what he might do to them within the cell. He was still the centurion that had driven them mercilessly. At such close quarters, he was even more menacing to them.

Lucius left the prisoners when he saw that he would not get anywhere. He had his proof. That was enough. Now he wanted to go back to the Sarmatian camp and see how Lunaris was getting on. He had wanted to see his stallion the day before but had been waylaid by Eligius' sudden appearance. He hoped, prayed, that Lunaris was not too badly injured, and that he would be the same as before.

When he arrived at the Sarmatian camp, Mar himself escorted Lucius to the area where the horses were cared for. Lunaris, he told him, was quartered by himself in a shaded area they had created with palm branches. He had been given fresh water constantly and had the care of a Sarmatian man who was a very skilled veterinarius, especially when it came to their own prized war horses.

"Your stallion truly is a wondrous creature, Tribune."

"Please, Mar, you may call me Lucius when we're away from the men."

"Fine then, Lucius. Your centurion outdid himself when he presented you with Lunaris."

"Yes. Alerio is my closest friend. He's saved my life on more than one occasion, including the other day. At any rate, I hope Lunaris will be fit and healthy again."

"My man informs me that the wound was located in such a position that it would not do any long-term damage. The Gods must have been watching over the both of you that day. It is unfortunate but true that most of the time, when a horse is wounded or lamed, it must be destroyed." Mar placed his hand on Lucius' shoulder. "Do not worry, Anguis. You will ride him again. The question is whether you will be able to sit yourself in the saddle as soon." Mar smiled, the creases in his face pushing against each other.

Lucius noticed that occasionally Mar and Dagon referred to him respectfully as Anguis. It seemed to him that his name, also another word for the symbol of their might, the dragon, was something they took very seriously. They noticed dragons everywhere, in symbols, in words, in thoughts and in actions. Although the mystery of these people seemed to be unravelling for Lucius, he knew as yet that there was still a great deal about them of which he knew little and understood even less.

"There he is, Lucius. Waiting for you." Mar stopped, indicating that Lucius should approach on his own.

In a circular pen, lying in the shade of the suspended palm branches, was Lunaris. Lucius walked hesitantly at first, not wanting to alarm him, but when the familiar shuffle of his footsteps reached Lunaris' ears, they twitched and his strong neck turned where he lay to see his master coming toward him.

"Lunaris," Lucius called gently as he moved through the gate into the enclosure. "I'm here boy. It's all right now." The stallion, his dappled coat matted with sweat, neighed softly, as if in surprise. He made to rise in the awkward manner it takes for a horse to get up from the ground. It took Lunaris a few moments to find his legs as he favoured the side on which the wound was located. Once he did get onto all fours, he moved slowly and without limping toward Lucius.

Lucius felt a lump in his throat as the muscular stallion, all trace of blood washed from his coat, came up to him, recognition in his large eyes. Lunaris' soft snout moved up and down Lucius' body, hesitating slightly over the areas where he had been wounded. When he had finished his inspection, he rubbed against his master with his strong neck.

Horse and rider stood silent, each happy to see the other alive and well. Lucius stroked his thick neck. "You seem well." For a few minutes he stood there before turning to walk to where Mar stood. He could feel Lunaris' hot breath on the back of his neck as he walked to the edge of the enclosure.

"Thank you for this, Mar."

"The Gods bless such close and loyal relationships between man and beast, Anguis. It may be that it was more Lunaris' love for you that kept him alive through that battle. I have never seen so loyal a stallion. I am glad to see you reunited."

"Me too." Lucius pat Lunaris on the head. "I'll see you later, boy. I have to go and talk to someone." Lunaris watched the two men walk away.

Once Lucius had taken leave of Mar, he passed through the tent rows of the cohort camp. Men smiled as he passed, more so with each day that elapsed since the day when they were attacked. The pain would be long lasting, as it is with all loss, but it would dissipate in time. It would not, however, dissipate for the man he was about to see.

Lucius found Eligius standing on top of one of the guard towers staring out at the desert. Eligius stiffened when his tribune came to stand beside him.

"He's out there somewhere, Eligius. He'll survive."

"Pff! What do you care? If you had things your way, Garai would be clapped in irons next to Maren awaiting military execution."

"You just don't understand, do you, Eligius. You're upset at being deceived by your own brother, I know, upset that he's in danger, of course. But you forget that he's done something bloody awful to one of us. I did what I had to. Why can't you see that?"

"I see a lot, Lucius. You've betrayed me as a friend. You should have told me what you knew. I could have talked him out of it."

"It was too late by then. Antanelis was already dead." Eligius shut his eyes as though to block out the words. Lucius continued, hopeful that he might reach him in that moment. "I loved Garai like a brother, Eligius, though you might find that hard to believe."

"Sometimes, Lucius, I wonder whether we were friends at all." Eligius' face hardened and he stared at Lucius and his purple-striped tunic. "You may be a tribune, my superior, and I'll obey your orders as such because I'm a Roman and a soldier like my brother. But that's all you are to me! You're no longer a friend."

"Why are you doing this?"

"Because Garai is my brother and you...you were my friend." Eligius stood back, cold, at attention. "May I be dismissed, Tribune?" he asked in an official tone of voice.

Lucius nodded, at a loss for words for one who evidently was not willing to listen. But what else could he say? Perhaps in time, he thought, it would wear off. Perhaps not. When Eligius had left to go about his duties, Lucius stayed there for a while staring out at a world of sand, wind and sun. He wondered whether Garai was alive or lying dead in the sand, alone and unmourned, for the vultures to prey upon.

Four days later, under a cloudy sky indicative of winter's coming, the cohort, along with the Sarmatian contingent, set out for Lambaesis. Riders scouted for miles in all directions surrounding the Roman column. At the head rode Lucius and Mar. Behind them, fluttering in the breeze, were their standards; Lucius' vexillum carried by Frontus, whose head was heavily bandaged, and the draconarius carried by Dagon.

At the centre of the marching column of men were the pack horses and the wounded troops who were as yet not fit enough to walk, and so passed the journey atop the horses of fallen enemies. As for the legionaries, the troops who had been part of either Garai or Maren's centuries were now divided evenly among Alerio, Eligius, Valerus and Pephredo. The signa of the previous two were wrapped in dark cloth and strapped to one of the packhorses; they were disbanded for the moment, humiliated by the actions of their centurions.

The way was slow going, but luckily uneventful. After three days, they approached the walls of Lambaesis. As they were riding, Lucius had been thinking once more of his wife. His mind had been preoccupied the past days but now that he had the time to contemplate matters as they rode, he wondered whether or not he should tell Adara to remain in Greece. Garai had escaped, but would he survive? How could he? Lucius turned in his saddle to look back at Maren and the other prisoners where they walked in chains, surrounded by twenty men from Alerio's century.

Lucius remembered Argus' name had come up several times and he wondered what role he had in all of this, wondered if his childhood relationship with him might blind him to his true nature and capabilities. No, he decided. He knew Argus better than anyone - what he was really like. He may be a Praetorian now but could he ever stoop to the level of a back-stabber in the shadows? At any rate, Lucius remembered, Argus was stationed in Rome, not Greece, nor Africa. He had always hated Africa.

The Sybil's message repeated itself in Lucius' mind until he was convinced it was the proper course of action. He had been told that Adara should be by his side, with him. Therefore, Lucius decided he would await the arrival of his wife with great joy and anticipation. First, however, there were matters to be taken care of. As they passed through the massive stone gates of the fortress, Lucius thanked Mar and Dagon for the escort, and left Alerio in charge of the men while he went directly to the Principia to see the legate and give his full report.

The tribune was admitted immediately to the legate's rooms where the military staff on hand were dismissed so that the two men could speak in private. Marcellus had a rough idea of what had happened with regard to the attack from the riders Mar had sent out after the battle. But, when it came to the true purpose of Lucius' expedition, he was in the dark. He fretted over the outcome and whether he had made a mistake in allowing the young Metellus to carry out his shaky plan.

When Lucius limped into the Commander's presence and saluted, Marcellus' jaw dropped at the sight of him. Bandages were wrapped thickly about Lucius' arms and thighs and there was a thick cut across his forehead. His lack of armour was evidently due to the need to lighten the burden upon his person so that the wounds would not open again. The only weapon the young man carried was a golden-hilted sword slung carefully across his back where it would not cause him any pain.

"By the Gods, Metellus! What in Mars' name happened to you?" The legate came around his table and moved a stool closer for Lucius.

"Thank you, Legate Commander." Lucius accepted the stool and sat down with a massive exhalation. Riding for so long had made him stiff. "I came straight here, Legate; we just arrived."

"Are your men being seen to?"

"Yes, sir. Centurion Alerio is seeing to the wounded and the prisoners."

"Prisoners?"

"The traitors, sir," Lucius stated. "Shall I make my report?"

"I think you'd better do so immediately. Tell me everything." The legate leaned back in his chair, attentive, curious and somewhat worried.

Lucius started from the beginning of the march, how he had the men drill and erect full marching camps each night. He related how none of the culprits suspected a thing up until the last moments when he confronted them. The legate listened to the exact description of the terrain, the rock face where the blood had been, the oasis and the pit. Lucius spoke of the giant palm and where the camp had been erected in relation to it and the oasis. All the protocol had been followed regarding the erection of standard marching camps and with this, the legate was pleased.

When Lucius began to talk of the day he confronted and accused the traitors with place and proof, and once he put the arrowheads and piece of bloody cloak on the legate's table, Marcellus' face darkened. Matters had been more serious than he had thought.

"And these men, Garai and Maren, your centurions, they attacked you when you accused them?"

"Yes, sir. Well, Garai attempted to flee but I managed to get a hold of him. Maren, who attempted to cut me down while my back was turned, was apprehended by Centurion Alerio."

"You have witnesses, I assume?"

"Yes, Commander. My vexillarius was standing nearby and several of the troops witnessed the scuffle and the attempt to flee."

"So, you were able to apprehend all of them? That was a good piece of work, Tribune."

"Not actually, sir." Lucius bowed his head, feeling a little ashamed. "When the nomads attacked we were taken completely unawares, even though the men at the camp had sounded the alarm. During the attack, Centurion Garai managed to steal a nomad mount. I'm sorry to say that he escaped into the desert."

"What of the others?"

"Centurion Alerio managed to restrain Maren and set a guard of men about him during the fighting. We have him now as well as four others from their centuries who attempted to flee. The signifiers, Gratian and Camilo, were slain when they attempted to aid their centurions."

Marcellus sighed in his chair and poured the two of them some wine. Lucius accepted it gratefully. Finally, the legate spoke.

"It's a bloody mess, Metellus. Are you sure you got all of the traitors, besides the one that got away?"

"I believe so, sir. Although a thorough search of the accused men's quarters may reveal more."

"See to it. Now, you know this Garai well. Do you think he'll survive out there?" This was something that evidently worried the legate a great deal from the look on his face, and the way his voice sounded.

Lucius thought for a moment, remembered what Dagon had said about the desert and what little chance Garai had of surviving.

"No, Commander. He won't survive. He has no food, no water. The sun is still intense at midday and there are still many nomads in that area according to the Sarmatians."

"I hope you're right about that, Metellus. To be safe I'll order all patrols to keep an eye out for this traitor." Marcellus made a note on a wax tablet then looked up again. "He has a brother in your cohort, does he not?"

"Yes, sir. Centurion Eligius."

"Did he know of the plots? Will he be any trouble?"

"He didn't know of his brother's treachery and he's extremely upset about the entire situation."

"But will he be any trouble?" the legate repeated the question.

"No, sir. I've spoken with him and though he resents me at the moment, I believe he'll continue to do his duty."

"Well," Marcellus began suspiciously, "I think it would be a good idea to have him watched carefully nonetheless."

"Yes, sir." Lucius finished his wine. "What about a trial, sir?"

"Yes. A trial will be needed soon. Now that you've completed your mission to the best possible extent under the circumstances, I see no reason why I can't approve your actions publicly and hold a military trial."

"When shall we hold it, sir?"

"The trial will be held on the Nones of November. Now, should it come to execution, which I'm sure it will for such actions, do you think these men deserve a proper death by sword or something else?"

"I'm not sure, sir. I haven't really thought about it yet." Lucius did not want to think about it, did not want the choice to be his. He hoped the legate would not leave it up to him.

"In my opinion, they don't deserve a soldier's death. Their actions were cowardly. So, in light of the way in which they brought down Centurion Antanelis, I'll have them taken out to the archery range beyond the walls for execution. The trial, of course, is more pretence than anything but it needs to be done properly. Do you agree with this course of action?"

"Yes, Commander. I do." Lucius tried to hold his courage for Antanelis, to see justice in the execution. He pictured his dead friend in the black pit. "I agree."

"Good. Now, you seem as though you could use some rest, Tribune. You and your men may have a short furlough until the trial. Heal your wounds and get well."

"Yes, sir." Lucius rose from his stool slowly and saluted. The legate seemed different for some reason. Lucius put it down to the seriousness of the situation. He had his duty, the legate had his own. As he was leaving, Marcellus called after him.

"Oh, and Tribune!"

"Yes, Commander."

"Good work, lad. Worthy of your name."

"Thank you, sir." Lucius forced a smile, turned and walked away.

In the days leading up to the trial of Maren and the four other men, Lucius, Alerio and the rest of the cohort were free to relax as each saw fit. Many of the men decided to go to Thamugadi for a bit of fun, while others decided to lounge around the base and make use of the gymnasium and the baths. Lucius slept, or attempted to, as much as possible. When not sleeping, he soaked his body in his private baths.

Lucius withdrew from duty for a time, going out of doors only to care for Lunaris and exercise his aching limbs. The skin around his wounds was tightening as they started to heal and so Loxias, the legion's head physician, gave him more of his ointments to speed the healing and stop the itching.

Mar made sure that a steady supply of the stinking broth was taken to Lucius every day too, occasionally going himself to check up on a man whom he had once thought an unlikely friend. Dagon and Alerio also came to visit Lucius and updated him on the men and how the legate was going about his investigation. The Commander had requested that Alerio, in order to allow Lucius time to heal, aid him and his staff in going through the traitors' quarters.

The barracks in which the two signifers and the other six men lived yielded nothing in the way of proof, once thoroughly ransacked. When it came time to go through the centurions' quarters, the results were quite different. Matching arrowheads had been found in Garai's quarters just as Lucius had said, as well as letters written in some sort of code that could not be deciphered.

In Maren's quarters, at the end of one of the barrack blocks, Alerio checked every corner, discovered every possible hiding place and when he had finished, they had a pile of letters that were not in code and yet remained unsigned. They spoke of a threat posed by the centurion Antanelis to plans that involved replacing the Tribune Metellus. These were evidently orders of some sort, curt and straight to the point. The letters also spoke of Senator Metellus in Rome and possible promises to Maren and Garai about advancement to the Praetorian Guard if the said plans were carried out successfully.

It was obvious to whom the letters had been sent; however, there were no other names mentioned in any great detail. The identity of the sender was distinctly missing. Alerio knew who had sent them and took the letters to Lucius. He recognised the writing at once as Argus' hand. The only problem was that Argus, as things now stood, was virtually untouchable in his role as a Praetorian. Lucius brought this to the attention of the legate who promptly refused to pursue any investigation into the so-called Praetorian known as Argus. Firstly, his name was not written anywhere and so there was no evidence that he had written the letters to the accused. Secondly, he was a Praetorian protected by the prefect. Plautianus' reach, Marcellus argued, was very far indeed. He was too powerful, too brutal to oppose with any hope of winning.

"I prefer to live my days to their full length," Marcellus said, "than go vainly after some Praetorian murderer. If we accuse one of them right now, we're done for. Doesn't matter how old or experienced. Far greater men's heads than mine have rolled away with their eyes wide and lifeless for opposing Plautianus. Leave it be, Tribune, for all our sakes, including your wife and unborn child."

Lucius was compelled to agree with the legate. Plautianus was too large a foe to take on. Even the empress was losing her battle behind the scene of imperial intrigue and death. He was reminded of the legate's advice long ago that he should remain a soldier and keep his nose out of politics and plots. So far, he had not excelled in that.

No word came of Garai from any of the patrols and after several days he was presumed to be dead. Eligius took it hard and spent much of his own time on the archery range where he and his brother had shared some of their final leisurely moments.

The prisoners awaited the day of trial silently, still refusing to answer any of the questions about the plots or the letters that had been found. Maren bided the time until his death with spite, stubbornness and wilful courage. He refused to say anything to Lucius or Alerio, and just knowing that it maddened them greatly made it all worthwhile to him. His laughter at seeing them approach his cell brought many a forceful blow upon his back and head, and yet he still refused to speak. Rather, he laughed like a madman, his deep blue eyes tossing like waves in the sea. Even in the final hours of his life, he did not turn to any god or goddess for solace, comfort or forgiveness. His heart was as cold and hard as tempered steel.

The Nones finally arrived and the men of the legion had gathered in the immense courtyard of the Principia for the sentence of the five traitors before them. The charges were read out loud for all to hear. The tale of Antanelis' death and the recent events at the oasis were described in detail. Gasps of surprise and disgust emanated from the mouth of many a veteran of the III Augustan. There were cries for justice and pleas to Nemesis. It was obvious that Antanelis had earned respect in the ranks. No mention was made of the Praetorians; the sole guilt of the crime was being assigned to the men who stood in plain tunics and chains on the flagstones of the courtyard.

Once the sentence was proclaimed, the legion marched out to the archery range where the guilty men were tied to stakes that had been driven into the ground that very morning, their hands behind their backs as they faced their frowning peers. Lucius had, for the first time since the battle, dressed in full armour along with his men. They stood in the front rows to watch the men who had plotted against their tribune and murdered one of their own.

Lucius stood silent beside the legate, his cloak hanging loosely behind him in the still, stale air. The gates of Hades were about to open then as he was reminded of a similar day in Sabratha when he witnessed the decimation of other men that had been assigned to his command, also traitors. His thoughts were broken by weeping as two of the condemned hung meekly by their bonds, tried to turn their backs so that they could not see the arrows coming at them. They were tied too tightly, however, and continued to plea for their lives, tears running down their ragged faces. Of the two others, one man shook uncontrollably while the other urinated where he stood as he anticipated the barbed arrows of the Syrian archers lined up before them.

Only Maren stood tall and still, unmoved by the whole charade as he saw it. He had always met the threat of death with indifference on the battlefield and now he did as he always had done. His dark eyes reached across the dusty ground to Lucius who searched for some sign of regret. There was no such sign. Lucius heard the archers notch their arrows and pull back on their bowstrings. Then, in that moment before death and departure from the world, Maren smiled evilly at him.

The arrows sped through the air like thunder before the expected crack of lightning. Every arrow found its mark and ended with a muted thud, the traitors riddled with four each. Maren's eyes glazed over and his black and grey head of hair collapsed forward as his body hung limply from the stake. It was done, but that image of Maren's punctured body would stick in Lucius' head for some time, the few seconds in which he yet strained to maintain his gaze on Lucius, and the trickle of blood that poured from the corner of his mouth as Death took him away.

That evening, as the bodies were burned all together and their ashes left to scatter to the dark, cold winds of night, Lucius returned to the confines of his quarters to contemplate the latest events that were to change his life and outlook. Much had happened, he hoped none of the same was to come. An ill feeling inside whispered that it was not over yet, that out there another threat yet loomed in the shadows, waited for a time to strike. He would have to be vigilant from then on, know his friends, and his enemies.

For the moment, the storm seemed to have subsided and there was light on the other side of the sea. Soon Adara would be with him and that thought alone provided him with the strength he needed. After making his offerings on the altar in his chamber, he went out into the courtyard to speak his wife's name to the night sky and thank the Gods for their guidance, their abiding sense of justice, and for the grace that allowed him to go on living.

Part II

RED LAMBAESIS

A.D. 203-204

XVII

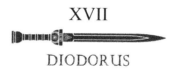

DIODORUS

"Tell me, Diodorus!"

"Tell you what, child?"

"Huh?"

"You must ask me a proper question, young Lucius, if you wish to obtain any information. If you do not, how can I, or anybody else for that matter, answer you?"

"I don't understand what you mean." The young boy kicked a small pebble as they strolled beneath the cypresses that lined one of the old man's favourite lanes leading to the forum. It was hot and his tunic was making him itchy, agitated. The old man looked askance at his young pupil as he stroked his long white beard in thought. It was always more difficult to teach during the summer months when young boys preferred to be playing in the fields or swimming in the rivers.

"You must not give up so easily," the old man said. "Let me try. Tell me your favourite colour!" He snapped his fingers, caused the boy to jolt. "Do you know what I just did?"

"You scared me!"

"No. I ordered you to give me information. But did you answer me right away?"

"No, Diodorus."

"Right. Now. Lucius, what is your favourite colour?"

"Blue, Diodorus. You know that."

"Aha! You see, I asked you a proper question and you were able to answer immediately; you were not shocked, or scared or offended."

"Yes. So?"

"When you order someone to give you information they are less likely to comply quickly or accurately. If you take your time, if you think before you speak, you will be able to obtain the information you seek."

The boy scratched his head thoughtfully, mulling over what his teacher had just told him.

"So, if I ask proper questions, I will waste less time in finding out things?"

"Exactly! You must also remember that people, be they senators or soldiers, prefer to be asked and not told. If you show other people respect in the way you address them, they will do the same for you."

"What about slaves?"

"Slaves are as human as everyone else. However, they do have their place in this world and so need to be told what to do from time to time. Yet, if you can, it is still better to ask them."

"I see. Should I also ask proper questions of philosophers?"

"Especially philosophers!" The old man smiled broadly behind his beard. "A philosopher is most likely to notice any mistakes you make in asking questions."

"I suppose if I had asked you a proper question in the first place, we would not have wasted all this time discussing proper questions, would we?"

"Ha! Ha! You are correct - impudent - but correct. However, since you are young and learning, none of this is a waste of time. Now, do you wish to ask me a question?" Lucius stopped, his hands clasped in front of his body like an orator before a speech.

"Yes, Diodorus. I would." He cleared his throat with a squeak. "During my lessons, why do we spend more time outside walking around than inside at a table?"

The old man smiled again. "We spend more time outside because there is much more to learn outside than there is inside. That was a good question."

"I am happy you approve. Only, I don't understand your answer."

Diodorus motioned for the boy to continue walking with him while he spoke, determined to make something clear to him. Today, it seemed, they would learn about learning.

"Why do we spend most of our lessons out of doors? Do you know why, Lucius?" The boy shook his head. "All right then. Do you remember what we studied two weeks ago at your home when it was raining very hard?"

"Hmm. I…I'm not sure. Was it something to do with Alexander the Great?"

"It was. But do you remember exactly what it was about him that we were talking about?"

"Um. No. I am sorry. I forgot."

"Very well then. Do you remember what we learned about that day two years ago when we sat beneath a tree to watch the crowds come out of the Colosseum?"

"Oh yes!" he began excitedly. "That was a fun day! We had been talking about how the world was made up of a great variety of people. People with different clothes, different looks, different ways of doing things. You told me that all of these were important because it is their differences that make the world beautiful. Yes, I remember that day very well. I also remember those two buffoons fighting over a girl!"

"Yes, well, forget the buffoons and the girl for the moment. The point is that you remember that day very clearly even though it was two years ago and you were only six years old. Correct?"

"Yes."

"You remember that lesson more clearly than a lesson you had at home just two weeks ago."

"Yes." Lucius hung his head, feeling quite badly about it, but Diodorus lifted his chin and smiled again. He smiled often when teaching Lucius.

"Do not be upset with yourself, Lucius. Your memory is not failing you."

"No?"

"Certainly not. In fact, it is behaving very admirably. Do you know why you might remember the one day better than the other?"

"Because...because it was more interesting." Diodorus frowned, his lips disappearing beneath the white fluff of his beard. Lucius felt badly for upsetting him but realised he had not when the philosopher began to laugh heartily.

"You are absolutely right!"

"I am?"

"Yes. It was more interesting. Do you know why?"

"Because we were outside and there was a lot to see. The sun was shining, people were laughing, fighting, singing and buying things."

"Does that answer your first question?"

"I think so. We spend more lessons outside than in because it is more interesting and there is more to see."

"Brilliant, young Metellus! Now, mark my words this moment." Diodorus stopped and the young man before him listened attentively, leaned closer so as not to miss a single word. "You can read scroll after scroll, every one that you can get your hands on - and you should -, but you should always remember that reading is no substitute for the things you will experience out here," he waved his hands in a big arching motion, "in the world." Lucius' eyes were wide with enthusiasm. "Out here, out in the vastness of the world, Lucius, there is more to learn than anywhere else. There are people and experiences, there is beauty and life and mystery. There is also death, but even *that* has something to teach you. Do you understand?"

"Yes, Diodorus."

"You must never stop learning new things. You can never know everything, but you can always strive to know more about people, places, the past and the present. The more you know, the better prepared you will be for your future. You must never be afraid of things you do not know or understand. That is very important. Instead, when you do not understand something you must do all you can to change that. You will appreciate life all the more for it." The old man stared at

Lucius, thrilled that his young charge was so enthralled and keen to hear more. "You have a question?"

"Yes. Should I become a merchant so that I can travel around the world and see everything?" Now, it was Diodorus' turn to look shocked.

"Ha! No, little one, not at all. I think…I know…you are meant for much greater things than commerce."

"What should I do then, Diodorus?" The boy looked puzzled, worried, and the philosopher put his hand on his shoulder as they continued to walk.

"I can not tell you what you will do. That is something you will be able to decide on your own when you become a man. Whatever you chose though, you will be good at it. Just be true to yourself, your family, and of course, honour the Gods as they are the ones who watch over us and guide us through to our destinies."

The old man and young boy strolled on out from beneath the trees, and turned into the forum where they seated themselves on the steps of the Curia Hostilia to watch the world go by in all its colour and glory. What Diodorus had said changed Lucius that day and from that point the boy looked at everything around him with a youthful cognizance and curiosity that made his world infinitely more interesting.

Young Lucius Metellus Anguis strove to understand and absorb every morsel of information that his tutor provided for his young eyes and ears. He was taught to see beyond what was visible - to analyse and understand what he saw or heard. Most importantly, to his own mind, Diodorus taught him to feel; to feel not only with his heart, but with the whole of his being, the mind, and every sense included. If Lucius was to be a man of the world, he had to be attuned to the world the way a tiger is attuned to his jungle environment. There was, the old Greek had told him, a voice inside everyone that one could either choose to ignore or embrace. This inner voice gave the ability to foresee things, anticipate dangers, and welcome unexpected gifts from the world without.

Diodorus also enjoyed enthralling his young student with tales of his travels to far-off places like Aegyptus and the lands of Persia where Alexander had won his fame. Most of all, however, the old man loved to relate to Lucius the places of his homeland, of Greece. He spoke of the Gods and their ancient sanctuaries: Dodonis, Delos, Delphi. He also related the tale of a place in Italy called Cumae and told Lucius that if he ever had the chance, he should make his way there, for it was another very sacred place of Apollo. Lucius listened to the tale of Aeneas and the Sybil in her dark cave, and he fought back the fear inside him that emerged as he was told of the oracle's extreme old age and her shrill voice.

Three times a week Diodorus would come to teach; whenever the weather was fair, they would go out of doors for the day to walk, sit, and observe. Lucius looked forward to these days with impatience. He sat in the atrium of the Metellus domus dressed and ready to depart as soon as the philosopher arrived.

One day, however, Diodorus did not show up because he was not feeling well. He sent word that he was going to remain at his home, so that he would not infect Lucius with whatever ailed him. It was a simple malady as it turned out, a result of old age and the season's change. Diodorus would be well in a few days. But Lucius, upon hearing that his lessons were cancelled for the day, was distraught. The young boy paced the entire household impatiently, upset that he was going to miss all there was to see. They were to go down to the river to sit in an area that was grassy, quiet, and peaceful.

Finally, toward midday, curiosity got the better of Lucius, and he sneaked out of doors by himself. He knew his way about the city well enough and also knew how to get to the grassy area by the Tiber where they were supposed to have gone. He went up to his room to get his cloak and decided to bring along the small wooden gladius he used to play legionary with Argus.

Stealthily, he made his way downstairs to the atrium careful not to disturb Alene, who was in the garden picking small flowers for their mother. If Alene spotted him, she would not let him go for fear that something might happen to him. He enjoyed her protectiveness but sometimes he was forced to find ways around it. He decided to bring back some different flowers for her from the river's edge - flowers she did not usually get to see.

The sun was bright that day, not a cloud in the sky as Lucius went along the narrow streets that bypassed the docks. At midday most citizens were indoors sleeping or eating their meals. Lucius however, enjoyed this time and delighted in the sun's warmth upon his face and neck as he picked his way along a narrow path beside the riverbank to the open green space he had been seeking. It was, he concluded, quite beautiful, and he could see immediately why Diodorus had wanted to take him there.

The space was large and little used, it seemed, as the grass was tall throughout; none of it was trampled underfoot except for where he had passed. It was private too. Cypress trees loomed at the back, away from the water, and willows slumbered down by the riverbank, their hair-like branches dipping into the bubbling water of the Tiber.

It was a good spot to practice his sword skills, he thought, and so he began to run about, dodging phantom enemies before cutting and thrusting into their soft bellies. He found he was quite good at it and was pleased with himself. He looked up for a moment and wondered about the far away places Diodorus had told him of. Did the land of Aegyptus share the same sky? Did Alexander know the Gods? Was the famous Greek warrior a god himself? Surely, no man could have done the things he did? Lucius wondered about all of this.

Eventually, he grew tired of fighting the enemy with his wooden gladius and laid himself down in the tall grass near the water to rest. Long green blades rustled in the breeze about his head, never bending or straining themselves too much under the wind's will. He noticed how they simply swayed, like a dance Alene would do when she was happy, her hair twirling about her head with her movement. The grass was like that.

It was like a spell really, something out of a dream: the sound of the grass, the water, the hum of the trees around him. Lucius sighed, his hands clasped beneath his head, and dozed off smiling. As he slept, he could still hear the gentle sounds of the space in which he lay, could picture the beauty around him, and feel how peaceful it was. Was this what Diodorus had meant? He listened to how the sounds changed, and yet the simple song of the world was the same in a way. That is, until it all stopped and there was no sound at all.

At first, he was startled and afraid. Was he still dreaming? He must have been; he hoped he was. The tall grass rustled behind him and there was a soft splashing in the water. Lucius remained flat on his back in the grass wondering what to do. Two sounds from two places. What to do? Slowly, he reached for the wooden sword at his side. He did not feel alone. He wondered who had come to this place where it seemed no one ever came.

If he were to run, it would have to be away from the water toward the trees where he could hope to find a way out. He knew he would have to be fast and roll to one side so that he could get off his back quickly. The grass would hide him momentarily. He decided to count to three, then, he would roll and run. *One...two...three...roll!* In a swift motion Lucius rolled to his left, jumped to his feet, and made a dash toward the trees with his sword raised in defence against whoever might attack him.

He did not get more than two strides before he was stopped dead in his tracks, unable to move. But it was neither foot nor fist that halted his retreat, but a sense that all was well, a look in the eyes that met his, brilliant, grey, telling eyes in which the stars shone though it was yet day. He said nothing, simply stared. No smile, frown, or indication of extreme emotion, just an intense observance. A giant bow was slung at the stranger's back, silver with arrows to match. It glinted in the sun. He was dressed oddly, all in white with a blue cloak that hovered about him as though it were weightless, a mirror image of the sky.

Lucius' heartbeat resounded in his ears. He tried to look back, to take in the appearance of the stranger before him, but he could not look upon him too long. The man moved slightly toward Lucius who tried to raise his wooden sword to point it at him but his arm would not obey. In his head, he thought a voice spoke to him. *Do not be afraid, little one. Drop your sword.* The wooden gladius fell from Lucius' hand into the tall grass and the man smiled.

"That is better." His voice was unlike any other he had heard before in the forum, on the senate steps, in the markets, anywhere. It was more pleasant, like the steady call of a horn blown from a high mountain top; a thing of comfort, almost familiar. "Out alone today, young Metellus?" he asked.

"Wh...what?" Shock shrouded the boy's face, but he stood still. "How do you know my name?"

"I know many things. I've been watching you play with that." He pointed to the wooden sword. "You're quite good with it."

"Thank you." Lucius was feeling less afraid and puffed up his little chest at the compliment. "My tutor says that I should balance my studies with physical activity. Playing legionary is my favourite thing to do."

"Hmm. Your tutor, Diodorus, is correct in that."

"You know him?"

"Oh yes. For some time."

"Do you also know my father, Quintus Metellus?"

"Yes." This time the tall stranger sounded unimpressed.

"I really should be getting back home now." Uncertainty crossed Lucius' face.

"Do not worry, little dragon, we won't harm you. We just wanted to say hello and share this nice patch of grass with you away from the stench of the city streets. Didn't we?" He called out, but not to Lucius. Suddenly Lucius remembered there had been two noises that had woken him and he spun around to look toward the water.

"Of course we did." There was laughter and a voice; a sound that was sweeter than any music made by man or bird. It was like the happy trickle of cool water in a fountain on a hot day. Lucius found himself laughing too, without having intended it.

A woman stood ankle deep in the water. She kicked her right foot to make a gentle splash and all of the tiny droplets that sprung into the air glistened like jewels in the sun. This new stranger was tall and lithe with hair the colour of golden summer wheat. Such was her beauty that, for the first time in his life, Lucius noticed clearly the sculpted mastery of the female form. But he had never seen the likes of her. To look upon her laughing and splashing in the clear water as the bottom of her white gown clung to her legs was pure joy. He smiled and did not want to stop, did not want to take his eyes away from her captivating gaze.

Where the man had beheld him with a keen observance, this woman looked upon him with eyes that sparkled with a joy that was mirrored in Lucius' own smile toward her. She held out a hand and the boy walked to meet her, but before he could feel her supple skin in his own hand, the man spoke from directly behind him.

"Do not let Love dazzle him too brightly, as yet. He is young and still has much to learn." Lucius knew the voice came from behind him; he waited for a hand to grasp his shoulder, but he could not tear his gaze from her. The hand withdrew though her smile remained as she continued to walk in the water. A pair of doves flew across the sky behind her right shoulder but without sound. "Tell us, young Lucius." He looked into the sky, fixed on something afar that Lucius could not spot. "What you were to study here in this place?"

The question took Lucius by surprise, but he was ready to answer nonetheless. If they knew Diodorus, then he would find out if he had answered correctly or not. He did not want to let him down. He thought for a moment and looked about.

"I was to study the world today."

"Study the world?" the man with the bow repeated. "And what were you to study in it?"

"The water, the trees, insects and birds, the sky above."

Love stopped, the water up to her thighs now, her voice clearly audible. "Have you observed these things on your own today?"

"Yes, my Lady," he answered shyly, daring to look at her more closely.

"And what have you decided about the world?" The woman, and the man, looked at him expectantly, still.

"That...the...world is a very beautiful place." That was all he could think to say. At that moment, it was the strongest thought in his mind. The young boy could only think of beauty, the kind you could see and hear.

"And what of War, young Metellus?" The strong looking man unhooked the bow from his back and strung it. Lucius admired its odd crafting, unlike any other.

"War, sir? What do you mean?"

"Is War not also a part of this world?"

"Yes. It is."

"What does that mean then?"

"I suppose...if the world is beautiful and there is war in it, then...war can also be beautiful?" The answer was uttered in uncertainty, and Lucius suspected he was wrong in how he had said it. "No, wait. The world is still beautiful even if there is war. War is exciting!"

"Exciting you say?" For the first time Love's smile disappeared briefly. "Men dying? Lovers torn apart and children left parentless?" The man held up his hand for silence and she stopped. Her smile returned to comfort the boy in whose face fear now was present.

"My sister is passionate about these things, about the preservation of beauty." He leaned on his great bow. "However, your answer is not incorrect. War is in the world of men and Gods. Exciting? Some may say that. A young man's point of view usually changes as the years go on and more and more blood is shed. But it is necessary. All evils go hand in hand with all that is good...and beautiful."

The young boy looked relieved but felt ashamed that he had angered the woman who now moved gently onto the shore, her skin dry and smooth. He turned his head to the sound of an arrow being notched. The man had taken one of his silver arrows, fixed it, and pulled the mighty bow back to his ear. His muscles strained as he pointed it to the sky and loosed. The sound was magnificent, like a note plucked on a lyre's string as the arrow shot into the heavens, glistening like a brilliant star across the sky. It was beautiful too, Lucius thought.

The two strangers stared at Lucius then, nodded to each other. The man stepped forward first and looked into Lucius' eyes. "We must be going now. The sun and moon continue onward and so must we."

"But...but..." Lucius found he did not want them to depart. Being around them filled something within himself. "Won't you stay? We can talk some more."

"It is not possible for now, but do not fear, young Metellus. We will meet again. *Never* fear."

"What should I do?"

"Do?" That took the man with the bow by surprise. "Until we meet again?" The little boy nodded vigorously. "You should continue to train your body and mind, fear nothing, dream, and above all things, honour the Gods."

"I will." Lucius bowed his little head, he did not know why. He felt a warm hand on his shoulder. When he looked up, the man had gone leaving only the woman standing before him on the river's edge; the crystal water caressed her feet. "Do you also have to leave?" Lucius asked sadly.

Yes he heard her say clearly though her lips did not move. She smiled radiantly as she approached him. "I must be gone also, but know that I am never truly gone, nor is my far-shooting brother." Lucius nodded, then froze as she leaned forward, her golden hair falling around his face, and kissed his forehead. He felt a cool comforting breeze on the back of his neck as he looked into her eyes, unafraid.

"Thank you." The words barely escaped his lips. She looked back to the water where its flow increased, and sound started to trickle back into Lucius' ears.

"I must go now." There was urgency in her voice. "We too will meet again but for now you shall not remember this, nor remember my touch." Lucius looked saddened, but the caress of her hand upon his cheek lightened his heart. He smiled again, overcome with sleep as he laid himself down in the tall grass. With a final glimpse of the boy, Love turned to the water and was gone upon the breeze that blows ever on.

The birds sang once again, a song for the evening. The leaves in the trees rustled, and the river gurgled as it rippled past. In the sky, the clouds had grown pink with the changing sunlight, the air cooler.

When Lucius opened his eyes, his return to wakefulness was slow and unwanted. He knew not how long he had lain asleep, but from the look of things it was late. He was about to get up from the ground when two doves fluttered high above where he lay in the grass. He then felt something on his leg near his ankle. His first reaction was to jump but then he knew that would not be wise. He fought back a sudden fear as he realised that a serpent had come to stay near him. He felt it slithering over his bare legs; the cool smoothness of it sent a shiver through his body as it passed, but he did not move. He waited until it was gone and then got up slowly.

Lucius wanted to grab his wooden sword and hit it, kill it, but something inside him held him fast and instead he watched it pick its sleek way amid the blades of grass. When he was sure it was gone, he picked up his sword and put on his cloak to leave. Suddenly, he realised he had forgotten something: Alene's flowers.

He looked around the grassy area, his eyes searched the clumps of colour that dotted the riverbank. Finally, he decided upon some bright delicate flowers for his sister and picked a handful of them. Knowing full well he would be in immense trouble if they noticed he had been gone so long, he darted off along the riverbank and the path to the docks. Before heading down the path to leave the grassy space, he looked back. Something made him smile and he turned to go home, humming happily the entire way.

The following week, Diodorus was well again. Lucius was grateful his tutor was no longer ill and though slightly tired looking, the old white-bearded man entered the atrium of the Metellus domus smiling kindly at his favourite student waiting impatiently on a stool for his arrival. The gentle Greek had no lesson planned for the day, having decided to allow Lucius to talk for a time about what he had been up to while he was ill, what he had read and thought in his absence.

After a short walk to the Forum Boarium, they seated themselves in the shade of an awning next to a farmer selling a variety of fruits and vegetables. Lucius asked whether they should seek another spot to watch the world go by, but Diodorus insisted that as it was his first day out of doors the musty smell of the manure from the cattle market was good for him. It reminded him he was still alive. So, as they sampled some juicy figs, Lucius began to ramble on contentedly about the world around them, the sky, the people, and the river beyond the forum.

Diodorus spent that entire day listening to the intoxicating enthusiasm of a child who had come to notice and appreciate the world about him, immune to doubt or disbelief, pessimism and lack of wonder. He thought how, this time, the teacher learned from the student while he viewed the world he so loved to talk about with fresh eyes, after several days of bed-ridden sickness. It was a gift Diodorus would never forget.

From that time on, their relationship was one of mutual respect and friendship; each was happy to learn from the other about what they knew. Age and experience flowed along with youth and enthusiasm for several years. Diodorus was very proud of Lucius who was approaching manhood with every new day.

Yet, as with all things, change became inevitable and the endless tide of life came and went. In the green Spring of Lucius' promising life and the cold Winter of his own, Diodorus passed to the world beyond to begin anew. Never again would Lucius hear the old man's shaky laughter, or converse with him in the midst of Rome's streets. His voice was muted then, except for the occasional memory that would whisper to Lucius' mind from the other side of the River.

It was a peaceful death, contemplative and painless. One day, Diodorus had felt extremely weak, frail, and tired. From there, the sensations increased such that he knew he should ready himself for the long slumber all must take. In his final days, he had himself seated in front of the window of his home that looked out onto one of the various forums and markets so that he could watch life go by as he awaited death. In those final days and hours, his favourite pupil, to whose home he had so often gone, now came to his own home to keep him company. Lucius spoke to him of his own promising life and read to him, not history or rhetoric, but poetry. He listened to poetry that revered the world about them: Nature, Beauty, Love and the Gods that made it all possible. The images of a lifetime flowed through his mind like acts in a play: sometimes sad, sometimes joyous, but always his very own.

Diodorus died peacefully in his sleep with Lucius Metellus Anguis at his side. When the time came, the young man of fifteen wished his friend farewell, placed a coin in his mouth, and went to notify the physician, a friend of Diodorus', who had been waiting dutifully in another room.

A monument was raised to the old Greek along the via Appia, the road he would have taken had he the chance to return to his beloved homeland. Many families came and went from there to show their appreciation for his presence in life but Lucius did not. He knew what Diodorus would have said: *Don't go crying to a slab of finely hewn marble when I die. Instead, go out, think of me, and think of what you learned from me during our time together.*

And so, Lucius spent his days out in the world admiring its beauty and variety as Diodorus did, and his nights indoors reading through the chests of precious scrolls that had been bequeathed to him by his tutor and friend.

XVIII

SODALITAS MORTIFERA

'Deadly Companionship'

The weather in Africa Province made it a place of contrasts during the first days of December. The elements vied with each other over the land in much the same way as beasts, men and gods had from the time of some beginning now lost to memory. The sea began its first assault on the sandy shores, threatening to push inland behind the wind. From all directions, the gusty air blew and battered the sandy earth shifting it, pushing it back, and piling it up, scarring it. Though forced to change, land and sand stood fast and met the next force that whipped across it.

In the skies, light and dark collided at dawn and dusk, one giving way to the other. In between, battle unfolded between cloud and sun, rain and wind. A never ending clash of wills ensued and to the victor would go the laurels of winter and power over the world below.

The echo of this confrontation seeped in everywhere, more so between two travellers locked together by fear and hatred, of each other, of their quarry, of the brutal man who had sent them into the desert together.

Argus and Brutus hated each other with a fervour that most men would not wish to keep up and that most beasts could not conceive of. Thanks to Plautianus, they were stuck together until the completion of their mission. It was because of Plautianus that they now found themselves on aged horses, dressed in rags, and travelling across the windy African void for weeks until they reached Carthage. The sea route was forbidden they were told, so as to maintain the secrecy of their mission and presence, but Argus suspected that the Praetorian prefect, now Consul, had insisted they go the landward route for his amusement, if not for their punishment. If either one of them had not complied, they would be lying in a ditch with their throats cut, their eye sockets empty after the crows' feasting.

They had only been journeying for two days but already the tension and distrust that existed at the outset had increased tenfold. As he rode, Argus wished he were back in Leptis Magna enjoying the comforts and services of the city and the women. It would be some time, he knew, before he would sleep on a comfortable bed between soft thighs. He turned in his saddle to see Brutus riding, staring at him, about twenty feet away.

"Keep up or we'll never get anywhere!"

"Fuck yourself, Praetorian!" Brutus spat back. He had not raised a hand against Argus, though he was not afraid of him. Instead he uttered nothing but obscenities and degradations. It was hard for Argus to stay his sword every moment.

"Just shut up, you lump of shit, and ride faster!" Argus pulled hard on the reigns of the pack horse that carried his belongings; on the beast were a bow and quiver of arrows, an extra sword he would give to Brutus when the time came, and a box with several phials of poison. Lastly, there was a round basket secured tightly with thick rope so that the lid would not come off; inside were two asps that he had purchased in the markets of Leptis Magna before they had set out. He made certain Brutus did not know of these or the poisons, for he most certainly would not approve of their intended use.

The wind picked up then, and Argus pulled the cloth that was tied around his neck up over his mouth and nose to block out the sand. He thought for a moment that he could hear Plautianus laughing on the wind and he cursed him beneath his breath. How had he known the truth about Quintus Metellus being his father? That had been something that Argus had wanted to keep to himself, to use as he chose against the senator. Before they had set out across the desert, Plautianus had questioned him every day about his willingness to undertake the mission, and his dedication to him and the Praetorians.

This mission would earn him a promotion, Plautianus had assured him, and allow him to live in luxury in Rome. The task ahead was not an easy one, but Argus knew he could do it. For too long, Lucius, his half-brother, had outdone him in everything; militarily, intellectually, and physically. Even the omens were consistently better for Lucius than for himself. Lucius had always been the preferred, legitimate son of Metellus and had now grown arrogant, had forgotten their one-time bond in favour of Ashur. He would pay for that. Change was in the wind and Argus could sense it, smell it, like a jackal that lifts its nose into the air and picks up the scent of blood - evidence of a creature that has been wounded and is ready to take down.

How would he do it when the time came? He had killed many men, even women and children, in order to make opponents suffer. Lucius was alone, that much he knew. It could not be some secretive means that he used, poison or a distant bowshot. He wanted Lucius to know it was him when he plunged the blade into his gut. He wanted to see the pain in his eyes.

Argus' thoughts were interrupted by Brutus who had ridden up beside him. "What are you thinking about, Praetorian?"

"None of your business."

"Fine."

"You ride in front now. I want to keep my eye on you."

"Ha!" Brutus twisted up his ugly scarred face and spat out the corner of his mouth. "I don't trust you anymore than you trust me, boy. I remember you, following that tribune's orders like a dog."

"You'd better keep your mouth shut if you know what's good for you," Argus warned under his breath, but Brutus ignored him.

"I remember the day you threw me down into that black fucking stench on the galley. Quite proud of yourself, you were."

"Bloody right! Now, if you don't ride on and get out of my face for a bit, I'll throw you into a mine next time."

Brutus smirked and began to ride on in front. "Don't fool yourself," he called over his shoulder. "You're as much a slave as me!"

Argus hated the man. He wished he could just slit his throat now and be done with it, but he knew that Plautianus was right; Brutus' rage, hatred and expendability would be useful. He would have to wait for the right moment when he could kill him, after he had served his purpose. For now, however, he was stuck in the middle of nowhere with him while Plautianus was in Rome with the rest of the Praetorian Guard, being made Consul. *After this mission, I won't have to live like this anymore. No more shit. A life of luxury*, he reminded himself.

Carthage, their destination for the time being, was a long way off. There would be many sleepless nights with one eye open and a sword in hand before they reached the city and comfort. He wondered if there were already messages waiting for him at the inn near the port where he was to make contact. He shook the thought from his mind; if he began to think of that now, he would go mad. There were, as yet, many more days of travel with Brutus' hateful face to endure, and so Argus pulled the hood of his black cloak over his head and plodded on, watchful of the scum up ahead. *I can't wait to kill him.*

Each night was the same and each day longer than the next, but after almost a month Argus and Brutus came within sight of Carthage. The journey had become easier when they had turned north, to the west of Tacape, leaving the boredom and desolation of the great salt lake behind for the cooler route along the sea. There, the weather too had grown more

412

hospitable, though distant clouds on the sea warned that that could change at any moment.

The tenement was located in the less desirable area near the port of Carthage; it was noisy, unbelievably filthy and dangerous. Most importantly, it was inconspicuous; much like the neighbourhood, little attention was paid to anything that went on there. Argus left Brutus outside in the street with the horses and went inside to make sure things were in order. It occurred to him that all of the dank places in which he usually awaited his orders smelled the same; a strange, pungent mixture of sour wine, urine and sweat-soaked woodwork. He approached the cracked wooden counter where a man made no attempt to hide his scrutiny.

"What do you want?" the man asked.

"Do you have anything for me?" Argus leaned on the wine-stained counter.

"What the hell are you talking about? Piss off!" The man stood up and his belly rested on the wood. Argus smiled. The man frowned like a confused hog, one nostril dripped a glistening stream to the corner of his mouth until he wiped it with his dirty hand. "You some kind of funny man looking for trouble?"

"*Vipera.*" Argus coolly gave the password Plautianus had told him about.

The man fell back down onto his stool. "Right...right. Sorry. Didn't know it was you," he mumbled. "Go on up. It's in order. No questions."

"About time, you piece of shit." Argus walked past him, spun and pulled out his dagger to rest on the man's stomach. "If you ever look at me again, I'll gut you right here. Got it?"

The man snorted in his shock and fear. "G...go...got it. Yes. Fine."

"Anyone leave anything for me here?"

"N...no...no, sir. Nothing." He looked away as Argus went up the stairs to check out their quarters.

I hope we don't have to stay here long, Argus thought to himself as he pushed open the door to the room. *I hate waiting.*

XIX

DONA AB MARI

'Gifts from the Sea'

Hadrumetum. It was here that Lucius stood and looked out from the port with worry as a massive wall of cloud and fog held sway in the distance, shrouding the sea from view. The conditions had turned in the Mare Internum and all ships had been either slowed, thrown off course, or made to turn back to their various points of departure.

Lucius and the two centuries commanded by Valerus and Pephredo had been in the busy port town for a week now. It was the third day after the Kalends of December already, and there was still no sign or word of the ship that Adara and Ashur were to arrive on. The dark, hovering wall out at sea did little to instill confidence or a peaceful frame of mind in Lucius or any of the other expectant people waiting daily on the docks.

The young tribune waited side by side with the local magistrate, harbour master, and a slew of merchants, the latter impatient for their cargo ships to return so that they could be sent out again laden with amphorae of precious olive oil bound for Rome. There was always a sense of urgency at this time of year, Lucius had been told, because the weather tended to be so unpredictable, and the final cargoes for the winter brought income to the merchants that would sustain them until the next sailing season. This thought did not help Lucius, who knew that the cargo he waited for was infinitely more precious and valuable than a load of oil, grain or wine.

Some time after the execution of the traitors in Lambaesis, around the Ides of November, Lucius had received an urgent letter by special messenger. It was from Publius Leander Antoninus. In it, Publius greeted his son-in-law warmly and notified him that they had secured passage for Adara and the others on a ship bound for Hadrumetum via Syracusae. He had journeyed with the captain on previous occasions and assured Lucius that he was a very able, wise seaman who had sailed the middle-sea from one end to the other without ever losing a cargo or falling prey to pirates. He had a swift, medium-sized merchant vessel whose sail bore the image of a tall cedar on a white background.

A tall cedar... Lucius' eye watched for it. The letter had said that the ship was expected to arrive in the first days of December, and so upon being granted the request by the legate, Lucius set out with two centuries to meet his wife and escort her back to Lambaesis.

Gaius Flavius Marcellus insisted that Lucius go early with the men on leave to attend the Ludi Plebeii in Thysdrus before making their way to Hadrumetum. His men, the legate insisted, deserved the time away. At the same time, Alerio and Eligius' men were given a furlough in which they attended the same games in Thamugadi. The official dates for the games were from the fourth to the seventeenth of November, but in Thysdrus, the Games always went a little longer than usual since people came from all over Africa Province to be entertained in the magnificent amphitheatre there.

Lucius, Valerus, Pephredo, some of the Sarmatians, and the rest of the men spent a week in Thysdrus. The games had been exciting with some of the best and most notorious gladiators in the Provinces coming out to perform. Many of the men made money on their bets, more lost, but all of them enjoyed the time off - the distraction helped them to forget a little more the tragedy that their cohort had experienced.

The men, however, were not accompanied to the arena by their tribune for more than two days, as Lucius spent most of his time at the Temple of Jupiter making offerings for a safe journey for Adara. He also spent time in the markets looking for a special gift for his wife. Saturnalia was approaching and this would be the only time he had to himself to get her something. Though a prosperous city, there was not much that caught Lucius' eye. There were vast amounts of pottery, spices, oils and other goods, but not quite exactly what he had in mind.

Finally, on a sunny day when the light from above reached into every stall and kiosk, Lucius was stopped by a flash from somewhere. He looked over a makeshift counter to see what it was that gleamed so interestingly. A short man with rings through both ears, curly black hair, and a simple striped tunic came over.

"Something interest you, sir?" The voice came in broken, thickly accented Latin. The big, but kind eyes peered up at Lucius.

"What is that, over there?" Lucius pointed to the half-covered item. Evidently, it was not meant to be on display. The gentle breeze must have pushed back the silk covering.

"Ah. I am sorry. That is not for sale."

"Is it not?" Lucius crossed his arms, knowing full-well the game that he was being drawn into. "Then why is it on your counter?"

"A mistake, sir. That item has journeyed far."

"If you say so. I was hoping to find something very special. Oh, well." Lucius turned and began to walk away.

"Wait! Wait, Man of the Tiber. I suppose..."

He feigns reluctance well, Lucius thought.

"...I suppose, sir, that you will appreciate this item. It was hidden and yet, you saw it. You have the eyes of a hawk."

This was going a little too far. Lucius knew he had him interested in selling.

"Very well. Let me see it." Lucius waited as the man turned, drew back the silk, and took up the item gently with a smaller piece of silk. He placed it on the counter between them and smiled as Lucius' face was lit up by the sun's reflection off it.

"Is it not beautiful?" The merchant stepped back to better observe the Roman's reaction.

417

"The workmanship is…not bad." *In fact*, Lucius thought to himself, *the workmanship is exquisite.* It was a golden arm bangle that circled three full times. Along it were intricate designs of golden granulation broken occasionally by brilliant pieces of lapis lazuli. At each end of the bangle were larger pieces of lapis delicately carved in the form of cobra heads.

Lucius picked it up, scrutinised it closely, as though he knew what he was looking for. The merchant's eye narrowed as he decided that this buyer required more information, and more prodding.

"It was made by an expert craftsman, a cousin of mine in Caesarea. It came from Palestine just three weeks ago. Every now and then he sends me his most precious work because he knows I have appreciative buyers here. Africa is much more sophisticated." Lucius looked at him, then back at the bangle, with an unsure look on his face. "My cousin uses only the purest gold, of course, and the lapis…imported directly from Aegyptus."

"How much?" The question hung in the air between them as the merchant mulled it over.

"A special price for you, sir. A thousand sestertii."

"A thousand?" Lucius could not believe the sum he just heard. "Thank you, but no." He turned to leave again and this time the merchant came around the counter and pulled on his arm.

"Wait, sir. Wait. I can see that you have a keen eye, and I would sell this item only to one who appreciates it as you do. Let us say eight-hundred and fifty sestertii."

"I'm waiting for a better price, my friend." The merchant began to sweat, not wanting to go any lower, but he knew that soon business would die down with the end of the games. This year there had been fewer wealthy Romans passing through than usual.

"Seven hundred."

"I'll give you six hundred and fifty sestertii for it." Lucius stood firm on that as the merchant's round head reddened.

"Six hundred and fifty?" Lucius nodded. "Too little."

"Very well." Lucius turned to leave, but before he could begin walking, he felt the man's desperate grip on his arm.

"Yes! Yes! Six hundred and fifty. All right." The man almost seemed upset, but he wanted to sell the item rather than hang onto it for gods knew how long.

"Done." Lucius removed his leather pouch from his tunic and pulled out the coins. The man smiled once his eyes fell on the money. "Here you go." Lucius dropped them into his hand with a jingle and picked up the bangle, carefully wrapping it in the deep blue silk. "A pleasure doing business with you."

"You are a thief, Roman!" The man made the obligatory curse. "But a generous one. Please come again!" he called after Lucius who was already on his way back to the inn where he was staying, to tuck the gift away carefully so that no one would find it.

When he arrived in his room, he unwrapped the bangle to look at it again. It was indeed one of the finest things he had seen and he could not believe the price he had paid. No doubt he could have paid less, but as it was a gift for his wife he did not want to haggle to the point of nastiness. Adara would love it and that was what mattered to him.

Lucius thought of the gold and lapis bangle as he waited in the harbour of Hadrumetum for Adara. The clouds had not shown any signs of clearing and he began to worry more now, wonder if he would have the chance to give it to her at all.

Off to one side there were shouts as a small, fast merchant vessel came to a stop at the far end of the docks. More shouts went up as a crowd gathered to see who it was. A tall, lanky man jumped immediately from the boat and came running to the grouping where the city magistrate and harbour master were still standing. The magistrate pointed in Lucius' direction and the sailor came running.

He was out of breath when he arrived but managed to speak. "Are...you...Tribune Metellus?" Lucius began to panic

419

inside, fearing the worst. The man's clothes were torn up, and the ship he had come in on seemed to be in rough shape.

"Yes, I am." Lucius looked at the man evenly. "You have news for me?"

"Yes, Tribune."

"Go on then." *Gods make it good news.*

"There has been a bad storm out at sea these past three days, and many ships are lost or adrift. Our ship managed to come through because we were faster but as we were making our way, we came upon a merchant ship."

"With a cedar tree upon the sail?"

"Yes, Tribune. They called over to us as we passed, and when we approached and told them where we were headed the captain asked us to deliver a message to you."

"What is it?"

"The captain said that they will be arriving tomorrow. They are waiting out the storm, and he has a feeling that it will clear briefly. All aboard are safe."

Lucius sighed and rubbed his face. Relief settled over him and he allowed the terrible thoughts that had been plaguing him to drift away. "You're sure about what he said?"

"Yes, sir. Word for word."

"Good. Thank you for the message." Lucius reached into his scrip, pulled out two silver denarii and handed them to the sailor. "There you go. For your pains."

"Thank you, Tribune." The man nodded a few times gratefully and went back to help unload his own small vessel.

"Thank you, Gods." Lucius said as he took one last look at the sea and went back to the inn to see Valerus and Pephredo and speak about orders for the following day.

That night, he did not sleep. Excitement, tinged with a bit of nervousness, kept him awake as he thought of what he would say to his wife whom he had not seen in months, how she would look to his eyes, and he to hers. No greater joy could he imagine then than holding her in his arms and not letting go for anything.

The fog and clouds had been thick, damp and grey for days and the seas choppy. But, the captain had sniffed his way clear of danger over and over again so that they had avoided the damages incurred by his counterparts elsewhere in the storm.

For the majority of the passengers stranded in the dark hull of the ship, the journey seemed ten times longer than it actually should have. Few ventured on deck and several had become ill. A separate area had been set aside for the women where they could have a measure of privacy in their discomfort. It was here, behind rough hangings that Adara and Alene waited out the storm and the difficult passage. Each in turn had been violently ill before becoming acclimatised to the ship's swaying. Carissa too had not been well, and Ashur did his utmost to make her comfortable along with the others, bringing them blankets and dried bread that the captain insisted would help.

Occasionally, Ashur would venture out on deck to ask the captain about their progress, for any sign that the storm was going to let up. Most times however, he was disappointed by the answers he received; either he was told the storm was getting worse, or he was met with annoyed silence when, as the sailors saw it, he interrupted their duties.

Each traveller was forced to find his or her own courage. Adara thought of seeing Lucius, as did Alene, eager as ever to see her younger brother and rejoin him with his pregnant wife. Ashur thought that being with Carissa would ease his impatience with the seas, but she was distant and not to find comfort in even his presence or the strong arms that he wrapped about her as they sat huddled in thick homespun.

Carissa thought only of Emrys. He had left Greece several weeks before they had, and ever since then she was inwardly lost without him. For years he had been there: a teacher, a friend, and a father. However, his insistence on leaving her in Greece to return to Rome and continue the work they had left unfinished was painful. She found herself alone, despite the fact she was now with a man that she loved beyond art or the joy of creating. Ashur was the only man that had ever enchanted and mystified her more than what she sculpted with her own hands. There was something about him that made her feel safe, but there was something sad in him too that she could also see in herself. They shared something certainly, but was it, she often wondered, enough? Could she leave behind the world she had known and loved, a world that included Emrys - kind, gentle Emrys - for a world that did not include him?

Ashur was not unaware of the thoughts tormenting Carissa, and it pained him greatly to feel so helpless. It was not a problem that could be solved with the point of a sword or any feat of martial prowess. All he could do was sit and listen and watch the young woman, who had taught him what love was, fall further into an oddly beautiful melancholy. Her eyes sparkled with tears in the night, and the shiver of her body against his in the dark made him feel strangely alive. He wanted to help her but had no idea how. That hurt him the most.

Suddenly, as if awakening to peaceful reality after a long nightmare, Adara, Alene and the others heard the sailors' voices shouting out. They rose from their beds to find that the ship had almost completely stopped its incessant dance upon crested waves. Ashur put on his cloak and went up to see what was happening. Apparently, a small ship had been sighted making for the coast, Hadrumetum as it happened, and the captain had signalled for them to approach. When finally they came close enough for speech, the captain asked them to take a message to the port for them. Immediately, Ashur went down to the women to tell them the good news that they would be arriving the following day and that the captain had given a message to a small ship to pass on to Lucius, who would certainly be waiting for them.

They were still surrounded by storm clouds in the distance and the captain wanted to make certain which way they decided to turn so that they would not end up in the storm again. Adara held her swollen belly lovingly, cried, and thanked the Gods for bringing them safely to Africa.

When day broke on the morrow, Adara and Alene helped each other to clean and prepare themselves for disembarkation. The air was very cool and there was as yet a slight wind but they nevertheless wanted to be on deck for their first sight of land. Adara, wrapped in her blue cloak and Alene, in a long green one, followed Ashur and Carissa topside where the captain greeted them and said that they were pressing on. There were still clouds ahead that prevented them from seeing the shoreline, but he knew it was there and pointed out the small pod of dolphins leaping about the ship's nose. Dolphins, he said, were a very good omen and would lead them safely to Hadrumetum.

After two hours during which those on deck filled their lungs with fresh air rather than the stale air of the hull, they found themselves in almost completely still waters thick with fog. It was a strange contrast compared with the violent realm through which they had been travelling for so long. All was quiet and shrouded; it was as though they had to pass through a middle world to reach their destination. Eventually, the wall of fog began to dissipate and transform into a vast wall of light as the sun on the other side burned away the darkness that held them. Finally, a thick beam of sunlight pushed its way through, then another, and another until the ship's prow emerged. Adara and the others had to shield their eyes from the sun's glare that deflected off a golden world of sand ahead.

Hadrumetum could be spotted in front of them and cheers went up from the crew as the sun finally poured across the entire deck. Adara and Alene looked on in wonder at a new world for both of them. Beyond sandy shores was a flat land of gold and green and even further, the flat gave way to hills and then mountains of muted earth, reds, and spotted greens. The ship turned toward the natural harbour where large numbers of people waited. On the north end of the city, in a larger open space, a large mass of ordered men stood in formation, several banners flying in the breeze at their forefront.

"Lucius!" Adara spotted the tall crimson crest of her husband where he stood waiting for her.

"It *is* him!" Alene agreed. "Oh, Adara, he'll be so happy to see you. I wonder how he looks after so long." Alene always wondered that, because every time she had seen him after a period of separation, he looked older.

When the sail with the cedar upon it finally emerged from the wall of cloud and fog, Lucius bowed his head silently to whichever god had brought the ship safely to port. He could see Adara immediately from her bright blue cloak and smiled. There were others around her; no doubt Ashur was the one in the black cloak. The other travellers must have been passengers heading for the same port.

Eventually, the ship reached the harbour and Lucius walked eagerly along the wooden quay to watch as his wife came closer and closer to him. He had asked that Mar, Dagon, Valerus, Pephredo and Frontus stay behind with the men so that he might greet his wife and friend first before being escorted back to the villa. His friends had, of course, willingly acceded to his wish and stood patiently beneath fluttering banners while the tribune welcomed his wife.

As the ship approached, Lucius' eyes met Adara's and they held each other's gaze, each wanting to smile, to cry, to yell out of sheer joy. It had seemed like ages.

Lucius had dressed himself in full armour, and Adara smiled when she noticed the hilt of the sword she had given him protruding above his shoulder. His helmet obscured his face slightly, making it hard to see, but his eyes gave her the welcome she had been dreaming of for so long.

The bustle began promptly the moment the ship was secured, and the dock filled with men who began unloading cargo, greeting friends and exchanging news. Ashur helped Adara down the gangplank onto the quay, followed by a woman in a hooded green cloak, and another woman. But Lucius kept his eyes on Adara and as they walked toward each other their hands were outstretched in anticipation of that first touch.

"My love." Lucius held her hands, kissing them gently before holding her face and staring at her to take in every inch. "Thank the Gods you're safe."

"I missed you, Lucius." She leaned forward to hug him, her arms wrapped tightly about his neck as she stood on her toes to reach him. All about them people moved and yelled and pushed in the chaos that accompanied the arrival of a ship in Hadrumetum, but they felt alone together like an island in the middle of a stormy sea. She kissed him tenderly on the mouth; both had feared they had forgotten the sensation of each other's lips. "Don't ever leave me again, my love. Never."

"Never again," he reiterated. "I'm never letting go." Then Adara tilted her head, the way he loved, and smiled as she looked down to her belly. "We're all here, safely." Lucius, wide eyed and smiling, put his hand beneath her cloak to feel her swollen belly. His touch made her shudder and she felt movement within. "Our child knows its father, I think."

Lucius was going to speak again, but Adara beat him to it. "I have a surprise for you," she said as she stepped aside to reveal the green-cloaked woman behind her, with her head down.

"What surprise?"

The woman stepped forward, raised her head and pulled back the hood quickly. "Alene!" Lucius stepped to her and picked her up in his arms so that her feet left the ground and her golden hair poured out of the cloak's hood. "What are you doing here?"

"I thought that I would see my pregnant sister safely to my little brother and that perhaps…" she smiled cheekily, "…I might stay with you for a time?"

"You can stay as long as you want!" Lucius clapped his hands loudly. "Gods, what a day!" Lucius then spotted Ashur coming down the gangplank and turned to Adara and Alene. "I'll be right back." He strode over to meet his friend, but before he could greet him he already had a sense that something was not right, that Ashur Mehrdad had changed. As Ashur approached, Lucius smiled a sad smile as he noticed that Ashur was older, a little hunched. The light that had once burned so brightly in his eyes was now faded.

"Lucius." Ashur stepped forward and embraced him. "We made it."

"Ashur. It's good to see you, my friend. Are you well?"

"Well enough. How are you?"

Lucius looked back at his wife and sister. "Better now. Much better. Carissa?" Lucius noticed her standing off to the side behind Ashur and went around to greet her. "It's good to see you as well." He kissed her hand. "I trust the Gods find you in good spirits?"

"They find me well enough, Lucius." That was all she said, her head hung low as she looked toward Ashur from beneath her hood.

"The journey was not an easy one." Ashur spoke again seeing Carissa's discomfort.

"Well, now you're all here, we can rest for a week before heading back to Lambaesis." They all stood together now. Lucius looked back to where the men stood a short distance off with a litter. He waved, and four men picked up the litter and began to move toward them.

"It seems my little brother has brought an escort for us." Alene put her hand on Lucius' shoulder.

"I've come with two centuries and some cavalry for the journey. I'll introduce you to some good friends shortly. For now, where are all your belongings?" He reached down to grasp Adara's hand in one and Alene's in the other.

Then there was a loud neighing, and the sound of stomping hooves upon wood. Lucius watched as a beautiful white

426

stallion was led off the ship. Adara went directly to the man who had the horse. Lucius followed. As soon as she approached, she took the bridle from the man and the stallion was calm again, if not a little unsteady, now that he was back on land.

"I decided to bring Phoenix with me. I didn't know when I would return to Greece." Lucius smiled as his wife stroked the animal's long nose. The animal calmed.

"He's beautiful, Adara." Lucius reached out to pet him but the stallion drew back. However, after looking him over, Phoenix seemed to decide that Lucius was all right and allowed him the contact as he, in turn, prodded the armoured man gently with his snout.

"He likes you. Good. Will there be room for him where we're going?"

"Of course. Lots."

"There's so much I want to ask you, Lucius...so much I want to say."

"I know, my love. Me too. For now, let's get back to the villa so that you can rest. Wait with the others while I give the harbour master instructions for your belongings." Lucius went over to the harbour master and indicated the two wagons that were approaching the quay. The man nodded and assured him that all their belongings would be brought safely to the villa. Lucius gave him some money and rejoined Adara and the others to help the three women into the litter. As he was about to close the curtains to give them some privacy Adara spoke up.

"Please, Lucius, can we keep them open? We've been confined for so long. A view will be a nice change. Is that all right? Is it safe?"

He thought about it for a moment and realised it would be fine. It was a short walk, and they could use the fresh air. "All right. Ashur, can you take Phoenix for me while I lead the way?"

427

"Of course, Lucius. Anything." Ashur took the bridle and walked behind the litter as they moved to join the two centuries of men and cavalry. He realised that he did not feel altogether comfortable with Lucius, and hoped that might change. Sometimes, when friends are parted for so long, they can change so much that they no longer seem familiar. Ashur hoped he was wrong, but inside he knew that at least he had definitely transformed.

"Would you look at that, Adara," Alene whispered into her ear. "By Apollo, those horsemen look strange."

"They do. And look at that banner." Adara spotted the draconarius held by Dagon. "It's in the form of a dragon." As they approached, Mar and Dagon dismounted and approached Lucius along with Valerus and Pephredo. Frontus went to stand directly behind Lucius, the vexillum hoisted high for all to see.

Adara and Alene looked on in wonder, never before having seen Lucius in his role as tribune. At once he seemed older, his voice louder, and his demeanour prouder. It seemed to the two women that many of the troops looked on with pride at Lucius' approach, and that even with a litter full of women, there was no break in discipline.

Their eyes were drawn to Lucius' own beautiful banner with the dragon upon it that ruffled in the sea breeze; they were somewhat taken aback when the man holding it turned to reveal a missing eye. Lucius, however, seemed to have great respect for his standard bearer as well as for the two heavily armoured horsemen who followed him up to the litter.

"Adara, Alene, Ashur and Carissa, may I present Lord Mar and Dagon of the Sarmatian auxiliary ala." The two men bowed deeply to the women who returned the greeting with polite nods. "We have fought together against the desert nomads. They saved my life," Lucius added.

"In that case, lords," Adara smiled, "it is our honour to meet you." Dagon blushed at her words, struck by the beauty of both women. Mar spoke for both of them.

"We have heard a great deal about both of you." He also gave a slight nod to Ashur and Carissa who were feeling more and more out of place. "The tribune has been waiting for this day for some time."

"We have been waiting for this day also for a long time, Lord Mar," Alene added. "We are grateful for your escort."

"It is our privilege, Lady Metella," Dagon said as he finally found his tongue.

The sun was getting low in the west now and Lucius thought it best that they get back to the villa. Mar and Dagon returned to their mounts, and Frontus brought over Lunaris. Adara gasped when she saw the stallion. Lucius looked magnificent atop the dapple grey steed, and as the wind picked up and whipped his crimson cloak to one side, he gave an order and Balbus sounded the cornu. The first century departed in front, and Lucius and the litter with Ashur next. The rear was brought up by the second century while the cavalry spread out on either side.

The villa was located amid the olive groves on the western edge of Hadrumetum. It was not immense, but after the sea voyage, anything with a proper roof and bed conjured luxury for Adara, Alene, and Carissa. Even Ashur expressed some gratefulness when he saw the simple bed that was to be his and Carissa's.

As Lucius was showing them around the buildings, he explained that the villa belonged to a friend of his Commander who had arranged for them to stay there until they were prepared to return to base. There was a large outdoor courtyard through which they had to pass to reach the main buildings. It had heavy wooden gates that could be barred safely during the night. Inside in a corner, there was an area to stable the horses comfortably; as it turned out, Lunaris and Phoenix seemed at ease with one another, eating their oats and straw side by side.

The main building contained several cubicula for sleeping and a decently appointed triclinium that opened onto a private garden. Two kitchen slaves and a steward had been left behind to care for the guests. Lastly, there was the bath house. Probably the most welcome sight for the weary travellers, the fires had been kindled so that it was ready for immediate use, and fresh linens laid out with a variety of scented oils and clean strigils.

"We'll have to thank your legate for this luxurious accommodation, Lucius," Adara said as she laid herself down on the bed in their room, her back aching from standing for so long. "I'm so tired." She yawned. "But I'm so happy to be with you. There were times when I never thought to see you again." Lucius struggled with the buckles of his cuirass in a corner near a small window as she spoke. "Here, let me help you with that."

"No I can do it. Rest, my love."

"Don't be silly! I've been looking forward to doing anything and everything with you and for you." She got herself up off the bed slowly and walked over to him. "I thought I'd die of pride seeing you today. So handsome a Roman. I married well." She giggled girlishly.

"I didn't do too badly myself. Do the buckles on the sides first." Adara began to unbuckle them while he held the heavy breastplate so that it would not fall. When it was loose he removed it, placed it against the wall and turned to face her. "Every time I look at you it's like the very first time."

"I feel the same." She nuzzled close to him. When she looked up again, she noticed the scar across his forehead. "Where did you get that?"

"Oh, that." He felt it with his hand. "My helmet cut into me during the battle in the desert that I mentioned."

"Does it hurt?"

"Not anymore." Lucius went over to the door to ask the steward if the baths were being used. They were not. "Come, let's get washed up before the meal. The others are finished with the baths."

Lucius began to remove his padded doublet. Adara sat on the edge of the bed, smiling as she watched. "I've been waiting for this." She winked and Lucius laughed. As he pulled his tunic up over his head, Adara's smile quickly departed and her eyes began to fill with tears.

"Oh, Lucius..." She wept and he knew why. He was thinner, still slightly weak looking, although not unhealthy. He was lashed with scars. "What happened to you?" She held one hand over her mouth, the other supporting her belly. "So many..."

"They look worse than they feel, my love. Don't worry. I'm better now." She looked over his body, so different, older and yet to her eyes, still beautiful.

"What happened out there?"

"I'll tell you later. For now, let's bathe." She acquiesced and they both went to the tepidarium in their thick robes. In the courtyard, a lit brazier cast shadows behind the columns that lined the covered walkways.

"The air smells differently in Africa," Adara mused, clutching his hand.

"*Everything* is different here, and much better now that you're with me."

With the doors to the baths bolted, they took in the long-missed sight of each other's bodies, washed and massaged each other in scented oils. Both had changed; Lucius had been severely scarred and Adara was now heavily pregnant. When he leaned down to caress her swollen belly and kiss her, she sighed as though she had been waiting for that moment forever.

In turn, Adara rubbed her husband down with oils and sponges from the sea, concentrating with great care on the harsh, jagged-looking cicatrices that had so marred his statuesque body. Their burning passions set aside for later, they contented themselves to hold each other in the warm soothing waters; to soak up the presence that had been so painfully missing.

431

Later, while Adara went into their cubicula to dress for the meal, Lucius found Alene strolling about the garden. He went directly over to her. She glowed in the moonlight as she smelled the foreign air, her head tilted upward, her eyes closed.

"You look like a goddess, sister," Lucius said calmly so as not to startle her. She opened her eyes and smiled.

"Lucius…this place."

"What about it?" He walked to her side to put his arm around her and look up with her at the star-dusted sky.

"It feels…strange to me."

"Strange?"

"Not in a bad way. I mean, well, like I have always been wanting to come here. I don't know how to explain it."

"I think I know what you mean. I feel the same way every time I look up at the moon, at a palm or at the desert. There's something mysterious and terrible about this land and yet…"

"…it's beautiful unlike any other place," she finished his sentence, knowing exactly what he was thinking. "We still think alike then?"

"Could you have doubted it?"

"No. Never." She was certain of it. "You know, there were times that I feared Adara would not be able to endure your absence."

"It was the same for me." Lucius looked at his sister with great love and pride and affection. "I missed you too, you know. More than I can say."

"We do still think the same then. Oh, Lucius, thank you for wanting me to stay with you. I won't be a burden, I promise. We've been apart too many years."

"You could never be a burden, Alene. You're my sister, I'm your brother. Nothing can ever change that or take it away from us."

She reached up and touched the scar on his forehead. "Just take care of yourself. None of us could bear to lose you." She sighed and held her little brother close. She remembered how she used to tower over him, his head reaching below the pit of her arm. She smiled at how things had changed, how it was now her head that rested beneath his shoulder as he held her close.

"There you both are!" Adara came walking up and Lucius helped her across some uneven ground. "The steward just told me that the meal is ready whenever we would like to eat."

"Are you hungry now?" Lucius asked.

"You must be joking!" Alene laughed. "Your Greek goddess-of-a-wife does nothing but eat these days."

"Try carrying around another person, you Roman beauty, and we'll see how hungry you get. No more eating like a sparrow." The two women giggled together as Lucius led them to the triclinium. He spotted Ashur and Carissa entering the courtyard and waved for them to join them. Ashur waved back and the two of them made their quiet way over to the door.

"Why can't we be alone, love?" Carissa whispered.

"Because, Carissa, I have not seen him in a long time. I should spend as much time with him as possible before he returns to Lambaesis."

"When will you tell him, Ashur?"

"Not now. Later. For now, let's enjoy their company." He kissed her forehead and put on a smile before entering the lamp-lit room and greeting everyone.

The dinner was a surprisingly quiet occasion in which Lucius did most of the talking in the form of answering questions about the legion, and the interesting group of Sarmatian warriors that had been there when the ship had come in.

When asked where the two centurions and the Sarmatian commanders were, he answered that they had insisted on giving the family time to reacquaint after so long, that they were content to remain in the town for the evening. One topic he avoided for the moment was the treachery in the ranks, its discovery and the subsequent outcome. He did not want to breach that, not before he confided it to Adara. If he was to relive that day, he wanted it to be for her ears only.

Carissa answered his questions about Emrys politely, in short sentences, though it soon became apparent that it was a topic to be avoided. Alene regaled Lucius with her impressions of Greece and Athenae and all of the wonderful items she had sent with Emrys for their mother. Lucius thought that she would be thrilled to receive such exotic things and wished he could have been there to see their mother open them.

Alene assured her brother that Antonia was absolutely thrilled about her going to Africa with Adara, that she had stressed her belief that it was a wonderful opportunity that Alene should not miss. Lucius thought that the adamance with which Antonia had supposedly said all this was slightly out of character. He knew that in the past, she always inserted a little compulsory, motherly guilt at being separated from her offspring. He was however, delighted that Alene was allowed to join him freely, without guilt or sadness. Besides, their mother still had her hands full with young Quintus, Clarinda and their father.

When they had finished eating, Lucius bid everyone a fond goodnight, made sure himself that the gate was barred and the horses cared for, before he joined Adara in their room. Several lamps were lit and Adara lay already fast asleep upon the bed, her dark, naked body half-covered by two layers of twisted sheets. Lucius smiled and stared at her, remembering how, for a time, he thought he would never see this happy day.

She was a sleeping goddess. Having traversed the dark depths of an untamed deep, she had finally come to rest on a sunlit, sandy beach, giving in to tiredness at last. Long, black curls wound themselves about her head, neck and shoulders. Lucius knelt beside the bed to admire her, careful not to disturb her peaceful slumber. One of her breasts protruded from the soft sheets, as did her slender arms and a long, soft leg. The kneeling Roman wondered if there had ever been such a beauty even among the Amazons.

Beneath the sheet, he could see the outline of their child within her. How would it be to be a father? He was determined not to make the same mistakes his father had made, mistakes that had led to their estrangement.

Adara moved slightly as he set aside his clothing and lay down beside her. Instinctively one of her arms reached for him and her green eyes opened slowly. "Tell me what happened, Lucius." She said softly.

"Tell you what, my love?" He knew the answer to that but wanted to be sure she was ready to hear it.

"About your men, the battle, everything. I want to know."

"You're not too tired for that?"

"No." She turned as best she could onto her side, placed her hand upon his chest and felt his heart pounding. "I need to know and you need to tell me."

"Yes. I do."

"I'm listening."

"Very well. Where do I begin? I killed a man in Leptis Magna…"

For what seemed like hours, Lucius unfolded all that had happened to him since the death of the Praetorian guardsman at his own hands. Adara listened attentively, sometimes fearfully, to what he told her. So much had happened to him since they had parted. How many times had he almost been killed, lost to her? More than she wished to count. Instead she decided to look at it as the number of times the Gods had spared him.

Lucius told Adara about Dido, though in no great detail, as he did not want to cause her undue worry. Adara was silent at this, jealous. She wondered if this woman really did save Lucius' life as he said. *Don't get angry*, she told herself. *We've just been reunited. This isn't the time to argue.* And so she nodded and listened, pushing back the painful thoughts that crept unwanted into her mind. She told her husband that she was grateful for Dido's help toward him and expressed a wish to meet her, to thank her for Lucius' life. She knew Lucius was a soldier, and she had heard stories about soldiers before, but she hoped that trust in her husband was not something she lacked, that her faith would never be misplaced or unwarranted.

When finally Lucius related to her how he and Alerio had discovered how Antanelis had died, Adara gasped. The terrible way in which the murder was carried out was wicked enough, but the thought that the same people, who had once been his friends, were prepared to murder him…well…she could not withhold her tears then, and Lucius comforted her. He spared her the details of battle and summed up by saying that the conspirators were all dead, most likely the one who had escaped too.

For Adara, that was a relief and now she was able to understand why Lucius had been so insistent that she remain in Greece. The situation had been far worse than she imagined. She could see the painful memories of his lost men weighing heavily on him. She kissed the scar on his arm where the arrow that could so easily have taken his life had cut into his flesh.

"What about the empress? Is she going to protect you still?"

"I don't think we can really count on her. She's in Rome and Plautianus is Consul now. She, above all people, must tread carefully."

"But Lucius, you killed a Praetorian," she whispered.

"And no one except the empress knows about it…no one alive, that is." Poor Drusus came to mind.

"Are you sure?"

"As sure as I can be."

Lucius held her in the crook of his right arm then and they fell asleep. For the first time in a long while, they each felt at home but it was not a home of timber and plaster surrounded by gardens and songbirds. Rather, it was the comfort and warmth of Love's embrace that cradled them together. Body and breath moved concertedly then as they moved to discover one another's body and sweet scent. The lamps in the room had burned away now. Carefully, slowly, they made love in the light of the single moonbeam that penetrated through the small, grated window in the wall across the room. The night was one they had each dreamt of in the loneliness of their mutual exile, one that was now a reality to be savoured, felt, thankful for.

The group had been at the villa in Hadrumetum for five days and Lucius announced to them that after two more they would set out on the journey across the sand and rock of Africa and on into Numidia. Provisions were being gathered by Valerus and Pephredo who also acquired a covered wagon that would allow the women to travel in greater comfort and protection.

Adara and Alene had enjoyed meeting Lucius' centurions and conversing with the Sarmatian lord, Mar. He had impressed them with his regal bearing, his strength and respect toward Lucius' own family. Dagon too had won them over to friendship with his praise of Lucius and also the tales he had to tell of the women warriors of Sarmatia.

In the five days, Lucius spent some time with Ashur, walking in silence along the shoreline with Carissa in tow; Ashur did not want to let her out of his sight. On the fifth day, Ashur came to Lucius without Carissa and asked if he would walk with him to the south-western edge of town. Lucius agreed but knew that something was amiss by the seriousness with which Ashur had asked. He had been withdrawn ever since their arrival and now, Lucius suspected, it was time to find out why.

Ashur walked in hesitant steps as they approached an area with a clear view of the desert to the south and west. Scattered palms swayed beneath a patchy sky and pools of sunlight lit the sands ahead like scattered puddles on a cobbled street. He stopped short beneath an olive tree, listened.

Lucius leaned against the tree, breathed deeply of the desert air mingled with scents of the nearby sea and felt alive, stronger than he had in a long while. His limbs no longer ached, his wounds no longer stung. He knew however, that it was not the same for Ashur. He had expected his friend to be overjoyed to see him, to see and feel the place where he had wandered, where they had met. He could not have been more wrong. Ashur took a hesitant step forward, peered out as if looking for something far away, listened even harder. Finally he spoke.

"Do you remember your childhood, Lucius?"

"Of course I do, most of it anyway. Why do you ask?"

"Do you enjoy your memories up to this point in your life?"

"Um, well, there are some things I suppose, which I would like to forget, like Argus, my father's harshness and lack of belief in me."

"I see." He did not speak again but stared out at the sands. Lucius wondered what Ashur was thinking asking such questions. He had made no response to Lucius' answer, was lost again in his thoughts. Lucius waited for him to speak again but he remained silent.

"It's out there, Ashur, waiting for you. You must have missed it my friend, the desert, the sun over Apollo's swaying palms." Ashur did not answer at first, showed no sign of having heard Lucius speak. After a time, he turned.

"This is as close as I can get to that outer world, Lucius. The desert is no longer for me."

"What do you mean? What are you talking about? Aren't you happy to be here?"

"No. I cannot hear anything, nor do I feel or see in this place." His eyes fixed on Lucius, tired and slightly wild at once. "I am no longer a servant of His. I don't wish it." The words were spoken harshly Lucius thought, irrationally.

"Adara mentioned something of your disillusionment with..."

"Disillusionment? Is that what she calls it?" He half smiled. "It's more than that, Lucius. Look at me! I'm old and weak now, tired, and why do you think it is so? Because, my dear Lucius, I have fallen in love. Apollo has turned his back on me for feeling."

"Carissa," Lucius acknowledged. "I had no idea that she meant that much to you. Is she worth it though, to suffer Apollo's anger?"

"Lucius, you above all others should understand Love's worth." Lucius felt humbled then. Had he so belittled Ashur's feelings toward the young artisan, her own feelings for Ashur? "You are blessed by Apollo, but I...I am no longer his servant. I cursed him in his own sacred sanctuary."

"If you entreat him, make sacrifices, He will welcome you back, both of you. It's where you belong. Look at you! You've aged, you're not yourself."

Ashur exhaled, frustrated, sad. "I don't care about *Him* anymore!" The air seemed stilled, clouds formed in the distance and Lucius prayed silently for protection against evil speech. "For as long as I remember I've given my life in service to Apollo, trotting to Hades and back protecting men who don't always deserve it." Lucius stepped back. "Of course, I do not include you among them. It is my privilege to have known you. But Lucius, I remember nothing else of my life except that when He spoke, I listened and obeyed. Now that I feel pain and age and the anguish of love and a measure of humanity...I am truly happy."

Lucius walked to his side and put his hand on his friend's shoulder. He remembered the first time they had met, the times Ashur had saved his life, the journey Ashur had made to Greece at his own request. He felt guilty, responsible. "Ashur, if you're happier now than you've ever been, why are you so full of anger?" The question rang true, struck a chord. Ashur knew the answer immediately.

"I'm angry...Lucius...because I must leave you for good." Ashur shook after saying the words and for the first time that he could recall, tears formed in his eyes as he looked upon a young man he had come to love as a brother and honour as a warrior.

Lucius at first was hurt by this, then confused. He realised however, that Ashur should be master of himself. If Carissa made him that happy he could not deny him that. Of course Ashur could do as he wished, without anyone's permission, but Lucius knew all too well that his own blessing would lift a titan's burden from his friend's shoulders.

"I know I asked much of you going to Greece, Ashur, but I'm very grateful for your protection of Adara and Alene. I only hope you didn't resent me for it."

"Resent you? That is not possible. What better, final mission than to protect your wife and sister and discover my own feelings of love along the way? It's funny though, that you were the one to make the request of me and not Apollo." He looked down at the ground, pushed some soft sand with his sandalled foot. "How often I've walked this land."

"Where will you go now?"

"To Rome with Carissa, to rejoin Emrys."

"Really?"

"Yes. Whereas I am prepared to move on to another path, Carissa has yet to learn from Emrys and I would not deprive her of that."

"She has seemed extremely distant since you arrived."

"Ever since she and Emrys parted ways in Athens, she has not been the same. Her heart is now clouded by guilt and remorse at her separation from the man who has been her only father."

"Then you have to go." Lucius tried to smile, be encouraging, but it proved difficult. "You go on to Rome with Carissa. I've brought along a fine escort of men and horses to take us to Lambaesis. We'll be all right."

"I know you will." Ashur stopped speaking, could see something in Lucius' eyes, something he had seen before but never asked after it. "What is on your mind my friend?"

440

"A question." Lucius now looked out at the desert, events lost in the dunes and moonlight.

"Ask it."

"From the moment we met, you've been an enigma Ashur. I've never fully comprehended your life, why you came to me. Of course I know that Apollo sent you and I understand why you must now chose to move on. But, if I don't ask the question now, the mystery of it, will always eat away at me. I know you and yet I don't know you, not really."

"Ask me, Lucius."

"I'm not sure it matters now but…" He did not know how to phrase it. How did one ask such a thing? He sighed, not knowing how else to pose it. "Ashur, you come and go as a ray of light, you move like the wind and fight like no other man. Are you truly immortal? Have you seen life through ages long past?" It sounded odd, unbelievable even, but Lucius remembered Diodorus having said that sometimes the deepest truths do indeed sound…ridiculous.

Ashur actually smiled but then his face became pitiable. "Those were not easy questions for you to ask, I know. Unfortunately, Lucius, I do not have an answer for you. I simply don't know." Lucius registered utter confusion and Ashur could see he was trying his utmost to understand. "You see, I remember little. My actions may seem impossible to you and others but I simply acted the way I felt I was supposed to, like breathing or chewing I suppose. I healed quickly when wounded, yes. However…much has changed. I have aged, as you pointed out, I feel pain and my wounds do not heal as they once did. Because I remember so little, it is impossible for me to say. I wish I knew. Were you to ask me years ago, I might have said yes, perhaps. But if you ask me now, which you are, the likely answer is no, I am not. That is why I must live for myself now. Perhaps on some distant road, I will find the answers to the questions that have plagued me for so long. I've seen the world, true, but not *seen* it. Do you understand?"

"I think so." Lucius looked on Ashur for the first time in the light of a man, a man who had his share of pain and fear, but was now confronted with his portion of joy and wonder. Perhaps he simply was just a man, vulnerable to the Gods' whims, to age, love, even death. Ashur had to find out and Lucius knew that. If he had indeed lost some part of his memory, he had a right to discover the truth. If Apollo had chosen him as a tool for a time, he had a right to know why. In the end, it was not something for Lucius to question.

"The wind is picking up and the desert is angry tonight," Ashur interrupted Lucius' thoughts.

"You're right. We'd better get back to the villa."

The two men turned and began the walk back to Hadrumetum. Both felt strange and yet comfortable, as though something between them had been settled. As they stepped onto the road that led west, Ashur stopped and took Lucius by the arm.

"I must say one thing to you Lucius."

"What?"

"Don't wish to forget any part of your past, be it Argus, your father or anything else, evil or good. I do not remember my own past and the unknowing of it has been painful. Your past...your memories...are a gift. Cherish them and don't forget, for they are what have made you the man you are today, a worthy, honourable man, husband, and soon-to-be father. I envy you your life, Lucius. Hold on to it and all it entails."

"I will." Lucius shook as he reached out to embrace Ashur Mehrdad one last time in friendship. "Thank you for having travelled the road with me."

"Thank you, Lucius Metellus Anguis."

The following day, Ashur and Carissa set out on the coastal road to Carthage where they hoped to find a ship to Ostia. Adara and Alene had awoken early to see them off with food for the journey, wishes to see them again in Rome and

442

emotional farewells. The two women had suspected that the two of them would leave at some point but were sad nonetheless, especially because of the sadness Ashur's departure caused Lucius.

Lucius had also risen early, saddled Lunaris and accompanied Ashur and Carissa alongside their wagon, for two miles up the road. When it came time for him to turn back, he wished them much love and joy and said that he hoped to see them again soon, though he inwardly doubted whether he would see them again at all. Once Emrys finished his work in Rome, they would no doubt be off to some other far corner of the empire, down some other road. He watched them roll into the distance, battered by the wind off of the sea.

When the day came for Lucius, Adara, Alene and their escort to return to Lambaesis, all were eager to get underway. The sun was out but there was an imminent change in the weather ahead. Lucius hoped that the Gods would grant them a safe and uneventful journey and made the appropriate offerings in the temples of Hadrumetum to this end.

The road would take them from Hardumetum to Sufetula and Thevestis and from there to Thamugadi and finally Lambaesis. The ground would be flat much of the way, through fields and groves, before giving way to the passes between the mountains. Trouble could rear up there, but Lucius knew that with two centuries and a contingent of Sarmatian cavalry, nobody would be foolish enough to attack them.

Valerus and Pephredo had acquired several wagons for the ladies' possessions as well as a very comfortable wagon for Adara and Alene, in which a multitude of colourful cushions had been placed along with blankets and furs for their comfort. Lucius' main concern was his wife's comfort as she was weeks away from giving birth, and he wanted the journey to be as easy as possible for her. Large leather hangings protected the sides and roof of the wagon from rain and wind but from the very morning they had set out, in the middle of the marching column of troops, the women had asked that the hangings be tied up when the weather was fair so that they could watch as they passed through this new, foreign world.

Adara and Alene were bewitched by the simple beauty of the land that Lucius had so often spoken of and gazed in amazement at its wonders, its mysteries, its barren beauty. As the wagon creaked along the Roman road west, Adara clasped Alene's hand in hers and imagined living there with Lucius at long last, the happiness they would all share and the child they would rear in a land of sun, wind and sand, a land where stars shed silver and blue light on endless dunes, and where Apollo's palms stretched and swayed to the sky.

XX

SATURNALIA

"I drink to Saturn! May He grant us all cheer, goodwill and a bountiful life worth living!" Flavius Marcellus held his large golden cup above his head as he made his final toast of Saturnalia.

"We drink to Saturn!" All the guests echoed their host's words, spilled some wine on the floor in offering, and drank. Marcellus then clapped his hands loudly, signalling the beginning of the banquet. Everyone eased onto plush dining couches as a small army of local slaves paraded into their midst holding trays piled high with fruit, bread, sweetmeats and numerous other delicacies from land and sea.

"Here, let me help you." Lucius reached out for his wife's arm to help her arrange herself amid the mound of cushions so that her now immense belly would not pain her during dinner. "There. Is that better, my love?" he whispered.

"Yes." Adara looked up at her husband and kissed his cheek lovingly, uncaring of the mass of men and women around them. "I feel enormous, Lucius."

"Nonsense. You're beautiful." Lucius settled next to her and looked around the room. "Look at all the admiring glances about the room. They've never seen such beauty."

"Don't lie before dinner, husband, or you'll get indigestion."

"Ha!" Alene giggled from the neighbouring couch when she heard this remark. "Oh, I'm sorry, Martia." She flushed red. "I overheard something my sister-in-law said to my brother."

"Not to worry, Alene," replied the tribune Sabinus' wife, smiling in the warmth of her unwatered wine. "The night is for merriment and laughter." She turned to her husband next to her. "Do you see, Tertius? Look how he coos over his pregnant wife! You never did as much for me."

"But – Lucius, you're going to get me and the rest of the men into trouble with our wives if you keep this up!" Sabinus tried to kiss his wife's hand but she pulled it away quickly, teasing him with a glimpse of the side of her breast.

"We are all willing slaves to Lady Venus, Tribune," Lucius answered.

"Indeed! But even at Saturnalia, the slaves have the day off." Everyone laughed at Sabinus' remark as Martia pulled the fold of her stola more tightly over her chest.

"No gifts for you this evening, my cheeky husband," she whispered to him. Alene tried not to laugh out loud.

All evening the Praetorium banquet hall was alive with laughter and song, resonant with praise for the hosts. Indeed, they had spared no expense. Their own slaves had been given the day off but, as it was an enormous undertaking to prepare food for the entire III Augustan senior staff and their wives, the legate had hired some local slaves to serve and prepare the food; many people of Punic descent chose not to celebrate the Roman festival, especially Punic slave owners who made a good deal of money on just such occasions.

As Lucius and Adara fed each other from a platter of stuffed kidneys, Alene looked about the assemblage at all the new faces she had come to know over the first week of their life in Lambaesis. The journey from Hadrumetum had proved smooth and uneventful, apart from the discomfort Adara sometimes felt in the heat of the wagon and the frequent stops that so many women in her situation require.

Camping beneath the stars of a foreign land was quite an adventure for Alene, born and bred in Rome beneath her parents' roof. She imagined what it must have been like for Lucius on campaign, a sky pocked with fiery lights. She envied him so many nights. As she popped black grapes into her mouth, her eyes fell upon one man sitting across the vast room, talking to no one in particular. He seemed distant, out of place and unused to such gatherings. When his eyes met hers, he smiled broadly and nodded in greeting, his black hair falling about his brow and his golden eyes flecked with brown spots. "I'll be back," Alene told Adara and Lucius as she picked up her cup and walked behind the rows of couches until she reached him.

"Hello, Alerio. Are you enjoying yourself?"

"Much more now that I have someone to speak with."

"May I sit with you?"

"The Gods take me to Hades if you don't."

Alene smiled and made herself comfortable on the other end of the couch.

"You aren't hungry? Your plate seems rather void of crumbs and bones."

"I haven't much taste this evening for kidneys."

"Me neither." They were silent a moment. Alerio flushed. They heard Adara laugh from across the room and noticed Lucius feeling her tummy. "I can't believe my brother is going to be a father."

"I know." Alerio looked at the couple. "He's waited so long to be with her. Quite the beautiful couple, aren't they?"

"Quite...perfect. In fact I think that the population of Lambaesis, no Numidia, has not seen such a beautiful woman before." Alene sipped her wine.

"Oh...I wouldn't say that."

She turned her head to see his golden eyes and as she smiled he turned to his cup, unable to look too long at her beauty.

"Thank you, Alerio." When she spoke his name she seemed to sing it.

He nodded his head as he moved his cup to his mouth to drink again. He felt oddly shy with her eyes brushing over him and pushed on with conversation.

"So, when will the world be blessed with a new Metellus?"

Alene looked across at Adara who smiled back. "The new midwife says that she should be due anytime within the next two months. Everything is progressing normally."

"Thank the Gods for that."

"Adara is strong and healthy, nothing to worry about as long as she continues to make her daily offerings to the Gods. She is favoured. Actually, Alerio, I'm more worried about Lucius."

"Lucius? Why?"

"He seems to have something always at the back of his mind lately. I think that seeing Adara in this state has made him realise what is about to take place in his life. It's her first child and he's worried for her. I see it in his eyes when he watches her."

"He hasn't said anything to me about it. I wouldn't worry about him too much. We both know that Lucius is strong."

"I suppose you're right." Alene looked a little sad and Alerio put his hand on hers. "I'm fine. It just occurred to me that you probably know Lucius better now than I do. Most of my memories are of him as a child when we were growing up. You've been with him for years. He's a bit of an enigma to me at the moment."

Alerio thought about what she said before speaking. "I don't think you have to worry about the sort of person he is. Lucius is always open and honest with his close friends and especially with you, from what he's told me."

"Really? What's he said about me?"

Now Alerio felt the heat rushing to his neck and head. "Oh, basically that you're perfect and that you've always given him the strength he needs."

"That's Lucius. Always exaggerating." Alene chuckled to herself.

"Lucius doesn't exaggerate."

"Do you, Alerio?"

"Never."

For the remainder of the feast, Alene lounged next to Alerio to enjoy the array of musicians and dancers that their hosts had hired for the entertainment. Lucius never left Adara's side and when she felt restless and hot he took her by the arm for a walk to the garden where the night air was crisp and refreshing. Above them was the sickle-shaped, ivory moon.

"It's beautiful here." She breathed deeply, filling her lungs with fresh air.

"Do you really like it? I haven't dragged you across the empire to a home you despise, have I?"

"Oh, Lucius. My home is where you are. That's all I need. Do you know how often I gazed up at the night sky and thought that I would rather be anywhere else than apart from you? Were you in the foulest place on this earth where legions had trudged, life there would smell as sweet as Attic honey if I were by your side."

Lucius grasped her hands and kissed them. "I've missed your voice, your face, your eyes...Apollo and Venus have blessed us. I'm glad you're here."

"Me too." Adara took two steps over to a full bush of yellow and white jasmine and bent over to smell the delicate flowers whose soft scent permeated the night air. "Wonderful! You know, Lucius, one would almost think we were back in Athens. What a beautiful garden."

"Thank you, my dear!" The joyous voice came from behind them, down the winding path, followed by two sets of footsteps. "Tribune, you always seemed drawn to our garden during banquets."

"Lady Sophonisma." Lucius bowed to the legate's wife as she came into view along the path with Martia in tow. "Martia," he acknowledged the second woman.

"I needed some fresh air, Lady Sophonisma," Adara began, her voice sweet. "My husband was good enough to bring me to your beautiful garden for a breath."

"It's quite all right, my dear." The older woman patted Adara's hand gently, like a mother. "I too wander out here when I can slip away from the banquets, especially when my husband and his officers are embroiled once more in the discussion of the merits of cavalry over infantry." She looked at Lucius. "Tribune, if I may borrow your wife's ear for a time you may want to return to the banquet and settle a dispute between the Lord Mar and my Gaius. They are boring the other diners to tears I fear."

Lucius smiled, looked at Adara and then back to his hostess. "I would be happy to, Lady." Lucius bowed his head and disappeared into the garden's shadows. A peacock squealed and there was a muted curse. Martia giggled.

"Oh, how my peacocks love to tease the guests!" Aelia Sophonisma mused. The three of them laughed as she led the two younger women to the circular sitting area amid the jasmine. "Now we are alone." She straightened herself where she sat next to Adara and took her hand. Martia sat across from them, smiling. " Lady Metella."

"Please, call me Adara."

"Very well. Adara. Martia and myself, as well as the other women, know what it is like to live in a military base and to try and raise a family in such an environment. It can be, to say the least," she waited for the word to come to her, "Martia, do help me."

"Lonely?" she ventured.

"Yes! Lonely. Unless you have other women about you who understand and can keep you company when your husband is away on patrol or campaign. What I am trying to say is that we are very happy to have you here with us, and that we are here for you. If you have need of anything, anything at all, I expect you to come to me, Martia or any of the other women for help."

"That is extremely kind of all of you." Adara inclined her head and smiled to herself. She knew that in Lucius she had all the help she would ever need.

"We know that Lucius," Martia began, "is, well, an extraordinary man to say the least, and gives you much attention but…"

"But," continued Lady Aelia, "he is after all, a man. And as a man there are just certain things that he cannot understand." Adara's brow creased ever so slightly at this but she listened and kept smiling. She knew this advice was well-intended. "You will be giving birth to your first child soon." She looked at Adara's swollen belly. "Very soon. And you shall need all the help you can get. You will need…Martia?"

"A woman's understanding?"

"Thank you, Martia. A woman's understanding of all the ailments, both physical and emotional, that accompany the birthing of a child."

Adara's first reaction had been to defend the slight upon her husband's care for her but then she realised that the two women before her were simply welcoming her into their fold. She was no longer in the heart of Athens or of Rome but rather at the far edge of the empire, in a land of which she had only heard tell tales of war up to the time she had arrived on the sandy shore. These women wanted to be her friends. It seemed obvious to her that their intent was nothing short of honest and sincere. She, and Alene for that matter, would find comfort together in this social circle. Adara cleared her throat and took a hand of each woman in hers.

"Ladies, you honour me *and* my husband by welcoming me so warmly to Lambaesis. The Gods' blessing upon all of you for such kindness. Thank you."

"You are most welcome, my dear. It will be nice to have such refined and decent young women here for a change," she said with a twinkle beyond her wrinkled eyes. "One who does not drink so much unwatered wine."

"I must protest!" exclaimed a rosy-cheeked Martia. "It was your wine servant. He is far too giving with his wine jug. Besides, not to drink the contents of my cup would be an insult to Bacchus!"

"Well, at least your piety remains intact," Lady Aelia chided happily. Adara laughed at the shocked look upon Martia's face as they followed the older woman back to the banquet. "Now, about your sister-in-law, Alene. Does she play tabula? Because we have a nice little women's club…"

"She said that? That I was *just* a man!"

"Don't look so wounded, Lucius," Adara laughed. "She was just being nice. Not everyone is as lucky as I am."

"Oh really?" Lucius smiled, could not help it. Somehow, Adara always had a way of making him smile. Her laughter, was contagious. "Well then, I thank the Gods that you think so." She pinched his buttocks as she helped him out of his toga. "Ouch!" he yelped.

"What's this? My great Roman warrior squeals when a woman pinches his bottom!"

"Squeal? Absolutely not! It was my war cry," he defended, rubbing his behind.

"I hope not for your sake. That wouldn't even scare off my little sisters."

He walked over to the washing table, splashed his face and dried it with one of the clean towels that Xeno had set out. Lucius had wanted to give him the day off as well but the old man had said that he wished to stay and make sure that all was clean and tidy for him and Adara when they returned.

After washing, Lucius helped his wife out of her gown and into bed where they lay next to each other. Since returning to base, he had gone back to training his body, overcoming his wounds, and Adara was happy to see his body's strong form returning once more after the weak, scarred sight that had first greeted her. "Do you think Alene enjoyed herself this evening?" he asked.

"I think so. She wasn't eating much but she seemed to be having a good time. Alerio was looking out for her at dinner. No need to worry about any of the single officers making advances."

"Good. I hope that she doesn't regret coming here." Lucius stared up at the ceiling.

"She doesn't, Lucius. Don't worry. In fact, the past days she's seemed happier than ever I think. Probably because she knows that you're all right; she doesn't spend her days worrying about her little brother now."

"Do you think she liked the necklace I gave her for Saturnalia? It suits her, don't you think?"

"Quite. She loves it. The green and red gemstones look beautiful with her hair." Adara traced a line along Lucius' hip, up his chest to his face. "I haven't yet given you your gift."

"Hmm. What could it be? Actually, I have a little something for you too."

"Me first!" she said as she reached beneath her pillow and pulled out something flat and rectangular, wrapped in red silk.

"What is it?"

"Open it and find out."

Lucius undid the silver thread and unfolded the piece of silk to reveal his gift. "Did you do this yourself?"

"Yes." she said proudly.

Lucius ran his eyes over every detail of his gift. It was a beautifully chosen piece of olive-wood in the centre of which was a painting. "I recognise this tree from somewhere."

"You were standing beneath it the first time I saw you, the night we first met in Rome."

"At the banquet - the date palm at the centre of the palace garden on the Palatine. You noticed me then?"

"Of course I did. How could I not?"

"But the room was so crowded and you and your family were going up to see the emperor."

"Lucius, my eyes fell on you the moment I entered that massive room."

He looked at the painting again, the delicate branches, the way the palm seemed to shudder as if some passing goddess had pursed her lips and blown into the midst of its green tendrils. "And you painted this yourself?"

"Yes. Mother taught me some of her secrets when we were in Athens, what types of paints and brushes to use, things like that. Do you like it?"

"Adara, it's beautiful." He kissed her gently. "I think we should hang it above the bed here."

"Good idea. We can sleep beneath our tree."

"Now it's my turn to give you your gift." Lucius got up and went across the room to a chest he had in the corner. He opened it and pulled out a package of saffron silk. Once back on the bed he lay down next to his wife. "Happy Saturnalia." Her eyes beaming, Adara accepted the gift. "Well? Open it."

She unwound the silk until a blue cobra head poked out, followed by coils of worked gold that ended in another blue head. "Oh, Lucius! It's gorgeous! You spoil me!"

"Not at all!"

"Will you put it on me?" Lucius took the bangle and slid it over her hand until it was past her elbow. With a little adjusting, it fit perfectly, the serpents settled around her with ease, coiling about her soft skin where they glistened in the lamplight. "It's so beautiful, Lucius, thank you."

"It's from Palestine and the lapis is from Aegyptus." He looked at her arm and smiled. "It looks as though it was meant for your arm alone." She smiled and leaned over to kiss him but her belly got in the way.

"After all these months I'm still not used to this enormous belly!" She laid herself back down and Lucius, smiling, leaned over to kiss her on the lips. Her hands caressed the straining muscles of his arms as her limbs slid smoothly up and around his neck like the serpents that were so lithely wound about her own arm.

There was the soft sound of wind, like subtle breathing, and of water gently lapping at a rocky shore the way the sea does in the heat of a summer's day, mixing different shades of blue the way a painter mixes on his palate. The sound of cicadas hummed in Lucius' ears and he awoke. *Where am I?* He felt something in the small of his back, a worn fragment of marble; he'd slept on the ground. His skin was darker than usual, he wore a chiton and a pair of unadorned sandals. It was hot. He looked around and found that he had been sleeping, huddled, in one of the rows of seats of a theatre. *The sea? How did I get here, wherever here is?* He ran up the steps to the top of the theatre to get a better view. *An island? But how...*

There was nobody around, not a soul. He was alone. *Hello!* he called out. All that came back was the sound of his own voice as it travelled through the marble seats, porticoes and back. He felt his heart tighten. *Adara?* He wondered where she was as he walked along the silent streets. A warm wind ruffled his hair and he shielded his eyes from the hot white of the sun. He heard something. *Whispers? Someone's here!* He walked faster, his sandals sliding on the smooth marble street as he passed temples and houses. The street opened up and he stopped, frozen.

Delos. Before him, brushing the air, humming, was the sacred palm. It sprouted out of the fresh lake, an island within an island. *How did I get here? Apollo...are you here?* Lucius walked along further, heard the whispers again; this time they sounded more like a muted roaring, soft and hollow. He turned and looked up at the row of lions, nine of them, watching him, silent sentinels. It felt permissible to approach.

His feet took him to the edge of the clear water where he heard a new humming, a woman's, a goddess? But still, he was alone. He felt tired then, moved to lie in the soft rushes along the shore. *So tired.* He closed his lids, his skin kissed by the hot air of godly summer as he succumbed to Delian sleep. *But where is she? Adara?...*

"Adara? Where are..."

"Lucius? Lucius? Wake up. I'm here."

"Huh? What?" The room was dark but Lucius could feel her familiar touch, her smell. "Adara?"

"I'm here. You were dreaming again."

"I was. I'm so glad you're here." He rubbed his face, tried to shake the hazy numbness of his mind. "I dreamt I was alone, on Delos, at the tree where Apollo and Artemis were born. I was the only one on the island. Nobody else. I was searching for you everywhere and couldn't find you."

Adara held him close, stroked his sweaty brow. "It was just a dream. I'm here with you now. You don't have to dream of losing me or being without me. I'm here and I'm not leaving." She did not know what else to say at the moment. Since she had arrived at Lambaesis, Lucius had been having such dreams almost every night. "You're just having trouble believing that we're finally together for good, that's all. The dreams will stop."

"I know, I know. This one was odd though. I wasn't afraid like in the others. It was peaceful, I saw the lions, the lake and the tree. It was beautiful."

"Maybe we can go there someday. I've never been."

"I'd like that." Outside, the sound of horns rang throughout the base. "Time to get up."

XXI

LUSTRATIO

'Purification'

The winter in Numidia proved a mild, sunlit season in which the men of the legion went happily to their drills and in which the women of Lambaesis gathered for gossip and talk in the gardens of the officers' quarters and the Praetorium. There was an odd, continued sense of merriment in the air, so much so that the time passed swiftly and unnoticed.

Adara and Alene spent their days getting to know the other women in whom they had found uncommon friendship, especially Martia and Aelia Sophonisma. Everyday however, without fail, Adara and Alene made their offerings to the gods and goddesses who could aid Adara in the weeks and days to come. Special offerings were made in the temples and on the altars to the goddesses of childbirth: Juno Lucina, Diana and Carmentis.

Joy indeed, but not without some far-flung, reticent fear that Adara had pushed to the back of her mind. She found comfort in the Gods she prayed to, in her husband's strong embrace, and in Alene's encouragement, but as the time approached, she began to grow nervous. She was very large and experiencing pains during the nights, so much so that Lucius made quarters for the midwife within their home.

With the arrival of Martius and warmer breezes from the south, the time was near for Adara to give birth. In a corner of the large cubicula that was the couple's bedroom, a newly made birthing chair had been set up along with fresh linens and basins for water. Still, Adara waited.

On a particularly sunny day, Dagon and Mar were off duty and had offered to stop by Lucius' quarters to see if either Adara or Alene wanted anything from Thamugadi. When they arrived to knock at the door they found it slightly ajar, screams emanating from somewhere within. The two Sarmatians drew their long swords and ploughed through the door into the courtyard where they were met by a severely panting Xeno, wringing his hands in front of the altar in the centre of the courtyard.

"Xeno!" Mar spoke. "What is going on here? We heard screams."

"Oh, oh, Lord Mar! It's time! Lady Metella has gone into labour and is ready to give birth. She is in much pain."

"Calm yourself, Xeno." The old man shuddered as more screams emanated from the cubicula. Alene came into the courtyard.

"Praise Apollo you're both here!"

"What can we do?" Dagon asked.

"Please, Dagon, go and get Lucius. I don't know where he is but he should be here to place something on the altar."

"I know where he is. Dagon, you go and get Lucius out on the parade ground. He's drilling the troops."

"Yes, Lord." With that, Dagon ran out of the door.

"Lore Mar," Alene began, her hair dishevelled, her eyes flashing, "would you be so kind as to call for Loxias the physician and notify Lady Sophonisma that it's time?"

"Right away, Lady. Now, go back to her. This is truly a day of days." Mar bowed quickly and set about his task.

"Lucius!" Adara's shrill cry punctured the courtyard and Alene ran back into the room.

"All's well, sister. He's coming, he's coming. I'm here for you." Alene put her head next to Adara's where she sat upright in the birthing chair. "Breathe love, breathe."

"It's almost time," the midwife said calmly as she rinsed her hands in one of the basins of hot water that Xeno had just brought in.

"Anguis! Anguis!" The troops on the parade ground all turned in wonder to see who the madman was on horseback speeding through all the orderly formations in a cloud of dust.

Lucius turned and felt something in his chest even before anything else was said. "Dagon! What is it?"

"It's time, Anguis!"

"By the Gods! Alerio!" Lucius turned to his friend. "Put someone in charge and follow after us!"

"Right!" Alerio ran to speak with Pephredo.

"Hop up, Anguis, hurry!" Dagon extended his arm for Lucius to grab and hoisted him onto his horse's rump. They sped off amid cheers from the cohort.

"Ahhh!" Adara moaned, exhausted. "Lucius…" she whimpered.

"He'll be here soon dear," said the legate's wife calmly from a corner of the room. "Martia, build up the brazier a little. We need more light." The younger woman stoked the fire and flames burst up, the flashing light revealing the sweat that poured from Adara's forehead. Alene patted her with a cloth, never leaving her side.

"Where is she?" Finally, Lucius' voice rang out in the courtyard, silencing all others. "Adara! I'm here, I'm with you!" He called out to comfort her but before anything else he placed a large bunch of rosemary on the fire burning next to the altar. "All you Gods, I beg you to protect her and our child. Keep them safe!" He watched blue smoke rise up to the sky and felt Mar's strong hand on his shoulder.

"She'll be fine, my friend. The Gods are watching over her." Another scream came from within.

"By Apollo, I can't stand this."

"Here, Tribune. Some water." Xeno set a basin for Lucius on a small pedestal table a few feet away. He helped Lucius remove his cloak and breastplate. After the dirt of the parade ground was washed from his hands and face, Xeno handed Lucius a towel to dry off and then poured him some wine.

"Lucius!" Alerio came rushing in, winded by his run. "How is she?"

"I don't know!" Lucius looked at the closed door. "I've never heard screams like that." He paced around the courtyard as Alerio, Mar, Dagon, Xeno and the physician Loxias watched, waited.

After what seemed an age of watching a female slave go back and forth with soiled linens and fresh water there was another cry.

"Lucius! Lucius! Come to me!" Adara's voice sounded desperate.

"That's it! I'm going in!" Lucius ran over to the door but was confronted by the legate's wife.

"No! No, Tribune! It is not proper!" She waved her hands violently, vainly, as though trying to frighten off a lion. "You will anger the Goddess! Men must not be present! No…"

"I must, Lady…" Lucius jumped around her and pushed his way through the door and into the fire-lit room where he spotted his wife, flanked by his sister. "I'm here, Adara, I'm here." He rushed to her side and grabbed her hand. "We're together, love." He whispered into her ear.

"You *must* push now!" the midwife commanded from where she was on her knees in front of the chair.

With every remnant of strength she could muster, Adara gripped her husband's and her sister's hands and pushed as hard as she could, her voice heaving a primal sound. "That's it!" the midwife cheered.

"Good, Adara! We're with you," Alene comforted as Lucius kissed his wife's forehead. Across the room, from the corner of her eye, Adara in her effort, thought she saw a flash of light and two bright, familiar faces smiling at her. A cool breeze whirled in the courtyard and shot through the door to fan her.

"Gods!" she cried out. Just then there was a wailing.

"And…there we go! Juno be praised." The midwife brought her arms up to reveal the soaking child as it wriggled.

"Adara! You've done it!" Lucius stared unbelievingly at the child held aloft by the midwife.

"Lady Metella, you have a son!" After cutting and tying off the cord, the midwife's helper cleaned the child and wrapped him in fresh linens. She turned to Adara.

"My Lady, would you like to hold your son?"

"Ahhhhhh!" To the surprise and shock of everyone present, including the men in the courtyard, Adara yelled out again.

"What's happening?" Lucius demanded as Alene took the boy from the helper. The midwife looked at Adara and bent down.

"Great Goddess!" she exclaimed. "There's another child!"

"Another?" Lucius looked questioningly at the woman, then at wide-eyed Alene. "Another child?"

"Lucius." Adara's voice was weak. "I can't…not again." She shook her head.

"You're not alone, my love. It's just us and the Gods above. For us, for our child, one last push." He pressed his cheek to hers. "Ready?" She nodded silently, dreading the effort.

"The child will not wait!" The midwife was now yelling. "Push, dear! As hard as you can, by Juno!"

With one long, drawn out effort, the second child came into the world and Adara wept with her husband, partly in gratitude for the end of the ordeal, but more so for the sight of the two children that had suddenly made them a family.

Holding the first child closely, Alene wept at the sight before her which reached deep into her heart and struck a chord that she hoped would never cease to ring out. The joy she felt for Lucius and Adara overwhelmed her and she smiled as she looked at the small bundle in her arms.

"Apollo be praised. Adara, you did it!" Just then, Lucius too thought he spied the two shining faces in the far corner of the room as he bent down to kiss his wife. The midwife then approached with the newly washed infant, likewise wrapped in clean linen.

"Your daughter, Tribune." She handed the baby to Lucius whose hands shook as he accepted his child. He felt extreme happiness mixed with awkwardness in a moment as surreal as any other he had experienced. It was simply overwhelming.

"A daughter?" He could not help but laugh for joy, glistening streams of reflected fire running down his cheeks as he and Alene held the children in front of their mother for her to admire and welcome them. They were beautiful, without question. The boy already had black hair upon his crown, and the girl slight wisps of gold.

"How do you feel?" Alene asked, stroking her sister's hair.

"I can't describe this." She breathed deeply, exhaustedly as her fingers caressed the tiny limbs of her children.

"The children appear healthy." The midwife stated as she removed the last of the afterbirth. "And you, dear? How are you feeling?"

"Tired. Very tired."

"That is normal," she stated matter-of-factly, "and will pass with sleep."

Lucius stepped up, smiling. "Thank you for your help. Gods bless you, lady," he said to the old woman.

"Think nothing of it, Tribune. She fought hard, your wife did. You should be proud." The midwife finished wiping her hands. "I have a good nutrix standing by in the room you set aside for me. She is healthy and full of milk…"

"No!" Adara interrupted. "Excuse me. No wet nurse. I wish to suckle the children myself."

"But, my Lady!" The midwife looked shocked. "It is not fitting for a woman of your station to do such a thing!"

"Makes no matter. I wish to do it myself." Adara appeared as her strong self again for a fleeting moment before exhaustion weighed on her lids once more.

"Very well," the midwife conceded. "I dare say the children will be the better for it. The nutrix is a tad on the chubby side and not as comely as yourself. But, if you should find that you do not have enough milk, let me know and I shall send her straight over to you."

"Fine. Fine," Alene butt in. "For now, I think we should get my sister cleaned up so that she may rest." The women in the room nodded. "Lucius?" Alene looked at him and smiled, noticed him awed by what had just happened. "Would you like to hold your children?"

"Yes, Lucius," Adara managed to say weakly. "Take them out into the daylight. Let Phoebus Apollo look upon them and bless them with his warmth." Lucius bent to kiss his wife.

"I love you."

"I love you too."

Alene held out the boy. "Here, take him." She placed the boy in the crook of Lucius' free arm. It felt strange to hold such small, fragile lives, their eyes cracked open ever so slightly as they felt their father's warmth, his beating heart.

"I'll write mother this evening," Alene said softly. "Go now, I'll take care of Adara." Lucius looked at the two women he loved most, how they smiled at him, and went to the door.

When the midwife's helper opened the door a crack of sunlight cut into the room, shedding light on Lucius' face. He blinked until his eyes adjusted and was met by the silent, smiling faces of his friends. For several moments however, he was alone, or at least it felt that way as he and his children breathed the Numidian air, looked up at the sky and felt the sun on their faces. The legate's wife came up to them.

"Two children? Tribune, the Gods' blessing upon your family." She smiled as she looked upon the young ones. "I shall go and see how your wife is doing." She hurried through the door behind him.

"Lucius?" Alerio whispered. "Two?" Lucius said nothing. He walked over to the small group of men holding his son and daughter, accepted the blessings each made out of love and respect, each to whichever gods he prayed. Pride swelled Lucius' heart as he walked about with his children beneath the sun.

Alerio could not believe the sudden change in Lucius; he seemed older but somehow stronger, as though he had emerged from that room, from screams in the darkness, a man instilled with new knowledge and vigour. The centurion looked to the door as the others crowded around Lucius. He watched for her to come out but she did not. She was surely busy. He wondered whether it was the joy of the occasion, the magnitude of the day, that made him question his own existence, made him want more. It was something he had never thought of before, had never really wanted until he met her.

"Alerio!" Lucius called over. "Come and see my children! By Apollo and Venus, they're beautiful!"

"And quiet too!" Mar observed. "I've never seen such quiet new-borns."

"What will you call them?" Dagon asked as Alerio brought his face close to the children, wondering what lay in store for them.

"Not sure yet, Dagon. I wasn't expecting two. At any rate, it's bad luck to name them until the proper sacrifices have been made and the usual nine days have elapsed."

"Quite right, Lucius. We have a similar tradition in our lands," Mar added.

"So we won't call them by any name until then?"

"No, Dagon, this is your final look for now. They shall rest and recover along with their mother for nine days and then, at the lustratio, to be held here, we'll announce them to you all."

"As it should be," Mar agreed. "But do you have the room for this doubly large family now, Lucius?"

"We'll find room."

Just then the door to the cubiculum swung inward and from the darkness emerged the legate's wife followed by Martia and then Alene. Lucius looked up and they smiled.

"She is asleep, Tribune."

"Thank you for coming today, Lady Sophonisma."

"My husband will be pleased for you." Lucius bowed slightly. "Come Martia. Lord Mar, would you be so kind as to escort us back to the Praetorium?"

"I would be honoured. Ladies. Dagon, come along." Lucius thanked them all as they moved to the door that led onto the via Principalis. Once they were gone, Xeno set about arranging some food in Lucius' meeting room for them.

"You two go ahead and eat," he said to Alene and Alerio. "I'm too excited to eat anything. I want to be with Adara.

"I've arranged a chair for you, Lucius, and a small, temporary bed for the children until we can have an extra cradle made."

"Thank you. Now, go ahead." Lucius moved toward the open door where he met the midwife who was coming out.

"Be quiet, Tribune. She needs her sleep. Soon enough the children will cry for milk and she'll have to wake."

"I understand. Xeno has set food aside for you in your quarters."

"Thank you. Now, go in and be with your wife and children." Lucius looked at the two bundles in his arms and went through the door.

Alene watched Lucius go and when she turned to speak to Alerio she found his eyes fixed upon her own. They said nothing but he reached out with one hand and brushed aside a long strand of her golden hair that obstructed her eyes. Even in disarray, after all that had happened that day, she was stunning. Alene took his arm as he led her to the study for some food and mellow wine.

The cubiculum was musty-smelling, brighter than it had been as the midwife's helper had built up all the braziers to combat the cool breeze that blew in beneath the courtyard door and the small, grated window on the far wall. Lucius lay the children on the bed Alene had prepared and covered them with a blanket. *They look similar*, he thought. Then he realised that was a strange observation. *Most babies probably look the same when they're born, don't they?* He did not know. This was the first time Lucius had held new-born infants, let alone seen them up close. Army life and war had not prepared him for this. He hoped he would be up to the task of being a different sort of commander: a father.

Adara slept more soundly, it appeared, than she ever had before. Her dark, curly tresses lay in a beautiful, tangled heap about her head like a sea nymph newly washed-up on shore after fighting a stormy sea. Her breathing was sound and steady and Lucius sat for a time just to watch her and the children, listen to the concerted breathing of his family.

"Thank you, Apollo." His voice was hushed. He got up from his chair and went to the altar behind him where the small statue of Olympian Apollo held his arm aloft. Lucius added incense to the small tripod that stood adjacent and lay fresh sprigs of olive and rosemary on the altar.

The children would wake soon, hungry and crying he supposed, and so he sat himself down next to them and his wife for a while longer to watch and listen. As he sat there, one question pressed on his mind. *What should the children's names be?*

Over the following days, Lucius found it extremely difficult to concentrate upon the usual duties that accompanied a man of his position and rank within the legion. Alerio helped as best he could, along with the other centurions, so that Lucius could have the time to spend with his wife and children and to prepare for the lustratio. Husband and wife thought long and hard about what names to give them, watching certain behaviour, taking in their features. No name seemed to describe them accurately.

Thankfully, the children were healthy and Adara was able to provide enough milk for the both of them. Neither lacked appetite. Whilst she slept and bonded with her baby boy and girl, Alene and Lucius wrote lengthy letters to the two families describing the event. They knew that Antonia, Delphina and

Publius Leander would be sad to have missed the births but hoped that they would have had the time to prepare themselves for the fact that they would not be present.

The rest of the time was taken up with the lustratio; an augur had to be hired to read the omens, a banquet had to be organised, and letters had to be sent inviting the few friends that were nearby. Lucius made a point of sending an invitation to Marius Nelek and his family in Thamugadi, including Dido, whom Adara had expressed an interest in meeting. He wondered how she was doing in her new home. As they would be the only people travelling from without the base to see them, Lucius informed them that he would find quarters for the whole family either in his own domus or somewhere else. When Lucius finished the letter, he leaned back in his chair. Alene seemed preoccupied, he thought. He reached out to take her hand.

"I don't know what we would do without you, Alene." She looked up, her face beaming as always. "I can't believe we spent all those years apart."

"Me neither, Lucius. I'm happier than I've ever been."

"Really? Are you so happy looking after your brother and his wife and now your niece and nephew?"

"Well, of course I am..." she paused, "but...I'm also happy because I..."

"Because what?" Lucius laughed, unused to seeing his older sister at a loss for words. She hesitated, held back.

"Ach! What's wrong with me? I guess it's just all the planning. What I meant to say was that I'm also happy because I'm getting to experience a new and wonderful land! I really do love...this place."

"I too have never been so happy. The world seems so full of possibilities now doesn't it?"

"It certainly does," she said beneath her breath as she gazed toward the courtyard for the tenth time in a few minutes. How could she tell him? She had never kept anything from Lucius, he had never kept anything from her. This was different though. "I think I'll go check on Adara and the children."

"I'll finish up this letter. Tell Adara I'll help her walk about the courtyard shortly. I have some ideas for names to share with her."

Alene put her stylus back in the glass inkpot, wrapped her green cloak about her shoulders and went out. *There must be an easy way to let him know*, she wondered.

Finally, on the day before the festival of Equirria in honour of Mars, the lustratio was to be held. It was the thirteenth day of Martius and the tribune's quarters where Lucius lived with his family had been washed and swept. Garlands of the first fragrant flowers that had begun by then to pop up in the rocky hills about Lambaesis had been hung.

Xeno rushed about the house arranging tables of food, settling the nervous animals that were to be sacrificed and making sure the extra cubiculum had been properly arranged for Marius Nelek, his wife and two children. Their companion, Dido, would sleep in a cot that had been set up in the meeting room behind a curtain. Soon Lucius emerged from his cubicula clad in is thin-striped toga, perfectly white and pressed.

"Tribune! If I may say so, you look like a Roman emperor."

"Ha, ha! Xeno, you may say so but not too loudly. I only wanted to look respectable for my wife and children today."

"Well you do, sir, truly."

"Thank you, Xeno. You will of course be joining us during the feasting."

"Me, Tribune? I couldn't possibly…"

"Of course. You're a part of our familia now."

"Thank you, Tribune. If I have the time perhaps I will manage a small morsel."

"Good. Now, is everything prepared?"

"Yes. The rooms are ready for our guests, the entire domus has been cleansed and prepared for the auguries, the sacrifices are…restless."

"That's normal enough, I suppose. They sense when the time is near. What about the food? Has the extra cook arrived to help you in the kitchen?"

"Yes. She is my cousin and so I know I can count on her to do a good job for you."

"Excellent." Lucius nodded his approval, rubbed his hands together. "I don't know why, Xeno, but I am actually quite nervous today."

"Do not fret, Tribune. It was a calm night and the Gods have set the sun to shining for you. Not a cloud in the sky. Do the Ladies Metella require anything for their preparations?"

"No, Xeno, I believe they're fine. They're just getting themselves and the children ready. Should be out shortly." It was still early in the morning and guests were not expected to arrive for the ceremony for three more hours and so Xeno went into the kitchens to help with preparations. Then, there was a light knocking on the outer door. "Don't bother, Xeno! I'll get it." Lucius moved across the courtyard to the door, uncaring that he was breaking protocol for once. When he opened it, he was greeted with a rushing onslaught to the legs.

"Tribune Lucius!" The girl clamped herself around his legs in a tight little hug.

"Lady Tulia!" He reached down and picked her up to rest on his arm. "I missed you, little one."

"We missed you too, Tribune Lucius." She smiled and kissed him on the cheek.

"It's good to see you. Lady Octavia," he bowed, "Aeneas. You've grown."

"Tribune Metellus." The young boy's voice had grown deeper since the last time they had met.

"And there he is!" Lucius embraced Marius Nelek. "My friend. The Gods smile on you always."

"One can only hope, Tribune. Congratulations! I must say we were all thrilled to hear of your news and receive this invitation. What a day!"

"What a day indeed. Did the guards help you with your wagon?"

"Yes. They took it away already. Our case is here. Not much needed for two days. We can't stay in your way for too long."

"Don't be ridiculous! You're welcome into our small, if not Spartan, home." Lucius looked beyond Marius briefly for her, for Dido, but she was not there. For a moment he was worried she had stayed away, but then that worry was put to rest when he heard the familiar jingle of jewellery.

"Tribune." Her voice was soft, shy and formal. Her eyes avoided his momentarily until he moved closer to her.

"I'm glad you came." She looked different, more elegant, having exchanged her rough silver jewellery for gold that she had fashioned herself.

"I would not have missed this." A hint of a smile crossed her lips but disappeared when voices came from across the courtyard.

"Ah." Lucius closed the door and moved away from Dido. "Friends, I would like for you to meet my wife, Adara Metella."

Clad in a brilliant blue stola with hints of red and gold, Adara came across the paving slabs to greet their guests. Her hair was done up in an elaborate braid which ended in a cascade of curls at her back. On her arm she wore the gold bangle and around her neck was a brilliant necklace of gold. Her smile made Tulia laugh and jump up and down.

"Welcome to our home," she said calmly. "We're most pleased you could come."

"Not as pleased as we are, Lady, to make your acquaintance after hearing so much about you from the tribune." Marius bowed deeply, surprising his own wife with a rare display of decorum.

"Thank you for having us, Lady Metella," Octavia said. "You honour us."

470

"And who have we here?" Adara looked down at the laughing little girl.

"I," she said in regal tones, "am Tulia."

"Welcome, Tulia." Adara bowed playfully to the little girl who returned the gesture. "And you, young sir, are Aeneas, correct?" The boy smiled shyly and nodded. "Welcome to our home." Adara was about to turn to Dido who stood in the back ground when Marius spoke out.

"By all the Goddesses! It can't be little Alene Metella?"

"Marius Nelek." Alene came out of her cubiculum wrapped in a yellow stola accented with fiery orange silk. "It is good to see you after so many years."

"Last time you were a little girl like Tulia here, with golden pigtails. Well, this is a wonderful surprise."

Alene noticed Dido standing behind everyone and realised she had interrupted. "You must all be parched after your journey here. Come, we've arranged a table with food and drink in the triclinium. Then, you can use the baths if you wish before the other guests arrive." Octavia came forward with the children to follow Alene who made sure to throw Dido a kindly smile. Marius followed after, knowing that Lucius would like to catch up on things with Dido. She had been quiet, ever since they had received the invitation.

There was an awkward silence for a moment before Lucius spoke. "Dido," he said softly, "this is Adara. Love, this is Dido, the woman who saved my life." There was an uncomfortable silence as the women's gazes met. Dido felt badly in her travelling clothes; the Greek woman before her shone like a goddess bathed in Castalian waters. She tried to smile, but Adara's brow seemed creased, displeased.

Adara tilted her head, observed her intensely. Dido wanted to turn and run. Was this the woman that Lucius, a man she had felt so deeply for, had chosen to wed? A single stream of tears ran down Adara's cheek, she turned and rushed back to the cubiculum, slamming the door behind her.

Dido felt terrible and Lucius was speechless. He never thought that Adara would behave in such a manner. "I'm sorry, Dido." He waved to Alene who had been watching. She came over. "I'll...I'll be right back," he said, panicked, before running after his wife.

Alene came to Dido's side and took her hand. The girl looked completely distraught. "Hello. I'm Alene, Lucius' sister."

"Ye...yes. Sorry. I...should...not have come, I think." They were some of the hardest tears she had ever to fight back. Alene felt for her.

"Don't worry about my sister-in-law. She's been quite emotional for a long time with the birth and having been away from Lucius for so long. She'll come around." Dido doubted that very much and was sad for Lucius. "Come," Alene said, taking her by the arm. "We've got some wonderful food and drink. You must be starving?" She led her to the triclinium. "I love your jewellery! Did you make it yourself?"

"Adara? What's wrong? Why did you run away like that?" Lucius knelt on the floor in front of his wife, her face buried in her hands. "What is it?"

"What is it?" she repeated, her hands revealing her sodden eyes. "She's beautiful! That's what it is. I can't believe you spent all that time travelling with her."

"What are you talking about?" Now Lucius was confused. "I told you what happened; Dido saved my life, Adara. In return I brought her to Thamugadi. Marius and Octavia took her in."

"Did you spend nights together?"

"On the road, yes, but-"

"You see? Oh, Lucius, I know that most women allow their men, especially if they are soldiers, the occasional company of other women, but I just can't take the thought of it. I've had all these horrifying thoughts ever since you told me about her and-"

"Wait!" Lucius stood up. Now he was upset, could not believe what she was saying, what she had thought since she arrived in Hadrumetum. "I wish you'd told me what you were thinking when the idea first popped into your mind. I would have corrected you then and there so that we could have avoided this mess." Lucius paced around the room, like a bull enclosed in an inadequate pen. He knelt down again and clasped her hands. "Listen to me, Adara. I love you and only you. I've never been with another woman since we met, never wanted to."

"But she's so stunning, Lucius. To spend so much time with her in dire circumstances, for so long…it's only natural that…"

"Hold on. You forget me. You also forget yourself. Have you looked in your bronze mirror lately? Because the woman I see in front of me is a goddess, unmatched in every way. Every night, every single starlit night, I would go for a walk and look up at the sky and speak to you. I know you could hear me, just as I could hear you. Even when we were attacked in the desert, it was your face that flashed before my eyes."

"Lucius, I want to believe you, more than anything."

"Then believe me. The only reason I took her to Thamugadi was because…I, the legion, may have been responsible for killing the only family she had left in the world. I swear on the lives of our children." That hit Adara hard, like a bucket of cold water on bare skin.

"Who was killed?"

"Her brother. The morning I left Cirta to come back to base I found her crying, shivering in the cold next to a pathetic grave-marker: her brother's. I couldn't just leave her there. Not after what she'd done for me. That's the reason I brought her to Thamugadi. She's a very kind girl who's had a terrible life. She needs friends, just as we all do."

Adara dried her eyes. *How could I have behaved so foolishly?* "I'm sorry. I…I had no idea. It's just that the thought of some other woman spending so much time with you while you were so far away from me, when I wanted more than anything to be close to you…it just didn't seem fair. I'm sorry I treated her so rudely. I feel terrible for thinking so badly of you."

"Stop now. I love you. As long as that's all cleared up, we're fine." Adara nodded and put her arms around him. "You can trust me with your life, my love. Never worry."

"I won't, not now. But what about Dido? She must feel humiliated."

"I'm sure Alene is taking care of her. It wouldn't hurt though for you to talk with her. Put her at ease. She looked really uncomfortable when they arrived." Lucius had not forgotten how Dido had felt for him before and knew that she must be very sad at the moment. "I'll go and see her."

"No," Adara said. "I will."

Dido did not feel like eating at all. She wanted to leave but what kept her there was her regard for Lucius. She still thought about him from time to time and seeing him that morning brought back all of her previous feelings.

When the knock came on the door of the room in which she was to sleep, she jumped. "Lucius?"

It was not Lucius, but rather Adara. Dido turned away, unable to look at her. *What does she want? I can't talk to her.*

"Dido?" Adara's voice was surprisingly gentle, easy and sympathetic. "Please forgive me for my treatment of you. I had no right." Adara moved across the room until she was next to Dido. She put her hand on the Punic girl's shoulder. Dido could feel it shaking a little. "You don't have to speak to me. I wouldn't blame you. I just wanted to explain myself, though there is no excuse. I was so far from Lucius, so very far, and I missed him. More than anything I wanted to be with him. When I saw you, how beautiful you are, my mind raced even more. I was jealous of the thought of all the time you and he had together, time I missed out on. Having met him, you must know what kind of man he is, how rare and wonderful?"

Dido turned to face her. She noticed that she too had been crying. "Yes. I do know what kind of man he is."

Adara nodded and took both of Dido's hands. "Thank you for saving his life. I owe you everything. I am *truly* happy to meet you. I swear by all the Gods that watch over us."

Dido looked upon the woman with new eyes. She meant what she was saying. She really was sorry. "Lucius, your husband," she corrected herself, "was never anything but a gentleman to me. He helped me find a new life but nothing ever happened between us."

"I know. I know. Please forgive me."

"I do." Before Dido could say another word, Adara had her arms tightly about her, kissed both her cheeks.

"I know that we'll be good friends!" She held Dido at arm's length and hugged her again.

Dido was overcome, shocked by what had just happened. Such a transformation in the woman she expected to hate her. She wept.

"Come. Let's go in to eat," Adara said when Dido had dried her tears. "We can get to know each other better. Will you come?" Dido saw the sparkle in those green eyes, the friendly warmth, and smiled back.

"Of course."

"Please, please call me Adara."

"Adara."

When the two women entered the triclinium together, they appeared happy and content. Everyone breathed an inward sigh of relief and Lucius held up his cup. "To family and friends!" He looked at everyone there, his wife and Dido last. "Welcome to our home."

The sun was at its zenith in the middle of the bright blue canvass of the Gods as the guests arrived for the lustratio of the two young Metelli. Xeno had been right. The Gods were pleased. Outside the tribune's quarters, two guards had been posted with a list of all the guests that were to be admitted.

Others, curious troops or families living outside the walls of Lambaesis were to be moved along.

Light seemed to sparkle on the paving stones of the courtyard at the feet of an almost silent assemblage. It was not an immense gathering, consisting only of close friends, comrades and superiors. Lucius' centurions, Alerio, Valerus and Pephredo were there, arrayed in full military dress; Eligius had declined the invitation. Mar and Dagon looked regal in their Sarmatian robes as they waited next to Marius and his family. Alene waited impatiently, a nervousness in her stomach.

To the left of the augur stood the legate and his wife and next to them was the camp prefect, Lartius Claudius. Three of the tribunes and their wives had come; Sabinus and Martia, Octavius and Laurissa and Ignatius and Jasmina. They had put on their finest togas and stolae.

The whispers were eventually drowned out by the cries of the young goat that the augur led forward and held upon the altar. The beast's heart beat uncontrollably, its eyes darting under the augur's tight grip. At the far end of the courtyard stood Frontus, holding Lucius' vexillum, and Balbus who waited for the augur's signal. The augur nodded and Balbus, taking in a deep, full breath, sounded a long, eerie note on the polished cornu that wound over his shoulder.

"Let the Gods bear witness to this sacrifice," began the augur, "and let them determine the rightfulness of this ceremony. Should it be allowed?" he asked in a mysterious tone of voice. The goat fought vainly as the knife approached and slit its throat. Its lifeblood ran red upon the altar as the augur cut through its stomach, poking and prodding, searching for the Gods' reply. Tulia let out a small cry but was quickly hushed by her mother. "The Gods say the ceremony may continue." He nodded to Balbus once more and another, higher note, was sounded.

The door to the cubiculum opened and out stepped Lucius holding his son and Adara holding their daughter. Everyone smiled except the augur who poured a libation on the carcass and ritually washed his hands in a nearby basin.

The couple walked in a circle about the courtyard, passing in front of each guest so that they might have a look at the newborns. When they had come full circle, they stood in the centre of the courtyard, next to the altar. Alene came forward to hold the boy next to Adara while Lucius stepped forward and accepted a clean blade from the augur. A small lamb was brought up and handed to Lucius who kept his breath steady and the knife hidden behind his back with one hand while he stroked it soothingly with the other. Its little ears twitched and its lids wavered as it relaxed.

Lucius then picked up the lamb and placed it upon the altar. His gaze moved skyward. "I offer this lamb to you mighty Gods, Jupiter, Juno, Minerva and Mars and to you Apollo and Lady Venus who watch over our family. Accept this offering in honour of my children. Let them live long in strength and wisdom." Lucius slit the lamb's throat, blood soaking its soft, white fleece, a few drops of which splattered the sleeve of his toga. Slowly, the lamb ceased its shaking.

The augur stepped forward to take the blade from Lucius and examine the carcass. Lucius poured a libation, washed his hands and from a small bowl he took a handful of powder which he then threw onto the fire in the tripod. A cloud of smoke rose up to the sky and the augur stepped back, his eyes on the blue above for a sign or omen.

As everyone present looked up, there was a shrill cry. "A bird!" observed the augur. Lucius strained to see, then his heart dropped within. It was a vulture circling overhead. "A vulture." The augur's voice was low, everyone gasped. "A bird of carnage, present in the aftermath of death and disaster. I fear this is not good."

Adara and Alene held the children close, the little boy began to cry out loud, but was soon soothed by his mother. "Wait!" The legate broke into the silence. "Another bird, no two!"

"By Jupiter," the augur exclaimed. "An eagle on the edge of the heavens. Sent down." Lucius looked at the augur and then back at the sky. "The other, a blackbird. The bird of Apollo himself!" Everyone watched in astonishment, fear and excitement. Three birds circling in the augur's vision: a vulture, a blackbird and an eagle. Then, it happened.

The eagle and the blackbird set upon the vulture, pecking at it as the three of them swooped in violent circles amid cries and screeches. Finally, there was one loud and final screech, followed by the body of one of the birds plummeting to earth. The augur gasped as his eyes followed the body. It fell like a rock, violent and fast, cast down by the Gods into the pool of the world.

"Ah!" Alene gasped as she felt something. To her horror, a drop of blood had fallen out of the sky and landed on her bare arm. She wiped it away quickly and covered the red stain with a fold of her stola.

For a moment, Lucius thought the bird would land directly on the altar but a gust of wind blew in from the west and sent it to the ground just outside the front door, onto the via Principalis.

Sabinus ran to the door and flung it open to see the vulture's mangled carcass lying between the two stunned guards who muttered prayers of protection. "It's the vulture!" the tribune confirmed. The augur looked back to the sky where the blackbird and eagle yet soared for a moment before departing to the right, back to their mountain reaches.

The augur muttered some more incantations and eyed Lucius warily. "This was a near disaster, Tribune Metellus," he warned. Adara grasped Alene's arm in fear of what else he might say. "However, it is obvious that the Gods hold you, and yours, in their favour and do indeed bless your children. But..." he looked back at the open door, "it appears that death will ever be a threat at your door. Protect your family, honour the Gods and, as is evident in the omens, your children will escape unscathed."

Lucius bowed, thanked Apollo, Jupiter and the other Gods for their aid; he wondered if it had not been the cool breath of Venus that had blown the carcass into the street and away from their home. Sweat was beading on his back beneath the folds of his toga. The priest looked to him and Adara. "You may now introduce your children to the world." With that he stepped back and Lucius and Adara, holding the children again, stepped onto a small platform that had been set up just behind the altar. Lucius cleared his throat to address everyone.

"Friends," He looked around the courtyard at all the faces. "I present to you our son." He held the child up for all to see. "Phoebus Metellus Anguis!"

Mar nudged Dagon with a smile. "We have a 'Shining Dragon' in our midst, nephew."

"Indeed we have, uncle." They quieted as Lucius accepted his daughter from Adara.

"And may I also present to you, our daughter, Calliope Metella!"

The gathering applauded the children and the choice of names for them. Now they were a recognised part of the world beneath the Gods' all seeing gaze. Once the ceremony was complete, family and friends gathered around the couple to admire the children and offer them gifts and blessings. The bodies of the goat and lamb were both taken to the kitchen to be prepared for the traditional feast that made up the final part of the lustratio.

The gifts varied in value and size, from a pair of cradles commissioned by the legate and tribunes, to carved wooden toys fashioned each by Valerus, Pephredo, Balbus and Frontus. Despite his missing an eye, Frontus had managed to carve an elaborate toy depicting a charioteer and his four-horse team. Lucius was stunned at this hidden skill in one of his men. Alerio had commissioned tiny chairs for the children which they would be able to use when they were slightly older.

As for Marius and Octavia, they presented Adara with beautiful fabrics with which she would be able to make clothes for the children. As an extra gift, Marius had made tiny rattles for each child out of smoothed and polished bronze. Mar and Dagon offered soft mattresses for the children's new cradles, the type they said were traditional in their homeland, as well as a carved ivory statue of a horse goddess they claimed was a protector of infants. Adara thanked the two Sarmatians with a smile as she held up the carving for Calliope to see. The child reached out with a shaky hand for the bright, white goddess.

Finally, Dido approached the couple and their children and knelt down to get a better look at Lucius and Adara's offspring. She was much better dressed now, more like a Punic princess than a road-weary traveller; her raiment was the colour of sand and sun with matching sandals. Her dark hair was curled and twisted into the tight, stiff locks that were traditional among her people.

"They're beautiful." Dido's face lit up when she looked upon them. The children grew silent.

"I think they like you," Lucius said. "What do you say, Adara?"

"The children are definitely smitten. Little Phoebus is smiling from cheek to cheek." Dido too smiled, felt a warmth coming from both children, a sense of welcome.

"I have something for both of you," she said in soothing tones as she pulled out two small leather pouches. "I made these myself." She showed the items to Lucius and Adara. "They will protect the children from all harmful thoughts, keep them safe." In her hand were two tiny blue eyes of lapis, set in brilliant gold and each attached to a silk thread."

"They're beautiful, Dido!" Adara said as she looked upon them. "In fact we have the same tradition in Greece. I'm most grateful that you have thought of this."

"You've outdone yourself, Dido. They're so small and delicate. It must have taken a long time."

"It is my pleasure to offer them to your children." She bowed her head as Adara hung them around the children's necks.

"Oh, those are striking!" Alene came up.

"I was wondering where you were." Lucius had noticed his sister's sudden disappearance after the ceremonies.

"I was just washing some dirt from my arm before I gave these to the children." Alene held out two tiny cloaks, one blue and the other green. "I made these for the children with some of the fabric I bought in Greece. I've attached an extra lining in each for winter. See, you can remove it."

"Sister, you're already spoiling your niece and nephew." Lucius laughed.

"Just you wait! When they're older, I'll take them shopping in the forum in Rome. *Then*, I'll spoil them!" Alene tickled Phoebus' foot. "By the way, I love their names."

"Yes, they're beautiful," Dido agreed. "What do they mean?"

"Well," Adara began. "Phoebus means 'shining'. We named him that because there is always a twinkle in his eyes, something lively and strong."

"And Calliope?"

"From the third day of life," Lucius explained, "Calliope seemed to be humming constantly, picking up sounds and turning them into song. If you listen now, you'll hear her." Dido put her ear close to the girl.

"I can hear her!" she said excitedly. Alene nodded, understanding now.

"So, you named my niece 'lovely voice' after the Muse of epic poetry?"

"Exactly."

"She's so darling!" Dido was still taken with Calliope and now humming, ever so slightly, along with her.

"Tribune." Xeno walked up to Lucius.

"Yes, Xeno."

"The feast is prepared."

"Very well. Thank you, Xeno." Lucius clapped his hands loudly to get everyone's attention. "Friends! I thank you all for your generous gifts. We are honoured that you have all come to join us this day. Now, we may all move to the triclinium where abundant food and drink await you."

As the triclinium was too small to accommodate everyone on couches, the room itself held large tables on which the food was placed so that the guests could pile as much or as little as they wanted upon their platters. Couches had of course been set aside for the legate and his wife who sat and conversed with Lucius and Adara about the day. The other guests mingled politely and ate as they pleased. The main topic of conversation was the appearance of the birds in the sky. While some had been made uneasy by that, the general consensus was that the outcome was favourable.

Marius Nelek, with Aeneas at his side, eventually found himself deep in conversations of war with the tribunes whose wives had gathered around Alene and Dido to talk of fashion and jewellery. Octavia, ever strong, took it upon herself to look after Phoebus and Calliope as well as Tulia who was amazed when her mother told her that she had once been as small as they. Mar and Dagon moved about the courtyard, speaking with everyone in turn and when finally Lucius had a moment for them they told him how greatly they admired the chosen names of his children, especially Phoebus.

"A truly powerful addition to the line of *Anguis*, my friend." Mar laid his hand on Lucius' shoulder. "You should be proud."

"I am. I'm also proud to count you among the guests here today. Your blessings are greatly appreciated."

"Think nothing of it, Anguis." Dagon smiled. "When I have children of my own someday, you shall be there too!"

"I would like that very much." Lucius smiled at the younger man's enthusiasm.

"Until then, *little fish*, you must do your duty and fulfill your vows before wandering into parenthood. You are still young. Now is the time for fighting."

"Yes, uncle." Dagon looked around, when his eyes fell upon Dido, he turned and said he wished to see the children once again.

Lucius was surprised at the sudden severity in Mar's voice, but brushed it aside. Perhaps he had his own plans for his nephew? After all, he was of royal blood, the last of a line. No matter what Rome had to say about it.

The guests laughed and talked into the starlit night. The courtyard rang with the music of a troupe that had been brought in from Thamugadi. The food was praised, as well as the company. Lucius smiled as he walked about the gathering and saw only laughing, contented faces.

Alene watched her brother and thought about how much their mother would have liked to be there. She should have been there, but it was not meant to be. Delphina and Publius too should have attended along with Adara's sisters. *Opposite ends of the empire and a sea apart; not always are paths meant to cross for every occasion,* she thought.

How her life had changed over the last year. Before going to Greece, she had remained in Rome for the whole of her life, never having seen anything apart from the family estate in Etruria. But since...she had lived a lifetime in a short period. She had seen mysteries, made friends, smelled the air of three different lands. She was surrounded by new people she had come to like very much, even...love. And now, she was blessed with a niece and nephew that she felt were as much a part of her as they were of Lucius. Alene Metella felt blessed indeed by the Gods and gave thanks to the stars. Then, when his voice came up beside her, she gave her thanks again.

XXII

EMRYS

It did not look right, the angle, the curve of the nose in the middle of the face. Not right at all. Outside in the street there was too much racket. The incessant noise that seemed to be drifting into the workshop was a constant nuisance, breaking in and out of his thoughts like the hands of a clumsy artisan, doing more and more damage. He found it hard to think that day.

Emrys walked over, slammed the door shut, and returned to where he had been working. The statue, yet another of the new Consul commissioned by the senate for some square in the city, was at best the work of an amateur. Not in twenty years had his work looked so poor. With a sigh, the sculptor moved backward to sit himself on his bench and study the image of the man before him. The eyes did not portray the frightening intensity so apparent in the Consul's eyes, his cheeks bulged overly and his hair seemed too long. The nose however, proved the most problematic.

The sculpture is there, Emrys thought. *I just have to uncover it.*

Usually, he could carve the nose so that it appeared so lifelike that it was as though one could hear the breath moving in and out of the nostrils, see the flaring. For a time, Emrys had told himself that it was no matter, that he did not like the man he was sculpting anyway and it would be no great loss if the work was not perfect. But that was not Emrys, or his way. He was in the business of carving, of shaping immortality. To create something less than perfect was failure and a denial of the gift the Gods had given him.

Things were just not right; his hammer and chisel felt heavy in his strong hands. The tools he always handled with such deftness now felt more like the great lumps of marble that he carved. He set the implements aside and reached into a bowl of pistachios on the table next to him; ever since his training in Greece all those years ago he had had a taste for them, the repetitive cracking of the shells helped him to think. He missed Greece, missed its rhythm, its smell, the way the sunlight captured every shape and brought the city alive. He missed Carissa.

Rome had changed since the last time he had walked its streets. A dark cloud seemed to hang permanently to dim Her beauty and there was a superficiality in the voices of the people, in their faces. Where citizens had once spoken their minds freely about politics or any number of events that occurred throughout Rome's vast empire, those same citizens now uttered only pleasing speech. None dared to voice an opinion contrary to the established power that roamed the marble halls of the Palatine; that power was not the empress or her sons, not even the emperor himself. Words were only spoken in the hope of self-preservation and anything else was relegated to the usual genial greetings that one offers daily in passing to another along the market stalls of the fora of Rome.

Emrys perused a list of orders he had received since his return from Greece. It was long and he knew that at the rate he was working, he would not finish on time. He scratched his head in frustration. His once brownish-grey hair was falling out, its colour now leaned more toward grey. He had not spoken to anyone either, save those who came to place orders. He felt that his voice was going unused, that he was perhaps hardening into one of his own statues and realised that he needed to get out. Work, such as it was, was finished for the day.

Having locked up his workshop, Emrys decided to make his way to the baths for a long soak and perhaps a massage. One thing he enjoyed about Rome was the number of baths available for use throughout the city, some small, others enormous. That day he decided to make his way to the Baths of Nero near the northern end of the Stadium of Domitian. It was a small complex but one that did not lack for elaborate decoration, frescoes, statuary, and colourful marble. It was also less crowded at midday, perfect for someone who wanted to be alone with his thoughts and who also had an aversion to the Roman tendency to soak communally, cheek to cheek with complete strangers.

The baths were not void of people but sufficiently quiet for a man to make his slow, solitary way through the various rooms at a pace which afforded him ample time for contemplation of whichever matters pressed upon his mind. After removing his clothing in the apodyterium, Emrys eased his way into the thickening mist of the gilded rooms and the waters of mosaic-strewn pools. A calm came over him as a morning of frustration and ill-humour washed away, replaced by a sort of pure serenity. He imagined he was a fresh, newly-cut block of Pentelic marble, that he could masterfully shape himself into something pure and strong to replace the clumsy amateur he now felt himself to be.

In the caldarium, as he drifted in and out of worldly consciousness, Emrys' mind travelled back to his homeland, to Britannia, to Dumnonia. During Martius, the first of the colourful flowers that heralded Spring would be dotting the hillsides, protruding from the cracks of moss-covered rocks. The grass would be full and green after the driving rains of Winter and the musty smell of burning peat would be rising up out of the hovels of those not fortunate enough to dwell within the walls of villas built by Rome. Still, it seemed a pleasant thought.

Emrys tried to recall the last time he had been in his homeland but it seemed too far in the past for him to remember, at least eight years, maybe more. *Someday I'll go back*, he promised himself as he lay upon a hard table in some anteroom, oiled and massaged by a monstrously hairy Cilician slave.

The late afternoon was warm and the pleasant sound of doves cooing in the cypresses made for a suitably lazy walk back to his small domus near the workshop. Market stalls were opening again after the midday rest and voices revived thoroughfares along his way. Emrys stopped at a small bakeshop to purchase two fresh pies stuffed with goat's cheese and vegetables.

He walked along, munching on his purchase, and noticed the presence of a great number of Praetorian troops as he neared the Forum Romanum. *The consul and prefect might be there*, he thought, and changed course to go down the street of the textile makers instead. The street was narrow and carried the scent of various ingredients used in creating an array of dyes; some smelled quiet lovely, others, not so. Roman textile makers were always trying to mimic the beauty of the east, much of the time without success.

Up ahead, Emrys spied a stall selling Greek materials; beautiful fabrics of deep blue, red and yellow with the traditional key fluttered in the breeze that swept down the lane. He stopped to observe. Overhead a woman yelled.

"Hymettos! Wake up! You have a buyer!" Emrys looked up to a plump woman leaning over the railing of a small balcony. She yelled again at a man snoozing happily behind the wavering fabrics. He jumped, jerked from his reverie.

"Huh? Oh! Yes, so," he began, scratching his groin as he came to, "you want to buy something?" He stood up and came around into the street to stand next to Emrys.

"No. No, friend, just admiring you wares, that's all," Emrys said politely.

The man looked up at the empty balcony. "He's not even here to buy anything! Mother! Ach." She was gone. The man turned back to Emrys. "I'm good enough to bring her here from Athens, to take care of her like a son ought to and what does she do? She nags and nags all day! Just hanging over the balcony cursing at me, good son that I am." The man waved his hands in the air dramatically, a player in some ancient tragedy. When the performance was over he smiled. "So, are you sure you're not interested in buying anything?"

"Quite sure, thank you. Actually, I recently returned from Athens myself." Emrys was hoping to entice the fellow into some sort of interesting conversation, not having spoken to anyone for days, but he was disappointed.

"Why on Earth did you go there?" the man asked. "Me, I've no need ever to return there. Boring city, Athens is. Too many intellectuals and artists trying to fancy up the place."

"Really?" Emrys frowned but the man was unperturbed.

"I tell you friend, the place to be is Rome. Sure, it's crowded and it smells, but you have everything you need right here. There's no need to go anywhere else."

"Hmm. You're right, my good man, it is crowded and does indeed smell." Emrys could not bear to remain in the man's company any longer. "I'd better be going."

"Oh? Well, if you have to." The man looked insulted. "Are you sure you don't want to buy anything? I'm having a sale, today and today only. *Very* special prices."

"I'm sure. Thanks." Emrys began to walk down the road, the man continuing to speak after him.

"Are you quite sure?" he yelled. "These fabrics are the perfect gift for a lady of quality!" Emrys kept walking but behind him he could still hear yelling.

"Hymettos! Did he buy anything?"

"No, mother! He didn't!"

"You let him get away? You're useless! We'll starve before too long!" said the husky-voiced woman.

"Mama, stamata!" he returned.

"AHH! You're going to kill me with your disrespect! Good mother that I am!"

As Emrys walked away from the welcoming family business he picked up the pace, eager to get away. Then he remembered the vendor's last words to him. *These fabrics are the perfect gift for a lady of quality.*

"In the name of the Gods! How could I have forgotten?" Emrys cursed himself. "Alene's presents for Lady Metella!" He rushed back to his home.

As Emrys dressed himself in a clean tunic and rummaged through the chest he had brought with him from Greece, he chided himself over and over again for having forgotten to carry out the task that Alene had asked him to perform, and which he had insisted was not a problem. In his sadness at Carissa's decision to be with Ashur and go her own way, Emrys had completely forgotten about the gifts of silk and other items that Alene had sent with him for her mother. He had delved into his work to forget his pain but in the process had forgotten everything else.

"Ah ha!" he exclaimed. "Here they are." He removed the beautifully wrapped packages from the bottom of his travelling chest and looked them over to make sure that they were not damaged or damp. They appeared to be in fine condition and so he set them aside on the small table by his front door.

Flustered by his ineptness, Emrys tidied his hair and made sure he was presentable for a meeting with the Metelli. It had been a long time since he had seen them and he hoped that he would find them well, that they would not be too surprised or put out by his sudden appearance. Usually, visitors to the old families of Rome were announced several hours beforehand, even days, but this could not wait and he had an errand to fulfill at the request of their eldest daughter. Besides, they had become good friends, especially he and Antonia. She had always been so welcoming and warm. A true Roman matron, genuine and hospitable. As he made his way to the home near the Forum Boarium, Emrys found himself quite excited at the prospect of a social evening with friends.

The door that had welcomed him so many times before seemed faded, its crimson colour flaked and chipping, the bronze knocker unpolished. His arms laden with packages hidden partly beneath his cloak, Emrys turned about before knocking. He felt eyes on him and wondered if someone was eyeing the bundles he carried. Sure enough, a man stood on the opposite side of the road doing nothing in particular. When Emrys looked, the man turned away and moved on. Emrys noticed a short sword hanging at his side. Time to knock.

It took some time for the door slave to answer. There were no voices within that Emrys could hear. A young, tired-looking woman opened the door a hand's breadth to see who it was.

"Good evening." Emrys smiled but the smile was not returned.

"Yes?" the slave asked.

"Uhm, would you please inform your Master and Mistress that Emrys the sculptor is here to see them."

"E-m-r-y-s, the sculptor?" the girl struggled with his foreign name.

"Yes, that's it." Emrys looked at the girl, recognised her. "Ambrosia, is it not? Don't you remember me?"

"Yes, sir, I do now. It's just that…"

"Ambrosia! Who's there?" A voice growled from a room just beyond the atrium. Emrys thought he recognised it.

"Wait here, sir, please." Ambrosia let Emrys just inside the door so that she could close it and scuttled to the door of another room to announce him. There was a ruffling of papers and some grumbling before she returned. "The master will be here momentarily," she said as she took his cloak and hung it on one of the wall pegs near the door.

"Is your mistress at home too? I have something for her from-"

"She is, sir, but…"

"Emrys, the sculptor! This is a surprise indeed."

"I hope I am not interrupting anything, Senator Metellus."

"Yes, well. You are here now," Quintus said smugly. "What can I do for you?"

"Well, Senator, as you know I accompanied your daughter to Greece. Although I am sure you know all of the wonderful news regarding her, your son and his own lovely wife, I also bring gifts for the Lady Metella from your daughter."

"Wonderful news you say?" Quintus' eyes lit up oddly as he outstretched his hand to lead Emrys into the house. "Come, let us have some wine and food and you can tell me all about your time in Greece. I'm very eager to hear of it." Quintus led Emrys to his study where he closed the door and seated himself behind his great desk with Emrys in the small chair before it, feeling uncomfortably like a suppliant.

"So, you say that my daughter is gone to Lambaesis with my son's wife who is pregnant?"

"Yes indeed, Senator. I do believe, Gods willing, that the baby has by now been born, or soon will be. But surely you already know this from the letters your daughter has sent you?"

"Of course I do. I just like to repeat things for my memory's sake." Quintus poured himself some more wine, neglecting to fill Emrys' cup. "And of course the man Ashur has gone with them."

"Yes, he has." It pained Emrys to be reminded. Quintus observed the artist sitting before him, swirling the dregs of wine at the bottom of his cup.

"And your apprentice? She was always with you before, was she not?"

"Hmm. She was, before. Yes. But now she too has gone to Africa."

"The young, useless they are, in all things. Should be locked up, the lot of them."

"I think that a bit harsh, Senator." Emrys was becoming upset now. *Who does he think he is, this frail, toga-clad man with his nose in the air?* "The young are our future and we should cherish them." As he said it, Emrys realised he had been hard on Carissa, not really allowed her to grow. "After all, we too were once young."

"What drivel!" Quintus looked disgusted, as though he smelled something terrible just then. "You are too idealistic, I think. Things were different when I was young; there was respect, decency." Somehow, Emrys thought that the man before him had forgotten the meaning of those words. "I say we should do away with children who disappoint, as was a father's right so many years ago. And if they are women, well, they should not be allowed out of doors."

"I cannot possibly agree, respectfully." In a short time, Emrys had come to hate that room, despise the man before him. Of course Quintus Metellus had always been cool with him, he was with most people, but something was definitely wrong. And where was the lady of the house? He had been there for an hour answering questions about Lucius, Alene and Adara without any sign of Antonia. The slave did say she was within. "Will the Lady Metella be joining us soon, Senator? I have been remiss in my errand to give her these packages from your daughter." He pointed to the bundles on a table next to him.

Quintus Metellus did not speak. He eyed the artist warily, believed he should be rid of him soon. "I am not sure she is prepared for an audience."

"I will not impose for long. My instructions were to hand her the gifts and give your daughter's love to her. I will leave after that."

"Very well. Ambrosia!" he yelled for the slave who came running.

"Yes, Master?" She opened the door hesitantly.

"Inform your mistress she has a visitor. Tell her to look…presentable. The children are to stay in their rooms. We shall be in the garden."

"Yes, Master." Ambrosia closed the door and ran upstairs.

"Come, Emrys. We shall wait in the garden where the air is fresh." Quintus got up and went out the door himself, leaving

Emrys to gather the packages and follow. One consolation, Emrys thought of as he walked in front of the row of Metellus ancestors, was that he would see the statues of Lucius and Adara, in his opinion some of his best work. Perhaps he would gain some inspiration from them?

As he entered the courtyard, Emrys was shocked at the sight presented to his eyes. What had once been a beautiful, welcoming garden, a place where he had enjoyed time with wonderful people, new friends, was now irretrievably run down. All the vegetation, flowers and delicate trees, were dead. The pathways, the mosaic in the midst of the garden, were dusty and unswept. It was obvious that this place was not used anymore. To make matters more painful, the statues that he and Carissa had created and brought to life were no longer there. There was no sign of them. Quintus smiled at the expression of sadness upon Emrys' face.

"I've found that the garden is a waste of time here. Someday, soon, I shall purchase a better house, a more luxurious one, on one of the hills. Perhaps the Caelian?" Quintus looked toward the stairs. "Where is the woman?"

"Quickly, mistress! You have a visitor."

"A visitor?" Antonia had been sitting by the window in her room, gazing up at the sky as she did most of the time of late. "Who is it?" she asked slowly, weakly.

"Emrys, the sculptor. He says he has gift for you from the Lady Alene." Ambrosia tried to sound cheerful enough to enliven Antonia. "He has been here for some time but…"

"My husband has kept him," she finished the sentence. "Quickly dear, help me with my hair."

Antonia straightened her long tunic and sat at her table looking into a bronze mirror to see her face while the girl arranged her hair more neatly. "They are waiting for you in the garden."

"The garden! That place is not suitable for guests. Oh no, what shall Emrys think of me? He has done this on purpose of course," she whispered, referring to her husband, "hoping that the darkness in the garden will hide my crooked face on this cloudy night. Go. See that the children are brought."

"He said they should stay in their rooms." Ambrosia looked down.

"Very well. At least set out some stools for us to sit on and light a brazier. I'm sure my husband has not deigned to offer our guest a comfortable chair. Go now." Ambrosia went out and Antonia finished arranging her hair before going down. She did not know why exactly she wanted Emrys to see her state. She so rarely had visitors. Perhaps she wished for him to see what she had been through, the scars that marred her face. But what could Emrys do? If anything it would be good to see a friendly face, even with *him* there.

"I'm always kept waiting within my own home. You see, sculptor? This is what women do. Stay here, I shall return shortly." Quintus stormed down the corridor to his office for his wine cup. He had developed the habit of drinking much wine, especially in the evenings when he was not with his fellow senators.

Ambrosia came around the corner with three folding stools which she hastily set up, motioning Emrys to one of them. He noticed how the girl moved with such fear all the time, like a beaten cat. "Thank you dear," he said. She then moved to the base of the stairs where she lit a small brazier, the flames of which jumped up and reflected off the marble. With the light, the form of Antonia Metella was revealed as she hobbled down the stairs on her bad leg.

Emrys laid aside the bundles and jumped up, a shallow gasp escaping his mouth. She limped toward him, trying as best as she could to walk proudly, as she used to. Her leg had become worse over the winter, and caused her more pain. She smiled, her jaw slightly askew. Not able to help himself, a tear ran slowly down Emrys' cheek to be lost in his thick beard.

"Lady?" his voice was hoarse.

"My friend. I can't tell you how happy I am to see your face." She looked over her shoulder to where Ambrosia stood, waiting to give a signal if Quintus appeared. "It seems ages," Antonia said, her speech slightly impaired because of the injury. Emrys knew he need not ask what had happened. A sudden rage came over him but was doused by the pity he felt for her.

"As you say, a long time." He took her hand carefully with both of his. Antonia fought back the tears that threatened to fall, the tender touch of a friend was a welcome oasis in that dark place, something all too rare.

"When did you arrive in Rome?"

"Some weeks ago. I regret, truly, that I have not come to see you sooner. Forgive me."

"There is nothing to forgive. Please sit." Antonia motioned to the stool and took one herself. She now whispered. "Have you said anything, anything at all, about Lucius and Adara, the child?" Her eyes were pleading.

"Lady, I'm afraid that I have said everything." Emrys felt a weight so heavy upon his shoulders he thought he would crumble where he sat. *What have I done?* Antonia's eyes shut tightly in despair and he soon realised that Quintus had known nothing, that she had been keeping the news a secret from him. For what reason, he did not know but Emrys felt the severity of the situation all too keenly. "Please forgive me. I…I did not know." Before Antonia could respond Ambrosia cleared her throat.

"Who lit this brazier?" Quintus demanded as he walked up.

"I had Ambrosia light it, husband," Antonia responded flatly. "It is a cool night."

"Yes, it is." he answered. "Did your friend here tell you wife, that our beloved daughter has gone to Africa? And that the girl Adara, is with child?"

Antonia threw her hands to her face, feigning surprise as best she could. "Alene gone to Africa? Really?" Emrys nodded, confirming for her. "And Adara is pregnant?"

495

"Yes, apparently she is. Did you know of this?" Quintus asked her bluntly, expecting her to panic, admit that she had known.

"I did not know. Oh how wonderful!" she said excitedly. "I do wish Alene would not be so remiss in her correspondence. Shameful of her to wait to tell us. It is likely she did not want us to feel badly about not being there for the birth."

"Quite." Quintus tried to figure out if she was lying or not. He had kept a tight leash on her, as he thought a paterfamilias ought to. No mail had come and if it had it was for him alone. He looked at Ambrosia who stood stalk-still, staring down at the ground. "At any rate, Emrys here apparently has some gifts for you from Alene."

Emrys picked up the packages and handed them to Antonia. Her eyes lit up. Gifts from her daughter. How happy she would be to open them later. "Thank you for bringing these to me, Emrys."

"It was no trouble at all, Lady Metella. I'm only sorry it took me so long to get them to you."

"Please, no apologies. You are here now. I shall enjoy opening these later."

"You can open them now," Quintus commanded.

"But I cannot see well enough here husband."

"You're not blind! Open them here, now."

Antonia looked down at the packages she held lovingly in her arms, so carefully wrapped. Alene always did take great care in wrapping things.

Without another word she undid the ribbon of the first bundle and slowly folded away the material to reveal a brilliant blue fabric, trimmed with a golden key and what appeared to be dolphins of an ancient design. Even in darkness the pattern was visible. "Oh! It's beautiful!"

"I remember the day Alene returned from the markets with that fabric," Emrys began. "She was so excited, certain that you would be able to make a beautiful stola out of it."

"Oh yes!" Antonia held it up, pressed it against her face. It was soft and smooth and smelled of jasmine. After a moment, she opened the other packages to find more beautiful silks and a small plaque with a fresco upon it depicting the Acropolis of Athens. It was more beautiful than she had imagined. "One more gift." Antonia looked at Emrys, who smiled as he caught a glimpse of the joy that had once flowed out of her luxuriant eyes. She gasped as she opened the smallest package.

Inside a small box of olive wood was a necklace made out of seashells, delicate seashells dipped in gold and threaded carefully together. "I had no idea such beauty sprung from Neptune's sea." She held them carefully in her hands, admiring them. Later she would try them on. "Thank you for bringing these to me Emrys."

"My pleasure."

Before another word could be said, Quintus spoke. "Well, it seems that our daughter has become quite cheap in her travels. Really, sending you second rate trinkets and imitation silks."

"I do believe, Senator, that they are of the best quality Athens has to offer." Emrys had to speak up.

"Indeed. The best *Athens* has to offer. Not saying much, is it?" Quintus rose, wine cup in hand, and waited by the brazier. "It seems, Emrys, that my wife is tired. The hour is late."

The sculptor continued to look at Antonia who remained expressionless as she held her gifts. He knew that it was time to depart. "You are right, Senator. It is late and I have imposed quite enough upon your hospitality" He turned to Antonia. "It is good to see you again, Lady Metella. You must come by my workshop and see my new creations."

"I do not think that is suitable," Quintus interrupted. "It is not a fitting part of the city for a senator's wife."

"At any rate. Thank you." Emrys bowed his head to her. "Perhaps I can call again?"

"You may leave, now!" Quintus' rudeness was tinted with anger. Emrys knew that if he persisted in that manner, Antonia would be the one to bear the brunt of it.

Emrys followed Quintus down the corridor and turned in front of the stairs to look at Antonia one more time. He could see her sad smile. He also heard a sniffling sound, but it was not coming from her. At the top of the marble stairs, in the darkness, two tiny faces stared back at him pleadingly. Young Quintus stood there with his arm around little Clarinda; their faces were wet with tears, their eyes begging him not to leave.

Feeling his heart would break, knowing that he could do nothing for the moment, Emrys turned from the stairs and the garden and went to the atrium where Ambrosia handed him his cloak.

"I hope you are enjoying Rome at the moment, sculptor." Quintus almost laughed.

"I have known Rome to be a better place in the past. There is too much fear."

"Ha! Too much fear from the fearful, the weak." The senator squared up to the artisan, though he was much smaller than Emrys. "I tell you, there is a new order in Rome and when all comes to fruition, the great families of the past will reign supreme. No more foreign blood will pollute our glorious city after that. Mark me."

"Good night to you, Senator Metellus. May the Gods bless your family and protect them." Emrys did not remain after that but went out into the street to leave the hateful man to his drink. As he walked, he realised that Quintus Metellus had been speaking of the new Consul when he spoke of a "new order" in Rome. Emrys only hoped the senator was wrong. He feared more for Antonia and the children and would not be able to sleep for the vision of their weeping faces tormenting his mind. He felt helpless as he went, knew that the following day he would have to finish the sculpture of a man that was admired by the senator, a despicable, dangerous and bloody man, a man even more hateful than the one he had just left.

After Emrys had left the house, Quintus returned to the garden to find Antonia carrying her gifts up to her room. "Just what do you think you're doing, woman?" he barked.

"Taking my gifts from Alene to my room. That is all." Her voice was timid, no trace of its former defiance.

"Oh no you don't. You don't deserve such things, especially after having kept information from me about Lucius and his whore."

"I kept nothing from you! I swear I did not know!" She knew her lie was entirely justified.

"I don't believe you!" he yelled. "It makes no matter. *I* know now. Give me those!" He pointed to the gifts.

Fighting back her tears with all her might, Antonia reluctantly handed the items over to him and turned to go upstairs. When she arrived at the top she looked down to see him smiling at her, laughing, as he held out a handful of Greek silk and dropped it into the brazier. The fabric contorted and shrivelled into a black heap. Quintus then tossed the fresco onto the ground where the plaque shattered.

"Now for this trinket!" He held the golden necklace above the flames, the fire lighting his smug, wrinkled face, and dropped them in. The gold began to melt into black ash and the shells beneath cracked. "Ha." He turned and went back down the corridor to his room and his drink.

When she was sure he was gone, Antonia let her tears fall without a sound within the walls of her room.

The following day, Senator Metellus strutted proudly through the forum after a lengthy session in the curia. The Consul had been there, and had spoken with him. He was very pleased with himself and reported that he had important news.

"Someone will come by your home this afternoon to pick up the document." That was all the Consul said to him but it was enough to lighten Quintus' mood, remind him of what was in his mind, his great importance. He was playing a role in the 'new order' of things.

When he arrived at home, the senator went directly to his room to write out the letter detailing his sons' whereabouts, his wife's pregnancy and any other information he thought would be useful to the Consul, and more importantly, useful to himself.

An hour later, there was a knock at the door. When Ambrosia made to answer it, Quintus stopped her and sent her away so that he could answer it himself. In his hand he held the small scroll with his seal on it. Waiting outside in the street was a man dressed only in black. He had a scar on his face that was just visible beneath the rim of his cloak's hood.

"Right on time. Very admirable of you."

"You have something for me?" the messenger asked gruffly and without ceremony. He looked about him. "Someone called here last night. Who was it?"

"It's no business of yours!"

"You're wrong, Senator. I have my eyes on you."

"How dare…" Quintus stopped himself, the man's hand was on his dagger. He knew that these Praetorian spies were untouchable, uncaring and unafraid. They were used to killing at any given moment and disappearing. "He was a sculptor. Someone who gave me the information I've detailed here for your superior. He may know more. I'll let you know when I find out."

"You do that, Senator." The man took the letter and tucked it in the folds of his clothing. "Anything else?"

"Just tell Argus that they are all together in Lambaesis."

The man in black turned without another word and disappeared down the street, the way he always did when Quintus gave him new information. He stood there for a moment muttering to himself. "Now, my bastard son, let's see if you're as good as you say you are." Quintus turned then and went back to his room, locking the door behind him.

Through the small crack of the adjacent door, the storage closet, small eyes peered from within, wet, angry eyes that could not believe what had just happened. On a stool within the large closet, before the statue of his brother and his sister-in-law, young Quintus Metellus felt his heart heaving in his chest, a sickness in his stomach.

He hid in that closet much of the time now, gazing up at the lifelike images of Lucius and Adara, praying that his older brother would come back to help them. That day, a part of him wished he had not been there, that he had not heard what was said. Their father was betraying his own blood to Argus. What would happen? He was young but he knew how terrible his father had become and fell to his knees as he grasped his brother's legs.

Argus was a bastard but their father favoured him now, was helping him against Lucius. He would tell their mother but how would she get word to Lucius? There had to be a way.

"Please stop this!" young Quintus whispered in the shadows as he grasped his head. The pain was unbearable, a never-ending pounding pressure. His vision failed then and he lost consciousness for a time.

When he came to, that evening, the young boy crept into his mother's room to tell her what he had heard and seen that day. More sleepless nights, more nightmares. She swore him to secrecy, by the dark gods in the cave in Etruria that he had told her about.

The sound of the hammer and chisel were absent yet again in Emrys' workshop in Rome. He had tried to finish the statue of the Consul but could not find it in himself. He wanted to hack the thing to pieces, but instead opted for a walk in the markets.

As he began to make his way toward the baths again, Emrys was stopped by an official-looking man, a man he had met before. Then he remembered; it was the fellow who had placed the order for the statue that he was having so much difficulty with. His deadline had passed and as he had accepted payment ahead of completion, the man was not happy when Emrys told him that it was not yet finished.

"Do not think you can swindle me, artisan!" the man threatened. "If you don't finish the statue in two days, the entire contents of your workshop will be confiscated and you will be locked up for good measure. Do we understand one another?" Emrys nodded, choosing not to speak. He would have liked to pommel the man then and there, to get out his frustrations, but that would have achieved little except for his execution.

Not at all in the frame of mind for the baths by then, Emrys turned around and made his weary way back to the workshop, determined to finish the damned sculpture no matter what. When he arrived, he found the door open. Cautiously, he pushed it, trying not to make it creak. The sight before him nearly caused him to faint.

"Carissa?" he said, his voice shaky. Before the statue of Plautianus stood the young woman. Her hair was longer and fell about her shoulders, only just, as her arms reached up with a hammer and chisel. She had just finished. "You always were better at noses than I." He smiled.

Carissa turned, also teary-eyed, and ran to embrace him. "I'm sorry," she cried into his chest as he held her tightly, lovingly. "I'm so sorry."

"Don't be. It is I who should be sorry." Emrys held Carissa's face between his strong, callused hands. "The Gods bless me for bringing you back."

Just then Ashur appeared in the doorway. Carissa had feared Emrys' reaction to his being there but was surprised. Emrys strode over to Ashur and grasped his forearm as a friend. "Thank you, Ashur Mehrdad. Thank you for this."

"It was her wish, Emrys. She was not happy without you." Emrys said nothing. He overflowed with joy and felt as though a lost part of himself had come home.

XXIII

MEMORIA EXCIDERE

'The Forgotten'

The streets of Carthage were deserted. The market stalls had closed up for the day and all that remained were the scraps of wilted vegetables and small pieces of fish that had slipped from various wagons and carts. It was feeding time for every stray dog, cat and street urchin, supper time upon the muddy paving slabs where pools of water and filth pocked the ways of the less wealthy districts.

Close to the sea, not far from the great harbour, the air stank of fish, and the sounds of dog and cat bounced off the walls of tenements, from the roofs of which angry residents tossed down broken pieces of pottery to shut up the whooping animals.

It had been raining for days. Off and on, heavy downpours crashed onto the city dampening everything, including people's spirits. This was the price of Spring, some said. Storms still raged above the swelling sea, the last vestiges of Winter. Soon, the sun would shine and the world would be transformed.

This sentiment however, was not shared by the weak, hobbling vagrant who fought away a group of hissing, scratching cats in the street that day. "Go away!" he yelled. "It's mine!" The rags that were his clothing were soaked like the rest of the world, torn and soiled. He had nothing except a piece of soggy, half-eaten bread and the piece of fish which he now wiped on his rags, having come out the victor in his struggle for supremacy with the rest of the residents of the alleys and dark corners of Carthage. At the bottom of the ancient, glorious city, was a foundation of misery.

With his feast in his clutches he walked along a narrow street that led to the western edge of the city and the amphitheatre. There were no games at the moment and in the arches of the amphitheatre he would be able to find shelter from the rain and the wind that swept off of the boiling sea. "Stop it!" he yelled, cursing the howling that was now ever-present in his mind. He hated wind, had had too much of it. Wind and dust and cold. "Hades! Hades! Hades!" His head twitched to one side uncontrollably, the scratches inflicted upon his legs by the cats stung and were swelling.

When he reached his makeshift home in one of the amphitheatre's smaller, hidden nooks, he nestled into the darkness to wipe the fish more carefully. Biting into it was not a treat but it would stop the pain in his stomach for a time. He found it was better eating in the dark, better not to see what he put into his mouth.

"Two days! Two days!" he muttered rhythmically. "No! Three! Wait, no, four!" He had not been there long, but three days in Carthage seemed like thirty. He scratched his head trying to remember something. "What was it? What was it now? Think!" He counted upon his fingers. "Two streets from the...from the...What? You can't remember? Idiot!" He slapped himself, choked on the soggy bread, and cried. His hands shook and his skin seemed to hang off his bones. "I hate him. I hate him. I hate him," he repeated. "Two streets...two...two...North! Yes, yes! North of...of..." His blue eyes flashed in sudden shock. "North of the harbour! Big harbour! That's it! Yes! Near the wall." He crawled back out into the rain. "Must go before I forget! Two streets north of the harbour, near the wall." The ragged man hobbled down the street back to the sea, repeating the words to himself the entire way.

As the bearded man stood at the window of the battered tenement, he cursed the rain, cursed the situation in which he found himself, cursed his orders. It seemed forever that he had been held up in that stinking place, a lifetime.

"Wait! That's all we've been doing for what, two months?" He looked behind himself at the ugly man sitting in the dark. It was a good idea to know where he was at all times.

"You talk too much, Praetorian!" said the other as he picked at some dried dates. "I thought you were best at waiting. Besides, anything is better than sitting in that dark pit again."

"Since when did you become so optimistic and patient?" He turned to face the man, his form outlined in the light of the window where he stood. He had grown bigger, stronger since they had been in Carthage; so much time on one's hands made for many hours on the palaestra of the baths.

"I don't mind waiting now. It gives me lots of time to think of what I'm going to do to him when we get him." He rocked his hips obscenely and ran his finger across his throat. "I'm going to take my time." His cracked and scarred lips parted in a grin.

"You'll do as you're told Brutus. Got it? Or you'll end up in that black pit again."

"Fuck you!" Spittle dripped from his mouth. "I wonder if you'd be so mouthy if you didn't have that blade levelled at me."

"If you keep things up you won't find out." Argus sheathed the blade and went back to the window.

"I'm going to the brothel!" Brutus said. "Don't say it again. I know I'm being followed at all times."

When he was gone, Argus slumped down into the chair he had placed near the window and set his sword against the wall. He had been telling himself for months that it would all be worth it once he had completed this mission for Plautianus. Until now however, it had only been extremely tiresome spending so much time with Brutus, sleeping with one eye open, his sword and dagger next to him.

The difficult thing was that there was a distinct possibility that he would need Brutus. His animalistic rage could prove useful, could be used as a distraction. Argus found himself thinking more often about how he would kill Brutus rather than the objective of his mission. *If only things weren't taking so long.*

When they had arrived in Carthage and he had checked in with some one of his local henchmen, Argus was given a message saying that he should wait before leaving Carthage. *Wait for what?* he had wondered. But there was no answer to that question. He considered moving if another month passed. In the meantime he had been training himself, keeping up his strength. He had also found a good brothel on the other side of town where the women were clean but not too expensive and were willing to do everything he wanted. He left Brutus to his own pursuits, mainly the brothel near the harbour, the one specialising more in boys.

To his own surprise, when Argus had arrived in Carthage, he had not found any messages from Maren or Garai apprising him of the situation. It had been a long time since he had heard from them but he put this down to Lucius' return to the base; they must have been more cautious so as not to give anything away. He knew they would not let him down in this. Maren, especially, was strong and secretive. Argus had a lot of eyes there, in that far away place. Nothing would be missed.

He scratched his bearded chin and yawned. Argus hated having the thing but he needed it to be fully grown in order to disguise himself when they did set out. The day was long, draining. Brutus would be gone for some hours ravaging the homeless brothel boys and so Argus decided to sleep for a time, with the door locked.

The rain pattered on the roof tiles the entire time and black and grey malformed clouds hovered and pressed down on the city walls. Argus slipped in and out of an uncomfortable, hazy sleep. At some point he heard a yelling out in the street but decided it was one of the local beggars, strayed from the port, and ignored it.

A short while later, there was more yelling and then a pounding on the door at the street, his door. Instinctively, Argus jumped out of bed, dagger in hand. The knocking stopped and there came the sound of footsteps on the stairs outside his door. *Damn Brutus!* he thought. *Idiot forgot to lock the door.* The footsteps stopped outside and then a foul smell came from beneath the door. *The vagrant! Bastard doorman's gone off again.* Argus thought he would let Brutus have it for leaving the door open. For the moment he would give the wretch outside the scare of his life.

There was a loud knocking on the door to the room, a moaning. "Are you in there?" the voice called. "You'd better be!" Before there was another knock Argus slid the bolt and flung open the door. He kicked his foot out first and made contact. There was a howl and a gasp. He jabbed his blade into the darkness of the hallway and it too found its target. There was a scream, cursing. "Hades! Hades! Hades!"

"To Hades with you then!" Argus said as he kicked even harder sending the man tumbling down the stairs where he knocked his head on the wall of the first landing. There was silence. Argus went back into the room to get an oil lamp and came back out, dagger extended at the heap on the floor as he moved closer to check if the vagrant was dead.

The smell was unbearable and he realised his attacker had shit himself when he fell. Argus moved the light closer. It was hard to make out any sort of a face because of all the dirt, the overgrown beard and hair. The man was thin, sickly. He bled profusely from the hand where Argus had stabbed him, part of a finger hanging off.

There was a wheezing sound. The man was breathing. *Still alive.* Argus wondered what to do. He could finish the job but then he would have to get rid of the body. True, no one would miss this vagrant, but he was sure that with all the racket he was making out in the street many people would have seen him come in the door downstairs. If he was alive, he could wait till he regained consciousness and then no doubt he would be more than willing to get out of there. Argus nudged him with his hobnailed boot.

"Hey! Wake up you son of a bitch! Don't make me cut you again." His threat was unheard and so he jabbed the dagger into the man's calf, just enough to sting.

"AHHH!" The vagrant flailed his arms hysterically, looked at his hand and then spotted the huge man standing two steps above him, blood upon his blade. "Don't hurt! Don't hurt…me. Where is he? Where is he?"

"What are you saying? Where's who?" Argus yelled at the weeping man before him.

"The man, the man! That's who!" Argus kicked him in the calf he had stabbed. "OW! No, no! Please…" he cried, "…the man. Don't kill me! Argus! Where is Argus?"

Argus' grey eyes shot wide and a pang of fear ran down his spine. He grabbed the man by the neck and pulled him off his feet, pounding him hard against the wall and pressing his blade to his neck.

"Who sent you?"

"Nobody send!"

"Answer me or I'll slit your throat right here! Who sent you?" The man could barely speak with the weight of Argus' arm on his windpipe.

"Argus! Where is Argus? Tell him…tell him Garai is here! Me! I'm Garai!" He lost consciousness. Argus caught him as he fell and tripped backward onto the stairs behind him. His mind spun and he felt ill as he held the stinking man. What did this mean? What's happened? He reached for the lamp and held it to the face next to him, and brushed aside the filthy hair. It was indeed Garai.

That night, with the door firmly bolted and Brutus in a room upstairs, Argus did not sleep. Instead, he sat in a chair gazing at the crumpled shadow of a man he had known, now lying in a stinking heap upon his own bed. He had bound the wounds he had inflicted on him and wiped the dirt from his face with a wet cloth so he could see the face more clearly in the light of extra lamps he had lit.

As he waited for Garai to wake, he thought a great deal, not about how to help him but rather how much he had given away and whether he should kill him or not. He decided that he needed to find out as much as he could first, then would decide.

Morning came and went and Garai yet slept. Argus had gone out to get food and drink when he awoke, but before leaving he had tied Garai to the bed frame so that he could not get away if he came to. The sun made an appearance that afternoon and Argus opened the windows wide to let the foul-smelling air out. The blankets on the bed would have to be burned after this. Brutus had knocked several times, wanting to enter but Argus had put him off, told him to go to the brothel again or stay in his room and wait. At this point he really did not care about Brutus.

As Argus sat at the window breathing the fresh air and eating, he heard a moaning behind him and then a panicked breathing. Garai struggled in his bonds.

"Wait! Don't make a sound, Garai. It's me Argus."

Garai's head flopped back on the bed and tears came to his eyes. "Argus? Is it you?"

"Yes."

"You look different…different…different."

"Calm yourself! You're talking like an idiot." Argus got up and paced the floor in front of the bed. Garai watched him. "What in Hades are you doing here?" Garai wept more. "Stop that! If you don't, I'm going to have to kill you!" Slowly, the weeping faded to a sniffle. Argus untied one of his hands and handed him a piece of bread. Garai held it to his face, sniffed it, devoured it.

"Oh, oh. So much has happened."

"What's happened?" Argus was getting more and more impatient but realised that this was going to take some time, especially if Garai's mind was not right. "Think, Garai. Think and tell me everything."

Garai shook his head as if trying to chase away the memories. His mind was cluttered and confused. He thought for a moment before speaking and then it began to come back to him in a rush, like a horrible flood. The oasis, he remembered the oasis…

Over the next hour, in a long, roundabout manner, Garai managed to retrieve the memory of what had happened, and he told Argus everything. He told him about the march to the oasis. Lucius had found out that they had murdered Antanelis because he had found out about Argus' own plan to kill Lucius. The tribune had set a trap for him and for Maren.

"What happened to Maren?" Argus was full of anger.

"Don't, don't know. Last I saw he was fighting with Alerio."

"What do you mean you don't know? You were there weren't you?"

"I fled, escaped."

"They didn't come after you?"

"No, they were too busy fighting the others."

"What others, Garai? Be clear about it. Try and remember."

"There was an attack. Garamantians, I think. Much confusion. I took a horse and escaped."

"So the cohort could have been wiped out?" Argus sounded almost excited.

"Maybe. They were outnumbered. I do know that Lucius was hit by an arrow."

"Where was he hit? Was it lethal?"

"I don't know. He fell." Argus breathed deeply. This could change things. If Lucius had been killed and the cohort wiped out it solved a lot of his problems. He wondered whether the

Gods had been so kind to him for once in his life. He looked down at Garai's tired blue eyes.

"What happened to you after that? After you fled the field to save your own skin."

Garai closed his eyes tightly, shook his head. He told Argus how he had ridden hard and fast into the desert, far, far into the desert. He spent many days riding east, he said, until he came to one of the small oases in the deep desert. He spent what felt like two days there, trying to figure out what to do, where to go. But, as he recounted the following experience he shook, twitched his head.

As he had slept one night, next to a pool of water, beneath a towering palm, Garai was knocked over the head and bound. When he awoke he was tied to that same tree, surrounded by several Garamantians, who, he assumed, had come from the battle or been following him. He could not understand their speech. He had been stripped down to his tunic, his own armour and weapons, shoes and the horse he had taken were now in his captors' possession. They inspected him, his strong build and seemed to decide he would fetch a good price. They haggled over who would be the one to take him to the slave market, wherever that may have been.

"How did you get away?" Argus stood there listening, arms crossed.

"There were only two who had decided to take me to…to…Sabratha maybe. Yes, I think I heard the word Sabratha. Or was it Tacape? Doesn't matter now. One night we camped somewhere among some rocks. One of my captors came to me in the night to fuck me. I resisted, kicked with my bound legs. He must have tripped or something because he fell and did not move. He had a dagger and I managed to lean against it and cut the ropes around my wrists. See?" Garai held up his free hand to show Argus several cut marks on his wrists that had occurred when the dagger had not found the ropes.

"What did you do to the other one?"

"I killed him as he slept. Then, I took a horse and rode fast as I could. I never was a good rider. The horse broke its leg among the dunes and so I had to walk. So much walking. So much wind too."

"Then you came here?"

"Yes. But along the way there were others who tried to…"

"That's fine." Argus was tired of the diatribe. "You're here now."

"Why do you have me tied up?"

"Because I don't know everything that's happened. You've gone a little mad and I don't think I can trust you."

"Don't kill me, please Argus!" he begged. "I…I…can tell you more! Yes! About Lucius, what he said about you." The threat of death seemed to clear Garai's head and a light seemed to spark in his eyes.

"What does it matter if he's dead already?" Argus asked, dashing Garai's hope of living.

"Do you *really* think *Lucius* is dead?" The question caught Argus off guard. They knew Lucius led a charmed life, always had. Argus hated him for it.

"What did he say about me?"

"He said. Hmm. Let me think, let me think. He said he knew about our contact with you and that he didn't care you and he had parted ways." Argus spat on the floor. He did not care either. "He…he called you a traitor, a coward, yes that was it, a coward who was…jealous…because you would never be good enough at anything."

"I'll kill him if he isn't already dead," Argus muttered to himself.

"He also accused Maren and I, in front of others, of treason and murder."

"Well, he's right there at least!" Argus laughed. "You are guilty of that."

"Because you asked us to!" Garai looked shocked.

"Don't be stupid! You wanted to move up the ranks too, just as much as Maren or any other grunt."

Garai looked away, knew that to be true. How things had changed he thought; months ago he did want promotion, so much so that he was willing to kill a friend. Now, what he would not have given for a bath and a warm meal, that is, if he left the tenement alive. He looked at Argus' back where he stood at the window.

"I can help you!" he said, trying to steady his voice. "You need me!"

"Oh really? Why do I need you? Tell me."

"Because, *if* Lucius is alive and we need to go to Lambaesis to kill him, then I know where to go, who to speak with."

"You forget that I was stationed there too. I know my way around."

"Yes but do you know who is loyal to us out of the men? There have been many changes made, promotions. I know a few men who will help."

"They'll be looking for you. I can't risk having you there."

"I can convince my brother to help..." Garai let that sink in. Eligius had never been a part of the plot, though he had never had a real problem with Argus. He lived to command his men, and gain status within the legion.

Argus now thought seriously about letting Garai live.

"Do you really think your brother will help us? Eligius has always been loyal to Lucius."

"He's more loyal to his family, to me. I can convince him to help us."

"*If* they are still alive," Argus stressed. "If they're not, I'll kill you myself."

"Yes. If they are still alive." Garai had not thought about that. He had missed his brother deeply, longed for his companionship in the desert, his best friend, his blood. "Eligius will help me," he said in a low, pensive voice.

"Fine. You live for now. But you need to recover before we do anything." Argus began to untie Garai, holding his breath from the stench. "First, we're going to the baths so you can wash the shit off yourself. Keep the beard, trimmed of course, as a disguise." Garai nodded, agreeing with everything. "You listen to me and do everything I tell you. If you make one wrong move, if you show any more signs of madness, I'll kill you. Got it?"

"Yes...yes. I understand." He stood up weakly, his legs shaking. Just then there was a harsh pounding on the door.

"Open up, Praetorian! I've had enough of this!"

"Who's that?" Garai recoiled like a frightened animal.

"That's our partner."

"There's another?"

"Yes." Argus went to the door and opened it.

Garai did not recognise the man at first. Indeed, he had completely forgotten about him long ago. Brutus entered the room, and looked suspiciously at Garai who instinctively backed away.

"Who's this smelly shit?" His voice was harsh on the ears and his breath smelled of wine.

"Garai, do you remember Brutus?" Argus moved next to Garai who searched through his memories, unable to place him. Both men had changed much in appearance.

"I want to know who this dirty cunt is, Praetorian." he demanded.

"This is Garai, Brutus. He was one of the centurions in our march across Africa."

"Not another one!" Brutus cursed and spat on the ground at the newcomer's feet. Garai could not believe it. Now he remembered, now he knew who the man was.

"But...but...he went to the galleys for treating with the nomads," Garai whispered into Argus' ear.

"So I did. Ha!" Brutus feigned a lunge at Garai who jumped back with a squeal. "Ha, ha, ha!" he laughed. "You'd better throw this beggar back, Praetorian. He won't do us any good." Brutus went and plopped himself down in one of the extra chairs on the other side of the room.

"Argus. Why is he here?" Garai asked nervously, remembering the beating Argus had given Brutus before throwing him into the hold of the slave ship in Sabratha. *He should be dead!*

"Shut up and listen. Orders from my superior. You understand? From the Praetorian prefect. You know who I'm talking about?" Garai nodded. "Good, then you'd be smart not to ask any more questions and just accept things as they are. We have to work with him and that's it! Unless you prefer the other option." Argus put his hand on his dagger.

"No, no. I'll do what you say, Argus."

"Good, now let's get you cleaned up and then we'll find you some decent clothes and a weapon. You'll need it around *him*." Argus nodded toward Brutus who chuckled to himself, enjoying the effect he had had upon Garai.

The three men spent an uneasy two weeks in the tenement together. Slowly, Garai began to regain his strength as well as his senses. Daily, he made the walk to the large bath complex to exercise his muscles. The process was not without pain or discomfort. He realised he would never regain even a shadow of his former youth and power. He had changed so much physically that he wondered if Eligius, if he was alive, would even recognise him in the thin, all-too-lean body he now inhabited.

As he toiled with the lifting rocks and was massaged by the slaves in the baths, Garai thought only of his brother and their separation and the man responsible for all the pain he had been through: Lucius Metellus Anguis. He had forgotten all the previous memories of goodness and friendship that he had shared with his former commander. It no longer mattered that they had bled together, that he and Eligius had owed their promotion to centurion to him. No, in Garai's mind, Lucius was only responsible for the break-up of the cohort from the time Argus left up until his ordeal in the desert. The fact that he now had to endure Brutus he also attributed to Lucius who, he thought, had been too cowardly to kill when he had the chance two years before.

Argus had warmed slightly to him but Garai knew that he had his own agenda and that if he put one foot wrong it would dash all chances of his seeing Eligius again. The lack of knowing was perhaps the most painful thing. If his brother were alive then he had a reason to go on putting up with Brutus and bowing to Argus' wishes. If Eligius was dead, then he had no reason to live, especially a life of shame.

Brutus on the other hand, regarded Garai with the disdain with which one looks at a crippled dog begging for scraps. Now and then he would kick at him, or spit, or curse. Garai was grateful that Argus had seen fit to give him a weapon whereas Brutus had none. As Garai gained in strength and managed to retrieve what confidence the Gods would grant him, he was able to face off against Brutus enough so that they each kept their distance. His hands seemed never to leave the handle of his blade however, and for good reason; there was something extremely disturbing about Brutus' eyes. The crack-lipped Egyptian seemed to have an evil in his eye that never ceased to burn. It appeared as though Brutus never stopped mulling over the carrying out of terrible acts in his mind and when he turned those hateful eyes upon Garai, the Roman thought he could hear the screams of those imagined victims.

On a sunny, early-Spring morning when the sea was finally calm and the winds had died down, Argus came bursting into the room where Garai had been eating a bowl of millet with some bread.

"Finally!" Argus said excitedly as he held up a sealed scroll.

"What's that, Argus?"

"What's up yours, Praetorian?" Brutus too came down the stairs and into the room.

"I met with one of the prefect's men who has just come from Rome with dispatches for the African network. He had something for me."

"Well? What does it say?"

"Wait, Garai! I'll read it myself first." Argus pulled his chair over to the window so that he was facing the others, preventing them from looking over his shoulder.

"Don't worry, Praetorian. I can't read your stupid letter anyway."

"You can't read? Figures!" Garai looked with contempt at Brutus now.

"Watch yourself, little boy!" he warned. " You won't be able to read either if I pluck out your eyes while you sleep." Garai continued eating his millet.

"Shut up, both of you!" Argus unrolled the scroll and read.

You know who you are,

I will be brief in this. I have obtained all of the information you require and expect your superior to reward me for my pains. The other day I discovered that the one you seek is indeed back in Lambaesis and doing well. His wife, and my daughter, have joined him there. Further, and this is something I think will interest you, the woman he is married to was with child and should have given birth by now.

Beware, the man Ashur also accompanied them. You know more about him than I. If this letter reaches you in time I expect you to use it well. The man you seek is no longer my son and the woman and child who are his have no relation to my family. Do your worst and do it well. No mistakes.

If you are successful in this and I receive my just rewards from your superior as agreed, then I might consider acknowledging you as my rightful son, and heir to my great family name. This however, remains to be decided.

If I receive more news, you will hear from me.

Argus rolled the scroll back up, clutching it tightly in his hand. His first reaction was to burn it but he stopped. *It might*, he thought, *be useful in the future*, an assurance against what was alluded to: acknowledgement.

For the moment, he pushed the thought away. Lucius was alive. His mission was on and therefore, the waiting was over.

"Well?" Garai asked. "What is it?"

"We're going to Lambaesis."

"He's alive?" Garai seemed almost overjoyed because it meant that his brother was likely alive also.

"Yes. And his wife and child are also there."

"Excellent." Brutus gritted his teeth and smiled through his scarred lips. Garai noticed that horrible look in his eye. "When do we leave and get out of this shit hole?"

"Two days." Argus got up and without another word went to make preparations.

And so, two days after the letter from Quintus Metellus arrived, from the hand of a Praetorian messenger, Argus, Garai and Brutus set out disguised as merchants with a single, small wagon and two mules. Their weapons were packed in the rolled carpets that were their wares.

The sun vanished and emerged intermittently behind clouds that blotched the sky. On that road west to Cirta, each man travelled in silence, each entertained his own individual thoughts; the thoughts of an assassin, of a brother and of an animal.

XXIV

SOL CADUCUS

'The Fading Sun'

It was early morning. The sun had just risen and cast its angled glow onto the face of the distant mountains beyond the sea of sand. A mass of tents, as well as several permanent huts or shelters, were huddled in a hidden recess of one rocky outcrop that seemed to spring out of the ground like some ghost of the underworld, the sort that parents talked about when children would not do as they were told.

Everyone was already about their business; best to do so before the sun was too high in the blueness above. When the little boy finished watching the sun rise into the swirling sky, he picked up his water-skin and began his walk to the well. This was his daily duty and he went about it in a sort of practised manner; the path he took, the way he carried the skin over his shoulder, the lightness with which he walked, all these indicated that he had done this many times before. Now, it all came without thinking. His mind was on other things.

He thought of being a warrior for his people. He remembered the tales his father recounted of warriors of past ages: Ramesses, Hannibal, Scipio and especially Alexander who had passed through the very area in which they lived. The boy's father spoke not only of their own people's heroes, their deeds, but of men of greatness from around the world who hailed from all peoples. *We are all men*, the words swept over the dunes whenever his father would utter them, *we are all men*. Of late, his kind-faced father told many tales of Roman warriors. "They are the rulers of our time," he would say, "and we must learn from them."

The boy remembered his father telling stories to many people, constantly writing upon papyrus sheets or clay tablets.

'Historian' was the word people used to describe him but the boy preferred to call him 'inspirer' for that is what he got from him. He wanted nothing more than to be like the men in the stories told to him beneath the full moon around the family fire. Today, to his surprise, he found the well surrounded by Roman soldiers. Perched on some nearby rocks he waited and watched. Their armour gleamed in the sun. They looked very impressive, their leader infinitely more. He looked like one of the many gods that were cut in stone in the Roman parts of town, the images before which people always laid flowers and dead animals.

When the soldiers marched off, the young boy made his way down to the well to fill the water skin and carry it back to camp where they would be waiting for him. Before leaving, he took a long drink for himself from a wooden ladle that was always there.

It was turning out to be a fine day. He loved the heat, loved the desert. Soon, they would be moving on to the place called Siwa. His father had said that it was time for "the Journey"; this was something their people had been doing for many, many years before he was born. It was not an annual journey but rather one that was made "whenever the call came from the God". Whatever that meant, the boy did not know; he was happy to go.

Smoke appeared ahead, screams were carried on the wind. The boy's heart leaped as fear flowed in his veins like a deadly poison. He ran and ran, tripping in the soft sand, scrambling to the top of the hill where he could see what was happening. A loud ringing deafened him as he peered through the black smoke and broken sunlight. Men were attacking their camp, men with long, curved blades that took the life of his people. An attack from the south, beyond the Roman lands.

"No!" he yelled, fumbling at his waist for his small dagger. "Stop!" The boy ran down the side of the dune, brandishing his knife. He spotted his father, on his knees before a man in black. He ran, screeching so loudly that his throat hurt, but he was too late. He arrived at his father's side just as he collapsed, head next to his body. "GODS!" he called out as he raised his little dagger and plunged it into the stomach of his father's murderer.

"Argh! I'll skin you!" the murderer yelled but dropped to his knees. The boy ran from him, ran as fast as he could, but then it happened. A hard knock from the side sent him flying into the soft wall of one of the tents. He scrambled, heard a yell. Crying, wailing, he ran again, looking back, ignorant of the rock face before him.

The world went black and all memory faded. The sight of his father around the fire, his smile, his mother's singing, all of it faded into a dark expanse from which nothing returned. Only the sight of grey eyes bright as stars and a wavering blue-clad arm reaching out. Darkness...

"NO!"

"*Minau? Minau*, wake up." Carissa shook Ashur where he lay sweating and weeping next to her in their small bed. "Ashur, it is only a dream. Wake up." Soon the crying subsided and he was sitting on the edge of their bed, his face in his hands with her arms about him. He shook. "Was it the same dream?" she asked.

"Yes. Always the same. The same screams, the same smoke, the same grey eyes looking into me." He breathed deeply. Carissa went over to a small table and dipped a cloth in the water of a bronze basin, dabbed the back of his neck, just below the deep scar that he had always carried on his head, hidden beneath his dark hair.

"The Gods are trying to tell you something."

"Please, Carissa! They are not."

"Why do you deny it?"

"Because the reality of it is far too confusing, and I cannot bear the burden of it. I wish only to live with you now."

"But this dream comes to you almost nightly. The same dream!"

521

Ashur rose from the bed, letting go of the artisan's hand to wrap himself in his long white robe. "I must be alone for a time. I shall be back, my love. I promise."

"I know. You always come back." Carissa watched as Ashur walked out. It was two hours before day and she lay herself down again, to sleep, to wait and to cry for the man she loved.

Since they had returned to Rome, since he had brought Carissa back to Emrys, Ashur had been happier than he could ever recall. The light that had once faded from Carissa's eyes had returned, as well as her smile. That is, until he had the dream and woke her in the night. At such moments, Ashur thought it best that he be alone with his thoughts, and the images the Gods were torturing him with.

He sat in his usual spot before the Temple of Apollo on the Palatine Hill, but he did not approach, did not dare. He did not know where else to go. Rome could be a large, lonely place. He sat and thought of his dream, of the boy and his father, of tents, of sand and of smoke. The blackness that followed was what truly frightened him. What happened to the boy? He felt a strong connection to him, to his father and the sounds of the woman's voice that always seemed to be there.

"It can't be," Ashur Mehrdad whispered to himself. "It can't be me!" Indeed, his greatest fear when that dream burst into his sleep was that he was the boy, that it was his father who was there, his family who was killed. Such a dream begged him to question his existence, a dream in the midst of a Roman world, dotted with Roman soldiers and structures. How could it be? If these were indeed memories, he wished they had never come upon him, for they were far too painful in their implied reality.

He looked at the empty square before the temple and remembered a happier time. He could hear the voices of Lucius and Adara's wedding feast, the laughter, the music. He remembered feeling a part of something, a family; oddly enough, this was a feeling familiar to his terrible dream also. By now, a new Metellus would have been born, yes, another dragon. He looked up at the fading stars, searching for the constellation, *Anguis*, for which his friend was named, but could not see it. The sun was rising.

As he walked back to Carissa, Ashur decided he would pay a visit to Antonia Metella and the children. She had always treated him with kindness. He could do this while Carissa and Emrys worked. He hoped however, that the senator would not be there during the day. He did not like Quintus Metellus pater.

Truth be told, Ashur had been thinking of the Lady Metella, young Quintus and Clarinda frequently. Emrys had told him and Carissa what he had seen when he had gone to deliver Alene's gifts. Ashur thought he at least owed it to Lucius to go and see what help he could offer, if there was anything to be done. It was certain, he thought, that Lucius did not know of this, nor Alene.

Seeing Antonia proved impossible, at least without causing her trouble. There had been races that day in the Circus Maximus, the streets rowdy with the fans of the victorious teams. Ashur pushed his way through the mass of people that dammed up the streets and the Forum Boarium until he was standing in front of the door he sought. Faded, run-down, as Emrys had said. Ashur knocked. No answer came. He knocked again...and again. Until the door creaked open slowly and two furtive eyes looked him up and down.

"Ah. Good day to you. I am here to see the Lady Metella."

"She is unable to see anyone," the girl said.

"Is she ill?" Ashur asked.

The girl shook her head.

"Tell her Ashur Mehrdad is here and wishes to pay her and the children a visit."

"Ashur...Master Lucius' friend?"

"Yes. May I enter?" Ashur moved forward but she held the door fast.

"Please, sir," she implored. "If you have any care for the Lady Metella you will not persist."

"Ambrosia," Ashur remembered her name, "what has happened here? Perhaps I can help?"

"No, sir. You can't."

"Why?"

"If anyone is seen entering the house the mistress will...the master will hurt her. I...I...can't say anymore." Ambrosia started to panic, her eyes looking momentarily over Ashur's shoulder. "You should not be here. There are spies everywhere," she whispered. Ashur did not need to turn around to know what was amiss. The girl's fear said much.

"Very well," he said loudly. "I am sorry I missed the Lady. Please tell her I called." Ashur then whispered so that Ambrosia had to lean closer to the door. "Who does the shopping for your household, Ambrosia?"

"I do. Why?"

"Tell your mistress I called and that if she has any messages for me to give them to you."

"What can I do?"

"I will be waiting in Trajan's markets every morning, near the Egyptian food vendors, for two hours from mid to late morning. I will give you any replies I have the following day. Understood?"

"Yes...yes. Now please go." Her voice was now quite desperate. Ashur could feel intense eyes on his back.

"I will call again some other time," he said loudly, before turning to leave. The door shut briskly behind him, the bolt slid home. As Ashur turned, he spotted the man dressed all in black, standing across the street, his eyes following him over the heads of passers-by. Another wave of Circus fans came down the street then and Ashur disappeared among them.

The following morning, the door of the Metellus domus opened and the slave Ambrosia, wearing a plain tunic beneath a simple brown cloak, came out and made her way down the street with her basket. She wore the hood up, not wanting to make eye contact with anyone as she went. Nevertheless, she felt the presence of the man in the street as she had come out. He was always there, watching and waiting. She did not like the way he looked at her. It frightened her greatly; Argus had looked at her that way the last time she had seen him.

It was a busy day at the markets and Ambrosia was grateful for the shopping throngs into which she was able to disappear for a spell, buying her way toward Trajan's Markets and the Egyptian food vendors. The letter she carried was safe beneath the cloth at the bottom of her basket, buried under a mound of fruit and vegetables.

As she approached the section of the markets she was looking for, the strong scent of foreign spices made her sneeze. The air was pungent, blue with the smoke of burning incense and roasting meat. The people looked strange to her also, not Roman. As she stumbled through the stands, she felt a hand grab her elbow. She jumped.

"It's all right, Ambrosia. It's me, Ashur. Come, let us get out of earshot." Ashur led the girl through the stands until they came to one selling chickens and other animals for sacrifice. "Numonius," Ashur addressed an offering seller standing in front of a draped carpet; the man had helped them in the past and was now a trusted friend of the Metelli.

"In here, friends." The man had a kind face, but that did not make Ambrosia feel any more comfortable with Ashur. Though she knew him, she was always wary of strange men in the market places of Rome, especially in such dark, out of the way corners as these. She sat down when told.

Behind the hanging carpet was a room lit by several lamps, a recess in the stone wall. Ashur sat down on a carpet, away from the girl so as not to make her nervous. Ambrosia had the basket at her feet.

"You are safe. No one can see you here, Ambrosia. Here." He offered her some dates but she shook her head, too nervous to eat. "What says your mistress? Do you have a letter for me?"

"Yes, sir. I do." Ambrosia fumbled around until she reached the bottom of her basket and pulled out a small piece of papyrus. "My mistress told me to give you this." She handed it to Ashur who unrolled it and read it on the spot.

Antonia had been surprisingly open in her letter. She said that as Ashur was a trusted friend of Lucius she could trust him with all that she said. Without going into too much detail about how things were at home with herself, Antonia Metella told Ashur that she was unable to leave the home, that she had been unable to receive guests. That would not change. The house was being watched by Praetorian spies, spies that were in constant contact with her husband. Ashur remembered Quintus Metellus speaking with the Praetorian prefect at Lucius and Adara's wedding feast.

He read on about Antonia's suspicions that her husband was providing the prefect's spies, Argus among them, with information about Lucius and his family. She was deeply worried about the child that would most certainly have been born by then. Lucius, Alene, Adara and the child were in grave danger, so Antonia believed and said as much. Quintus Metellus had sent a letter after he discovered that they were all together in Numidia.

I beg you, Antonia had written, *do not worry for me and the children. We will survive. However, Lucius must be warned! He will need help. I have done what I can in this but I beg you, Ashur, will you go to Numidia to help my son? Will you help him and my daughters and grandchild? Darkness is closing in on them. Argus has much hatred in his heart and I fear he will stop at nothing. His superior is master of Rome, an evil man who lures others with false promises, including Argus and my husband. I care only for my children, Ashur. Please help. Antonia Metella.*

The hasty scrawl of the letter ended abruptly, its words a call for help that pierced Ashur's heart. How could he go back after just having arrived? He had bid Lucius farewell, fortune in his own life, on his own path. How could he diverge once more from his *own* road, a road he had chosen to travel with Carissa?

Ashur held the papyrus over one of the flames in the small room, between the tips of his fingers until it burned away.

"Do you have a reply for my mistress?" Ambrosia asked hesitantly. Ashur was silent. He needed to think on the matter.

"The Lady Metella cannot send messages to Africa?"

"No, sir. She says that everything is read before being sent now. The spies…" her voice trailed off. "Besides, the master does not allow her to send any kind of correspondence. She can only contact you through me."

"What else do you know?"

Ambrosia looked down at the ground for a moment then spoke. "The master has turned terribly cruel and has beaten my mistress and young Master Quintus."

"How badly?"

"Very badly, sir." Ambrosia began to weep. She had said too much. She had been told not to say anything of their own dire situation. "The truth is, sir, my mistress and the children are well enough if they do not cause a disturbance. It's the matter in the letter that she says is most important. More important than anything."

Ashur looked at the pile of ashes upon the stone floor. "What should I tell her, sir?" Ambrosia asked again.

"Tell her that I must think about this. Remind her that the Gods themselves watch over her son and daughters. For myself, I am alone in this world except for the one I have vowed not to leave."

"Does that mean you will not help?"

"It means I must think on it. Come back here in two days for your shopping and I will give my answer. If you see

527

Numonius out front, as he is today, then you know it is safe. He will recognise you. He is a friend of Lucius'."

"Yes, sir. I'll be here." Ambrosia picked up her basket as Ashur stuck his head out from behind the hanging carpet to check that there was nobody suspicious about.

"You had better get back before they realise you are gone too long. I shall be waiting here for you. Remember, two days."

"I'll be here." Ambrosia pulled her hood over her head and went out with her basket of vegetables and fruit and disappeared again into the marketplace. Numonius turned to Ashur.

"Is the tribune in danger, Ashur?"

"Yes. He is, Numonius. Grave danger, I fear."

"Can I help? Please tell me, what can I do for him?" Numonius' genuine will to help Lucius, a man he had not seen for some time but who had been touched by his goodness, humbled Ashur.

"There is only one person who can help him."

"Who's that?" Numonius demanded, full of worry for the young tribune. Ashur did not answer him.

That evening Ashur sat down to a simple meal with Carissa and Emrys to discuss matters. He had been keeping them abreast of what was happening. They knew of his visit to the house and the presence of the same spy that Emrys had seen before. Carissa had been worried for Ashur; meeting in secret with the slave of a senator carried a heavy punishment, especially when that senator was one of the new Consul's supporters.

"What did the girl say, Ashur? Did she have a message from Lady Metella?" Emrys decided to ask first since Carissa was caught up in studying Ashur's sullen face as he gazed at the flames of the lamp on the table.

"She did have a message from her mistress."

"What did it say?" Carissa asked.

"Lady Metella said that she feared for the safety of Lucius, Alene, Adara and the new child. She said that after Emrys visited," he nodded to Emrys, "the senator sent a letter informing the Consul's spies of Lucius' whereabouts and who is with him. She fears he stressed the presence of the baby too." They were all silent.

"This is all my fault. Gods!" Emrys slammed his fist on the table. "How could I have been so stupid? He was asking me all those questions."

"It's not your fault," Carissa soothed vainly. "How were you to know what had been going on behind those walls? You were away, we all were. She didn't even tell Alene."

"Lady Metella is a strong woman," Ashur said. "She would have wanted to keep Alene safe if things were ill at home. If she had told Alene, she would have come back to Rome and would be in the same situation her mother is in now." Ashur put his hand on Emrys' shoulder. "It is not your fault."

"Soothing words from either of you will not help in this. Not now." Emrys was distraught, the image of Antonia's broken face haunted him. "A lot of good it does Alene and the others now, being in Numidia! Plautianus has surely notified his spies. He's eliminating anyone who could be a threat to him now or in the future. Quintus Metellus has bought himself favour with his son's own life. Lucius and his family will be killed."

"But how can they get to Lucius and Adara when they are living inside the legion's base?" Carissa asked naively.

"My dear," Emrys explained, "they can get at anyone, anywhere, anytime. I've seen the reach of this man all over the empire, especially here in Rome." He turned to Ashur. "Did Lady Metella say anything else?"

Ashur was silent. He did not want to say but knew he had to eventually. "I am to meet with the slave girl again tomorrow to give the Lady Metella an answer."

"An answer to what, Ashur?" Carissa asked, her voice a whisper.

"She has asked, no, begged me to go back to Numidia to warn Lucius and help him." Emrys was silent and Ashur could not look into Carissa's eyes as she stared at him, two big, beautiful orbs of sadness changed to glassy pools as the words sank in. "I haven't said yes," Ashur stressed. Nobody spoke.

"How can you think? Both of you!" Carissa's eyes finally closed and the tears ran in rapid streams. "Lucius is in danger! Our dear friends, those who brought us together, brought *you* together, are in danger."

"It's not that easy, Emrys," Ashur defended.

"By all the Gods above and below, it most definitely is!" Emrys was up and standing by now, ready to chide them some more but he realised the pain they both must be feeling. The anguish of love separated could be more terrible than anything. "Listen to me," he said more gently. "I see how you both feel for each other. I'm not ignorant of love. Indeed, it was taken from me long ago and I wish more than anything that I could have it back." They were both looking at him now. "But by Venus, a love plagued by guilt is a tainted love, a painful love. If they die and there was something that any one of us could have done to stop it, then it must be done! Surely you can see that? Trust me, you don't want to look at each other day after day only to see the faces of the people you could have saved but were too selfish to save."

Carissa got up from the table and ran into the next room, her face buried in the blanket on the bed. Ashur followed, leaving Emrys standing in the dimly-lit room.

"I don't have to go, *Minau*," Ashur said, his face in her soft hair as she wept, her body heaving with her cries. "I will stay here with you and we will live long, be happy together. I don't have to go." Ashur stroked her hair, her back. "I don't have to go."

"But you do." Carissa sobbed as she turned around to face him, her lashes thick and wet. "You *must* go, my love."

Ashur heard what he had not expected to hear, did not want to hear. However, it was what he should have heard, the words spoken from the lips of a woman he had fallen in love with, a strong, loving and truthful woman.

"Carissa..." he said her name, his voice shaking as she held his head between her artist's hands, looked closely at him and kissed him sadly upon the lips. "I love you beyond life and time," he whispered, her arms gripping his body more tightly than ever before.

On the arranged morning, Ashur awaited Ambrosia once more in the Egyptian quarter of the markets. It was less busy that day and he could see the girl coming from a distance, her head cloaked. She walked with a hurried step and a greater degree of nervousness. She came running, looking behind her.

"Ambrosia, come!" Ashur waved, took her hand. "What's wrong? Is someone following you?"

"Yes." She was panting. "Yes. The man outside the house, the one in the street all the time. I think it's him."

"Come. Let's get behind the carpet before he sees you." Ashur began to lead her in when Numonius spoke.

"Too late," he whispered. "He's coming. I'll get him close, Ashur. You be ready." Numonius looked about to see who was present and slid a long, thin dagger up his tunic sleeve, the sort of dagger he used to bleed livestock. For the moment, there was no one else except another merchant who was sleeping behind his counter down the way. Ashur pushed the girl behind the carpet.

"Stay there and don't make a sound." Ambrosia huddled herself in the dark, frightened and shivering. Outside she heard voices.

"You there!" The determined footsteps ended in a gruff voice. "Where's the girl that was just here?"

Numonius looked at the man, then looked around, his arms upraised in ignorance. "What girl? There's no girl here, only me, my lazy friend there," he pointed to Ashur who was pretending to sleep on the ground next to them, "and my chickens. Do you want to buy one?"

"Buy what, you idiot?"

"A chicken of course. The Gods favour the pious, my friend. When was the last time you offered a live sacrifice to Father Jupiter?"

The spy reached out and grabbed Numonius by the collar of his tunic and put his dagger to his throat. "Listen, swine! In the name of the Consul, I demand you tell me where that girl is. I saw her with you not moments ago!"

Before Numonius could speak again, Ashur's dark hand came up to grab the spy's dagger hand and cover his mouth. Numonius' own dagger unsheathed itself from his sleeve.

"Here she is pig!" He drove the dagger into the spy's left side, pushed it deep. The man squirmed, his legs kicking violently as Ashur dragged him behind the carpet and slit his throat in the dark with his own blade. Outside Numonius checked that no one had seen anything. Everything was clear.

Ambrosia ran to the back corner of the small dark room when she had seen Ashur's silhouette despatch the spy. She sunk to her knees, wringing her hands and turning her head away. Ashur took a spare carpet and covered the body for the moment.

"He's dead. Nobody saw what happened." Ashur approached her but she shook more the closer he came. "Listen, Ambrosia. We don't have much time. Do you have another message from your mistress?"

After a few moments Ambrosia calmed herself and tried to answer Ashur, averting her eyes from the bulging carpet. "My mistress does not have another message for you. I was told to bring her your answer. That is all."

"Very well." Ashur kneeled down next to her. "I'll tell you my answer so that there is no evidence of what I'm going to do." The girl nodded, listened carefully. "Tell her that I am going to warn Lucius and that I am leaving tomorrow. I will travel day and night until I reach him. Do you understand?" Ambrosia nodded again. "Now, as for what has just happened. You saw nothing, heard nothing." Ashur spoke slowly so she would not miss anything. "When you left the house to do your marketing, the man was standing there as usual if anyone asks about him. Apart from that, you simply did your shopping and went directly back to your mistress. Can you remember this?"

"Yes," she said as she pulled her hood over her head once more.

"Good. Let me check if it's safe for you to leave." Ashur poked his head out through the carpet.

"It's clear," Numonius whispered.

Ashur signalled to Ambrosia to come out and as she did, she paused next to him. "My mistress did have one thing she wanted me to tell you."

"What?"

"She said to say 'Thank you' and that she never doubted that you would help."

"Tell your mistress I will do all that I can for her, and them."

Ambrosia gave a fleeting smile and then her cloaked form dashed off into the markets with her basket. Ashur stood there for a moment, watching her, then turned to Numonius.

"I need you to do something for me."

"I told you that I would do whatever would help the tribune and his family."

"I need you to dispose of every piece of *that* back there." Ashur motioned to the carpet.

"Done. One of my old cows died this morning. She was too old to offer as sacrifice, too tough to eat. I was going to chop her up and take her out to my cousin's farm. He uses the meat to attract the wild boar thereabouts. I'll do the same for our friend back there."

Admittedly, Ashur was shocked that a man so friendly and gentle as Numonius could do such a thing so casually. However, he was grateful for his help. "Thank you, Numonius." Ashur prepared to leave.

"Fortuna guide you," he said to Ashur.

"If She will, friend." Ashur returned the smile and made his own way through the markets. He had one more stop before returning home to prepare for his journey.

The square before the Temple of Apollo was quiet, the silence broken only by a flock of doves that had come to drink at a small puddle in the middle of the white marble of the paving slabs. The birds scattered at Ashur's approach. A part of him wished to fly with them but he felt compelled to do this last thing before leaving.

For his whole life, what he could remember of it at least, he had felt close to Far-Shooting Apollo. His presence had once given him succour, like sunlight in the dead of a cold winter, it had been all pervading. He stood in the middle of the square, looking up at the steps, the towering columns that supported the pediment. Ashur knew he had turned his back on the god he had always served and believed in. He needed him and was humbled, afraid, cold in the shadow of the temple. He could not bring himself to move forward then, as he thought about it, knowing that he did not deserve Apollo's aid.

"Ashur?" The soft voice arrived without warning. Ashur turned around.

"Carissa? What are you doing here?"

"I thought you might be here, that perhaps I could help."

"I don't think that even you could help me in this. Carissa, my legs will not move because I am no longer worthy to approach." The girl came forward and took his hand in hers.

"Ashur, my love. It is time for you to make peace with Him." He knew her words to be true, felt it. "Let me go with you." She began to lead Ashur forward, up the stairs and through the great bronze doors.

It felt strange inside, strange and familiar. The smoke of incense embraced the two as they moved through it like fog upon a glassy pond. Fires flickered in the wings. Behind them, a priest stood watching. He recognised Ashur, but said nothing.

Apollo and his muses stared down at the two as they came to a stop before the great altar. "I'll be right here. Go ahead, my love." Carissa stepped back a few paces to allow Ashur the time he needed and to say her own prayers for him. Although she would not say it, she was deeply afraid.

Ashur Mehrdad gazed up for a long time and then fell to his knees in supplication. In the slightest of whispers, he spoke. "Mighty Apollo. I have been wrong, my faith not as it once was and for this I am truly sorry. I beg for your mercy, for your forgiveness of my...my being human. For I now realise that is all that I am. Human. I am grateful to you for all that you have given me in this life, and though I do not remember much of it, what I do remember I shall cherish always. I thank you for the dreams you have sent to me, what you have shown me. I realise therein that you have indeed been speaking to me and not been silent. I was blind. Someday I hope to understand fully the images in my mind.

"Tomorrow I leave down an unknown road. I am afraid, afraid that you will not be with me, that I will not succeed. I ask for your aid so that I may help Lucius Metellus Anguis and his family who honour you above all. Make me strong to this end, fast as the warm winds in summer, so that I may help him, reach him before it is too late. Whatever may become of me, I beg you to protect Carissa. I want for nothing more and I put myself at your mercy." Ashur thought for a moment and realised he had forgotten an offering. His heart beat quickly. Behind him Carissa was looking up at the God and his muses as she prayed for her love.

Ashur then felt at his side. He did indeed have something to offer and approached the main altar. As he reached the top step, he removed the small curved dagger from his belt and placed it on the altar. "This is all I have to offer to you, Mighty Apollo. Please accept it. I have had it for as long as I can remember, from the time you reached out to me in the darkness and spoke my name."

Ashur stepped backward several paces until he was beside Carissa and bowed deeply, his hands crossed upon his chest. "I honour you," he said before turning around and leaving the temple.

The night had been calm and the morning had passed too quickly. Carissa, wrapped in a thick cloak, clung tightly to Ashur's arm as they waited for the remaining cargo to be loaded onto the barge that he was to take down river to Ostia. Emrys stood to the side.

"Which route will you take, Ashur?"

"I'll try to find a ship to Hippo Regius or Rusicade. It will be much faster than going through Carthage."

"Hmm. Quite." The sculptor thought for a moment. "You shouldn't have trouble finding a ship. Spring is here and the seas are swelling less. Here, take this." Emrys handed him a bag of coins.

"What's this for?"

"A little extra for some folk goes a long way down there."

"I cannot accept this Emrys. Keep it for the two of you."

"Please, friend. Accept it." There was a sense of finality about the way he said it; he would not take 'no' for an answer. "There's not much that I can do to remedy the mess that I've caused. It's the very least I can do to help. Please." Emrys' face was sad but determined. Ashur knew that he was blaming himself.

"Thank you." Ashur bowed and took Emrys' hand in friendship before turning to Carissa. The two of them walked to the edge of the dock, just beyond the edge of the barge. The clouds and light traces of early morning reflected in the water. Ashur wondered what he could say to make her feel better, some comforting words to dry her eyes.

"I love you. I will come back to you, *Carissa*." Her name left his lips just as the tears left her eyes. Ashur hugged her tightly, felt her touch, inhaled her scent, tried to remember the feeling of her hair against his face.

"Apollo watch over you, my love." She tried to control her emotion but could not. All her life she had been outwardly emotionless, a silent artisan who expressed herself in her work. No amount of chiselling, hammering or polishing could channel the anguish of that moment, the worry.

"All aboard for Ostia!" the captain called out as the final passengers made their way up the ramp and onto the barge.

Carissa then took something out of a fold in her cloak, a simple, straight dagger, and tucked it into Ashur's belt. She knew he would need it, having given his own in offering. He kissed her one last time, and was gone. The barge drifted out and, caught in the current, drifted away.

"He'll be back, my dear." Emrys tried to console her. "He's a strong, skilled man. He'll be back." Carissa said nothing, simply nodded her head and pulled her hood over to hide her face for the walk back to the workshop.

That afternoon, Carissa, in her silence, began a new sculpture, one that required no sketches, no designs. She knew the shape and form by heart. While the memory of him was still fresh in her mind, Carissa began to sculpt Ashur Mehrdad, the only man who had ever truly won her heart, the only man she would ever truly love beyond creating.

XXV

NEX

'Death'

Late Spring in Numidia that year was a time when the Gods were temperamental. Clouds born in the highest peaks thundered down out of the mountains and onto the unsuspecting plains. Lashings of rain soaked the land and in turn coursed through the arteries of rocky riverbeds to feed the rest of the world on the edge of the deep desert. This lifeblood rushed down out of the previously snow-capped teeth of the world where the locals said their Punic gods had taken refuge after their fall to Rome's Pantheon.

The sun too, under the command of Apollo, burnt through the aftermath of rain and cloud to pour light and warmth into every fissure. Like the blazing rivers of fire that are wept by volcanoes, those sleeping Titans whose wrath is fierce, no stone was left unturned. A desert land, a land of sand and dust and sky above, was preparing for the summer months. Still, hues of emerald, silver and lemon yet lingered, for it was a time of comfort, of joy and of ease.

Lambaesis. Lucius had never thought he would enjoy being there as much as he did in the weeks following the birth of his children, Phoebus and Calliope. The tribune's quarters had become a smaller, crowded home in a short period of time but it did not matter to him or the rest of the family living there. The happiness they shared was a gift. All worries had melted away as with a great thaw, they way snows disappear in the northern parts of the empire.

Lucius had returned in earnest to his duties; the parade ground beckoned and his troops needed to be seasoned for the campaigning months of summer. He felt at ease once more upon Lunaris whose stable was now adjacent to Phoenix, Adara's own stallion. She had not gone out to ride him yet, but had been sure to visit him in the stables and see that Lucius, or one of the Sarmatians, exercised him once a day.

In her own heart, Adara felt as though she had found her place in life, that she was where she was meant to be, and enjoyed every moment between herself and her children. She found she could spend entire days with them and, though exhausted, the smile never left her face. Phoebus' strong personality made her proud, and Calliope's constant rejoicing eased her heart and dulled the pangs she felt for the rest of her family away in Athens. Her parents would have received the letters by now. Her mother would finish the mural she had begun prior to her daughter's departure for a strange land.

Always there, ever ready for her sister and her nephew and niece, was Alene. She too had come to enjoy life at the base, the sense of family she had regained with Lucius and Adara and the trusted friends she had made. Things were actually quite good, not as claustrophobic as she had expected them to be. There were plenty of women around the base to socialise with and Thamugadi was but a few hours distant; they had already been to visit Marius Nelek and his family since the lustratio.

For Alene, there was another reason that made life at Lambaesis more than bearable: Alerio. They had grown close since her arrival, both smitten from the time they met, though they had not expressed this fully until the birth of the children. Strange how such events push hesitant emotions into the foreground of life from an unknown or denied existence. As a result of this, Alerio passed over the threshold more often than any other. Adara had spotted this immediately but had said nothing to Lucius at Alene's bidding; they were not sure how he would take the news. Though he loved them both dearly, he had always been protective of Alene. For the moment at least, it was decided that he need not know the extent of their attraction.

Therefore, as Adara and Lucius enjoyed life with their newborn children, Alene and Alerio cultivated their emotions in private, both wanting to tell Lucius of it, but neither knowing how. For the moment, life took on a comfortable pace and routine that was pleasing to all. Days of warmth and of sunlight were more plentiful, nearing their summer permanence.

On such days, Adara would go out in the early mornings to walk with the children by herself, a time to bond with them, stretch her legs and breathe before the dust that seemed to surround the base clouded the air. Her presence became known to the guards that were posted regularly around Lambaesis, the form of her long blue cloak and her singing voice as she hummed to the children.

Lucius had been worried at first, tried to dissuade her from going out of doors alone but she had insisted on it, maintained that she needed the time to herself and could not remain indoors from morning until evening when he returned from drilling the troops. In the end, they agreed that she could go if it were before most of the base was awake and if she kept herself covered, the hood of her long cloak pulled up over her head to hide her face. They were, after all, in the midst of a military base full of men, many having raped their way from one burning city to another. Lucius took comfort in the fact that most of the men who had gotten to know him and his wife, respected her and were even protective of her. If she stayed along the via Principalis, all would be well.

One morning, while Adara was walking, Lucius sat in the triclinium with Alene enjoying a leisurely breakfast of fruit, bread and cheese. He noticed that she was unusually quiet and asked her what was wrong.

"I had a terrible dream last night," she began. "I dreamt that mother was crying."

"Why was she crying?"

"I don't know but her face looked different, like I couldn't really see it clearly." Lucius moved to Alene's side and put his arm around her.

"You've been away from her for a long time, that's all. You feel guilty."

"I don't know." She looked down at the stone floor.

"You know, I had the same sort of dreams when I was away on campaign for the first time."

"Really? You never told me that."

"I suppose I just didn't think it something to worry about. I had similar dreams about you." Lucius smiled. She looked more beautiful these days, happier. "I missed you more than anyone when I was away. I always felt safer with you around."

"I didn't know, but I'm glad to hear it. I feel safer with you here too." Alene put her arms around him tightly, wanted to tell him about Alerio but decided against it.

"If you feel so badly about being away, Alene, then you can return to Rome. I know you miss mother. Perhaps you even miss little Quintus and Clarinda?"

"They're probably much grown since the time we left. You haven't really been there to get to know them over the years Lucius, but our little brother and sister are good and can be kind-hearted. Mother has even written to me how they've grown as close as us."

"Well, I'm glad to hear that at least. But my offer still stands. If you want to go back to Rome I can make sure you get there safely. Though, I really don't want you to go."

Alene half-smiled. She didn't want to leave, for several reasons, and so decided to push her dream aside, forget about it. "I don't want to leave, Lucius. I want to stay here with you."

"Phew!" Lucius gasped, relieved. "For a moment I thought you wanted to. We won't be in this little domus for too long. I promise, that if it's decided absolutely that I will be posted permanently to Lambaesis then we'll purchase a villa somewhere near Thamugadi, a place with trees, larger baths and a proper peristyle garden. You can help Adara decorate it."

"I'd like that very much. Imagine, my brother the tribune taking care of me." They laughed, enjoying the thought of a larger home.

Then there was a humming in the courtyard. Adara had returned with the children and appeared in the doorway of the triclinium. Lucius went over to kiss her and take the children from her so that she could sit and have some food. He was already in uniform, ready to leave, but remained a little longer with his children, placing them on one of the couches and tickling their tiny feet. The women chuckled to see such a fierce looking man behaving like such a child himself.

"Did you enjoy your walk today?" Alene asked.

"Oh, yes. It really is beautiful here before the day gets too hot and too dusty. The children seem to like it too, their eyes are wide open at all the new things they see. Today I took them to the stables to see Lunaris and Phoenix."

"A little far from the via Principalis, I'd say." She pretended not to hear Lucius' chiding.

"Did the horses frighten them?" Alene looked worried for the children.

"No, no. Well, at first Phoebus started to cry, being so close to their warm breath, and the horses got a little nervous. But, little Calliope began to sing and calmed them all down. Oh! That reminds me, Lucius. I saw Dagon in the stables."

"What did he say?"

"He said that they were setting out on a long patrol westward and wouldn't be back for a few weeks. They wanted to see you before they left."

"I'd better get going then so that I don't miss them." Lucius picked up the children and gave them to their aunt who held them gently in the crook of each arm. Lucius kissed Adara. "Have a good day, all of you. If I have a chance I'll come back at midday. If not, I'll see you this evening."

"Be careful on the parade ground, Lucius," Adara said as she did every morning before he left.

"I will, I will." He winked at Alene.

"Was he always this cheeky?" Adara asked, amused.

"Always." Alene remembered.

Travelling as a merchant was never his favourite disguise, worse so because in Africa and Numidia there were hundreds of other merchants upon the same road at any given time. At the very least, blending in was easier. It was the actual selling that Argus hated, that and the fact that all merchants upon the roads stayed together in large camps overnight for safety's sake. This would have been fine if they were indeed merchants, but as they were not, Argus, Garai and Brutus had to keep up appearances and find ways of talking trade with those who nosed into their business around the various fires that burned in the night among the wagons and tents.

It was in this fashion, hidden among the ripples of an ever-flowing caravan from the coast, that the three men made their way to Thamugadi. Argus thought endlessly of the task ahead, how they might gain access to the base, how they would be able to get at his quarry without being caught. A base with a garrison of over five thousand men was not the easiest infiltration he had ever been faced with. Plautianus had set him to many tasks in many places, quiet homes in Rome, villas scattered about the countryside, silent harbour master's homes in Ostia or whorehouses in Brundisium.

As leader of this expedition, Argus also fretted over how to handle Brutus when the time came. The man was a bitter animal uncaged, dangerous and unpredictable. He was somewhat comforted by Garai's presence though he was still unsure of how far he could trust him; his anger at Lucius for what had befallen him could be used to their advantage. Deep down, though he would not admit it to himself, Argus felt the strain of commanding two men and grudgingly wondered how Lucius had been able to command almost five hundred. He convinced himself that he could have done better than his half-brother, that it was in part due to his own help that Lucius had been able to stay alive for so long. Now, he would end that life and he was amused by the thought of telling Lucius he was his brother, just before he slit his throat.

Garai found himself lost in his own thoughts. He wanted to let Eligius know he was alive and embrace him as he had longed to. Poor Eligius, thinking that he was dead all this time, that he was the last of their family's sons. Garai felt sure that he would be thrilled to see him. If only he did not have to tag along with Argus and that swine, Brutus. He wanted to make Lucius pay for what he had done. The unease he felt between Argus and Brutus seemed to be increasing and he did not want to be caught up in the storm that would most certainly rage between them at some point. Of course he would help Argus, but what would happen after Lucius was killed? Eligius would help keep him safe. Yes.

"Hey! You can't do that!" cried the voice of a date merchant in the wagon next to theirs as they creaked down the road.

"Bugger off, you! You've got plenty." Brutus spat the pits at the man from whom he had just taken a branch of dates. The man had been ready to protest some more but the look in Brutus' eyes told him that would not be a wise move.

"What do you think you're doing?" Argus had come up to Brutus, hand on his dagger. "Keep a low profile or you'll sleep in the ditch tonight, a long dark sleep. Got it?"

"Ease up, Praetorian. A man's got to eat, doesn't he? Besides, he won't miss it." He pointed at the cart of dates where the merchant looked back in disgust. "He's got a wagon full of the things."

"I warn you, pig!" He was clearly worked up, tempted to make swift use of his dagger. Brutus simply laughed as Argus moved away to walk at the front of the wagon. He knew Brutus was beyond care or fear and that *that* could be a problem.

Three days later, the merchants reached Thamugadi at mid-morning, beneath a yellowing sky. The smoke of the bath houses was a welcoming sight and the two Romans relished the thought of a bath to wash the dirt from themselves. Argus decided that they should not all enter the town at once and so he left Garai, Brutus and the wagon in a quiet grove outside the east gate of the colonia while he went in to find a landlord with suitable accommodation and not too many questions.

The town was busy, too busy at that time of day and Argus moved about the marketplace asking a casual question here and there about places to stay. Eventually he decided on a quiet street in the south-east corner of the town. There, he found the place that had been recommended. He knocked on the door and a groggy, middle-aged man answered.

"What do you want?" the man asked, his breath foul.

"I was told you had a small place to let short-term." Argus towered over the man who, when he noticed the stranger, seemed much more awake.

"Nope, not me. My cousin has the place. This is his."

"When will he be back?"

"Oh, not for some time, friend."

"I was told there was a place to let."

"There is. I can let it to you. My cousin Cato is off doing whatever it is he does on his long trips. He left me in charge."

"How much is it?"

"Well, that depends. How many of you are there?" The man was in the mood to bargain. Argus was not.

"Three."

"Hmm. Three eh? Well, let's see. I'd say one denarius each per week." Argus tried not to laugh as he took out his purse. The man regretted not asking for more when he saw how heavy it was.

"Fine," Argus said. "But first, show me the rooms."

"Follow me." The man closed the door behind him and went three doors down the street to an entrance with a rotten, wooden door. He put in a rusty key and opened it. It was dusty and dark and stank of urine in the entrance. Argus followed him upstairs to where there were two rooms on the second floor and another on the third. It was bare and dusty but it would do. "So? What do you think?"

"I think this place should be burned down and you with it." The man jumped. "But," continued Argus, "I'll give you four denarii a week if you don't ask any questions and if you don't speak to anyone about us. Got it?"

The man gulped. "Yes…yes."

"If you speak about us then I'll have to kill you." Argus smiled seeing the fear in the man's eyes. "You know how it is for us merchants. The carpet business is nasty. I don't want people to know I'm here to undersell all the others before I get down to business."

"Of course. Understand. Well, here's your key." Argus plopped the four coins into the man's hand. "I'll leave you to settle in then." He stumbled backward and bumped his head on a low beam. When the man was gone, Argus opened all the windows to air the place out and then went back to the wagon to get Garai and Brutus.

"I've found a place," he said gruffly. "Let's get moving."

"The men did well today," Lucius addressed his centurions in his study during their weekly meeting. "The new drills are coming together and we've become a cohesive unit again." He did not say it of course, but what he meant was that they were back to normal since that day in the desert months ago. It had shaken the men. Many had suspected their fellows of foul play, but it seemed the trust and camaraderie had returned now and Lucius was pleased. In a corner of the room, Eligius stood with his arms crossed, listening but never saying a word. If Lucius asked him a question he answered with as few syllables as possible.

Lucius was silent and Alerio took over for the moment. "The legate's next inspection of the legion is in five days so we had better make sure that every tarnished buckle is polished, every torn strap repaired."

"That's right," Lucius added. "I want the men to look their best for the legate…all the time in fact. I know they're getting bored, but summer will be upon us soon and so will the raiding season. Enjoy the peace for now."

As Eligius listened to this, he realised that since becoming a father, Lucius had lost any interest in battle, patrols or other martial pursuits. He could not stand being in the same room with him, could not wait for the meeting to be adjourned. He waited patiently, his helmet under his left arm, while Pephredo and Valerus asked their usual array of precise questions as to the plans for what remained of the cohort.

"I don't know anything at the moment. For now, let's just be glad that we can stay in one spot. We're finally accepted here in the III Augustan."

"One more thing isn't that right, Tribune?" Alerio reminded Lucius.

"Of course. I almost forgot. You and the men can have the day off tomorrow." There were cheers of delight from Valerus and Pephredo but Eligius remained silent. Days with leave were no longer a pleasure, not without his brother. "That's all. Dismissed."

Eligius, followed by Valerus and Pephredo, went out and into the courtyard to the main door. The two younger men greeted Adara as they walked past her, grinning from cheek to cheek. Eligius nodded.

"He's not improved in manners much," Alerio said of Eligius when the others had gone.

"Nope. I don't expect he will either. Would you?"

"I like to think that I would but, I'm my father's only child. I suppose my opinion doesn't count for much." Lucius pat him on the shoulder.

"Ach. Let's leave that for now." They made their way into the courtyard and the fading light. "Will you eat with us tonight?"

"How can I resist? The new cooks in the mess aren't the greatest. Xeno's creations are much better."

"Excellent. I'll see you later." Lucius saw Alerio out and then went to bathe himself. He coaxed Adara into joining him, while Alene played with the children and thought of reclining next to Alerio at the evening's meal.

The day of leave that Lucius had given the men happened to be the day when merchants from all over the surrounding area pitched their tents and stalls along the road heading out of the eastern gate of Lambaesis. Lucius had tried to arrange leave on such days as it gave the men a chance to spend some of their remaining wages after the compulsory deposit for each soldier in the vault.

Early morning was accompanied by the cries of various sellers calling out the sales of the day that should not be missed. Eligius always went to buy things earlier than most since he hated the crowds that formed along the road later in the day. Still, he was not the first. Many of the men and women who lived in the vicus that had grown around the base's walls were there to shop also, some to sell.

There were many merchants that day, he noticed, a large variety of goods; fruit from the north, pots and pans, spices, clothing, tools, incense and carpets. As Eligius picked through a pile of used, lost and stolen military paraphernalia, he heard a voice further down the rows of stalls. It sounded strange to his ears and he followed the sound of it. Walking past the outstretched arms and special offers of the merchants, he spotted an odd looking wagon parked below a lone olive tree. There were several people around that particular merchant looking at the array of colourful carpets that had been spread out upon the ground for viewing.

"If you don't like the price then piss off!" the merchant yelled. Not the best way to attract business, but there was something about that voice. Eligius held his breath and waited, hidden, until the would-be customer left in frustration.

"Carpets! Carpets from the East!" the voice yelled out half-heartedly. Eligius approached from the side until he was standing next to the covered wagon where the merchant was fiddling with a bundle on the other side.

"Ga...Garai?" his voice was shaking. The merchant lifted his head and Eligius turned in embarrassment, seeing the thin, bearded man before him. "Sorry. My mistake," he began to say.

"Haha!" The merchant ran over to him and grabbed him. "You *are* alive!" The merchant shook him violently, peering into his eyes. "Eligius? It's me, Garai!"

"Garai? Is...it...you?" He tried to look past the thin body and the thick, rough-looking beard. "It can't be..." He began to sob, felt his knees weaken beneath him.

"Eligius, my brother! It's me. I've come back for you." Garai embraced his brother and both wept tears of joy, ignorant of the nosy people looking on.

"The Gods bless us. But how did...I thought you died out there!"

"Almost." Garai then told a stunned Eligius about what had befallen him, the torturous road he had taken to get back to him.

"I can't believe you're here. The Gods have answered my prayers. But why are you set up as a merchant? I would have come to meet you elsewhere. You shouldn't be here you know. If they catch you they'll execute you like they did Maren." Garai paused at that. He then told Eligius his other purpose for being there, who he was with.

"Argus?" Eligius whispered. "He's here?"

"Yes. And with that swine of a cavalry officer from Sabratha, Brutus."

"What are you doing with them, Garai?"

"It was the only way that I could get back to you. Besides, don't you want revenge?"

"Revenge? Against who?"

"Lucius, of course!"

549

"Sshh! Keep your voice down. What do you mean?" Garai then told him of Argus' orders from the prefect that he was to dispose of Lucius and in return they would all receive high-ranking commissions in the Praetorian Guard.

"You're mad! I can't help you in this!"

"But you're my brother! Lucius would have had me killed."

"Because you conspired against him and killed Antanelis! Please, Garai, just leave, go home to northern Italy and never come back here."

"I can't do that. I owe Lucius. Besides, Argus will kill me if I don't help. Please, Eligius! Help me!"

"No! No, I can't." Eligius got up to walk back to base, his head spinning with what he had just been faced with, his stomach sick with emotion. Garai picked up a large bundled carpet and followed him. "Leave me alone! Don't come in with me, Garai."

"I'm not leaving you, not now. No one will recognise me like this. Just say you bought this from me and that you're having me carry it back to your quarters for you."

Eligius wanted to say no and run but before he knew it they were passing beneath the large, open gates and he was telling the guards that he had purchased the carpet. They walked down the via Principalis, Garai with his head down, the carpet slung over his shoulder. Eligius' eyes darted back and forth searching for anyone to avoid. Just then there was a voice from the street that led to the stables.

"Good morning, Centurion," said the cheerful, soft voice. Eligius turned to see Adara standing there in her blue cloak, the children held close to her breast.

"Lady Metella," he said formally. "Good morning."

"I see you've bought a new carpet for your quarters. It's beautiful."

It was hard for him not to like her, he wanted to move on.

"Oh, ah, yes. I did."

"Good idea. I'm sure your centurion's quarters are a bit grim sometimes." She smiled from beneath her hood but her smile faded when the merchant's eyes fell upon her. His gaze was piercing, intense and studying. "Well, I had best be going," she said. "The tribune will be waiting for me and the children. Good day to you."

"Good day," Eligius replied before continuing on down the street.

"Is that Lucius' wife and children?" Garai asked.

"Yes. I should have known better! She's out here early, every morning by herself walking with the brats."

"Every morning?"

"Yes. Now would you shut up and keep your face down! Walk behind me." Eligius nodded greetings to a few of the men as they passed, utterly relieved that none of them paid much notice to the hunched carpet merchant behind him. Once they were safely inside his quarters, Garai dropped the carpet and Eligius bolted the door.

Later that evening, when Garai returned to Thamugadi, he gave his report to Argus that he had made contact with Eligius. Argus was pleased at this, but not as pleased to hear that Eligius was reluctant to help.

"Don't worry," Garai tried to sound convincing. "He'll help us."

"He'd better!" Argus sat in a rickety chair in the corner.

"There's more!" Garai sounded excited.

"What?"

"I saw Lucius' wife and children."

"You did? Where?" There was a sudden fire in Argus' eyes as Garai told him what she looked like and that Eligius had said that she often went out in the mornings to walk with the children. "And she wears a blue cloak you say?"

"Yes. Out all by her lonesome too. Pretty girl actually." Garai sat back and ate a piece of bread, pride imprinted upon his face.

"You did well, Garai. Just keep working on your brother. If he's not cooperative then he's dead. He might alert Lucius."

"I said don't worry. I'll handle him."

Back in Lambaesis, Eligius sat alone in his quarters, wondering what to do, praying for guidance. Garai needed his help and he knew that Argus would kill him if he did not help him. But how? He couldn't warn Lucius; that would mean his brother's life, an arrow through the neck on the archery range, like Maren. The only way to help Garai out of this was to keep him from coming back to Lambaesis, maybe even speak to Argus, and if he wouldn't listen, kill him. He paced back and forth waiting for day but knew that it was impossible. He could not wait. He had to go to Thamugadi. Garai had told him where they were staying in case he decided to help them. So, wearing plain crimson breeches and a tunic the same colour, he slung his gladius over his shoulder and threw on his cloak.

Luckily, two of Garai's former men were in charge of the eastern gate that night, men he knew would let him through without question. He did not care if he was not back in time for drills, all he cared about was Garai and getting him away from Argus and Brutus alive. The night was cold, the moon hidden by clouds that seemed to be rolling in from afar.

Eligius arrived at the gate and gave his men the watch-word for the evening.

"Scythia," he said to the guard.

"That's the right word, sir. Are you sure you want to go out there this time of night?" The trooper tried not to sound too insubordinate but the situation was rather odd.

"Are you questioning me?" Eligius rose to his full height and got into the man's face so that he could feel his breath.

"No! No, sir!" The man stood at attention.

"I can't sleep and I need fresh air!" Eligius barked. "Do I have your permission, soldier? he said sarcastically.

"Yes, sir...I mean, I meant no disrespect, sir!"

"Good. I won't be long. Stay awake while you're out here."

"Yes, sir." The other trooper opened the smaller door that was built within the larger gate and Eligius went out into the darkness beyond the walls.

Despite the lack of ample moonlight to travel by, Eligius found it easy to follow the road. He jogged along the edge of the cobbles so as not to attract attention with the clicking of his hobnails. His heart raced. He felt that his brother was in danger, and the thought of losing him again was unbearable. He owed it to his family. Eligius thought about the farm on which they had grown up together, green fields and glades of oak, fresh flowing streams of cool water.

It seemed to take forever to reach Thamugadi, but eventually the faint glow of torches atop the walls came into view two miles distant. He decided to stop to catch his breath and drink some water at one of the small roadside shrines. By his reckoning, there were about three more hours to daylight.

"Gods, do not desert us," he said to the cold night air as he pressed on toward the city.

When he arrived, he was pleased to see that the western gate was open and moved through it.

"Hold there!" came a voice from the shadows. "What do you want?" An older man levelled a long spear at him.

"Good evening, friend. I'm here to see my cousin. I've got word that he's in town. He's a merchant." Eligius hoped the man would believe him.

"Where's he staying?" the man asked suspiciously.

Eligius thought for a moment then remembered. "The house of Cato, at the south-eastern edge of the town."

"Oh, the rental place." His voice was now flat and uninterested. "Cato's not there you know. It's being run by his idiot cousin, stupid fellow, he is."

"I'll avoid him. Thanks." Eligius went on down the street until he reached the crossroads and then turned in to the south-eastern sector to search for the house.

When he found it, he stopped to catch his breath. He had not been prepared to see Argus. In his haste he had thought only of Garai. And what of Brutus? He remembered the man vaguely, knew he was not to be trusted. He knocked twice on the door and waited.

There was no answer. He knocked louder this time and after a few minutes he heard creaking steps within. Eligius felt uneasy, his gut told him that he was being watched the entire time. Indeed above him, in a dark window, he could swear he saw the shape of someone's head. The door opened slowly, and a shadow spoke.

"Eligius. How long has it been?"

"Argus?" Eligius whispered. Argus' voice gave him chills. It sounded much different than he recalled. "Where's Garai?"

"Upstairs of course. He's been waiting for you."

"I need to talk with him…and you."

"Then come upstairs, friend. Let's catch up on things." Argus turned his back and went up slowly. "Bolt the door behind you Eligius," he said as he turned into a room at the top. Eligius moved up the stairs cautiously. It was quiet except for some mumbling coming from the room. He reached the top and pushed open the door.

The sight that met Eligius' eyes horrified him. As in the nightmares of a child, he felt terror, an urge to cry.

In front of a window at the other side of the room, Garai was tied, hands and legs, to a chair. He was gagged and blood ran from a great cut across the side of his head. Tears ran down from his swollen eyes when his brother appeared in the doorway.

Eligius reached for the handle of his short sword but before the blade was completely drawn he felt a sharp blow to the back of his head and went down, face first, to the floor. He had not checked behind the door. Brutus' boot came crashing down upon his wrist and there was a loud crunching sound. Eligius screamed in pain, was hauled up onto his feet and winded by a punch to his stomach. Garai struggled in his chair but could not free himself. Brutus laughed and Argus came over to Eligius and sat him in another chair next to the table with a flask of wine and some cups.

"I don't know if it was such a good idea for you to come here tonight, Eligius." Argus spoke but all Eligius could do was look at his brother by the window. "If you yell out, Brutus will slit Garai's throat. So, you'd better sit and listen." Brutus went behind Garai and held Eligius' own sword to Garai's throat. "Now. What are you doing here?"

"Garai told me you needed my help, so I came." There was no point in telling the truth now. Eligius hoped he could fool Argus for the moment.

"Hmm. So you want to help me then?" Eligius nodded. "You're going to help me kill Lucius and his family?"

"Yes. I'll help you." Argus backed up to take a look at Eligius.

"You look worried, Eligius. Truth is, Garai told me that you were reluctant to help us. But, he was convinced that he would be able to change your mind." He stared into Eligius' eyes. "Somehow, I doubt that. Garai's an idiot. Did he tell you he was mad when he stumbled through my door in Carthage?" Eligius looked at Garai whose eyes pleaded with him for forgiveness for being so stupid. "He was. Mad as a Syrian soothsayer."

"Just untie my brother, Argus, and I'll tell you what you want, do whatever you want."

"You think *I'm* mad? You'll tell me first. Then you'll help me. Then I'll let him go."

"Let us go and I swear I'll help you."

"You're not too bright, are you, Eligius? If I let you go, what's to stop you from going back and telling Lucius? In the morning I'll have half the legion banging down my door. No. Answer my questions." Eligius nodded. "Good. I've been told that Lucius lives with his wife, two children, and his sister in his tribune's quarters. Is that correct?" Eligius nodded. "Good.

Maren is dead and so are the others who were going to help me, is that also true?"

"Yes. They were cut down in battle or executed afterward."

"Right. Now, this Greek bitch that Lucius has married. Garai said that you told him she goes out for a walk alone with her babies, every morning. And she always wears a long blue cloak to hide herself?"

"Yes, she does."

"Do the troops know who she is?"

"Yes. Everyone knows the officers' wives, especially Lucius' wife."

"Good. Now we're getting somewhere." Argus paced the room, aware that Eligius was looking about but not moving, not daring to budge while Brutus held his blade to Garai's throat. "One more thing, then you can go. Are your centurion's quarters in the same location within the base or have they moved you to another barrack block?"

"I'm in the same place as before, Argus."

"Good."

"I have a question for you." Eligius stared at him, aware also of Brutus.

"What?"

"Why are you doing this? Sure, Lucius was a bit annoying at times but he was never so awful as to deserve this. Why do you hate him so much?"

"Strange words coming from a man who's just betrayed him like the rest of us."

"I said I'd help you. I'm just curious. You've changed a lot."

"I have changed. I'm smarter." Argus stood over him. "But, since you're so curious, I'll tell you. I hate him because he owes me and will never admit it. He's always played high and mighty with me from the time we were little shits up until I left the cohort. He's always thought he had the upper hand but now, things are different. I'm going to make him see."

"Is that all?" Eligius thought he spied a trace of doubt in Argus' expression, thought to weaken him a little.

"Is that all?" Argus repeated. "No. But the rest is none of your fucking business." With that, Argus nodded to Brutus and before Eligius could react, the blade of the gladius had cut deep into Garai's throat so that there was an audible gurgling from the wound.

"NO!" Eligius watched as the life drained slowly from Garai's wide, shocked, eyes. He reached for the flask of wine on the table and wheeled it at Brutus so that it hit him in the face and he fell back into the window, cursing. "Garai!" Eligius lunged for his brother, tried desperately to stem the flow of blood. He could hear laughing behind him as Argus stepped up.

Eligius spotted his sword where Brutus had dropped it, reached for it and began to swing upward when he was stopped instantly, unable to control any muscle, the strength gone from his limbs. Argus' sword was imbedded in his chest and he fell gasping into Garai's bloody lap. The last sound Eligius heard was his own, final breath. Then, darkness.

"You touch that sword, Brutus, and I'll kill you too." Argus levelled his dagger at Brutus who had regained his feet and was reaching for the gladius on the floor. His face was cut from the shards of broken ceramic that were now scattered on the floor. "Go sit down over there." Argus pointed to the chair next to the table and Brutus went over and sat down to observe what was partly his own handiwork.

The bodies of the two brothers lay lifeless in a spreading pool of blood. Argus looked at them without regret, thinking about what his next move would be. He looked at Eligius' clothes and his hair; it was still blonde but much longer than it had been. Then, Argus smiled and looked over at Brutus.

"How good are you at removing the scalp from a body?"

"Done it a few times," he stated matter-of-factly.

"Here." Argus tossed him a small dagger. "Get to it."

557

The night had faded away by then and the streets were lit with a heavy grey as clouds roiled thickly above the world. Distant claps of thunder shook the ground, causing nestled birds to screech and take flight. It began to rain.

XXVI

MANES FAMILIAE

'The Dead of the Family'

The downpour continued into the afternoon, holding out against the sun and soaking the search party as they swept the area surrounding the base. Lucius, his cloak clinging uncomfortably, had some words with the optio he had assigned to lead one of the groups. The man saluted and went back to it.

The crest of the tribune's helmet dripped water onto his face as he entered the Principia and was admitted to the legate's office. Lucius saluted, hung his sodden cloak on a peg and went over to the commander.

"Still no sign of him, Legate."

Marcellus leaned back in his chair, his brow a series of deep crevices. "Has he ever missed drills before, Tribune?"

"No, sir. Never. Eligius has always been prompt when it came to duty."

"Has he shown ill feeling toward you since the affair with his brother?" Marcellus eyed Lucius. "Tell me the truth, Metellus."

"Yes, sir. I mean, he has been doing his duty. He is only withdrawn when it comes to me. He takes his orders, carries them out. That's all."

"You're no longer amicable."

"No, Legate. In fact, Eligius is now an outsider among the centurions."

"I see." Marcellus rose from his chair and rubbed his hands over the brazier in the corner of the room. "Damn cold for this time of year. So, the guards that were on duty said that he'd gone out because he was tired and couldn't sleep. Does he have a wife outside the walls?"

"Not that I know of, sir." Lucius was sure of that at least.

"Is he a whoremonger?" The question was blunt but Lucius could see that this might be a possibility.

"No more than any other soldier, Legate."

"I want you to expand your search to Thamugadi. Have some men inquire at the brothels. I don't care if you have to torture a few slaves to find out where he is. I just want to know what in Hades has happened to him. You stay here though, in case he comes back. If he does, I want him detained. Is that clear, Tribune Metellus?"

By now Lucius knew that the legate was not angry at him, simply determined, serious about the situation.

"Absolutely clear, sir. I'll keep you updated regularly."

"Good. It may be as simple as he got caught out in this storm and is waiting it out."

Lucius saluted, put his cloak back on and went to meet with Alerio who had gathered the other centurions in his meeting rooms. Adara, Alene and the children had been told to stay in their rooms or the triclinium for the day.

"Still no sign of him?" Alerio asked as Lucius entered the room.

"No. Nothing. Legate thinks he may have been caught in the storm and is waiting until it's finished."

"What do you think, Tribune?" Valerus asked.

"I don't know anymore. Eligius hasn't been himself since Garai disappeared. He never said anything about a wife to you did he, Alerio?"

"Not to me. Either of you know?" Alerio turned the question over to Pephredo and Valerus. They shook their heads.

"Well, for the moment I have to stay here at base. If he comes back we're supposed to detain him. I know it's a shit job, Pephredo, but I'm sending you and your men to Thamugadi to ask around. Check the brothels and get permission from the local magistrate to torture any slaves if you have to. Though, I'd prefer not to have to do that."

"What about me, Tribune?"

"Valerus, when your men get back from searching get them warm again, give them some food and then send them back out. Alerio's century will stay here and take up the search tomorrow if we need to."

"It's a shame the Sarmatians are away on patrol," Alerio pointed out. "This would go a lot faster if they were here to help."

"You don't need to tell me that. No sense thinking about it now. They're gone for a couple of weeks." Lucius rubbed his temples, the aching in his head was getting worse and worse. "Dismissed for now. Get to your individual tasks and report tomorrow morning."

"Tribune." Valerus and Pephredo saluted and went about their business. Alerio stayed behind for a moment as he always did.

"I'll take care of the horses for you this evening. You look like Hades."

"I feel like it. Adara's not feeling well either. Not sure if we had bad meat. She's resting and Alene is taking care of the children."

"Well, get some rest. I'll keep an eye out."

"Thanks." Lucius felt his head pounding and poured himself some watered wine.

"Should I come back later?" Alerio knew that Lucius was not up to it but he wanted the chance to see Alene again, to sit in the same room with her.

"No. Not tonight. Just come by tomorrow morning."

"All right then." Lucius did not notice the disappointment in Alerio's voice. "Sleep easy, Lucius."

"You too."

Alerio put on his cloak and went out into the courtyard, closing the door behind him. The rain smacked on the paving stones and trickled down the sides of the small altar in the centre. The sky was still grey and the temperature seemed to have dropped even more.

Alene spotted Alerio from the triclinium and ran out to see him, avoiding the pooling water in the courtyard.

"Are you staying for the evening meal tonight?" Fresh drops of rain hung from the ends of her long lashes.

Alerio tried hard not to take her close to him.

"No. Not tonight. He's not feeling well and I take it Adara isn't either?"

"No. She's not. She needs to get outside everyday or else she feels confined. The children are crying more too without the fresh morning air. More likely for Lucius and Adara it's the stuffed liver they ate last night."

"Terrible stuff that." Alerio made a funny face and Alene laughed. *How can she dazzle even on the dullest of days?* he wondered.

"I would like to see you later." Alene's voice lowered to a whisper and she nudged him. "What if I come to your quarters?"

"I don't know."

"Oh, it's fine. The children sleep in Lucius and Adara's cubiculum anyway. Once they're all asleep I'll slip out. I have a key to the bolt." Alerio knew it was a bad idea, but he wanted to see Alene alone more than anything. Every moment he was away from her was an agony, an agony he had never felt before and wanted to feel always.

"I'll be out in the street to walk with you about the third hour of night. Is that good?"

"Perfect. I can't wait."

The covered wagon moved uneasily along the muddy ground as the rain came down. It was not safe to take the road at this time with all the troops travelling along it to Thamugadi. They had made a hasty retreat from the town and the apartment of the man called Cato; Argus knew that the bodies and blood would begin to smell soon enough. Furthermore, he could not risk the chance that some neighbour might have heard something of the struggle the night before.

While Brutus got wet driving the wagon, Argus sat in the back among the carpets, thinking out his plan. He had had Brutus remove Eligius' hair and clothes hoping that if someone came upon the body, it would take them longer to identify it. They had left both brothers bloody and naked in the middle of the floor, faces slashed. Their clothes were hidden under a loose floorboard. That was one less thing he had to worry about. The next was how to get into the base.

He remembered the small vicus that had grown up around the walls of Lambaesis. It was a disorderly gathering of dwellings and some tents. The wagon could be hidden there. The gates of the base were closed just before sundown when all civilians were cleared out for the night. Argus remembered this being a particularly hectic time of day with people coming out and troops going back to base. Many of the troops had brown cloaks like Eligius'. They would be looking for his blonde hair but not the brown cloak. Too many men wore such things. He decided that if he could lose himself in the mass of people, he could get in and make his way to Eligius' quarters. That is, if he was extremely careful. He would have Brutus wait outside the gates. It would depend however, on whether the sun would shine or if the rain would continue.

Shortly before dark that night, the wagon pulled up to a secluded spot among the tents and hovels of the settlement and Argus donned the brown cloak beneath which were hidden a short bow and some arrows. People were already filing through the gates, as were some of the troops who had been shopping or visiting outside. The rain had finally ceased but the ground was sodden and muddy.

"Brutus. I'm going in," Argus whispered from the back of the wagon. "If the sun is out in the morning you either make your way to this gate or the southern gate. Got it?"

"I've got it, Praetorian. What about you?"

"I'm going to spend the night in Eligius' quarters if I can and then in the morning I'll watch for them." Brutus smiled wickedly and Argus did not know if he smiled at the thought

563

of killing them or him. *He won't have the chance*, he told himself as he walked toward the gate.

The guards on duty seemed unbothered by the massive, two-way exodus of people passing in and out of the fort. People's spirits seemed to lighten as the rain clouds dispersed and the air was filled with chatter. With the hood pulled over his head and his back hunched slightly, Argus blended in with the crowd and passed beneath the guard towers before the gates were barred for the night.

It was strange being back. A lifetime ago, when he was second to Lucius. *Not anymore,* he thought, *not now.* He avoided the via Principalis and made his way down the smaller lanes of the base to find Eligius' quarters. There were troops everywhere but they were more concerned with cooking or heading to the baths and various clubhouses. Barrack doors were swung open and the smell of food emanated from them as groups of soldiers who lived together prepared their evening meals in small kitchens. Argus tried to ignore the smell, the growling in his stomach, as he walked carefully along the puddles dotting the lanes.

Unfortunately, there were two troopers guarding Eligius' quarters, waiting to apprehend him in case he returned. Argus peered from around a corner for a second before picking up a pebble on the ground. He held his breath and lobbed it over their heads so that it made a sound around the other corner opposite them. When they went to investigate, he ran for the door, opened it and went inside.

Silently, he slid the bolt home on the door so that if someone tried to enter he would have some warning. He had to keep quiet. As the centurion's quarters were at the end of the barrack block, there was a small window through which some fresh air passed. From where he crouched down in a corner, covered in blankets, Argus was able to keep an eye on the window for daylight.

He unbuckled his sword and dagger and placed them on the ground next to him along with the small recurve bow and arrows he had hidden beneath his cloak. He tried to sleep but the room was uncomfortable, more so because it reminded him of the darkness of the room in which Plautianus had broken him. That was one memory he could not shake and no matter how much he convinced himself that he was strong-willed enough to beat it, it still made him feel like weeping. So, eyes resting, Argus waited out the night beneath a blanket, and listened to the hours of the watch being called out by the men on duty.

In the tribune's quarters it was quiet. Adara had not eaten that night, and Lucius had eaten only a small portion with Alene while the children slept.

Alene had decided to cook for her brother the broth that their mother had always made for them when they were ill. He ate it happily and felt slightly better though he was extremely tired.

"Long day?" she asked.

"Very."

"Still no word about the centurion?"

"Nothing yet."

"What could have happened to him? Centurions don't just go missing like that do they?"

"Certainly not. I have no answers, Alene." Lucius drank more broth and had a small piece of bread. "Thank you for this. I feel much better now."

"Works every time!" she said proudly. "Of course it's mother's recipe, not mine."

"Have you had word from her lately?"

"No. Although I'm sure she has received our letters by now about the children." Alene wrinkled up her face in a sentimental smile. "She'll be so proud to see you with them. They're so beautiful." Lucius said nothing, just thought about what it would be like the next time he saw their mother and how happy she would be to have an even larger family.

"It's too bad she wasn't here."

"We can't control everything. She'll be content once she sees them. I'm sure there's a messenger on his way here with a letter from her containing a thousand questions. 'What colour is their hair? Do they have all their fingers and toes? Does one of them look like me?' That's what she'll say." Lucius laughed at Alene's perfect imitation.

"It's frightening how well you do that." He leaned back in a massive stretch, unable to control his yawn. "I'm sorry, Alene. I've got to get some sleep now. I'm sure I'll feel wonderful in the morning though. Are you turning in?"

"No, no. I think I'll stay up and read one of the more poetic scrolls in your collection." Lucius walked over to her.

"That's fine. I'm so tired I won't hear a thing." Lucius leaned over and kissed her on the cheek. "Good night. I'll see you in the morning." Alene felt a pang of guilt.

"Lucius," she said, causing him to turn around in the doorway. "Sweet dreams. I love you." Lucius seemed confused by these sudden words but was happy to hear them.

"I love you too. Sleep well."

Alene did indeed read for a short time after Lucius had turned in for the night. It was extremely quiet when she stepped out into the courtyard in her green cloak, turned to silver in the moonlight that was now falling instead of rain. The last remnants of cloud were blown away in thin wisps. She hoped Alerio would be waiting for her by now. She crept toward the main door that led onto the street, unbolted it and stepped out. He was there, waiting for her. Alene carefully bolted the door and followed Alerio back to his quarters

Luckily, no one saw them as they went and both were relieved once the door was closed behind them. Small lamps burnt everywhere, painting the stone walls with golden light. A sweet incense burned in a small tripod in a far corner of the second room and soft smoke swirled as Alerio took Alene in his arms and kissed her.

That night they felt blessed to have found something that had seemed to both a lost cause. Love had eluded them until they had met and now a dream had come to fruition. After making love, they lay upon the small bed, Alene humming, wrapped in the warm fold of Alerio's embrace.

When the cock crowed early that morning, Alene realised that she had fallen asleep and started with a jump.

"Alerio, wake up." She ran her hand over his black hair, waiting for his golden eyes to open.

"What is it?" he rubbed his eyes, roused from the deepest sleep he had enjoyed in years.

"I have to get back quickly, before Lucius is up." Alene rose from the bed and stepped reluctantly into her clothing. "I wish we could stay here all day."

"Me too." He swung his legs over the edge of the bed and helped drape her cloak about her shoulders. Her golden hair was in disarray, her beauty overwhelming. "How am I going to concentrate today? You have undone me, you goddess!" He kissed her.

"You'll just have to invite me back is all." She smiled. "Do you have immediate duties?"

"Yes. I've got to take the horses for a good run before getting the men up. We've got to continue looking for Eligius."

"Well, I hope you'll try not to forget me."

"Impossible! Do you want me to walk you back?"

"Nobody will be out and about yet. I'll be fine. I'm as quiet as a mouse." Alerio opened the door and went out to see if anyone was there.

"All right," he whispered. Alene came out, her hood over her head, and kissed Alerio one more time as they tried to pry themselves apart. "I'll see you later."

"The sooner the better." Her eyes glistened as they took him in, her smile stopped his heart. "Bye." Her voice was a soft breeze as her cloaked figure turned and disappeared around the corner.

Alene was extremely careful as she went. It would not do for her to be seen alone at this time. It would do less for the sister of a tribune to be out unescorted. Last night she did not care. *It's worth it!* she told herself. *What a wonderful man.* He was not of a great family but what of it? When one felt as she did then, all sense of 'right' and protocol was dutifully dismissed in her mind.

She came onto the via Principalis where muddy puddles had been created by all the rain the previous day, dotting the way between the larger paving stones of the main thoroughfare; the last stars of night were reflected prettily in the little pools as she hopped nimbly over them. She felt giddy as a young girl with Spring ribbons in her hair. She wanted to laugh out loud but knew that at any moment someone might walk out onto the street. She quickened her pace and before she knew it she tripped.

"Oh no!" she cried. Alene lay sprawled in one of the muddy pools of filth, her green cloak soaking and patched. She was upset, but it would take more than that to dampen her spirits. She got herself up, she made sure the key had not fallen and continued on to the door a few feet away.

Luckily, no one was stirring yet. Alene carefully locked the door behind her and crept over to her room. Inside she washed in a basin of cool water and put on a fresh stola. Her cloak was the worse off and would need a good cleaning before it would be presentable. Unable and unwilling to sleep now, she hung her dirty clothing on a wall peg to be washed later.

She wondered what Alerio was doing then, if he was thinking of her. *How can I keep all this a secret?* She felt the need to tell someone. Adara knew of her feelings for Alerio. If anyone would understand, she would. She tiptoed over to Lucius and Adara's cubiculum, cracked the door and peered in.

"Alene?" Adara's voice whispered out of the darkness. "Is that you?"

"Yes, sister. How are you feeling?"

"A little dizzy, but better. Can you come and take the children for me? I'll feed them in another room so that Lucius can sleep a little longer."

Alene opened the door and moved across the room carefully to Phoebus and Calliope's cribs. She went out as Adara put on a long tunic and a robe. With Lucius sleeping and the door closed, the two women settled down in Alene's room with some food and drinking water from the kitchen. While Adara fed the children, she spoke to Alene.

"What are you doing up so early? Usually I'm the first one up." She noticed the huge smile upon her sister's reddening face. "Uh, oh. You've been up to something, I think. Out with it!"

"I didn't sleep here last night."

"You didn't?" Adara's eyes bulged. "You naughty girl!" Unable to concentrate, she pulled Calliope away from her breast. "By Venus! What was it like?"

"Adara!" Alene was shocked. "You're not angry?"

"Of course not. I could see it coming I suppose."

"It was wonderful. I can't wait to see him again." She noticed a sombre look cross Adara's face.

"You know, Alene, if Lucius finds out he'll be very upset. He thinks you tell him everything."

"I do. I always have. This is the only thing I have ever kept from him. It's the only thing I've ever wanted to tell him more than anything else."

"I'm happy for you both. And *proud* of you! How un-Roman a thing to do!" Adara giggled like a little girl. "Don't let anyone else find out though. The gossips in the base would have a field day with this. Lucius wouldn't be able to hold his temper if anyone spoke ill of you."

"I know. I'll be careful." Alene picked up little Phoebus who promptly grabbed hold of her nose. "Oh, Adara! I'm so happy, I can't sit still."

"I'm sure. That beautiful, rosy hue on your cheeks won't go unnoticed." Adara put her hand to her head, feeling dizzy again.

"Are you still unwell? I'm not sure you should be out of bed yet."

"I'm fine, but I don't think the children will get their walk today." Adara looked out the half-open door of Alene's room to see the first traces of sunlight streaking the sky. "It's going to be a beautiful day I think. Sorry little one," she said to Calliope as she bounced her on her knee.

"I can take them for a walk!"

"Oh, you don't have to, Alene. They can wait another day."

"Nonsense. We should take advantage of the beautiful sky and fresh air. Besides, their amita wants to spend some time with them."

"Are you sure?"

"Absolutely! I promise I'll stay on the via Principalis like you do." She held Phoebus up to her face. "Do you want to go for a walk with me, nephew? The sun is shining." Phoebus laughed with her and jostled his little hands.

"Let me get their blankets so they don't get a chill." Adara gave Calliope to Alene and went out.

"Ach!" Alene remembered.

"What is it?" Adara came back into the room.

"I just remembered my cloak is filthy and wet. I tripped in a puddle when I was coming back here from...*Alerio's*," she whispered his name.

"Oh." Adara stopped. "You know Lucius likes us to be covered when walking around the base."

"I know. Maybe just this once it will be fine. Please Adara, just a little time with my niece and nephew."

Adara waved away her worry. "Ah, you're right. It'll be fine. Just keep it short."

"I will." Alene laughed as she bounced the children on her knees and Adara went to gather the children's blankets.

Once the children were wrapped and held safely in their auntie's arms, Adara went with Alene to the main door to see her out. Adara closed the door again. "No wait Alene. I'm nervous about you walking around the base uncovered with the children. Take my blue cloak," Adara offered. "Xeno cleaned it for me yesterday and scented it with wild flowers."

"If it makes you feel better."

"It does. I'll be right back." Adara went to her cubiculum to get the cloak, came back and put it over Alene's shoulders.

"Thank you. I promise I won't fall this time and get it dirty." Alene smiled and cooed at the children as she went out into the street and Adara closed the door behind her.

Alene was happy for the small amount of light that now made the street and all the puddles clearly visible as she carried the children in her arms. Several people were up now and those that knew the tribune's sister greeted her warmly. The children always seemed to make even the most fearsome grunts smile as they passed. The young Metelli had been adopted by many as a good omen, the birth of healthy children always being a blessing.

She had kept the hood up, as Lucius had asked Adara to do, but found that she could not see that well. *Never mind,* she thought, *if Lucius wants me to wear it I will.* "It's going to be a perfect day!" she said to the children as they smiled up at her. She heard footsteps all around now, the base was indeed waking up, the street becoming more and more crowded. She wanted to look around to see who was behind her but thought it no more than the usual troopers making their rounds of the base first thing in the morning. She was growing accustomed to the regular rhythms of life there.

Alene arrived at the southern gate of the fort. The doors were open but no guard was visible aloft. It was not uncommon for the gates to be opened during the day to allow traders and troops returning from patrol to enter. She spotted a century of men making their way to the parade ground already.

The sun felt good upon her face and she was reluctant to return so soon. The children were smiling and she was enjoying life very much that morning. "What do you say, little ones? I'm feeling rebellious today. Shall we be daring and venture out of the base to that nice little grouping of palms over there?" Alene looked out. It was not that far. A short walk and then quickly home. "Yes? I think so too. Let your mother and father eat a peaceful morning meal." Alene looked around her to see if anyone was watching. Nobody was watching and those who were about were standing on sentry duty up the street. She passed through the gate and left the road.

The sky above was rippled with red and white as the sun rose higher and higher. It was mesmerising and Alene could not take her eyes off of it as she walked casually along with the children. "Look at how beautiful the world can be." She turned to show them the sky. "There is so much I shall teach you. I'll make sure Lucius gives you a life outside of the home, so you can see all the wonders I only ever heard about until recently."

The trees were not far ahead now and Alene continued to walk at a leisurely pace. Far to her left was a small, covered wagon with a man sleeping at the front. *Some kind of merchant out to enjoy the sun,* she thought. The sky was indeed stunning.

The sudden footsteps behind her became audible across a patch of dry dirt.

Argus had learned to walk carefully but it was impossible to maintain absolute stealth upon the rocky surface. Alene pulled the hood closer over her head and walked more briskly toward the trees, unsure of where the footsteps were coming from. She was afraid to look. The steps stopped as the merchant in the wagon awoke. *Good,* she thought, *I'm not alone.* "Isn't it nice here children? Breathe the fresh air." She cradled the babies nervously and looked toward the merchant who was holding something shiny. He was running toward her.

There was a loud banging upon the main door of the courtyard, an aggressive, urgent banging that caused Xeno to cut his finger as he diced some vegetables in the kitchen. "I'm coming, I'm coming." The old slave made his slow way over to the door. The banging continued until he slid the bolt. "What is it?"

A man burst through the door, knocking Xeno over, and ran across the courtyard to where the voices of Lucius and Adara emanated from the triclinium.

"Lucius! Lucius!"

The tribune, wearing only a tunic and boots, jumped from his couch to face the doorway and the man standing there.

"Ashur?" Lucius looked upon him, his face flushed and panicked, dried saliva crusted around his mouth. "What in Apollo's name are you doing here?" Lucius' voice was a mixture of shock, anger and unknowing fear.

Ashur tried desperately to catch his breath, to speak what he had travelled hundreds of miles to speak. "Lucius...listen to me! Argus is here! He's here! He and his spies have come to kill you, your wife and your children!"

"What?"

"Lucius?" Adara's voice was panicked. "What's happening?" Ashur looked at her, his eyes relieved momentarily.

"Oh, Gods! Alene and the children!"

"Lucius!" Adara was shaking as Lucius turned to her.

"Adara, stay here with Ashur! Lock the door behind me!" Lucius ran to their room where he grabbed the sword his wife had given him and his gladius. As he ran across the courtyard to the main door he threw the gladius to Ashur who caught it. "Ashur stay here with her! Keep her safe!" Lucius disappeared out the door, his striding footsteps echoing off of the buildings that lined the via Principalis to the southern gate. Ashur bolted the door and put Adara in a room with Xeno.

Alene held the children closely as she began to run further along a small ridge of rocks. She wanted to scream but could not find her voice. The children cried but she could not comfort them as sudden fear overcame her.

"Apollo protect us," she cried, stinging tears running down her cheeks onto the children's faces. There was a loud, distant snapping sound behind her and then a pain in her back that sent her face down into the rocks so that she and the children collapsed beneath the blue cloak.

The shot from the small bow beneath his brown cloak had been well placed by Argus who stood a long way off. He grinned when the woman went down in a screaming, blue heap. He looked around to see if anyone had seen. No one. Brutus was almost at the body now and Argus went to meet him.

"Ah, what have we here? A little fresh meat?" Saliva slithered out of the corner of Brutus' cracked lips as he tossed aside his cloak and stood above the woman. Argus was still a ways off. It was time for his own fun.

It was dark beneath the cloak and Alene tried not to crush the crying children beneath her shuddering body but her strength was fading. It was hard to breathe and she tasted blood trickling from her mouth. She felt a pulling on the cloak that choked her where it was tied at the neck. Desperately, she tried to cover the children. The cloak ripped and came off, her blonde hair poured out. There was a pulling at her legs and she tried to kick. Then extreme pain as the arrow in her back was prodded. There was laughter.

"What?" Argus was stopped dead in his tracks. "Blonde hair?" Brutus was pulling at the woman who clung to life, her sobbing almost deafening. In that moment he realised who it was and all the rage and hatred in him turned to fear and weakness. "Alene?" he could not believe it but his thoughts were answered above her cries.

"Alene! Alene!" Lucius ran out of the gates as fast as his legs would carry him. As if in some terrible nightmare his

574

every stride got him nowhere nearer to the horrible sight before him. The huddled blue mass beneath a dark looking assassin. Out of the corner of his eye he spotted a figure in brown running away. "AHHHHH!" Lucius willed himself to move faster and faster toward Alene and the children, unsure if they were dead or alive. "Get away from them!"

Brutus turned toward the wildly yelling man who was fast approaching, a long blade swinging above his head. "Finally," he said to himself as he recognised Lucius; for a long time he had thought of nothing else but that face. From behind a rock with his bow strung, Argus sat shaking uncontrollably as he watched Brutus and Lucius charge toward each other like battling furies. "Tribune!" Brutus yelled. "I'll kill you and finish off your wife and children!"

Lucius did not hear him. His body went through the motions of defence and attack, but all he could see was Alene lying on the ground, shaking. Brutus' blade found a mark on his thigh and he went down, rolling immediately. A blow came straight down upon him and he held it with his sword, struggling against the man standing above him. The eyes, he recognised the eyes.

Lucius kicked upward with all his strength and Brutus went down, over his head. The clash of metal reached the ears of the men who had just topped the walls of the base and a horn rang out.

Lucius was roused by this and got to his feet. He cut and thrust and hacked away at Brutus who stumbled backward, unaffected by each new gash in his flesh. There was a whizzing sound and Lucius felt a stabbing in his calf where an arrow had hit. Another one missed his head. "AHH!" Brutus' blade broke under the harshness of Lucius' crazed attack. The second blow took off the assassin's arm.

Brutus looked confused and stood swaying upon his feet. He looked at Alene's body and smiled. "They're dead!"

With tears running down his face, Lucius swung his sword and cut clean through Brutus' neck. The body wavered for a second and then fell with a thud. Another arrow just missed Lucius from the rocks, but he paid it no heed. He ran to Alene's side, the arrow in his calf unnoticed now in the face of far greater pain.

Men charged out of the base and spread out. Argus, his opportunity lost, his strength and will to kill gone, ran away up the rock face. A lone horseman charged over from the western edge of the fort, having seen what was happening.

"Alene. Please, Gods. Alene." Lucius' shaking hands were afraid to touch or move her. He stroked her dirty hair. "I'm here Alene. You're safe now." Lucius heard a muffled crying and realised what it was. Carefully, his eyes blinded by tears, he lifted his sister onto his lap as he knelt. Her eyes were still open, looking at him, but blood poured from her mouth. The children were safe.

"L...u...cius..." she managed to say.

"Don't speak, Alene. Don't speak." He cradled her, realised she had saved them.

Tears ran from her eyes to mingle with the blood. "Lu...cius...the...chil...dren?"

"They're safe, Alene. Please don't speak. Save your strength." She tried to smile. The children were safe. Alene shook her head as Lucius looked into her eyes. The life was leaving her, he knew this look. It was infinitely more painful to see it in her face. "Stay with me, Alene, please. I need you." Her body shook as she tried to speak.

"Love...Lucius. I...love." Her eyes held his momentarily until a cry came from behind him where Alerio had jumped down from Lunaris. Alene's eyes looked from her brother to him briefly and then closed.

The world went into a whirling spin in that moment, an unmatched storm of emotion not equalled by any mortal, titan or god. Lucius tried to will her back to life, prayed to every god of good that he knew, with every ounce of will, but when he opened his eyes to look at her he knew she was gone.

Lucius stood up, laying her down gently first and looked up at the red, dawning sky and the dark rocks above.

"ARGUS!!!!!!!!!!!!"

Lucius screamed out with a pain that arose from an inner deep within his blood, and the heads of the Gods themselves wheeled round in horror where they stood in their far reaches. Apollo and Venus wept in anger and sadness and warlike Mars shook his head in dismay; the gaze of all three was now turned on the figure of Lucius crouched over the body of his sister and behind him, Alerio.

A terrible feeling came over Adara and Ashur as they waited without word beneath the darkening pallor of the sky. Several times she had tried to get out, her worry too great, but Ashur and Xeno had held her back. She knelt on the cold stones in front of the courtyard altar, her eyes staring up at the sky, her heart quickening at the sound of a distant horn.

"Ashur, something's happened. I can feel it! You must go and help Lucius, please!" Ashur could feel it too but he knew that Lucius would want him to stay.

"I cannot. We must stay here." He felt helpless waiting, but had no choice. It seemed hours before any word came.

"Tribune? Tribune, listen to me," Flavius Marcellus said as he lifted the crying children from the dirt. He stood above Lucius where he knelt in the clotted sand beside Alene's body. Lucius did not move or speak as he held her lifeless hand. The legate had been called out when no one else was able to persuade Lucius to return to base. Troops had been scouring the area for the other assassin in the meantime, but none had been found. "Tribune Metellus!" The legate's voice was much louder now. "I *order* you to return to base." Lucius looked up at his commander, his eyes shot and pained. "I am sorry for your family, Tribune," his voice was kinder now, "truly sorry. But you must not leave her here. The sooner the rites are carried out, the better it will be for her. Do not linger with her in this place. Please, come."

Lucius nodded, understanding what Marcellus had said, but he would not let anyone help him up, not even Alerio who had stood by the entire time, staring glassy-eyed down at Alene. Lucius had difficulty moving, as part of the arrow was still embedded in his calf. He did not care about the pain as he lifted the body up, wrapped in the cloak, and carried it back to base. He stared at Alerio as he passed, willing him not to speak or come near. He could not deal with *that*. He had seen Alene look at him.

The legate walked alongside Lucius, carrying the two children, grateful that they had been spared. He wondered how this would affect Lucius and what he would have to do with him.

There was a knock upon the door and Ashur ran to peer out of the small, barred hole to see who it was. His fears had not been wrong. Lucius came limping in and went directly to the room that had been Alene's. Adara could not move close for she knew what had happened and collapsed in a wailing mass against the altar. Next, through the door came the legate, accompanied by the sound of crying.

Adara looked up. *They're alive! Thank you Gods!* she screamed inwardly and ran over to take them from Marcellus.

"They're fine, Lady Metella, but I fear for your husband." He looked at Adara who could not contain her tears.

"What has happened?"

"It seems they were attacked by some assassins. The tribune's sister was killed but...she had covered your children with her body to keep them safe." He paused, realising this was not the time to discuss. "That is all I know for now. I will send someone over from the collegia funeraticia to help. Our funeral club at the base is a noble one." He turned to leave. "I'm sorry for your loss." The legate went out the door, leaving Adara, Ashur, Alerio and Xeno staring at the closed door of Alene's cubiculum. "I want two men guarding this door at all times!" the legate ordered the men outside. *I've lived too long to have seen a day like this.*

Adara was afraid to enter the room, but she knew that Lucius would need her. She tried to compose herself but found it almost impossible, especially as the reality of what had happened began to set in; Alene was gone. "Ashur," Adara said. "Can you go two doors down and ask for the Lady Martia to come here?"

"Of course." Ashur went out into the street and was back shortly with Martia who had already heard what had happened.

"Adara? Are you all right?"

"Martia please, look after the children for me while I help Lucius." She could not believe what was happening. Martia understood, took the children, and went into the other room. Adara looked at Alerio and Ashur. "You two stay here."

"But I want to see her..."

"Alerio, please. Not now. He's not ready for this." Alerio nodded, tears running down his cheeks. Ashur realised, recognised, what he felt.

So much pain, so quickly, Ashur thought. He cursed himself for not having been faster, for betraying his trust. *Had I left but one day earlier...* He knew it was no use. He had been too late, and as a result a friend was dead. He and Alerio sat with their backs against the altar and waited.

After bringing fresh clothes and two basins of water to Adara, Xeno, shaking and upset, went into the kitchen to busy himself, crying as he cut the food. *She was such a lovely girl.*

When Adara opened the door, she found Lucius kneeling next to Alene's bed where he had lain her body. He spoke in whispers she could not understand, either praying for her or talking to her. The sight struck Adara hard as she moved to Lucius' side and knelt, unbelieving of her own eyes. She held her husband's trembling hand and they leaned against each other and wept for their departed sister.

"Come, Lucius. We have to wash her. I've brought the coin, the nicest aureus we had." Lucius nodded silently and together they began to remove the blood-stained clothing. They washed her body, the skin no longer soft and warm but cold and unfamiliar. Gently, Lucius rounded the corners of the eyes and mouth with the wet cloth, Adara combed the hair. When they had finished the painful deed, they dressed her in her favourite yellow stola and placed the golden coin in her mouth.

They stepped back to look upon her. Lucius finally spoke. "She saved our children."

"I know." Adara fought back another wave of tears. "She loved them very much."

"The Gods have damned us, Adara. Turned on us." Adara looked fearfully at her husband.

"No, Lucius. They haven't. Don't say such things. Some things are even out of Their control. Alene saved our family, and we must honour her for it." *Be strong. He needs you now.* "We have to see to the rites of passage."

"I know...I know." He sighed, unwilling to face anyone or anything outside of the door of the room in which they now stood.

"Alerio is outside with Ashur."

Lucius bit his lower lip, a feeling of betrayal coming over him. He had seen Alene look at Alerio. Her last look. "I don't want to see him."

"Lucius, listen to me." Adara put her hands on his face. "He loved Alene. She loved him too."

"Why didn't she tell me?"

"She wanted to, more than anything. She just didn't want to hurt you or your relationship with Alerio. He is in much pain too." Lucius remained silent. "I'll tell him to come back tomorrow. For now we must cleanse ourselves with incense and oils. It's not good to be so close to death." Lucius shot her an angry look. "Alene would want us to be protected, Lucius."

He knew she was right. Alene would want them to cleanse themselves properly. It was not good to be in the presence of death, to touch it. Lucius felt he had been around it for ages, but it had never been like this, so painfully close. Adara went out into the courtyard. It was night already and Ashur and Alerio still waited. The men from the funeral club had already come and set up a table with flowers in the courtyard where the body would lie until the funeral. When Martia emerged from the far room to tell Adara that the children were asleep, Adara thanked her from a distance and told her to go home.

"I'll come by tomorrow," Martia said as she went out.

"Alerio." Adara turned to him. He looked beaten and tired.

"Can I see her now?" he pleaded.

"Tomorrow will be best. Go back to your quarters and rest."

Alerio wanted to burst through the door, ignore her, but he knew that it would only make matters worse. Without a word, he left and made his way to one of the mess halls to drink and try to forget.

That night, Ashur slept in the extra cubiculum while Lucius and Adara washed themselves and went to bed, sleepless in a changed home. Lucius wondered when the nightmare would end but knew better than to lead himself into a world of false hopes. During the night, the children awoke crying and he rose from bed to hold both of them, to calm them. He realised the gift Alene had given them, the sacrifice she had made and thanked the star-pocked sky for her courage. He hoped she could hear him.

The following day, Lucius rose early to a clear sky. He felt Alene's presence, knew that her shade would be restless and pained. It was his duty to see that everything was prepared. After arranging her on the table amid flowers, trying not to look too much at her silent form, he went directly to the funeral club to find that the legate had already instructed them to give him whatever he wished. In truth, the legate felt partially responsible, as this happened under his command. It was only right that he help to an extent. The more personal arrangements he left to Lucius and his family.

Alene's body would lie beneath the sky amid scented flowers for the whole of that day and night. There would be nine hired mourners as well as someone to play the lyre, Alene's favourite instrument. The following day, the procession would go from the tribune's quarters to the ustrinum, the cremation site on the western side of the base where three times three sacrifices would be made. Three chickens, three goats and three lambs would be offered and then consumed in the feast for the assembled mourners.

The man in charge of the club was used to dealing with people who were not quite present, their minds wandering in thought alongside the deceased. He was patient, understanding.

"She was a Metella?" he asked. Lucius nodded. "Will the imagines be included in the procession?" Lucius looked at the man and shook his head. The imagines were the wax mask representations of their illustrious ancestors that had, in the distant past, been worn by living family members who rode along in a chariot.

"No," Lucius answered. "There are no imagines." It was the right of those who had held curule magistracies to have the imagines in their processions, but Alene was a woman and the masks that they did have were in Rome. Besides, it had been a long time since the masks were worn in the funeral of a Metellus. Lucius knew that his ancestors would be watching, looking down on the funeral not of a senator or magistrate, but of a strong, beautiful, loving woman that any Metella could only hope to emulate.

"Very well, Tribune. I shall arrange for everything." The man took some notes on a wax tablet. "What about an urn?" The thought pained him but Lucius said that he would like a circular, studded urn made out of bronze just as his ancestors had used in far away Etruria. "When would you like the procession to take place?"

"Tomorrow. Late in the morning."

"Everything will be ready, Tribune. Do not fear. The aedituus of the Temple of Jupiter in Thamugadi will have the animals ready and waiting on site. Will you be performing the sacrifices by yourself or would you like the services of the popae to do it for you?" This was too much to think about. Lucius' head spun but he forced himself under control.

"I'll do it myself." He then thanked the man and went out.

Lucius moved dazedly through that day, nodding to greetings and condolences, answering questions, but never truly knowing what was happening. He felt Alene's restlessness at all times and tried not to fear the lemure of his sister. Those who died before their time were said to be the most dangerous. He could not believe that of Alene though, would not believe it. *You'll be free soon, Alene. I promise*, he thought as he walked.

A short time later, he found himself face to face with Alerio who had been standing outside the door of the tribune's quarters. He stopped, saw the pleading eyes of his friend but also a steely determination he had not seen before. Lucius remembered what Adara had told him and it hurt, but he knew that if it were true, Alene would want it so. He said nothing to Alerio, simply nodded, opened the door and let him in.

The courtyard was smoky with incense, a sort of mist hovering around Alene's yellow-clad body among the flowers. Alerio moved forward slowly, one hand over his mouth, the other outstretched as if she would take it at any moment. Lucius decided to go to Adara and leave Alerio alone as he knelt beside the shell of the woman he loved.

After an hour, Lucius emerged from their cubiculum when he heard the bolt of the main door sliding open. He walked over to Alerio, whose eyes were wet with grief, and stopped him.

"Tomorrow, my friend, you'll walk in the procession with us." Lucius held his forearm firmly and Alerio, trying to hold his head up, nodded.

The day before the funeral, Ashur knew that his presence would only create confusion and so he had gone for a long walk to feel his feet in the sand of a desert he had never thought to see again, a land he had not wanted to see again. Carissa would be thinking of him, hoping he had succeeded. He felt as though he had failed everyone and begged the sand, sun and sky for forgiveness. Adara had asked him to follow with them in the procession, but Ashur did not think himself worthy of it. In the end, however, he agreed, hoped that his presence would not anger Apollo, or Alene's shade. He knew that every day from then on would be difficult.

The next morning, Lucius, dressed in a simple black toga, awoke early again to see that the body had remained unmolested during the night. It was strangely pristine. As the sun began to rise, he said a silent prayer and waited for the others.

The day passed in a blur, like a mirage on a scorching day. There were not many people present, but enough for honour. He, Adara and the children, Alerio and Ashur had followed directly behind the body as it was carried through the streets of Lambaesis to the pyre that had been erected in the ustrinum. The mourners did their job well in their wailing and tearing of clothes and the sound of the lyre was like a feather on a breeze. It would have pleased Alene.

The body was placed on the pyre and Lucius stepped forward to perform the sacrifices. He knew that many thought it improper for a member of the family to perform the act personally, but he owed it to his sister to do it as it was done long ago. Nine animals fell one by one, the sound of their suffering drowned out by the gentle lyre. Their blood was then caught in a large dish by the priest who poured it on top of the altar before the remains were roasted for the feast.

Around Alene were placed some of her favourite possessions: scrolls of poetry, glass phials of oil, a small vase and other items. Over her body was placed a rich fabric that she had brought from Athens, one she had intended to make clothing out of.

All present waited as the torch was held in readiness. Lucius approached the pyre and poured libations of wine, honey and milk around the body. He then placed a bunch of flowers next to his sister's head and spoke lowly. "I know you always liked the flowers I would give you, Alene...I hope you like these. Thank you for saving my children. I'll never forget what you've done. I'm sorry you couldn't tell me about Alerio. He is a good man and I'll try to comfort him as you would want me to. I also vow to you, upon your pyre...that I will kill those who are responsible for this and when it is done I'll erect a beautiful monument to you...I love you, sister." He looked his last upon her, touched her hair. She was still, calm and beautiful.

Lucius extended his shaking hand to accept the torch, lit the pyre and stepped back to stand beside Adara and the children. The flames moved quickly, a sound of crackling mixing with the sounds of mourning and the lyre as sparks were swept up into the sky. Gods and men watched the body as it was consumed by the fire and turned to dust, as all things eventually do. Lucius looked up at the infinite blue ceiling above and knew that Alene was appeased and that they would never truly be without her.

Nine days of mourning had elapsed and the cena novendialis, the feast in which the dead of the family, di parentes, continued to be remembered, was held in the sunlit courtyard of Lucius' quarters. Sacrifices were made and healing began as they feasted around the shiny bronze urn. Inwardly, everyone said what was left unsaid and tried to come to peace with a changed life. In a way, Lucius and Adara were happy that every time they looked at their children they would remember

Alene and her life. It was in Phoebus' bright eyes and in little Calliope's song.

The healing would take long however, and Lucius would not forget his vow. When he was of the mind to do so without getting angry, he sat down with Ashur who was finally able to tell him everything he knew about his mother, his younger brother and sister and his father. As Lucius listened, he knew that things went far beyond Argus to a person whom it would be suicide to cross or kill. Gaius Fulvius Plautianus controlled Argus, and his own father. He would have to think on this.

Lucius left Ashur. He felt angry with him, but knew it was unfair to feel that way. Had Ashur not come when he did, the children and Adara would be dead too. He left Adara, Alerio and Ashur with the children and went to the table in the meeting room.

Three lamps burned around the piece of papyrus that he had laid out. Lucius slumped down in his chair and dipped the stylus into the inkpot. With a deep breath, he began to write words that did not come easily, words to someone far away whom he did not want to hurt and for whom he was greatly afraid. It was the most difficult letter he would ever write.

Part III

THE HYDRA'S HEADS

A.D. 204-205

XXVII

METELLA

Toward mid-summer, the nights were unbearably hot, the days even hotter. The city stank more than usual during this latest wave of heat. There had been outbreaks of malaria further down the Tiber in some of the smaller settlements where the water was more stagnant and marshy. The baths within the city were busy from morning to night as most of the citizenry thought it much more comfortable to remain there than in their own steamy tenements. A couple of fires had broken out in the city but they had been quickly brought under control. Nobody wanted another fire.

The air was especially foul near the Forum Boarium where the smell of baking excrement from the cattle market was a permanent nuisance. Quintus Metellus opted to spend as much time as he could within the cool marble walls of the curia or at the baths, while his wife and two youngest children were confined to the hot, bathless house. Antonia felt weakened by the oppressive heat and tried to maintain a sanitary home by having the children wash themselves in small tubs of cool water. She did the same, although the large open spaces of Rome's baths were never far from her mind.

Worry had been a permanent state of mind for her for weeks now. Weeks since Ashur had raced off. Weeks without word of what had happened to her family. Her prayers were constant and everyday grew lengthier, more intense in their pleading tones. She could bear being beaten by her husband, locked up in a home that was falling apart, she could even bear the constant stench wafting in from the streets. But, she could not bear *not* knowing.

Ambrosia met constantly in secret with Carissa and Emrys on market days. The sculptors had not had any word from Africa either but they always enquired after Antonia and the children's well-being and supplied them with foods they could not acquire, herbs for little Quintus' headaches or extra oils and sponges for washing. It was also easier for Ambrosia of late to bring things home since her master was out most of the time.

Antonia had asked Ambrosia to warn Emrys and Carissa not to come near the house as it was under constant surveillance by the Consul's lackeys. She even spoke in whispers within the walls of her own home. Young Quintus and Clarinda walked in silence now, in fear, never playing or laughing as they used to; it broke their mother's heart to see them in such a state. The tutors had stopped coming to them long ago, forbidden by their father who, believing his entire family had turned on him, had ceased to pay for any services. Therefore, when Quintus was gone to the senate or baths, Antonia took it upon herself to read to them from scrolls she had hidden away for safekeeping.

Everyday, she and the children escaped for a welcome spell as she spoke to them of far away green hills and wine dark seas, of beasts and battles. She read to them of great men and women who had overcome incredible odds and horrific circumstances. Clarinda listened in gaping amazement while little Quintus seemed stirred by what he heard. He listened so intently that by the end of the story his head hurt so badly that he needed another mixture to help him sleep immediately. He did not regret it though, and came back for more as soon as he was awake again.

Antonia too found comfort in her readings, in the strong women who had come before her; she vowed not to let her own situation defeat her. But oh, how she wished for news from Africa. After so long, so many nightmares.

One market day, as usual, Ambrosia returned from her shopping with a basket of wilted vegetables and soft fruit. The heat, she had told her mistress, was destroying most of the produce. The prices for any food that was fresh and firm had risen beyond the means provided by Quintus senior. Antonia despaired as she limped to peer over the edge of the basket the slave had placed on the kitchen counter.

"Things have still not improved?"

"No, mistress. Prices are very high and it was difficult to get to the stands that were not trying to cheat people. Shoving and pushing everywhere."

"We will make do. Did you get the herbs for my son's headaches?"

"Yes, mistress, and something else!" Ambrosia's voice rose excitedly but she quickly checked herself. "Is the master within?" she whispered.

"No. He is not. What is it, girl?"

"Carissa brought me a letter today. I think it's from Africa." The slave held out the letter and Antonia grabbed it.

"I shall read this in my room. See to the children, Ambrosia."

"Yes, mistress."

Antonia walked faster than she had in a long while until she reached the stairs, went up and entered her room. She shut the door behind her. Rays of sunlight penetrated the small window on the far wall and she went to sit in the small chair before it to read the letter. There was no seal upon it, only a hard glob of wax, but she hoped it was from her son.

"Please, Gods, let them be alive," she said as she broke the wax and unrolled the papyrus.

From Tribune Lucius Metellus Anguis
To Antonia Metella

Dearest Mother,

This is not a letter that I know how to write. I remember that you always told me the Gods had granted me special gifts, that I stood apart from others. Writing a letter such as this is not, I believe, what They had in mind. Nor is the gift of strength to protect our family. I know of your ordeal and it gives me great pain to think of you, Clarinda and little Quintus in such a state. Why did you not tell us sooner? I would have come to you. Suffice it to say that Ashur has reached us with your message, yet only just in time. Adara, the children, and I are safe.

Antonia noticed odd markings upon the papyrus as she read and realised they were tears, her son's tears. A name was distinctly missing from the letter and she felt fear grip her heart with an iron fist.

Mama, Alene is dead.

A loud cry burst forth from Antonia's lips and her crooked jaw. Her eyes pooled over making it hard to read further. Ambrosia and the children burst through the door but Antonia did not notice them. They froze and watched.

Forgive me mother for not being stronger. I have let you, and Alene, down. I should have been able to protect her, keep her safe. The Gods have taken her from us and there is nothing I can do to get her back. I wish I could call the black boat back to shore. I have never felt so helpless. Please know that Alene died a hero and was braver than ever I was. She saved the lives of my children by sacrificing her own.

Antonia wept. Was it possible that the world should become so dreadful? She had only ever wanted to protect her daughter, had kept her away from Rome for that very purpose but now…now…*oh Gods.* Alene was taken from her.

I know that anything further I say will be of little comfort to you. But, know that Adara and I have seen that Alene was properly taken care of so that she will honour the Gods' halls.
I swear, by the blood that is in my veins, I will avenge her death one way or another. Everybody here feels in part

responsible for her death. The truth is that I am the one who is responsible. It is my task.

When I am able, I shall return to Rome and do what needs to be done. My father has gone too far and I do not care any longer about the price of what I must do. He must pay for this, and those he has helped must also pay. You know the people I speak of.

A sudden sense of dread came over Antonia as she realised what her son was saying and she knew that if he carried it out he would be damned, executed under Roman law, leaving his wife and children alone in the world. Alene would not want that. Antonia shuddered at the thought of her daughter upon a burning pyre.

I will do all that I can to return to you soon, mother. I will bring Alene home to you and bury her with honour in the place she was born. You will soon be free, I promise. Pray for my sister and I hope that someday you can find it in yourself to forgive me.

Your loving son, Lucius

"It is not your fault, my son. The Gods know whose fault it is." Antonia bent her head and let her tears fall. She felt a hand on her arm.

"Mama? What is it?" Young Quintus stroked her arm. Her tears were different this time, came from somewhere else.

"I will tell you soon, but not now." Antonia ran her hand along her younger son's cheek, her finger along the pulsing vein on the side of his brow that caused him so much pain. "Go and read to your sister, Quintus. I need to be alone." Quintus left his mother sitting by the window where she cried and looked up at the sky for hours. She began to mutter things as he closed the door but he could not understand what she was saying.

"I tell you, Popeius," insisted Senator Metellus to his colleague on the steps of the curia overlooking the Forum Romanum, "things are definitely looking up for Rome, and for us."

The old senator looked at Quintus curiously, wondered what was going on in that head of his. "You are in a jovial mood today, Metellus. Do you know something I do not?"

"My dear Senator," Quintus clapped his hands, "do you not feel the life pulsing through this city at the moment, the hope?"

Popeius was doubtful, but decided to play it safe. "I am afraid I do not have your sight in this, Metellus. Perhaps it is my age. The years are passing by and the weight upon my shoulders is increasing when it should be lifted completely."

Quintus ignored the old man and looked out over the forum. People walked in silent, orderly rows, heads hung low. No disturbances, no upstarts voicing ridiculous opinions.

"Ah!" Popeius spotted another senator. "Senator Dio! Would you speak with us for a moment?" Cassius Dio smiled at the old man and turned toward them. "Let's ask Dio here what he thinks."

Quintus huffed, unable to tolerate Dio and his Greek ideas.

"Senators," Dio greeted them warmly. He knew Popeius well and recognised Quintus, though they were not on friendly terms. "I trust I find you both well."

"Well enough, Senator, thank you. Senator Metellus and I were just having a discussion about these times we live in. He insists that Rome has never been better and that things are looking up for us. Old as I am, I cannot see this. You are younger than both of us. What do you think?"

Dio clasped his hands behind his back as he was wont to do and thought about it for a moment. This was not the greatest place to discuss personal opinions on the state of Rome, not these days anyway. "That is a difficult question and an interesting observation, especially for one who has always been such an outspoken Republican." He smiled at Quintus who smirked. "Rome has definitely changed, that much is true."

"Would you not say it is for the better, Senator Dio? I have found that there is finally some hope for this empire of ours."

"Only time will tell, Senator Metellus. History and the Gods shall judge us all." Popeius nodded in agreement. "For now I am happy to enjoy a beautiful summer's day while eating a honeyed pastry."

"Oh ho! That sounds like a marvellous idea!" Popeius licked his lips. Dio noticed Quintus' annoyance and admittedly, enjoyed it.

"That reminds me, Senator, how is your son, the Tribune Metellus? It has been a long time since his name has graced forum talk. Is he still in Africa?" Quintus scowled, his pleasant mood gone. Dio's face was passive.

"Yes, he's in Africa...last I heard. To be honest gentlemen I do not speak of him. He has no respect for his family."

"Nonsense, Metellus," Popeius chided. "The lad has grown into a strong Roman. Really Senator, you are too hard on the boy."

"I'm afraid, Senator Popeius, that you are wrong. He was a disappointment, and an embarrassment. Nothing more."

Dio thought it curious that he should say Lucius 'was' anything. "And how is the rest of your family? I swear," Dio chuckled, "ever since my wife met the Lady Antonia she has tried to emulate her every action."

"My wife is at home, as a true Roman matron should be."

"Is she still ill? I heard somewhere that she has been quite ill for some time."

"Oh, I do hope Lady Antonia is getting better," Popeius sighed. "She is such a lovely woman. Senator," he spoke to Dio, "you should have seen the way she turned heads when she would walk through the forum with the senator years ago. My, my. How time goes by."

"I'll ask you not to speak about my house so disrespectfully!" Quintus snapped.

"I'm sure, Senator Metellus, that Senator Popeius meant no disrespect, did you Senator?"

"Not at all!" Popeius was truly hurt by this accusation. Quintus was silent for a moment then turned to leave.

"I have to go now, gentlemen. I have an appointment. Until tomorrow." Both men nodded politely at Quintus as he made a rude retreat toward the other side of the forum. Dio leant Popeius his arm and they made their way down the stairs.

"By Jupiter, I meant no disrespect!" Popeius continued to proclaim sadly.

"Of course you didn't, Senator," Dio comforted as they walked, looking back over his shoulder to where Quintus stormed down a small lane. "Now, how about those honeyed pastries?"

"Oh ho! What a lovely idea!" Popeius forgot immediately about the conversation.

Quintus Metellus did indeed have an appointment of a sort, but not with an important client or trader who was ready to buy olives from the estate. He made his way down some of the lesser-known lanes to an area along the Tiber. There, he stormed through a pink door without knocking.

"Oooo! Senator? You're early today!" A buxom red-haired woman walked out from behind a table. She had layers of makeup upon her face and wore very little. She smelled heavily of jasmine and spice as she came over to lead Quintus into a cushion-clad lounge.

"Not now, Sabina! Where's the girl?" He looked down the long, dark corridor where smoke bounced off the walls and swirled around the emanating sounds.

"She's with a customer. Like I said, you're early." The woman moved closer to Quintus and stroked his cheek. He frowned. "What say you try me out this time? I'm more...willing...to experiment. Anything you want." Quintus brushed her hand aside. "Fine." The woman thundered back behind her table. "I don't know why you prefer that little stick of a girl. Just make sure there are no bruises on her when you leave. I have other paying customers."

Quintus waited for a few more minutes, pacing the floor like a distraught animal. He stopped when he saw a man, a rich merchant, coming down the hallway, arranging his clothes. The man smiled at Quintus who frowned down his nose at him.

"She's done!" Sabina said. Quintus strode into the smoky hallway.

He did not bother to knock at the door, and when he opened it he saw her. On the edge of a ruffled bed was a girl of no more than eighteen years with yellow hair and white skin. She sniffled as she dipped a sponge in a basin of water and ran it between her legs. She hadn't noticed Quintus enter the room she was so lost in her thoughts. She often escaped into another world while she was working. It helped in a way. She tried to concentrate on her home far, far to the North.

"Stop that crying!" Quintus said, causing her to drop the sponge on the floor and jump up.

"I'm not ready yet-" she began to protest but the slap across her face stopped her words. She fell onto the bed and sniffled some more. This one always hit. She always dreaded his arrival. Without another word, Quintus tossed aside his clothing and took what he was paying for. Her crying hurt his aching head to distraction, so he picked the sponge up off the floor and shoved it in her mouth.

By the time Quintus returned home from the baths, it was dark outside. The cool night breeze had begun to blow away the stink of the hot day and the Forum Boarium was quiet again. His head had ached ever since he had spoken with Popeius and Dio on the steps of the curia. "Damn them!" Quintus said to himself as he walked. He decided he would add their names to his list for the Consul as soon as he was home.

The house was pleasantly quiet to his ears, as it always was these past months. He decided it was filthy though, as he walked past the door slave directly to his office. Fortunately, he was rarely at home; he could stand a little filth in passing. At the large table in his office, Quintus sat down and pulled out a wax tablet he had in a small drawer. On it were the names of people in Rome that he believed, were enemies of the state. *Plautianus will thank me for this some day soon*, he thought to himself. Once he had pressed the names of Popeius and Dio into the wax, he started going over other papers.

Antonia had spent the entire day at her window, thinking of her daughter who was never coming back to her. The wells of her tears had dried up, leaving only a stony determination at the bottom. She yet had three children and two grandchildren who were in danger. She thought of her own family; was it not a great one too? She was a descendent of the Antonii, no lesser a family. Far away, she could feel the searching eyes of her parents and others, willing her to be strong for what family she had left.

When the echo of the home's slamming door rang through the house and her husband's footsteps sounded the way to his hateful room, Antonia awoke from her shrouded thoughts. She went into the room next to hers to make sure that the children were asleep and told Ambrosia that she was to remain with them, no matter what.

It was difficult for her to make her way down the stairs without making a noise, but she did, despite her limping. She had put on a black stola and arranged her dark hair high on her head. She passed the busts of the ancestors, her son's ancestors, and asked them to see the right in what she was thinking. Alene was not coming back. She thought of the story she had read to the children three days ago, the story of Iphigeneia and her father Agamemnon. He had sacrificed his own daughter to achieve his own ends. Her husband was not an Agamemnon, but Alene was dead and the Gods could not change that.

Alene's mother walked down the marble corridor, the letter in hand, and pushed open the door. Her husband was hunched over a pile of letters, sipping wine from a samian goblet. He barely noticed her until she slammed the door.

"What in Hades are you doing here, woman?" Antonia said nothing, stared directly at his smug face. "Well? Are you deaf?"

"No, husband. I am not deaf."

"Tell me what you want or you'll get a slap."

"Your taunts don't frighten me, Quintus, not anymore." He stared icily at her, his fists clenched. "We need to talk."

"There's nothing to talk about."

"By Apollo, there most certainly is." Antonia moved forward and Quintus slammed his stylus down on the table, crossed his arms.

"All right. Make it quick." He motioned to the chair like he did to all of his clients.

"I shall stand," she said plainly. Her heart was beating quickly in her chest, but she thought of Alene and pressed on. "What has happened to you?"

"To me?"

"Yes, to you. You have become an animal, Quintus. Do you know how many years it has been since I have seen the man I once loved? How many years it has been since his eyes have taken me in? How many years has it been since you have looked upon our children with the pride that a parent should have?"

"Spare me the sentimental tripe!" He emptied his cup.

"I used to be proud to be your wife, but now I am ashamed. I am ashamed that I have allowed you to treat our children so cruelly," her voice caught in her throat as she said it. "I am ashamed that I have allowed you to disgrace this family with your dealings."

"*I* disgrace this family? How dare you!" Quintus was on his feet for a moment but sat back down.

"Yes. The only one who has brought honour to this family has been Lucius and…and Alene."

Quintus spat on the floor.

Antonia continued. "I have brought shame to this house, to my own family for allowing things to have gone this far. I can forgive your incessant drinking or your violent temper. I can even forgive your having had Argus, your bastard, live beneath this roof all those years. But I cannot forgive your actions against our children!" Antonia's voice had risen but she brought it under control and held out the letter.

"What is that?"

"Read it!" Antonia placed it in front of him on the table. Quintus unrolled the scroll and read. His face was unmoved, cold. His head hurt again, more than before. When he finished he looked up, chuckled.

"So stupid. All of them."

"Is that all you have to say?" A fire burned in Antonia's eyes, a strength to well up within her frail body.

"What else is there to say?"

"You arranged for the murder of your own son and his family!"

"So I did."

"You killed our daughter!" Antonia was shaking now, trying with all her will to stay strong.

"I didn't. If she was stupid enough to get in the way, it's her own fault. I'll give Argus another chance and if he succeeds. Then, perhaps, I'll have a son again. Not before!"

Antonia could not believe her ears. It was now obvious that Quintus planned to acknowledge Argus as his son in Lucius' place, making him heir to everything, including the name.

"Don't stand there like an idiot, Antonia! If you're finished you had better get back to your room and stay there. I have work to do. More work now that I know this!" He held up the letter and threw it at her.

"You are a coward!" Her voice was stony and strong.

"What did you say, woman?" Quintus pushed back his chair so that it fell behind him. He began to walk slowly around the table, fists clenched.

"I said you're a coward. You are no Metellus, nor a Caecilius...and you are certainly not an Anguis."

"Damn you, woman," he said through gritted teeth. She continued, ignoring his words, ready for a beating.

"You are nothing but a lowly coward, Quintus. That is all." His fist flew quickly to her chest and she stumbled backward into the door.

"I *am* a Metellus! I'm paterfamilias! I'll kill you for saying such things!" he began to stride toward her.

Blood trickled from Antonia's mouth where she had bitten her tongue as she stumbled. "You're nothing! Coward!"

Quintus lunged at her and wrapped his hands about her throat, squeezing with all his might.

Antonia did not try to scream with the few moments of strength that were left in her body. Instead she reached into the folds of her black stola. Alene's face floated in the air beyond Quintus as he tried to wring the life out of her. Antonia finally grasped the dagger's handle and plunged it into her husband's abdomen.

At first, Quintus did not feel it, and he continued to choke her. She withdrew the blade awkwardly and drove it into his side this time. His grip loosened and he stumbled back to lean on the chair, clutching at his stomach and side. The air began to fill her lungs again and without hesitation she let out a scream as she jumped at him wielding the dagger.

"Gods damn you!" she yelled as she stabbed and stabbed and stabbed.

Quintus' body slumped over the edge of the client chair and then onto the floor in a bloody heap at Antonia's feet. She gasped for air again as she felt his blood soaking her feet on the mosaic floor, the mortared cracks filling with crimson waste. She made herself look at what she had done, was unashamed of it. When she was certain that he was dead, she dropped the dagger on the pathetic mass, turned and walked proudly from the room.

For the first time, Antonia fully understood the story of Iphigeneia. She felt strong like her mother, Clytemnestra. Agamemnon had sacrificed her daughter and she had killed him for it. Only, there was no goddess, no huntress that had come down out of the skies to save Alene.

Antonia stood in the garden looking up at the night sky. *It is a beautiful night,* she thought. The breeze caressed her face and neck and she felt the well within herself fill once more. "For you, Alene," she whispered, tears flowing down her cheeks.

XXVIII

VOCATIONES

'Summons'

Alene's death brought an end to summer within the walls of Lambaesis, but especially within the walls of the domus of Tribune Metellus. There were whispers among the men of the legion that the young tribune was cursed by the Gods, that ill omen followed him wherever he went, including those associated with him. The smoke that rose from the courtyard where he and his family lived was an incessant reminder of the death of beauty. The distinct plume that wafted skyward was in fact emanating from the tripod Lucius had set up in honour of his sister; in it burned an array of incense day and night. The routine of this vigil gave some comfort to Lucius, Adara and the few friends who would come through the door to add something to the flames. On the outside however, it was a source of discomfort to the superstitious ranks; Lucius was annoyed by this, the legate disturbed.

When Mar and Dagon had returned from their wide ranging patrol, both men had been shattered at the news of what had happened. Dagon tried to hold back tears he had never shed and Mar's kingly exterior crumbled to reveal a deep, regretful sympathy for Lucius and his family. Without care of superstition or possible contact with a vengeful lemur, both men came through Lucius' door daily to lend their support and their friendship. Lucius was glad of their presence and the strength that they leant him.

As for Alerio, work and duty were the order of the day. The pain he experienced had hit him hard. Though he did visit Lucius and Adara, his main concern was soldiering. He was reincarnated into a hard-nosed centurion. War had been his life before and now it was again. So long as he stayed busy, he was able to forget his pain.

Ashur, who had been ill for some days after that terrible day, was yet with Lucius, Adara and the children. The life, the enthusiasm and the mystery that had once dwelled within him were long departed, leaving him sad and weakened. He and Lucius did not speak of the past anymore, only the day and what it held. Ashur's thoughts drifted constantly to Rome and Carissa and the hope that she would not be disappointed with him for having failed. A return to Rome was what he most wanted, and what he most dreaded. Lucius had only so much energy within to ease his friend's heart and mind. His real concern was for his wife and their two children.

With the death of her new-found sister, Adara was suddenly a woman alone, the vibrant, laughing spark within her struggled to stay alight. Lucius vowed to himself that he would never allow it to burn out, that he would do all in his power to keep his family together. For Adara, her children became her life. She spent her days nursing them, cherishing them. Always, within the little domus, her voice could be heard as she sang to them, her voice soft and loving. When Alene had departed, little Calliope had ceased her singing and Phoebus had awoken nightly, screaming. After a few weeks that all passed. Calliope began to sing with her mother and little Phoebus' nights became soft and sleepy once more.

At the end of every day, before returning home to Adara, Lucius would check for letters from Rome. Every day he was disappointed. There had been no word from his mother, from Emrys or from Carissa. They had received a long sad letter and offers of help from Publius and Delphina in Athens but nothing from Rome.

When Lucius was summoned to the Principia by the legate one bright, windy day, he was on the parade ground drilling the troops. He had been sitting upon Lunaris, lost in thought when the trooper came up to him and told him the Commander wanted to see him 'immediately'. Rarely did Marcellus demand to see anyone immediately, viewing drills as the most important duty an officer had day-to-day. Lucius set off directly.

He reigned in at the entrance to the Principia and handed Lunaris' reigns to one of the guards. There was another horse in the courtyard, dirty and travel-worn. A groom was brushing it down and feeding it when Lucius walked by. He noticed that the animal was clad in ornate harness, a beautiful, fast-looking stallion.

Without saying a word, Lucius was admitted to the legate's offices where he found his commanding officer sitting at his desk, head heavy. Lucius saluted, waited to be spoken to.

"Sit down, Tribune," the legate said, his voice even.

"You wanted to see me, sir?"

"Yes." Marcellus had had much on his mind the past weeks, one of those things being the young tribune. He walked around his desk and sat on its edge. The young man looked up at him, the dark circles under his eyes betraying sleepless nights and heavy worries. "Metellus," the legate began, "I've been thinking quite a bit lately about you and your place in the legion."

"Yes, sir?" Lucius was suddenly worried. Marcellus had never spoken to him in such a sad tone.

"I don't know if I've said it to you personally, Tribune, but I am truly sorry for what has befallen you here in Lambaesis. It's unforgivable and I pray that Jupiter will bring justice on the men responsible for it." Lucius bowed his head, feeling that familiar weight of worry upon his shoulders. "You're an excellent, talented commander in the field. You have a bright future ahead of you, I'm sure. You are also a good lad and...I have actually come to see you as what I had hoped my son would have been, had he not died long ago."

Lucius looked up into the old man's eyes and caught a momentary glimpse of feeling in an otherwise hard, battle-worn face. "I don't know what to say, Commander."

Marcellus put up a hand. "Say nothing. That is something between the two of us. I'm fond of you and, at times, you've been an asset to this legion."

"At times, sir?"

"Yes. I have seen you inspire your men and when they don't know I'm listening I've heard them speak of your valour, your strong sense of leadership. All the tribunes have told me about this. But…lately, things have been different."

"I know. I'm sorry, Legate."

"Don't be sorry, Metellus. You can't control everything that happens. The Gods do that and when they set their minds upon something, there is little that you or I can do about it." Marcellus got up and walked to the back wall where various pieces of weapons and armour hung as reminders of battles won or lost. "Sadly, there are times in a commander's career where he *can* do something. In a way, these times are more difficult than the times when one's hands are tied.

"I'm not sure I understand, sir."

"I've had reports from many of the other officers that your presence here is…well…a distraction to the men. Please, don't speak. Let me finish. I myself have seen men distance themselves from you along the road, your cohort's drills are suffering, and there is constant talk that you've fallen out of favour with the Gods. Now, both you and I know that that is complete rubbish of course, but our common rank and file are a superstitious lot. You know as well as I what happens when they're not fully concentrated on the task at hand." Lucius nodded. "Discipline breaks down, and if we were to be involved in a battle when that happened, we'd be wiped out."

"I know that, sir, believe me, and I would not endanger my men or any others for any reason. Let me talk to them," Lucius pleaded. "I can convince them that they will not suffer from being around me."

"Perhaps you would have done, in the past, but this time it's different, Tribune. The men are afraid. There have even been rumours that a young woman's ghost has been seen by the night watch, roaming the base at night." Lucius felt his heart tighten up. "Death's a funny fellow for soldiers. At a distance they talk of facing him down, challenging him, but when he approaches out of the dark, without warning and takes someone, even the toughest grunt is reduced to a quivering infant."

"What do you propose, Legate?" Lucius did not know what else to say. Marcellus had evidently made up his mind beforehand, had thought about this very conversation. Besides, Lucius knew he was right. He could feel the fear, see it in the eyes of his men and others.

"A few weeks ago, I wrote to the emperor to apprise him of the situation." Lucius' eyes betrayed his shock and embarrassment. "You have your duties, Tribune. I have mine. I informed the emperor of what had happened, the impact of it and how things stood at the time. Today a messenger has arrived with a reply."

Lucius wondered for a moment if it might have been another Praetorian spy in disguise. "Do you know if this man is legitimate, sir? I mean, what if the letter you sent, or the emperor's reply, was intercepted?"

Marcellus shook his head painfully. He knew it was exactly that sort of paranoia that affected an officer's performance in the field and felt genuinely sorry for Lucius. "I know this man. He's been the emperor's personal messenger for years and is completely trustworthy. He is...how shall I say this...untouched...by certain powers in Rome." Lucius knew what he meant by this. "This man only carries the most valuable of messages directly from Severus' hand to the intended recipient."

"May I ask what the emperor wishes to do with me?"

"You may, but not yet. The messenger has also brought letters for you. Two to be exact. He says he can only hand them to you. I have read mine. You will read yours first and then we'll talk some more." Marcellus clapped his hands and a guard showed the messenger in. Lucius stood, his helmet beneath his left arm, cautious of the stranger.

"Tribune Metellus?" The man was tall, strong-looking, with quick eyes and a deep voice. His clothing was ornate but he was heavily armed and looked as though he knew how to use the weapons he carried. He was not Roman, nor was he African. Lucius thought he recognised the accent then realised it was similar to the empress'. He was Syrian.

"Yes," Lucius replied. "You have dispatches for me?"

"I do." The man stepped forward and Lucius put his hand out to receive the missives. The messenger placed them into the tribune's hands with a certain amount of ceremony. He had completed his duty by delivering them directly. Lucius looked at him. "I must remain to see that you have opened the larger of the two and read it."

Lucius broke the wax seal on the papyrus and moved next to a brazier along the wall to read it. He recognised the hand.

For Tribune Lucius Metellus Anguis
From Julia Domna, on behalf of your Emperor,

Hail Tribune,

I have given this message into the hands of my trusted cousin to bring directly to you. You need not give him a reply.

News has reached me here in Rome about what has happened to you in Numidia. I am very sorry for your loss. Your legate has informed the emperor of the situation and as a result you will receive new orders from him. However, I wish to speak of something more, something for you and you alone. There has been an incident here in Rome. I do not know if you have been told already. Unfortunately time and circumstance require me to be blunt. Your father, Senator Quintus Caecilius Metellus, has been murdered within his own home.

The legate and the messenger watched Lucius' face as he read. They noticed the look of disbelief that crossed his features as he held the paper closer.

I know you must be shocked by this news. More shocking is who has committed the crime. Your father was killed by your mother, Antonia Metella. Luckily, I was told of this by the sculptor, Emrys, before certain other parties in Rome, and was able to send trusted people. Your mother has been placed under arrest within her home and your brother and sister are living with a family friend. I am afraid things must be this way for the moment, but take comfort.

Comfort! Lucius thought. *What Comfort?*

There is a way out of this, a way to save your mother and the rest of your family. I cannot outline anything in this letter. To put it plainly, your presence in Rome is required as soon as is possible. Once here, you must come to us. If you help us, we can help your family and bring to justice those who are responsible for your sister's untimely death.

You must be secretive in this and you must also bring one of your most trusted men. Your legate will have instructions as to this also. I cannot say any more on this matter.

Your Empress, Julia Domna.

Lucius dropped his hands at his side and stood gazing into the flames of the fire. Marcellus walked over to the messenger while Lucius was lost in thought.

"I must be going now," the messenger said. "My duty is fulfilled and I have a long journey ahead."

"I understand. Lartius, the camp prefect, will give you any supplies you need for your return journey."

"Thank you, Commander." The man turned to Lucius who looked back at him. "Farewell, Tribune." Lucius nodded absently, looked at the second letter in his hand. The man left and Marcellus poured them both some wine.

"Have a seat, Tribune." Lucius moved dazedly to the chair and sat, still gazing at the letter. "You don't have to tell me what you read. I'll tell you what I know and what I have been ordered to do." Lucius forced himself to look away from the letter and pay attention to the legate. There was a look of pity in the man's eyes and Lucius did not like it. Too much pity could suck the life out of a man.

"I've been informed of what has happened in Rome. I'm sorry about your mother and father. I am assured that your mother is safe enough for the moment. You know this?" Lucius nodded. "Good. In view of the effects of events here on the men, I've been told that I must relieve you of duty for the time being."

"Relieve me of duty?" Lucius raised his voice but the legate's look brought him back down.

"Calm yourself. You're still a tribune, simply unattached to this legion. You are of Equestrian rank and therefore entitled to certain things. The emperor knows your value as a commander and appreciates a good soldier. He won't dismiss you completely. However, it seems that you are needed for something in Rome. I don't know what. I'm a soldier and there are certain things I don't need to know. Thankfully. Suffice it to say that you are to pack up all your belongings and your family and leave Lambaesis. Your men will stay here as part of the III Augustan."

Lucius could not believe it. The look on his face betrayed the sadness he was feeling, the insult. He had been to Hades and back with his men and now they were being taken away from him. To be an officer without men to command felt empty.

"I know this hits you hard, Tribune. Gods know I understand, but events have been set in motion that are once more beyond our control. I have a feeling that you have some business of your own that you need to see to. All I can do is bid you a fond farewell, thank you, and wish you well as you stand among the lions and wolves of Rome. Look at me." Lucius looked him in the eyes. "Stay strong, Metellus, don't be rash. You're still a man of honour. *I* don't believe the Gods have turned on you."

"Haven't they, sir? I'm not so sure anymore."

"No, they haven't. I'm sure of it. Keep your wits about you and never lose sight of the gifts they have given you. Behind the blood and the darkness, the Gods often leave us precious gifts. You just have to fight your way through to them."

Lucius nodded.

"When should I leave, sir?"

"You can leave in one month. You know your men so you can take care of any appointments or promotions before you leave." Lucius nodded. "My orders are also to relieve one of your most trusted men to go with you. I've no idea why but I think I know who it should be."

"Me too, sir."

"Good. I know Alerio is your best friend in this place."

Lucius sat there for several moments in silence, thinking of all that was happening so quickly, so soon. Part of him was happy to leave Numidia but another part of him dreaded returning to Rome and facing what lay in store for him there. He rose from the chair, placed his helmet upon his head.

"It has been an honour serving under you, Legate Commander." He saluted Marcellus sharply.

"The honour has been mine, Metellus. Gods willing, our paths will cross again someday." Lucius felt a great sadness then, knew that this would be the last personal moment he would have with Marcellus. He thought it odd that he felt so much for a man whom he had feared when he first arrived in Lambaesis. Now, this old soldier that many had warned him about was bidding him a very fond farewell, saying that he hoped to see him again. Lucius tried to remember Marcellus that way instead of the leather-skinned brute that commonly ordered floggings for men who fell out of step on the march. For all Marcellus' years of brutal service, Lucius gained some hope from the fact that he had come through it all with his dignity and some measure of kindness intact.

"Thank you, Commander."

"Back to Rome? Why, Lucius? What's happened?" Adara laid the children down in their cribs and came to sit next to her husband. He told her about the empress' letter and the other letter from Emrys in which he told Lucius what had happened. Ambrosia had run to tell Emrys and Carissa. The children were safe with the Lady Claudia, and the empress' men had Antonia under arrest in her own home, more for her own protection. Officially, Emrys said, she was under arrest. He had seen her and said she appeared calm and very quiet. Quintus' body had been buried in the family mausoleum, along the via Appia. Apparently, though she was not present, Antonia had not wanted her husband to go to the other side without an honourable burial.

"Poor, poor Antonia." Adara was afraid for her mother-in-law whom she had grown to love very much. Inwardly, she felt nothing for the departed senator; he had been nothing but cruel to Lucius and apparently to his wife and children, as well as rude to her own family. "But what does the empress want you to do?"

"I don't know. All she said is that if I want to help mother and the rest of the family I was to report to her in Rome."

"But to leave Lambaesis?"

"It's out of my control. Besides, we have to bring Alene home."

"I'm afraid, Lucius." Adara stood and paced nervously. "I'm afraid for the children and you. Argus is still out there, isn't he?"

"Yes, he is." Lucius raged at the thought. "That's why I must go to Rome. The empress might be able to protect us."

"Oh, don't be naïve! She doesn't care about us. She wants something."

"Most likely, but so do I. I want to help mother and if I can, get to those who killed Alene."

"You know Alene would never want you to do such a thing."

"I know." Lucius was silent. Adara was right, but he knew he had no choice.

She came and sat beside him, put her arm around him.

"You know I will follow you anywhere, Lucius, don't you?"

"Yes."

"Whatever you decide, I'm with you. I said I'd never allow us to be parted again and I meant it." She paused. "Have you told Alerio and Ashur about this?"

"Not yet. I'll tell them tonight at dinner. Are Mar and Dagon eating with us tonight too?"

"Yes. Dagon came by earlier to tell me."

"Good. They'll want to know."

Lucius left Adara to arrange things with Xeno for the evening meal while he went to the baths to ease the day's tension and think on what lay ahead. Looking at the steaming water, he wondered if life would ever be calm and glassy like the early-morning sea in summer or whether it would be a sea of endless winter, lashing him with stinging waves.

Mar and Dagon were speechless on their couches while Alerio sat stern-faced and lost in far-away thoughts. The meal had been magnificent but it was little comfort in the face of the news they had just received. Ashur too was silent, hoped that Carissa was safe; he held a secret admiration for Antonia and the strength and selflessness she had shown.

"When do you leave, Anguis?" Mar's voice was calm, sad.

"One month. Already, I've been relieved from duty."

"Hmph!" Dagon was disgusted. "I thought Roman troops were the toughest. No Sarmatian would shudder when death was near."

"It's hard to explain, Dagon," Lucius eased.

"After all you've given to those men!" Alerio spoke for the first time. "I can't believe I didn't see this coming."

"We've had a lot on our minds, Alerio."

"I know, Lucius, but...by Mars, they should stand by you."

"They've stood by me through more than I can ask of them. I'm no Alexander. Besides, the legate is right. Without discipline, the legion and the frontier it protects are in danger. I don't want to be the one responsible for that. My duty is to Rome...and my family."

"I wish we could go with you, Anguis." Dagon pounded his fist on the couch but Mar put his hand on his nephew's arm.

"We all wish that, Dagon, but we are all Rome's servants and we go where we are needed," he looked sad, "and where we are told."

"You're needed here most of all, Mar." Lucius tried to comfort him. "Besides, where we're going it's a different sort of battlefield. Heavy cavalry wouldn't be of much use."

"You are right, Anguis, but trusted friends would." Lucius nodded. "Well, the least we can do is to provide you with a safe escort to the sea. I'll speak to the legate about it."

Xeno entered with more wine and a platter of honey cakes and fruit. When all their cups were full, they toasted each other, their friendship, their gods and their future. Though nobody said it, they each knew that it was the last time they would enjoy such a meal and such company for a long time to come and hoped that the following month would pass slowly.

When October and its windy chill emerged from the tail end of summer, the time had finally come for Lucius, his family, Alerio, Ashur and their escort to depart from Lambaesis. Much of the legion had turned out to see the tribune off and saluted

Lucius as he passed, giving him the respect he deserved and had earned, as a parting gift.

Valerus and Pephredo were left in charge of the remainder of Lucius' cohort along with another man named Paulus, whom Alerio had appointed to centurion of his own men. In front of the Principia stood the legate, flanked by the other tribunes of the III Augustan. Each man remembered doubting Lucius when he had first arrived but realised that they were bidding farewell, with mixed emotions, to a skilled commander and a true Roman. Lucius saluted them all as he passed and was touched to see the kind look that Marcellus gave to him as he and Adara passed, a look of hope, of wishes for a bright future.

As the massive gates heaved open, three horns sounded from the battlements. Lucius felt his heart beating hard and his throat tighten up. Despite all that had happened in that place, he regretted leaving it.

Front and rear of the column, the Sarmatian banners were flying high in the autumn breeze along with Lucius' own banner which he had been allowed to keep as a symbolic gesture that he would someday return to his command. He rode Lunaris beside one of the wagons in which Adara and the children rode. There were cushions and blankets piled up for their comfort and for the protection of the large wooden chest that carried the urn containing Alene's remains.

As the road turned north, in the direction of Hippo Regius, Lucius reined in on the side of the road to look back one last time at Lambaesis. Its walls stood tall and strong as the horns rang out for him one last time in that land of red rock and sand. He would miss the desert, the legate and Xeno. The old slave had been greatly saddened by Lucius' departure. In return for his loyalty, Lucius had given him a bag of silver denarii to buy his freedom if he wished. Truth was however, that with Lucius, Xeno had never felt like a slave, but rather an old friend. He had wept when Lucius told him he was leaving, knew that his years would not be enough to allow him to see him or Adara again or their children grown.

The week before, Lucius had gone with Adara to Thamugadi to bid farewell to Marius Nelek, his family and Dido. Lucius had decided not to tell Marius about what had happened in Rome, simply saying that his orders had changed and that he had been re-assigned. Marius put it down to Emperor Severus' compulsive reorganisation of the legions and left it at that. The children were sad to see Tribune Lucius go but there was none sadder than Dido. She had been given a new life by Lucius, a new beginning.

Lucius had told her in private. At first Adara had been dismayed by this but realised that Lucius was telling Dido exactly what had happened and that that was why they were leaving. She was afraid for Lucius, Adara and the children and said that she would pray to her Punic gods every day for their safety. She tried not to let her past feelings re-emerge, she had grown adept at masking them. Her tears however, were not to be withheld.

When it came time for Lucius and his family to leave, Dido had found it difficult to speak, unable to find words to express her sadness at seeing them go, saying goodbye to him. She kissed the children, who wore the gifts she had made them. When Lucius walked up to her to say his farewell, Dido looked him in the eyes, placed her hand upon his chest, and ran inside without another word. There were no words.

"We'll watch over her, Lucius," Marius had said. "She's family now, and family's the most important thing in this mess of a world."

"Yes, it is," Lucius agreed, feeling his wife and children next to him. "Thank you, my friend."

"Safe journey to all of you. May the Gods love you."

So many farewells in so little time. People, places, friends and comrades. Lucius thought of them all as he looked his last upon Lambaesis before turning Lunaris and riding to the front of the column and a view of the road ahead.

XXIX

IMPERIUM URBANUM

'A Polite Command'

After a few days at sea, the solid ground of Ostia was a welcome sight, an even more welcome feeling beneath one's feet. The port was busy, as usual, and it took some effort for Lucius to arrange a secure unloading of all their baggage, including Lunaris and Phoenix, who stumbled around a bit until they found their own land legs.

Adara was probably the only one who had enjoyed the journey; she had not realised how much she had missed the sea, its colour and its smell. While Lucius arranged for slaves to help with their belongings with the harbour master, Ashur and Alerio stayed with Adara and the children next to the stacked trunks and crates. Ashur kept his wits about him, never having liked the port and the innumerable sticky-fingered characters who were likely to take the clothes off of one's back before they were noticed missing. Alerio was quiet, as he had been the entire voyage, watching over the chest that contained the urn.

"Has Lucius decided how we are to get to Rome and where you will stay?" Ashur finally asked Adara during a lull in crowd movement around them.

"I think he was going to arrange for land transport to Rome. I believe we're going to stay at the house."

"Really? I would have thought that with Antonia under arrest it would be impossible." Ashur did not like that idea at all.

"That's what I told Lucius but he says it's his right as a Roman citizen and heir to his father, that he should be able to remain in his family's home."

"There must be another way," Ashur pushed. "The children would be…affected…by what has happened there." Adara did not answer. She had not thought of that.

Finally Lucius returned, sweating and frustrated at the chaotic mess that always accompanied bureaucracy at port. He was followed by a gang of slaves and a freedman. They stood by at a distance until the hired wagons arrived.

"Everything all right?" Ashur asked his flustered friend. Alerio looked up and walked over to Lucius.

"Ach. What a mess. There's no better logistic organisation than in the army. When you don't have it you sure miss it." He waved a hand in the air. "Anyway. I managed to hire some wagons and these slaves here to carry everything."

"Perhaps we should hire a bodyguard too, Lucius," Adara said casually. Lucius paused, thought about it.

"You're right. We should have an escort. I saw some for hire on the other side of the harbour. I'll be back." Lucius turned to walk away but was stopped by a man on his other side. Ashur's dagger and Alerio's sword were out before anything was said but Lucius put up his hand the second he recognised the man.

"Tribune Metellus." It was the messenger who had come to Lambaesis. The man nodded in greeting.

"You? What are you doing here?"

"I think it would be best, Tribune, if you kept your voice down." The man casually looked around. Lucius noticed that his clothes were less elaborate this time. Ostia was always crawling with spies.

"Fine," Lucius whispered. "What are you doing here? I didn't know that you were to meet us."

"My mistress thought it would be a good idea."

"Your mistress? You mean your cousin."

"Yes. She is that also. She has asked me to accompany you, your family and your friends to a villa where she believes you will be safe during your stay in Rome." Lucius shook his head.

618

"I plan to stay in my family's home while we are in Rome. Thank your mistress for me." The man inhaled patiently through his nostrils and looked more intently upon Lucius, unperturbed by the presence of Alerio and Ashur on either side of him.

"That is quite impossible, Tribune. My mistress has seen to your mother's safety as she remains inside your family domus but, your own safety cannot be guaranteed as yet. I cannot say any more except that you must come to this place I speak of. My *cousin*, wishes for me to assure you that you will be safe there."

"One moment." Lucius stepped back to talk with Alerio and Ashur.

"Who is this, Lucius?" Alerio whispered.

"He's the empress' personal messenger. I've met him before."

"Can we trust him?"

"I think so."

"What else *can* you do?" Ashur asked.

"Not much. Now that I think about it, maybe being in the city is not the safest thing." Lucius scratched his head. "We'll go with him but let's be ready for anything." They both nodded and Lucius turned back to the messenger. "We'll go with you. You're sure this is a safe place where we are headed?"

"Yes, very safe, Tribune. My mistress has seen to everything personally."

"Fine then. I'll have the slaves load up the wagons."

"That won't be necessary."

"Why not?"

"Because I have already arranged for a barge to carry all of us to our destination." The messenger began to walk to the other side of the docks where a man on a barge waved to him.

"All right. Let's go. Lucius motioned to the slaves to load the baggage onto the barge instead. They all made their way on board. Alerio stayed behind until all the baggage was safely loaded and then joined the rest.

"Shove off!" the captain of the barge called out to his mates as they scurried to untie the ropes and push the barge down the Tiber toward Rome.

It was a peaceful journey down river. The water was oddly calm and the first of the autumn leaves fell gently upon the surface. Birds sang in the trees and the sun began to make its way past midday in its westerly arc. Adara sat under a shelter with the children, while Lucius tried to calm the horses who were not at all happy about being on another boat. They reminded him of his Sarmatian friends whom he had left behind on the sandy shores of Numidia.

He hoped that he would see Mar and Dagon again. They had grown extremely close in the time they had spent together, become friends upon whom Lucius could count if ever he was in need. Unfortunately, the duties of empire dictated that they should not be together for whatever lay ahead in Rome. Lucius remembered the uncharacteristic look of worry upon Mar's face when they had parted ways. The noble Sarmatian was, always had been, wary of Rome and her ways. In private he was pessimistic and doubtful of the trustworthiness of the empress and her people, but there was little he could do or say besides telling Lucius to be cautious of everyone that crossed his path.

Lucius thought of this and looked at the empress' cousin where he stood at the front of the barge, staring straight ahead along the shore. He walked over to him, not unnoticed by Ashur or Alerio.

"You have not given me your name," Lucius told the man.

"It is not permitted for me to give you my name." The man smiled knowingly.

"And why is that?"

"My duty carries much responsibility, and even more danger. The fewer people who know about me, the better."

"I know you are the empress' cousin."

"It was her prerogative to reveal that information. I trust her judgement."

"I see." Lucius leaned on the railing of the barge. "She said that she wanted to see me when I arrive in Rome." The man nodded. "When will that be? Is the place where we are going to stay within the city?"

"The place where you will be staying is just outside the city. As for your meeting with my mistress, I will let you know when it is time for you and your centurion to meet with her."

"Very well." It was obvious to Lucius that he was not going to get any more information out of this fellow. One more question came to his mind, more of a curiosity. "Did you know the empress' man Drusus?"

The messenger shot Lucius a quick, pained, revealing look. He stared down at the black water where the barge caused ripples at the prow. "I did know him...well."

"He was very good to me in Africa." Lucius remembered the short, friendly man that had kept him safe in Leptis Magna.

"Drusus was a good man, and a good friend."

"I am sorry he is gone." Lucius tried to comfort, feeling guilty for having brought it up.

"Many are." The messenger said no more about Drusus or anything else for the time being and Lucius returned to sit with Adara and the children who were dozing calmly under the small shelter, the slow lumbering of the barge having lulled them to sleep.

A short time later, the captain began to shout out orders to his crew and Lucius went to the front of the barge to where the messenger was still standing, signalling to a group of men gathered on a small, private jetty hidden among leaning trees. They appeared armed but were calm as the barge approached and the ropes were tossed to them. Lucius noticed how un-Roman they appeared.

"If any harm comes to my family, messenger, I'll slit your throat." Lucius was unnerved by the armed men but the messenger spoke calmly, despite the threat.

"Do not trouble yourself, Tribune. These men are some of my mistress' personal Syrian guard. You will be well protected." He pointed to the trees where the hill sloped upward; only just visible were several men with bows, forming a defensive perimeter on what appeared to be an estate of sorts.

"I see. Forgive my hastiness."

"I understand, Tribune. You have all been through much. Your caution is understandable. My mistress only wishes to help." The messenger jumped onto the jetty and had some words with the men there who all turned toward Lucius, Adara and the others, and bowed. Lucius nodded back. Meanwhile, Alerio and Ashur's eyes were scanning every inch of the place.

They were on a thickly wooded estate along the Tiber. No buildings were visible yet as the party followed the messenger up a neatly paved pathway, the luggage and horses following after. Once they cleared the dark trees and came to the top of the embankment, a vast, one-storey complex came into view. It was surrounded by high walls and other trees all around. There were several slaves waiting outside as the guests were brought up.

"The entire household staff has been handpicked by my mistress," the messenger said to Lucius and Adara. "They have been told to see to your every need while you are here." He turned to the head slave. "Are the baths ready for our guests?" The slave nodded once. "Good. You may bathe if you wish before the evening meal." Lucius was very impatient and stepped forward to lead the man aside.

"When may I see my mother?"

"Oh, that will not be possible."

"No? Then when am I to meet with the empress?"

"You, and your centurion, will be called upon soon. I will come and take you to her when the time comes."

"How do we get to the city? We have friends there."

"I'm afraid that none of you can leave the estate." Lucius began to protest but the man raised a pleading hand and lowered his voice. "You see, Tribune, you are *not* supposed to be here, in Rome. The fewer people who know this, the better it will be for you."

"How long must we stay here?"

"I do not know. Rest assured that here you are safe and will want for nothing."

That was it. Lucius knew the man was finished. Before he realised it, they were being ushered into the villa.

The building was simple and elegant with long marble corridors, frescoed walls and choice pieces of statuary in niches throughout. There were several courtyard gardens with fountains and fruit trees. As they walked through the buildings to their various rooms, Lucius noticed that all of the servants were Syrian. His suspicions eased. Luckily, the estate was well protected. He wondered exactly how far they were from the city.

The rooms that were given over to Lucius and Adara faced onto a private garden where the sound of a trickling fountain reached their ears. Fresh, scented linens had been set out and their baggage had already been placed in an adjacent room so that they would not worry about its whereabouts. Lucius checked immediately for the wooden chest with the urn; it was there, safe.

Adara laid the children on a smaller bed next to the large one and turned to Lucius. "What's happening here, Lucius?"

"Apparently, we have to remain on the estate."

"For how long?"

"I don't know. All he said was that we were to stay here and that nobody in Rome is to know of our presence."

"I don't like this secrecy. You're a Roman tribune! You should enter the city with pride to meet with your empress."

"Not this time." He realised she did not fully realise the severity of the situation. He was not sure he did either. "I'm here to help mother and to avenge Alene. The empress said she would help me."

"But Lucius…" Adara crossed the room and made sure the door was closed. "She doesn't care for you, or us," she whispered.

"She does more than the Consul."

"Lucius, I'm frightened. This is Rome now, not Athens, or Leptis Magna, or Lambaesis."

"I know." He put his arm around her. "I also know that I don't have a choice. Whatever she asks of me, I will have to do." Adara could not hear anymore. She rose from the edge of the bed and walked through the arch that led into the garden. She would not be able to spend long in that place, a strange villa outside Rome where the nights would be dark and silent and they were surrounded by strangers. It was more like a prison than a home. She reached out gently and felt the soft edges of a delicate jasmine blossom where it ran along one wall of the garden.

She missed Alene and remembered her love of the jasmine bushes in Athens. Adara shook her head and fought back the frustration she was feeling with Lucius. She knew he was only doing what he thought was right. She spied their children dozing on the bed and knew that Lucius' hands were bound. In Rome, one needed powerful friends to survive, especially when they protected one against powerful enemies.

Her mother and father came into her mind then, her sisters too. For them, life would be simple; shopping in the Agora, taking care of the estate, her mother painting. Nothing complicated, nothing dangerous. Here in Rome, however, one could not take a step without the fear of setting one's foot upon the tail of some viper that would strike to kill instantly and without regret. Adara knew that she could not bear to remain calm behind high walls. She had to do something to help her family, something that would ensure their safety to a greater extent. After thinking about it for several minutes, she decided that she would get to know each and every one of the household staff and any of the guards she met. She would be kind and grateful for their help, so kind that they would see her and the others as more than just guests. She wanted to cultivate their loyalty to the empress so that they would be loyal to her and Lucius while they were there. If the servants could be trusted, then at least they might be safer within the walls of the estate.

After bathing, Lucius, Adara and the children, Ashur and Alerio reclined in the large triclinium for a sumptuous meal, an extremely welcome change from the simple fare of sea travel. Ashur and Alerio said that their quarters were very comfortable. They wanted to know what was happening, so Lucius told them what little he knew.

Ashur was dismayed at having to remain there as he had planned on going into the city to stay with Carissa.

"What can I say, Ashur? This is what I've been told. Those are my orders." Lucius could see that his friend was upset at being confined by his orders but knew that if Ashur were to be seen in Rome it could go badly for them. Alerio on the other hand was calm, his mind fixed on the task they had been called to perform, whatever it was. All he hoped was that it would be a chance for revenge.

While the men talked carefully of the situation, out of earshot of the slaves that were waiting upon them, Adara began her own mission of endearing the household servants to them. Two of the serving women had seemed curious about the children and Adara had bidden them over so that she could speak with them and discover their names. They were not very fluent in Latin but knew Greek perfectly well, and so they were doubly happy to be speaking with the new guest in a language in which they were more comfortable. They cooed as little Calliope began to hum and stayed as long as they could to listen before their next duty required them to leave.

That night, after a filling meal, the empress' guests settled down in their individual quarters to sleep and be left with their own thoughts, of family, of duty, of loves near and departed. It was dark and quiet outside, and the October winds brought a cold white mist that cloaked the outer world.

Two weeks passed and they were well into November. Impatience became a daily companion for Lucius as he waited for his summons. Every morning he would rise, bathe and ask the house steward for any messages and every morning he was told the same thing. "Sorry, Tribune. Nothing today."

Adara had settled as best she could, having gotten to know most of the Syrian staff on the estate so that they were greeted kindly and respectfully around every corner and never had to ask for anything. The children were growing quickly and beginning to crawl about the garden where Adara spent much of the day with them. It had come to a point where she felt safe in the private garden and took advantage of any sunny days tinted with warmth.

Being forced to find some way of occupying their own time, Lucius, Alerio and Ashur took it upon themselves to train with each other every day on the sprawling grass of the estate. It was essential that they stay fit and keep from being bored to death. Having no gymnasium in which to exercise, the men kept their sword and shield arms in shape, sparring with each other one on one, two on one in various combinations. Lucius also exercised Lunaris and Phoenix daily, giving the stallions the chance to run and jump and socialise with their human counterparts.

One afternoon, while Lucius and Adara were enjoying a light meal in the private garden and playing with the children, there was a knock upon the door. Lucius grabbed his sword where it leaned against a tree and went to answer it.

"Yes? Who is it?"

"Tribune. I have a message for you." Lucius recognised the voice and opened the door to see the empress' cousin standing before him.

"I was beginning to think we had been forgotten." Lucius tried to hide any sign of anger he was feeling.

"Not at all, Tribune. You are remembered."

"You have a message?"

"Yes. My mistress will be here shortly, with Caesar Antoninus, to speak with you." Lucius felt his heart jump in his chest and his nerves prickle in his stomach.

"Whe...when?" The messenger smiled at Lucius' surprise.

"This evening."

"Why here? I thought that my centurion and I were to go into Rome when they called."

"Things have changed. My mistress will be here this evening to join you for dinner. I have already instructed the servants and they know what to do. You are asked to be prompt."

"Very well. I shall be ready."

The messenger nodded. "Good. Now, Tribune, if you will excuse me, I must see that all of the guards on the estate are briefed and prepared for this evening." The man turned and went down the marble corridor to go about his business.

Lucius shut the door, feeling suddenly very nervous. Adara came up to him holding the children in her arms. "Who was it?"

"The empress' messenger."

"Has she called for you to go into the city?"

"No." He looked her in the eyes. "She's coming here tonight...with Caracalla."

Adara said nothing but Lucius could tell she felt as nervous as he did. She had not met privately with either of them. Lucius on the other hand had spoken privately with the empress before. It was Caracalla that made him nervous; he had always felt ill-at-ease in the presence of the emperor's first son. More so now because Adara would be there too. Silently, Lucius and Adara set out the clothes they were going to wear.

Oil lamps and braziers had been lit all along the corridors, and mouth-watering scents wafted from the kitchens as Lucius and the others stood at the main entrance of the estate to greet the empress when she arrived with her son. Beneath his toga, Lucius felt his heart pounding. It was cold outside, but he felt as though it was mid-summer. Adara stood beside him wrapped in a saffron stola, the children in her arms. She did not want to leave them alone and thought that since they were quiet they would not offend. Next to them, Alerio stood in a plain white toga he had not worn in a long time, and Ashur next to him, in a long blue tunic with an ornate belt about his waist.

There came shouts from outside and then the sound of a heavy iron gate creaking open. Torches appeared in the darkness beyond, held by rows of bodyguards whose swords and buckles jingled as they entered the front courtyard. They surrounded two large litters each carried by eight Syrian slaves. All the colours were dark, Lucius assumed, to maintain cover in the night. The litters were carefully set down and the curtains of the first one pulled aside by two slaves. A pair of legs swung outward, belonging to an old man, neatly dressed in a crisp, white toga. He said nothing but turned and held out a hand.

From out of the darkness within came a dark, jewelled hand draped in purple silk. Golden sandals came lightly to the ground and out came the empress, her face veiled. Out of the second litter emerged a husky figure, outlined by a full-length cloak of black wool. There were immense shoulders beneath and the pommel of a sword protruded from the front. He grunted, stretched and turned to come over to the empress who took his arm.

As they approached, the old man in tow, Lucius and the others bowed respectfully, waiting for a word. The empress stopped in front of Lucius and pulled back her veil. "You may rise." Her voice was soft and as Lucius met her gaze he felt more at ease. Caracalla stood back for a moment, waiting for another man who was coming out of the litter.

"Augusta," Lucius said reverently. "We thank you for bringing us here to safety. I am your servant."

"Tribune Metellus. It has been a long time since Leptis Magna." She smiled slightly and then her gaze moved to Adara. "And Lady Metella."

"Augusta. We thank you for your kindness." Adara bowed again and little Phoebus squealed. The empress laughed affably.

"I congratulate you, my dear, on such beautiful children." The empress acknowledged Alerio and Ashur while Caracalla strode up to Lucius with a man who had a tough, scarred face and wore a gladius close to his body.

Caracalla pulled back the hood of his long cloak and smiled, but only very slightly. He looked different, Lucius noticed. His hair was tightly curled and he had a fuller beard than before. There were new creases across his brow and he seemed stronger, his confidence bordering on arrogance. Lucius bowed as he approached.

"Caesar. It is an honour to see you again." Lucius did not know quite what else to say and hoped it would go over well. Caracalla smiled beneath his beard, came forward and clasped Lucius' forearm like a soldier.

"Tribune Metellus!" His voice was uncommonly friendly. "Good to see you here. You have our thanks for coming." Lucius could only smile and bow again. Caracalla continued. "You have my congratulations on the birth of your children too." He smiled at Adara who bowed slightly. He looked at Alerio and Ashur who bent at his gaze. "Gentlemen." Caracalla stepped back and motioned to the two men that had accompanied them. "This is my tutor, Euodus." The old man bowed. "And another one of our esteemed men of the legions, Saturninus." The soldier nodded, forced a rough smile.

Lucius greeted both men, wondered what they could possibly have been there for. They followed the empress and

Caracalla down the corridor to the triclinium where steaming platters of meats and breads awaited them beside beakers of wine.

The meal had been one of pleasant, veiled converse. Lucius suspected they were building to more weighty matters which they would breach once the meal was finished. There had been no music or poetry performed by slaves at this small banquet, the setting much more exact, planned. The empress had reclined at the head couch along with her son. Lucius and Adara sat next to them. Adara had tried to maintain converse with the empress much of the time so as to avoid the discomfiting gaze of Caracalla that would occasionally break through his friendly exterior. Fortunately, Lucius was able to remain locked in conversation with the young Caesar most of the time, covering all manner of military topics in desert warfare. The extent of Caracalla's knowledge quite astonished Lucius.

Alerio had slight conversation with Saturninus across the table and Ashur debated lightly on philosophy with the prickly old man, Euodus. The empress had been very kind and genuine to Adara over the entire evening, giving her tips as to what to expect after the children's first year of life. She even remembered Publius and Delphina and asked after them.

Julia Domna reclined on her own couch, amid purple folds and gold jewellery. Her hair was the same as always: tightly wound and bound close to her head in an ornate swirling pattern. Her fine features looked more beautiful when she smiled, which was often, it seemed to Adara, and her eyes relaxed the listener. Because of this, it was all the more evident that things were about to change when the empress' features tightened and her smile departed. Caracalla took notice of this and set his cup aside, crossed his arms and waited for his mother to speak.

"I think that it is now time for us to come to the business at hand." Julia Domna turned to Lucius. "Tribune, we will require the presence of you and your centurion."

Lucius nodded and Adara rose with the children. It was obvious that she was not to be included in the remainder of the evening. Ashur felt Caracalla's cool gaze upon him, and rose from his couch to go out with Adara. As they went down the hall, the sound of the closing doors behind them, Adara asked Ashur to remain with her and the children in the garden. He agreed, knowing that she did not wish to be left alone in a house where the young Caesar was in attendance.

"Now, gentlemen. I know you have many questions." The empress looked at Lucius. "I know you have been through much and that you wish to put an end to certain doubts you might have. We want the same thing. First of all, Tribune," the empress said as she actually reached out and touched Lucius' arm, "let me say that we are deeply sorry for the pain your family has experienced. We are sorry for the loss of your dear sister and for the situation in which your mother now finds herself."

Julia Domna and Caracalla watched as the effects of what was said showed on both Lucius and Alerio's faces. There was still much pain there, much anger. Lucius nodded, acknowledging the wishes. Euodus and Saturninus sat silently in the background. The empress continued.

"Now. A great deal has happened in Rome while you have both been away. You both know Gaius Fulvius Plautianus." Lucius and Alerio nodded. "Of course you do. We all know him. What you will not have seen are the thousands of statues of him adorning our city, more than of our emperor. You will not have heard the public prayers made to him in all the squares and temples. You will not have seen the fear in the faces of citizens as they walk the streets of Rome. It is no great secret that the Praetorian prefect and consul is Rome's most powerful and most dangerous man. He is dangerous not only to yourselves and the Roman people, but also to our own

631

family and the whole of the empire." The empress stopped speaking and looked to Caracalla to continue.

"Gentlemen, it's widely known that I have always despised Plautianus. He has used my father, fouled the reputation of my mother with false rumours and betrayed the trust of the Roman people. I despise him even more now for what he has done to the empire which the emperor, my father, has always sought to preserve with the help of men such as you, men who have bled and given their lives for the sake of Rome." Caracalla got up from his couch and circled the room like an orator. "The emperor, has been misled by his cousin Plautianus, and it is up to the rest of us to come to his aid. The scoundrel has harmed all of us in one form or another, most recently you, Tribune Metellus."

"Sire?" Lucius was not sure where all this was leading.

"Yes, Tribune. It was Plautianus who corrupted your father, the late Senator Metellus. It was Plautianus who sent spies to kill you and your family in Numidia. It was Plautianus who was, is, responsible for the death of your sister, Alene Metella."

Lucius felt the heat beneath his toga again, his anger rising. *Why is he saying all of this?* Alerio was not so skilled at hiding his anger and slammed a fist on his couch, bringing an understanding smile to Saturninus' lips.

"It is true, now I think if it." Lucius knew that Plautianus was behind everything. All their pain. He had felt the evil from that first encounter with the man, the hate.

"Of course it's true, Tribune. That's why we have brought you here." Caracalla sat down again, feeling a thrill of excitement.

"But, sire, begging your pardon, but why have we been waiting so long in this place? I was expecting our summons much earlier." Lucius' question was impertinent. The empress answered.

"You see, Tribune, we had planned on seeing you sooner, but much has happened in the past two weeks in Rome."

"What, my Lady?"

"The emperor's brother, my uncle Geta," Caracalla continued, "has made the journey to the other side in the last two weeks. He was never one to grovel to or be fooled by Plautianus. On his deathbed, my uncle spoke to the emperor about Plautianus' treachery, something nobody ever dared to speak of to the emperor for fear of Plautianus. Only I was in the room with them at the time. My father listened to his own brother. Only yesterday he erected a bronze statue of my uncle in the Forum Romanum. Furthermore, as a result of what my uncle said, the emperor has taken away many of Plautianus' powers in the provinces."

"Of course," the empress began again, "Plautianus, knowing my son's dislike for him, blames him for this. I feel his own life is in danger now."

Caracalla made a dismissive sound and waved his hand as though he was declining more snails at a banquet.

The empress continued. "I do not share his slight appraisal of the situation. Plautianus has many spies, as you know. He is still dangerous. We believe he is planning to assassinate the emperor and my sons."

Lucius found it difficult to care after what had happened to Alene, but he knew it would be wise to look shocked and upset. "I can't believe he would be so bold!"

"He would, Tribune. He'll stop at nothing to gain even more power." Caracalla bared his white teeth.

"Have your spies tortured any of Plautianus' men to get this information?"

"We have something more solid than a tortured slave's testimony. Saturninus here," he motioned to the seated centurion, "is one of ten centurions, he says, that were approached by Plautianus to carry out the assassination." Lucius looked at the man who nodded gravely. "Being a good Roman, Saturninus brought the letter to my tutor, Euodus here, in the hopes that he would warn me. He did." Euodus nodded.

"What of the other nine centurions?" Lucius asked. The three other men looked at each other while the empress sipped her wine.

"They would not identify themselves and we couldn't risk approaching them without alarming Plautianus." Caracalla crossed his arms and stared at Lucius.

"But sire, the word of one centurion against the Praetorian prefect and consul of Rome... Would it be believable to the emperor and the senate?"

"The senate must be left out of it. Plautianus has purchased most of them. But, you are correct. The word of one man will not do. That is why we need your help, both of you."

The room was silent. Lucius glanced over at a still-faced Alerio, at Saturninus and Euodus, and back to Caracalla and the empress. "What can we do?"

"Tribune," the empress spoke finally, "you, and your centurion," she nodded to Alerio, "are the only men we can trust in this. You yourself hail from one of Rome's greatest families and you, above all others, know what Plautianus is capable of."

"But what, Augusta, can *I* do to sway the balance? I myself am marked by Plautianus and his spies. The moment I enter Rome, I'll be killed."

"We would see you safe, as we are now." It was a reminder, not an answer. "What you can do is simple enough, though it requires great courage, something you do not lack." Lucius leaned forward to listen. He was confused, his head spinning as he tried not to miss a thing. "You and your centurion must swear that you were approached by Plautianus' agents, like Saturninus here, to kill the emperor."

She stopped speaking for a moment. Lucius tried not to look aghast, afraid. "The emperor has always admired you, men like you. Before him, you will swear that you said no to the assassination plot and that because of your refusal, Plautianus sent men to kill you, your wife and your children and that it ended with the death of your sister."

"I don't know that I'll be believed..."

"Don't worry so much, Tribune," Caracalla said. "It doesn't matter if that is not exactly the way things happened. The fact is that Plautianus *is* responsible for the death of your sister and for your mother's current imprisonment." Lucius looked at him, wanted to ask what it had to do with his mother but Caracalla's eyes were challenging. "If you do this, Tribune, you will avenge your sister, you will free your mother and you will help us. We shall not forget it."

"The fact is, Tribune, that because of my husband's brother's brave words on his deathbed, Plautianus' position is temporarily weakened. The Gods have presented us with an opportunity. You can help us, but at the same time you can help your family. Your name will be lauded in the streets of Rome and your mother will be free again. I am sure that we could avoid her trial being held in the criminal courts; the Questiones are not very lenient when it comes to murder. Of course, we all know that she did it to save her family, that is not in question here. Things could however, be made easier for her if she were tried as the Honestiores, as is the right of the Equestrian class. I would see to it personally that she be given comfortable exile rather than the prescribed punishment."

For the first time all evening, the empress' voice was hard and unwavering. Lucius knew that if his mother was not exiled from Rome she would be executed as the law prescribed. He knew he was not being given a choice. All eyes in the room were upon him. He looked at Alerio who nodded. He was up for it, no questions, but Lucius knew he had much more to lose. If he said yes there was a chance that Plautianus would find out and have him killed. Then Adara and the children would be alone and his mother executed anyway. If he said no, his mother would be dead and he, Adara and the children would probably not live out the night. He already knew too much.

The empress saw him thinking and reached out again with her perfumed hand. "Do you remember Leptis Magna?"

Lucius looked up, concealing the surprise on his face. He remembered that she had said she wished to help him and did. He also remembered that she was the only one who knew that he had killed the Praetorian guardsman there. She smiled sympathetically, but Lucius could not be sure what she was referring to: the fact that she had shown she was willing to help him or the fact that she knew of his guilt.

Lucius knew that he had to agree and hoped that he was making the right decision. He did want to help his mother. He did want revenge for Alene's death. He had vowed it. Also, now that he thought of it, this was a chance for him to restore the honour of his family name after the damage his father had done to it. He was the pillar holding up the ancient temple of his ancestors and he could either stand strong or crumble and let the world about him collapse.

"What do you say, Tribune?" Caracalla was growing impatient. "Are you going to help us?"

Lucius stood up, stepped back to look at all of them and bowed deeply to the empress and her son, his right hand over his heart. "I am your humble servant, yours to command."

"As am I," Alerio said as he too rose and bowed.

Caracalla nodded his approval and the empress rose from her couch, smiling broadly, her face dark and radiant.

"You honour us with your loyalty, both of you," she said. "And now, we must return to Rome before Plautianus' men discover our whereabouts.

"Before you go, Augusta…" The empress turned her dark eyes to Lucius. "When shall you require us?"

"We shall summon you when the time is right. For now, remain as you are. Train, take care of your beautiful wife and children, and above all maintain your resolve in this. I will see that your mother is safe for as long as it takes."

Caracalla walked over to Lucius and clasped his forearm again. "When this is all over, Metellus, I won't forget your help." Somehow Lucius failed to see the comfort in the words.

"Sire." Lucius bowed and Caracalla went out, following after Saturninus and Euodus.

"Do you think he suspects anything, Euodus?" Saturninus asked the old tutor as they got into the litter.

"No, Saturninus. I don't. Remember, not everyone will say anything for a bag of gold." Saturninus laughed as they got up into the litter.

Inside, Lucius escorted Julia Domna down the dimly-lit corridor to the main entrance. She had given him her arm as they walked but had not said anything more for several paces.

"I will see that your family is well protected, Tribune. That I promise."

"I am grateful, Augusta," Lucius said formally. She stopped then and turned to him.

"It is I who am grateful, Tribune." Julia Domna then leaned forward, pressed her lips to Lucius' cheek. The scent of body oils enveloped them. He remained still, knew he could not back away without insulting her. "Do take care," she whispered as her lips pulled away slowly and she replaced her veil over her head. He bowed low and watched her form recede into the darkness outside. The curtains of her litter closed behind her.

Servants scrambled about to open the gates quickly and let the bodyguards and their charges through. The gates were closed just as quickly and the torches outside dimmed. Alerio came to stand beside Lucius.

"Looks like we're in deep now, doesn't it?"

"Too deep, I'm afraid," Lucius replied.

"Well, I'm going to bed now. I'm beat after all the intrigue. See you tomorrow for training?"

Lucius nodded. As he walked the corridors back to Adara and the children, he felt as though he was drowning, utterly devoid of the ability to tread water. Politics had always been a deep, dark water to him and now he had been pushed in headlong, from the highest precipice. To survive, he would have to stay calm and not flail about losing strength. Most of all he would have to keep a wary eye for predators that might spring out of some hidden crevice to devour him and his entire family.

XXX

GAIUS FULVIUS PLAUTIANUS

Saturnalia passed without incident in the streets of Rome that year. As was the custom, all the shops had been closed for the duration of the festival and gambling was permitted in public. The Praetorians had maintained a strong presence throughout the festivities causing many of the usual rabble-rousers to tread much more carefully. If any brawls or disagreements over gambling debts broke out, they were put to an end quickly and without mercy. This threat meant that the old year went out calmly and carefully.

Januarius opened with its usual glumness. A grey pallor coloured the sky above Rome, her buildings and monuments echoing the drabness, their glint dulled. Citizens entered the phase in which they hoped for an early spring to bless them with warmth and sunlight and the smell of fresh flowers in the markets. There was also a dearth of games to be had and the lack of entertainment in the amphitheatres meant that amusement had to be sought elsewhere. At night, cloaked figures walked the cobbled streets, hugging the walls of alleyways and temples on the way to brothels or other nocturnal houses. Roaming gangs hoped to test their metal against one another in some chance meeting before the Urban Cohorts were alerted to their disturbance.

The consul and Praetorian prefect of Rome had his own daily duties to attend to. Gaius Fulvius Plautianus began his days in the Praetorian camp to the north-east of the city, where he heard reports from his commanders and held private meetings with his spies. The latter were his eyes and ears across the empire and he dedicated inordinate amounts of time to hearing the reports of their activities everywhere, from the senate to the smallest dockside fishmonger in Pelusium. Some of his men had gone unheard from for some time, but this was

ADAM ALEXANDER HAVIARAS

not unusual; the collection of information and execution of duties for his spies could be a long and tedious process.

Besides, Plautianus was experiencing discomfort in Rome and was still raging privately at the withdrawal of some of his former duties. His involvement in the supply of grain and other imports from the provinces had been restricted, leaving a few less aurea in his coffers. It was, he knew, a temporary situation that would change once a little time had passed and he managed to regain the emperor's full attention.

For the moment, the Guard were well in control of the city and more importantly, loyal to him. That, he knew, made him untouchable. He walked with certainty among the rows of stone barrack blocks within the camp, acknowledging salutations everywhere and enjoying the traces of fear seen in men's eyes as he passed. If he could instill fear in the Praetorians, he could instill it in anyone. Before leaving his offices in the Praetorian camp that morning, his daughter Plautilla came in, her eyes red and watery as usual. She had her habitual bodyguard wait outside for her and dismissed her father's scribes as she entered. Plautianus looked on her with annoyance, having told her not to order his people around.

"Father!" she burst into the room. "I must speak with you."

"Plautilla…how many times have I told you not to come to the camp? Damn it, girl! You disobey incessantly." He knew he would have had anyone else executed on the spot for ignoring orders or speaking out of turn, but when it came to his daughter he could naught but acquiesce. She reminded him too much of her mother. He rubbed his eyes, tired already with the day. "What is it?" he asked her, pointing to a chair.

Plautilla walked over, threw back her cloak and sat down. On one wrist, a slight bruising was visible. He waited for her to explain what had happened, though, he suspected. "I hate him, father! I can't stand it anymore." Tears began to rim her eyes again. She was not a beautiful girl, in fact she was quite plain for all the jewels and fine clothing that bedecked her body.

"What has Caracalla done this time?" He was growing more and more angry with stories about the young Caesar, especially since Caracalla had conspired to have some of his duties revoked. "Tell me."

"When I came back to the palace last night from a party at lady Jemela's, I went searching for him. I wanted to tell him that people at the party were laughing at him."

"Why would you tell him that?"

"Because he despises hearing such things! Anyway, I went looking for him and when I came to our own chambers I found him engaged with three of the new slave women I had bought for myself just last week!"

"Did you confront him?"

"Of course I did. I'm your daughter, aren't I?. I went up to him and told him he was a whoremonger and that indulging with dirty slaves was all he deserved."

"What did he say?" Plautianus tried to retain the anger bursting within. He hated it when Caracalla treated his daughter this way, wanted to wring his neck. The marriage had been a politically expedient one at the time it was made, but the young Caesar was becoming too bold, too blatantly insulting of Plautilla. For Plautianus, she was the only family he had or really cared about.

"He laughed at me and so did the slaves! They resumed their orgy and left me to watch. I began to hit him and he rose from the bed and slapped me. He grabbed my wrist very harshly and threw me out of the room into the hallway." Plautilla broke down, felt her wrist where it was swollen and blue.

"Gods! I'll have his head on a spike!" Plautianus slammed his fist down on the table. He got up and paced the room. It was good that she had sent his scribes away. He did not want anyone to see him like that, ever. He went over to Plautilla and rubbed her shoulders. "I'm sorry you have to go through all this my dear, but you'll just have to grin and bear it for now."

"Grin and bear it? How can you say that?"

"We don't have a choice right now. The emperor is doubtful of me at the moment, thanks to your husband. Now is not the time to insult either of them."

"How much longer do I have to go on like this?" Her face was wet and pleading, pathetic. It hurt to see her in such a state. It had been bad before, but not this bad.

"Trust me. Not long. Soon. I'll think of a way to get rid of him soon. I just need time."

"Can't I get away from Rome until then? I can go home to Leptis, or even to Cyrene. Please, father!" She grasped his hand and shook it, kissed it.

"No. That's impossible, Plautilla. You have to remain here. If you go, it will arouse suspicion. I need you to be close to me. If you are far away then I can't concentrate on other matters without worrying about you."

Plautilla seemed to deflate of all strength and hope, nodding her head in agreement like a priestess inhaling oracular fumes. Silently, she rose from the chair. Her father picked up her cloak, draped it around her shoulders and kissed her forehead. "When I am emperor, we can do whatever we want with the world."

"Yes, father. I know." Plautilla moved to the door and went out into the courtyard where her bodyguards were waiting. Plautianus followed and they cowered at the site of him.

"Take her back to the palace."

"Yes, Prefect!" The head bodyguard saluted as the slaves picked up the litter and carried Plautilla back to the palace complex. Plautianus watched them go out of the gate and sighed to himself. Something had to be done.

"Is something wrong with your daughter, Prefect?" Before even turning to see who was speaking, Plautianus swung a hard, heavy fist around which landed square in the middle of the face of one of his scribes. The man reeled, papers flying into the air all about him.

"How dare you speak about my daughter!" he snarled. "Guard!" A burly Praetorian came running from his post on the other side of the courtyard. "Take him outside the walls and kill him! I don't want to see his face again except when you bring me his head."

"Yes, sir!" The man saluted and hauled the squirming scribe up from the ground as he begged for his life through a muffled, bloody nose.

Plautianus went back inside to be alone for a while before he had to attend the senate meeting in the curia. He imagined how good it would feel to do to Caracalla what he had just done to the scribe. "Someday, I'll have his head," he muttered as he poured himself a draft of date wine.

Dusk crept in upon the world with a swiftness that was accelerated by the thickset clouds that continued to cover the seven hills of Rome. These clouds, riding in on the north wind, caused the priests of the Temple of Jupiter to stand and stare as they made their final offerings on the Capitol. It was just past the mid-way point of Januarius, the time when the chill of winter could be felt in the bones; not a comforting thing when the omens were ill as well. Some of the birds that had been sacrificed in the temples of Rome had proven to be bloodless when opened. Also, a strange, never-before-seen bird had been seen flying above the city for several days; it was an odd, ugly looking bird and those who saw it quickly turned their heads away.

The priests also fretted over word from one of the harbour towns that a sea-monster had come upon the shore where it attacked and killed one of the local magistrate's hunting dogs. Before the beast could be slain, it disappeared back into the winter sea. The strange goings-on were on the lips of many citizens in the taverns of Rome. The most superstitious fled the city while the rest remained, happy for a bit of fresh news, whatever form it might assume, to break the winter doldrums.

For Lucius and Alerio, all that mattered was that they were on their way to Rome. For weeks they had waited, an eternity. When the messenger finally arrived, summoning them to the empress, Lucius was both relieved and fearful. The time had come; he would have to leave Adara and the children behind and tread the dark road where wolves slept in shadows. He dreamt of eyes in the dark, of never seeing Adara, Phoebus and Calliope again.

For Adara, she had known the day would come, that the life she was destined to lead with her husband was not to be a quiet, predictable one. She feared greatly for Lucius, but he had explained to her all that was said, all that they stood to lose if he did not go. After weeks of anxious waiting, the dark covered wagon came for them, to take the two men into the heart of Rome.

While the messenger waited for the men to prepare themselves, Lucius prayed above the wooden chest containing the urn. On it he had placed the statue of Apollo, the small altar and the eagle feather from his youth. When he finished, Adara helped him to strap on his armour. The images of the dragon upon his cuirass, greaves and cheek pieces shone with their usual brilliance and the red horse-hair crest fluttered tall and proud. They had been told to come armed; Lucius had both his gladius and his dagger strapped to his sides and over his back was slung the sword Adara had given him. She checked three times, assuring that every buckle and strap was secure.

"There," Adara said as she stood back to look at him. He was strong and beautiful, she thought. She hoped he was strong enough, and that the Gods would protect him this time if any. He made to speak but she stopped him. "Shh. Please, my love. No goodbyes." Tears rimmed her eyes as she looked over to the children. "You'll come back to us, no matter what happens. Right?"

"I will." Lucius leaned over and kissed her. "Gods, I love you, Adara."

"I love you, my Anguis. Now go, and come back." Lucius kissed her once more, smiled at the children as they rolled about on the large bed, and then, ripped himself away.

Down the corridor, Lucius spotted Ashur's outline in the shadows and a raised hand of farewell. He nodded to him, put his helmet on his head and strode out to the wagon where the messenger and Alerio were waiting for him. They only had a short time before the guards at the city gates were changed over. The gate they were headed for was commanded by a trusted man, but only for two more hours.

The wagon moved at a quick, steady pace. The road was quiet and untravelled that time of night. The glow of the city could be seen clearly where the light reflected off of the low-lying clouds and along the walls, torches flickered where guards stood on sentry duty. Lucius noted that as they approached their particular gate, many of the torches were out, making it dark.

"I've arranged that, so we may approach unnoticed by the adjacent guard posts along the walls." The messenger spoke in a very low voice. Lucius heard strain this time, even in his usually steady tone. "Do not speak or show yourselves as we pass through. Our man will admit us but we don't want to alert the other sentries. All right, get down. We're approaching." Lucius and Alerio crouched down inside the wagon and pulled a large, black leather tarp over their heads.

"Halt, and state your business," came a strong military-sounding voice. The messenger answered.

"Making a delivery of wine to the Markets of Trajan."

"A bit early to be making deliveries, no?"

"I have many deliveries to make and I like to get an early start before the streets are too crowded with wagons. Last time I lost four amphora of wine!"

"Well, we can't have that now, can we?" The guard's voice was calm. "Move along."

The wagon creaked through and Lucius and Alerio heard the massive city gates close behind them.

While Rome drifted in its usual uneasy sleep, the black wagon rolled along smaller, darker streets so as not to attract attention. They moved on in shadows, their hearts pounding. Lucius knew they had entered the city from somewhere along the western bank of the Tiber but he was not sure which gate it had been. Shortly after entering they had crossed a bridge and he wondered if they were in the vicinity of his family's home.

It seemed an age since he was last in Rome, an age since he had walked her streets and markets freely, forever since he had enjoyed a day in the Circus Maximus. He strained to hear or smell anything familiar but Rome was foreign to him in that moment, the air beneath the heavy, damp leather tarp stuffy and confining.

Beside him Alerio breathed heavily; he always hated being confined. However, he had been nothing but determined since the empress' visit. In his full armour, Alerio had settled down in the bottom of the wagon, his mind upon their objective.

Just as the two men were beginning to stiffen in cramped discomfort, the wagon slowed and came to a halt. It was extremely dark, wherever they were. Lucius and Alerio gasped and breathed deeply when the messenger threw back the tarp. He put his finger to his mouth for them to remain silent while he looked around.

"Be ready for anything," Lucius whispered to Alerio as he unsheathed his gladius.

"I'm ready."

A few moments later the messenger returned to the back of the wagon. "Come down, quickly." They could barely hear his voice. When they got down from the wagon, Lucius could feel grass under his feet. It seemed that there were high walls all about them and the only light he could see was up.

As they followed the man amid tall shrubs and trees, Lucius realised that they were at the very base of the emperor's palace, behind the Circus and the Septizodium from which the play of water was loud enough to stifle any noise they might have accidentally made. They reached the wall of the palace foundations and the messenger stopped.

"The empress and young Caesar are expecting you in the palace. It is not safe to take the way through the gardens because there are too many Praetorians there." He turned around and got down on his knees, feeling for something. He pulled on a rope that had been hidden beneath the grass somewhere and lifted.

Lucius and Alerio watched in amazement as the messenger opened a small door in the grassy earth; there was a dim light in the darkness below. The messenger turned to them. "Go now. This is the only way in. Follow the passageway until you reach an iron door. When you get there knock, three times."

"Three times," Lucius repeated.

"Yes. They are expecting you. Saturninus will be waiting there." Lucius sheathed his sword again so that he could feel in the dark with both hands. Alerio watched him go first. "Go now. Go," the man said to Alerio, obviously desperate to close the grassy door before someone spotted them.

When they reached the bottom of the stairs, there was a muffled thud above as the messenger closed the hatch. A single torch burned at the far end of the passageway and the two men fixed their eyes on that point. They made their way through the dark, hunched as they went.

When they reached the far end, Lucius knocked. There was a momentary pause and then noise on the other side as someone began to unbolt the iron door. Lucius placed his hand on his dagger. The door was pulled hard from the other side causing the rusty hinges to creak and grind. A torch and a sword blade showed themselves first and then Saturninus' scarred face.

"Finally." He smiled, sly and toothy. "I was beginning to think you'd been stopped after all." He backed away so that Lucius and Alerio could come out of the passage and then closed and bolted the iron door behind them. "I'm to take you upstairs. Come this way." Saturninus walked on and Lucius and Alerio followed. They were at his mercy now.

The corridors they followed were not ornate in the least. Simple brick wall after brick wall until they went up two flights of narrow steps and reached plastered, painted corridors. Lucius noted how narrow the passages were, decided that they must still be in a lesser-known, secret part of the edifice. Severus had built a massively tall palace; it would not have been unbelievable to have such unknown ways throughout the complex.

After climbing several flights of stairs, they reached another door. It was painted red and Lucius guessed that it must lead onto the upper levels. His heart suddenly pounded as his nerves grabbed hold inside. Saturninus turned and eyed both of them.

"We're going in and we're going to wait. You," he pointed at Alerio, "will stay with me and you, Tribune, you will go through another door."

"Why?" Lucius eyed the fellow.

"Because that's what you've been ordered to do." Lucius looked doubtful. "Don't worry your pretty little heads lads, the three of us are in this thing together. We have the same orders, for tonight at least. Now let's go." Saturninus opened the red door and they followed.

The room in which they found themselves was small, warm and well lit. There were no windows but it was well decorated with coloured marble floors and painted walls. Saturninus pointed to a door on the other side of the room and Lucius made his way over, glancing back over his shoulder to Alerio whose golden eyes were taking everything in.

Lucius opened the door and went through. The first thing he noticed was the smell of cooked food and incense. Sitting alone on the far side of the room, was Caracalla.

"Come in, Metellus, come in," he said without looking up. Lucius walked over to him and saluted. "Sit down and have some food if you like."

"Thank you, sire." Lucius sat but did not eat.

"Not hungry? Butterflies in your stomach I suppose." Caracalla laughed to himself. "Not to worry, Tribune. After tonight we will be rid of the pain in my side." For the first time he turned his eyes on Lucius. "I've called you here because I want you to know what will happen tonight."

"I'm listening, sire." Lucius made sure his voice sounded strong and unafraid.

"Good." Caracalla sat up on the edge of the couch. "Only just in the last half hour, the emperor has summoned Plautianus to the throne room on urgent state business. He will come and he will be alone, without any of his guards. You know the reason you are here, correct?"

"Yes, sire. I am to swear that I was approached by the Praetorian prefect to murder the emperor and that I said no."

"Exactly. And, when you said 'no' to him he sent men to kill you and your family." Lucius shuddered, seeing the trace of truth in that last statement. *Alene!* his heart cried out. They had grown up together, not far from where he now stood. Caracalla stared at Lucius. "Are you listening, Tribune?"

"Yes, sire."

Caracalla was, in truth, doubtful of Lucius' determination to carry out the task at hand.

"Do you remember what this man has done to you and your family?" Lucius was silent, stared into the man's hard eyes beneath a creased brow. "He bought your father who beat your mother. He had his spies, men who had been your friends and enemies, sent across the desert to kill you, rape your wife and murder your children. This dog, is the man responsible for the arrows that stuck into your sister's body."

Why is he saying all of this? Stop! Stop! Stop! Lucius boiled with anger inside as all of the pain of what Caracalla said re-emerged to torture him. His face and neck coloured in anger and frustration beneath his helmet.

Caracalla smiled. He had achieved what he wanted to with so few words. It was easier to threaten or anger men who had much to lose.

"I doubt if many people hate Plautianus as much as I, Tribune, but I'm certain that you are one of them and are willing to do whatever it takes. Am I correct?"

"Absolutely!" Bloody images passed through Lucius' mind. He clenched his fists and his breathing increased.

"Keep your voice down, Tribune. Few people know you are here. And save that anger for when it is needed. Now, this is what will happen. When Plautianus is brought before the emperor I will be there, with my father and my brother. My mother will be with my bitch-of-a-wife, Plautilla, keeping her well away. Charges will be laid against Plautianus. He will deny them of course. Then Saturninus, yourself and your centurion will be presented as witnesses along with the letter in Euodus' possession. That should be enough to condemn the bastard and strip him of all his power."

"That's all, sire?" Lucius would be amazed if things went so smoothly. He had to ask if there was not more to it.

"Not exactly. Plautianus is a friend of the emperor's and he has a honeyed tongue that always seems to get him out of the direst of situations. Do not be fooled by him. Remember that this *is* the man who killed your sister."

"I know, sire."

"Good. If he begins to sway the emperor I will need to provoke him. What I want you to do is to be ready for anything that might happen. You and the other two are hardened warriors and your duty is to your emperor. You must be ready to do *anything*. Do you understand? Anything at all." Caracalla said no more, simply observed Lucius and was pleased at the cold look that met him.

"I'll be ready, sire."

"Good. Go back into the other room now. Wait. That is all. It won't be long now. Euodus will come and get you when it is time."

Lucius saluted and went back to join Alerio and Saturninus who was briefing the centurion on what to do.

Caracalla finished his meal and then promptly made his way to his own quarters to ready himself. If the evening played out the way he hoped, Rome would be a very different place when the sun rose.

"Urgent state business?" Plautianus questioned the Praetorian who had brought the message from the palace. "Is that all they said?"

"Yes, Prefect. There is some sort of crisis in the provinces to the north and I believe the emperor wishes to consult with you as Consul before he takes action."

"I don't remember hearing anything about a crisis." Plautianus scratched his head and tapped his fingers on the table where he sat.

"Apparently the messenger only just arrived, sir. He had ridden for days and went directly to the emperor."

"Where is the man now?"

"In the infirmary. They say he's unconscious."

"When does the emperor require my presence?"

"Immediately, sir. With all haste."

"Very well. Where is my daughter this evening?"

"She is dining with the empress, as they do every week."

"Gods. The days do pass quickly. I thought she had yesterday. Ready my mule. I don't feel like trudging across the entire Palatine on such a cold night. Have the guards gather out front."

"Yes, Prefect!" The man snapped a salute and left Plautianus to dress for his audience with the emperor. Something bothered him greatly but he did not know what it was. He had been very tired lately, especially since Plautilla had come to him. Anger tended to drain him these days and he had noticed more than a few hints of white cropping up on his head of black hair.

The prefect had been going over piles of dispatches the whole evening in his villa on the northern edge of the Palatine hill. It was late now and being called out at this time of night was annoying and inconvenient. Still, he knew that he had to remain on the emperor's good side more than ever now, especially since the young Caesar had connived to have some of his powers taken away. It was a temporary situation but one that required some nursing if he were to come through unscathed.

He was dressed in a few minutes, having opted to wear a gold and black cuirass, black boots and leggings. It was cold out and so Plautianus reached for his thicker cloak that was almost purple in colour.

The guards were assembled in the courtyard, waiting. The prefect and consul stopped at the door, went back to the far wall and took down the gladius the emperor had given him; a sword with a keen edge, an ivory handle and a golden hilt and pommel.

"Move out!" he yelled at the men who awaited him in the swirling winds. Plautianus walked up the mounting block and sat atop the young mule that he always used to go about the Palatine and to the forum. The beast groaned as the weight of the tall man settled on its back. The gates opened and the troops marched out onto the street that led to the palace, forming a square around their master.

The stomp of the men's hobnailed boots, that was usually so audible wherever they went, was lost on the howling wind that night. Many torches had been blown out, or their flames blown to thin, horizontal lines along the street. Plautianus looked up ahead at the palace where it loomed ominously over the gardens, pathways and other buildings. *This had better be urgent!* he thought to himself.

Finally, they arrived at the gates of the palace complex. They were closed and there were several guards on the other side.

"Open the gates!" Plautianus' centurion called out. The gates did not open.

"What's going on there?" Plautianus finally bellowed, feeling cold. "Open the gates! The emperor has asked for me!"

He kicked his mule to the gates where a tall, thickly-built guard stood. "Are you going to open the damned gates or do I have to batter them down?" Usually, a threat from the prefect would cause any trooper to tremble and obey, but the man before Plautianus was calm.

"The gates are open to you Consul, of course, but *only* you are to be allowed entrance." Plautianus eyed the man, wanted to wring his neck.

"Why in Hades do they have to stay out here?"

"Orders, sir. That's all. The emperor has already ordered extra guards on duty for your protection while you are here."

"I don't believe this!" Plautianus knew that he was on the verge of making a scene, appearing afraid to go in alone with so many eyes watching him. He could not appear weak. "Very well." He turned in his saddle to face his men. "Stay here and wait for me. I won't be long."

The gates opened and Plautianus rode through and up the path that led to an outer courtyard. The gates closed behind him, leaving his men outside, peering confusedly through the shadows beyond the gate.

The prefect noticed that there were indeed extra guards all over the place. They saluted him sharply. One of them took the reins of his mule when he dismounted. He gave the beast a slap and began to stride up the grand staircase to the main palace entrance.

As he went up the steps he heard an odd sound and turned around to see the mule lying on the ground. He ran back down. "What did you do to my mount, trooper?" He grabbed the trooper who had been holding the reins.

"No...nothing, sir, I swear." The man trembled. "She just dropped dead!" Plautianus saw that the man was just as shocked as he was.

"What about you?" He turned on the other guard who had been there.

"It's like he said, sir. The mule just fell down as soon as you went up the steps."

Plautianus did not know what else to say. The emperor was waiting on him. "Get me another mule for the way back!"

"Yes, sir!" they said. Plautianus turned and went back up the stairs. The two of them looked warily at the body of the dead mule and backed away from it, determined neither one was going to touch it.

Inside the palace, the marble corridors that led to the throne room glistened with the light of evenly spaced braziers. Plautianus handed his cloak to a guard who followed him. His footsteps smacked the gleaming floor as he went and several slaves scurried out of the way to let him pass.

Finally, he reached the gilded doors that led into the throne room. It was oddly quiet for a time of crisis and urgency. Two more guards knocked as he approached, there was a voice from within and the golden doors swung open.

"Gaius Fulvius Plautianus, Consul of Rome and Prefect of the Praetorian Guard!" a steward announced formally. Plautianus pushed past him and into the emperor's presence.

The vast marble room was exceedingly bright and cold. Plautianus noted several people seated or standing around one man.

Septimius Severus sat on his gold and ivory throne on the highest dais, quiet as he looked down on Plautianus, his one-time friend, his kinsman. To the emperor's right sat Caracalla and to his left, Geta. The emperor was dressed all in purple and gold. Caracalla wore his finest gold and black armour and his long black cloak that spilled about him like a pool of dark water. He stared intently at Plautianus. Geta fidgeted as usual.

There were others too. Beside Caracalla, stood his tutor, Euodus, with a rolled papyrus in his hand. Next to Geta stood the renowned jurist, Aemilius Papinianus, in a crisp white toga. There were other minor attendants scattered here and there but Plautianus deemed them unimportant. However, far to his right, near the great arched windows, stood three men.

He could not see them, who they were, without turning fully about. He kept his gaze upon the emperor.

"Your messenger said that I was needed on urgent state business?" Plautianus' voice was loud in that room, strong, confident and defiant. For years, men all over the empire had cowered at his mention.

The emperor sat straight in his throne, his face calm but intent. He rubbed his curled beard, succeeded in stifling one of his coughing fits. He was determined not to appear weak this day.

"I *have* called you here on urgent state business. But first, let me tell you about a dream I had last night." Plautianus looked puzzled for a moment but listened. He was used to Severus' whimsical talk of dreams and stars. "Last night, I dreamt of my former foe, Clodius Albinus. I dreamt that he was still alive and that he was still plotting to kill me."

"Albinus has been dead for some time, sire," Plautianus said flatly.

"Of course. I defeated him. But!" The emperor's voice was strong, as it had once been, and sent chills down the spines of those loyal to him in that room. Lucius knew that from where he stood near the windows, he was looking upon the strong, powerful emperor he had known before. The emperor who had come out the victor in a bloody civil war, the emperor who had crushed the former Praetorian Guard. The emperor who had finally conquered Parthia. "But!" Severus continued. "The spirit of men such as Albinus, men who want to see me dead, goes ever on. Alas, it is the fate of all emperors to have such enemies. That is why only the strongest of emperors remain alive."

"I know that you are strong, sire." Plautianus did not know where Severus was going with this but he knew he could not stand silent. The implications of what was being said were too serious. "It is with the help of men such as I that you have risen to these heights of power, men who are loyal to you and you alone."

"Loyal! LOYAL!" The emperor's voice crushed the walls. He calmed himself, wanting to maintain his dignity, show no fear or emotion. "You speak to your emperor of loyalty? The men of my legions, are loyal. My wife and sons, are loyal. The stallions in my stables, are loyal."

"As *I* am and always have been, sire." Plautianus took two steps forward but was stopped as Severus held up his hand to be handed the scroll which Euodus had been holding. Caracalla moved to the edge of his seat.

"I have something here that I would like to read to you and all these people." The emperor unrolled the papyrus, cleared his throat and began to read. "I read this word for word,

'To Centurion Saturninus
Of the XIII Gemina Legion

I write to you because I have been told that you are a man who knows the value of power and that you are one to give your loyalty accordingly. I need not remind you who, in this vast empire, holds the true reins of power, who controls the will of the senate.

The time has come for a decision. The most powerful man of the Roman world must be emperor and at the moment, he is not. The time will soon come when strong men such as yourself will need to make a decision. You can either support the current, false emperor, or, you can support one who is truly destined to wear the Purple and lead you.

Septimius Severus has known his day and must now be disposed of for the good of the empire. I have enlisted the help of nine other men who will help me in this. You can be the tenth. If you agree I will not forget it. The rewards for ridding us of this upstart will be far beyond your imagination. When Severus falls, you can be one of those who will rise with me.

It is in your interest to reply as soon as is possible to this request. My men will be standing by for your answer.

*Your Praetorian Prefect, Consul and soon-to-be Emperor,
Gaius Fulvius Plautianus.'"*

The emperor finished reading and the entire throne room
was still. Lucius could hear Saturninus breathing beside him,
Alerio too. His own heart pounded and his blood rose up as he
looked across the vast marble floor at the man who was
responsible for all of his pain. He would never see Alene again
because of him. In a moment he would testify against him. It
was not a lie, it was justice, the Gods' will that had given him
this chance for revenge.

"It is even in your hand. I recognise it." The emperor held
up the scroll. "Tell me why, Gaius?" Severus' voice was mild,
his features soft but unhurt.

"Sire, I did not write that letter or any other like it. It is a
forgery."

"Is it now? Most of the ten men to whom you wrote similar
letters would not come forward or identify themselves publicly
for fear of you. However, three of them, three brave and loyal
men have come forward and they are here today to swear that
you sent them such letters."

"What men, sire?" Plautianus' voice was angry and biting.

"The first is the one to whom you wrote this letter.
Centurion Saturninus, step forward." Saturninus marched
smartly toward the throne to stand to the side, between the
emperor and the prefect. He saluted the emperor. "Centurion,
do you swear before all these witnesses that this letter was
addressed to you?"

"Yes, sire! It was put into my hands by the prefect's own
Praetorian messenger."

"And did you agree to this heinous act?"

"Absolutely not, sire. My loyalty is to my emperor and
none other. I felt it my duty to report this."

"You may step away." Severus nodded and Saturninus
saluted and backed away to stand once more to the side.
Plautianus leered at him.

657

"This is preposterous! The man is lying. Only an incompetent fool would send such a letter by messenger, no less ten letters."

"Silence. There are yet two more witnesses. Centurion Alerio of the III Augustan legion. Step forward."

As Alerio moved forward, Lucius could see the sweat beading on his brow. He walked over, perfectly straight, the horizontal crest of his centurion's helmet wavering in the heady air. He saluted and stood to attention.

"Centurion. You say that you received such a letter?"

"Yes, sire. A Praetorian messenger came to Lambaesis to approach me in secret and give me the letter."

"Do you have this letter, Centurion?" Alerio was silent for a moment and could feel Plautianus' burning gaze to his left.

"No, sire. I do not." Caracalla eyed Alerio viciously for a moment. "I burned it, sire."

"You burned it? Why, Centurion?"

"Because, sire, such a letter is an offence to the Gods themselves, an ill omen. To have it close to me was dangerous."

"Very admirable of you, Centurion, you may step back." Alerio saluted and moved back to his position.

"Very admirable?" Plautianus laughed. "Very convenient I think, sire. Someone," he looked at Caracalla, "has made all of this up to make you look like a fool."

Just then, a guard came in and waited for the emperor to see him. He was waved over and came close to the emperor's ear. He whispered something and was dismissed, disappearing back through the golden doors.

"Speaking of omens, Gaius. It seems that even the stars are not in your favour."

"What?" asked Plautianus.

"I have just been informed that as you mounted the steps of my palace, your mule dropped stone dead where you left it. None of the guards will go near it for fear of contaminating themselves with your guilt."

"It is not an omen, sire. Merely chance, a coincidence having nothing to do with my innocence."

"You are wrong, Gaius. The Gods speak to us through such omens. They speak to us on the winds. Their will is known to us in the movements of the stars."

"I'm innocent of any crime!" Plautianus proclaimed. The emperor was silent and glanced over at the third witness. Despite the distance and his ailing eyes, he knew who it was by the armour he wore.

Lucius could feel his gaze even from across the vast room. His eyes were fixed on Plautianus as he waited to be called.

"Tribune Lucius Metellus Anguis! You are our third witness. Come forward," the emperor commanded.

Standing tall, feeling strong, Lucius moved through the next few moments in a dreamlike haze. The golden glow reflected off of the walls, the sound of his footsteps, the hushed whispers from some of the others as he approached; it all seemed unreal. For Lucius, in that moment, what was reality was the presence of his emperor, the evil man who had wronged his family, the weight of the sword at his back and the harsh voice of Nemesis as she whispered in his ear. Somewhere distant, in the far away reaches of his mind and memory, he could hear Alene weeping.

Lucius stared into Plautianus' eyes before turning to the emperor and saluting. The dragons glimmered on his armour as though made of fire, and the crest atop his helm bristled like the hair of an enraged, wounded beast. Plautianus recognised the name, the armour, and noted to himself in the back of his mind that Argus had failed, but that was quickly forgotten as Severus addressed the young tribune.

"I see that my prefect's greed has tried to reach to higher ranks. Tell us all, Tribune, did *you* receive a letter from this man?"

Lucius could see Alene's face in the golden light that lit the room and it hardened him, gave him strength. "My Emperor, I did indeed receive the self-same letter from the prefect of the

Praetorian Guard, Gaius Fulvius Plautianus. I swear, that I was approached by his agents with the letter. These same agents tried to persuade me to help murder you, sire."

"And what did you say to the prefect and his agents, Tribune?"

"I said that I would never help him, sire. I said I would rather die than betray my oath to my emperor." Lucius looked up at the emperor, believing what he said, the emperor believing him.

"Your honesty and strength are an example to us all, Tribune and-"

"Sire, I..." There was a collective gasp as Lucius interrupted the emperor.

"You have something else to add, Tribune?" Severus remained calm.

"Forgive me, sire, but yes, I do. When I said no to the prefect's demand for help in your murder, he sent his spies to kill me, my wife and my two children." Lucius looked to his left at Plautianus whose eyes stabbed aggressively at him. "He did not succeed in that, sire, but...he...his men, murdered my sister, Alene Metella, in cold blood." Lucius found it hard to say anything more.

Severus looked with pity upon the young tribune. "You have our sincerest regrets, Tribune. It upset us greatly when we were told of this atrocity." His gaze moved from Lucius and pity to Plautianus and disgust. "Why did you wish to do this to me? Why did you conspire to have me killed? Are you a coward?" Lucius remained at the left foot of the dais, not having been dismissed. "Answer me!" The emperor's voice shattered the silence and peeled away all dignity Plautianus had left. His face was now openly hostile toward the emperor.

"This is an outrage! For years, I have served you, held you up and protected you. You call me a coward? It is you who are the coward, not I!" Plautianus was now pointing at Severus but the emperor remained calm still, as though watching a cornered animal in the Colosseum. "How dare you take the word of two lowly centurions and a miserable tribune from a decrepit family over mine, your countrymen, your cousin! We have been through so much and *this* is the measure of your gratitude?" Caracalla watched intently, pleased with how things were going, knowing that his father was not being swayed by the prefect's words, not this time.

"You speak well, Gaius," the emperor said, "but not nearly well and honestly enough."

"You are not worth the sand on my boots!" Before Plautianus could utter another word or react, Caracalla, like an enraged leopard, sprung from the dais, took Plautianus' sword from his side and punched him with a heavy fist square in the face. Plautianus fell to the floor, his nose broken and Caracalla raised the sword he had taken high above his head.

"I have dreamt of this," he muttered to the fallen man.

"CARACALLA STOP!" Caracalla's arm froze in mid air as his father's voice commanded him to stop. "No, my son, no. Do not kill him."

Caracalla stared down at Plautianus and stepped back. He spat at the man who rose from the floor spitting blood. As the young Caesar mounted the steps to his chair, Plautianus pulled a dagger from the sleeve of his tunic and rushed.

Before he had gone two steps, Lucius, with the speed he had trained for all his young life, drew the sword from his back and cut him down, slicing into the prefect's thigh. The prefect stumbled with a fierce cry, made to throw his dagger at the emperor, but was stopped when Lucius' blade plunged into the unprotected pit of his arm. As the prefect swayed, bleary-eyed on the end of the tribune's sword, all Lucius could hear or see was Alene. Plautianus spat blood at him and he twisted his deadly blade violently, one more time before the body fell in a bloody mass on the marble floor before the emperor and his sons.

"By the Gods! What a mess!" Geta covered his mouth in disgust, the first words he had said all evening.

Lucius stood there, solid and still, looking down when Caracalla spoke.

"Take his beard to my wife!" Caracalla said.

Saturninus ran over, his dagger drawn and proceeded to cut the black and white beard from Plautianus' face.

Severus looked on, silent too. He had no words for this, for such a scene, for such deserved punishment. *The stars are against you cousin*, he thought.

"Away with this filth! To Hades with him!" Caracalla ran down the dais and began to drag the body across the floor to the high windows of the palace. Alerio came quickly to his aid, grabbing the neck of the man he had hated. As the body was dragged, a shiny crimson trail slithered behind it on the marble. The two men hoisted the heavy body and flung it from the window so that it fell into the darkness far below the palace and onto the streets of Rome.

In a far room on the other side of the palace, Saturninus burst through the doors of the triclinium where the empress was dining with Plautilla. His hands were bloody and a wicked grin spanned his face.

"Here's your Plautianus!" the centurion said as he tossed the bloody beard onto the floor in front of them.

"NO!!!!!!!!!!!!!!!! FATHER!!!!!!!!!!!!!" Plautilla's screams rang through the entire palace. Her father was dead. On the couch next to her, Julia Domna breathed a sigh of relief, sipped her wine, and put her arm around the crazed young woman.

News of Plautianus' fate spread through the city like a torrential storm in which his bloody, broken body was carried on waves of arms of screaming citizens until it was washed ashore on the steps of the senate. The mob howled so that their uproar could be heard down every street and in every room.

Once the people had seen the body, the emperor ordered his guards to bring it back to the palace where it was cleaned and made ready for burial outside the city walls.

"The dead are to be treated with respect," he had stated. After that, he ordered a convening of the senate and all her members. As the crowds milled about the forum buildings, there was a clash of rumours as to how the prefect had been killed and who had killed him.

While the city cheered over the body of Plautianus, Lucius stood alone in the immense, rooftop garden of the palace. He still wore his blood-spattered armour from the night before and felt an oddly peaceful numbness within. He had wanted to go back to Adara immediately but had been told that it would not be safe for him until the city had been brought under control. The prefect had had many followers in Rome, especially among his guard, and they needed to be weeded out.

A gentle breeze blew out of a white and sapphire sky, rustling the palm under which he stood, where Alene had first introduced him to Adara at the imperial banquet. It seemed only yesterday. He could hear people cheering and singing in the streets. Revenge was a bitter-sweet song that had him speechless. *Would Alene have wanted this?* It was difficult to say. Alerio had told him that they had done the right thing, the Gods' will. He was not so sure. Now, Alerio was off helping Caracalla with some other duties while Lucius was left waiting again with his thoughts and his uncertainty. Of one thing he was certain though, and that was the fact that his family was safe. *In the end, isn't that all that matters?* He contented himself with that thought for the moment. He had to.

He looked down at his breastplate and chipped away the dry blood that had clotted on the image of the dragon, scratched it with his nail. Then, he heard footsteps. At the far end of the garden, a slave caught his eye. He bowed as a purple figure brushed past.

Julia Domna approached the tribune, smiling, not overly much but just enough to show that she was pleased. She took in Lucius' pallid face, contrasted with his bloody armour, and felt for him. He bowed deeply as she approached.

"Rise, Tribune, rise."

"Augusta."

"I am sorry I have kept you waiting here for so long, Tribune. You must want to return as soon as possible to your wife and children." Worry crossed Lucius' face. He knew that Adara must have been quite fearful without any news. "Do not worry, I have sent my messenger to inform her that you are well and safe."

"Thank you, my Lady."

"I know this has been a difficult night for you, as it has been for all of us. I wanted to thank you personally for your help and your bravery."

"I was doing my duty, Augusta."

"Nevertheless. I sincerely thank you. The emperor has informed me of what happened, how you cut Plautianus down before he could kill either him or my son." She looked at the blood on Lucius' chest and arms. "He was an evil man. Rome is better now that he is gone."

"I'm sure it will be, my Lady."

"Yes. I also want you to know that you may stay at my estate along the river for as long as you wish, until you decide what you would like to do."

"Thank you." Lucius had few words at the moment as the empress looked at him expectantly.

"I suppose that you would like to cleanse yourself and offer prayers before anything else."

"I should, yes."

"I have had rooms prepared where you may wash. While you do so, my servants will clean your armour for you. When you have finished, my guards will escort you to the Temple of Apollo if you wish."

"Thank you, my Lady. You are too kind."

"Not at all, Tribune. We owe you a great deal for what you have done. I keep my promises." The empress turned to leave, then stopped. "Oh, before you go, there is someone who would like to see you."

"But, my Lady, I am not presentable. I feel badly enough looking like this for you."

"I am certain, Tribune, that this person will not mind in the least." Julia Domna gave Lucius a smile and turned toward the far door as it opened. There were several footsteps before Antonia came into view with Clarinda, young Quintus, and Ambrosia behind them.

The empress stood back as Antonia limped across the floor, unbelieving of her own eyes. Lucius' voice caught in his throat and his eyes burned with tears as he took in the sight of her. Despite her battered appearance she managed to smile through her own tears and crooked jaw as Lucius came toward her.

"Mother?" He stopped just a few feet in front of her, reached out and took her trembling hands.

"My son, my boy." Antonia's strength began to melt away, even before the empress, and she wept to see her first-born in front of her. "Lucius." She did not care about the blood on his chest as she held him close and felt his arms hold her. "Praise Apollo, you're safe. Thank you, Gods."

"Everything is well now, mother. I'm here." Lucius realised he was making quite an assumption in the presence of the empress, turned to see her smiling.

"It's quite all right, Tribune," Julia Domna said, moved by the scene between mother and son. "It has been arranged. Your mother is free to leave her home. But, for appearances' sake, she must be banished from the city of Rome for at least one year. We cannot set too lenient a precedent. After that she may come and go as she likes."

"I am grateful, my Lady." Antonia did her best to bow and the empress held up her hand.

"Do not thank me, Lady Metella. Thank your son. He is the hero of Rome at the moment. However, as I told him, he should not remain within the city. You may join him at my estate for the time being, until you decide where you will spend the next year."

"Lucius!" Clarinda and Quintus could not stand back any longer and rushed up to their big brother. They stopped, the sight of him slightly frightening.

"Are you both all right?" Lucius asked, kneeling down to look at them.

Clarinda nodded emphatically making Lucius smile. He looked over at young Quintus, noticed the scar on the side of his head. Lucius held out his hand and his younger brother took it strongly, his eyes watery. Lucius knew only little of what had happened to him, but he did know that it had been difficult.

"Thank you for taking care of mother and Clarinda, brother."

"I tried, Lucius."

"I know." Lucius hugged his brother. "You're not alone anymore."

"Tribune," the empress interrupted, "if you would like, I can arrange for your mother and the children to collect their belongings. I will have a large wagon ready to take you all out of the city after you have cleansed yourself and visited the temple."

"Thank you, my Lady. I shall not take long."

"My men will look for you outside the Temple of Apollo."

Lucius kissed his mother, brother and sister and told them he would see them soon. "Ambrosia." Lucius turned to the slave girl where she stood timidly to the side.

"Yes, Master?"

"Ashur told me what you did for us." The girl dropped her head, embarrassed. Lucius took her hand in his. "Thank you."

With that, everyone followed the empress out and went their separate ways to meet again later in the day.

While Lucius washed the blood from himself in the palace baths, the emperor, Caracalla and Geta sat before the senate.

The long room, filled to capacity, was silent. Outside in the forum, the Roman people chanted for their emperor. When the emperor rose to inform the senate what had happened, he made no accusations against Plautianus. Instead, he spoke of the deplorable weakness of human nature and man's inability to remain pure under the strain of excessive honours.

Severus blamed himself for so loving and honouring Plautianus, a man he had known and cared for since boyhood, a man he had trusted, a man who had betrayed him beyond redemption.

The emperor ordered all statues of Plautianus throughout the city and the empire to be either broken or melted down. He informed the senate that all of Gaius Fulvius Plautianus' amassed wealth would be put into his own, personal coffers. No one dared oppose despite the fact that it was widely rumoured that the sum was roughly a billion sestertii.

Two new Praetorian prefects were appointed to replace Plautianus: the Syrian jurist from Emesa, Aemilius Papinianus, and the former prefect of Aegyptus, Quintus Maecius Laetus. The men accepted the honour dutifully as well as the fact that the military authority that had once belonged to the prefect of the Praetorian guard was now severely restricted. Being a jurist, Papinian was pleased with the vote that the prefect's judicial powers be amplified beyond the hundredth milestone from the city of Rome.

When this business was concluded, the emperor became silent and stared at all of the faces crowding the senate. It was a look they knew well from the end of the civil war, and now they saw it again. Many men in that room had given their loyalty to Plautianus and they were not to go unpunished. Caracalla stood up at his father's command and unrolled a long papyrus from which he read the names of the proscripted.

Among the condemned was an intimate of Plautianus by the name of Coeranus who claimed that he was not that close to, and had kept a safe distance from, the prefect; he would be watched closely. A man who did not get off so easily was Caecilius Agricola, a man known by many to have been a great flatterer of Plautianus and a contemptuous scoundrel. He was sentenced to death and the very night before his execution he cut his veins with the shards of a drinking cup that was said to have cost two-hundred-thousand sestertii. He died on the pieces.

Many others were sentenced to death in a great cleansing of the senate, young men and old, and many more throughout the empire would follow. When it was announced that Plautianus' daughter Plautilla and her younger brother Plautius were to be banished to a remote part of the empire, a smile crossed Caracalla's face. He had never liked his marriage to the woman and now, he was free of her.

When the senate was dismissed, many went out into the world refreshed and relieved. Others, hung their heads and prayed that nothing that they had done for Plautianus when he was alive would be found out, come back to haunt them and strike off their heads. Severus felt the fear emanating from every man as he left, and enjoyed it. It was that very fear that would keep them in line for the time being and push them to grant whatever he wished.

Outside in the sun, on the steps of the curia, Senator Dio watched the crowds dissipate and his colleagues make their way home to the various quarters of the city. He had sat enthralled through the entire proceedings. He knew some of the men who had been sentenced to death, knew it was their own fault. He also knew that those same men who had cowered to Plautianus, taken his money and done his bidding, had not loved the swine anywhere near as much as the very emperor who had condemned them to death.

However, to say this would be folly. It was a thought to be kept to oneself, not even to be written privately. Dio descended the marble steps, made his way through the crowd to get himself a honeyed pastry and make his way home, happy to be alive. As he went, he wondered, *Who really killed Plautianus and where are they now?*

Outside the Temple of Apollo on the Palatine Hill, Lucius was happy to see Numonius. The vendor's tables were set up, his animals restless. When he saw the tribune approaching, he smiled and shook his hand, happy to see him alive.

"Fitting that I should see you here, Tribune. Thank the Gods you're safe!"

Not wanting to go over the entire ordeal, Lucius thanked him for his help with Ashur and bought a thick bunch of rosemary and some scented oil to give as offerings.

"No chicken today?" Numonius asked.

"No. I'm not in the mood for the sight of blood. Gods bless you, my friend."

"And you, Tribune." He watched Lucius go up the steps of the temple and disappear inside. Content now, able to breathe having seen Lucius alive, Numonius packed up his things with a smile and went home singing.

Lucius did not know what to say when he arrived before the altar. The priest had greeted him kindly and bade him take as much time as he liked. He thanked him and placed his offerings upon the great altar before the statue of Apollo.

"Please, Mighty Apollo, cleanse me and purify me of the deed I have done this night. Grant my sister and my family peace now that it is over. I honour you above all others and would never disgrace you." Lucius wept then. He felt a warmth inside his soul that he thought had departed for good the night before.

He opened his tired eyes to look up at the powerful god and his Muses. Far-Shooting Apollo stood before him in the swirling smoke of fire and offerings. His arm was outstretched, his hand held above Lucius' head. The kneeling man could feel words of comfort and peace within, and his heart lightened.

The Muses smiled and sang behind Apollo whose voice was the sound of his own lyre. *Rise young Metellus. Rise and be strong. Rise.*

Lucius felt as though he was helped up, lifted by power and light and song. "Thank you my Lord. Thank you." He backed away, smiling and standing tall as the God vanished into smoke and fire.

Outside again, Lucius was met by his mother, the children and Ambrosia. "Come," he said. "Let's go." They followed the empress' guards who led them safely out of the city to the peaceful estate where Adara waited for him. The sun was bright in the western sky and Lucius looked at it, felt the warmth upon his face. Above the golden orb, an eagle sang and whirled, reveling in its flight.

XXXI

RECONCILIATIO

'Reunion'

Adara ran as quickly as she could through the corridors of the estate buildings, her heart pounding, desperate sounds of pained relief escaping her lips. One of the Syrian slave girls followed her as best she could with the two children in her arms; Adara had come to trust her with them and she did not want to trip as she went.

There were many voices in the courtyard. Ashur was already there, standing in the main doorway, smiling. There was a mass of guards too, standing in two orderly rows beyond two large wagons. Adara stopped next to Ashur.

"Is it?"

"Yes. He's back." As Ashur said it, Lucius appeared from between the wagons and came directly toward them. Adara ran to meet him.

"You're safe!" She flung her arms around him, her thick cloak enveloping them both. "I was so afraid!" She buried her face in his neck. He could feel her tears. "I was so afraid."

Lucius held his wife tightly, his eyes closed, her scent familiar and soothing. "I'm fine now, my love. It's all over."

"The messenger told us part of what happened, about the prefect being..." she paused. "Were you there, Lucius?"

"I'll tell you about it later, in private." Just then, Antonia and the children emerged from the shadows and Adara turned to them.

"Praise Apollo you're all safe." Adara went straight to Antonia and hugged her warmly, not saying anything about her worn and battered appearance. That too, was done with. "I've been so worried for you," she looked at Clarinda and Quintus, "all of you." Adara knelt down and hugged the two children at once. Quintus winced, his head hurting again, but he was happier than he had been in a long time.

While Ashur greeted Lucius, grateful for his safe return, and then Antonia and her children, Adara took her own children from the slave girl and stood beside Lucius, waiting. Antonia stopped when she saw them, her voice lost in emotion.

"Mother," Lucius said, smiling, "come meet your grandchildren." Antonia covered her mouth with a trembling hand as she approached. Adara held them up so that Antonia could see them in the dim, evening light.

"Children this is your avia." Tears formed on Antonia's lids as two pairs of bright eyes gazed up at her. "Avia, this is Phoebus, and this is Calliope."

"Oh, my dear," Antonia kissed Adara's cheek, "they're so lovely. The Gods have blessed you." In that moment, as she accepted them into her arms, Antonia knew that this is what she had suffered for. The two children before her, the family about her, they were the reason for her actions. No regrets now, not ever. "Quintus, Clarinda, come and see your niece and nephew." The two children approached hesitantly, unsure of the two tiny people.

Clarinda giggled as she caught wind of Calliope's singing and little Quintus opened his eyes wide and laughed when Phoebus took hold of his nose and squeezed. He shut his eyes to the pain in his head.

"Mother?"

"Yes, Clarinda."

"Does this mean that I'm an auntie?"

"Yes, it does. You are now an auntie and Quintus is an uncle."

"Really?" Quintus could hardly believe that. "Am I not too young to be an uncle, Lucius?" He looked up to his big brother.

"No. You're just right, little brother. You're their uncle." Quintus looked back down again at the children.

672

"I will help to protect you both," he said to his niece and nephew. Phoebus grabbed his nose again. Evidently, the child had already developed a great interest in his uncle's nose.

"Come everyone. We'll get you to your rooms and then we'll eat." Lucius turned to the head slave who stood patiently by. "Are their rooms prepared?"

"Yes, Tribune. My mistress sent the order with her messenger this morning that we should be ready for more guests."

"Good." Lucius felt his mother's grasp on his arm.

"Lucius," she whispered. "Before I do anything else, I must be with my daughter." Lucius nodded. "Where is she, so that I might be alone with her?"

"I'll take you to her." Lucius informed Adara of where he and Antonia were going so that she could take care of the others, and led his mother to their rooms and the private garden.

"Inside everyone!" Adara called as she was followed by the rest of the family and Ashur.

In the private garden just off of their room, Lucius set a brazier, next to a comfortable chair covered in blankets. Antonia sat down with some difficulty, waving aside Lucius' concern; he had not seen how she had been coping for the months since her first beating. She was used to it.

As Antonia waited, Lucius removed the wooden chest from one of the inner rooms and carried it out. He placed it on a low table in front of his mother and undid the latch.

"It's a beautiful urn…" Antonia's voice caught in her throat. "You made a good choice."

"I knew it was what you would have chosen. Alene too."

"Yes." Antonia looked upon the bronze urn, reached out and opened the lid. Lucius turned away. *Is this really my beautiful daughter?* "Please leave me with her, Lucius. I'll be fine."

Lucius kissed his mother's head, placed his hand upon the urn and went out of the garden. The flames of the brazier flickered and were reflected in the polished surface. When she was sure that her son was gone, Antonia reached into the urn to feel its contents. It was soft and smooth. *A good cremation.* Carefully she shook her hand clean over the urn, closed the lid and wept the tears she had been saving for just that moment.

When Antonia finished, she called for Lucius who had been waiting in the corridor outside the rooms the entire time.

"I'm going to have Emrys and Carissa create a perfect monument to Alene," Antonia said as Lucius closed the chest and carried it back safely inside.

"I had thought the same thing," Lucius agreed. "But where?"

"I'll think about that for a while. It has to be perfect and as I'm not to be in Rome for the next while..." her voice faded. She had not really thought about her exile at all, had only brought a few essentials to the estate. She watched as Lucius placed the chest down and said something beneath his breath, kissing the smooth surface before getting up.

"Tell me, my son," his mother asked. "Was it your hand that cut Plautianus down last night?" For a moment, Antonia radiated strength.

"Yes, mother. I killed him."

"Do not be ashamed of your actions!" she insisted. "You did it for all of us."

"As you did, mother." He hugged her then, an understanding between them.

"Yes. As I did."

After everyone had bathed and refreshed, dinner was served in the triclinium. It was unbelievable that they were dining together, after so long. There was a feeling of familial warmth between them, but also much hesitation; after all of the time, distance and pain, it was difficult not to think about all that had

Killing the Hydra

transpired, the people who were distinctly missing from the affectionate fold. They kept the conversation light for the sake of the children who had been through enough, but it was hard not to notice that even the babies were more silent than usual. After the sweets were brought out and Quintus and Clarinda had had their fill, Antonia told them to get to bed. Both agreed, Clarinda because she was so tired and Quintus because the pain in his head had worsened over the evening. Ambrosia went with him to prepare the mixture he drank to ease the pain for sleep. When they were gone, Lucius turned to his mother.

"Are his headaches that bad?"

"Worse than you can imagine. That boy has been my rock through this entire ordeal. But, I worry about him." Antonia told them about the doctors drilling holes in his head to relieve the pressure but it never seemed to be working.

"I can't believe all that's happened to you." Lucius covered his face, as if to block out the thoughts his imagination conjured. *They've suffered so much. I should have been there.* He still could not get used to his mother's slurred speech as she struggled to push words through her crooked jaw.

"Let's not talk about it anymore." Antonia knew that there were other matters that she did have to talk about and turned on her couch to face her son next to her. "What about Argus, Lucius?"

The name was one Lucius had hoped never to hear again, but he knew it would crop up at some point, that he could not escape it. This was the last time he would talk about that terrible day. "He got away mother. I was more concerned with getting to...he got away."

"So he is still out there?"

"Yes. I should have killed him when I had the chance."

"No!" Antonia stopped herself. "I'm relieved you didn't."

"Why? Why, by all the Gods?"

"Lucius there is something you need to know." Antonia placed her hand on his. "Argus is...was...your father's son."

675

Everyone was silent and all that could be heard were the flames of the oil lamps set around the room.

"Is this some cruel joke?" Disgust and rage creased Lucius' face.

"No, Lucius. Argus' mother and your father, well, I don't need to tell you. But it's true. That is why he came to live with us after his parents died. He was using that fact to blackmail your father."

"I can't believe this." Lucius hung his head. The shame of it!

"Your father had planned on naming Argus his heir if he succeeded in eliminating you, but that will not happen now."

"Mother, this is a heavy blow."

"Yes. It was especially for me, but now, you see why I am relieved that you did not kill him?"

"Why? I hate him! He deserves to suffer."

"Lucius dear, if there is one thing the Gods cannot abide or forgive, it is a fratricide. Your hands must be clean in this. His master is dead, that is enough. Now, he will have nowhere to go, no one to answer to."

Lucius was silent. He knew that nothing could change the fact that Argus was his half-brother, no matter how much he willed it so. He had to accept it and pray that he would never see him again.

"Your mother is right, my friend. Apollo blesses you, as does Venus. You can't risk their anger by killing your own brother. Think of your family."

"I do!" Lucius shut his eyes, embarrassed that he snapped at Ashur. "Forgive me. I do think of them. Last night was for my family." He looked to his wife whose glassy eyes betrayed sadness for his pain. He kissed her hand. "Well, it seems the Gods do indeed have a life of surprises for us. Now, other more pleasant matters. Your exile!" Lucius looked at his mother.

"Lucius!" Adara chided.

"It's all right, dear," Antonia laughed. "I am glad for some remnant of humour. To be honest, I would like nothing better than to get away from Rome. The recent past is just too painful."

"You could go to Greece and my parents!" Adara suggested excitedly. "They would love more than anything to have you."

"It sounds lovely, dear, but I'm afraid that I couldn't impose all my belongings upon them. Besides, it would remind me too much of Alene and I want to think of Greece in the way she described it to me."

"Firstly, mother, I suppose we should discuss what we have. My army pay is good, but now that I'm temporarily relieved from duty..."

"I wouldn't dream of taking your money. You have earned it and besides, you have a family of your own to care for. No, financially we are sound."

"How so?" Lucius asked.

"While I was kept under guard, alone in the house in Rome, I had the time to go through all of your father's papers. It seems he had been investing in trading companies around the empire."

"Really?"

"Yes. Of course he was going to keep it all to himself and then pass it on to Argus. But legally, now, all inheritance goes to you as first-born, and the rest of us."

"What about the estate in Etruria?"

"It seems that the estate has been doing exceedingly well. The olive yield is wondrous and the wine much sought after. I suppose that's the reason for the connections with all of these trading companies." Antonia was thoughtful for a moment.

"Mother, why not go to live in Etruria, on the estate?"

"What?"

"Why not? The empress said that your exile was only from the city of Rome." Antonia smiled. She had always loved the estate there, the peace and quiet. The children loved it too.

677

"But it needs so much work and...there are so many memories." She knew this to be true. It had been in Quintus' family for generations.

"We can all help to fix it up." Adara was excited at the prospect, never having seen the estate itself. "Lucius doesn't have any pressing duties at the moment and it's close enough to Rome if he needs to attend to anything."

"You are quite right, my dear. What do you think, Lucius?"

"It's your exile mother, spend it where you wish. You may have a few extra tenants in the meantime."

"Done!" Antonia clapped her hands, thrilled at the images that flowed through her mind. "Do you want the house in Rome for yourselves?" She looked at Lucius and Adara questioningly.

Ashur, sitting off to the side was feeling out of place. Carissa was in his thoughts.

"I don't think so mother. After all that's happened there...I think we should sell it."

"Very well. Actually, now that Plautianus is gone, the property prices should go up. We'll make an excellent profit." Lucius wondered if that were true. If it was, they would indeed make a lot of money.

"I'll take care of the sale of the house for you, mother."

"Thank you."

At the pause in the conversation Ashur rose from his couch. "I think, my friends, that I shall go back to Rome now."

"Really, Ashur? Are you sure you want to do that with all the people in the streets? There might be rioting."

"I have been away from Carissa for too long, and she will need to know that I am well. My place is with her from now on." Ashur's face was sad and tired as he stood there. He longed to go.

Lucius went over to his friend. "Thank you for staying here and watching over them for me. You're my greatest friend." He embraced him like a real brother.

"For you, *Anguis*, for you."

Adara helped Antonia up off the couch as she saw her struggle to rise. She too wanted to express her sincerest thanks.

"I wanted to thank you, Ashur. You have given me…" she looked over at Lucius, Adara and the sleeping babies on the couch behind them, "…everything. You are a dear friend."

Ashur hung his head, ashamed at the kind words, still strangled by his guilt over Alene's death.

Antonia lifted his head, her hands on his cheeks. "It was the Gods' will, Ashur. You did all that you could. Had it not been for you, none of us would be standing here." Antonia Metella then hugged Ashur like a son and he felt her truth, the honesty of her words and feelings. He wept.

He wiped his eyes, went toward the door and turned. "You are all my dearest friends. The blessings of Apollo be with you always." Bowing in gratitude for their love and kindness, Ashur Mehrdad turned and went down the long corridor until he was outside. When the gate was opened for him, he stepped onto the road and went back to Rome and Carissa.

Two weeks later, all the preparations had been made. Lucius had succeeded in selling the house near the Forum Boarium for a hefty sum which pleased Antonia greatly. Twenty slaves and their overseers had been hired along with a train of wagons to move the contents of the Metellus household to the estate in Etruria. There was an air of excitement among the family, a sense of new beginning.

Emrys, Carissa and Ashur had come by especially to move the statues of Lucius and Adara that had been shut in the closet for so long. One of the arms had broken off of Adara's likeness, as well as Lucius' nose. "They can be fixed," Emrys had said matter-of-factly as the slaves slowly, carefully, brought them out of the closet and laid them in the thickly padded bed of one wagon. The sculptor's watchful eyes never left them. He, Carissa and Ashur would act as escort to the belongings until they arrived at the estate.

Lucius and the others had been notified by the empress' messenger that they would have a Praetorian escort the entire way to Etruria. He was wary of having Praetorians guide them the whole way but the empress had said in her letter that there would be someone he trusted among them. His curiosity peeked, Lucius waited in the courtyard of the estate for the arrival of the troops.

Soon enough, the stomping of hobnails upon the paving slabs of the road could be heard loud and clear. Orders were shouted as the gates swung open. Lucius was shocked to see a century of men file into the large courtyard, their brown armour and red cloaks filling the space, the clink of weapons and shields concerted. At their head, the centurion held a thick, gnarled vinerod with pride, as though with the practice of years.

The man turned and began to walk in Lucius' direction. When he stopped, Lucius was speechless and the centurion laughed at his expression, careful for his men not to hear him.

"Alerio?" Lucius had known that Alerio had been helping Caracalla with certain duties in the city but this was more than unexpected.

"Tribune Metellus!" Alerio saluted, crisply, as he always had done. "Your escort to Etruria has arrived."

"When the empress said that our escort would be led by someone I trusted, she wasn't joking."

Alerio came closer. "Aren't you pleased, Tribune?" He smiled, his golden eyes twinkling in the sunlight.

"Most pleased, my friend. So, I suppose that you'll be close, garrisoned at Rome?"

"Indeed. That way I can keep an eye on you." Alerio turned to see some of his men straining their necks to get a look at Lucius. "Back in line!" he barked, pointing the vinerod at them.

"What's all that about?" asked Lucius.

"Oh they're just trying to catch a glimpse of the powerful brute who killed Plautianus."

"They know who did it?" Lucius' voice was a whisper.

"Of course they do. Everybody knows. Of course no one is positive. Rumours really, this one just happens to be true. Don't worry, you've got me looking out for you now in the city." Lucius nodded gravely, ill-at-ease with this bit of rumoured fame.

"What's done is done. I'd have no other Praetorian looking over me. How are the new prefects?"

"They seem to be honest men. Time will tell. Being a jurist, Papinian knows the law and tries to obey it. Laetus is a typical administrator. In the end, what do I know? You can never tell with politicians."

"I think the emperor planned it well this time."

"Most likely. Actually, he speaks of you often, how grateful he is to you."

"Who, the emperor?"

"You really showed your metal that night, Lucius."

"Yes, well. I did it for other reasons."

"I know. I just wish I'd been able to help you with that. Still, it was something to throw the bastard out the window." Lucius felt a little uncomfortable with Alerio's lax view of the events but they each had to deal with it in their own way. He too had lost Alene.

"Anyway, I'm happy for your promotion. Congratulations, Centurion."

"Hey. Don't fuss in front of the men." Alerio winked. "Are you ready to leave?"

"Just about. I'll go in and see what's happening. The wagons are already loaded."

"Very well, Tribune," he raised his voice. "I'll get the wagons and men turned around and formed up."

"You do that, Centurion. I'll be with you shortly." Relief washed over Lucius. He could trust Alerio with their safety.

"Yes, Tribune!" Alerio saluted, turned on one foot and went back to prepare his men for departure.

It had not taken long to travel to Etruria; the roads were clean and clear and the weather likewise. With a Praetorian escort, all other travellers quickly edged themselves onto the side of the road when they met them, making the going more brisk, especially outside of the city.

Before leaving, Lucius had sent a courier on ahead to inform Numa, the estate's steward, that they would be moving in permanently. He would have his work cut out for him, no doubt. The entire villa would have to be cleaned and swept from top to bottom, clean linens placed in every room for the family and their guests, the baths would have to be scrubbed and the stables prepared for Lunaris and Phoenix; the list went on and on. Lucius specifically mentioned that all trace of his father's belongings be put in crates and set in one of the outbuildings for him to go through at a later date. He did not want anything to remind them about Quintus Caecilius Metellus, a man who had done them no amount of honour and caused a whole world of pain.

As for the estate, it may well remind them of Quintus for a short time but Lucius realised that, as a true Metellus, that land and everything on it, was his by right of birth. His ancestors had dwelled there for hundreds of years and now it was his. There was much that he wanted to do to it, changes he dreamed of making. However, he could not be sure how long he would be allowed to remain there before duty called him back. For the moment, he was happy to care for his family and try to heal the wounds that had been inflicted upon each of them.

As the party travelled along the via Flaminia and then the via Cassia, Adara marvelled at the rolling green beauty of the countryside about them. If Greece was dry and sweetly scented, Etruria was soft and magical. It was damp, true, but what beauty! So much to look at. When the wagon train and troops turned westward down the minor road to follow a small river, Adara wondered what lay in store and was unable to remain in her seat. Her head peered out of the wagon's leather flaps and Lucius laughed as he saw her poking out.

It had been ages since Lucius had been to the estate, and now he was back. He went over certain pleasant childhood memories of long summer days spent running down the hills and rolling in the grass, plunging into the cool, gurgling stream. He hoped his own children would have the same joy. They would have plenty of olives this time of year; it would not have been long since the crop was brought it. He could taste them, feel the smoothness of the estate's wine wetting his lips. He hoped Alerio would be able to share an amphora with him. Perhaps not this time; duty no doubt called him back to Rome.

After a short time, rising smoke became visible. "The baths!" Lucius said to himself as he rode, slapping Lunaris' thick neck. "You'll have plenty of green grass to eat and space to run around, boy!" Lunaris neighed in reply.

Soon, the small bridge came into view as they cleared the trees along the river.

"Oh my!" Adara gasped as she sighted the villa atop the cypress-clad plateau. She turned to Antonia. "It's beautiful!" Antonia looked up too and remembered how the place once was, how she hoped it would be. "What's that up there, on the mountain top?" Adara pointed to one of the high peaks beyond the vineyards. Young Quintus poked his head out next to hers.

"Sister, that's where the gods of the mountain live."

"Gods of the mountain?" She was still feeling warm from being called 'sister'.

"Yes! There is an ancient tomb of our ancestors up there, under the tall trees in the middle."

"Really? Will you show me, Quintus?"

He thought about it for a moment, remembered the last time he had been up there and quickly shook the memory. "Of course I will! I know the way very well and the gods there know me. I'll keep you safe."

"I never doubted it, little brother." Adara ruffled Quintus' hair and the boy smiled, uncaring of the pain it caused his head.

As the wagons crossed over the bridge, Lucius rode on ahead to see who was there. It appeared that Emrys, Carissa and Ashur had already arrived and had begun the process of unloading. Lucius could also spot Numa's short stocky form as he scurried in and out of the house, doubtless wondering where he could put everything.

The tribune charged up the long winding path to the plateau, his red cloak flapping behind him, turning the heads of all the slaves working in and around the fields as he went. He felt like a child but knew all too well that he was now master of this estate and would have to behave like one. He could not wait to get into the bathhouse.

"Greetings, friends!" Lucius called out, dismounting as Lunaris skidded to a halt. "You travelled quickly." Lucius embraced all three of them.

"The statues are safe, Tribune, as are all the busts of your ancestors."

"Glad to hear it, Emrys, although I'm even gladder if you are all well."

"We are, Tribune," Carissa said shyly. Ashur smiled and Lucius winked at him playfully; his friend seemed much happier.

"Come now, you two, we're friends. If my troops aren't with me, call me Lucius. Agreed?"

"Agreed!" Emrys laughed heartily and slapped Lucius on the back. He saw someone approaching from behind him. "Ah, here's your man." Lucius turned to see the estate steward.

"Numa! How long has it been?" The small, but strong man, smiled nervously.

"Master Lucius...erm...Tribune...I hardly recognised you. It's been many years. Welcome home."

"Thank you, Numa. It seems you have everything in hand, as usual. Are you well?"

"Very well, Tribune. It's been a mild winter here in the hills; Ceres and Mars the Father have blessed our crops."

"Excellent. And your wife Prisca, she is well?"

"Yes, Master. She'll be shocked to see how much you have grown."

"I'm sure." Lucius took Numa by the arm and led him aside while the others continued unpacking. "Listen, Numa. As I said in my letter, a lot has happened to everybody. We have been through a very painful few months."

"So I understood from your letter. As you asked, I have removed all of your father's belongings and put them in a back corner of one of the storage buildings. They are locked."

"Good man. Now, my mother especially requires all the love and attention we can give her. She has had the worst of it, along with Quintus and Clarinda. But mother however, is a hero to our family. Remember that, and do not be shocked when you see her. She does not look the same." The little man's eyes studied his master's face intently and he knew that he was absolutely serious.

"I understand, Master. We will take care of her."

"Good." Lucius looked to where the wagons were approaching with the troops. "Here they are." The two of them walked over to meet the wagon with Antonia, Adara and the children. Lucius helped Adara down and then his mother, who had trouble with the long drop from the wagon. Ambrosia held out the children to Adara and Quintus and Clarinda jumped down themselves.

Antonia looked around the place, the life flowing through it already, and smiled. Numa stood before her, calm and steady, though his glassy eyes betrayed the sadness he felt at seeing her.

"Mistress Metella. It's so good to have you here!"

"Oh Mistress!" Prisca came running up. Lucius grinned as he saw her, still rosy-cheeked and plump as ever. "Oh Mistress! It's so good to have life in this place again." Antonia smiled and returned the greetings fondly. She had always liked the two of them. Then Prisca spotted Adara and the children where they were next to Lucius. "Ooooooo! I can't believe my eyes!" Numa covered his face in mock shame and Antonia laughed as Prisca went over to Adara and Lucius. "Little Master Lucius?"

"The same, Prisca."

"It's 'Tribune' now, wife!" Numa barked.

"How are you, Prisca?"

"I'm fine now, 'Tribune'. And who is this?" Adara tried not to laugh as the woman turned her attentions on her and the children.

"Prisca, Numa, this is my wife, Adara Metella, and our two children Phoebus and Calliope."

"Ooooooooooooooo!" the two servants sighed collectively. "A whole new family!" Prisca clapped her hands. "They're beautiful. But their names sound so foreign? They're not Roman names, that's for certain."

"No, Prisca. They are not. The Lady Adara is from Athens. The children's names are Greek."

"Oh! My dear you must be absolutely freezing!" Prisca began to fuss.

"No really, I'm quite fine thank you." Before Adara could say another word Prisca had grabbed a blanket from the wagon behind her and thrown it about Adara's shoulders, leaving the beautiful Greek woman astonished and now far too warm.

"There! That's better. Keep the little cherubs warm too!" She cooed at the babies, her hands twisting in a jerky dance that Lucius remembered from his own childhood. "Oh ho! By the heavens above! This one sings! A blessing upon the house!" Prisca bobbed up and down for joy, grabbed Antonia's hand and Adara's arm and led them into the house talking as she went. "Come, everyone! The baths are warm and the food is almost ready!" Lucius laughed as they went into the house, Adara looked back over her shoulder as the portly woman pulled her along.

"Please forgive Prisca, Tribune," Numa said. "She has been quite low since the family stopped coming here all those summers ago. I have not seen her so happy in years."

"There's nothing to forgive, Numa." Lucius put his arm around the old man. "Why don't you show my friends to the baths?" He gestured toward Emrys, Carissa and Ashur. "And please show Ambrosia here to her room. I want her to be in the house with us, not in the slave quarters down the hill."

"Very good, Tribune." Numa turned, smiling to Ambrosia. "Come, dear. I'll show you where you will sleep."

When Numa had gone in with all of them, Alerio came up behind Lucius.

"So? How does it feel being all the way out here, master of the house?"

"Feels strange. Good too. It's going to take some time, but I think we'll manage."

"Your servants are funny. I wish mine back in Rome was as interesting."

"Where are your men?"

"Oh, they're setting up camp down on the other side of the river. There's just enough room. Tomorrow, we'll head back."

"Do you want to stay in the house yourself?"

"No. Better not." Alerio looked into the distance where his men had already outlined the perimeter of their camp and were pitching the tents. "I should camp out with them. I haven't won their full obedience and respect just yet."

"You'll be a tribune before you know it!" Lucius laughed.

"Naw! Primus Pilus would suit me fine."

"First centurion of the Praetorian Guard, eh? I'm sure you'll make it my friend."

"We'll see. It really is beautiful here." Alerio looked around, smelled the fresh air.

"Sure you can't stay for a time?"

"Positive. Have to get back to Rome and besides, I've had enough of the wilds for the time being." The two men were silent for a few moments.

"So, when will I be seeing you again?"

Alerio smiled, reading his thoughts, also feeling the emptiness of having to say goodbye.

"I'll be back soon. I'm also your official messenger now. I may need a little getaway from the city now and then. You'll see me, Lucius. Don't worry."

"I won't worry. I'll look forward to it, Centurion."

"Good! Now I'd better be getting back to my men. We'll leave before sunup tomorrow."

"Safe journey back to Rome, Alerio." The two men clasped forearms tightly.

"Thanks. Now, you get in there are take care of that beautiful family of yours."

"I will." Lucius watched Alerio turn and walk down the path to the river. When he had gone fifteen paces, he called out to him. "Alerio!"

He spun around. "What?"

"Alene couldn't have picked a better man to love." Alerio nodded, his face softened for a moment, then continued to walk down the hill to his century.

XXXII

NEMESIS DETEGEBAT

'Nemesis Unveiled'

A month passed and the family was finally beginning to settle into life on the estate. The nights were chilly and the wind had a different sound but the days bore mostly sun. When it did rain, it was loud and heavy, but in the storm's wake, a glorious rainbow always arched across the sky to fall into green hills.

The villa bustled with the sound of works, changes that Antonia wanted to make immediately; walls were painted in lighter, more uplifting colours, the upper loggia was reduced by half the size with the creation of extra rooms on that level. One of the rooms on the upper level was to be Lucius' study; he did not want to use the same room that his father had and so a newer, larger one was created. The old study was turned into a store room.

Ashur, Emrys and Carissa had stayed the entire time to help in the work too. When Paentalia, the festival of the dead at Rome, began in the middle of February, work on Alene's monument was underway. Emrys and Carissa had designed a beautiful memorial which they began immediately the day the three massive blocks of marble arrived from the warehouse in Rome. They knew they had to work quickly for Alene had gone unburied for too long. Those that died too young were feared as they were said to haunt the family dwelling and those within. For this reason, Emrys and Carissa, with Ashur's help, worked almost day and night to finish it. This time, there was no lack of inspiration and the work went fluidly.

After two weeks, the monument was finished, leaving the artisans exhausted but proud of their work. Emrys went into the house to see Antonia.

"Antonia."

"Yes, Emrys." She put down a scroll of poetry she had been reading.

"We've finished it."

"By Apollo, you've worked quickly! Are you pleased with it?"

"Very. I just wanted to know where you would like it."

Antonia thought about that for a moment and then it came to her. "I think it should stand down by the river, between the bridge and the apple and plum orchard."

"It should work. The ground is not too soft there."

"Alene used to pick flowers by the water's edge when she was a child." Antonia smiled to herself.

"Would you like to see it before we set it in place?"

"Hmm. No. I'd like to look upon it where it will remain."

"Very good. We'll finish polishing it up and then tomorrow morning we'll set it in place. With your permission, I'll ask Numa to assign several of the slaves to help with it. It's quite large and we need many hands to move it."

"Whatever you need is yours. Thank you, Emrys."

"You're very welcome." The sculptor held her gaze for a brief moment. *Such a strong woman*, he thought, as her face eased into that smile he never thought to see again. "I'll get back to work then." Antonia nodded slowly to him and went back to her reading as he left the room.

The following morning, the monument was set in place along the bank of the small river that flowed at the boundary of the Metelli lands. The sun was shining and the birds were revelling in the opening of spring and new warmth in the hills.

A large yellow cloth was draped over the monument and reached to the ground on either side. As the family looked upon it, they marvelled at its size. It appeared to be no less than five feet in height with awkward shapes sticking out the sides. In front of the monument a deep hole had been dug, big enough for the chest containing the urn to fit inside, and there to remain. On a small table were offerings to the departed: flowers, milk, honey and scented oils.

As soon as Antonia arrived with Adara and the children, Lucius asked Emrys and Carissa to remove the fabric to reveal the work.

The first thing to strike everyone was the brilliant mass of purest white marble as it stood among green grass and purple flowers. Then, it came to life. It was a tall rectangular altar that scrolled at the top corners. At the bottom were three steps. All eyes were then drawn to the façade to see an image of Alene walking before them, the likeness something only Emrys and Carissa could have achieved.

The young woman walked barefoot among budding flowers, dressed in a stola, with a long cloak that seemed to be blowing in some unfelt breeze. Her hair cascaded down her shoulders and back and she smiled serenely, unencumbered by worry or pretence. Above her, in the sky, was an inscription

Here lies Alene Metella
Daughter, Sister, Aunt
Beloved of Apollo
Alas, too young to leave…

"It's as though she is here with us…" Antonia said quietly, a tear creeping down her cheek.

"Who are those two men on the sides?" Clarinda asked, pointing to the images of two warriors on either side of the monument. They were kneeling, leaning against the sides of the altar, their hands almost reaching for Alene as she walked in flowered fields that continued up from the real flowers at the base of the steps. The men's eyes were closed beneath their crested helmets, their solemn longing and pain felt by anyone who looked upon their still forms.

Lucius realised that one vaguely resembled Alerio and the other, himself. Adara held him close, their eyes burning again with memory. She noticed that only the image of Alene was lifelike, clear.

After several minutes, Lucius and little Quintus picked up the chest with the urn and placed it in the hole. Emrys and Ashur then filled in the hole, making sure that the lead pipe coming up out of the ground was straight and free of obstructions. With that, libations could be offered directly to the departed in the other world.

Antonia rose, a thick bunch of flowers in her hands, and approached the altar. She placed the flowers on the top with some effort and then knelt down in front of the image, running her shaking fingers over her daughter's face, stroking her hair. "Apollo watch over you, my child."

Each of the family made their own prayers and offerings in turn and then began to make their way back up to the villa for a special meal in honour of Alene. As they walked, Lucius put his hand on Emrys' shoulder.

"You are truly a master, my friend, both of you." Carissa smiled too, pleased with the work they had done.

"We could only hope to aspire to the perfection that she had achieved, Lucius. She was a marvel."

They walked on in silence back to the house. When Lucius was on the upper level of the villa, in the room that was to be his study, he leaned over the railing of the loggia and found that he could see Alene's monument clearly, like a perfect white pearl in the grass. All around it swirled apple blossoms from the orchard, decking it with white and pink petals that blew on into the river and floated away.

With the lengthening of the days and the increasing warmth, Lucius had begun to rediscover the place of his youthful summers. It was a rediscovery made all the more pleasant because he now had Adara to share it with. Every morning, they were able to leave the children with their grandmother to ride around the estate.

These were to be some of the happiest times of their life together, full but fleeting moments brimming with joy and laughter and a sense of peace with which few mortals are ever blessed. Phoebus and Calliope had passed their first year of life without any problems to their health, and Lucius and Adara thanked the Gods for it. Indeed, the children were growing stronger and more beautiful by the day. Both had their parents' stature, and dark hair was thick upon their heads. They were the darlings of the estate and never wanted for any measure of attention, especially from their parents.

One day, little Quintus was thrilled when his older brother awoke him early in the morning to see if he wanted to go riding with them up to the top of the mountain to see the ancient tombs. The young man opened his eyes, squinting as he lay in bed, wondering if his head would start to reel the second he rose. It had been very sore the previous night; Lucius knew to be very gentle when waking him. Quintus eased his feet over the edge of his bed and pushed himself up.

"It doesn't hurt right now." He smiled, relieved. "Let's go!"

"I'll go and meet Adara at the stables, Quintus. Meet us there when you're ready."

"All right, Lucius. I won't be long. I just need to get dressed and put on a cloak. Can I bring my bow?"

"I don't see why not. You've been practising a lot lately, so I'm told."

"I find that I'm quite good with it." Lucius smiled at his little brother, not remembering a time when they had got on so well.

"I'll see you at the stables." Lucius closed the door behind him and went to meet Adara.

He had, in fact, been the one who had given Quintus the bow and specially made arrows. He remembered when he had taken it from one of the bandits who had been waiting to attack him and Dido on the road to Cirta. At the time, he had thought of learning to use it himself. Instead, Lucius had decided to make a gift of it to his brother. Quintus needed to learn the use of at least one weapon and the clang of sword blades gave him unbearable headaches. The bow seemed the perfect alternative and happily, the young man had become quite adept at it. He could skewer a hare on the move at a good distance or bring down a duck as it took off from the riverbank.

It did not take long for Quintus to meet Lucius and Adara and soon they were trotting gently up the trail that led past the vineyards and on up the sloping mountainside, zig-zagging their way along the path and through the trees to the top. As they rode, Quintus gazed up at the tombs where they were just visible through the still-bare foliage of the trees. He had not been there for a long time and once more tried to shake the memory of the last time he had gone into the darkness of the tombs.

"What's wrong, brother?" Lucius asked as they rode.

"I was thinking, Lucius. I don't think I want to be called 'Quintus' anymore."

"Really? But that's one of our ancestral names."

"I know. But it was also father's name and I don't much like the thought of sharing it with him. I'm not even the fifth born!"

"Hmm. I see your point."

"What would you like to be called?" Adara asked, her face making him smile as always.

"Well, I know that I should keep one ancestral name at least. After all, many of our forbears were very noble." Lucius nodded in agreement. "Maybe I should just go by 'Caecilius'. What do you think?"

"I think it's a good name. These days, many of the big families don't even use three names anyway. 'Caecilius Metellus' works well for you. What do you think, Adara?"

"I think it sounds very manly. Quite suitable for you, brother." The young man sat up straight and proud in his saddle, going over the sound of it in his mind.

"Caecilius it is then! But you keep your three names, Lucius. It suits you better."

Lucius laughed. "Oh, I will *Caecilius*. I'm a bit old fashioned when it comes to longer names."

"Look! There it is!" Caecilius trotted on up ahead as the tomb came into sight and was already off his horse by the time Lucius and Adara caught up with him. Lunaris reared as Lucius brought him up on the hollow-sounding earth.

"What is it, boy? Whoa!"

"What's wrong with him?" Adara stroked Phoenix who was also spooked.

"I don't know. He doesn't usually disobey like that." Lucius stroked the stallion's neck and muzzle, whispering softly to him. "There, there now. Shh. Good boy." He turned to Adara. "I think we'd better tie them up. We won't be up here too long. Quintu…Caecilius, did you bring the torch?"

"It's already lit! Come on inside!" Caecilius was already within, the glow of the torch lighting up one of the four passages that led to the inner chamber.

"Stay close to me, Adara. It gets a little tricky at times." Adara took Lucius' hand and he led her inside, his other hand instinctively on the handle of his sword.

Their voices echoed in the dampness of the rocky tomb. Adara found herself hoping that the giant cypresses growing out of the mound above them would not cause the entire roof to collapse.

"Caecilius," Lucius called out, "come back. We can't see anything. Bring the torch." Lucius moved along, feeling with his feet as he went. Adara was silent behind him, her palm sweaty in his. "There you are!"

They finally reached the central chamber and found Caecilius standing in the middle. He held the torch out and was looking into one of the corners.

"Look here, Lucius."

"What is it?" They all looked at a small pile of dirty clothing, a jug of water and what appeared to be strips of salted meat. There was a black spot on the floor where a fire had been lit and Lucius knelt to put his hand over it. "This isn't that old!" The smell of stale urine permeated the air.

"Looks like someone's been staying here," Adara said, backing up until she hit a wall. The sound of Lucius' sword coming out of the scabbard was soft in the dim tomb.

"Careful, sister!" Caecilius warned. "Don't disturb the niches in the walls. Sometimes snakes sleep in them."

"Snakes?" Adara quickly came forward. "Lucius," she looked to where he was poking the items on the floor with his blade, "let's go now. I don't like this place."

"Me neither. We should be going. Brother, lead the way while I have a look in the other rooms. Here, give me the torch." Caecilius handed Lucius the torch and led Adara out of the tomb to the light.

Lucius held the torch and his sword straight out in front, poking them simultaneously into each antechamber. The bones of his ancestors were still in their eternal sleep and he muttered a prayer to them, not wanting to disturb their spirits.

When he had checked all the chambers, Lucius emerged from the other side of the mound and made his way around. Green grass and red poppies were a welcome sight after the dank greyness of the tomb's interior.

"Did you find anything else?" Adara asked.

"No. Whoever is staying there is gone now. I'll tell Numa to notify all the workers to be on the lookout for strangers. Let's get back to the villa. I'm starving and I need a bath after that."

The three of them mounted the horses and made the slow journey down hill and back to the stables. It took about an hour to go back down and by the time they arrived they were all famished. They dismounted in front of the stables.

"I'll take care of the horses, Lucius," Adara said, reaching for the reigns.

"You don't have to."

"I want to. I enjoy brushing them down."

"All right. We'll see you up at the house." Lucius kissed her cheek and led Caecilius to the villa.

"Is Centurion Alerio coming to visit any time soon, Lucius?"

"Actually, he sent a letter not long ago saying he might drop by soon. He's got a lot of duties to attend to so I don't know how long he'll be able to stay."

"I can stay for a week! If you'll have me?" When they looked up, Alerio was standing in front of the villa, out of uniform, wearing a crimson tunic and leggings beneath a brown cloak.

"Well! This is unexpected!" Lucius clasped his arm. "I didn't think I'd see you for months!"

"Needed a break from the city." Alerio looked guilty.

"Ah. I see. So you've come to the wilds for a little relaxation?"

"Pretty much. Yes. How are you, Quintus?"

"Erm. It's Caecilius now," Lucius corrected Alerio gently.

"Oh. Forgive me. *Caecilius*. All is well?"

"Yes, Centurion Alerio. Very well."

"I'm off duty little man. Just 'Alerio' for now." Caecilius smiled and ran inside to tell his mother of their visitor. Alerio turned to Lucius. "I saw the monument as I rode up." He glanced down the hill. "It's...beautiful..."

"It is, isn't it?" Lucius wondered if Alerio recognised his likeness on the side of the monument.

"How are Emrys, Carissa and Ashur?"

"Oh, they're fine. They returned to Rome shortly after the monument was finished. Emrys had a lot of work to catch up on and Ashur and Carissa needed a little time alone, I think."

"Of course." Alerio looked around momentarily. "Where's Adara?"

Down in the stables Adara took her time brushing down the horses, taking extra care of Phoenix whom she felt she had neglected for too long after the birth of the children. She hummed as she worked and the horses' ears twitched to her music, content with her soft voice.

"There you go, Phoenix. All clean. You like it here, don't you?" The horse bobbed its head up and down. "Good. I knew you would. All this green grass everywhere and…what was that?" There was a sound near the stable door, as though a piece of wood had fallen. Adara closed the door to Phoenix's stall and walked to see who it was.

"Tellus? Is that you?" She called the name of the stable-master, walking over to his little room. "I wanted to ask you if you could… AHHHH!" The old man was sprawled on the floor, his neck opened and bleeding from a knife cut across it. As she ran to the door someone caught her arm and she felt cold steel rest against her throat.

"That's enough screaming now," said a deep voice. She tried to struggle but could not break free of the man's powerful arms. "Where's Lucius now? Tell me or I'll cut your throat."

"Did you hear something?" Lucius asked.

"Was it one of the children inside?" Alerio looked around.

"I don't think so." Lucius seemed to be feeling out, into the wind. Something was wrong and he had a sudden pang of fear. "I'd better check on Adara." He began to walk down the hill but was stopped dead in his tracks as Adara appeared along the path, her face fearful and her lithe neck marred by a slight cut along it. A large bearded man held a dagger to her and pushed her forward. "Adara!" Lucius yelled.

"That's far enough, Lucius!" the man yelled. His eyes spotted Alerio behind Lucius, sword drawn and ready. "Either of you move, she's dead!"

"Whoever you are, you'd better let her go or I'll gut you!" Lucius was raging, struggling to hide the fear that threatened to overwhelm him.

"All talk as ever! You're pitiful!"

"Look here. I have no quarrel with you. I don't even know you. Just let her go and you can be off without any trouble." The man seemed further angered by this.

"Do you think that's what I want? What I want is this place! You're on what's supposed to be *my* land!"

"You're mistaken friend," Alerio said from behind Lucius. "This is the tribune's land and you're trespassing."

"Shut your mouth, Alerio! Before I cut out your tongue! You two are responsible for everything I've been through, and now it's time you had yours."

"By the Gods," Lucius exclaimed. "It's Argus."

"Ah! Finally, you recognise me! I suppose you managed to convince yourselves that I was dead or that since Plautianus was dead I would simply forget all about *you* and go off and hide somewhere."

"I owe you an arrow, Argus!" Alerio said.

Lucius waved him off. His main concern at that point was Adara. Her eyes searched his as she wondered what to do.

"What do you want, Argus?" Lucius asked again.

"I want you to suffer. You always had the better of it when I should have shared in everything you ever had. It was my right! Do you know why?"

"I do know why, Argus. We're brothers. I know." Argus' face panicked and he let out what sounded like a growl. He had hoped to shock Lucius with this news. "Our father is dead, Argus! Gone before he could change any documents, before he could wipe us out of existence and put you there in our place."

Argus pressed the blade harder to Adara's neck. Lucius stepped forward but stopped as more blood began to trickle down her skin. "I guess there's just one thing to do then!" Argus gripped his prisoner tighter and angled the blade upward. "ARRRGGG!"

There was a whistling sound and Argus loosened his grip momentarily, giving Adara a chance to run. She pushed him backward and lunged up the hill crying and into Lucius' arms. Off to the side, behind one of the cypress trees, Caecilius

Metellus stood with another arrow notched in his bow. Argus grit his teeth as he felt where the first arrow had grazed his calf muscle.

By this time, most of the slaves had come around to see what was happening and Prisca helped Adara who held her throat by the door. Alerio began to move to one side and Caecilius on the other.

"I can kill him, Lucius!" Caecilius sighted along his arrow to Argus' chest.

"No! Wait! Alerio no!" Lucius waved both of them down and stared at Argus. He looked different; his hair was long as was his beard, he appeared strong and capable but his grey eyes looked wild and unpredictable. "What is it you want now Argus? Do you want to try and kill me?" Argus stood up. "Now's your chance. Let's get it over with. You and me. Isn't that what you've wanted for years?"

Argus eyed Lucius and spat. "I'll enjoy cutting your throat so that your pretty little wife can watch."

Lucius did not answer, simply tossed his cloak onto the ground and drew his sword as Argus drew his. He tried to ignore Adara's pleading behind him, begging him not to fight.

The two men crouched into fighting stances and circled each other like animals. "Let's see what you're made of," Argus said as he made the first attack.

The sound of clanging blades reached Antonia's ears within the house and she limped to the upper loggia to see what was happening. "Oh, Gods! Please not this!" She leaned on the railing to watch her son and Argus fight in the midst of a circle of onlookers, like the ancient combats on the tombs of fallen warriors.

Lucius realised that Argus had learned a lot more in his time with the Praetorians and struggled to keep his odd attacks from coming too close to his skin. Argus laughed as Lucius stumbled back, his effort apparent on his face. Lucius tried to think of some way to penetrate and break his attacks and remembered briefly how Ashur used to move, spinning in the air like a storm in the desert. Before he could try something, Argus lunged again in a run across Lucius' path and cut his prey's chest diagonally.

"AHH!" Lucius yelled in pain as he felt one of his pectorals rip. Argus laughed again.

"That's it! Cry like a baby! The way they all do before I kill them! Blade or bow, it doesn't matter, they all cry the same!" Argus circled Lucius who pivoted where he stood.

Lucius didn't have the energy for a quick attack and many blows so he decided to try and lure Argus who was preparing for another charge. It came with great force and speed, Lucius could see the blade with his own blood on it coming for him a second time. As Argus extended in his attack, Lucius parried in a lighting-quick spin so that his attacker's own momentum sent him quickly by. As Lucius came out of the spin he extended his own arm and walloped the back of Argus' head with the flat of his blade, sending him face down into the dirt. Lucius ran as best he could over to Argus' sword and kicked it away.

He reached out and grabbed Argus by the hair and dragged him back to the middle of the circle, flipped him over and levelled his sword at his throat.

"You got lucky, Lucius," Argus spat blood that leaked into his mouth. "You know I'm better than you."

"The only thing I know, Argus, is that you've always been an animal. You're not a man. You're not a Roman. You're nothing." Lucius could feel the urge to plunge the blade deep into Argus' face, mutilate him as he had done to so many. He could feel his mother's eyes on him from behind, Adara's too. *Not a fratricide!* He heard within himself. *The Gods will have their way!*

Lucius raised his sword above his head. "AHHHHHHHHHHH!" he swung down with all his might and slammed the flat of the blade against the side of Argus' head, sending him into unconscious darkness.

Antonia leaned over the balcony, thanked the Gods for keeping her son from such a crime, no matter how deserving Argus had been of the punishment.

Lucius turned and went straight back to Adara. Alerio bent over Argus with Caecilius to the side, his arrow still pointed at the limp body.

"He's still alive! Why didn't you kill him?"

Lucius turned to Alerio, his face the one that had commanded respect from hundreds in the field.

"You take him! I don't care where, I don't care what you do with him! My children won't have been fathered by a fratricide." Alerio smiled, and began to draw his dagger. "No, Alerio! Not here. Take him as far away from my land as possible, to Rome if you wish. Throw him to the mob, dump him in a stream. I don't care and I don't want to know." Alerio nodded, shocked by Lucius' harshness and what he saw as his sentimentality, but happy that he was the one to choose the method of Argus' demise. "Numa!" Lucius called the steward. "Get one of the extra pack horses and some rope for Alerio so he can take the bastard out of here."

"Ye…yes, Tribune! Right away!"

Three days had passed and Lucius began to wonder what Alerio had done with Argus. A part of him cursed himself for not having killed Argus himself, but he knew that it would have been a bad omen for his family and for the place in which they had made their new home. He had felt the slickness of enough blood upon his hands and did not want to add a brother's blood to it, even a half-brother.

The cuts on Adara's neck had been superficial and with herbal compresses that Prisca had prepared, there would be no physical scarring. She did however, awake in the night for several days after the event, screaming and grasping her throat. Lucius thanked the Gods that things had not been worse and suspected that Far-Shooting Apollo was guiding Caecilius' sight on that morning.

The stable-master's body had been horribly mutilated, the head just barely hanging from the body. The room was immediately purified and the body buried in the small necropolis for slaves on the far-western edges of the estate. Numa had seen to a suitable monument made of wood.

After a few weeks, everyone began to reclaim their own individual sense of normality and return to the peaceful day-to-day lives that they had all come to love and accept. Only Ambrosia still felt the torment of that day. She had loved Argus, long ago, and as he and Lucius had fought so brutally she had been torn. When Alerio carried his body off, tied to the back of a horse and bound for Rome and certain death, she cried and cried until tears no longer came. She had always held some reserve of hope that Argus would mend his ways and come back to her, apologise, but when he was carried off in defeat she realised that it was not the Gods' will that she should be happy with him. She had to be content with other things in life, but not love. Never love.

Summer was fast approaching and the estate was alive, the sun melting away all traces of horror and gloom. Lucius and Adara continued their morning rides together. The estate flourished. Merchants came to see if he was willing to offer them more of his crops of olives and stores of wine since they had done so well with his goods the year before.

When merchants did come, Lucius turned to Numa and the stocky man promptly went into a haggling business mode of behaviour. Lucius trusted him to do things as he had always done, with loyalty, wisdom and sometimes a heavy hand on the scales.

He finally had the chance to set up his own study, unpack all of his scrolls, weapons, and items he had gathered from around the empire in his first years of service. Publius Leander, Delphina and the girls would be arriving soon to stay with them for the summer, to see their grandchildren. He wanted every room in the villa to look perfect and his room was the last to be addressed.

Lucius leaned on the railing of the upper loggia and looked out over the land, the hills, the trees. The sun was high and bright, the sky blue as the summer sea. Down below, Adara, Antonia, Caecilius and Clarinda played with Phoebus and Calliope in the grass, giggling and singing and enjoying the day. His wife looked up at him and he waved, feeling the warmth of her smile before he turned back into his study.

He had set up a large campaign table in front of an arched window and on the opposite wall was a massive pigeonhole case for all of the scrolls that Diodorus, his beloved tutor, had left to him years ago. In the corner to the left of the table, the armour of his ancestors gleamed brightly upon its wooden frame. Above it stood the vexillum, the dragon emblazoned upon it.

Lucius pushed past the crates and chests of items to the wall opposite the entrance of the room where he had set up an altar. The powerful image of Olympian Apollo stared knowingly into the young man's eyes and Lucius thanked him. There was nothing in particular for which he expressed his thanks, simply a general sense of gratefulness in life, of fulfilment, of good fortune. After lighting some incense in offering, he moved to one of the boxes he had brought from Numidia, carefully removed a wide, clay dish with a cover and put it upon the table in front of the window.

He glanced over at the vexillum again, thought he could hear the sound of horns and drums, and removed the clay top of the dish to reveal the soft sand he had brought with him. Lucius Metellus Anguis sank both hands into the dish to feel the soft cool contents fall between his fingers. He gazed out the window at the green hills, listened to the laughter of his family.

He was a long way from Lambaesis now, far from sand, and swaying palms.

EPILOGUS

A.D. 207

After the death of Gaius Fulvius Plautianus and the executions of his staunchest supporters throughout the empire, absolute control fell once more into the hands of Septimius Severus and his sons, Caracalla and Geta. The emperor was not a favourite among the senators of Rome, indeed he never had been, but to the Roman people, Severus was a man of utmost generosity and power. These two highly prized qualities meant that he had the loyalty of the people and hence, was master of Rome.

Always at her husband's side, always in his ear, Julia Domna too held the reigns of power firmly in her grasp. She had almost lost them, lost the battle that had taken place behind closed doors and performed smiles, the battle fought by slaves and spies, loyal soldiers, and those other men whose values could be bought for a bag of denarii.

Whenever she had the luxury of time alone, Julia Domna would make her way to the throne room of the palace and stand at the window where her fiercest foe had been thrown down into the jaws of Hades. She had not been there to see it, but, as she leaned on the marble railing with the city before her, she tantalised herself with images of Plautianus' limp body being dragged across the floor and tossed out of the high window like a pile of rubbish.

She had hoped that her troubles would end with the demise of the Praetorian prefect, his successors being much easier to control, but it was not as she hoped. With Plautianus gone, her sons, Caracalla and Geta went wild. Rumours reached her ears of sexual abuses upon women and boys, embezzled money and close associations with the gladiators and charioteers of Rome, among the lowest of society.

The two young Caesars argued constantly with each other and their squabbles were notorious. The most brutal of their disputes culminated in a chariot race between the two of them; seven times around the hippodrome they sped, cheered by the unscrupulous men with whom they held company. It was said that they raced with great ferocity, neither willing to back down or accede to defeat. The turns were tight and deadly and they lashed each other as they went. Before a winner was determined however, Caracalla was thrown from his chariot at such an intense speed that upon landing the sound of his leg breaking could be heard by most of the onlookers.

The emperor was furious, especially that this happened at a time when he was still deeply involved in his cleansing of the senate. Therefore, while Caracalla mended, Severus carried out his duty and convicted and killed the last of the senators who had supported Plautianus as each was discovered. He even ordered the execution of the much-admired, aged Quintillus Plautianus, a noble whose death shroud, which had already been made, fell apart at the execution. The fibres of the fine material simply crumbled before all eyes prior to the execution and upon seeing this, the gentle greybeard was heard to have said: "What does this mean? I suppose it means that we are late."

There were other such cases of victims of informers, some old, some young. As in all times of proscription, the opportunists were out in force to eliminate any of their own personal opponents, be they harmless old men living out their days in the countryside or young men of Rome heedless of their creditors' demands for payment.

Such were the goings-on in Rome in the two years after the fall of Plautianus. Often-times word would even reach Lucius' ears in Etruria about what had been happening and every time he said, "Thank the Gods we're not in Rome."

In the two years that he and the family had been living in Etruria, Lucius had devoted much of his time to enriching his knowledge of the inner workings of the estate. As head of the family, he knew that he should take responsibility for the family's welfare and prosperity. In truth, he had never thought that he would find so much enjoyment in working the land and overseeing the wine and oil production, but he did. Every day he set out with Numa to make the rounds of the estate, to learn who did what jobs and how.

The rest of his time was shared between training and time with Adara and the children. Phoebus and Calliope were into their third summer of life and were thriving; so much in fact that they had to be under constant supervision. As they ran and jumped, so too did they learn to disappear in a flurry of giggles only to be found in the most unlikely of places. Usually, singing would bring Calliope out of hiding, Adara wandering the corridors and gardens of the villa humming the tune the children's aunt used to sing.

Phoebus on the other hand, proved more difficult to find, and it was not unusual for Lucius to be walking in the orchard or among long grass when a small beast resembling his son would dart out and grab hold of his boots. It came to the point where Lucius eventually decided to leave his sword in the house for fear that he would be unduly surprised by Phoebus. He found it difficult to be angry with either of his children however, decided that a little freedom of youth was warranted at such a young age; the estate was safe and it was their own.

It was on a hot, sunny day in Junius that Lucius' perception of his newly discovered peace and place in the world changed. For long, he had felt the approving gaze of Apollo and gentle breath and Lady Venus; they had been pleased and rewarded him. But the God of War was restless. His face hidden for too long behind the sun, Mars began to peer over the hills and march across the land with the sound of horns in his dusty wake.

Lucius had been practising manoeuvres on Lunaris out on the vast field between the villa and the river, charging back and forth as he attacked the elaborate array of wooden dummies he had constructed. Just up the hill, watching, Antonia, Adara and the others were enjoying a summer picnic in the long shivering grass.

The feel of the exertion and the hot sweat that dripped down his face felt good. He found that the hard labour of the estate, combined well with his training, gave him a connection to his war-like ancestors who also farmed in times of peace, until the call to arms came.

Lunaris charged and reared and spun at Lucius' command, almost dancing about the field. Then it seemed a wind picked up, hot and breezy from the south. Lucius rode to the river's edge and stopped to listen, his eyes closed. He could hear it on the wind, the howl of a familiar standard.

Up the hill, Antonia and Adara looked about for the storm clouds that no doubt accompanied the thunderous clamour, but could see none. The earth seemed to rumble as the storm came closer and closer and Lucius recognised the song. He had thought of it often and smiled.

Charging up the road from the via Cassia was a large force of cavalry, scales glinting in the summer sun. They roared as they approached, striking fear into the hearts of everyone except for Lucius who knew what it was. At the head of the column, the draconarius howled and tore through the peaceful air, its long fluttering tail extending into the men behind it. They stopped at the bridge over the river and a single rider rode forward to meet Lucius, his face covered by a cavalry mask.

Lucius smiled. "What's all this about, soldier?" The heavily-armoured man nudged his stallion forward to stand next to Lucius and flipped up his mask.

"It's about seeing long-missed friends, Anguis!"

"Dagon!" The two men clasped forearms, each smiling from ear to ear, sweat and dirt glistening on their brows. "What, in Epona's name, are you doing here?"

"Well, I've never actually seen Italy and, as I have a good friend who lives here, I thought a visit was warranted."

"You're a terrible liar, *little fish*, but I'll accept that reason as much as any. You've got yourself quite an escort for a simple visit..." Lucius rode round to see the hundred and twenty mounted warriors, many whom he recognised. They saluted him and he returned the courtesy. "What's the news? Where's Mar?"

Dagon was silent.

"Barta!" Dagon called to the standard bearer.

"Yes, Captain!" The man's horse came to the edge of the bridge.

"Set the horses to graze in that field opposite while I speak with the tribune."

"Yes, sir!" The man turned his horse and shouted orders to the other riders.

"We need to talk, Anguis." Lucius led Dagon up the hill toward Adara and the others who had been watching with mingled fear and curiosity.

"Dagon!" Adara exclaimed as they dismounted. "What a surprise to see you!"

"It is good to see you too, Lady Metella." Dagon bowed to Adara and to the others.

"Mother," Lucius began, "this is my good friend, Dagon. We fought together in Numidia against the nomads. He saved my life on that occasion." Dagon waved his hands humbly.

"No more than Anguis would have done for me, Lady."

"I am happy to meet you, Dagon," Antonia said.

Caecilius walked up to stand beside Lucius, his eyes staring at Dagon's scaly armour. Dagon smiled at him.

"And I take it this is the younger Metellus?"

"Yes, sir," Caecilius said proudly. "I'm Caecilius, Lucius' brother."

"I am happy to meet you, Caecilius."

"I like your armour very much!" Caecilius was excited.

"Thank you. It is the armour of my homeland."

"Dagon is from Sarmatia," Lucius added, "but was posted in Numidia." Dagon nodded. "You're a long way from base Dagon. Shall we go inside and eat? The baths are warm." Dagon reached into a deep pouch that hung from his saddle.

"Perhaps after, Anguis. For now, I bring news that cannot wait."

"What is it? Shall we go into my study?"

"There's no need. It concerns your family in a way. First of all, I must tell you about Mar."

"What, Dagon? Tell me." Lucius could see the young man holding back intense feelings.

"Mar, my uncle and lord, is dead." Lucius could hear Adara gasp behind him and he reached for her hand.

"What happened?"

"We were out on patrol far to the south when we were ambushed by a combined force of Garamantians and Numidian rebels. We fought them back of course, killed most of them but not before Mar was struck by a stray arrow."

"Gods." Lucius felt great sadness at this, pictured the noble Sarmatian's face.

"It was not a serious wound, more of a scratch really, but the arrow happened to be poisoned. The physician Loxias could not devise a remedy in time and Mar died in his sleep three nights later."

"I'm sorry, my friend." Lucius put his hand on the younger man's shoulder. "He will be missed."

"You were in his thoughts, Anguis, in his final hours. He always spoke fondly of you." Dagon held out a scroll with the imperial insignia on it and gave it to Lucius. "This brings me to the other purpose for this visit. Mar knew he was going to die. He called the Legate Marcellus to his chamber..."

Lucius read over the letter and when he was finished he looked up, his eyes betraying his disbelief and surprise.

"What's the meaning of this?" he asked.

"It contains your new orders and confirms your promotion." Dagon stood straight.

"Promotion?" Antonia said from where she stood.

"What promotion, Lucius?" Adara leaned closer to him.

"It seems that I've been promoted from my rank as Tribunus Angusticlavius to Praefectus of a cavalry ala, by order of the emperor."

"Praefectus. What an honour!" Antonia exclaimed proudly.

"To be exact," Dagon began, "prefect of a Sarmatian cavalry ala." He looked down the hill to where the field glittered with scale armour. "Those are your men down there, *Praefectus*."

"But that should be your command, not mine. Why was *I* chosen for this?"

"It was Mar's suggestion to the legate that if he were to die, you be the one to take his place. He didn't think I was ready for command yet, said that he would rest easier in the green fields on the other side of the eternal river if he knew that you were with me." Dagon looked at Lucius, his face friendly and accepting. "I agreed with him, Anguis. I can't think of another man, after my uncle, whom I would rather serve under. Do you accept this?"

"Of course I do. It'll be an honour to ride with you and your countrymen."

"Good. I'll go notify the men of their new commander and then, I'll take you up on that meal."

"I'll be waiting here." They watched Dagon ride down the hill at breakneck speed and then everyone turned to Lucius.

He was in shock. Mar was dead and because of his kind words to the legate, who passed them on to the emperor, Lucius now held one of the most sought after ranks in the career of the Equestrian class. There were very few positions for ala commanders and Lucius knew that the highly prestigious appointments were reserved for the best and ablest men. He also suspected that the help he had leant to the empress and Caracalla must have had something to do with it. Lucius read over the letter again; it was signed by the emperor himself.

"Lucius?"

"Yes, Caecilius."

"Does this mean you'll be going away now?"

"I don't know, brother. Most likely, yes."

Then Adara took Lucius aside briefly, having remembered something. "I can tell there's much doubt in your mind. I see it. Do you suppose this is a gift?"

"It is. I know. I just don't feel right about taking Mar's place."

"I know, but I just thought of something. Remember the Sibyl's words?"

"What about them?"

"*They will come to you as thunder!…Use them…know them. Upon the grassy mound.*" Adara repeated the words that so often haunted her thoughts. "Look around you Lucius, look at this place where Dagon has just come to you." Lucius looked about at the green grass and the plateau on which the villa sat amid the hills. He looked down the hill at the men as they made their camp on his land.

"By Apollo, Adara. You're right." He sighed deeply, knowing the implications of his appointment, wondered if they would be returning to Africa after all. It was an honour, a command that allowed a larger degree of independence and was accompanied by no less glamour. "Come, let's go inside. Over dinner, we'll find out more from Dagon. Here he is."

The young Sarmatian rode up the hill and dismounted with a jump. "The men are happy you've accepted, Anguis. I told them you would come down to meet with them tomorrow."

"I look forward to it. For now, let's go inside and talk some more." Lucius put his arm around Dagon as they walked.

"The children have grown up quite a bit," Dagon observed.

"You have no idea," Lucius answered as he led him inside.

Over a wonderful meal, Lucius was apprised of all that had happened since he left Africa. The attack in which Mar had been struck was one of several incidents, all of which had been stomped out thoroughly. Dagon had seen Alerio in Rome apparently, and so the centurion knew of Lucius' imminent promotion.

When they had eaten their fill, Dagon reclined, echoing his departed uncle's grace. "I suppose that we had best get on with the training as soon as possible, Anguis. There's much for you to learn about Sarmatian tactics."

"There will be plenty of time for training." Lucius sipped his wine.

"No. Not really much time at all."

"What do you mean? We can train back at Lambaesis."

"Anguis, we're not going to Lambaesis."

"You're not blunt enough for a Sarmatian, my friend. Spit it out."

"Your other orders are to prepare your cavalry ala for the coming campaign." Dagon handed Lucius another scroll.

"Campaign?" Adara and Antonia stared worriedly at the two men. It was something they had all been dreading in the last two years, but knew that the day would come at some point.

"Yes, the emperor is planning a massive campaign."

"Where?"

"Britannia. North of the Wall. Caledonia to be precise." Everyone was silent. Lucius hung his head, stared into his wine cup and swirled its contents. He felt Adara's hand on his thigh.

"Britannia." Lucius let out a deep breath. It was a long way from the peaceful home he had come to love. Like his ancestors, he would have to leave his lands, unsure of when, or whether, he would return. "When do we leave?"

"Six months. The emperor wants to land the main force there in the new year but we are to go on ahead to get things rolling."

"Where will the emperor land?"

"At Eburacum, according to Alerio."

Lucius knew that more than just the eyes of the people in the room were upon him at that moment. He could feel the presence of Apollo behind him, the warmth of Venus beside and before him, the fateful gaze of Mars, waiting. Lucius stood up from his couch to face them all, the statues of his ancestors lit by torches in the courtyard outside, not far off. He raised his cup.

"To Gods, Goddesses and Heroes."

He could see and feel them all.

Thank you for reading!

Did you enjoy *Killing the Hydra*? Here is what you can do next.

If you enjoyed this adventure with Lucius Metellus Anguis, and if you have a minute to spare, please consider posting a short review on the web page where you purchased the book.

Reviews are a wonderful way for new readers to find this series of books and your help in spreading the word is greatly appreciated.

The story continues in *Warriors of Epona*, and the next Eagles and Dragons novel will be coming soon, so be sure to sign-up for e-mail updates at:

www.eaglesanddragonspublishing.com

Newsletter subscribers get a FREE BOOK, and first access to new releases, special offers, and much more!

Become a Patron of Eagles and Dragons Publishing!

If you enjoy the books that Eagles and Dragons Publishing puts out, our blogs about history, mythology, and archaeology, our video tours of historic sites and more, then you should consider becoming an official patron.

We love our regular visitors to the website, and of course our wonderful newsletter subscribers, but we want to offer more to our 'super fans', those readers and history-lovers who enjoy everything we do and create.

You can become a patron for as little as $1 per month. For your support, you will also get loads of fantastic rewards as tokens of our appreciation.

If you are interested, just visit the website below to go to the Eagles and Dragons Publishing Patreon page to watch the introductory video and check out the patronage levels and exciting rewards.

https://www.patreon.com/EaglesandDragonsPublishing

Join us for an exciting future as we bring the past to life!

AUTHOR'S NOTE

Killing the Hydra was a difficult book to write. The world and experiences into which I had thrown Lucius in *Children of Apollo* led him into a labyrinth haunted by many antagonists. Each time Lucius defeats one enemy, another appears.

The Roman Empire in the early third century was not a safe place for honest men. This is a particularly dangerous time for Lucius who has tried, unsuccessfully, to distance himself from politics. Life was cheap in ancient Rome, and those holding the reins of power thought little about using soldiers and others for their own ends.

It is also a fascinating time of change, for during this period the Roman Empire is at its greatest extent, having incorporated aspects of the religions and cultures of the many peoples now under the rule of the Caesars. The Severans are also the first non-Italian dynasty to sit on the imperial throne.

As my main source for this period, I have once more opted for Cassius Dio (c. A.D. 164-230) and the text of his *History of Rome*, particularly books 76-77. Dio lived during the events that are occurring around Lucius and was actually at the imperial court.

Septimius Severus, though a strong emperor in some ways, was, at that time, in ailing health. He was expertly manipulated by his friend and kinsman, Gaius Fulvius Plautianus, who was prefect of the Praetorian guard as well as consul.

Plautianus was the most powerful man in the empire, and Dio describes the lengths that Plautianus went to to amass so much power and wealth. He used threats, torture, terror, and manipulation, and had a spy network with an infinite reach.

All feared the Praetorian prefect and it is, I believe, Severus' main failing as emperor that he trusted his kinsman so implicitly.

Dio quotes a letter Severus had apparently written in which he says: "I love the man [Plautianus] so much that I pray I die before he does."

It is perhaps fortunate that Caracalla and the empress, Julia Domna, were waging their own private war on Plautianus. They had reason to. The Praetorian prefect harassed the young Caesar who was married to his daughter, Plautilla, at every turn. Plautianus' spies notified him of every move Caracalla and his mother made.

Dio describes the way in which Plautianus had "mastery in every way over the emperor, that he often treated even Julia Augusta in an outrageous manner; for he cordially detested her and was always abusing her violently to Severus."

However, Julia Domna was a highly intelligent woman, and an astute politician. Caracalla was close to his mother and, though rash, he was no coward. It would have been imperative for the empress and her son to enlist their own network of spies and allies.

The character of Drusus, the empress' spy and cousin, is fictitious. However, the Syrian contingent at court was large, and it is not inconceivable that family members would have been among Julia Domna's most loyal supporters.

Lucius and his family find themselves enmeshed in this behind-the-scenes war that was raging between the empress and Plautianus. Lucius is indebted to the empress for the help she gave him in Leptis Magna. It is an historical truth that those indebted to people in power will eventually be called upon to make good on those debts.

In *Killing the Hydra* I have tried to remain true to the history as Dio relates it. Even though Dio's account is likely tainted by his personal dislike of the Praetorian prefect, the story he relates as history for the fall of Plautianus was just too good not to use.

According to Dio, Caracalla did indeed plot with three centurions, one named Saturninus, to overthrow Plautianus with false accusations. It was an opportune moment for Julia Domna and her son. The emperor's brother, Geta, had recently accused the Praetorian prefect as he lay on his death bed with Severus at his side.

Severus' trust in Plautianus had taken a hard hit, and so the Praetorian prefect was brought before Severus to answer for himself, however false the allegations might have been.

The only liberty I have taken in this crucial episode is that I inserted Alerio as one of the three centurions, and of course Lucius, a tribune, as the third accomplice. Both characters certainly had the motive after all the pain that Plautianus and his agents had caused. Lucius was already indebted to the empress, and so it seemed like a perfect fit.

A new introduction to the *Eagles and Dragons* series in Book II is the Sarmatian cavalry *ala* led by Mar and his nephew Dagon. The latter are both fictional characters, but the Sarmatians themselves were very real.

The Sarmatians were a Scythian-speaking people from north of the Black Sea, whose culture and military force thrived from the fifth century B.C. to the fourth century A.D. when their borders were broken by invading Huns and Goths.

These ancient warriors are fascinating. The Sarmatians were a nomadic Steppe culture whose heavily armoured cataphracts were the elite cavalry of the age. Their battle standard was the *draconarius*, a dragon-headed banner that roared in the wind. The men and horses wore scale armour that struck fear into the enemies they would ride over with ease, and because of their armour, they looked like lizards, or the dragons they so revered. Sarmatian women were also trained to ride and fight!

When the Sarmatian forces came up against Rome's legions and finally suffered a crushing defeat against Marcus Aurelius in A.D. 175, things changed. The Romans knew a good thing when they saw it, and so the heavy Sarmatian cataphract was made a part of Rome's auxiliary forces, the first wave of recruits numbering eight thousand. These warriors came fully equipped, with their own larger mounts, and were sent to various hotspots around the empire, including Britain.

I do not know if any Sarmatians were active in North Africa during the early third century, but with Severus' erratic distribution of forces, it is not implausible. Look for an even bigger role for these warriors in Book III, *Warriors of Epona*!

Killing the Hydra is a sprawling novel that takes place in sites from North Africa, such as Leptis Magna, Thugga and Lambaesis, to Athens, Etruria, and of course Rome.

Rome and Athens are two of my favourite cities in the world, and I encourage anyone with an interest in ancient history to visit both. In these places one can really feel and understand the majesty of the classical world.

For the North African locations in *Killing the Hydra*, I have had to rely on topographical maps, city plans, photos, and other secondary sources for places like Leptis Magna in Libya, and Lambaesis in Algeria. Due to modern conflicts in these areas, travel would not have been a smart move on my part.

However, apart from Athens, Rome, and Etruria, I was able to travel through the Sahara desert in Tunisia and visit the ruins of the Roman city of Thugga.

Thugga is, of course, where Lucius meets the Punic prostitute, Dido, who saves his life. Dido is fictional, but the brothel where she worked, beside the public latrine, is real, and today visitors can still see the many small *cubicula* about the peristyle of the courtyard.

The ruins of ancient Thugga are vast and incredibly well-preserved. I have never seen a site like this. As one strolls from the magnificent theatre, past the Capitol, and down the fully paved road to the brothel and beyond, the ghosts of Roman and Punic dead are there, whispering in one's ear.

It is incredible that Rome built such cities so far away from its beating heart. When I see places like Thugga, I realize how truly far the arm of Rome reached.

One more location in the book that I should mention is the Sahara desert itself, where much of the action in *Killing the Hydra* takes place. I love the desert and ever since my travels over the dunes, through the canyons and oases, I can't stop thinking about it. The desert's sparse beauty is captivating. It is a gift, and one that, for the writer, is an infinite blank page for the imagination. You feel like anything can happen.

As I walked over the dunes and felt the soft sand slip through my fingers one handful at a time, as the sun set red in the distance, Lucius' story played out before me. Many of the ideas and scenes for Books I and II came to me there. Not many places can affect a person so, or inspire art with such simplicity.

At the end of *Killing the Hydra*, Lucius receives orders to go to another far corner of the Roman Empire. He will leave the desert and Rome far behind now, and go with his troops to Britannia, where yet another war is to be waged.

Lucius Metellus Anguis will return in the third book of the Eagles and Dragons series, *Warriors of Epona*.

For discussion on the history and archaeology of the Roman Empire during this period, as well as photos and more, go to https://eaglesanddragonspublishing.com/the-world-of-killing-the-hydra/.

Adam Alexander Haviaras
January, 2014
Toronto, Ontario

GLOSSARY

aedes – a temple; sometimes a room

aedituus – a keeper of a temple

aestivus – relating to summer; a summer camp or pasture

agora – Greek word for the central gathering place of a city or settlement

ala – an auxiliary cavalry unit

amita – an aunt

amphitheatre – an oval or round arena where people enjoyed gladiatorial combat and other spectacles

anguis – a dragon, serpent or hydra; also used to refer to the 'Draco' constellation

angusticlavius – 'narrow stripe' on a tunic; Lucius Metellus Anguis is a *tribunus angusticlavius*

apodyterium – the changing room of a bath house

aquila – a legion's eagle standard which was made of gold during the Empire

aquilifer – senior standard bearer in a Roman legion who carried the legion's eagle

ara – an altar

armilla – an arm band that served as a military decoration

augur – a priest who observes natural occurrences to determine if omens are good or bad; a soothsayer

aureus – a Roman gold coin; worth twenty-five silver *denarii*

auriga – a charioteer

ballista – an ancient missile-firing weapon that fired either heavy 'bolts' or rocks

bireme – a galley with two banks of oars on either side

bracae – knee or full-length breeches originally worn by barbarians but adopted by the Romans

caldarium – the 'hot' room of a bath house; from the Latin *calidus* caligae – military shoes or boots with or without hobnail soles

cardo – a hinge-point or central, north-south thoroughfare in a fort or settlement, the *cardo maximus*

castrum – a Roman fort

cataphract – a heavy cavalryman; both horse and rider were armoured

cena – the principal, afternoon meal of the Romans

chiton – a long woollen tunic of Greek fashion

chryselephantine – ancient Greek sculptural medium using gold and ivory; used for cult statues

civica – relating to 'civic'; the civic crown was awarded to one who saved a Roman citizen in war

civitas – a settlement or commonwealth; an administrative centre in tribal areas of the Empire

clepsydra – a water clock

cognomen – the surname of a Roman which distinguished the branch of a gens

collegia – an association or guild; e.g. *collegium pontificum* means 'college of priests'

colonia – a colony; also used for a farm or estate

consul – an honorary position in the Empire; during the Republic they presided over the Senate

contubernium – a military unit of ten men within a century who shared a tent

contus – a long cavalry spear

cornicen – the horn blower in a legion

cornu – a curved military horn

cornucopia – the horn of plenty

corona – a crown; often used as a military decoration

cubiculum – a bedchamber

curule – refers to the chair upon which Roman magistrates would sit (e.g. *curule aedile*)

decumanus – refers to the tenth; the *decumanus maximus* ran east to west in a Roman fort or city denarius – A Roman silver coin; worth one hundred brass *sestertii*

dignitas – a Roman's worth, honour and reputation

domus – a home or house

draco – a military standard in the shape of a dragon's head first used by Sarmatians and adopted by Rome

draconarius – a military standard bearer who held the draco

eques – a horseman or rider

equites – cavalry; of the order of knights in ancient Rome

fabrica – a workshop

fabula – an untrue or mythical story; a play or drama

familia – a Roman's household, including slaves

flammeum – a flame-coloured bridal veil

forum – an open square or marketplace; also a place of public business (e.g. the *Forum Romanum*)

fossa – a ditch or trench; a part of defensive earthworks

frigidarium – the 'cold room' of a bath house; a cold plunge pool

funeraticia – from *funereus* for funeral; the *collegia funeraticia* assured all received decent burial

garum – a fish sauce that was very popular in the Roman world

gladius – a Roman short sword

gorgon – a terrifying visage of a woman with snakes for hair; also known as Medusa

greaves – armoured shin and knee guards worn by high-ranking officers

groma – a surveying instrument; used for accurately marking out towns, marching camps and forts etc.

hasta – a spear or javelin

horreum – a granary

hydraulis – a water organ

hypocaust – area beneath a floor in a home or bath house that is heated by a furnace

imperator – a commander or leader; commander-in-chief
insula – a block of flats leased to the poor
intervallum – the ditch between two palisades
itinere – a road or itinerary; the journey

lanista – a gladiator trainer
lemure – a ghost
libellus – a little book or diary
lituus – the curved staff or wand of an augur; also a cavalry trumpet
lorica – body armour; can be made of mail, scales or metal strips; can also refer to a cuirass
lustratio – a ritual purification, usually involving a sacrifice

manica – handcuffs; also refers to the long sleeves of a tunic
marita – wife
maritus – husband
matertera – a maternal aunt
maximus – meaning great or 'of greatness'
missum – used as a call for mercy by the crowd for a gladiator who had fought bravely
murmillo – a heavily armed gladiator with a helmet, shield and sword

nomen – the gens of a family (as opposed to *cognomen* which was the specific branch of a wider gens)
nones – the fifth day of every month in the Roman calendar
novendialis – refers to the ninth day
nutrix – a wet-nurse or foster mother
nymphaeum – a pool, fountain or other monument dedicated to the nymphs

officium – an official employment; also a sense of duty or respect

onager – a powerful catapult used by the Romans; named after a wild ass because of its kick

optio – the officer beneath a centurion; second-in-command within a century

palaestra – the open space of a gymnasium where wrestling, boxing and other such events were practiced

palliatus – indicating someone clad in a pallium, a sort of robe for rituals

pancration – a no-holds-barred sport that combined wrestling and boxing

parentalis – of parents or ancestors; (e.g. *Parentalia* was a festival in honour of the dead)

parma – a small, round shield often used by light-armed troops; also referred to as *parmula*

pater – a father

pax – peace; a state of peace as opposed to war

peregrinus – a strange or foreign person or thing

peristylum – a peristyle; a colonnade around a building; can be inside or outside of a building or home

phalerae – decorative medals or discs worn by centurions or other officers on the chest

pilum – a heavy javelin used by Roman legionaries

plebeius – of the plebeian class or the people

pontifex – a Roman high priest

popa – a junior priest or temple servant

primus pilus – the senior centurion of a legion who commanded the first cohort

pronaos – the porch or entrance to a building such as a temple

protome – an adornment on a work of art, usually a frontal view of an animal

pteruges – protective leather straps used on armour; often a leather skirt for officers

pugio – a dagger

quadriga – a four-horse chariot

quinqueremis – a ship with five banks of oars

retiarius – a gladiator who fights with a net and trident

rosemarinus – the herb rosemary

rusticus – of the country; e.g. a *villa rustica* was a country villa

sacrum – sacred or holy; e.g. the *via sacra* or 'sacred way'.

schola – a place of learning and learned discussion

scutum – the large, rectangular, curved shield of a legionary

secutor – a gladiator armed with a sword and shield; often pitted against a *retiarius*

sestertius – a Roman silver coin worth a quarter *denarius*

sica – a type of dagger

signum – a military standard or banner

signifer – a military standard bearer

spatha – an auxiliary trooper's long sword; normally used by cavalry because of its longer reach

spina – the ornamented, central median in stadia such as the Circus Maximus in Rome

stadium – a measure of length approximately 607 feet; also refers to a race course

stibium – *antimony*, which was used for dyeing eyebrows by women in the ancient world

stoa – a columned, public walkway or portico for public use; often used by merchants to sell their wares

stola – a long outer garment worn by Roman women

strigilis – a curved scraper used at the baths to remove oil and grime from the skin

taberna – an inn or tavern

tabula – a Roman board game similar to backgammon; also a writing-tablet for keeping records

tepidarium – the 'warm room' of a bath house

tessera – a piece of mosaic paving; a die for playing; also a small wooden plaque

testudo – a tortoise formation created by troops' interlocking shields

thraex – a gladiator in Thracian armour

titulus – a title of honour or honourable designation

torques – also 'torc'; a neck band worn by Celtic peoples and adopted by Rome as a military decoration

trepidatio – trepidation, anxiety or alarm

tribunus – a senior officer in an imperial legion; there were six per legion, each commanding a cohort

triclinium – a dining room

tunica – a sleeved garment worn by both men and women

ustrinum – the site of a funeral pyre

vallum – an earthen wall or rampart with a palisade

veterinarius – a veterinary surgeon in the Roman army

vexillarius – a Roman standard bearer who carried the *vexillum* for each unit

vexillum – a standard carried in each unit of the Roman army

vicus – a settlement of civilians living outside a Roman fort

vigiles – Roman firemen; literally 'watchmen'

vitis – the twisted 'vinerod' of a Roman centurion; a centurion's emblem of office

vittae – a ribbon or band

ACKNOWLEDGEMENTS

It is surreal to me that I am sitting down to write the acknowledgements of a second novel when the launch of the first was not so long ago.

So much goes into researching and writing a book of this length. I have stood on the shoulders of titans along the way and so a great many thanks are due.

To my Parents, Stefanos and Jeanette Haviaras, I am grateful for starting me off on my love of history and travel with that first great journey across the Atlantic and the subsequent mountains of books I asked for in the aftermath.

The Roman Empire is a vast and varied world in which to create a story. I would not have survived without my good friend, Andrew Fenwick of Dundee, whose knowledge of Roman weapons and tactics have always been an inspiration and whose passion for the subject is absolutely contagious.

As I have said before, I am not a Latin scholar. And so, the deepest debt of gratitude goes out to a few people who have helped review my Latin, no doubt with much academic discomfort to themselves. A massive thank you to Kostis Diassitis of Athens who gave me linguistic aid during the writing of my first two books.

To historians Tom and Eleftheria Crouch for being my Latin and HTML cavalry in a time of need, despite the increasingly busy schedule brought about by an ever-growing family. My appreciation to you both truly runs deep. Once again, if there are any errors in the use of this ancient language they are of my own making.

To my dear friend, Maria Carmen Brunello, Renaissance woman and expert beta reader, thank you for your enthusiasm and artistic passion which truly inspire.

No writer can expect to go very far without a fantastic editor with a keen eye and for this I must thank Shannon Donaldson whose editorial prowess during a final read of the book made all the difference.

To Professor Dennis J. Tini of Detroit, an Italian of great musical renown, I offer heartfelt thanks for an endless supply of encouragement and enthusiasm. Many a writer wishes for such a vocal champion of their work.

Sincere appreciation to poet, Jenn Blair, for her encouraging words, and to Derek Murphy of Creativindie.com, my many thanks for his vision and creation of such moving cover artwork for my books. It is indeed a pleasure working with you.

I should also tip my hat to Richard Lee and the folks at the Historic Novels Review for giving independent publishers and authors a venue for expert review. Not all publications or websites are so far-sighted and so I give my sincere thanks.

Writing can be a lonely adventure and during my own journey I have, at times, felt like Lucius Metellus Anguis venturing into that unknown desert. However, the solitude that goes with writing and publishing has been greatly alleviated by all the indie writers and artists online who share and provide helpful input without end. You are all amazing and if the rest of the world sought to help others as much, we would be living in a near-perfect place.

Of course, there would be no books without all of the wonderful readers around the world who supported and reviewed *Children of Apollo* and *Killing the Hydra*. I thank you all for reading and for the wonderful interactions we have had via e-mail and online.

To my girls, Alexandra and Athena. Thank you for always brightening my day and lightening my heart. I love that we are 'making books' together! You both inspire me at every turn.

Finally, to my superstar wife, Angelina, who is always there for me. Thank you for your unwavering confidence and for watching my back when the demons approach. Your killer editing, as ever, makes me a better writer, and your love is a wellspring that makes me a better human being. With all my heart, I thank you for believing in me and inspiring me. The gods do indeed smile on mortals from time to time and for that, I am eternally grateful.

Adam Alexander Haviaras
January, 2014
Toronto, Ontario

ABOUT THE AUTHOR

Adam Alexander Haviaras is a writer and historian who has studied ancient and medieval history and archaeology in Canada and the United Kingdom. He currently resides in Toronto with his wife and children. *Killing the Hydra* is his second novel.

Other works by Adam Alexander Haviaras:

The Eagles and Dragons series

A Dragon among the Eagles (Prequel)

Children of Apollo (Book I)

Killing the Hydra (Book II)

Warriors of Epona (Book III)

Isle of the Blessed (Book IV)

The Stolen Throne (Book V)

The Carpathian Interlude Series

Immortui (Part I)

Lykoi (Part II)

Thanatos (Part III)

The Mythologia Series

Chariot of the Son

Heart of Fire: A Novel of the Ancient Olympics

Saturnalia: A Tale of Wickedness and Redemption in Ancient Rome

Titles in the Historia Non-fiction Series

Historia I: Celtic Literary Archetypes in *The Mabinogion*: A Study of the Ancient Tale of *Pwyll, Lord of Dyved*

Historia II: Arthurian Romance and the Knightly Ideal: A study of Medieval Romantic Literature and its Effect upon Warrior Culture in Europe

Historia III: *Y Gododdin*: The Last Stand of Three Hundred Britons - Understanding People and Events during Britain's Heroic Age

Historia IV: Camelot: The Historical, Archaeological and Toponymic Considerations for South Cadbury Castle as King Arthur's Capital

STAY CONNECTED

To connect with Adam and learn more about the ancient world visit www.eaglesanddragonspublishing.com

Sign up for the Eagles and Dragons Publishing Newsletter at www.eaglesanddragonspublishing.com/newsletter-join-the-legions/ to receive a FREE BOOK, first access to new releases and posts on ancient history, special offers, and much more!

Readers can also connect with Adam on Twitter @AdamHaviaras and Instagram @ adam_haviaras.

On Facebook you can 'Like' the Eagles and Dragons page to get regular updates on new historical fiction and fantasy from Eagles and Dragons Publishing.